ALSO BY STRINGFELLOW BARR

The Will of Zeus
Mazzini: Portrait of an Exile
The Pilgrimage of Western Man

THE MASK OF JOVE

STRINGFELLOW BARR

THE MASK OF JOVE

A HISTORY OF GRAECO-ROMAN
CIVILIZATION FROM THE DEATH
OF ALEXANDER TO THE DEATH OF
CONSTANTINE

J. B. LIPPINCOTT COMPANY
PHILADELPHIA AND NEW YORK

For permission to quote from copyright material, thanks are due:

to G. Bell & Sons, Ltd, for a passage from *The Homecoming of Rutilius Namatianus,* translated by G. F. Savage-Armstrong (London, 1907)

to The Clarendon Press, Oxford, for passages from *The Works of Lucian of Samosata,* translated by H. W. and F. G. Fowler (Oxford, 1905); reprinted by permission of the Clarendon Press, Oxford

to Columbia University Press for passages from Salvian's *On the Government of God,* translated by Eva M. Sanford (New York, 1930), pp. v, 5, 7-8

to J. M. Dent & Sons Ltd: Publishers, for passages from Virgil's *Aeneid,* translated by Michael Oakley

to Grove Press, Inc., for passages from *The Poems of Catullus,* translated and with an Introduction by Horace Gregory (New York, 1956), copyright © 1956 by Horace Gregory, published by Grove Press, Inc.

to the Harvard University Press for passages from the various Loeb Classical Library volumes cited in the Notes, pp. 541-576; reprinted by permission of the publishers and The Loeb Classical Library (Cambridge, Mass.)

to Houghton Mifflin Company for lines from Sulpicia and Tibullus in *Latin Poetry,* translated by L. R. Lind (Boston, 1957)

to Indiana University Press for passages from Ovid's *Metamorphoses,* translated by Rolfe Humphries (Bloomington, Ind., 1955), and from Ovid's *The Art of Beauty, The Remedies for Love, and The Art of Love,* translated by Rolfe Humphries (Bloomington, Ind., 1957), and from *The Poems of Propertius,* translated by Constance Carrier (Bloomington, Ind., 1963)

to The Jefferson Medical College of Philadelphia and Mr. John M. Rankin for passages from *The Civil Law,* translated by Samuel P. Scott (Cincinnati: The Central Trust Company, 1932)

to Purdue University Press for passages from *The Idylls of Theokritos,* translated by Barriss Mills (West Lafayette, Ind., 1963)

to the Society for Promoting Christian Knowledge for passages from Volume I of Eusebius's *Ecclesiastical History,* translated by H. J. Lawlor and J. E. L. Oulton (London: S.P.C.K., 1927)

to Mr. Willis Kingsley Wing, A. P. Watt & Son, and Penguin Books Ltd. for passages from Apuleius's *The Golden Ass,* translated by Robert Graves (Harmondsworth, England, 1951); reprinted by permission of Willis Kingsley Wing, copyright © 1951 by International Authors N. V.

Thanks are also due for permission to quote the following:

From *The Aeneid* by Virgil. Translated by Michael Oakley, 1957. Everyman's Library Edition. Reprinted by permission of E. P. Dutton & Co., Inc.

From the New Testament in the translation of Monsignor Knox, copyright 1944, Sheed and Ward Inc., New York. With the kind permission of His Eminence the Cardinal Archbishop of Westminster and of Burns & Oates.

Passages reprinted from *The Satyricon* by Petronius, translated by William Arrowsmith, by permission of The University of Michigan Press; copyright © by William Arrowsmith 1959

Lines from Helen Rowe Henze's translation of *The Odes of Horace* are reprinted by permission and are copyright 1961 by the University of Oklahoma Press.

FIRST EDITION

PRINTED IN THE UNITED STATES OF AMERICA

LIBRARY OF CONGRESS CATALOG CARD NUMBER: 66-12338

To Another City

PREFACE

THIS BOOK continues the narrative of *The Will of Zeus*, which was published in 1961. In that volume I tried to picture the development of Greek culture from its origins to the death of Alexander the Great in 323 B.C. In *The Mask of Jove* I have tried to experience with the reader the further development of that culture, now perhaps better described as a civilization, down to the death of the Emperor Constantine in A.D. 337. This second and final volume therefore includes what historians have commonly called the Hellenistic and Roman periods of classical civilization. I wanted to make the story in these two volumes an intelligible whole composed of two parts, each of which would also be an intelligible whole in its own right. I have therefore sometimes used recapitulations in *The Mask of Jove* rather than assume that my reader was familiar with *The Will of Zeus*. But it is a sort of recapitulation, I believe, that inheres in a civilization conscious of its past and a sort I had already chosen to use within the narrative that each volume contains. If some of these repetitions annoy the reader, I would remind him that every civilization is in no small measure a matter of remembering.

Like *The Will of Zeus*, *The Mask of Jove* is a narrative, not an argument, a drama in which I have again allowed the actors to tell the story in their own words whenever available documents permitted. Again, therefore, my quotations are often long. When I have thought my own comments might be useful, I have made them in the notes. In this second volume as in the first, I have placed all notes in the back of the book. The number affixed to each note occurs twice and only twice in this volume: once in the section devoted to notes, pages 541–76, and once in the text itself at the point to which the note applies.

Though its geographical focus is Rome, *The Mask of Jove* is not intended to be a history of Rome but a history of Hellenic civilization. But since Rome conquered the countries where that civilization flourished, since she partly adopted it, adapted it, and in some measure transmitted it to her less civilized provinces in Western Europe and North Africa, since she defended it with her legions and organized its laws, Roman actions and Latin literature play deceptively lengthy roles in this history. Again, the Christian and Jewish communities were largely foreign bodies in the Graeco-Roman Cosmopolis. But the Christian community, which emerged from the Jewish, was the embryo of a Greek-speaking Byzantine civilization, ruled not from Rome but from Constantinople. The growth of this embryo within the womb of Hellenic civilization, therefore, also plays a deceptively long role in this history. Its Caesarian birth as a Christian empire becomes in some sense the death of Hellenic civilization and the end of the story narrated in *The Will of Zeus* and *The Mask of Jove*. Although some of my readers may believe that they worship the true God in their church or synagogue, while the gods worshiped in the temples of ancient Greece were false gods imagined by their worshipers, I have chosen not to make this distinction in either volume of my history but rather to respect the faith of pagan, Jew, and Christian and in consequence to relay their accounts of religious events. My own religious views have seemed to me not a matter these two volumes should be concerned with.

As in *The Will of Zeus*, so in this volume the spelling of proper names offered problems. To these problems I have deliberately added another by giving preference to contemporary place names over their ancient equivalents, both in maps and text. For various reasons I have occasionally given both. In the maps all city names not in current geographical use are italicized. Finally, I have used traditional English spellings of modern foreign place names: Marseilles rather than Marseille, Nimwegen rather than Nijmegen, Treves rather than the German Trier or the French Trèves, and Trebizond rather than the Turkish Trabzon.

Many scholars who read Greek and Latin will disagree with me on my choice of translations and with each other on which translations I ought to have chosen. As in *The Will of Zeus,* I have favored the Loeb Classics wherever I found no compelling reason against doing so. They offer the reader a reputable Greek or Latin text to consult and an English translation facing it in one readily available edition. Because many dates in ancient history cannot be fixed with complete precision, phrases such as "c. 99" in the Chronological Summary are necessarily frequent. Although the dates in this volume run from the mythical founding of Rome in 753 B.C. to the death of Constantine in A.D. 337, I have rarely thought it necessary to add letters to dates except during a few decades when the reader might otherwise be confused.

Although work on the subject covered by *The Will of Zeus* and this present volume began in 1935, it has been only for the past eight years that it has had the first claim on my working time and that I have had the full-time help of a research associate. For these precious years I thank the Old Dominion Foundation, which repeatedly extended its grant to Rutgers University for this purpose; Rutgers itself, which showed great consideration in adjusting my teaching load; and the Librarian and staff of Firestone Library, Princeton University, for their continued hospitality to my work in a field where few other libraries could offer comparable opportunities.

I owe thanks, for various forms of help in my writing of this second volume of my history, to Baldwin Barr, Scott Buchanan, Francis Fergusson, Everett Gendler, Mary Frances Gyles, Arno Mayer, Stewart Richardson, and George Stevens. I am grateful for their advice; but, since I did not always follow it, none of my failures can be fairly charged to any of them. The role of my research associate, Cary T. Peebles, in helping me to plan the work, to select translations, to draft my own translations where none in English was available or where a legitimate change in phrasing would better correspond with the context, and in furnishing illuminating editorial advice on call, has been crucial to whatever power the book may have to speak directly to the mind of the reader. Finally, I must mention the many students I taught over more than forty years. Their insights convinced me long years ago that Socrates was right in his apparent assumption that one person can teach another only if he is constantly ready to learn from him and that the condition for teaching is full intellectual encounter.

STRINGFELLOW BARR

March 15, 1966
Princeton, New Jersey

CONTENTS

ILLUSTRATIONS

(between pages 192 and 193)

MAPS

Drawn by Guy Fleming

THE GROWTH OF THE ROMAN THING
BY THE DEATH OF AUGUSTUS IN 14 A.D.

▬ ▬ ▬ Imperial Frontiers
◎ Cities having a population
of over 100,000 about 218 B.C.

ATLANTIC
OCEAN

GERMANS

BOHEMIA

Teutoburg Forest

Elbe R.

Rhine R.

Danube R.

ILLYRIA

• LYONS

Rhone R.

NÎMES •

MARSEILLES •

Ebro R.

• TARRAGONA (Tarraco)

E T R U R I A

MODENA •
BOLOGNA •

ANCONA •

ROME ◎

SAGUNTUM •

LATIUM

EPIDAMNU
[Dyrrachiu

CAPUA •
PUTEOLI •   • NOLA
I. of Capri

CANNAE •
APOLLONIA •
TARENTUM •

MA

• CADIZ

(New Carthage) CARTAGENA •

M E D I T E R

MAGNA GRAECIA
[Great Greece]

EPI

R
MESSINA •
AGRIGENTUM •
A
N

ACTIU

UTICA •
CARTHAGE
ZAMA •

SYRACUSE •

E
A
N

ROME

MILES
0   10   20   30   40   50

ROMAN TERRITORY ABOUT 500 B.C.

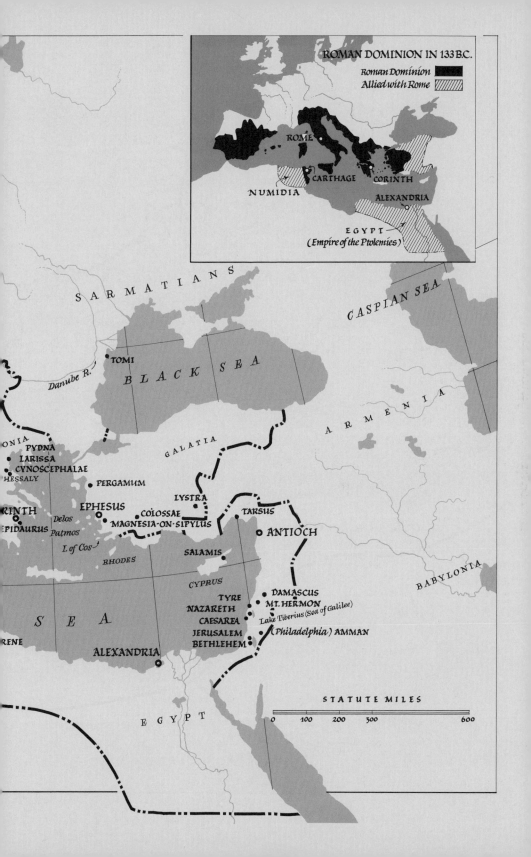

ROMAN DOMINION IN 133 B.C.

Roman Dominion
Allied with Rome

ROME

CARTHAGE   CORINTH

NUMIDIA

ALEXANDRIA

EGYPT
(Empire of the Ptolemies)

SARMATIANS

CASPIAN SEA

TOMI

BLACK SEA

Danube R.

ARMENIA

ONIA

GALATIA

PYDNA
LARISSA
CYNOSCEPHALAE
HESSALY

PERGAMUM

LYSTRA

TARSUS

RINTH
EPIDAURUS

EPHESUS

COLOSSAE
MAGNESIA-ON-SIPYLUS

ANTIOCH

Delos
Patmos
I. of Cos

BABYLONIA

RHODES

SALAMIS

CYPRUS

DAMASCUS

MT. HERMON
Lake Tiberius (Sea of Galilee)

TYRE
NAZARETH
CAESAREA
JERUSALEM
BETHLEHEM

SEA

(Philadelphia) AMMAN

RENE

ALEXANDRIA

STATUTE MILES

EGYPT

0   100   200   300   600

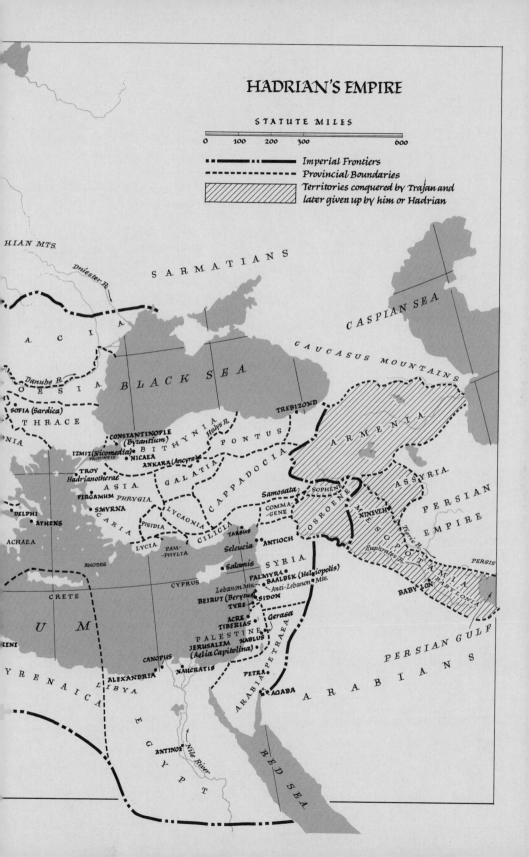

HADRIAN'S EMPIRE

STATUTE MILES

0   100   200   300   600

— · — · — · — Imperial Frontiers

— — — — — — Provincial Boundaries

Territories conquered by Trajan and later given up by him or Hadrian

HIAN MTS.

Dniester R.

S A R M A T I A N S

CASPIAN SEA

A   C   I   A

Danube R.

C A U C A S U S   M O U N T A I N S

OESIA

B L A C K   S E A

SOFIA (Sardica)

ONIA

THRACE

TREBIZOND

CONSTANTINOPLE
(Byzantium)
IZMIT (Nicomedia)
PROPONTIS   NICAEA

BITHYNIA
Halys R.
ANKARA (Ancyra)

PONTUS

A R M E N I A

ASSYRIA

TROY
Hadrianotherae

GALATIA

CAPPADOCIA

Samosata
SOPHENE

OSROENE

NINEVEH

P E R S I A N

ASIA
PERGAMUM   PHRYGIA

COMMA-
GENE

MESOPOTAMIA

DELPHI
ATHENS

SMYRNA
CARIA
LYCAONIA

Tigris R.

E M P I R E

ACHAEA

PISIDIA
CILICIA

TARSUS
Seleucia   ANTIOCH

Euphrates R.

Babylonia

PERSIS

RHODES

LYCIA   PAM-
PHYLIA

Salamis

PALMYRA

BABYLON

CRETE

CYPRUS

SYRIA

BAALBEK (Heliopolis)
Lebanon Mts.   Anti-Lebanon Mts.
BEIRUT (Berytus)   SIDON
TYRE

U   M

ACRE
TIBERIAS   Gerasa
PALESTINE
JERUSALEM   NABLUS
(Aelia Capitolina)

PERSIAN GULF

RENE

CANOPUS

A R A B I A N S

YRENAICA

LIBYA

ALEXANDRIA   NAUCRATIS

PETRA

ARABIA PETRAEA

AQABA

ANTINOE
Nile River

E   G   Y   P   T

R E D   S E A

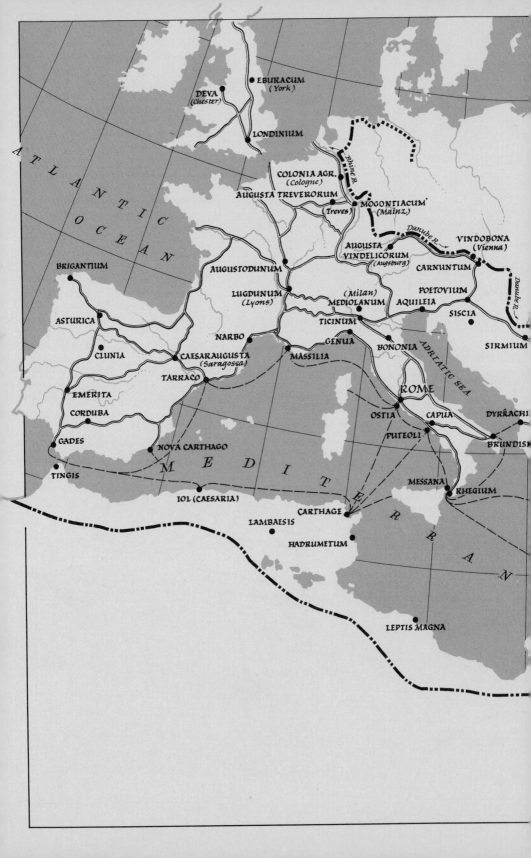

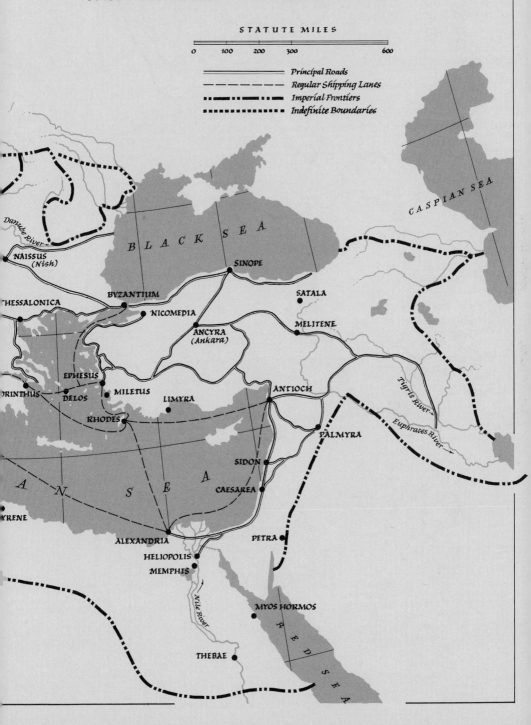

THE CHIEF ROMAN ROADS AND
SHIPPING ROUTES IN HADRIAN'S DAY

STATUTE MILES

0   100   200   300   600

——————— Principal Roads
– – – – – Regular Shipping Lanes
▬▬▬▬▬ Imperial Frontiers
■■■■■■ Indefinite Boundaries

CASPIAN SEA

Danube River

BLACK SEA

NAISSUS
(Nish)

SINOPE

THESSALONICA

BYZANTIUM

NICOMEDIA

SATALA

MELITENE

ANCYRA
(Ankara)

Tigris River

EPHESUS

Euphrates River

ORINTHUS

DELOS

MILETUS

LIMYRA

ANTIOCH

RHODES

PALMYRA

A   N   SE   A

SIDON

CAESAREA

YRENE

ALEXANDRIA

PETRA

HELIOPOLIS

MEMPHIS

Nile River

MYOS HORMOS

RED SEA

THEBAE

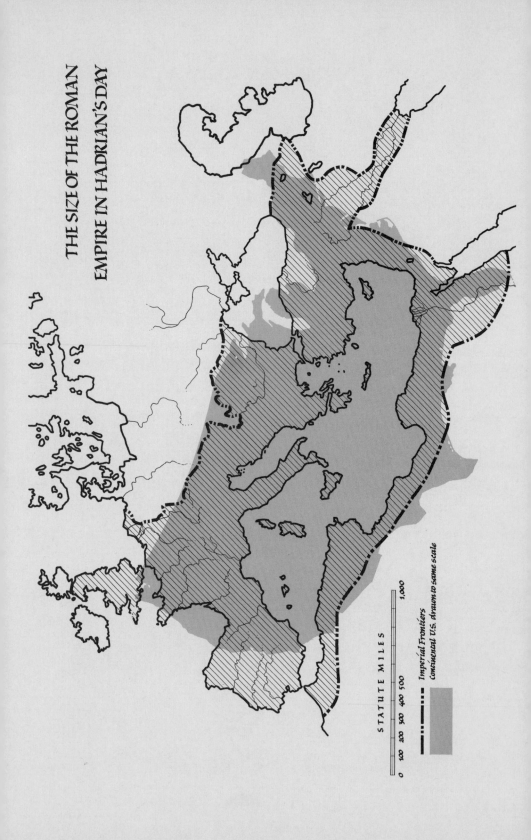

THE SIZE OF THE ROMAN
EMPIRE IN HADRIAN'S DAY

STATUTE MILES

0   100 200 300 500   1,000

Imperial Frontiers

continental U.S. drawn to same scale

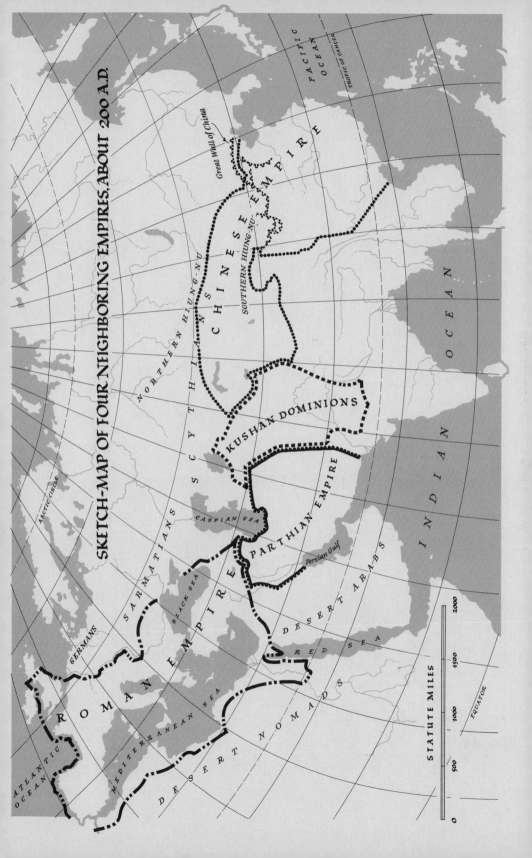

SKETCH-MAP OF FOUR NEIGHBORING EMPIRES, ABOUT 200 A.D.

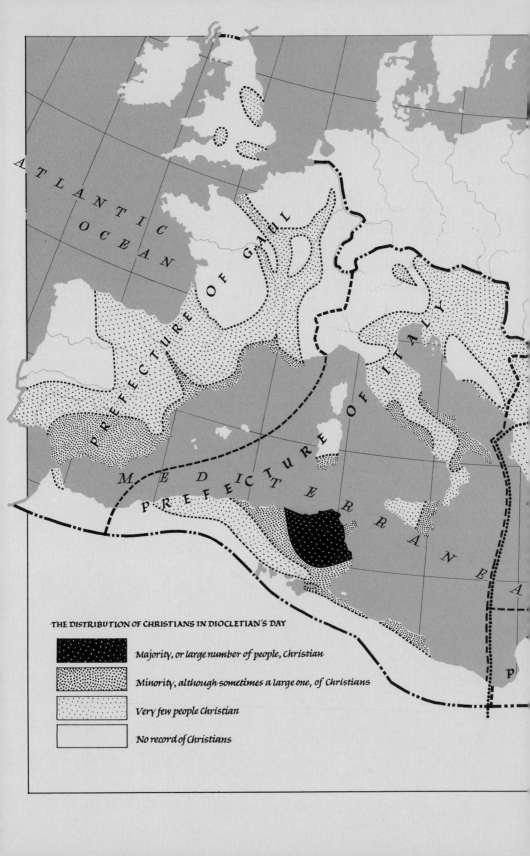

THE DISTRIBUTION OF CHRISTIANS IN DIOCLETIAN'S DAY

Majority, or large number of people, Christian

Minority, although sometimes a large one, of Christians

Very few people Christian

No record of Christians

THE EMPIRE IN DIOCLETIAN'S DAY

STATUTE MILES

0   100   200   300   600

·—·—·—·—·—·—·—· Imperial Frontiers
- - - - - - - - - - - Limits of Prefectures
················· Approximate Linguistic Boundary
Between Latin West and Greek East

CASPIAN SEA

BLACK SEA

AFRICU...

S E A   O F   T H E   E A S T

...FECTURE

Scipio, beholding this city, which had flourished 700 years from its foundation and had ruled over so many lands, islands, and seas, as rich in arms and fleets, elephants, and money as the mightiest empires, but far surpassing them in hardihood and high spirit (since, when stripped of all its ships and arms, it had sustained famine and a mighty war for three years), now come to its end in total destruction—Scipio, beholding this spectacle, is said to have shed tears and publicly lamented the fortune of the enemy. After meditating by himself a long time and reflecting on the inevitable fall of cities, nations, and empires, as well as of individuals, upon the fate of Troy, that once proud city, upon the fate of the Assyrian, the Median, and afterwards of the great Persian Empire, and, most recently of all, of the splendid empire of Macedon, either voluntarily or otherwise the words of the poet escaped his lips:—

> The day shall come in which our sacred Troy
> And Priam, and the people over whom
> Spear-bearing Priam rules, shall perish all.

Being asked by Polybius in familiar conversation (for Polybius had been his tutor) what he meant by using these words, Polybius says that he did not hesitate frankly to name his own country, for whose fate he feared when he considered the mutability of human affairs. And Polybius wrote this down just as he heard it.

—Appian, THE PUNIC WARS VIII, 132

Cities, my friend, die just like men. . . .
—Lucian, CHARON 15

THE ROMAN THING

When ALEXANDER THE GREAT lay dying at Babylon in his thirty-third year, he had conquered the Persian Empire and opened it to Hellenic commercial expansion. By this year, 323 B.C., his dominions extended to the Danube on the north; to the Arabian desert, to the First Cataract of the Nile, and to the Sahara in the south; in the east, at least in theory, to the Indus River and beyond it in West Pakistan; to the Adriatic on the west. Like his father, Philip of Macedon, he was both King of Macedonia and the officially elected leader of most of the city-states of Mainland Greece, south of Macedonia. Unlike his father, he controlled Greece-in-Asia as well. The whole eastern basin of the Mediterranean, the cradle of Greek culture, was his. But the western basin was not, although its coast had been sown with Greek colonies from the eighth century on. Beyond the numerous Greek cities of Sicily, beyond the many Greek cities that caused men to call southern Italy Great Greece, lay Greek cities on the southern coast of France and even on the coast of Spain. In this Western Greece stood such wealthy and powerful Greek cities as Syracuse on the east coast of Sicily and Tarentum on the Gulf

 3

of Taranto, the instep of the Italian boot. In the western basin of the Mediterranean there likewise stood, near the site of modern Tunis, the rich commercial city of Carthage, founded by Phoenician traders four centuries before, and ever since those days in partial control of Sicily. It was Carthage that guarded the Strait of Gibraltar and the secret sea route to the tin mines of Cornwall: the Mediterranean craftsmen who made bronze weapons, bronze armor, bronze tools, and even bronze statues paid well for tin to mix with their copper. The Etruscan Empire had once controlled the western coast of Italy from the Arno River to the Bay of Naples, and also much of the Po Valley. Now it had largely crumbled under pressure from the north by Celtic barbarians, under pressure from the south by the small Roman Republic and her Latin allies. Rome had also extended her tight network of alliances to include some of the Greek cities of Campania. Campania was the fertile coastal plain around Naples, itself a Greek colony.

After the young Alexander's lightning conquest and sudden death, reports were circulated that he had planned to conquer the western basin of the Mediterranean. Alexander's own words and his own acts all suggested that he wanted, in some sense of the phrase, to conquer the world, the *kosmos*. Although he was explorer as well as conqueror, a true map of the world was at that time quite out of the question. Even had such a map existed, he was too good a general and too good a statesman to follow a blueprint of empire without knowing the military and political realities with which he would have had to cope. Both his old tutor, the philosopher Aristotle, and Aristotle's master, Plato, had seen in the *polis*, or small city-state, the largest political unit able to become a community worthy of civilized men. It seemed obvious to Aristotle that a polis of 100,000 citizens was no longer a community in any but a barbarian sense. Athens, for example, included in her great imperial days scarcely more than 40,000 free male citizens, exclusive of perhaps twice that number of women, children, resident aliens, and slaves. In those days Athens had become not merely a commerce in commodities for the bodies of men but a commerce in ideas that fed their minds. She had become a great conversation between thinking men, a communion with the immortal gods, and a symphony of poetry, drama, music, dance, painting, sculpture, and architecture. Her small size had enabled the Athenians to deliberate in common for the common good.

There seemed but two ways open to the Greek polis. It could remain small enough to foster the intense community life that had created Greek culture. Or it could lose its human purpose and become a despotic and sprawling empire. But Alexander faced a new and practical problem. He longed indeed to hellenize his rough Macedonians. He longed to spread Hellenic civilization through the cosmos he was conquering and organizing; to make that cosmos into a new and wider polis, a cosmopolis. Not Alexander, but commercial enterprise, had created that cosmos; and it could not continue to flourish in a state of anarchy. When he returned from India to Babylon, the cosmos he was trying to shape had to be built from the ancient cultural debris of fallen empires: the Persian, the Median before that, the Chaldean, the Assyrian, the Hittite, clear back to the Babylonian and the Egyptian. The Macedonia he had inherited and the hundreds of tiny Greek polises scattered around the eastern basin of the Mediterranean had now been multiplied by him into many Macedonias and into more polises, polises he himself had founded as foci of Hellenic civilization, expanding now throughout most of the Middle East. His dream of a Hellenistic cosmopolis would sooner or later also have dictated the absorption of the colonies that had made the western basin so largely Greek. Whether he faced that fact before his death was never clearly established: in any case, he had plenty of other business and much more urgent business to face. At Babylon he contracted fever and died, but the problem of locating Cosmopolis and organizing it politically could not possibly die. The tiny Greek polis, whether Athens or another, had indeed created a kind of society that would haunt the imagination of man, but the insistence of the polis on absolute political sovereignty had made a cockpit of Greece and of much of the Mediterranean world, had spread the cancer of class war, had deformed the very dream of what a polis could mean. Law and government must be toilsomely constructed in the cosmopolis Alexander sought, or the violence between each polis and its neighbor and between rich and poor within each polis would brutalize Hellenic civilization beyond recognition.

Less than a year before Alexander's death, he had held at Opis on the Tigris River a great feast. Some nine thousand guests, Macedonians, Persians, and others, broke bread together, drank wine together, and sang together one paean. And Alexander publicly prayed for harmony and fellowshop in his half-built, polyglot empire, an empire that occupied portions of three continents and opened them to the ideas, the language, the art, the crafts, and the commerce of Hellas. It had taken him nine

5

months of siege-craft to subject the city of Tyre and thereby to break Phoenician sea power in the eastern Mediterranean. His frontiers in Africa already reached temptingly toward Tyre's powerful daughter, Carthage; and Carthage appeared to be the strongest sea power in the western Mediterranean. Had he lived to subject Carthage, could any other power in the West have prevented him from gathering into Cosmopolis the Greek cities that studded the coasts of Sicily, southern Italy, and even southern France and northeastern Spain? Regardless of whether Alexander explicitly hoped to do this, the logic of events would have put pressure on him to move westward, if only because land-hungry and trade-hungry Greek colonists had carried Greek culture westward some five centuries before he had been born. The task now was the organization of the Hellenic world and its partly hellenized neighbors. That task necessarily included the world of Western Greece beyond the Adriatic.

But this task Alexander's premature death bequeathed to his successor or successors. According to tradition, when those at his bedside asked him to whom he left his throne, he answered, "to the strongest."[1] He was also reported as predicting, perhaps in allusion to the magnificent athletic contests he had recently held at the funeral of his beloved Hephestion, that on his own death there would be a great funeral contest. In the eyes of many of his subjects, Alexander was the son of Zeus. It is true that on this point the Greeks displayed skepticism. But a weakened Greek religious tradition still recognized that the god Apollo really was the son of Zeus and that in his oracles delivered at Delphi Apollo spoke the will of Zeus. It recognized that those oracles often yielded the same cryptic and ambiguous meanings as did those words ascribed to the dying Alexander. For the Greek word Alexander used for strongest also meant best. Would Alexander's heir be merely the strongest or also the best? This oracular style Socrates had respected, apparently because it challenged men to question further and to think through their purposes before they acted.

Tradition does not record that anyone who heard Alexander bequeath his Cosmopolis to the strongest sought to learn at Delphi whether the strongest might also be the best. The rash of murders that usually accompanied a royal succession promptly broke out in Macedonia. The great funeral contest which the dying Alexander predicted was fought out between his most powerful marshals. The contest was indecisive, and it lasted for nearly two centuries. During most of that time, descendants of the Macedonian marshals ruled as kings, the Antigonids in the European

6

portion of Cosmopolis, the Seleucids in the Asian, the Ptolemies in the African. In each of these three kingdoms, the monarch maintained a mercenary army of Greeks and Macedonians and a predominantly Greek civil service. Each monarch warred with the others partly for glory but in considerable measure from economic motives: for markets, trade routes, tax revenues. This period of intermittent civil war in Cosmopolis would eventually be known as the Hellenistic Age. While the Hellenistic kings fought, Apollo and the other gods watched their futile struggle and prepared an all but unknown state in the West to claim the prize, to inherit Cosmopolis. At least, this destiny was implicit in the traditions which slowly grew up in this not very highly civilized republic in the West, the *Res Publica Romana.*

According to this western republic's own traditions, the mother of Rome's founder was the daughter of a nearby king, whose father dedicated her, while yet a virgin, to a temple. There Mars, god of war, violated her, and she gave birth to twins, Romulus and Remus. Like so many other folk heroes, including Moses and Cyrus the Great, the unwanted baby brothers were exposed. They were placed in some sort of small casket and cast adrift on the Tiber River. But the gods brought them to shore and a she-wolf suckled them. Although the wolf was an animal sacred to Mars, it should be pointed out that the word *lupa*, Latin for she-wolf, was also a word for prostitute, so that maybe the two bastard brothers were suckled, if not borne, by a prostitute. In any event, the two outcasts founded two settlements close together. The one that Romulus founded, Rome, endured. She welcomed exiles, refugees, and robbers as to a kind of asylum, and together they raided a nearby settlement of Sabines, and kidnaped wives for themselves. Romulus became Rome's first king, and six other kings followed. In the end, Tarquin the Proud, an Etruscan, violated the wife of a noble, whereupon the nobles drove him out and proclaimed a republic, the Res Publica Romana, literally the Roman Public Thing.

But the Greek world told other tales about how Rome had come into being. The Greeks related that some of the adventures of Odysseus had occurred in Italy, and some Greeks claimed that Odysseus had a bastard son by Circe, the witch-goddess with whom Odysseus had lain. This happened at the Circean promontory halfway down the coast from Rome to Naples, where Circe had changed Odysseus' men into swine. And this son by Odysseus Circe named Romus, and this Romus founded Rome. Still other Greeks sought the origins of Rome, not in the *Odyssey*, but in

7

the *Iliad*. There[2] they read Posidon's speech to the gods concerning Aeneas. Posidon predicted that this human son of the goddess Aphrodite would escape the fall of Troy and "be king among the Trojans, and his sons' sons that shall be born in days to come."[3] The Greeks read also how[4] Posidon saved his life when he was fighting Achilles, as once before[5] Apollo and Aphrodite had saved him. The Greeks concluded that after Troy fell, Aeneas led a band of survivors to Sicily and then to Italy. Perhaps he was the true founder of Capua, the oldest Greek colony in Italy. In any case, he founded Rome. Or a son of his named Romus did. Or a daughter named Rome. This Greek account of Rome as a reborn Troy was widely accepted by the Romans themselves within two or three decades of Alexander's death. Finally, Greeks were capable of assuming that Rome was just another Greek colony, a northern extension of Great Greece, which the Romans called *Magna Graecia*. For instance, according to Plutarch, one of Plato's pupils wrote not long after 390 B.C., when the Gauls sacked Rome, that

> out of the West a story prevailed, how an army of Hyperboreans had come from afar and captured a Greek city called Rome, situated somewhere on the shores of the Great Sea.[6]

As history, this medley of often contradictory traditions may have left much to be desired; but as poetic myth it was eloquent of Rome's growing confidence that she could turn obscure origins into proud achievement, appalling defeat into triumphant victory, a human wolf pack into an ordered society; and all because the gods had chosen her. The god-fearing refugee, Aeneas, had taught her, too, to fear the gods; and that those Romans best served the gods who best served the Res Publica, the Public Thing. The Roman Thing had been carved out of this western wilderness by a saving remnant from across the sea. Neither men with ideas, such as the Greeks, nor writers of great tragedies or of unseemly comedies, nor dancers nor musicians nor lyric poets nor philosophizing pedants could have done so much. Neither Greek athletes lolling in shameful nakedness nor the sculptors who loved to make statues of them; neither insolent democrats nor self-seeking aristocrats nor luxury-loving kings could have done it. It could only be done by the sober, severe, modest, disciplined people of the toga. These could be unbreakable in defeat, moderate and just in victory, precisely because they had been chosen by the gods themselves for a manifest destiny. It was their mission to rule more frivolous folk. That they should do so was the will of *Jupiter Optimus Maximus,* Jupiter Greatest and Best. Once handed this commission, and once having bound themselves by relations with him that were contractual, punctilious, and formal, they had set to work. To this labor, therefore, they were bound by their religion. Was not *religio* etymologically a binding together? Was not their word for law, *lex,* also a binding? To accomplish their task, they must acquire power and authority, over themselves and over others. And since their task lay, not in the sky where Jupiter reigned, but here on the south bank of the Tiber, near the west coast of Central Italy, they were determined to deal with the concrete, the practical, the here, the now, and always with things: with men, arms, land, farm tools, seed, flocks, herds, money. Even empty space was a thing, at least in the metaphor of the poet Ennius, who wrote of "the piled spaces of the ether."[7] The total of what they built or seized would be the Roman Thing, the Res Publica, the Republic. It was this Roman Thing, rather than the invisible gods who had willed it, that they passionately loved. They would love it, defend it, extend it, and die for it. But because their religion bound them to do so, they would do it gravely and with dignity. They would govern it, along with those whom it subjected and bound to itself by solemn treaty and by law. They therefore gave themselves to war, to law, and to labor on this land of theirs.

As to the actual history of the Roman Republic, from the time that Romulus, or Aeneas, or somebody else established *Roma Quadrata,* Foursquare Rome, to the time when Alexander the Great lay dying in Babylon, not much is precisely known. But, legend aside, the history of Rome had much in common with the histories of Athens or Sparta and indeed of the average Greek polis. The Romans, like the Greeks, were herdsmen speaking an Aryan tongue, who had come down from the north in war bands led by chieftain kings and had imposed their language on the agricultural people they settled amongst. The Latin the Roman spoke was distantly kin to the Greek the Hellene spoke. The alphabet the Roman used was adapted from the Greek alphabet, which Rome borrowed from Greek traders or indirectly through her Etruscan neighbors. For these Etruscans, who were commonly thought to have migrated to Italy from Lydia in Asia Minor, had borrowed much from the Greeks they traded with, including the Greek alphabet. The Roman kings consolidated villages into a small city-state. At Rome, as in Greece, the king was chosen by a small class of warriors, who composed his council. In Athens these aristocrats were the Eupatrids, the Well-

9

fathered; in Rome they were the patricians, those citizens who were descended from the *Patres*, or Fathers, who headed their respective clans. The kings whom these nobles chose were formally acclaimed by the humbler members of the polis gathered in a popular assembly.[8] The king was commander-in-chief in time of war, high priest and therefore intermediary between his people and their gods, and the judge who interpreted and applied their laws to the wrongdoer. In Rome as in Greece, settled life brought a shift from monarchy to an aristocratic republic, a shift that was far from reflecting a popular revolt. For example, in Roman tradition, the body of the common people, known as the plebs, looked to Romulus to protect it against the rapacious patricians; the patricians were charged with murdering Romulus;[9] and they could quiet the plebeians only by reporting that Romulus had been whisked up to heaven by the gods. And, just as it was a patrician who murdered the last Roman king, so it was patricians who proclaimed Republican liberty.

In the Roman Republic as in Athens the law was unwritten. In the Athenian republic, only the Eupatrid could interpret the will of Zeus and the lesser gods and enforce it in Athens as human law, just as in Rome only the patrician could interpret the will of Zeus, whom Romans knew as Jupiter, or Jove. In both instances the lower class loudly demanded written law. According to an Athenian saying, Dracon wrote his laws in blood. Similarly harsh law was written at Rome in the Twelve Tables by the Decemvirs, a special commission of ten patricians who for a while ruled the city. In Rome as in Athens, the burning issues were the redistribution of land, or at least the abolition of mortgages; and the scaling down of interest on debts, or the abolition of the creditor's right to imprison or enslave his insolvent debtor. The Twelve Tables, Rome's first written law, even provided that creditors with claims against the same insolvent debtor might carve up his body and divide it among them.[10] The plebeians were so indignant with the continued rule of the Commission of Ten that they seceded from the Res Publica, gathered on the nearby Aventine Mount, constituted a sort of plebeian republic within the Roman Republic, and created new officials called tribunes. The persons of these tribunes were declared inviolable and they were charged with representing the interests of the plebs and with negotiating with the patrician Senate and the two patrician consuls. The consuls were annually elected administrative officers who had replaced the king, just as the annually elected archon had replaced the Athenian king.

The so-called Aventine Secession and the *de facto* establishment of a plebeian legislative chamber occurred about 449, about a century and a half after Athens had given Solon emergency powers to reform her laws and avert a class war. Not even Solon's wise provisions had prevented Pisistratus from setting up a tyranny, a tyranny that did much to rescue the poor of Athens from economic and legal oppression. But another development also helped Athens to create political democracy. The farm land of Attica was not rich, and its poverty steadily urged Athens to take to the sea, to commerce, and to industry.

At the time that the Roman plebs solemnly assembled on the Aventine, Athenian democracy, led by Pericles, was at the height of its glory. It was perhaps not by chance that the Aventine Mount, where the plebs took their Sacred Oath to defend themselves against oppression, was the site of a trading community. Four similar secessions occurred, always to the same site. Among the traders on the Aventine were Greeks, and those Greeks can scarcely have been ignorant of the revolutions that had converted so many Greek cities from aristocracy to democracy. Rome, however, was ill fitted to make that transition. Under the late monarchy she had developed a little local industry, but she did not take to the sea. The pottery she bought from Athenian and Corinthian traders she could pay for in salt from pans at the mouth of the Tiber, timber from upstream, slaves captured in constant wars with her neighbors. The volcanic soil in her valleys was far richer than Attic soil, and her farmers, patrician and plebeian alike, could grow plenty of spelt, a species of wheat admittedly better suited to making porridge than to making bread. In the nearby hills Rome had good pasture for cattle. Finally, throughout the fifth and a part of the fourth centuries, her constant wars with her neighbors tended to cut her off from intercourse with the world beyond and from any large-scale exchange either of commodities or of ideas.

For these reasons Rome turned in on herself, as Sparta had done somewhat earlier. Like Sparta, she was oligarchical in politics, inland and not maritime, proud of her simple living, not much given to art, unfriendly to speculation, harsh of wit, grave of manner. But she was unlike Sparta too: no legendary laws of Lycurgus forbade her governing class to own land privately or to amass what money they could get hold of. And though her poorer peasants were cruelly ground down, they were not state serfs like the Spartan Helots, shut out entirely from the political community. Moreover, while the Spartan spent his whole life in training for war and abstained from labor, the Roman patrician of the early Republic was proud to farm with his own hands. Sparta strove to exercise the hegemony of the Peloponnese. But once she had acquired neighboring Messenia, she tried to hold hegemony by maintaining a highly trained standing army rather than by wars of conquest, if only because of the specter of an uprising of Helots at home. Rome, however, managed to be at war almost constantly and to make war pay: in booty, in money indemnity, in land, and in allied manpower available for the next struggle.

Yet the Roman Republic was not a militaristic state in any simple sense. To a large extent Rome was forced by time and place to learn war. For this She-Wolf stood guard over Latium and its tiny Latin cities, at the Tiber River, the southwestern frontier of powerful and wealthy Etruria. She bore the brunt of Etruscan assault, as her son Horatius bore the brunt when single-handed he held the wooden bridge across the Tiber until his comrades could escape and then himself plunged, armor and all, into the river and swam to refuge. Nor was it merely the hammering might of Etruria and the quarrels over land with her Latin neighbors that taught Rome war. Always she remembered the Celtic tribesmen whom she called Gauls, who had come down out of the north about 390, had overrun Etruria, had captured and sacked Rome. Nearly four centuries later the historian Livy recorded that memory. He told how they approached the city while "their wild songs and discordant shouts filled all the air with a hideous noise."[11] He told how a terrified Roman army fled before this horde, which proceeded to burn Rome. He told how

> a thousand pounds of gold was agreed on as the price of a people that was destined presently to rule the nations. The transaction was a foul disgrace in itself, but an insult was added thereto: the weights brought by the Gauls were dishonest, and on the tribune's objecting, the insolent Gaul added his sword to the weight, and a saying intolerable to Roman ears was heard,—Woe to the conquered.[12]

When Camillus, whom the Senate had appointed dictator, drove the Gauls out of the country, Rome lay ransomed but burned, and

> the tribunes . . . were urging the plebs unceasingly to quit their ruins and emigrate to a city ready to their hand at Veii . . .[13]

for the Romans had recently captured and sacked that Etruscan city and had sold its inhabitants into slavery. Camillus, now hailed as the Father of his Country and its Second Founder, then declared to the popular assembly that

> you will find that all things turned out well when we obeyed the gods, and ill when we spurned them.[14]

Moreover,

> We have a City founded with due observance of auspice and augury; no corner of it is not permeated by ideas of religion and the gods; for our annual sacrifices, the days are no more fixed than are the places where they may be performed.[15]

In Camillus' view Rome was not a disembodied idea. The gods who prescribed through official channels what sacrifices should be made also prescribed time and place. The Roman Public Thing was no abstraction; it was rooted in time and place and could extricate itself from neither. It was an incarnation of the will of Jove, and Jove worked in history by issuing orders to Rome. Rome must obey.

When the victorious Camillus had conquered, he did what all Roman conquerors did whenever the Senate gave its sanction: he triumphed. A Roman triumph was in those days no mere personal vaunting. Camillus would don a special toga, painted over with gold stars. He would hold an ivory scepter and would wear a wreath of laurel. He would be driven in a four-horse chariot, preceded by twenty-four lictors. Each lictor would bear the fasces, that is, bundles of rods bound about two-edged axes. Those fasces were the symbol of Rome's authority and of her power to flog and even behead in order to enforce her law. A servant would hold a heavy gold crown above Camillus' head; and to protect him from the irreligious arrogance the Greeks called *hybris*, another servant would whisper to him repeatedly: "Look behind thee; remember thou art a man."[16] Armed with this warning, he could with impunity appear here and now with his hands and face painted vermilion to match the vermilion face of the statue of Jove in the temple of Jove. This statue was made of simple terra cotta in the ancient Etruscan manner and was housed in a wooden temple sheathed with terra cotta tiles. Camillus, at this crucial moment, was the special agent of Jove. The chariot was driven from the Field of Mars to this simple temple of Jove, preceded by the prisoners of war and the booty. According to tradition, the booty borne in the triumph of Camillus included the thousand pounds of gold which the Gauls had recently collected as ransom for the City of Jove. Last came the victorious army, further tempering the dangerous exaltation of Camillus by hurling humorous gibes at him. Time triumphed and place triumphed, and this was clear from the lifelike waxen images, carried in this procession, of the ancestors of Camillus, which would ordinarily grace his home. These ancestors too had served this city, not merely cities in general; they had served not merely in general but at some moment of history, in some hour of Rome's dire need. Through them, through Camillus, and through Rome, the will of Jove had repeatedly intervened in human history.[17]

The memory of Rome contained this triumph along with many others over foes less deadly than the barbarous Gauls: with their Latin neighbors, with the wealthy Etruscans, with the warlike Samnites from the Apennines to the southeast who kept preying on the rich plains of Campania and on Rome's ally there, Capua. For twenty-one years, from 325 to 304, Rome fought these mountain tribes and their Etruscan allies as well, and in the end she triumphed. For eight years, from 298 to 290, she fought the Samnites again, while she beat off attacks from the north by Etruscans again, by Gauls again; and again after a bloody struggle she triumphed.

Along with her Second Founder, Camillus, and along with Horatius at the Tiber bridge, Rome could remember her other military heroes, who served the will of Jove because they served the will of his She-Wolf City. In the early days, when Rome had driven out her last king, the Etruscan Tarquin, and when the Etruscans besieged Rome, a young Roman noble named Mucius Scaevola stole into the Etruscans' camp and tried to slay their leader, Porsena. He was captured and Porsena threatened to burn him alive.

> Whereupon Mucius, exclaiming, "Look, that you may see how cheap they hold their bodies whose eyes are fixed upon renown!" thrust his hand into the fire that was kindled for the sacrifice.[18]

Porsena released him.

If one believed her ancient legends, Rome had a right to infer that it was her devotion to the gods as much as the courage of her sons that defended her from extinction by the enemies who ringed her round. Indeed, *devotio* meant among other things a formal sacrifice, made in order to bind the gods to help the city. In 362, in the middle of the Forum, the central market place of Rome, the ground suddenly gave way and left a deep chasm. The soothsayers announced that the city could not hope to endure unless the Romans offered up on that spot whatever constituted the city's chief strength. What could that thing be? Clearly, cried a young soldier named Marcus Curtius, that thing was Roman arms and valor.

> A hush ensued, as he turned to the temples of the immortal gods which rise above the Forum, and to the Capitol, and stretching forth his hands, now to heaven, and now to the yawning chasm and to the gods below, devoted himself to death. After which, mounted on a horse caparisoned with all possible splendour, he plunged fully armed into the gulf; and crowds of men and women threw offerings and fruits in after him.[19]

Twenty-two years later, the consul Publius Decius Mus, when battle with the Latins was going against the Romans, devoted himself even more correctly, for Marcus Valerius, a state pontiff or priest, was conveniently near. Decius called out to him in a loud voice:

> "We have need of Heaven's help, Marcus Valerius. Come therefore, state pontiff of the Roman People, dictate the words, that I may devote myself to save the legions." The pontiff bade him don the purple-bordered toga, and with veiled head and one hand thrust out from the toga and touching his chin, stand upon a spear that was laid under his feet, and say as follows: "Janus, Jupiter, Father Mars, Quirinus, Bellona, Lares, divine Novensiles, divine Indigites, ye gods in whose power are both we and our enemies, and you, divine Manes,—I invoke and worship you, I beseech and crave your favour, that you prosper the might and the victory of the Roman People of the Quirites, and visit the foes of the Roman People of the Quirites with fear, shuddering, and death. As I have pronounced the words, even so in behalf of the republic of the Roman People of the Quirites, and of the army, the legions, the auxiliaries of the Roman People of the Quirites, do I devote the legions and auxiliaries of the enemy, together with myself, to the divine Manes and to Earth."[20]

Then he armed himself, vaulted onto his horse, and plunged alone into the thickest of the foe, where a rain of missiles brought him death and the gods a heavy obligation. The enemy was instantly terrified and the Roman army was inspired with courage. The Romans, "their spirits relieved of religious fear,"[21] pressed on.

Livy even relayed an ancient account of how this man's son, of the same name, also devoted himself at the battle of Sentinum in 295, in which a Roman army routed the Gauls and ultimately drove them back into the Po Valley. This second Decius was devoted with the same form of prayer and in the same habit his father, Publius Decius, had commanded to be used, when he was devoted at the Veseris, in the Latin war; and having added to the usual prayers that he was driving before him fear and panic, blood and carnage, and the wrath of gods celestial and gods infernal, and should blight with a curse the standards, weapons and armour of the enemy, and that one and the same place should witness his own destruction and that of the Gauls and Samnites,—having uttered, I say, these imprecations upon himself and the enemy, he spurred his charger against the Gallic lines, where he saw that they were thickest, and hurling himself against the weapons of the enemy met his death.[22]

These ancient tales that Livy included in his history had been passed down from generation to generation, perhaps embroidered, to inspire in the young a devotion to Rome. But, accurate or inaccurate, they are eloquent of the Romans' scrupulous observance of religious formulae. The gods were a constant and terrifying threat to Rome. The Romans were especially terrified by extraordinary portents and prodigies, and most of all on the eve of battle. Before engaging, they, like the Greeks, demanded favorable auspices, and if they fed the sacred chickens and the chickens refused to eat, they were willing to lose a military advantage rather than risk battle. In the days of the kings a snake was seen in the royal palace, and the king was so terrified by the portent that he determined to consult the oracle of Delphi. And

not daring to trust the oracle's reply to anybody else, he sent two of his sons, through strange lands, as they were then, and over stranger seas, to Greece.[23]

In 397 when the lake in the Alban Wood rose to a suspicious height, they sent to Delphi for advice. They were sensibly ordered to drain off some of the lake; they would then capture Veii; after that, they should bring an ample gift to Delphi and stop neglecting their ancestral rites. Later, during the Samnite Wars, the Republic consulted Delphi again and was ordered to set up two statues. One should be a statue of the wisest of the Greeks; the other, of the bravest of the Greeks. The Romans did so, in the Forum, choosing Alcibiades as the bravest and Pythagoras as the wisest.

These consultations with Delphi and these statues of Alcibiades and Pythagoras were far from meaning that the Roman Republic in any real sense shared Greek culture. True, the Roman alphabet, Rome's adoption of coinage in place of barter, and even the Greek traders on the Aventine Mount were contacts. And as the Roman Alliance spread down the Italian peninsula, the Greek influences the Romans most felt were those in southern Italy and Sicily: Pythagoras had taught in Croton in the sixth century and Alcibiades had helped lead the Athenian armada against Syracuse in the fifth. Rome had got rid of her last king only some nineteen years before the Athenians in 490 conquered a Persian force at Marathon. At Athens, Aeschylus, Sophocles, and Euripides had each won a first prize for tragedy before the Decemvirs wrote the first Roman laws, in the Twelve Tables. While Athens was building the Parthenon and Phidias was sculpting and Aristophanes was mocking the follies of war in his comedies, Rome was doggedly conquering or reconquering Latins, Gauls, and Etruscans, as well as Greek cities in southern Italy. During the fourth century, when Plato and Aristotle were teaching, when Epaminondas of Thebes destroyed Spartan hegemony, when Demosthenes delivered his *Philippics* against Philip of Macedon, and when Philip won control of Greece, Rome was fighting thirteen wars, some of them desperate struggles. These wars preoccupied Rome for about sixty-four years.

Always Rome's two basic problems were to impose peace on her neighbors and to secure the *pax deorum,* literally the peace of the gods. This covenant with the gods involved, as Cicero would write long afterward, fear and ceremonial rites.[24] It was the task of the college of pontiffs, the state priesthood, to keep, or restore when broken, this pact with the gods. It was the task of the other officials of the Republic to obey the will of the gods as construed by the pontiffs and by their subordinate augurs, haruspices, and soothsayers. It was the task of private citizens to obey the will of the officials of the Roman Republic. And in each family it was the task of a man's wife, sons, daughters, daughters-in-law, grandchildren, and slaves to obey the Father of the Family, who sacrificed to the domestic deities, the Lares and Penates, on behalf of every member.

This was Roman discipline: unyielding authority and ungrudging obedience. The long chain of command began with Jove, father of gods and men. His will must be obeyed. Homer had declared in the fifth line of the *Iliad* that all that happened at Troy happened in order that the will of Zeus, the Romans' Jove, should be fulfilled. But the Greek word for will that Homer used was *boule,* a word associated with plan and counsel. The Roman word was *voluntas,* whose root meaning was simply wish or desire. The Greeks loved their gods, and the exquisitely beautiful statues they

17

made of them gave solid proof of their love, as did the conversations they reported holding with those whom their sculptors carved or molded. But the Roman gods were distant, somewhat impersonal, and sometimes mere abstractions. They were vague forces often called *numina*, and *numen* originally meant the nod of a god's head. That nod must be obeyed, reverently, decorously, decently. "Towards the gods," wrote an early Latin poet, "you should be scrupulous, but be not superstitious."[25] *Religio* was legalistically correct worship; what the Romans meant by *superstitio* was worship that involved an unseemly display of emotion such as some Asian cults exhibited. The Roman in general used his religion to discover at what hour and at what place he could safely do something he himself already willed to do. He even tried like the two Decii to use the correct incantation, which would compel the gods to help him get what he himself willed. The Roman's own *voluntas* chose the end and chose the gods as means. This was what Xenophon did when he consulted the Delphic oracle about joining the Ten Thousand in Asia, and what Socrates held to be misuse of the oracle.[26] But then, Xenophon was a noble, a soldier, a man of action, and a voluntarist; and so were the heroes Rome remembered and celebrated in story.

Socrates, who placed speculation and contemplation higher than practical action, was fond of distinguishing between two forms of argument in which men engage. One was eristic, in which each opponent tries only to win,[27] and to impose his own opinion. The other was dialectic, in which the basic purpose of both opponents was not to impose an opinion but to discover truth. When Socrates questioned Apollo at Delphi, he questioned dialectically, in the sense that he hoped that he himself, at least, would think and learn. Xenophon questioned eristically, to find the means appropriate to his own humanly chosen end, to serve his own *voluntas* and not the *boule* of Zeus as declared by Apollo, son of Zeus and guide to men. That was how the Romans consulted their gods. And why not? They were practical men. When they went to court for a client, they went, not to understand justice better, but to win a case. When they went to war, they learned, not what Achilles learned, but how best to win future wars.

When Rome's long struggle with her neighbors had apparently ended in her favor, the Greek world of Alexander sent the Italian peninsula not wisdom or philosophic inquiry but force. About 338, some two years before Alexander succeeded Philip as King of Macedon, Tarentum, a Greek port inside the heel of Italy, called in a Spartan king to defend it against the hill tribes of Lucania, but he was defeated. A few years later Tarentum appealed to Alexander, King of Epirus, uncle and brother-in-law of Alexander of Macedon, then warring in Asia. Alexander of Epirus crossed the Adriatic with an army, fought the hill tribes, and also gained control of most of Magna Graecia. But Tarentum came to distrust its rescuer, and in the end he was killed by Lucanians. A third appeal brought over Cleonymus, son of a Spartan king, with a third army of mercenaries, but the Tarentines soon quarreled with him and he returned to Greece.

Rome, too, had been drawn into the affairs of Magna Graecia. Capua and other Greek cities in Campania sought and obtained a Roman alliance against the predatory mountain tribes of Samnium, in the southern Apennines. This of course embroiled Rome with the Samnites, who had previously helped her against the Gauls. In 321, two years after Alexander the Great died in Babylon, a Roman army of 20,000 men was trapped by the Samnites in the Caudine Forks, a defile in the southern Apennines, and was forced to surrender. But by now Rome and her Latin Allies could draw on a free population of probably 750,000:[28] she increased her levies and raised her field army to between 35,000 and 40,000 men. She also borrowed from Samnite tactics.

In the third century, the Academy Plato had founded and the Lyceum Aristotle had established still flourished in Athens but found a rival, the Museum, which Ptolemy I set up in Alexandria for teaching, research, and literary work. The Museum became the center for the extraordinary flowering of mathematics and natural science that made the third century the great period of the Hellenistic intellect. Rome spent this third century fighting seven wars, which covered about seventy years. The first of these struggles was the Third Samnite War, ending in 290.

In 281 Tarentum, fearing Rome's intrusions into the affairs of Magna Graecia, called in another king of Epirus, named Pyrrhus, with 25,000 men. In the Hellenistic world he was generally considered the ablest commander of his day. Pyrrhus met a Roman army at Heraclea. His phalanx of pikemen could do nothing against the Roman infantry, whose tactics were more flexible and who were already celebrated for "perseverance and endurance."[29] But the horses of Rome's cavalry were terrified by his elephants, and Pyrrhus outflanked the Roman infantry and won his battle. The Romans showed no sign of discouragement, and Pyrrhus sent an envoy to Rome to try negotiation. According to later tradition, this envoy reported that the senate impressed him as a council of many kings, and that, as for the people, he was afraid it might prove to be a Lernaean hydra for them to fight against, since the consul already had twice as many soldiers collected as those who faced their enemies before, and there were many times as many Romans still who were capable of bearing arms.[30]

At Asculum, a year later, the elephants nearly won for Pyrrhus again, but the Roman infantry fell back on their fortified camp. Magna Graecia had gone over to him; so had the Lucanians and the Samnites. He marched into Latium, got within fifty miles of Rome, and tried to detach Rome's Latin allies, but to no avail. He proved he could outgeneral Rome, but it did him no good. His losses were heavy, Rome's manpower was indeed a hydra, and, when some of the Greek cities of Sicily invited Pyrrhus over to help them drive out of the island their centuries-old enemies, the Carthaginians, Pyrrhus promptly sought glory in Sicily. When, however, the Greeks there began to quarrel with him and when his allies in Magna Graecia, now hard pressed by Rome, begged him to return, he left for Italy again. There the Roman army made the interesting discovery that elephants, if wounded by javelins, had a way of losing their heads and trampling their own army. When at last it became apparent that Pyrrhus could liberate neither Greek Sicily from Carthage nor Magna Graecia from Rome, he salvaged eight thousand of his infantry and five hundred horse, went home to Epirus, recruited some Gallic mercenaries, and attacked Macedonia. After many adventures he met his death in 272 in a street battle in Argos.

Eight years later, Rome had again subjected all of Magna Graecia. She now controlled the whole of Italy south of the Po Valley, which she still called Cisalpine Gaul, or Gaul this side of the Alps. Pyrrhus had won many victories over her troops, but they had all turned out to be Pyrrhic victories. He was the last of the four military adventurers who had led their mercenaries out of Alexander's Hellenistic Cosmopolis to liberate the Western Greeks, in Magna Graecia or in Sicily, from neighboring tribes, from Carthage, or from Rome. It was symbolic of Rome's success that the year before Pyrrhus was killed in Argos, King Ptolemy of Egypt, one of the three most powerful states in Cosmopolis, entered into a treaty of friendship with the Roman Republic. The Roman Public Thing had constructed a network of alliances with all the cities and tribes of peninsular Italy, alliances which guaranteed Rome money-tribute from many of them and immense military manpower. Many of them had been forced also to surrender land, on which Rome planted military colonies. Those colonies answered two purposes: they made it risky for Rome's allies to revolt against her control, and they helped to satisfy the land hunger of her own growing population. The same two objects had been served in the fifth century by the cleruchies, or military colonies, of imperial Athens.

Nevertheless, land hunger remained a problem, as it had in most of the Hellenistic world. In that world, industrial processes lacked power-driven machinery and could find a mass market only in a very restricted sense. Industry could therefore employ few hands. Trade, it is true, played a larger role. But early Rome left foreign trade in the hands of the Etruscans, the Greeks, and the Carthaginians. Perhaps the first treaty the Republic signed with Carthage, in 348,[31] stipulated that Carthage should not pillage the coast of Latium, but it reflected no Roman interest in sharing Carthaginian markets. Indeed, when Rome moved from barter to coinage as late as 451, she issued only heavy copper coins, and she never issued silver coin until 269, when Pyrrhus had been driven out of Italy, when Magna Graecia had been reintegrated into the Roman system of alliances, and when trade with Magna Graecia made silver coin necessary. In Rome almost everybody worked on the land, or owned land that others tilled for him, either for a wage or as slaves. Of those who were landless, most sold their labor to those with land.

The Roman Republic, like the early Greek republics, had been a community of farmers centered on a market town. With two or three acres of the soil of Latium in his possession a man could make a living and still serve in the army during the summer dry season before returning home for fall planting. Wars were an off-season occupation, and in the early days a natural supplement to farming, since they included lifting cattle, seizing the enemy's harvest, acquiring slaves for farm hands, and even acquiring some more good earth. It was not until 403 at the siege of Veii that a Roman army wintered in the field.[32] Nevertheless, smallholders with large families often could not provide their sons with enough land to become prosperous smallholders themselves. Even with sufficient land they often had too little capital, whether in cattle, seed, provisions, or cash, to weather bad seasons. They therefore fell into debt and lost their farms to more prosperous neighbors. The economic gap between the patrician landowner and the plebeian steadily increased as big farms devoured neighboring small farms. As early as the sixth century, King Servius had to pare down the estates of the nobles, who had illegally taken possession of state lands. And wealth was so unequally distributed that this same Servius

> called the rich "money-givers," because they paid the expenses of the State, and named those who had less than 1,500 denarii or nothing at all except their own persons, "child-givers."[33]

The Latin word which Servius used for child-givers was *proletarii*, because what these proletarians could give the Republic was *proles*, offspring.

From the beginning of the Republic, the land question and the related problem of debts were the very stuff of politics: of the Twelve Tables which the Decemvirs drew up, of the Aventine Secession of the plebs from the Roman Public Thing, of the constant class tension in Rome, of the development of constitutional theory and practice. The repeated secessions of the plebs made explicit the class war in the Republic. But what distinguished that war from the wars that tore so many of the Greek republics in two was that Rome found means to institutionalize the latent violence in her class structure by uniting all her citizens in wars that subjected and exploited their neighbors.

King Servius had found it no longer possible to exclude plebeians from the honorable profession of arms. He therefore instituted the census, so as to determine which citizens had enough money to equip themselves for military service. War brought the plebeians a share of the pillage and sometimes an allotment of public land, surrendered by the vanquished. The hero Cincinnatus was supposed to have said in 480 that

> We are somehow fated to enjoy the favour of the gods in larger measure when warring than when at peace.[34]

Even so, the plebeian had every practical reason to long for political equality with the patrician. He learned early that, even if he helped win land with his sword and even if he won land laws that promised him an allotment, the patrician often managed legally or illegally to get land, while the plebeian got none. The various popular assemblies were organized in such fashion as to make his vote worth less than that of the patrician, or their decisions were subject to ratification by a Senate dominated by patricians, or the exodus of plebeians to military colonies left the assemblies in the hands of a demoralized urban proletariat, or the tribunes of the plebs were corrupted by the patricians. The secret ballot was not introduced until 139 B.C., and accordingly the patron-client relationship gave the patricians partial control of the plebeian vote. Most high offices were long closed to plebeians, so that it was mostly patricians who administered the laws. Finally, priestly offices were the monopoly of the patricians, and Rome's priests had a way, when legislative reforms were brought up, of adjourning debate on the grounds that the auspices were unfavorable. Although the plebeian was considered good enough to die for the Republic, he was legally forbidden to intermarry with patricians.

In 445, according to Livy, a tribune of the plebs, Gaius Canuleius, proposed to sanction intermarriage. Although one of the grievances of the plebs was that patricians preyed on the wives of plebeians, the idea that the offspring of such a union might be classed as a patrician horrified the Senate:

> What tremendous schemes had Gaius Canuleius set on foot! He was aiming to contaminate the *gentes* and throw the auspices, both public and private, into confusion, that nothing might be pure, nothing unpolluted; so that, when all distinctions had been obliterated, no man might recognise either himself or his kindred. For what else, they asked, was the object of promiscuous marriages, if not that plebeians and patricians might mingle together almost like the beasts? The son of such a marriage would be ignorant to what blood and to what worship he belonged; he would pertain half to the patricians, half to the plebs, and be at strife even within himself. It was not enough for the disturbers of the rabble to play havoc with all divine and human institutions: they must now aim at the consulship. And whereas they had at first merely suggested in conversations that one of the two consuls should be chosen from the plebeians, they were now proposing a law that the people should elect consuls at its pleasure from patriciate or plebs.[35]

At the very time when these opinions were finding expression in the senate, Canuleius held forth in this fashion in behalf of his laws and in opposition to the consuls: "How greatly the patricians despised you, Quirites, how unfit they deemed you to live in the City, within the same walls as themselves, I think I have often observed before, but never more clearly than at this very moment, when they are rallying so fiercely against these proposals of ours. Yet what else do we intend by them than to remind our fellow citizens that we are of them, and that, though we possess not the same wealth, still we dwell in the same City they inhabit? In the one bill we seek the right of intermarriage, which is customarily granted to neighbours and foreigners—indeed we have granted citizenship, which is more than intermarriage, even to defeated enemies;—in the other we propose no innovation, but reclaim and seek to exercise a popular right, to wit that the Roman People shall confer office upon whom it will. What reason is there, pray, why they should confound heaven and earth; why they should almost have attacked me just now in the senate; why they should declare that they will place no restraint on force, and should threaten to violate our sacrosanct authority? If the Roman People is granted a free vote, that so it may commit the consulship to what hands it likes, if even the plebeian is not cut off from the hope of gaining the highest honours—if he shall be deserving of the highest honours—will this City of ours be unable to endure? Is her dominion at an end? When we raise the question of making a plebeian consul, is it the same as if we were to say that a slave or a freedman should attain that office? Have you any conception of the contempt in which you are held? They would take from you, were it possible, a part of this daylight. That you breathe, that you speak, that you have the shape of men, fills them with resentment. Nay, they assert, if you please, that it is sinning against Heaven to elect a plebeian consul."[36]

But, Canuleius persisted, as if addressing himself to the Senate,

Who can question that in a city founded for eternity and of incalculable growth, new powers, priesthoods, and rights of families and individuals, must be established? Was not this very provision, that patricians and plebeians might not intermarry, enacted by the decemvirs a few years since, with the worst effect on the community and the gravest injustice to the plebs? Or can there be any greater or more signal insult than to hold a portion of the state unworthy of intermarriage, as though it were defiled? What else is this but to suffer exile within the same walls and banishment? They guard against having us for connections or relations, against the mingling of our blood with theirs. Why, if this pollutes that fine nobility of yours—which many of you, being of Alban or of Sabine origin, possess not by virtue of race or blood, but through co-optation into the patriciate, having been chosen either by the kings, or, after their expulsion, by decree of the people—could you not keep it pure by your own private counsels, neither taking wives from the plebs nor permitting your daughters and sisters to marry out of the patriciate? No plebeian would offer violence to a patrician maiden: that is a patrician vice. No one would have compelled anybody to enter a compact of marriage against his will. But let me tell you that in the statutory prohibition and annulment of intermarriage between patricians and plebeians we have indeed at last an insult to the plebs. Why, pray, do you not bring in a law that there shall be no intermarrying of rich and poor? That which has always and everywhere been a matter of private policy, that a woman might marry into whatever family it had been arranged, that a man might take a wife from that house where he had engaged himself, you would subject to the restraint of a most arrogant law, that thereby you might break up our civil society and make two states out of one. Why do you not enact that a plebeian shall not live near a patrician, nor go on the same road? That he shall not enter the same festive company? That he shall not stand by his side in the same Forum? For what real difference does it make if a patrician takes a plebeian wife, or a plebeian a patrician? What right, pray, is invaded? The children of course take the father's rank. There is nothing we are seeking to gain from marriage with you, except that we should be accounted men and citizens. Neither have you any reason to oppose us, unless you delight in vying with each other how you may outrage and humiliate us.[37]

And so the commons are ready, consuls, for those wars you deal in, be they feigned or genuine, if you give them back their right of intermarriage, and make this a single state at last; if you enable them to coalesce, to unite, to merge with you in domestic alliances; if the hope of attaining honours is held out to strenuous men and brave; if they are granted a share in the partnership of government; if, in the enjoyment of equal liberty, they are allowed to govern and obey in turn, with the annual change of magistrates. If anyone shall prevent these reforms, you may talk of wars, and multiply them in the telling; but nobody will give in his name, nobody will take up arms, nobody will fight for haughty masters with whom he has no association in the honours of the state nor in the marriages of private life.[38]

The law permitting intermarriage probably passed. If it did, little if any intermarriage apparently resulted, at least for a long time.

The role of war in maintaining the patricians in power was by 406 as obvious as the use of religion to accomplish the same result. According to Livy, the plebeian tribunes

persistently declared that it was the plebs with whom the senators were chiefly at war; them they deliberately plagued with campaigning and exposed to be slaughtered by the enemy; them they kept at a distance from the City, and assigned to foreign service, lest they might have thoughts, if they remained peaceably at home, of liberty and colonies, and might agitate for public lands or the free use of their votes.[39]

Again, in 380, the tribunes accused the Senate:

from Antium the legions had been marched to Satricum, from Satricum to Velitrae, from there to Tusculum; now it was the Latins, the Hernici and the Praenestini who were threatened with attack, more out of hatred of Rome's citizens than of her enemies. The object was to wear the plebeians out with service and give them no time to take breath in the City, or leisure to bethink them of liberty or to stand in the assembly, where they might sometimes hear the voice of a tribune urging the reduction of interest and the removal of their other grievances.[40]

More than once the tribunes of the plebs vetoed a military levy until they had extorted some measure of reform. For example, in 378, the censors, elected to investigate debt, suddenly announced that the Volscians had crossed the border.

> Yet with all this alarm, the danger from abroad was so far from restraining dissensions at home, that on the contrary the tribunes but acted with the greater violence, in exerting their powers to block the levy; until the senate submitted to their terms, and agreed that till the war was finished no one should pay a war-tax or give judgment in a case of debt.[41]

There were of course some conservatives like Appius Claudius always ready to suspect that the plebs would be content if their tribunes did not constantly, from motives of personal ambition, stir them up against their betters. Or, as Claudius himself put it to the plebs in 403,

> Indeed they are like quack-salvers seeking employment, since they desire that there should always be some disease in the body politic, that there may be something which you may call them in to cure. Pray, are you tribunes defending the commons, or attacking them?[42]

But pillage and pay did more than Claudius could do to preserve the loyalty of the plebs. In 406 the Senate had taken the initiative in providing modest pay for soldiers who had always previously served at their own expense as embattled farmers, in the hope, at most, of pillage or land. Although plebeian pressure steadily opened offices to the commons and even resulted by 367 in the election of a plebeian consul, the plebeian voter usually voted for patrician candidates rather than for men of his own class. Partly, the old, aristocratic, conservative traditions of an agricultural society held the plebeian voter in line. Partly, the somewhat chilly dignity of the patrician could thaw in the most flattering way when he put on the especially whitened toga, the *toga candida*, as a candidate for office, and solicited votes. Partly, the patrician still cherished a group of family retainers, or "clients," whom he defended in the law courts, protected generally, and even helped financially when the need arose; and this relic of a semifeudal rural society was exceedingly useful in mustering votes. And yet, despite these obstacles, high offices continued to be opened to plebeians. Nevertheless, by 300, two brothers with the name Ogulnius, both of whom were tribunes, proposed a law that would allow successful plebeian candidates to enter even that holy of holies, the state priesthood, so long and so jealously guarded by the patricians. They

> proposed a law, that whereas there were then four augurs and four pontiffs and it was desired to augment the number of priests, four pontiffs and five augurs should be added, and should all be taken from the plebs. . . . But since they were to be added from the plebs, the patricians were as distressed by the proposal as they had been when they saw the consulship thrown open. They pretended that the gods were more concerned than they themselves were: the gods would see to it that their rites should not be contaminated . . . They . . . beheld their adversaries . . . in full possession of all the things for which they had striven with dubious prospects of success—repeated consulships, censorships, and triumphs.[43]

Appius Claudius, the intransigent patrician, of course spoke against this new outrage. But Publius Decius Mus spoke also: of how his father, a plebeian, had made the gods heed his prayer for the Roman army when he devoted himself in a battle with the Latins and thereby won a Roman victory. Then he cried to Claudius that

> our . . . tribune . . . has not desired to oust you patricians, Appius, from your places, but that men of the plebs may help you in the administration also of divine affairs, even as they help you in other and human matters, to the measure of their strength.[44]

And it was Decius, not Claudius, who won.

The long years of war that gave the Roman Republic control over peninsular Italy and that witnessed four armed interventions launched from the Hellenistic world gave Rome the appearance of having remained what the Romulus legends declared her: a city of outlaws and robbers suckled by a she-wolf, a city of lovers of violence. But that appearance was deceptive in one respect. Certainly any Greek who was fond of etymology might be pardoned for noting that the Greek transliteration of *Roma, Rome,* happened conveniently to be a Greek word for violence. Certainly the temple of the god Janus, which was opened only when the Republic was at war, had, according to tradition, never been closed but once.[45] Certainly violence played an enormous role in Rome's history: though she won some of peninsular Italy by diplomacy, she won most of it by the sword. Within the city the relation of patrician to plebeian was one of tension, often one of brutal oppression tempered by last-minute compromise. As for the relation between free man and slave, this, as in democratic Athens, was necessarily a relation of force, and the Roman was a more brutal master if only because he had perhaps less imagination than the Athenian. Witnesses to that brutality are the successive slave revolts that Rome put down, in 501, in 499, in 498; whereas before the Roman conquest Athens seems to have experienced none, except at the Sunium silver mines during the Peloponnesian War. In 419 bands of slaves marched on Rome in an unsuccessful effort to burn it. Moreover, at various times Rome's allies tried in vain to throw off her control. In the allied cities the populace would often have preferred independence, if Roman armies had not been available to the Roman patriciate to maintain local oligarchies like itself in power.

In short, the City of the She-Wolf controlled peninsular Italy largely by organized violence. On the other hand, the violence of intruders from the Hellenistic world, such as Pyrrhus, tended to be aimless, even if its declared purpose was to liberate the Western Greeks from barbarous neighbors, from Carthage, from Rome. The She-Wolf's depredations did bring order. She protected the cities of Italy, whether Latin, Italic, or Greek, from pillaging mountain tribes; Etruria, from the Cisalpine Gauls. She protected the cities from each other. In each city she protected men of substance from revolution. She charged a good commission, in the form of military support, for her services, whether or not she fixed the rate too high. She pacified Italy at a time when the Hellenistic world was still torn by war, both foreign and civil. Whether or not Jove really commissioned the Roman people to rule, they were rapidly on the way to becoming "the strongest" people in the whole Mediterranean basin, and thereby to claiming Alexander's Cosmopolis. The only power that stood a chance of preventing Roman domination and of claiming that heritage was Carthage.

Rome's generals were mediocre strategists, if only because they were not professionals like Pyrrhus: Rome's armies were commanded in the field by her consuls, whose tenure of office, unless they were re-elected, was but one year. One result of this rotation was that outgoing commanders often distorted their strategy rather than leave the credit of victory to a military successor who was also a potential political opponent at home. The armies themselves were less highly trained than mercenaries of the sort that Pyrrhus brought over from Epirus. But the Roman soldier had the perseverance and endurance that the historian Appian later described; he had the *constantia* or steadfastness, that Livy[46] described, which his enemies impolitely called *pertinacia*, or stubbornness.[47] This steadfastness sprang from harsh discipline, high morale, and perhaps an undeveloped imagination. The morale sprang in large part from the Roman's sense that his city was commissioned by the gods to establish and extend law and order. And since Rome had abundant and growing manpower, the soldier knew that when an army was destroyed or ambushed a recruit would replace him, that Rome had a way of losing the first battle but winning the war.

The same soldier believed that he was fighting for the right, because aside from war Rome's central passion was law, a law that bound her to the gods, that bound the gods to help her against her enemies, and that bound each citizen to his fellow, each soldier to the man who fought at his side. Rome's memories of the monarchy included Numa, who had supposedly learned wisdom from the Greek philosopher Pythagoras before he became King of Rome.[48] Once chosen King,

> he prepared to give the new City, founded by force of arms, a new foundation in law, statutes, and observances.[49]

And when Livy had set down the hazy traditions of the monarchy and had come to the establishment, about 508 B.C., of what from his point of view was the aristocratic Roman Republic, he wrote with pride that

> laws superior in authority to men will henceforth be my theme. This liberty was the more grateful as the last king had been so great a tyrant.[50]

Half a century later the Romans reportedly dispatched an embassy of three men

> on a mission to Athens, with orders to copy the famous laws of Solon, and acquaint themselves with the institutions, customs, and laws of the other Greek states.[51]

Solon, the poet, merchant, traveler, and thinker, had declared his intention of joining might with right, of somehow marrying economic and political power with justice. But what Rome wanted from Athens was practical, tested institutions, customs, and laws. She therefore felt her way, improvising solutions, naming consuls to replace her kings, praetors to run her courts, quaestors to handle her finances, aediles to supervise necessary public works, censors to take the census and later to regulate morals. Her constitution grew by such improvisation, by constant adaptation to new needs. This process she kept steady by her love of precedent and her reverence for the *mos majorum*, ancestral custom. As her earliest epic poet put it,

> On manners and on men of olden time
> Stands firm the Roman State.[52]

If there was injustice in the Roman Republic, perhaps Rome was less interested in a high consideration of justice than in public order and in the incontestable authority of the Republic. The aristocracy that ruled her had never been torn by the family vendettas that tore the aristocratic republics of Greece. The class struggle had often been tense but had never turned into civil war. Both patrician and plebeian were guided by an instinct for legal procedure, for compromise, and at least in theory for the sanctity of property, especially private property. Rome was deeply convinced that her dealings with other states were just and that treaties with other states were sacred, as contracts at home between citizens of Rome were sacred. She was convinced that she herself punctiliously observed her treaties as she did her contracts with her gods, which achieved and maintained the Pax Deorum she so prized. Some of her foreign victims were less sure of Roman virtue. Pontius the Samnite demanded of her:

> Will you never, when you have been beaten, lack excuses for not holding to your covenants? You gave hostages to Porsinna—and withdrew them by a trick. You ransomed your City from the Gauls with gold—and cut them down as they were receiving the gold. You pledged us peace, on condition that we gave you back your captured legions—and you nullify the peace. And always you contrive to give the fraud some colour of legality.[53]

But Rome showed skill in construing inconvenient treaties and inconvenient contracts, and she had no intention of putting herself in the Samnites' shoes. She was sure enough of her own virtue to judge her own case against Samnium; no idea of legal conflict of interest deterred her. The will of Rome, commissioned by Jove to carry out his will, was guided by no intellectual search for justice, since Rome was herself the earthly source of justice. Over and over, when some half-defeated general attempted to negotiate with his Roman opponent, the Roman insisted that he first lay down his arms and submit to the good faith of the Roman people.

The half-defeated general might demur that he would then be helpless in negotiation. But the Roman would calmly insist. For how could justice be done until the source of justice, which was Rome, had been secured? Once the enemy laid down his arms, Rome usually granted surprisingly moderate terms. The conquered enemy was then offered a treaty: in exchange for obedience he got protection. What was more, the She-Wolf allowed him to join a wolf pack that grew ever larger. Of course, he might later regret his lost freedom. But it would then be too late; for if he rebelled and broke his treaty, then Rome remembered what the Gallic chieftain had said to her when she herself lay helpless: "Woe to the conquered!"

More and more, amongst Rome and her allies, appeal to arms was giving way to appeals for redress under Roman law. The peninsular empire that Rome now headed resembled in some ways Rome herself. Both were strongly hierarchical. The Roman patrician hoped to win his way by popular election from aedile to quaestor to praetor to consul to triumphator, in order that his portrait bust in wax might one day take its place with those of his more famous ancestors in the *atria*, or patios, of his descendants' homes. This *cursus honorum*, or race for honors, he could win only by serving the Roman Thing, the concrete embodiment of the Greek idea of the common good. His means of winning were the sword and the word; courage and skill in battle, skill in rhetoric. He was therefore schooled primarily in fighting: on the battlefield, in the law court, in the public assembly. As time went on, even the despised plebeian was permitted to enter that race. As a "new man" he would not inspire the deference that Rome accorded to those of famous patrician lineage, but his descendants might hope to inspire it.

Service to the Roman Thing judged not only the race for honors among Roman citizens but the race for honors among all states within the Roman Alliance. Thus most of the cities of Latium received important civil rights under Roman law, including the right to vote in Rome under certain conditions. The cities of southern Etruria and of the Sabine country, which were farther from Rome and less familiar with the Latin tongue, were accorded the same civil rights as the Latins, but no Roman suffrage. Taken together, Rome and all these other cities included about a million inhabitants. All these cities were subject to the same military draft and the same taxes as Rome herself. The cities and tribes of the rest of Italy were bound to Rome by separate, permanent treaties and were called Allies. They were forbidden to make treaties with other states, so that in effect Rome controlled their foreign relations. They were required to furnish troops when Rome made war, and these troops served under Roman generals. The Greek states on the coasts of southern Italy were exceptions: these furnished only ships and crews. None of the Allies paid taxes of any kind to Rome. These Allies, as distinguished from the more closely federated states, contained some two million inhabitants. Thus the Roman Alliance was formed of various classes of city-states, arranged in a roughly concentric pattern of both rights and duties under Roman law. But it was possible to move upward from one class to another.

The whole structure of the Alliance invited a kind of Cursus Honorum among communities as among individuals, a competition under law for full participation in the Roman Thing. This was something the Athenian Empire had not offered. Nor had any other Greek state. On the other hand, the attempts of the Greek states to discover and apply the federal principle as equals never tempted Rome. She did not desire to join freely with her neighbors to create a new and better city of man, since she was certain that what concretely existed on the Tiber was more worthwhile than any imagined city could be; and besides, she was already bound by religion to the gods themselves. She started, not from Alexander's idea of Cosmopolis, but from a Thing. And with pride she watched the Thing grow. She did not start from the idea of law, but built on the actually operating laws and courts and institutions of her early past, anchored securely to the practical experience of her chief citizens, the Mos Majorum, the custom of their ancestors. But although Rome's treatment of her Allies did invite a Cursus Honorum among them for participation in the Roman Public Thing, Rome always assumed sole right to judge that competition. As early as 340, delegates from a group of cities known as the Latin League, restive under Rome's tightened control, demanded of the Roman Senate that the Roman Alliance be an association of equals:

> One consul should be chosen from Rome, the other from Latium, the senate should be drawn in equal proportions from both nations, there should be one people and one state; and that we may have the same seat of empire and the same name for all, by all means let this rather be our city, since one side must make concessions,—and may good come of it to both peoples!—and let us all be known as Romans.[54]

Immediately, a Roman consul turned indignantly to the statue of Jove and cried,

Hear, Jupiter, these wicked words! Hear ye, Law and Right! Shalt thou behold, O Jupiter, alien consuls and an alien senate in thy consecrated temple, thyself overpowered and taken captive? Are these the covenants, Latins, that Tullus, the Roman king, made with your Alban forefathers, that Lucius Tarquinius afterwards made with you? Remember you not the battle at Lake Regillus? Have you so forgot your old disasters and our goodness to you?[55]

Rome did not wait for the Latins to declare war. Two years later she conquered the Latins, dissolved their league, and dealt strictly with its member cities. They again entered a Cursus Honorum, but once more it would be Rome who would decide on promotions.

Meanwhile, although the Republic's long struggle in the fifth and fourth centuries had limited her intellectual growth, her artistic achievements, and even her economic development, yet the order she established allowed the Etruscans to the north to carry on their metal and ceramic industries; the goldsmiths and silversmiths of Latium to flourish; and Magna Graecia to manufacture its bronzes and its imitations of the painted pottery of Athens. Etruscan and Greek artists even beautified the Roman Forum itself. A few statues of Roman heroes like Camillus appeared there; and near the Forum in 296 Rome set up a bronze statue of the She-Wolf, suckling the rejected twin babies,[56] the Founder of the Roman Thing and his less famed brother. Though Rome herself was not a sea power, she protected many allies, especially in Magna Graecia, who were. Though by Greek standards she was not highly civilized, she was at least civilization's protector.

By 264 peninsular Italy had been pacified. True, to the north the Gauls still held the Po Valley; to the south there still stood powerful Carthage on the African coast, dominating not only her rich agricultural hinterland but southern Spain, Corsica, Sardinia, and western Sicily as well. In 289 a corps of discharged Campanian mercenaries, who called themselves the Sons of Mars, had seized Messina, which they used as a base for plundering other Sicilian towns nearby. In 264, involved in a quarrel with a Carthaginian fleet, they appealed to Rome for help. After some hesitation Rome sent a small relief expedition. Carthage reacted: what had started as a local clash quickly spread into a full-blown war between the only two great powers in the western Mediterranean. Rome made an alliance with the King of Syracuse, closed the Strait of Messina to Carthage, and seized Agrigentum, a Greek city on the southern coast of Sicily that Carthage was planning to use as a landing base. The Sicilian possessions of Carthage lay invitingly open, and Rome attacked them. She shortly discovered, however, that to conquer them she must break Carthage's control of the sea. Rome got only modest naval help from her seafaring allies in Magna Graecia. Even to cross the narrow Strait of Messina the Roman army had been forced to borrow boats from these allies. Carthaginian ships attacked this convoy, and one Carthaginian ship ran aground. She was a quinquereme: a warship with some fifty oars, and five men to an oar. The Romans seized her and promptly used her as a model from which to construct some hundred and fifty ships, a larger fleet than Carthage then had.

The new ships were not very well built and they were slow; but "someone suggested to them," as a help in fighting, "the engines which afterwards came to be called 'ravens.' "[57]

When a Carthaginian ship approached, the Roman ship could close in, the raven would grapple, and the dogged Roman landlubbers could board the enemy and fight it out hand to hand, as they had done the length of the Italian peninsula. It looked as if Carthage's superiority in naval strategy might be canceled out, as if the leading land power of the West could drive from the sea the leading sea power of the West, simply because "someone" had apparently converted the sea into dry land. In 260, off the north coast of Sicily near Mylae, the Roman ravens grappled and the Roman swords won. The battle of Mylae was followed by the battle of Ecnomus, this time off Sicily's south coast. The ravens won again.

Rome, with her characteristic instinct for the jugular and with her new control of the sea, now struck at Carthage itself. The invader's prospects seemed good: although the commercial oligarchy that ruled Carthage employed experienced and sometimes brilliant generals, their army of mercenaries seemed unlikely to stand up to Roman infantry. A Roman army landed in Africa, seized the town of Tunis as a base of operations, and approached Carthage. But then the mercenaries of Carthage, well drilled in Greek tactics by the Spartan who commanded them, outmaneuvered and all but destroyed the Roman army. Miracles were multiplying: Rome had beaten Carthage twice by sea; now Carthage had beaten Rome on land. But the sea presented one problem with which not even ravens could grapple. While a Roman fleet was transporting the remains of the badly mauled Roman army back to Italy and was escorting captured enemy vessels as well, a storm arose and the sea struck. Most of Rome's navy was destroyed. The proclivity of Roman admirals for obstinately fighting it out with storms, as Roman marines successfully fought it out on deck with other men, brought three similar disasters during the years that followed.

By 249 Rome had to pause for breath. Two years later Carthage sent a young commander named Hamilcar Barca to Sicily. For a while his superior strategy sorely harassed Rome's forces there, and he even made raids on the coasts of Italy. But Carthage gave him too little support either to hold its possessions in Sicily or to carry the war to Italy. A new Roman expedition against Carthage itself soon threatened, and Carthage sued for peace. In 241 she surrendered everything in Sicily that Rome's ally, Syracuse, did not possess; and she undertook to pay a heavy war indemnity. The Punic War had ended in victory for Rome after a bitter struggle of twenty-three years.

By Hellenistic standards the war had involved huge forces: both sides used land forces of as many as 50,000 men and naval forces of 70,000. The misplaced audacity of Roman admirals, confronted by the threat of storms, was such that Rome lost more men and ships at sea than did her defeated opponent. But when the sea did not fight for Carthage, Rome outfought her on the sea. Moreover, the great merchants who governed Carthage respected money too much to give their armed forces the financial support they needed, whereas Rome made every sacrifice necessary to win. The fact is that a wealthy oligarchy, accustomed to use war only to promote trade and profit, was pitted against the Roman people, accustomed to impose its will by force of arms.

The shortsightedness of business calculation led to even further catastrophe: the Carthaginian government haggled over the arrears in pay due the mercenaries who had returned from Sicily; the mercenaries mutinied; worse, they raised a rebellion of the Libyan subjects of Carthage. Rome, with her instinctive distaste for rebellion of any sort, behaved correctly: she permitted Carthage to recruit other mercenaries in Italy and she refused an offer by the mercenaries who garrisoned Sardinia to turn on Carthage and deliver the island to Rome. Meanwhile Carthage, which had relieved Hamilcar Barca of his Sicilian command, in its present desperate plight assigned to him the task of putting down the mutinous mercenaries and the Libyan revolt. Hamilcar was distrusted and feared in Rome, and Rome immediately seized Sardinia. When Carthage protested this breach of the peace, Rome declared war, refused arbitration, demanded further indemnity and the island of Corsica too. Carthage, powerless for the moment, complied; but Rome's actions strengthened the democratic war party that backed Hamilcar and weakened the ruling oligarchy's normal policy of peace and profit.

Rome now controlled not only Italy from the Strait of Messina to the Po Valley but all the island approaches to Italy. It is true that Syracuse remained independent and ruled a handful of cities nearby, but Syracuse was an ally of Rome. Carthage held only her North African possessions and a strip of southern Spain. Rome quickly put down native uprisings in Sardinia and Corsica. She stood supreme as the champion of all the Greeks in the western Mediterranean and indeed of all its other civilized peoples outside the dwindling realm of Carthage.

That Rome's protective function was a necessary one was quickly put to the proof. In 225 a coalition of tribes from Cisalpine Gaul suddenly invaded neighboring Etruria with an army of some 70,000 men. But by now Rome and her allies together could draw on a reservoir of more than 700,000 infantry and 70,000 cavalry. She therefore promptly took the field with three armies totaling 130,000 men and maneuvered the Gauls against the Etrurian coast at Telamon. There the Romans with javelins broke the frightening charge of the Gauls, fought them hand to hand, and destroyed them almost to a man. It was a victory for civilization against the half-civilized warriors of Cisalpine Gaul, supplemented by mercenaries from the even less civilized Transalpine Gaul, or what is now, roughly speaking, France. This time the Romans decided to put an end once and for all to the Gallic danger, or at least to any that might start from the Po Valley. They conquered Cisalpine Gaul and planted military colonies to pin it down. They built a military road across the Apennines to Rimini on the Adriatic Sea, and another from Rome up the Tyrrhenian coast to Pisa. They established naval stations on the gulf of La Spezia and at nearby Genoa. In 227 they had converted Sicily, except for the small area ruled by Syracuse, into a province, their first; and they made a second province of Corsica and Sardinia. They now governed directly, or controlled by alliance, approximately the territory of modern Italy.

Unless Hamilcar's party found some way to revive Punic power, the Romans had constructed a remarkably secure empire, protected by the Alps and the sea. More fatefully, this empire included nearly all the Greek states in the western Mediterranean, states which Alexander's Hellenistic Cosmopolis had never included. For the Roman Alliance took in Magna

Graecia and Sicily. The Greeks in these areas were the most civilized people in the Roman confederacy, and their civilization would inevitably radiate through the non-Greek peoples on whom Rome had imposed order, a kind of order which the Western Greeks themselves had never succeeded in imposing. Greek commodities, Greek ideas, Greek art forms were free to travel. Greek naval architects, Greek seamen, and Greek engineers would supplement Roman military perseverance itself. Not all the Roman soldiers who attended Greek theaters in Sicily or gazed at the exquisite Greek temples or even observed with a farmer's eye Greek scientific agriculture would forget their lesson. Rome herself, largely isolated from Greek culture during Athens' great fifth century and much of the fourth, was now open to the spell of that culture. Inevitably, Rome's efforts to borrow Greek culture sometimes missed the point. For example, when a Roman consul captured the Greek city of Catania in Sicily, he sent back to Rome a sundial. Though inaccurate for Rome, it was used for ninety-nine years before an accurate one was designed and placed beside it.[58]

The City of Man that Rome had built was not a despotic empire but at least in theory a confederacy of free republics. Yet because of the Roman army, this confederacy appeared to be more secure than any of the three great Hellenistic kingdoms to the east, more secure from rebellion within, from invasion by civilized neighbors, or from any onslaught by the restless sea of nomadic and barbarous tribes to the north.

Was not this to be "the strongest"? Was not this robbers' lair or Trojan remnant clearly destined by Jove himself to rule the Cosmopolis which Alexander strove to found? Or must this robber-remnant endure still further trials before it could consciously strive to claim such a heritage?

COSMOPOLIS ACQUIRES
A RULER

WHEN ISOCRATES OF ATHENS advised Philip of Macedon in the mid-fourth century to lead the quarreling little states of Mainland Greece in a crusade against their secular enemy, the vast Persian Empire, his project promised three possible advantages. It would direct the violence in Greek hearts against a common foe instead of against Greek neighbors. It would rescue Greece-in-Asia, those rich Greek states which studded the coastlands of Asia Minor, from their Persian masters. And it would open up rich Asian lands for Greek settlement. This in turn might relieve population pressure on the poor soils of Mainland Greece and thereby diminish the dangerous tension between rich and poor.

When Philip was murdered and Alexander led the Hellenic crusade against Persia and when the great Persian Empire fell, the violence remained in Greek hearts, whether as rivalry between polis and neighboring polis or as hatred between rich and poor. The political freedom of the Greek cities in Asia Minor soon turned out to be illusory. But the conquest of the Middle East clear to the Indus Valley did open up a vast area to Greek immigrants. Some of them found land. Many found other opportunities. Nearly all the states into which Alexander's newly conquered empire promptly crumbled were ruled by Greek-speaking Macedonians rather than by Greeks. But the administrators and mercenary soldiers whom these rulers employed were mostly Greeks or hellenized natives. The businessmen who took over trade routes, shipping, and manufacturing were mostly Greeks. The philosophers, teachers, scholars, writers, and artists who graced the courts of the rival Macedonian monarchs or found a following in the major cities were also either Greeks or hellenized natives. In short, the whole area was supplied with a new Greek upper class, supported by the labor of the conquered natives. Hellenistic skill, Hellenistic intelligence, and Hellenistic love of money ruled Cosmopolis and spoke a common cosmopolitan tongue. That tongue was the dialect of Athens, the wellspring of Hellenic culture, with some admixture of the Ionic forms of the Asian coastland; and it was Isocrates, more than any other writer, who had adapted it for general use. If it lacked the high beauty and poetic depth of Aeschylus or Sophocles, it was at least simple, precise, and flexible. It met admirably the needs of an energetic society, eager for material comfort, nostalgic for a culture that had passed its prime. Maybe this culture could add grace and ornament to a higher standard of living than had ever been enjoyed by the poets, painters, sculptors, architects, and philosophers who had created such a culture. The new language now spoken was one that an educated Asian or Egyptian of native stock could learn far more quickly and easily than the Greek language in which the great age of Hellas had expressed its ecstasy and its agony. This new language of the Hellenistic Age was called the *koine*, or common, dialect.

Along with a common upper-class tongue, Cosmopolis acquired immense booty in gold and silver, which had been hoarded by the Persian emperors but which Alexander largely minted into coin. Although the disintegration of Alexander's vast domain into a number of states robbed Cosmopolis of the advantages of a common currency, nevertheless many states used the standard which Alexander had borrowed from Athens. The monarchs who ruled this new, extensive, middle-class society were themselves thoroughly middle-class. Many of them resembled the enterprising Ptolemy II of Egypt, who owned business enterprises, developed Egypt economically, made wars for commercial advantage, and dynastic marriages to the same end. Wars were now fought largely for profit, and profit was sought in order to hire mercenaries with whom to make more wars of the same sort. It was a system which the oligarchy that ruled Carthage would have perfectly understood. It was also a system which had begun to appear in Mainland Greece even before the death of Plato.

The commercial revolution now under way led Alexander's successors to continue eagerly Alexander's search for trade routes. Seleucus I of Syria planned to dig a canal from the Black Sea to the Caspian, since he had heard that a sort of northeast passage furnished a water route from the Caspian to India and the India trade. Ptolemy II of Egypt repaired the ancient Pharaonic canal which connected the Nile with the Red Sea and sent an agent to the court of Asoka, the Buddhist Emperor of India. Asoka in his turn sent missionaries to the Hellenistic kings of Syria, Macedonia, Epirus, Egypt, and Cyrene. Asoka's father, Amitrochates, the son of the conqueror Chandragupta, had written to Antiochus I of Syria

> to purchase and send him grape-syrup, figs, and a sophist. And Antiochus wrote back: "Figs, to be sure, and grape-syrup we will dispatch to you, but it is against the law in Greece to sell a sophist.[59]

Ptolemy also tried to capture the Arabian caravan trade that brought spices and incense to the Nabataean cities beyond the Dead Sea. To intercept this trade, he founded Philadelphia, now called Amman. Ptolemy III explored the Red Sea coast of Africa clear to Somaliland, built forts along the route, patrolled the Red Sea against pirates, and thereby gained access to elephant country. Hellenistic armies laid great store by elephants, as the Romans learned when they had to drive Pyrrhus out of Italy. Ptolemy VII provided a Greek captain named Eudoxus with a Hindu sailor who knew the habits of monsoons and who guided Eudoxus by sea to India. After a second journey there, Eudoxus quarreled over his share of the proceeds and left for his home in the Greek city of Marseilles. Traders in Marseilles then combined with traders, probably Greeks, from the Roman colony of Puteoli to commission Eudoxus to circumnavigate Africa. He sailed, but never returned. Marseilles sent another Greek sailor, Pythias, through the Strait of Gibraltar to Cornwall, where he saw tin mined. Then he sailed around Scotland and along the north coast of the continent as far as Heligoland, an old amber district. In short, the desire for profit, for more things to sell, was pushing the Greeks to learn more about the strange countries beyond the bounds of Alexander's empire.

As educated Greeks extended their experience in space and attended more and more to things, especially to those things that satisfied bodily appetites, their inward glance grew rare and dim. Their gods slowly faded. Perhaps these gods, when transplanted to Babylon and Egypt, where other gods had immemorially ruled, had been so deeply associated with the soil of Greece that their worship became merely one form of a self-conscious culture. Or perhaps, quite simply, the Greeks had not seriously invited their own gods to follow them when they set out to make their fortunes in new kingdoms. For by Alexander's time many educated Greeks worshiped the Olympic gods more as a matter of good form than from any genuine faith in their existence. Even the initiate into one of the more intimate Greek mystery religions eventually found less in it to free him from sin or lead him safely to a world beyond death. More and more the sophisticated Greek bowed to *Tyche*, or Chance, who seemed to be governing the world, if indeed any god governed it. Or he flirted with Babylonian astrology or the Egyptian cult of Sarapis and Isis. But, especially in Egypt, which cherished an ancient tradition of divine kings, the Hellenistic Greek did offer a kind of religious worship to men, at first to the dead Alexander and finally even to his successors while still alive. Among the Greek ruling class this worship was, it is true, scarcely more than formal, but at least it prudently stimulated in the natives loyalty to a throne that guaranteed Greek privilege.

It might have been expected that the early Greek's communion with his gods, lovingly expressed in the exquisite statues that his sculptors molded or carved, would be replaced by the love of ideas that had shaped Greek philosophy; that religious worship might at most yield place only to philosophic speculation. But before long speculation flagged too. The Academy which Plato had founded continued to teach logic and epistemology; but if it still cultivated the critical dialectic of Plato, it had somehow lost his illuminating faith in the human intellect. With this went an increasing interest in moral philosophy and a decreasing ability to build any such philosophy that would prove adequate. The Lyceum which Aristotle had founded passed to his pupil Theophrastus, who did excellent work in botany. Moreover, not content with collecting and classifying plants, Theophrastus even collected and classified men: he portrayed brilliantly the various human types in his *Characters*. He studied

41

political science and wrote a treatise on jurisprudence. Later the Lyceum specialized in natural science and then turned to historiography.

A number of new philosophic schools sprang up in Greece during the Hellenistic Age. Pyrrhon of Elis taught a quite complete intellectual skepticism, which urged men to doubt everything so as to achieve a kind of indifference to life. At its worst, Pyrrhon's doctrine invited Hellenistic man not to think so as not to worry. More popular was the view of the Cynics, a name derived from the Greek word for dog. For Diogenes, the most celebrated Cynic, though not the founder of the Cynic tradition, was nicknamed the Dog for his shameless behavior in public.[60] Diogenes, an immigrant to Athens from the coast of the Black Sea, met the increasing artificiality of Greek life by teaching that morality and happiness lay in rejecting social conventions and returning to nature. Learn, he urged, to reduce your needs to the barest animal necessities and thereby to live in freedom. His followers preached this doctrine in the market place to anybody who would listen. Their idiom, like that of Diogenes, was sharp and full of tang.

Diogenes had certainly turned his back on the chase for wealth, but he had displayed neither the love nor the gentleness toward others, nor the intellectual ardor either, of Socrates. "A Socrates gone mad"[61] was the verdict of Plato. Socrates had accepted death rather than flout the laws of his polis and flee into exile. It was rumored that Diogenes had fled his native polis under accusation of financial corruption. Socrates had served his polis by risking his life on the battlefield and by risking it again in civil office. When Diogenes was asked where he was from, he answered "I am a kosmopolites."[62] A citizen of Cosmopolis: he may well have been the first Greek to use the term cosmopolitan, with all its ambiguity. For Cosmopolis posed a dilemma. On the one hand the sovereignty of each little polis seemed to generate anarchy in the Hellenic community, the kind of anarchy that produced explosions like the Peloponnesian War. That anarchy in turn had placed an intolerable strain on each small polis, a strain which produced the horrors of revolution in Corcyra and in many another polis. On the other hand, if the polis yielded its sovereignty to a government of all Cosmopolis, could life offer more than universal obedience to a benevolent despot like Alexander? Must it not be, as his deathbed speech suggested, rule by the strongest? The Greeks who fought for freedom at Marathon, at Thermopylae, at Salamis, at Plataea, and at Mycale were fighting to prevent just such despotism. Socrates,

Plato, and Aristotle all looked on the polis as a community of persons. They rejected a collectivity of men, ruled by fear and greed, as animals must be ruled, or ruled perhaps as money-grubbing subjects, slaves of a Chief Slave. They rejected a collectivity of civilized cosmopolitans, able to turn out a poem on Thermopylae but unwilling to fight for a freedom they no longer knew how to use. If this career of money-making failed to satisfy the generations that followed Alexander's death, they could of course join the followers of Diogenes the Dog, the Cynic. They could give up their possessions, live in a tub as he had done, live a dog's life. Or, as Diogenes might have put it, they could give up their struggle for position and power, embrace poverty, and thereby find the only freedom available, the freedom of their own minds and the freedom to scoff at those who still struggled for money and power. Otherwise, go flatter money and power and let the Cynics say of the whole Greek Cosmopolis what Diogenes had once said of Athens, that

> it had better go to the vultures rather than to the flatterers, for the latter devour good men while they are still alive.[63]

But although the wandering Cynics who preached their doctrines on street corners won some acclaim, they never won an important following. A much larger number were attracted by another philosopher, eager to guide men to happiness. The Athenian Epicurus set up a formal school, like the Academy and the Lyceum. He taught his disciples in his own garden and it was as the Garden that his following came to be known. His central thesis was that pleasure should be the guiding principle of life. This ethical position he bolstered by adopting the atomist materialism of Democritus and a not too rigorous logic. As to religion, the gods are remote and do not bother with human affairs. Man's will is free. Knowledge comes to us only through the senses; and in a way all sense perceptions, visual, auditory, olfactory, gustatory, are special cases of touch. A man is only a special concourse of atoms affected by other concourses of atoms. Likewise, "all good and evil consists in sensation"[64] and we should choose or avoid a thing according to whether it conduces to

> the health of the body and the [soul's] freedom from disturbance, since this is the aim of the life of blessedness. For it is to obtain this end that we always act, namely, to avoid pain and fear.[65]

43

Epicurus was careful to point out that the wise man does not choose pleasures that later bring disproportionate pain. Prudence can guide us away from lust.

> Wherefore prudence is a more precious thing even than philosophy: for from prudence are sprung all the other virtues, and it teaches us that it is not possible to live pleasantly without living prudently and honourably and justly, [nor, again, to live a life of prudence, honour, and justice] without living pleasantly. For the virtues are by nature bound up with the pleasant life, and the pleasant life is inseparable from them.[66]

Unlike Diogenes, that somewhat surly recluse and citizen of the world, Epicurus loved his friends and was greatly loved by them. And he declared:

> Of all the things which wisdom acquires to produce the blessedness of the complete life, far the greatest is the possession of friendship.[67]

Death is not to be feared, since it is merely the final dissolution of self. The punishments after death which some Greeks feared cannot occur. Unharmful pleasures of the body and a gentle peace of mind combine to make the wise man happy. Hedonism and quietism guided the Epicurean.

Still another philosophic school arose. Its founder was another immigrant to Athens, this one from Cyprus. Zeno came to trade, and remained to study. He was at first a Cynic, but eventually started lecturing in the so-called Painted Porch, or *Stoa Poikile*, and his school became known therefore as the Stoa, or Porch. The Stoics became bitter critics of the Epicureans' hedonism and denounced the Garden as a pigsty. Instead of inviting the Greeks to forget the gods and to withdraw from the confusion and clamor of Cosmopolis, the Stoics rejected pleasure as the guide to human happiness and chose duty and endurance instead. Logic was useful only to help discover this arduous path. Physics disclosed chiefly flux and change. The knowledge a man primarily needed was moral philosophy.

All these practical philosophies of life were Socratic heresies, and the men who founded these later schools spoke often of Socrates. But Skeptic, Cynic, Epicurean, and Stoic in their separate ways and for different reasons were all at first anti-intellectual. Cosmopolis was losing its faith not only in its traditional gods but in ideas. This loss of faith was turning philosophy into moralizing or into disengagement.

Perhaps it was inevitable that intellectual life should flourish at its most real in the field of mathematics and natural science. Since philosophic speculation had flagged and genuine political life was abdicating before force and money, the human world was becoming less and less intelligible. The Greek mind accordingly turned to the high intelligibility of mathematics. On the other hand, with even philosophers showing less and less faith in ideas, the problem was apparently not how to escape from the shadowland of Plato's cave to the light of the sun, from things and opinions to ideas and knowledge, but how to examine these shadowy things more carefully and see whether mere perceived matter was as unintelligible as Plato had thought. Many Greek intellects therefore turned their attention from politics to natural science.

Nobody had urged the study of mathematics with more insistence than Plato, but Plato followed Pythagoras in seeing more applications of mathematics than the Hellenistic mathematician was looking for. In general, the latter applied it only to matter. Finally, although the Greek mathematician reached high and magnificent abstractions, he reached them not by means of algebra[68] but through geometry. His Greek word *geometria* meant earth measurement, or surveying, before it came by extension to mean the abstract principles that lay back of this earthy art. He quickly discovered how fruitfully the principle that he discovered by abstract thought could be applied to concrete things.

The mathematicians and scientists for the most part left Athens to the humanists and adjourned to Alexandria where Ptolemy II was establishing a research center called the Museum, or home for the Muses. Here scholars found royal fellowships, a royal library that shortly became the leading library of Cosmopolis, the simple material the scientists required, ample time for research, other scientists to work with, and the agreeable distractions of the largest city in the Greek world.

One of the first scholars to teach at Alexandria was Euclid, whose *Elements* of plane and solid geometry collected, ordered, and developed into a coherent whole what the Greeks were already doing in those sciences. But his work also explored by purely geometric methods ratios and number theory. Archimedes of Syracuse, who studied in Alexandria, wrote on the geometry of plane curves, came close to solving the problem of what ratio the diameter of a circle bears to its circumference, and considered that his crowning achievement was to find the ratio of volume between a cylinder and an inscribed sphere. Archimedes also developed a sand reckoner, a system of notation capable of expressing any number up to that number which modern arithmetical notation would require 80,000 million million

45

ciphers to express.[69] Apollonius of Perga published a work on conic sections, examined by geometric methods. Hipparchus, a Bithynian, developed by geometric methods a new mathematical science, trigonometry. No doubt, if the Greeks had developed an algebraic notation, they could have gone even farther in their odyssey among numbers and magnitudes. But they stuck to their more vividly sculptural, more architectural, more obviously aesthetic science, geometry. Moreover, they often envisaged numbers as geometrical groups of dots. In this geometrical world a man could view with the mind's eye alone the cause of a reflected splendor that every man beheld in the rectangular temple, its cylindrical columns, its triangular pediment, in the circular setting sun or sliced sphere of the waning moon which illumined them, and even in the graceful curves of his own wine jar or lamp. There was the same adventurous play of the mind that had immortalized the poetry of Hellas and later its philosophy. It was perhaps in mathematical thought more than in any other activity that the third-century Greek best displayed what remained of his old joyous love of freedom under law and that he best vindicated Aristotle's ringing declaration that all men by nature desire to know.[70]

Small wonder that the Hellenistic scientist wanted to know how far off the circular blazing sun and the pale moon were; why most stars seemed fixed in relation to each other, while some of the biggest or closest were *planetai*, wanderers. And so, paradoxically, he brought his science of geometry, of earth measurement, down from the heaven of order which only the mind's eye could see, to the nearest thing to order that other men beheld, the sky on a clear night; and he called the wandering planets to account. Did they in fact revolve around our stationary earth guided by a complex system of concentric spheres? Eudoxus of Cnidos had said that they did. But Heraclides Ponticus had suggested to Aristotle that Venus and Mercury revolved around the sun and that the earth rotated daily on its own axis. Aristarchus of Samos went further and hypothesized that all the planets revolved around the sun. He was promptly denounced by Cleanthes, who had succeeded Zeno as head of the Stoic school in Athens, for Aristarchus' suggestion ran counter to certain views of conventional religion concerning the planets. It was Aristarchus also who wrote *On the Sizes and Distances of the Sun and Moon.* Lacking the instruments that he needed in order to get correct answers, he nevertheless did what mathematics could do with only the human eye for lens. Hipparchus, too, measured the distance between the earth and the moon; his answer, thirty-three times the diameter of the earth, was almost correct. Hipparchus also located accurately some eight hundred and fifty stars. He calculated the length of the solar year with an error of only six minutes and fourteen seconds; and he missed the length of the lunar month by only one second. As for the queer behavior of the planets, there was already a theory, perhaps developed by Apollonius, that they moved on so-called epicycles, which in turn moved on cycles around the earth. It was as if a fixed point on the rim of a small wheel seemed not to move in the regular circle that well behaved stars ought to follow, but only because the small wheel turned on an axle which was in itself fixed to the rim of a larger turning wheel. This hypothesis did much to save the appearances, to account, that is, for the phenomena which the eye, unaided by a telescope, in fact observed.

Even in Aristotle's day there were scientists who were convinced that the earth was a sphere, not a disk. But it remained for Eratosthenes, the versatile head librarian of the Museum, to measure its circumference and to come within two hundred miles of finding the correct answer. He also was the first Greek to lay out on a map a grid of latitudes and longitudes, although his meridians, given his lack of accurate clocks, could be only approximate. Eratosthenes also reasoned, by correlating the tides of the Atlantic and Indian oceans, that Asia, Africa, and Europe combined to form a huge island. To the Greeks, accustomed for centuries to live on the shores of an almost tideless sea, the tides in both these oceans had long been matter for wonder. Then Seleucus of Babylonia had detected a correlation between the phases of the moon and these tides. In addition to geography, Eratosthenes wrote on literature, historical chronology, mathematics, astronomy, philosophy, and even composed a number of poems. The specialized scholars of the Museum were so annoyed by their head librarian's versatility that they called him a second-rater and a Jack-of-all-trades.

Geography was not the only terrestrial science to summon matter to trial by mathematics. Archimedes of Syracuse applied mathematics to mechanical and hydrostatic problems. He discovered the basic principles of the lever, the pulley, the screw. He invented the compound pulley; was credited by later tradition with the so-called Archimedean screw, which was used to raise water for irrigation and to drain sumps in the mines; and he devised novel and effective engines of war. Ctesibius of Alexandria, who flourished perhaps a century later, was credited by sub-

47

sequent tradition with a taximeter, an air gun, a water organ, and a water clock, and he may have been the first Greek to invent a rotary steam engine.[71]

Greek medicine had won fame ever since the practice and research of Hippocrates of Cos in the time of Socrates. A considerable medical literature was ascribed to him.[72] Earlier, in Greece as elsewhere, medicine had been largely religious in character, although it also made heavy use of herbs. In Greece the god Asclepius was a renowned healer, with headquarters at Epidaurus but with temples elsewhere too. His followers, the Asclepiads, used fresh air, hydrotherapy, massage, and gymnastics. A favorite method of healing involved the patient's sleeping overnight in the temple, where dreams could come to help him regain health. But although Hippocrates was an Asclepiad, the writings ascribed to him are thoroughly secular. Hippocratic medicine carefully studied the typical course run by each disease, in order to aid the diagnostician. Its therapy turned first to regimen; to diet, exercise, baths. Its second line of defense was drugs. Only in dire necessity did it turn to surgery. Its strength lay in painstaking observation and in the knowledge that the body possesses enormous powers to heal itself, provided the doctor removes impediments to that process. What the Hellenistic doctors added especially to Hippocratic medicine was greater knowledge of anatomy. This they acquired through dissecting animals and human cadavers, and the Museum at Alexandria became famous for its medical research. Moreover, by dint of exploring the human anatomy, they made a good beginning on human physiology. They discovered the function of the brain, dissected out the nervous system, and recognized the function of the heart. Major operations were successfully undertaken, although the surgeon had at his disposal no stronger anesthetic than opium. Cities as well as kings appointed official doctors, and some of these public health officers won high respect for their profession, especially by their selfless service during dangerous epidemics.

Although the thinking that went into Greek mathematics and science was higher than the thinking that was going into philosophy, it too declined signally by the second century. For one thing, there was no adequate technology to furnish inventions that might have enabled scientists to observe natural phenomena more accurately and in greater number. It is true that Greek society was now organized to make money, but capital made its profits by commerce and finance, by the improvement of agriculture, and only in minor degree by industry. Although, given the cost of transportation, many long-distance traders preferred to deal in expensive articles for the rich, the steady growth of cities required transport of such basic necessities as grains and olive oil. The banker found his profit through loans to the merchant; the large landowner and the usurer found theirs by loans to the poor. The rich found an ample supply of labor to exploit, whether slave, freedman, or low-wage freeman. The industrialist likewise had little incentive to adopt labor-saving inventions. The mechanical ingenuity of scientists produced scholarly playthings rather than technological innovations. Technology therefore failed to support pure science.

The problem of the man of letters was more difficult than that of the scientist. Like the Greek athlete, the Greek writer tended to become a professional. In the great fifth century, an Athenian who wrote tragedies or comedies spoke to his polis, a group of free citizens, rich and poor, joined in joyous festival to honor a god. Written for the polis, his drama was in a high sense political. It usually concerned the common good of some polis. By implication it concerned the common good of all men everywhere. The actors were amateurs, fellow citizens of their audience.

By the third century, that sort of audience was gone. The theater was now handsomer, with marble or stone tiers instead of wooden ones for the audience to sit on. The actors were a professional troupe that went on tour from city to city to the four corners of Cosmopolis. The gods were dead, or in any case less accessible. What was there to talk about? Already in fourth-century Athens Menander, the most admired comic poet of the Hellenistic Age, talked about individuals and contemporary human types and love intrigue. For the boisterous obscenity of Aristophanes, he substituted sly innuendo; and for the common hopes and fears of the polis, an entertaining picture of private lives. Menander had great technical skill; he was a close and accurate observer of the life around him: what he said put no undue strain on either the intellect or the emotions of his audience; it was, indeed, highly cosmopolitan. Yet something was missing, perhaps some sense of high significance. Maybe it was not consciously missed by the audiences of his day.

Hellenistic society achieved tragedy neither in real life nor in any memorable way on the stage, but since it was in any case an audience of culture consumers rather than of culture makers and since it was exceedingly proud of the culture other and earlier Greeks had made, it solved the problem of presenting Greek tragedy in characteristic fashion: it sponsored theatrical revivals. Again, perhaps because it enjoyed the emotional outlet of pathos rather than the Aristotelian catharsis of tragedy, it revived Euripides far more often than Aeschylus or Sophocles. Besides, a new humanitarianism found a resonance in Euripides' greater interest in social evils; a growing preference for the concrete particular over the general and essential led this new audience to relish his interest in individual psychology and his skill at characterization, the same kind of interest and skill that Menander offered them in comedy.

In the third century, a rapidly growing literacy furnished an increasing reading public for books. This widespread literacy among the Greek governing class was in part due to the rise of public schools, supported financially either by the public treasury of a Greek polis or by endowments from the rich. Egypt's papyrus plant furnished the paper scrolls which made Alexandria the center of the publishing industry. In default of printing presses, the publisher hired copyists, and he could count on well-edited master copies from the pens of professional scholars at the Museum, busily engaged in authenticating texts, in textual criticism, in making compendia and excerpts for those who wanted their culture in a hurry, in making lists of famous Attic orators or of the Seven Wonders of the World, and of course in carrying on scholarly vendettas. By the mid-third century, the Museum contained between 400,000 and 500,000 papyrus scrolls and was still growing. These editors were paid by the royal treasury; living authors were paid not by the publisher but by a patron, usually a royal patron; hiring copyists and finding customers, therefore, were the publisher's chief costs. Pella, the royal capital of Macedonia, and Antioch, the royal capital of Syria, also maintained libraries. The little kingdom of Pergamum in Asia Minor possessed an impressively well-stocked royal library, but when Egypt cut off its supply of papyrus Pergamum, which had long raised sheep to supply its textile workers with wool, promptly turned to sheepskin as a substitute for papyrus. The Greeks called this durable writing material *pergamene,* or parchment. But papyrus remained standard. Finally, Greek women now enjoyed greater liberty; endowed schools for girls began to spring up. Women therefore began to buy books, and authors began to adjust their writing to women's interests and tastes.

Besides putting their culture on shelves and annotating it, the Hellenistic Greeks wrote many more books than their ancestors did. Aristoxenus of Tarentum, a pupil of Aristotle's, was credited with four hundred and fifty-three works, including learned treatises on music. The Stoic, Chrysippus, scored seven hundred. Callimachus, poet, scholar, and cataloguer of the Museum library, wrote some eight hundred. He was considered the greatest poet of his day. As with so many Hellenistic writers, his poems were technically skillful, full of learned allusion. Since he often wrote in a clever style about gods in whom neither he nor his reader believed, inevitably much of his poetry was frigid. Callimachus invented the miniature literary epic. But the muse of epic poetry had long since vanished. It was in briefer poetic flights like the epigram that he and the other new poets excelled. There was genuine pathos, for example, in the epigram Callimachus addressed to his friend, the elegiac poet, Heraclitus of Halicarnassus:

> They told me, Heracleitus, they told me you were dead:
> They brought me bitter news to hear and bitter tears to shed.
> I wept, as I remembered, how often you and I
> Had tired the sun with talking and sent him down the sky.
> And now that thou art lying, my dear old Carian guest,
> A handful of gray ashes, long, long ago at rest,
> Still are thy pleasant voices, thy nightingales,[73] awake
> For Death, he taketh all away, but them he can not take.[74]

Western Greece furnished the Hellenistic Age with one of its most celebrated poets, Theocritus of Syracuse. Theocritus was not only born and reared in Sicily: he immortalized the Sicilian countryside. True, his search for a patron led him to Alexandria, where certain poets were trying to compete with Homer by attempting long epics. Theocritus would have agreed with one of the goatherds in his bucolic poems:

> How I hate the stonemason who tries
> to build his house up as high
> as the top of Mount Oromedon.
> And I hate those cocks[75] of the Muses
> who challenge the Chian nightingale
> with their foolish crowing.[76]

The country songs of Theocritus were short. They were written, not in the Attic koine spoken by educated city folk, but in the Dorian dialect of Syracuse, an ancient colony of Corinth. His country songs turned nostalgically away from the cities to the countryside, which so many city readers remembered from their childhood. And although Greek poetry had traditionally focused on man, or on man and his gods, these idylls of Theocritus lovingly recalled the trees and the flowers and the bees, and the lizards sleeping in the sun. Simple shepherds and goatherds declared their uncomplicated love to pouting country wenches, of course in verse. They held formal singing matches with each other and won as prize a shepherd's pipe or a conch-shell horn, while the heifers and the she-goats danced in the tender grass.

Theocritus wrote about the gods also, cherished now as delicate literary myths. He wrote about children, who no longer appeared to the Greeks as primarily imperfect, unripe, and hence defective men and women, but as sentimentally charming. They had the charm of the reader's own lost childhood, of his nostalgia for the lost youth of Hellas. The gods whom poets like Theocritus wrote best about were pictured in their infancy. The hero who became a god, Heracles, appears as ten months old, strangling with his soft little fingers two frightful serpents who planned to eat him. Now he shows their dead bodies to his father and capers in his pretty, childish glee. In another poem Eros, the god of love is very young:

> One day a wicked bee
> stung thievish Eros when he
> was stealing honey from the hive,
> and pricked his finger-tips.
> He was in pain, and blew
> on his hand, and danced up and down,
> and stamped on the ground.
> And he showed his hurt to Aphrodite,
> and complained that so little a creature
> as a bee could inflict so mighty
> a wound. But his mother laughed.
> "Aren't you like the bees—so little
> to inflict such mighty wounds?"[77]

For two little children he wrote this epitaph:

This maiden went to Hades ere her time, in her seventh year when life was scarce begun: poor child, she sorrowed for her brother who tasted the cruelty of death, an infant of twenty months. Ah, hapless Peristere, how near at hand for mortals has God set grievous trouble.[78]

For the faithful nurse of a little boy he wrote another epitaph:

> Little Medeius built by the wayside this memorial for his Thracian nurse, and inscribed upon it "Here lies Cleita." She will have her recompense for her upbringing of the lad. How so? In that she will still be called "faithful."[79]

He wrote an inscription for another statue. It was the statue of the poet Epicharmus, a famous writer of comedies in the fifth century, and it stood in the theater at Syracuse. Theocritus wrote:

> Dorian is the speech and Dorian too the man—Epicharmus the inventor of Comedy. In thy honour, Bacchus, since he was their fellow-townsman, the folk that dwell in the splendid city of Syracuse have set him here, in bronze, not flesh and blood. Fitting it is that they who recall his words of wisdom should recompense him, for many precepts serviceable for the ordering of their lives did he utter to the young. Much thanks to him therefore.[80]

Haunted by the glorious past of his culture, Hellenistic man had now substituted this culture for the religion which had largely produced it; at least some writers, therefore, inevitably wrote history. That none of them equaled Thucydides was also inevitable. Thucydides had watched the Peloponnesian War half destroy Hellenic culture. And he had seen it not as pathos but as a vast and terrible tragedy. He had lived when the tragic sense of life was still strong in Greece. In the absence of this tragic sense, some Hellenistic historians fell back on mere, useful accuracy; some fell back on mere, antiquarian rhetoric. Hellenistic historiography reached its peak in Polybius, a second-century Achaean statesman from the city of Megalopolis. Polybius set himself the formidable task of narrating the rise of Cosmopolis. That is, he wanted to write a world history, meaning the rise of a politically united universal society, inhabiting the lands around the Mediterranean. With some justice Polybius despised the academic historians who thought that all the historian needed was access to a good library, if not to the library of the Museum in Alexandria. Like Herodotus centuries before, Polybius traveled widely to check what facts he could on the spot. But he suffered from a grave disadvantage. Herodotus had dealt with the hybris or arrogance of Xerxes and of his vast empire, and with Xerxes' catastrophe. Thucydides had traced the rise of the Athenian Empire, its hybris or arrogance bred of power and of substituting violence for reason, and the Empire's resultant fall. Polybius proposed to recount the rise of a set of human institutions without recounting, what he could not in his century recount, their necessary fall. Polybius half recognized this problem when he discovered later that he would have told his story differently had he known the sequel. Without seeing his story's correlative end he could not wholly understand his subject: he could only recount a story of apparent success or else a story of a human enterprise that did not aim high enough to achieve significant failure.

As to the declamatory rhetoric that now defaced most histories, it was defacing poetry and other kinds of writing too. The art of rhetoric had once helped statesmen like Pericles to persuade a free assembly to a given course of action. It was a necessary part of the art of deliberation. As fully sovereign, self-governing communities disappeared, the oratory of statesmanship grew futile, less cogent, more strident, until Plato's verdict seemed vindicated: that the art of rhetoric was essentially the art of flattery. As more and more Greeks used words not to advance understanding but to coax, frighten, or sell, or merely to titillate the emotions, the demagogue and the merchant, the panegyrist and the mere exhibitionist took over; and rhetoric polluted both genuine thought and genuine feeling. Among those who turned away from rhetoric and insisted on inquiry were, notably, the mathematicians and natural scientists, although, even of these, many sank intermittently into fruitless and noisy polemic. Research scholars in literature, toiling at the Museum, often did valuable work and were especially apt at the kind of scholarly polemic that made full use of rhetorical devices.

> Timon of Phlius, the satirist, calls the Museum a bird-cage, by way of ridiculing the philosophers who got their living there because they are fed like the choicest birds in a coop: "Many there be that batten in populous Egypt, well-propped pedants who quarrel without end in the Muses' bird-cage."[81]

Or was this merely the normal reaction of a practicing sophist and satirist to academic and literary roosters, roosters whom scholarly rancor often impeded in the search for truth?

During the Hellenistic Age the fine arts followed essentially the same path as literature. That path was already clearly marked out before Alexander died. As with the poets, so with the artists the gods became more purely human; the virtuosity of the artist and the generosity of

54

the patron both loomed larger; the artist's brush or chisel sought the specific, either the rich and powerful or the weak, the small, and even the deformed, either the voluptuous courtesan or the doting mama. Both sculpture and painting were more often literary than before; they more often told a story. They confined themselves less to man and exhibited a sort of romantic naturalism that glorified animals and plants. A society that had once demanded immortal statues of their immortal gods now erected statues of divine monarchs or of local plutocrats, in gratitude for their public benefactions. Statues of individual men quickly multiplied. What those who paid for them wanted was not a vision of their essential and hence shared humanity. It was rather a faithful, often literal record of their uniqueness if not of their eccentricities and peculiarities. The result was an imposing gallery of portraits as eloquent of their age as its new interest in biography. The bronze or marble faces of many leaders of Cosmopolis recorded both their love of power and their spiritual alienation.

The new wealth of the Hellenistic world expressed itself in a building boom, and architects naturally flourished. Mainland Greece, however, found itself in something of an economic backwater; the new burst of building affected it very little except when the cultural piety or diplomatic rivalry of the kings supplied porticos to the holy island of Delos, or a new library and gymnasium or new colonnades at Athens, or caused Antiochus IV to resume building the huge temple of Zeus which an Athenian tyrant had started centuries before at the foot of the Acropolis. So many young men had left Mainland Greece to seek their fortunes as mercenaries or administrators or traders or artists or writers in Greece-in-Asia or in Alexandria and so many families in Mainland Greece avoided rearing children that many of the older cities of Greece were declining. Their power to build had to depend largely on gifts from abroad. But the new or growing cities in Asia built abundantly, sometimes handsomely, often ostentatiously. The city planner joined with the architect to secure at least a few wide and often parallel streets and vistas; and these made the ancient, crooked streets of the more famous old cities like Athens look both quaint and inconvenient to the prosperous tourist or the student eager to study in the city where Socrates, Plato, and Aristotle had taught. The new cities had at least some streets partially paved. Pergamum enforced street-cleaning on householders. Alexandria, Pergamum, Syracuse, and this time even Athens built closed drains in at least the principal streets. The water supply of Alexandria reached the city through underground pipes. Pergamum even boasted of water brought under pressure by aqueduct and purified in filter beds before being distributed through the street pipes.

The arch became, perhaps under the influence of Babylon, a feature of architecture for use in gateways or repeated in arcades. The vaulted ceiling appeared, though as yet only in basements. Temples and palaces were built, and much larger gymnasia and theaters. Alexandria had a royal park; its suburb, Canopus, enjoyed public pleasure gardens; and Antioch had a famous garden suburb named Daphne on the banks of the Orontes River. If no architect achieved the exquisite harmony of the Parthenon, many helped to give Cosmopolis grace and charm and to make it a pleasant city of man, in some ways even for a poor man, in most ways for the rich.

The tired philosophic skepticism of this middle-class paradise, its interest in Babylonian astrology and Egyptian magic, its restless search for foreign gods like Isis and Sarapis to replace the old gods of Olympus, all reflected a certain inner and often unconscious anxiety. Its thirst for diversion, for the trivial but novel in literature and art reflected an unconscious emptiness and boredom. A marked migration from countryside and hamlet to towns and to great cities was a further symptom of a loneliness and loss of community that drove men to huddle. Nevertheless, it offered, at least to its Greek governing class and its hellenized natives with money, more physical comfort, more bustle, wider travel, more physical pleasure, more business opportunity, more chances to get rich, to secure power, to win applause and acclaim, than the tiny cities of old. These compensations went a long way to keep a man's mind off his vain anxieties, to alleviate inner boredom, and to exorcise inner loneliness. Besides, although the few with a sense of high significance could hardly expect Cosmopolis to produce an Aeschylus in tragedy or an Aristophanes in comedy, a Phidias in sculpture or an Ictinus in architecture, yet the *Oresteia* and the *Birds* could still be played and there was a brisk tourist trade to Athens to see the famous monuments the guidebooks described. A cultivated man could in some sense possess these riches of the spirit as part of Hellenic culture. Indeed, Hellenic culture was a spiritual capital on which Cosmopolis might hope to live for some time. Meanwhile it made up in size or splendor for anything it might lack in significance. It could produce splendid monuments to wealth. For example, the rich trading city of

Rhodes erected the Colossus, over a hundred feet high, standing beside the entrance to its busy port. Never had the Greek artist or literary man been more handsomely financed, whether by monarch or wealthy city or rich private customer. If religion, philosophy, art, and literature no longer guided Greek society, they at least ornamented it and gave it a reflected radiance. If Hellenistic man was less deeply and importantly human than his ancestors, at least he was more humane. If his polis, his city, was less satisfying as a community, at least he was more urbane. In his rules of warfare, in his public benefactions, in his increasingly scientific outlook he was, according to his own lights, or to most of them, more civilized. When cities suffered natural catastrophes, they frequently received economic aid from their neighbors. Thus, in 224, when an earth-quake threw down the Colossus of Rhodes along with the city's walls and arsenals, the shrewd Rhodian merchants

> made such sound practical use of the incident that the disaster was a cause of improvement to them rather than of damage. . . . by laying stress on the greatness of the calamity and its dreadful character and by conducting themselves at public audiences and in private intercourse with the greatest seriousness and dignity, they had such an effect on cities and especially on kings that not only did they receive most lavish gifts, but . . . the donors themselves felt that a favour was being conferred on them.[82]

How this Cosmopolis could defend itself, whether from strife between rich and poor or, metaphorically speaking, from civil wars between its many sovereign states or from barbarians beyond its borders, was one of its gnawing anxieties. In most states the rich managed to keep the poor in order, although there were a good many revolutions and the consequent dispersion of political exiles or refugees seeking foreign assistance for counterrevolution at home, for recovery of their property, and for revenge. The three major powers, Egypt under the Ptolemies, Syria under the Seleucids, and Macedonia under the Antigonids, constantly conspired or fought against each other to dominate desirable trade routes or merely to maintain a precarious balance of power. The minor kingdoms of Pergamum and Bithynia, both in Asia Minor, struggled to survive. Some of the Greek city-states, like Rhodes and Sparta, managed to retain their independence. Two groups of such states in Mainland Greece had tried to secure a measure of independence from their powerful neighbor, Macedonia, by forming confederations. The Second Achaean League, in the Peloponnese, achieved a kind of common federal government. The Aetolian League, north of the Gulf of Corinth, was its jealous rival. Members of the Aetolian League had never participated fully in the culture which had flowered in Athens and Corinth and other Greek states under the stimulus of Greece-in-Asia in the sixth century. Neither league was able to unite all Greek cities or even those in Mainland Greece.

In the third century, wars, therefore, were still fairly frequent. True, there was increasing disapproval of the custom of sacking a city and then selling its inhabitants into slavery. The armies of the three great powers were composed of professional mercenaries, more given to outmaneuvering than to slaughtering. But there was plenty of pillaging and quartering of soldiers on civilians. And the disorder bred highway robbery on land. On sea it bred the pirate and the privateer, and one Greek word served to designate both. Aetolian law provided no punishment for them, even when they preyed on the ships of a nominal ally. In short, comfort-loving Cosmopolis still lacked the security which a single, strong government could have given it, the sort of government Alexander had hoped to establish. Meanwhile, as the successors of Persia's Asian empire, the Seleucids tried to reconquer Thrace or Palestine, or hold the Greek cities on the coast of Asia Minor, or even to march on Persia's former province, Egypt. Macedonia tried to hold Mainland Greece and win Asian territory which Philip of Macedon had claimed. The same economic needs which had driven the Pharaohs of the New Empire more than a millennium before to war in Palestine and Syria now drove the Ptolemies: timber from Lebanon to build ships, caravan routes from Arabia to control. All three dynasties longed to control the trade routes of the eastern Mediterranean. Syria and Egypt recruited mercenaries from the Greek cities. All three royal courts sent rich gifts to Apollo's holy temple at Delphi, and to Athens, traditional seat of the Greek culture which all three strove to exemplify. And since the Greek cities still yearned for their ancient sovereignty, a cliché of the power struggle was a proclamation of aid to liberate the Greeks, meaning the Greek cities under the rule or hegemony of a rival great power.

The peace and order of Cosmopolis were also constantly threatened by the barbarians on its perimeter. Its African lands were relatively safe behind their deserts, although Carthage needed watching until the First Punic War robbed her of her naval superiority. But the Seleucids had inherited a heterogeneous collection of provinces from what is now the western coast of Turkey, clear to West Pakistan. Already by 304 Seleucus I had yielded the Indus Valley to the Emperor Chandragupta, who from his capital at Patna, far away on the Ganges, dominated half of India. Chandragupta had built that empire partly with the swords of Greek mercenaries. Between 250 and 225 the Seleucid monarchy lost control of the northern fringe of what are now Iran and Afghanistan. Alexander the Great had been forced to conquer the Persian Empire or else face rivals for his new-won throne. He also longed to reach the Ganges and proceed to the Stream of Ocean, which he expected to find at its mouth. As a result, he extended Cosmopolis too far eastward. He had annexed lands that could not be assimilated to Hellenic civilization, and some of the colonies he founded failed to survive. To unite the Greek-speaking world he would have had to yield much in the East and conquer much more in the West, notably Sicily and Magna Graecia. Eventually Cosmopolis lost to the Parthians not only the whole Iranian plateau but even Babylon.

It was Pyrrhus of Epirus who tried to rescue the Western Greeks, those in Magna Graecia from Rome, and those in Sicily from their ancient enemy, Carthage. But the year after he landed in Italy some of the Celtic tribesmen whom the Greeks called Galatians suddenly burst through the Macedonian frontier of Cosmopolis, gutted Macedonia, and reached the pass of Thermopylae, the Hot Gates. Here an Athenian general with some 30,000 men from many Greek cities waited. But the Galatians outflanked them, as the Persians had outflanked Leonidas and his Three Hundred two centuries before, and marched on the wealthy temples of holy Delphi. Again Apollo defended his own, as he had done against the men of Xerxes' army: again rocks broke off from Mount Parnassus. Again a sacrilegious enemy fled. Again some of the Greeks saw divine figures helping them to rout the barbarians. The Galatians butchered the inhabitants of an Aetolian village, but Aetolian troops cut them up, and those who survived fled through Macedonia to Thrace.

A second column of Galatians entered Cosmopolis by the Thracian border. There some of them settled. But in 278, the very year Pyrrhus abandoned Magna Graecia to the Romans and sought adventure in Sicily, a third column of Galatians crossed into Asia Minor and marauded through the rich cities of Greece-in-Asia. They raided another famous temple of Apollo's, this one at Didyma, near Miletus. Eventually, they settled in what came to be called Galatia, and lived as a military aristocracy on tribute from the native farmers and the hellenized towns. They continued to speak Celtic. They sometimes took service as mercenaries. But before long they were again terrorizing Asia Minor. In 230 Attalus, King of Pergamum, routed them and for a while they were quiet. For a long time they served as mercenaries here and there and won a reputation as fighters, mutineers, and inveterate plunderers. All cities were terrified of them and regarded their frenzied way of fighting and their lack of discipline with the same mingled horror and scorn that the Romans felt for the Gauls who lived on both sides of the Alps. Meanwhile, Macedonia strove to hold the barrier against Paeonian and Dardanian to the north and the violent, piratical Illyrians who bordered the Adriatic.

In the western Mediterranean likewise the borders of Hellenic civilization were threatened: until the First Punic War, by Carthaginian mercenary armies in Sicily; by Gauls behind the thin line of Greek cities on the south coast of what is now France; and by the mountain tribes of Iberians behind the Greek cities from the Pyrenees to the Ebro River. After the First Punic War, Carthage slowly advanced northward up the Mediterranean coast of Spain, as she sought to compensate for the loss of Sicily, Sardinia, and Corsica to Rome by building a new empire. Spain was rich in the metals for which the merchants of Carthage could always find a hungry market.

But there was also something more dangerous to the western Greek world than Gauls or Spanish Iberians or even Carthaginians, or at least more dangerous to the cherished sovereignty of such Greek cities as democratic Tarentum. This dangerous thing was the relentless, methodical drive of Rome, expanding her military alliance down the Italian peninsula until it swallowed Magna Graecia and all of Sicily except the little that Syracuse held. Indeed, the independence of Syracuse was merely nominal. For short of possible intervention by Carthage, Syracuse was at the mercy of her powerful ally on the Tiber.

Nearly half a century after Rome drove Pyrrhus and his remaining mercenaries out of Italy and back across the Adriatic to his kingdom of Epirus, the pirates of Illyria had so harassed Italian shipping in the Adriatic that in 229 Rome made war. The next year, Teuta, Queen of Illyria, submitted. She promised to end the piracy, to limit the area of Illyrian navigation, to pay a tribute, to yield control of all Greek cities. Rome established a protectorate over the Greek cities of Corcyra, Apollonia, and Epidamnus. The Roman commander then sent envoys to notify the Aetolian and Achaean Leagues that they had cleared the Adriatic for merchant shipping, and the Greeks expressed their gratitude by admitting all Romans to the Isthmian games and to the Eleusinian Mysteries. Romans were not accustomed to competing in athletic and literary contests and they frowned on mystery cults like that of Eleusis. But the honor now accorded Rome for protecting Greeks against barbarians had high symbolic value. It suggested that she was looked on as a member of the Panhellenic community. In 219 Illyrian piracy flared again, and Roman troops under Aemilius Paullus not only put it down but subjugated a portion of Illyria. This newest eruption of disorder from the Greek Cosmopolis in the eastern Mediterranean finally led Rome to seize a considerable beachhead in that world. She was keeping order in the narrow sea which separated that world from the western world of Italians and Greeks, the latter tightly allied with Rome.

From the various peoples she conquered and forced to enter the Roman Alliance, Rome learned. As one of her own historians later wrote,

> Our ancestors . . . took their offensive and defensive weapons from the Samnites, the badges of their magistrates for the most part from the Etruscans. In fine, whatever they found suitable among allies or foes, they put in practice at home with the greatest enthusiasm, preferring to imitate rather than envy the successful.[83]

Moreover, in 240, the year after Rome had ejected Carthaginian power from Sicily, Rome had introduced Greek tragedies and comedies at her festivals, and a veteran of the First Punic War could see plays that reminded him of those he had first seen when encamped near some Greek town or other in Sicily: tragedies by Euripides, comedies by Menander, mimes by Theocritus. By the third century Plautus and by the second century Terence were adapting or loosely translating Greek comedies into Latin. By keeping their settings Greek they avoided the fate of Naevius: Naevius had attacked a faction of Roman patricians in a play and was imprisoned.

Meanwhile Rome noted that the man who was extending the power of Carthage from a narrow strip on the southern coast of Spain northward towards the Ebro was precisely the ablest and most daring general in her recent war with Carthage. The growing empire of Carthage in Spain brought Carthage not only important revenues from Spanish mines but gave her access to an immense reserve of hard-fighting native manpower, available as mercenaries. When Hamilcar died in Spain, his son-in-law

Hasdrubal took over. From him Rome managed in 226 to exact an agreement that the Carthaginians were not to cross the Ebro in arms. Nevertheless, the originally Greek city of Saguntum, which was well to the south of the Ebro and near the site of modern Valencia, had already placed itself under Roman protection. In 221 Hasdrubal was murdered, and his army chose a twenty-eight-year-old son of the great Hamilcar named Hannibal. Two years later Hannibal besieged Saguntum. Rome was busy in Illyria; Saguntum resisted for eight heroic months, then the city fell. Rome demanded that Carthage hand over Hannibal, Carthage refused, and once more the two giants of the western Mediterranean prepared to go to war.

Rome had kept her naval superiority ever since the First Punic War. She now planned to invade Africa, while a smaller army was sent to Spain to contain Hannibal. But suddenly Rome and the whole Greek world heard that Hannibal had crossed the Pyrenees with a polyglot mercenary army of 50,000 men, 9,000 horse, and 37 elephants; had passed through southern France, ferried his troops across the Rhone before an army on the way to Spain under the consul Cornelius Scipio could prevent him, fought his way against local tribesmen across the Alps, and called on the Gauls of the Po Valley to rise against their Roman conquerors. In September, 218, on the Ticino River, a northern branch of the Po, he confronted Scipio, who had returned by sea to Italy to meet him. Hannibal had lost half his forces in the terrible passage of the Alps and now had less than 20,000[84] men. But he still had a force of superb cavalry, and Scipio was beaten. Meanwhile, Rome recalled her main army, under her other consul, Sempronius, from Sicily, where he was preparing to attack Carthage. In December, Sempronius met Hannibal on the Trebia, a southern branch of the Po, and was overwhelmed. Over 60,000 Gauls now joined Hannibal. Even so, since Rome's allies swelled her forces to some 700,000 foot and some 70,000 horse, Hannibal's strategy was not to assault Rome until by political warfare he had detached as many of her allies as possible. To that end he treated Roman prisoners harshly and released allied prisoners without ransom. By 217 he caught another consul, Fabius Maximus, in a narrow pass near Lake Trasimene in Etruria and slaughtered or took prisoner some 30,000 men.

It was now clear that Rome was dealing with a master strategist whom no Roman general could match. Fabius, given dictatorial powers, determined to gamble on the loyalty of Rome's allies, to evade massive encounters, to harass Hannibal when he could safely do so, and so to wear him out. His strategy won him the title of the Delayer and a line in the epic poem Ennius wrote on the Second Punic War: "One man by delaying restored for us the Thing."[85] But in 216 two new consuls, Aemilius Paullus and Terentius Varro, also amateur generals, attacked Hannibal near Cannae, between the modern cities of Foggia and Bari, in Apulia, some miles west of Bari. Rome experienced a defeat costlier in manpower than she had ever before known: with some 40,000 men Hannibal all but annihilated a Roman army of at least 50,000. In Etruria he had lost the sight of one eye and all his elephants but one. As for the Celts, or Gauls, whom he had recruited in the Po Valley,

> Fearing the fickleness of the Celts and possible attempts on his life, owing to his establishment of the friendly relations with them being so very recent, he had a number of wigs made, dyed to suit the appearance of persons differing widely in age, and kept constantly changing them . . .[86]

During his long campaign, Hannibal

> had with him Africans, Spaniards, Ligurians, Celts, Phoenicians, Italians, and Greeks, peoples who neither in their laws, customs, or language, nor in any other respect had anything naturally in common. But, nevertheless, the ability of their commander forced men so radically different to give ear to a single word of command and yield obedience to a single will.[87]

Hannibal claimed that he used the strategy of Pyrrhus. But, alas, he had inherited from him the frustration of winning Pyrrhic victories. No Roman general had appeared with enough imagination to learn from Hannibal what Hannibal claimed to have learned from Pyrrhus. But Rome had the manpower, she had ample provisions, and until Cannae her alliance held; Carthage was lukewarm in its support of Hannibal and sent him reinforcements of only 4,000 men. Yet, even after Cannae, Rome never wavered. Before the year was over she had replaced her army, in part by promising freedom to those of her slaves who would enlist. She refused to negotiate, even for the ransom of Roman prisoners, and Hannibal sold them as slaves; some 2,000 went to Greece.

Even before Cannae, Greece was watching. Philip V of Macedonia and the Achaean League were at war with the Aetolians; but when news of Hannibal's great victory at Lake Trasimene arrived, Philip was at Argos to celebrate the Nemean festival.

A little after he had taken his place to witness the games a courier arrived from Macedonia bringing the intelligence that the Romans had been defeated in a great battle, and that Hannibal was master of the open country. The only man to whom he showed the letter at first, enjoining him to keep it to himself, was Demetrius of Pharos. Demetrius seized on this opportunity to advise him to get the Aetolian war off his shoulders as soon as possible, and to devote himself to the reduction of Illyria and a subsequent expedition to Italy. The whole of Greece, he said, was even now and would be in the future subservient to him, the Achaeans being his partisans by inclination and the spirit of the Aetolians being cowed by what had happened during the war. An expedition, however, to Italy was the first step towards the conquest of the world, an enterprise which belonged to none more properly than to himself. And now was the time, after this disaster to the Roman arms. By such words as these he soon aroused Philip's ambition, as I think was to be expected in the case of a king so young, who had achieved so much success, who had such a reputation for daring, and above all who came of a house which we may say had always been inclined more than any other to covet universal dominion.[88]

Later, when Philip and his Achaean allies conferred with the Aetolians, Agelaus of Naupactus warned of what the Second Punic War meant to the Greek world:

It would be best of all if the Greeks never made war on each other, but regarded it as the highest favour in the gift of the gods could they speak ever with one heart and voice, and marching arm and arm like men fording a river, repel barbarian invaders and unite in preserving themselves and their cities. And if such a union is indeed unattainable as a whole, I would counsel you at the present moment at least to agree together and to take due precautions for your safety, in view of the vast armaments now in the field and the greatness of this war in the west. For it is evident even to those of us who give but scanty attention to affairs of state, that whether the Carthaginians beat the Romans or the Romans the Carthaginians in this war, it is not in the least likely that the victors will be content with the sovereignty of Italy and Sicily, but they are sure to come here and extend their ambitions beyond the bounds of justice. Therefore I implore you all to secure yourselves against this danger, and I address myself especially to King Philip. For you, Sire, the best security is, instead of exhausting the Greeks and making them an easy prey to the invader, on the contrary to take thought for them as for your own body, and to attend to the safety of every province of Greece as if it were part and parcel of your own dominions. For if such be your policy the Greeks will bear you affection and render sure help to you in case of attack, while foreigners will be less disposed to plot against your throne, impressed as they will be by the loyalty of the Greeks to you. If you desire a field of action, turn to the west and keep your eyes on the war in Italy, so that, wisely biding your time, you may some day at the proper moment compete for the sovereignty of the world. And the present times are by no means such as to exclude any hope of the kind. But defer your differences with the Greeks and your wars here until you have repose enough for such matters, and give your whole attention now to the more urgent question, so that the power may still be yours of making war or peace with them at your pleasure. For if once you wait for these clouds that loom in the west to settle on Greece, I very much fear lest we may all of us find these truces and wars and games at which we now play, so rudely interrupted that we shall be fain to pray to the gods to give us still the power of fighting with each other and making peace when we will, the power, in a word, of deciding our differences for ourselves.[89]

Polybius pointed out in his history that in one and the same year Ptolemy IV of Egypt overwhelmed Antiochus III of Syria and seized the area of Palestine and modern Lebanon; that Hannibal won his victory near Lake Trasimene; and that Philip, with one eye on Hannibal and the Romans, made peace at his conference with the Aetolians. Polybius therefore saw in this one year a sort of confluence of separate local historical processes and the start of a world historical process, guided by Rome.

It was at this time and at this conference that the affairs of Greece, Italy, and Africa were first brought into contact. For Philip and the leading statesmen of Greece ceased henceforth, in making war and peace with each other, to base their action on events in Greece, but the eyes of all were turned to the issues in Italy. And very soon the same thing happened to the islanders and the inhabitants of Asia Minor. For those who had grievances against Philip and some of the adversaries of Attalus no longer turned to the south and east, to Antiochus and Ptolemy, but henceforth looked to the west, some sending embassies to Carthage and others to Rome, and the Romans also sending embassies to the Greeks, afraid as they were of Philip's venturesome character and guarding themselves against an attack by him now they were in difficulties.[90]

The crushing defeat of the Romans at Cannae decided Philip to accept a treaty with Carthage. It decided other things: Capua, second city of Italy, seceded from the Roman confederacy. Syracuse, now under a new king, allied itself with Carthage. The Samnite hill tribes and the hill tribes of Lucania went over to Hannibal. Many cities of Magna Graecia went over. The Roman confederacy seemed to be crumbling at last. Moreover, Rome, defender of oligarchies everywhere, heard with horror that the oligarchies she defended were threatened:

> One malady, so to speak, had attacked all the city-states of Italy, that the common people were at odds with the upper class, the senate inclining to the Romans, the common people drawing the state to the side of the Carthaginians.[91]

But in the very first year after Cannae, Claudius Marcellus, who had fought in the First Punic War and had then won renown by pacifying the Gauls, defeated Hannibal at Nola. Hannibal's new-found allies were unwilling to give much help. No help came from Spain, where his brother Hasdrubal's forces were pinned down by Publius Scipio and Publius' brother, Gnaeus. The two Scipios fought their way clear to southern Spain. Philip of Macedonia tried to transport troops to Italy to aid his new ally, Hannibal, but Roman warships appeared and he abandoned the attempt. Then, in 214, Marcellus crossed to Sicily, crushed a Carthaginian force that had come over to relieve Syracuse, and in 213 laid siege to Syracuse by land and by sea. From the sea his ships attacked with scaling ladders, but strange, newfangled machines appeared above the seagirt fortress wall and dropped massive stones into his ships. Grappling hooks on derricks lifted the prows of his ships high above the water, then suddenly let go and let the plunging ships submerge. A Roman land army was getting the same treatment: the iron claws were even grasping Roman soldiers, lifting them high in the air, and then letting them plunge to earth. Luckily for the Romans, a traitor let the Romans in. There was a vast haul of loot, including many beautiful statues and paintings. According to tradition, a Roman soldier found an old man all alone, working on a mathematical problem, oblivious of the pillagers. A soldier ordered him to come with him. The old man refused to do so until he had completed his demonstration, and the soldier was angered and stabbed him. It was Archimedes, the famous mathematician.[92] He had been persuaded by his kinsman the King of Syracuse to interrupt his mathematical studies long enough to devise powerful engines for siege warfare. These were the machines that had held the Roman forces at bay for eight months. They were Greek theory holding practical Roman force at bay. When Roman force interrupted Greek theory, Archimedes had already designed the tomb he desired. It recorded nothing of his war machines; only a cylinder with an inscribed sphere and the ratio between their respective volumes. A Roman historian later wrote that the Romans' early assault on Syracuse

> would have met with success if one man had not been at Syracuse at that time. It was Archimedes, an unrivalled observer of the heavens and the stars, more remarkable, however, as inventor and contriver of artillery and engines of war, by which with the least pains he frustrated whatever the enemy undertook with vast efforts.[93]

This Roman writer either did not know or did not care that a Roman soldier had robbed the Greek world of one of its ablest mathematicians. That Archimedes' mind loved and grappled with abstract ideas or even that it knew the motions of the heavenly bodies was less "remarkable" than that here on earth he had made things, things that could grapple with other things.

In 211 Rome's allies in Greece, the Aetolians, tried to persuade Sparta to help them in a war against Macedonia. A Greek ally of Philip's objected. He pointed out that it was Macedonia who protected the Greeks against the northern barbarians:

> But now Greece is threatened with a war against men of a foreign race who intend to enslave her, men whom you fancy you are calling in against Philip, but are calling in really against yourselves and the whole of Greece. For just as those who when imperilled by war introduce into their cities garrisons stronger than their own forces for the sake of safety, repel indeed all danger from the enemy but at the same time subject themselves to the authority of their friends, so do the Aetolians contemplate doing. For in their anxiety to get the better of Philip and humiliate the Macedonians, they have without knowing it invoked such a cloud from the west as may, perhaps, at first only cast its shadow on Macedonia, but in time will be the cause of great evil to all Greece.
>
> All Greeks, therefore, should foresee the approaching storm and especially the Lacedaemonians.[94]

In the same year that heard this warning, the Romans were besieging Capua. Hannibal tried and failed to relieve the city. He tried another method: he marched on Rome and camped within a mile of its gates. But Capua remained under siege; as for Rome, he had not assumed he could take that. He ravaged the neighborhood and withdrew to southern Italy;

Capua fell to Rome. In Spain the two Scipios lost their lives, so Rome sent out their son and nephew, Publius Cornelius Scipio, who crossed the Ebro and in 209 laid siege to New Carthage at the site of modern Cartagena. Scipio inspired his soldiers by hinting that he had a special relation with the gods. When he took New Carthage in four days from his arrival,

> he was greatly elated and it seemed more than ever that he was divinely inspired in all his actions. He began to think so himself and to give it out to others, not only then, but all the rest of his life, from that time on.[95]

Divinely inspired or not, he failed to prevent Hannibal's brother, Hasdrubal, from crossing the Pyrenees, reaching the Po Valley, and inciting another rising of the Gauls. Hannibal marched northward to meet him. In 207 a Roman army caught Hasdrubal near Ancona and defeated him. The Romans threw his head among Hannibal's Carthaginian pickets, and Hannibal read the sign: there would be no reinforcements either from Spain or Gaul. Again he withdrew to southern Italy. The next year Scipio captured Cadiz and drove the last Carthaginians from Spain. He had improved his time in Spain by secretly slipping over to Africa and forming an alliance with Masinissa, a dispossessed Numidian prince. There they concerted plans: Masinissa would aid the Romans if they attacked Carthage; Rome would restore him to his throne.

Scipio returned to Rome, was elected consul, and went to Sicily to prepare an attack on Carthage. In the same year, Hannibal's youngest brother, Mago, landed at Genoa with what was left of the army which Scipio had driven out of Spain. Scipio landed an army in Africa, defeated a Carthaginian army, and threatened Carthage. Carthage hastily recalled Hannibal and Mago from Italy. In 202, near Zama, and fairly near the site of modern Tunis, Hannibal sued for peace and offered generous terms. But Scipio demanded unconditional surrender. It was Carthage, he stated, not Rome, that was responsible for both the First Punic War and now this Second. He added that

> The gods, too, had testified to this by bestowing victory not on the unjust aggressors but on those who had taken up arms to defend themselves.[96]

The next morning Scipio addressed his troops. He told them,

> if you overcome your enemies not only will you be unquestioned masters of Africa, but you will gain for yourselves and your country the undisputed command and sovereignty of the rest of the world.[97]

This time Hannibal was weak in Numidian cavalry, and Scipio, thanks to Masinissa, was strong. Something very like the battle of Cannae took place; but this time Hannibal, not Rome, was the victim. The battle of Zama ended the Second Punic War, and Hannibal knew it. Indeed, it was on his advice that Carthage surrendered. Hannibal escaped to Carthage. After Zama the Roman army "billowed in booty."[98]

The Greek world knew that the Roman Public Thing was now the leading great power of the Mediterranean. Part of the peace terms bound Carthage not even to make war on her neighbors without the permission of Rome. Rome engaged in an orgy of pillage and massacre in those cities in Italy which had gone over to Hannibal, and her violence measured the fright that Hannibal's genius had inspired in her. Besides, her latest lesson in violence had lasted for seventeen years and she had had time to learn it well.

With the help of the Aetolian League and of King Attalus of Pergamum, the small forces Rome could spare for her war with Macedonia had imposed by 206 a moderate peace on Philip V. It was her first real exercise in one of the Eastern powers' favorite games: liberating the Greeks. If any Greeks then knew what Polybius later learned, they knew one of the most interesting sources of Rome's power. She had of course succeeded for many reasons. She had manpower, resources, great devotion to the Republic. Her citizen armies fought against invaders, invaders who were mercenaries. Besides the fact that Carthage, a traditionally maritime state, had never regained the naval superiority that Rome had snatched from her in the First Punic War, the powerful businessmen who governed Carthage had never really wanted the war which Hannibal precipitated. The stolidity that marked the Roman character made the foot soldier in the legions less liable to panic than he otherwise might have been. That same stolidity hampered Rome in the strategic use of cavalry, and it produced generals who learned little or nothing from Hannibal's mastery of ruse and ambush. Only one Roman general really learned from observing Hannibal, the man now called Scipio Africanus. Even when he was still in Spain, he was using Hannibal's methods, those methods that Pyrrhus had brought from the Hellenistic world in the East.

But what really fascinated Polybius and what he considered Rome's prime source of strength was the organization of the Roman army. The army insisted on the right kind of noncommissioned officer. Those who trained it wish the centurions not so much to be venturesome and daredevil as to be natural leaders, of a steady and sedate spirit. They do not desire them so much to be men who will initiate attacks and open the battle, but men who will hold their ground when worsted and hard-pressed and be ready to die at their posts.[99]

This tenacity compensated in part for amateur generalship. The straight, paved Roman roads that spread through Italy made for mobility. The military colonies of Roman citizens served as sentries and advance guards when trouble came. But the real triumph of organization was the Roman camp. Polybius informed his Greek readers that the military tribunes in charge of a field army

take both the Romans and allies and pitch their camp, one simple plan of camp being adopted at all times and in all places.[100]

Greek camps, Polybius reminded his readers, vary in shape and arrangement and adjust themselves to the terrain; but not the Roman camp.

The whole camp thus forms a square, and the way in which the streets are laid out and its general arrangement give it the appearance of a town.[101]

Also,

as everyone knows exactly in which street and in what part of the street his tent will be, since all invariably occupy the same place in the camp, the encamping somewhat resembles the return of an army to its native city. For then they break up at the gate and everyone goes straight on from there and reaches his own house without fail, as he knows both the quarter and the exact spot where his residence is situated. It is very much the same thing in a Roman camp.[102]

As a Roman general once explained to his army, a field camp on campaign was

a second home for the soldier, its rampart takes the place of city walls and his own tent is the soldier's dwelling and hearthside. Should we have fought like nomads with no abode, so that, whether conquered or conquerors, we might return—where?[103]

The camp was surrounded by a ditch, which was backed by a stake palisade, but these stakes were better adapted to making a strong barrier than were the stakes the Greeks used. Finally, the camp was closely guarded by sentries. If one of these sentries slept or was negligent, thereby endangering the whole camp,

A court-martial composed of all the tribunes at once meets to try him, and if he is found guilty he is punished by the bastinado. This is inflicted as follows: The tribune takes a cudgel and just touches the condemned man with it, after which all in the camp beat or stone him, in most cases dispatching him in the camp itself. But even those who manage to escape are not saved thereby: impossible! for they are not allowed to return to their homes, and none of the family would dare to receive such a man in his house. So that those who have once fallen into this misfortune are utterly ruined. . . . Thus, owing to the extreme severity and inevitableness of the penalty, the night watches of the Roman army are most scrupulously kept. . . .

The bastinado is also inflicted on those who steal anything from the camp; on those who give false evidence; on young men who have abused their persons; and finally on anyone who has been punished thrice for the same fault. Those are the offences which are punished as crimes, the following being treated as unmanly acts and disgraceful in a soldier— when a man boasts falsely to the tribune of his valour in the field in order to gain distinction; when any men who have been placed in a covering force leave the station assigned to them from fear; likewise when anyone throws away from fear any of his arms in the actual battle. Therefore the men in covering forces often face certain death, refusing to leave their ranks even when vastly outnumbered, owing to dread of the punishment they would meet with; and again in the battle men who have lost a shield or sword or any other arm often throw themselves into the midst of the enemy, hoping either to recover the lost object or to escape by death from inevitable disgrace and the taunts of their relations.

If the same thing ever happens to large bodies, and if entire maniples desert their posts when exceedingly hard pressed, the officers refrain from inflicting the bastinado or the death penalty on all, but find a solution of the difficulty which is both salutary and terror-striking. The tribune assembles the legion, and brings up those guilty of leaving the ranks, reproaches them sharply, and finally chooses by lot sometimes five, sometimes eight, sometimes twenty of the offenders, so adjusting the number thus chosen that they form as near as possible the tenth part of those guilty of cowardice. Those on whom the lot falls are bastinadoed mercilessly in the manner above described; the rest receive rations of barley instead of wheat and are ordered to encamp outside the camp on an unprotected spot. As therefore the danger and dread of drawing the fatal lot affects all equally, as it is uncertain on whom it will fall; and as the public disgrace of receiving barley rations falls on all alike, this practice is that best calculated both to inspire fear and to correct the mischief.[104]

If the Roman paid a heavy price for failure to do his duty, he could confidently look for rewards provided he did that duty well: a spear if he wounded an enemy in battle, a crown of gold if he scaled the wall of a besieged city, honorary gifts from the consul in command if he shielded or saved a fellow soldier. Finally,

> the recipients of such gifts, quite apart from becoming famous in the army and famous too for the time at their homes, are especially distinguished in religious processions after their return, as no one is allowed to wear decorations except those on whom these honours for bravery have been conferred by the consul; and in their houses they hang up the spoils they won in the most conspicuous places, looking upon them as tokens and evidences of their valour. Considering all this attention given to the matter of punishments and rewards in the army and the importance attached to both, no wonder that the wars in which the Romans engage end so successfully and brilliantly.[105]

Part of this brilliance and this success was loot; and loot, like sentries, had to be under law.

> I have already stated at some length in my chapters on the Roman state how it is that no one appropriates any part of the loot, but that all keep the oath they make when first assembled in camp on setting out for a campaign. So that when half of the army disperse to pillage and the other half keep their ranks and afford them protection, there is never any chance of the Romans suffering disaster owing to individual covetousness. For as all, both the spoilers and those who remain to safeguard them, have equal confidence that they will get their share of the booty, no one leaves the ranks, a thing which usually does injury to other armies. For since most men endure hardship and risk their lives for the sake of gain, it is evident that whenever the chance presents itself it is not likely that those left in the protecting force or in the camp will refrain, since the general rule among us is that any man keeps whatever comes into his hands. And even if any careful king or general orders the booty to be brought in to form a common fund, yet everyone regards as his own whatever he can conceal.[106]

Polybius' panegyric on the Roman army and the Roman camp became justly famous. But he did not make wholly explicit one striking difference between Greek and Roman. The Greek, like the Roman, craved a polis, a city-state. Plato's *Republic* reflected this longing. Aristotle, also, wanted the polis to be small enough to meet man's deepest needs. Socrates' pupil, Xenophon, conducted a kind of self-governing polis of ten thousand Greek mercenaries through the heart of an enemy empire, a polis in flight. And Aristotle's pupil, Alexander the Great, dreamed of Cosmopolis.

Rome did not dream. She started with Foursquare Rome. She methodically conquered other cities; made of them subordinate allies; later incorporated some; seized land and planted military colonies, little Romes. In a sense her field armies never left Rome, since their ideal was always to pass the night in a foursquare, fortified camp, one in which each man knew his own street and his own tent. Her generals could feel that they fought beneath the walls of Rome itself. From that safety they might strike an enemy too imprudent or too lazy to re-create his polis wherever he went. The Roman encamped polis of course looted when it could, as did Foursquare Rome. But both tried to bring some semblance of law, of coordinated action, even into the looting; and both found they got more loot that way.

The Greek Polybius read Plato's *Republic* and looked at Rome. For him, Plato's *Republic* was an idea; Rome was a thing, a *res*. A *res* is *realis*, real; an idea is not real. It is but a statue, and not a living, breathing man.[107] Nor could living Sparta, even with its famous laws of Lycurgus, compete. Those laws were good enough so long as the Spartans stayed home.

> But if anyone is ambitious of greater things, and esteems it finer and more glorious . . . to be the leader of many men and to rule and lord it over many and have the eyes of all the world turned to him, it must be admitted that from this point of view the Laconian constitution is defective, while that of Rome is superior and better framed for the attainment of power, as is indeed evident from the actual course of events. For when the Lacedaemonians endeavoured to obtain supremacy in Greece, they very soon ran the risk of losing their own liberty; whereas the Romans, who had aimed merely at the subjection of Italy, in a short time brought the whole world under their sway, the abundance of supplies they had at their command conducing in no small measure to this result.[108]

Polybius was not the only educated Greek to praise ideas and to prefer the Roman Public Thing, to praise freedom but to long for power.

After winning the Second Punic War, Rome subjugated the unruly Gauls of the Po Valley once again, this time for good. She temporarily pacified Hither, or northeastern, Spain; Farther, or southern, Spain; and even the Lusitanians, in what is now Portugal. As protector of the Greek city of Marseilles, she conquered the Ligurian raiders on the French Riviera and put down rebellions in Corsica and Sardinia. The Ligurian campaign embroiled her with various Gallic tribes in southern France and she ended up with a new province stretching from the Rhone to the Pyrenees. She subdued the Istrians, at the head of the Adriatic. Most of these Gauls and Spaniards and Istrians were uncivilized men, who liked danger but lacked discipline, or who pillaged camps and got hopelessly drunk at crucial moments, or whose "uncultured natures" and ignorance "of all etiquette"[109] made the Romans, now partially hellenized, feel as civilized as the men of Athens herself. The uncultured men were barbarians, the word so many Greeks applied to Romans. Such men sometimes made Romans laugh, and sometimes, as in Spain, they suffered nameless Roman atrocities and acts of treachery, which might have disturbed the Senate if they had taken place in Italy, even against Hannibal.

Rome's own understanding of her success did not include the treachery and broken faith her generals showed in Spain or even the strategy and ruses and ambushes that Scipio learned from Hannibal. Rome believed she owed her success to the courage, perseverance, and discipline of her infantry; to the perseverance of the government that sent them out, that held the city until those who conquered and survived could return to their city; and to force rather than to diplomatic maneuver and negotiation. They believed that the Trojans, whom they claimed as ancestors, had never been conquered in a fair fight; Greek deceit and ingenuity had caused the fall of Troy. They already believed what their poet Lucilius would write a few decades later: "Force is life, you see: all we do, force forces us to do."[110] Another Roman poet, Ennius, who fought in the Hannibalic War and composed an epic on it, wrote:

> He who has conquered is not conqueror
> Unless the conquered one confesses it.[111]

And when Aemilius Paullus had beaten the Ligurian raiders and the tribesmen asked for terms, he replied "that he did not negotiate for peace except with people who had surrendered."[112] Paullus was acting out what Ennius merely wrote. The demand for unconditional surrender was common Roman practice and effectively expressed Lucilius' point that force is life. Polybius recognized that force had served Rome well, although better against men than against storms, which wrought such havoc on her admirals in the First Punic War:

> The Romans, to speak generally, rely on force in all their enterprises, and think it is incumbent on them to carry out their projects in spite of all, and that nothing is impossible when they have once decided on it. They owe their success in many cases to this spirit, but sometimes they conspicuously fail by reason of it and especially at sea.[113]

From two other directions than from the lands inhabited by barbarians there loomed possible dangers. Rome's inveterate enemy Hannibal had now got the better of the Carthaginian oligarchy and had considerably cleaned up corruption in the government. Moreover, although chased out of Sicily, Sardinia, and Corsica by the First Punic War, and chased out of Spain by the Second, Carthage was enriching herself again, both by her ancient skill in trade and by her application of Greek scientific agriculture to her rich hinterland. She paid off her war indemnity with alarming speed.

The other danger to the new Roman peace was Philip V of Macedonia, who had allied himself with Hannibal in the tense period that followed Rome's disaster at Cannae. Philip had been a good king in those days, much admired in Greece. Now he had changed. He had taken to preying on Aegean merchant ships and, when he captured towns, he reverted to the ancient practice, now despised by many Greeks, of selling the inhabitants into slavery. Rhodes and Pergamum made war on him, and needed help. So they invoked what Philip's erstwhile Greek defender had warned the Spartans was "a cloud from the west," a cloud that would "be the cause of great evil to all Greece."

The cloud in the west, or at least the Senatorial portion of it, saw the chance of a useful preventive war. Despite the unfavorable reaction of the people, the Senate managed in 200 to send east some 30,000 men, including a modest fleet. Most of the Greeks stood aside. As was usual in their wars, the Romans made a poor beginning; but in 197 Titus Quinctius Flamininus caught Philip's army at a group of sharp-topped hills in Thessaly called Dogs' Heads, or Cynoscephalae. His legion dexterously outflanked the less maneuverable Macedonian phalanx, and the Roman short sword ended the Second Macedonian War. Once more somebody had liberated the Greeks.

The Aetolians had fought at the Romans' side, although after Cynoscephalae they were accused of plundering Philip's camp instead of helping the Romans to cut down the fleeing enemy. When the victorious Romans returned for loot there was none left. Having stolen the loot, the Aetolians spread the word, flattering to the vanity of their fellow Greeks, that it was also they who had won the victory. Flamininus was furious. The Aetolians wanted Philip deposed, but Flamininus answered them:

> Brave men should be hard on their foes and wroth with them in battle, when conquered they should be courageous and high-minded, but when they conquer, gentle and humane. What you exhort me to do now is exactly the reverse.[114]

Moreover, said Flamininus, only Macedonia stood between Greece and "the lawless violence of the Thracians and Gauls."[115] Phaeneas, one of the Aetolian negotiators, objected that Philip would make Macedonia a threat to her neighbors again.

> Flamininus interrupted him angrily and without rising from his seat, exclaiming, "Stop talking nonsense, Phaeneas; for I will so manage the peace that Philip will not, even if he wishes it, be able to wrong the Greeks."[116]

Flamininus made a separate peace with Philip, who was forced to free all the Greek cities he held, destroy his fleet, and pay an indemnity. But the Aetolians were shocked that Rome should have given the enemy such moderate terms and suspected double dealing.

> For since by this time bribery and the notion that no one should do anything gratis were very prevalent in Greece, and so to speak quite current coin among the Aetolians, they could not believe that Flamininus's complete change of attitude towards Philip could have been brought about without a bribe, since they were ignorant of the Roman principles and practice in this matter, but judged from their own, and calculated that it was probable that Philip would offer a very large sum owing to his actual situation and Flamininus would not be able to resist the temptation.
>
> If I were dealing with earlier times, I would have confidently asserted about all the Romans in general, that no one of them would do such a thing; I speak of the years before they undertook wars across the sea and during which they preserved their own principles and practices. At the present time, however, I would not venture to assert this of all, but I could with perfect confidence say of many particular men in Rome that in this matter they can maintain their faith.[117]

At the Isthmian Games of 196 a herald proclaimed that the Roman Senate and Titus Quinctius Flamininus had liberated the Greeks. Flamininus then dedicated shields at Delphi, with the inscription:

> O ye sons of Zeus, whose joy is in swift horsemanship, O ye Tyndaridae, princes of Sparta, Titus, a descendant of Aeneas, has brought you a most excellent gift, he who for the sons of the Greeks wrought freedom.[118]

He also dedicated a golden wreath to Apollo, with another inscription:

> This will fitly lie on thine ambrosial locks, O son of Leto, this wreath with sheen of gold; it is the gift of a great leader whose descent is from Aeneas. Therefore, O Far-darter, bestow upon the god-like Titus the glory due to his prowess.[119]

Greece was delirious with joy that this son of ancient Troy, this descendant of Aeneas, founder of Rome, this lover of Greek culture, had liberated the Greeks. And he had done it with no Greek help except that from the Aetolians, who were boastfully overstating the aid they had given him. The Greeks showered Flamininus with honors.

But there was of course a price. Flamininus saw to it that all Greek cities should be governed by oligarchies. Then he took his army back to Italy. This son of Aeneas thereby won the best of both worlds, or thought he had done so. He was the Liberator of Greece, and he really did love Greek culture. Also, Greece was now an area he confidently expected to be politically pro-Roman.

Flamininus also declined to let the Achaeans keep the island of Zacynthus, near the mouth of the Gulf of Corinth. He tried to convince the Achaeans that they were actually better off without it. So long, he explained, as the Achaeans stayed inside the Peloponnese, they were like a turtle withdrawn inside his shell; but if they acquired territory outside it, they would be as exposed to attack as a turtle that sticks his head or legs out. The Achaeans either were convinced or thought it wise to appear convinced. Rome kept Zacynthus, an island well beyond the shell of Italy; but then Rome was a much bigger and more powerful turtle than Achaea.

It was not as simple as Flamininus assumed. Antiochus the Great, the Seleucid King of Syria, whose Aegean coast was Greek, could scarcely relish Rome's entry into the centuries-old competition of liberating the Greeks. The Aetolian League, thoroughly disgruntled by Flamininus' high-handed settlement after the Aetolians had helped him to defeat Macedonia, now invited Antiochus to liberate the Greeks whom the Romans had liberated. Meanwhile, Hannibal's oligarchic enemies at Carthage informed the Roman Senate that Hannibal was conspiring against Rome with Antiochus. When the Senate sent a commission of inquiry to Carthage, Hannibal fled, and ultimately he did go to Antiochus. Scipio Africanus, fearing the combination of Antiochus' resources and Hannibal's generalship, urged the Senate to make Greece a province; but Flamininus the Liberator saw that this would merely prove that the Aetolians, who were now claiming his liberation of the Greeks was unreal, were right; and he won the Senate to his view. Hannibal advised Antiochus that he could never defeat the Romans in Greece,

> where they would have plenty of home-grown corn and adequate resources. Hannibal therefore urged him to occupy some part of Italy and make his base of operations there, so that the Romans might be weakened both at home and abroad. "I have had experience of Italy," he said, "and with 10,000 men I can occupy the strategic points and write to my friends in Carthage to stir up the people to revolt. They are already discontented with their condition, and mistrust the Romans, and they will be filled with courage and hope if they hear that I am ravaging Italy again." Antiochus listened eagerly to this advice, and as he considered the accession of Carthage a great advantage (as it was) for his war, directed him to write to his friends at once.[120]

But Antiochus did not attempt Italy, and no help ever came from Carthage. Antiochus landed in Thessaly with an advance guard of 10,000 men. But, except for his Aetolian allies, the Greeks were still infatuated with Rome and for once they did not want to be liberated. Philip V took sides with Rome. Again, despite much grumbling at Rome against another military draft, the Senate in 191 sent an army, under the consul Acilius Glabrio, to Thessaly. He met Antiochus at Thermopylae. One of his military tribunes, Marcus Cato, detoured the pass as a Persian detachment had done in 480 in order to attack the Spartan defenders from the rear. The Aetolians could not stop Cato, Glabrio scattered Antiochus' army, and the King fled to Asia. He did not believe the Romans would follow. But Hannibal insisted to Antiochus that

> In Asia and for Asia itself there would soon be war on land and sea between him and the Romans, and either the Romans, seeking dominion over the world, would lose it or he himself would lose his kingdom.[121]

Next year Scipio Africanus was sent out, nominally under his brother, a consul; he crossed Macedonia, Thrace, and the Hellespont; and in 190 he defeated Antiochus at Magnesia-on-Sipylus. Antiochus surrendered to Rome all of his European conquests and all of Asia Minor west of the Taurus Mountains, agreed to a large indemnity, and agreed also to give up Hannibal. Rome pacified the troublesome Galatians, and thereby won the acclaim of Greece-in-Asia. But this time Rome liberated only some of the Greek cities. Others she turned over to her allies, Pergamum and Rhodes.

Hannibal escaped to Prusias, King of Bithynia. It was Flamininus, the Liberator of Greece, who demanded Hannibal's extradition. When Prusias' troops surrounded him, Hannibal called for the poison he had long kept at hand.

> "Let us," he said, "relieve the Roman people of their long anxiety, since they find it tedious to wait for the death of an old man. Neither magnificent nor memorable will be the victory which Flamininus will win over a man unarmed and betrayed. How much the manners of the Roman people have changed, this day in truth will prove. Their fathers sent word to King Pyrrhus, an enemy in arms, commanding an army in Italy, warning him to beware of poison: these Romans have sent an ambassador of consular rank to urge upon Prusias the crime of murdering his guest." Then, cursing the person and the kingdom of Prusias and calling upon the gods of hospitality to bear witness to his breach of faith, he drained the cup. This was the end of the life of Hannibal.[122]

Hannibal Barca was about sixty-five when he took poison rather than grace a Roman triumph. When he was still urging Antiochus to fight the Romans, he told him how his hatred of Rome had started. When he was only nine years old, his father Hamilcar was preparing to lead an army from Carthage to conquer Spain. His father made the official sacrifice. Then he asked the boy whether he would like to accompany him to Spain. When Hannibal begged to be taken,

> his father took him by the hand, led him up to the altar, and bade him lay his hand on the victim and swear never to be the friend of the Romans.[123]

Whether Hannibal's report to Antiochus was true or false historically, it was true poetically. He spent a lifetime striving to overthrow Rome. Besides being the most brilliant military leader of his time, he twice displayed considerable statesmanship: once, by detaching many of Rome's allies in Italy; and again, after his defeat, by reforming the constitution of Carthage.

But he offered Cosmopolis nothing, except freedom from Rome. Cosmopolis, however, was ripe for a common government and law, and until it got them there would be a power vacuum. It was that vacuum that kept sucking the Roman Public Thing into all of Italy, into Sicily, into Illyria, Macedonia, Greece, and now Asia, and the momentum of this thrust carried Rome also into Spain, Portugal, southern France, and eventually North Africa. Sometimes the Senate and sometimes the popular assembly hesitated. No doubt, ambitious consuls sought glory, impoverished plebeians sought booty, and both groups were hungry for land. No doubt the contractors who furnished the army, the merchants who followed it and bought up booty, the financiers who loaned money usuriously to those who were vanquished and must pay tribute, all pushed towards war. But all had one, powerful argument: there was always a quarrelsome, lawless community just beyond the newest frontier. So the Thing kept spreading. No other center of power showed the slightest chance of filling the vacuum. What a Rhodian said at a slightly later period was already true: that the Greeks might as well give up "currying favour with kings," since the Roman alliance was

> the only alliance in the world at that time which was secure whether through power or trustworthiness.[124]

Certainly it was not Carthage, which wanted only to buy and sell in the world as it was. In a real sense, therefore, although Carthage had a good moral case against Rome, Hannibal fought against history. With all his brilliance, courage, and determination, he had no answer to the most urgent question history asked: who would organize Cosmopolis? The Roman Public Thing showed no signs that it could state the question. It merely met one concrete problem after another and was content to carry out what it was sure was the will of Jove.

In 179 Philip V of Macedonia died. Eight years later his son and successor, Perseus, prepared to drive Rome out of the Balkan peninsula. He began by making alliances with neighboring tribes of barbarians, by enlarging his army, and by befriending bankrupts and debtors in the Greek cities, a class dissatisfied with the oligarchs whom Flamininus had placed in power in those cities. By 172 Eumenes, King of Pergamum, had warned his Roman ally that Perseus was preparing to strike. Many Greeks were recovering from their love affair with Flamininus. Prosperity was still passing by Mainland Greece for fairer fields in Asia, and the poor especially were teased by the idea that Perseus might prove the newest *deus ex machina* to liberate the Greeks, this time from the cloud in the west.

When King Perseus began the Third Macedonian War in 171, it started off true to form with bungling Roman strategy and a severe Roman defeat near Larissa in Thessaly. But some of the King's more prudent advisers urged him to negotiate a peace while his position was strong. Envoys were sent to Roman headquarters and presented an offer to evacuate all places he had won and to pay the same annual tribute Philip had paid. The Romans deliberated. Then,

> It was unanimously decided to give as severe a reply as possible, it being in all cases the traditional Roman custom to show themselves most imperious and severe in the season of defeat, and most lenient after success. That this is noble conduct every one will confess, but perhaps it is open to doubt if it is possible under certain circumstances. In the present case, then, their answer was as follows. They ordered Perseus to submit absolutely, giving the senate authority to decide as they saw fit about the affairs of Macedonia.[125]

Even when Perseus made several increasingly favorable offers, the Roman demand for unconditional surrender stood firm.

Meanwhile, when news of Perseus' brilliant victory had spread through Greece, the popular, democratic support he enjoyed in the Greek cities, "which had been for the most part concealed, burst forth like fire."[126] Polybius thought this reaction of the poorer Greeks could have been reversed. If somebody

> had reminded them even briefly of all the hardships that the house of Macedon had inflicted on Greece, and of all the benefits she had derived from Roman rule, I fancy the reaction would have been most sudden and complete. But now, when they gave way to their first unreflecting impulse, the delight of the people at the news was conspicuous, hailing, as they did, owing to the very strangeness of the fact, the appearance of some one at least who had proved himself a capable adversary of Rome. I have been led to speak of this matter at such length lest anyone, in ignorance of what is inherent in human nature, may unjustly reproach the Greeks with ingratitude for being in this state of mind at the time.[127]

If only Perseus had used his bulging treasury to subsidize potential allies and to distribute modest bribes to kings and key statesmen, then no intelligent man I suppose would dispute that all the Greeks and all the kings, or at least the most of them, would have failed to withstand the temptation. Instead of taking that course, by which either, if completely victorious, he would have created a splendid empire, or, if defeated, would have exposed many to the same ruin as himself, he took the opposite one, owing to which quite a few of the Greeks went wrong in their calculations when the time for action came.[128]

As to the leaders, a Roman historian later wrote:

> Some were so enraptured with the Romans as to undermine their own influence by their unrestrained partisanship; a few of them were attracted by the justice of Roman rule, most were moved by the thought that if they displayed some especial service for the Romans they would become powerful in their own states. Another group were toadies to the king; some, because of debt and despair of their own fortunes if no change should occur, were driven headlong to the overturning of everything. Some were upset by their own windy instability of character, since the breeze of popular favour turned in Perseus' direction. A third group, which was also the worthiest and wisest, if merely a choice of a dominating superior were offered them, preferred to be under the Romans rather than under the king; but if they had a free choice of destiny in this respect, they wished neither side to become the more powerful through the downfall of the other, but rather that, the strength of both sides being unexhausted, peace on terms of equality should continue; thus the situation of the free states with respect to the two powers would be most advantageous, since one power would always protect the weak against wrongdoing by the other. With these sentiments they watched silently from a safe position the contests of the partisans of either side.[129]

Meanwhile, Perseus won several victories and began to erect triumphal columns to commemorate them. But in the fourth year of the war the consul Aemilius Paullus, an experienced veteran from the Spanish and Illyrian theaters, was assigned the Macedonian command. Paullus restored discipline in the demoralized Roman army. Then in 168 he backed Perseus against the seacoast at Pydna, withstood the first shock of the famous Macedonian phalanx, and again the short sword broke a phalanx and won a war. Before returning to Rome, Paullus noted the triumphal columns Perseus had begun to erect; then, "finding them unfinished, completed them and set statues of himself on them."[130] The Roman conqueror of course visited Olympia to see the sights. The Greek Polybius reported later that when Paullus saw the statue of Zeus he was awestruck, and said simply that Pheidias seemed to him to have been the only artist who had made a likeness of Homer's Zeus; for he himself had come to Olympia with high expectations but the reality had far surpassed his expectations.[131]

But Livy, reporting the same incident, wrote that Paullus

saw many sights which he considered worth seeing; but he was stirred to the quick as he gazed on what seemed Jupiter's very self. Therefore he ordered a sacrifice prepared larger than usual, just as if he had been going to sacrifice on the Capitol.[132]

Zeus, after all, was identified with Jupiter Capitolinus. Having demonstrated to anti-Roman Greeks that he was fully capable of appreciating the past glories of Greece, Paullus examined the path to heaven itself, where he saw not only objects of beauty but more practical things. He

went to Athens, which is also replete with ancient glory, but nevertheless has many notable sights, the Acropolis, the harbours, the walls joining Piraeus to the city, the shipyards, the monuments of great generals, and the statues of gods and men—statues notable for every sort of material and artistry.[133]

Perseus, who had escaped from Macedonia, tried to stipulate before surrendering that he be guaranteed at least

the title of king, while Paulus urged him to entrust himself and all he had to the discretion and mercy of the Roman people.[134]

Perhaps Perseus did not know that it was Paullus who had told the Ligurian tribesmen "that he did not negotiate for peace except with people who had surrendered." The prediction of the Aetolians to Flamininus had come true. Philip V had lost the Second Macedonian War but had not been deposed. He had planned revenge. His son and successor had provoked the Third Macedonian War. And now at last Rome did depose a king of Macedonia, which is what the Aetolians had asked her to do nearly three decades before. She also divided Macedonia into four states, separately exposed to what Flamininus had called the lawless violence of the Thracians and Gauls.

Next, while Greece watched with horror, Paullus, on orders from the Senate, unleashed his army on Epirus. Although Epirus had done little to aid its Macedonian allies, Paullus plundered its towns and villages and sold 150,000 Epirotes into slavery. The loot that reached Rome was so huge that all Roman citizens were henceforth exempted from all direct taxation. A thousand leading citizens of the Achaean League, including Polybius, were deported to Italy as hostages and detained without trial in Italian cities for sixteen years. Two of Rome's allies, Pergamum and Rhodes, had backed off and tried to play mediator. They were punished. Just as Macedonia was carved into four independent republics, Illyria was carved into three. All seven of these puppet republics paid a moderate land tax to Rome. Perseus and his leading officials were deported to Italy. Paullus, to the astonishment of his contemporaries, kept none of the loot for himself except Macedonia's royal library. He died poor.

Rome was at last free to intervene in a war which her ally, Egypt, had prepared to wage against Antiochus IV of Syria. Antiochus had invaded Egypt, had crowned himself king, had issued coinage, and was now approaching Alexandria. Four miles from the city a group of envoys from the Roman Senate, led by Gaius Popilius, met him. The Romans bore with them a Senate decree that Antiochus must call off his war against Egypt.

> As they approached, he greeted them and offered his hand to Popilius; whereat Popilius handed him the tablets containing the decree of the senate in writing, and bade him read this first of all. On reading the decree, he said that he would call in his friends and consider what he should do; Popilius, in accordance with the usual harshness of his temper, drew a circle around the king with a rod that he carried in his hand, and said, "Before you step out of this circle, give me an answer which I may take back to the senate." After the king had hesitated a moment, struck dumb by so violent an order, he replied, "I shall do what the senate decrees." Only then did Popilius extend his hand to the king as to an ally and friend.[135]

From all over the eastern Mediterranean came deputations and embassies to Rome, eager to secure backing for their projects: cities sought help against cities; political factions, against their opponents; even the kings came. The Senate was bewildered. Its growing suspicion that it might be easier to conquer than to govern was now amply confirmed, and inevitably the Senate fumbled many complex problems. It was a pleasant interlude to have Prusias, the Asian king who had betrayed Hannibal, furnish comic relief:

> At the same time King Prusias also came to Rome to congratulate the senate and the generals on what had happened. This Prusias was

a man by no means of the royal dignity, as may easily be understood from the following facts. In the first place when some Roman legates had come to his court, he went to meet them with his head shorn, and wearing a white hat and a toga and shoes, exactly the costume worn at Rome by slaves recently manumitted or "liberti" as the Romans call them. "In me," he said, "you see your libertus who wishes to endear himself and imitate everything Roman"; a phrase as humiliating as one can conceive. And now, on entering the senate-house he stood in the doorway facing the members and putting both his hands on the ground bowed his head to the ground in adoration of the threshold and the seated senators, with the words, "Hail, ye saviour gods," making it impossible for anyone after him to surpass him in unmanliness, woman-ishness, and servility. And on entering he conducted himself during his interview in a similar manner, doing things that it were unbecoming even to mention. As he showed himself to be utterly contemptible, he received a kind answer for this very reason.[136]

This account by Polybius scarcely did justice to King Prusias. The liberty cap and the Oriental salaam were judiciously combined. The cap might have reminded the savior gods who comprised the Roman Senate of the delirious joy at the Isthmian Games when Flamininus declared the liberation of Greece. The salaam acknowledged that not only Main-land Greece but western Asia Minor recognized Roman power; in Asia Minor the salaam was from of old the authentic way to recognize sov-ereign power. And Prusias was not alone. The whole Greek-speaking world vibrated in resonance with the greatest accumulation of money and military might that it had ever encountered.

On the other hand, it is at least conceivable that Prusias was simply satirizing the Roman habit of liberating the Greeks by requiring uncon-ditional surrender to the will of Jove.

Nearly two decades after the conquest and partition of Macedonia, an adventurer named Andriscus announced that he was really Philip, the brother of Perseus, and that he was therefore the rightful King of Mace-donia. Like Perseus, this pseudo-Philip promised help to the debtor class in Greek cities. Rome hastily sent over a first detachment of troops, and when Andriscus defeated it, many Greeks again felt a wave of hope. But more Roman troops of course arrived. In 148 the Fourth Macedonian War ended in a crushing defeat for Andriscus. He was captured; graced a Roman triumph; then was executed. This time the whole of Macedonia, to which Thessaly and Epirus were added, was made a Roman province, the first one to be organized east of the Adriatic. A military road was built from Apollonia on the Adriatic straight eastward across Macedonia to a gulf of the Aegean.

In either 157 or 153, Marcus Cato served on an embassy Rome sent to Carthage. He was shocked by the speed with which Carthage was recovering from the Second Punic War. On his return he made a practice of ending every speech he gave in the Senate with the statement, "In my opinion, Carthage must be destroyed."[137] Cato was then about eighty years old.

Born of plebeian stock, Cato had served in the Second Punic War as a young man, had risen to the rank of consul, organized Roman rule in southern Spain, and performed brilliantly at Thermopylae when the Romans defeated Antiochus of Syria. In 184 he was elected censor. He became perhaps the most famous censor Rome ever had, and he labored tirelessly and ruthlessly to suppress the growing luxury of Roman life. He

> made mock of all Greek culture and training, out of patriotic zeal. He says, for instance, that Socrates was a mighty prattler, who attempted, as best he could, to be his country's tyrant, by abolishing its customs, and by enticing his fellow citizens into opinions contrary to the laws.[138]

He denounced Greek philosophers, Greek physicians, Greek cooks. But in his old age he studied the Greek language; and the maxims and proverbs he loved to utter were often literal translations from the Greek.[139] He farmed; wrote a handbook on farming, which was considered the first major prose work in Latin; denounced literature and published copiously. Though he hounded usurers, he loved money, drove his slaves hard, practiced stern thrift, and announced

> that a man was to be admired and glorified like a god if the final inventory of his property showed that he had added to it more than he had inherited.[140]

His wit was the barbed wit of a Spartan. Once to a fat man of the Equestrian Order he cried:

> Where can such a body be of service to the state, when everything between its gullet and its groins is devoted to belly?[141]

He prosecuted many men, persuaded others to prosecute, and was himself prosecuted nearly fifty times. The last time Cato was very old, and he remarked to his judges that

> It is hard for one who has lived among men of one generation, to make his defence before those of another.[142]

While still a young man, he had become the most widely praised orator of his day,

> distinguished by such sagacity and eloquence that the Romans called him Demosthenes for his speeches, for they learned that Demosthenes had been the greatest orator of Greece.[143]

The comparison might more fitly, perhaps, have been made with the trenchant Phocion, whom Demosthenes called his meat cleaver. Cato's celebrated and typically laconic advice to other orators was "Stick to the point, and the words will come."[144]

In 149, Cato got his chance to destroy Carthage. Masinissa, King of Numidia and Rome's ally, began conquering and annexing territories held by Carthage. Carthage, forbidden by treaty from making war, appealed to Rome. The Senate proved evasive. Carthage tried vainly to defend her territories. The Roman Senate had been waiting for an excuse to destroy Carthage, chose to consider that she had violated her treaty not to make war, and declared war on Carthage. The Senate then sent to Sicily one consul with an army and the other consul with a navy. These were given secret orders to raze Carthage. Desperate, the Carthaginians sent another embassy to Rome with full powers.

> The Senate was convened, and told them that if, within thirty days, the Carthaginians would give to the consuls, who were still in Sicily, 300 children of their noblest families as hostages, and would obey their orders in other respects, the freedom and autonomy of Carthage should be preserved and they should retain their lands in Africa. This was voted in public, and they gave the resolution to the ambassadors to carry to Carthage; but they sent word privately to the consuls that they should carry out their secret instructions.[145]

The Carthaginians, with much foreboding, sent the children.

> When the consuls received them in Sicily they sent them to Rome, and said to the Carthaginians that in reference to the ending of the war they would give them further information at Utica.[146]

The consuls crossed to Utica and received another Carthaginian embassy, which appealed to "that morality in which you claim to be pre-eminent."[147] And the Carthaginians reminded the consuls that Carthage had promptly sent the children as demanded by the Senate's decree:

> It was a part of this decree that if we would deliver the hostages Carthage should remain free under her own laws and in the enjoyment of her possessions.[148]

If they really wanted peace, came the reply, then they should surrender all their weapons and engines of war; Rome would protect them against a threatened attack from without by rebels. So the Carthaginians fetched to Utica complete armor for some 200,000 men, countless javelins and darts, and about 2,000 catapults. Then Censorinus, one of the consuls, congratulated them and added,

> Bear bravely the remaining command of the Senate. Yield Carthage to us, and betake yourselves where you like within your own territory at a distance of at least ten miles from the sea, for we are resolved to raze your city to the ground.[149]

At last Carthage seemed helpless. The ambassadors begged for mercy, adding the reminder,

> Romans, you desire a good name and reputation for piety in all that you do, and you profess the virtue of moderation in prosperity, and claim credit for it from those whom you conquer.[150]

To which Censorinus replied:

> What is the use of repeating what the Senate has ordered? It has issued its decrees and they must be carried out. We have not even power to defer what has already been commanded. If we had imposed these commands on you as enemies, Carthaginians, it would be necessary only to speak and then use force, but since this is a matter of the common good (ours, perhaps, to a certain extent, but yours even more), I have no objection to giving you the reasons, if you may be thus persuaded instead of being coerced. The sea reminds you of the dominion and power you once acquired by means of it. It prompts you to wrongdoing and brings you thus into disaster. The sea made you invade Sicily and lose it again. Then you invaded Spain and were driven out of it. While a treaty was in force you plundered merchants on the sea, and ours especially, and in order to conceal the crime you threw them overboard,

until finally you were detected, and then you gave us Sardinia by way of penalty. Thus you lost Sardinia also because of the sea, which always begets a grasping disposition by the very facilities which it offers for gain.

Through this the Athenians, when they became a maritime people, grew mightily, but fell as suddenly. Naval prowess is like merchants' gains—a good profit to-day and a total loss to-morrow. You know at any rate that those very people whom I have mentioned, when they had extended their sway over the Ionian Sea to Sicily, could not restrain their greed until they had lost their whole empire, and were compelled to surrender their harbour and their ships to their enemies, to receive a garrison in their city, to demolish their own Long Walls, and to become almost an inland people. And this very thing secured their existence for a long time. Believe me, Carthaginians, life inland, with the joys of agriculture and quiet, is much more equable. . . .

In brief, you will understand that we do not make this decision from any ill-will toward you, but in the interest of a lasting concord and of the common security . . . This is what we told you beforehand, that Carthage should have her own laws if you would obey our commands. We considered *you* to be Carthage, not the ground where you live.[151]

Censorinus then dismissed them.

The ambassadors returned to Carthage. There were riots. The Carthaginian senate declared war and freed the slaves to help defend the city. The citizens worked day and night to forge new weapons. For a while the Romans besieged the city in vain. Scipio Aemilianus served as military tribune in the besieging army and distinguished himself. The historian Polybius, since 151 no longer a hostage, was with him.

Scipio was the son of Aemilius Paullus, who had won the Third Macedonian War. But Paullus had given him for adoption to a friend with no sons; the friend was the son of Scipio Africanus, who had won the Second Punic War. The young Scipio had sought out Polybius and had invited him to be his intellectual and moral mentor. Polybius reported that

The first direction taken by Scipio's ambition to lead a virtuous life, was to attain a reputation for temperance and excel in this respect all the other young men of the same age. This is a high prize indeed and difficult to gain, but it was at this time easy to pursue at Rome owing to the vicious tendencies of most of the youths. For some of them had abandoned themselves to amours with boys and others to the society of courtesans, and many to musical entertainments and banquets, and the extravagance they involve, having in the course of the war with Perseus been speedily infected by the Greek laxity in these respects. So great in fact was the incontinence that had broken out among the young men in such matters, that many paid a talent for a male favourite and many three hundred drachmas for a jar of caviar. This aroused the indignation of Cato, who said once in a public speech that it was the surest sign of deterioration in the republic when pretty boys fetch more than fields, and jars of caviar more than ploughmen. It was just at this period we are treating of that this present tendency to extravagance declared itself, first of all because they thought that now after the fall of the Macedonian kingdom their universal dominion was undisputed, and next because after the riches of Macedonia had been transported to Rome there was a great display of wealth both in public and in private.[152]

In 146 Scipio was elected consul and directed to complete the capture and destruction of Carthage. He restored discipline in the badly demoralized Roman army, cut off the city's line of supply, and after six days and nights of street fighting accepted the surrender of Carthage.

Scipio, beholding this city, which had flourished 700 years from its foundation and had ruled over so many lands, islands, and seas, as rich in arms and fleets, elephants, and money as the mightiest empires, but far surpassing them in hardihood and high spirit (since, when stripped of all its ships and arms, it had sustained famine and a mighty war for three years), now come to its end in total destruction—Scipio, beholding this spectacle, is said to have shed tears and publicly lamented the fortune of the enemy. After meditating by himself a long time and reflecting on the inevitable fall of cities, nations, and empires, as well as of individuals, upon the fate of Troy, that once proud city, upon the fate of the Assyrian, the Median, and afterwards of the great Persian empire, and, most recently of all, of the splendid empire of Macedon, either voluntarily or otherwise the words of the poet escaped his lips:—

> The day shall come in which our sacred Troy
> And Priam, and the people over whom
> Spear-bearing Priam rules, shall perish all.

Being asked by Polybius in familiar conversation (for Polybius had been his tutor) what he meant by using these words, Polybius says that he did not hesitate frankly to name his own country, for whose fate he feared when he considered the mutability of human affairs. And Polybius wrote this down just as he heard it.[153]

Carthage was razed, imprecations were uttered against any who should settle on its site, and the remnant of Carthaginians were sold as slaves. But when news of the destruction of Carthage reached Rome, the Romans "poured into the streets and spent the whole night congratulating and embracing each other."[154] Cato could not savor the victory: he had died in the first years of the war at the age of eighty-five, hating and fearing Carthage to the end.

In 151 Rome had sent home from sixteen years of Italian exile some 300 of Polybius' Achaean fellow hostages. About 700 had died in exile. The cities of the Achaean League were in ferment. At Corinth the industrial and commercial working class longed to get rid of Roman domination: it was Rome that everywhere, in the name of law and order, helped the oligarchies to block social reforms. The final collapse of both Macedonia and Carthage in the same year set the Greeks to arguing about the growth and merits of Roman power:

> Both about the Carthaginians when they were crushed by the Romans and about the affair of the pseudo-Philip many divergent accounts were current in Greece, at first on the subject of the conduct of Rome to Carthage and next concerning their treatment of the pseudo-Philip. As regards the former the judgements formed and the opinions held in Greece were far from unanimous. There were some who approved the action of the Romans, saying that they had taken wise and statesmanlike measures in defence of their empire. For to destroy this source of perpetual menace, this city which had constantly disputed the supremacy with them and was still able to dispute it if it had the opportunity and thus to secure the dominion of their own country, was the act of intelligent and far-seeing men.

> Others took the opposite view, saying that far from maintaining the principles by which they had won their supremacy, they were little by little deserting it for a lust of domination like that of Athens and Sparta, starting indeed later than those states, but sure, as everything indicated, to arrive at the same end. For at first they had made war with every nation until they were victorious and until their adversaries had confessed that they must obey them and execute their orders. But now they had struck the first note of their new policy by their conduct to Perseus, in utterly exterminating the kingdom of Macedonia, and they had now

completely revealed it by their decision concerning Carthage. For the Carthaginians had been guilty of no immediate offence to Rome, but the Romans had treated them with irremediable severity, although they had accepted all their conditions and consented to obey all their orders.

Others said that the Romans were, generally speaking, a civilized people, and that their peculiar merit on which they prided themselves was that they conducted their wars in a simple and noble manner, employing neither night attacks nor ambushes, disapproving of every kind of deceit and fraud, and considering that nothing but direct and open attacks were legitimate for them. But in the present case, throughout the whole of their proceedings in regard to Carthage, they had used deceit and fraud . . .[155]

In 147 Critolaus, commander of the Achaean League's armed forces, had got himself proclaimed dictator, and marched against Heraclea, a city near Thermopylae that had seceded from the Achaean League and now counted on Roman protection. Democrats from Thebes and other cities of central Greece joined Critolaus' expedition. The consul Metellus routed this army and threw it back on Corinth. Another popular leader, Diaeus, improvised reinforcements with some 1,500 freedmen and slaves and met at the Isthmus a Roman army under a new consul, Mummius. The Greek democrats fought hard but were crushed. Anti-Roman leaders were punished with death or confiscation; the Achaean League was dissolved and oligarchies were restored in its member cities. Considerable self-government was salvaged by many cities, but there was no longer any question who controlled Greece. Athens had not participated in this democratic war for independence, and in theory remained completely free.

Rome's handling of revolutionary Corinth was more drastic. Corinth, like Carthage, was razed to the ground, and in the same fateful year, 146. Its inhabitants were sold into slavery.

Where is thy celebrated beauty, Doric Corinth? Where are the battlements of thy towers and thy ancient possessions? Where are the temples of the immortals, the houses and the matrons of the town of Sisyphus, and her myriads of people? Not even a trace is left of thee, most unhappy of towns, but war has seized on and devoured everything. We alone, the Nereids, Ocean's daughters, remain inviolate, and lament, like halcyons, thy sorrows.[156]

Corinth was an ancient and wealthy city, and the haul of loot was tremendous. Polybius witnessed the final catastrophe and witnessed too the contempt of the Roman soldiers for the works of art. He "saw pictures thrown on the ground with the soldiers playing draughts on them."[157] The sack of Syracuse sixty-six years before had furnished an admirable precedent for converting valuable sculpture and paintings into military loot. At Rome the taste for such things had grown. Other Greek cities besides Corinth were looted, but Corinth was wealthier than most, her artistic tradition exceedingly long, her destruction thorough.

As a somewhat Romanized Greek and a conservative, Polybius had watched with horror and disgust this rising against Rome and against government by the Greek propertied class, a rising that was partly a hopeless war of independence and partly an outbreak of class war. He reported that during the Achaean war of 146,

> Some arrested others to surrender them to the enemy as having been guilty of opposition to Rome, and others informed against their friends and accused them, although no such service was demanded of them at present. Others again presented themselves as suppliants, confessing their treachery and asking what their punishment should be, in spite of the fact that no one as yet demanded any explanation of their conduct in this respect. The whole country in fact was visited by an unparalleled attack of mental disturbance, people throwing themselves into wells and down precipices, so that, as the proverb says, the calamity of Greece would even arouse the pity of an enemy, had he witnessed it. In former times indeed they had erred gravely and sometimes entirely come to grief, quarrelling now about questions of state and now betrayed by despots, but at the time I speak of they met with what all acknowledge to be a real calamity owing to the folly of their leaders and their own errors. The Thebans even abandoned their city in a body and left it entirely desert . . .[158]

To Polybius it seemed clear that Rome's control of the western Mediterranean and of an increasing portion of the eastern as well, and her obvious domination of the rest, were "the finest and most beneficent of the performances of Fortune."[159] And indeed to a Stoic like Polybius the speed and sureness of Rome's rise did wear a providential air. As early as 195, only two years after Flamininus so dramatically liberated the Greeks, Smyrna had consecrated a temple to the City of Rome and, as time went on, many other cities followed suit. Some of this was perhaps no more than prudent flattery, but the flattery agreed in effect with what Scipio Africanus had claimed at his conference with Hannibal on the eve of Zama: that the gods fought for Rome. And flattery found its uses. For example, the Acarnanians reportedly appealed to the Roman Senate to make the Aetolians

> withdraw their garrisons from the cities of Acarnania, and to allow those to be free, who alone, of all the people of Greece, had not contributed aid to the Greeks against the Trojans, the authors of the Roman race.[160]

But many Greeks, out of their humiliation and resentment, chose to believe the Romulus legend about Rome rather than the Trojan. A later historian wrote that the great majority of Greeks were ignorant of Rome's history and believed

> that, having come upon various vagabonds without house or home and barbarians, and even those not free men, as her founders, she in the course of time arrived at world domination, and this not through reverence for the gods and justice and every other virtue, but through some chance and the injustice of Fortune, which inconsiderately showers her greatest favours upon the most undeserving. And indeed the more malicious are wont to rail openly at Fortune for freely bestowing on the basest of barbarians the blessings of the Greeks. And yet why should I mention men at large, when even some historians have dared to express such views in the writings they have left, taking this method of humouring barbarian kings who detested Rome's supremacy,— princes to whom they were ever servilely devoted and with whom they associated as flatterers,—by presenting them with "histories" which were neither just nor true?[161]

The hellenized courtiers of Perseus, who later became King of Macedonia, gibed at the Roman barbarians. Some

> would poke fun at their manners and customs, others at their achievements, others at the appearance of the city itself, which was not yet made beautiful in either its public or its private sections, others at individual leaders . . .[162]

Even Polybius, with his admiration for Rome, thought that many Roman leaders had pillaged a culture they could not comprehend. This was true not only of Sicilian sundials. According to Athenaeus, Polybius reported that

> Lucius Anicius, the Roman praetor, upon conquering the Illyrians and bringing back as his prisoners Genthius, the king of Illyria, and

his children, in celebrating games in honour of his victory, behaved in the most absurd manner. . . . For having sent for the most celebrated scenic artists from Greece and constructed an enormous stage in the circus, he first brought on all the flute-players at once. These were Theodorus of Boeotia, Theopompus, Hermippus and Lysimachus, who were then at the height of their fame. Stationing them with the chorus on the proscenium he ordered them to play all together. When they went through their performance with the proper rhythmic movements, he sent to them to say they were not playing well and ordered them to show more competitive spirit. They were at a loss to know what he meant, when one of the lictors explained that they should turn and go for each other and make a sort of fight of it. The players soon understood, and having got an order that suited their own appetite for licence, made a mighty confusion. Making the central groups of dancers face those on the outside, the flute-players blowing loud in unintelligible discord and turning their flutes about this way and that, advanced towards each other in turn, and the dancers, clapping their hands and mounting the stage all together, attacked the adverse party and then faced about and retreated in their turn. And when one of the dancers girt up his robes on the spur of the moment, and turning round lifted up his hands in boxing attitude against the flute-player who was advancing towards him, there was tremendous applause and cheering on the part of the spectators. And while they were thus engaged in a pitched battle, two dancers with musicians were introduced into the orchestra and four prize-fighters mounted the stage accompanied by buglers and clarion-players and with all these men struggling together the scene was indescribable. As for the tragic actors Polybius says, "If I tried to describe them some people would think I was making fun of my readers."[163]

Although Rome had trouble converting Greek musical concerts of this sort into gladiatorial contests, the Hellenistic East faced similar problems in reverse. For at least a century Rome had witnessed gladiatorial combats commonly given at funeral games in honor of the great. In 175, eight years before the battle of the Greek flute players rejoiced the praetor Anicius, Antiochus Epiphanes, son of Antiochus the Great, came to the throne of Syria. Polybius called him Antiochus Epimanes, or Madman, because of his eccentric conduct. It was this Antiochus IV whom Popilius sternly ordered out of Egypt. But the Madman contributed substantially to cultural exchange between Rome and the Hellenistic East. For he not only gave spectacles in the Greek style with an abundance of Greek theatrical artists; a gladiatorial exhibition, after the Roman fashion, he presented which was at first received with greater terror than pleasure on the part of men who were unused to such sights; then by frequent repetitions, by sometimes allowing the fighters to go only as far as wounding one another, sometimes permitting them to fight without giving quarter, he made the sight familiar and even pleasing, and he roused in many of the young men a joy in arms. And so, while at first he had been accustomed to summon gladiators from Rome, procuring them by large fees, finally he could find a sufficient supply at home.[164]

Despite the reputation the Romans had among the Greeks for anti-intellectualism and aesthetic vulgarity, Polybius knew that his friend Scipio and Scipio's circle at Rome had largely outgrown both these vices. Moreover, he was convinced that the Romans had a discipline and an understanding of the uses of power that the Greeks had always lacked. For example, although sophisticated Greeks might scoff at what they considered Roman religiosity, Polybius had seen it work:

But the quality in which the Roman commonwealth is most distinctly superior is in my opinion the nature of their religious convictions. I believe that it is the very thing which among other peoples is an object of reproach, I mean superstition, which maintains the cohesion of the Roman State. These matters are clothed in such pomp and introduced to such an extent into their public and private life that nothing could exceed it, a fact which will surprise many. My own opinion at least is that they have adopted this course for the sake of the common people. It is a course which perhaps would not have been necessary had it been possible to form a state composed of wise men, but as every multitude is fickle, full of lawless desires, unreasoned passion, and violent anger, the multitude must be held in by invisible terrors and suchlike pageantry. For this reason I think, not that the ancients acted rashly and at haphazard in introducing among the people notions concerning the gods and beliefs in the terrors of hell, but that the moderns are most rash and foolish in banishing such beliefs. The consequence is that among the Greeks, apart from other things, members of the government, if they are entrusted with no more than a talent, though they have ten copyists and as many seals and twice as many witnesses, cannot keep their faith; whereas among the Romans those who as magistrates and legates are dealing with large sums of money maintain correct conduct just because they have pledged their faith by oath. Whereas elsewhere it is a rare thing to find a man who keeps his hands off public money, and whose record is clean in this respect, among the Romans one rarely comes across a man who has been detected in such conduct . . .[165]

Did even Polybius misread the Romans in this matter? Of course, the Roman patricians did constantly use their gods to control the plebeians. To an intelligent, educated, worldly Greek like Polybius these patricians were to be congratulated on their cynicism. But was it not Polybius himself who elsewhere declared that Scipio the Elder had first claimed to be in the confidence of the gods merely to give his soldiers confidence and had ended by believing his own story? Most Roman leaders showed considerably less sophistication than Scipio; was it so certain that they did not believe their own stories? If the gods, and notably Jove, willed that Rome should first win in battle and then rule by law, was it not good for Rome to fake the auspices in order to shut off dangerous debate in a plebeian assembly, and was not what was good for Rome admittedly good for the gods? Perhaps Plato would have preferred the cynicism of a Polybius to the unexamined religion of the Roman patriciate. Plato loved truth and considered the lie on the lips not quite so evil as the lie in the soul. But Plato did not love power; Polybius did. So did Rome; and Rome's elaborate ritual for securing the Pax Deorum, that peace of the gods which profits men, may have been as necessary to her morale as was her deep conviction that Romans were more moral than other men.

Polybius was especially impressed with the Roman device for leading young men to emulate the deeds of their ancestors:

This image is a mask reproducing with remarkable fidelity both the features and complexion of the deceased. On the occasion of public sacrifices they display these images, and decorate them with much care, and when any distinguished member of the family dies they take them to the funeral, putting them on men who seem to them to bear the closest resemblance to the original in stature and carriage. These representatives wear togas, with a purple border if the deceased was a consul or praetor, whole purple if he was a censor, and embroidered with gold if he had celebrated a triumph or achieved anything similar. They all ride in chariots preceded by the fasces, axes, and other insignia by which the different magistrates are wont to be accompanied according to the respective dignity of the offices of state held by each during his life; and when they arrive at the rostra they all seat themselves in a row on ivory chairs. There could not easily be a more ennobling spectacle for a young man who aspires to fame and virtue. For who would not be inspired by the sight of the images of men renowned for their excellence, all together and as if alive and breathing? What spectacle could be more glorious than this?[166]

Polybius, who had defended Roman integrity when the Greeks suspected that Philip V had bribed Flamininus to combine his victory with moderate terms of peace, also pointed out that at Rome "absolutely no one . . . ever gives away anything to anyone if he can help it."[167] The aunts of Polybius' friend Scipio could not believe Scipio's banker when he insisted that Scipio wished an inheritance to be remitted to them before it was due. "And this," wrote Polybius,

> was quite natural on their part; for not only would no one in Rome pay fifty talents three years before it was due, but no one would pay one talent before the appointed day; so universal and so extreme is their exactitude about money as well as their desire to profit by every moment of time.[168]

Cato would scarcely have condoned this profligacy on the part of his political opponent, Scipio, and may indeed have seen in it another sign of his corruption by Greek ideas. But Polybius, who admired Scipio's generosity, who thought the Romans were close with money, but who considered them scrupulous about bribes, came to admit sorrowfully that the Greeks' suspicions of bribery were growing less absurd as more and more Romans began to sell the immense power they now held in conquered lands.

Some Greeks toadied to this power. Some, like Alexander the Aetolian, wanted the Romans to go home. Some, like the famous warrior Philopoemen, who commanded the forces of the Achaean League in the days before Rome overthrew the League and razed Corinth, opposed obedience to Rome only so long as it was premature. Philopoemen told the Achaeans that

> they must not think he was so stupid as to be incapable of measuring the difference between the two states, Rome and Achaea, and the superiority of the Roman power. . . . "But if we ourselves, ignoring our own rights, instantly without protest make ourselves subservient, like prisoners of war, to any and every order, what difference will there be between the Achaean League and the people of Sicily and Capua, who have long been the acknowledged slaves of Rome?" Therefore,

he said, either they must confess that with the Romans justice is impotent, or if they did not go so far as to say this, they must stand by their rights, and not give themselves away, especially as they had very great and honourable claims on Rome. "I know too well," he said, "that the time will come when the Greeks will be forced to yield complete obedience to Rome; but do we wish this time to be as near as possible or as distant as possible? Surely as distant as possible."[169]

By 146, when Rome erased both Carthage and Corinth from the map and had already liberated the Greeks of the eastern Mediterranean, there was no power left that was strong enough to liberate them again. Whatever liberty the Greeks could hope to enjoy would have to be secured under Roman law. The propertied class at least had the guarantee of public order, which interested them perhaps more than justice. As the leaders of a subject people, they could indulge in discreet sneers at their barbarian masters. Or they could cooperate with the Romans and seek preferment. They could even make money out of Romans by copying antique paintings to adorn the walls of Italian villas or antique statues to adorn Italian gardens. In short, they could purvey culture, as they had previously purveyed it to the royal courts of Alexandria, Antioch, Pella, Pergamum, and lesser capitals. Many of them could even purvey it in Rome itself, where lectures on rhetoric were in great demand from a governing class of statesmen, lawyers, and generals. Even lectures on philosophy, especially Stoic philosophy, attracted Romans who approved of culture as an adornment to power.

To Romans of the old school like Cato, the influx of Greek ideas felt as demoralizing as the influx of Greek art, Greek cooks, and Greek luxury in general. The political opponents of Scipio Africanus, when Scipio was in Syracuse during the Second Punic War, denounced his love of Greek ways. They

> kept censuring even the personal appearance of the general-in-chief, as not even soldierly, not to say un-Roman; that wearing a Greek mantle and sandals he strolled about in the gymnasium, giving his attention to books in Greek and physical exercise; that with equal indolence and self-indulgence his entire retinue was enjoying the charms of Syracuse . . .[170]

In a poem by the satirist, Lucilius, a Roman praetor in Athens rebukes his friend Albucius for his un-Roman behavior:

You have preferred to be called a Greek, Albucius, rather than a Roman and a Sabine, a fellow-townsman of the centurions Pontius and Tritanus, famous and foremost men, yes, standard-bearers. Therefore I as praetor greet you at Athens in Greek, when you approach me, just as you preferred. "Good-cheer, Titus," say I in Greek. "Good-cheer" say the attendants, all my troop and band. That's why Albucius is foe to me; that's why he's an enemy![171]

The truth is that many Romans were nettled by the obvious superiority of Greek culture; at the same time they found the Greeks whom they encountered in the flesh unworthy descendants of the men who had made the name Athens a holy and mysterious word. True, when Rome conquered these Greeks, she looted not only their paintings and statues, their actors and dancers, but even the tongue the Greeks spoke. The loot somehow remained hauntingly foreign. Rome even changed her own poetry from the strong, accentual rhythm of Saturnian verse to the relatively unaccentual hexameter in which heroic Greek verse had been written since Homer. With a kind of noble pathos the epitaph which Naevius composed for his own tomb declared:

> If it were right for the immortal ones
>   To mourn for mortals,
> Then for the poet Naevius would mourn
>   The Goddesses of Song.
> And so when unto Death's own treasure-house
>   He was delivered,
> Romans no longer did remember how
>   To speak the Latin tongue.[172]

Naevius fought in the First Punic War, and his account of it was Rome's first epic. The poet Ennius came from Calabria in Magna Graecia, though he fought for Rome in the Second Punic War. His tragedies were adaptations of Euripides. He, too, wrote an epic, *The Annals*, a sort of Roman history in hexameters. From then on, the literature that sprang up in Latin was always subject to the pull of Greek. In a certain sense, it was the Greeks and not the Romans who were the aggressors, not merely because men like King Pyrrhus had led Greek mercenaries over to Italy, but because the splendor of Greek literature forced Roman writers to borrow, and perhaps to borrow too early.

Rome commonly saw in Greek dialectic mere contentiousness, which could be best settled by something like court procedure under the authority of a judge. "Well," says a Roman in a dialogue,

> I remember that my friend Phaedrus, when I was in Athens, told me the following story about your friend Gellius. When, after his praetorship, he went to Greece as proconsul and had arrived at Athens, he called together the philosophers who were there at the time, and urgently advised them to come at length to some settlement of their controversies. He said, if they really desired not to waste their lives in argument, that the matter might be settled; and at the same time he promised his own best efforts to aid them in coming to some agreement.

And another Roman replies:

> It was said in jest, Pomponius, and has often raised a laugh: but I should really like to be appointed arbiter between the Old Academy and Zeno.[173]

No doubt what Gellius said was indeed said in jest, but it wittily reversed the Socratic formula that free philosophical speculation is necessary to any wise practical action. The intellectual loot the Roman wanted was not the knowledge of how to speculate on ends but how to use means; not philosophy but rhetoric. In another dialogue, Antonius, a famous orator, could both rightfully and admiringly refer to Greece in the century that followed the destruction of Corinth as "that most famous factory of rhetoricians"[174]; and budding Roman statesmen flocked to such places as Athens and Rhodes. There they could learn how to persuade men to vote or to fight, to convict or acquit, always provided that the anti-Greeks in Rome could not label these foreign-educated statesmen un-Roman. Antonius' contemporary, the orator Crassus,

> did not so much wish to be thought to have learned nothing, as to have the reputation of looking down upon learning, and of placing the wisdom of our own fellow-countrymen above that of the Greeks in all departments; while Antonius held that his speeches would be the more acceptable to a nation like ours, if it were thought that he had never engaged in study at all. Thus the one expected to grow in influence by being thought to hold a poor opinion of the Greeks, and the other by seeming never even to have heard of them.[175]

Indeed, Antonius remarked:

I always considered that a speaker would be more pleasing and acceptable to a nation like ours if he were to show, first, as little trace as possible of any artifice, and secondly none whatever of things Greek. And at the same time I considered that, with the Greeks undertaking, professing and achieving such marvels, and promising to reveal to mankind the way to understand the profoundest mysteries, to live rightly and to speak copiously, it would be brutish and inhuman not to lend an ear, and, though perhaps not venturing to listen to them openly, for fear of lessening your influence with your fellow-citizens, yet to pick up their sayings by eavesdropping, and keep a look-out from afar for their talk.[176]

More than half a century after Mummius razed Corinth, Athens, no longer rich and powerful but dependent substantially on tourists and students for a living, drew Romans to herself as she had always drawn Greeks. Her popular leaders in the third century

used to declare by way of flattering the Athenians that while all other things were common property of the Greeks, the road which led men to Heaven was known only to the Athenians.[177]

Apollo himself was said to have proclaimed Athens "the hearthstone of Hellas, the town-hall of Hellas."[178] But by 91 B.C., the orator Crassus could say admiringly:

At Athens erudition among the Athenians themselves has long ago perished, and that city now only continues to supply a lodging for studies from which the citizens are entirely aloof, and which are enjoyed by foreign visitors who are under the spell of the city's name and authority; nevertheless any uneducated Athenian will easily surpass the most cultivated Asiatics not in vocabulary but in tone of voice, and not so much in the correctness as in the charm of his way of speaking.[179]

These Athenians, who alone knew the path to heaven and could speak of it with charm, maintained their nominal independence from Rome for sixty years after the destruction of Corinth. But then Athens somehow stumbled onto the path which led to defeat and foreign subjection. How could this be? Such a question could not baffle a Roman statesman for a second: her fall was due to her foolish dream of democratic self-government, of free and equal men seeking through debate the common good of the community. For

all the states of the Greeks are managed by irresponsible seated assemblies. And so, not to discuss this later Greece, which has long been troubled and vexed by its own devices, that older Greece, which once was so notable for its resources, its power, its glory, fell because of this defect alone—the undue freedom and irresponsibility of its assemblies. Untried men, without experience in any affairs and ignorant, took their places in the assembly and then they undertook useless wars, then they put factious men in charge of the state, then they drove most deserving citizens out of the country. But if these things were wont to happen at Athens at a time when Athens was pre-eminent, not only in Greece, but almost the whole world, what chance of considered action do you think there was in the assemblies in Phrygia or in Mysia? Men of those nations often throw our own assemblies into confusion. What, pray, do you think happens when they are by themselves? Athenagoras of Cyme was flogged because he dared to export grain during a famine.[180]

What a glorious custom and practice we inherited from our forefathers—if only we had retained it! . . . they were wise and scrupulous men, and they gave no power to the mass meeting, such was their will.[181]

It is remarkable how gladly those men to whom our symbols of power are hateful, our name bitter . . . how gladly they seize the chance for retaliation when it is offered! Remember, then, when you hear Greek decrees that you are not listening to evidence; you are listening to the vagaries of a mob, you are listening to the utterance of fickle men, you are listening to the uproar of the ignorant, you are listening to a frenzied assembly of the most fickle of nations.[182]

As to decrees by popular assemblies, a Roman court ought to ignore them as testimony:

I deny that what you call decrees are testimony at all. It is a howl of the needy, a kind of chance emotion of a Greek assembly.[183]

Despite the mutual misgivings and distrust that marked the relations between Greek and Roman in the second half of the second century B.C., the Hellenistic Cosmopolis had acquired a ruler. For weal or woe it had at last become a Graeco-Roman world. It was this fact, planned by neither Greek nor Roman, that the historical insight of Polybius had grasped. To that world the Greek would contribute what was left of his religious understanding, his love of philosophic inquiry, his artistic skill and aesthetic sensibility, his literary capacity, his genius for mathematics and mechanics, his skill in commerce, industry, and navigation, his wit and gaiety and courtesy in human intercourse. To that world the Roman would contribute his passion for law and order, his military tradition, his persistence, his ability to organize. With Carthage, enemy first of the Western Greeks and then of Rome, finally out of the way, the Graeco-Roman world faced only one great power on its borders, the Parthian Empire. For the rest, her neighbors were mere barbarians, hard fighters but divided by tribalism, explosive but undisciplined. From the Atlantic Ocean to the Aegean Sea lay Roman provinces, in Europe and in Africa. From the Aegean to Parthia lay vassal states or helpless neighbors. East of the Adriatic the upper class, their local rule backed by Roman power, spoke Greek. West of the Adriatic the dominant upper class either spoke Latin or were learning to speak Latin, even in the Greek cities of Sicily, southern Italy, and southern France. Many upper-class Greeks in the East had learned, or were learning, to speak Latin. And many upper-class Romans had learned or were learning to speak Greek. A multitude of Greek slaves, taken in war, were living in Rome and throughout Italy. And numerous Greek artists painted or sculpted in Rome; numerous Greek philosophers and rhetoricians lectured there. Prominent Romans studied in Athens or Rhodes. Cosmopolis developed steadily toward a single City of Man. How real a polis it might become depended largely on whether Rome could transmute conquest by force into enforceable, but also intelligible, law.

3

VIOLENCE AND RHETORIC

IN 133 Tiberius Gracchus was elected a tribune of the
Roman people. Earlier in that same year Scipio Aemilianus, who had
destroyed Carthage and had wept over the possible fate of Rome, had
starved the Spanish city of Numantia into capitulating. Tiberius had taken
part in the siege. The victory brought an apparent end to the long series
of guerrilla insurrections that had marked the Roman occupation of
Spain, an occupation that had now lasted for seventy years. That same
year, 133, Attalus III died, bequeathing his kingdom of Pergamum to
Rome. In doing so he added to the already immense wealth which Rome
had won by her wars in Macedonia, Greece, and Asia Minor. But whereas,
except for war indemnities and new taxpayers, that wealth had previously
been loot and had in large part been pocketed by generals and soldiery,
the new bequest belonged legally to the public treasury and left undeter-
mined who would benefit by it. In 135 a bloody slave insurrection broke
out in Sicily, covertly aided by free but poor peasants. In 134 slave insurrections broke out at the silver mines in Attica; on Apollo's holy island of
Delos, the center of the slave trade for the whole Mediterranean; in the

kingdom of Pergamum; in Italy; and even at Rome. Except in Sicily the slave insurrections were quickly suppressed; but the praetors in Sicily and later a consul successively failed against an army of slaves soon swollen to at least 60,000, and only in 132 was the Sicilian slave revolt suppressed.

The father of Tiberius Gracchus was a plebeian who had distinguished himself in Spain both as general and as colonial governor. The mother, Cornelia, was a patrician, the daughter of Scipio Africanus, Hannibal's conqueror in 202. One of Tiberius' sisters married Scipio Aemilianus, under whom Tiberius was serving when Carthage was destroyed in 146. Indeed, Tiberius was reported to have been the first man to scale the city wall. Cornelia shared the two Scipios' interest in Greek culture, and both Tiberius and his younger brother Gaius were educated by Greek tutors, especially by a hellenized Italian Stoic from Cumae named Blossius and by a Greek exile and rhetorician from Mytilene named Diophanes. From the Stoic philosophy of Blossius the two boys learned that the individual citizen's interests must be subordinated to the common good of society, and from Diophanes they learned what every politically ambitious Roman wished to know, the art of oratory.

When Tiberius went out to Spain to serve in the siege of Numantia, he passed through Etruria and noted with dismay that the large estates of the rich, with their slave labor, were crowding the Roman peasant farmers off the land. In Spain he observed a decline in the quality of the Roman legionary. He inferred that it was tough, hard-working, self-disciplined yeoman farmers who had won Cosmopolis for Rome, and that without this human material the Roman army, as he knew it, was doomed. It was when he returned to Rome, somewhat under a cloud because of a military disaster for which he was in fact not responsible, that he was elected tribune. With the advice of several leading Senators, including its senior member, Appius Claudius, who happened to be Tiberius' own father-in-law, Tiberius promptly introduced in the popular assembly a law for land reform. In effect his law required landowners to vacate all land which they had occupied beyond 300 acres, a limit already set by a law they had largely ignored. To coat the pill Tiberius provided that landowners might also retain another 150 acres for each son. What remained would be distributed to smallholders for a modest quitrent. In formidable orations he appealed to the people for support:

> The wild beasts that roam over Italy have every one of them a cave or lair to lurk in; but the men who fight and die for Italy enjoy the

common air and light, indeed, but nothing else; houseless and homeless they wander about with their wives and children. And it is with lying lips that their imperators exhort the soldiers in their battles to defend sepulchres and shrines from the enemy; for not a man of them has an hereditary altar, not one of all these many Romans an ancestral tomb, but they fight and die to support others in wealth and luxury, and though they are styled masters of the world, they have not a single clod of earth that is their own.[184]

The Senatorial landowners then used one of their favorite stratagems: they persuaded another of the tribunes, Marcus Octavius, to veto the proposal. Tiberius induced the popular assembly to depose and replace Octavius, and the law was passed. A land commission, consisting of Tiberius, his brother Gaius, and his father-in-law Appius Claudius, was set up and began to make allotments. Tiberius passed an act by which revenues from newly bequeathed Pergamum could finance his resettlement. The rich landowners were furious. Only once before, ninety-nine years earlier, had a land law been submitted to the popular assembly without first receiving the approval of the Senate. As for the assembly's deposition of one of its own tribunes, there was no precedent for that. It was even argued[185] that, when Tiberius presented himself for a second term as tribune, he was breaking a recent statute. But, while it may be true that with more political tact Tiberius could have got his land act peacefully enforced, it may also be doubted. From the terrible Second Punic War onward the Senate had steadily usurped power. The rich men who largely composed it were the only group with enough capital to restore the devastated countryside and moreover they had power enough to hold what they had illegally seized. The rich desperately clung to the land they had grabbed, if only because its revenues enabled them to engage in political life and because running for office was getting steadily more expensive, what with clients to assist and what with costly entertainments if proletarian votes were to be won.

Of the yeomen who had once farmed Italy, many had been killed in battle or were hopelessly uprooted and demoralized. Many had moved to the cities, especially to Rome, where they became debtors to the rich, or clients of the rich, or both. Many no longer knew any trade but war and pillage. Besides, the wheat tithe from Sicily had ruined their kind of farming; the new cattle ranches in southern Italy and the new olive orchards and vineyards were beyond their means either to buy or to operate; and the huge increase in slaves, captured in Rome's wars, crowded them out of the labor market. In fact, these economic changes suggested that Tiberius' land reform came too late to bring about the end he sought. Those proletarians who had no intention of farming soon lost interest in his reforms. Farmers who had come to the city to vote for land reform now faced the season of harvest: they returned to their farms. Some of the Senators who had favored Tiberius' law were turning against him in favor of their own economic class, and even the other tribunes were ceasing to support him.

Tiberius was determined to win re-election and to consolidate his land reform. He summoned his partisans to protect him on election day. A scuffle ensued. The Senate was convoked. Scipio Nasica, chief priest of the Republic and leader of those who opposed Gracchus and who charged him with desiring to become tyrant of Rome, demanded in the Senate that the consul Publius Mucius Scaevola, a famous jurist who had helped Tiberius draft his land reform, put down the tyrant. Scaevola replied that he would put no citizen to death without trial. Nasica thereupon sprang up and cried: "Let those who would save our country follow me."[186] A group of Senators followed him. The crowd gave way respectfully. Scipio Nasica and his supporters seized clubs and fragments of broken benches, killed Tiberius and a large number of those who defended him, and threw their bodies into the Tiber.

> On the subject of the murder of Gracchus the city was divided between sorrow and joy. Some mourned for themselves and for him, and deplored the present condition of things, believing that the commonwealth no longer existed, but had been supplanted by force and violence. Others considered that their dearest wishes were accomplished.[187]

Scipio Nasica, the ringleader, was conveniently sent on a mission to Asia Minor. The group that dominated Rome economically had reasserted by force and violence their right to dominate it politically.

However, the Optimates, or Best People, as they called themselves, dared not abrogate the land-reform act. The murder of Tiberius and the death of his father-in-law, Appius Claudius, left Tiberius' younger brother Gaius as the sole commissioner. Two new commissioners were added. Gaius Gracchus was in fact a more formidable opponent of the rich squatters than his brother. He was less doctrinaire, more coolheaded, a rougher but even more effective speaker, more deft in acquiring and manipulating power. The land commission was naturally meeting difficulties, not least among Rome's Italian Allies, where much of the land lay.

Gaius first ran for the tribuneship and won handily. To relieve the misery of the poor at Rome, to block the speculators in wheat, and to make sure that the city plebs would have an interest in backing his program of reform, Gaius proposed a monthly ration of grain for each Roman citizen at a fair price. One of his fellow commissioners, Fulvius Flaccus, helped him get this measure adopted. Then Gaius Gracchus found a loophole in the law forbidding the re-election of tribunes, and got himself re-elected. He had bought the support of the plebeians; he now planned to buy the members of the Equestrian Order. These were called *equites*, or knights, because knights had been rich enough to report for military service on their own mounts. However, the term knight now connoted a most unknightly occupation, finance. The Equites organized joint stock companies and undertook many functions for the Republic, which would otherwise have had to maintain a civil service. They bid for contracts to collect taxes and then lent money at high rates to the persons who had to pay the taxes. They bid for war contracts; they bid on highways, on aqueducts. They had contacts in the Senate in order to influence foreign policy. If Gaius Gracchus could get the support of these businessmen,[188] he could split them off politically from the Senate. Those Senators who were assigned to rule provinces as proconsuls often interfered with the Equites' ruthless exploitation of the provincials. Since cases of such exploitation came before the courts on which only Senators served, Gaius knew what would win over the businessmen: he proposed that the courts be transferred from the Senatorial Order to the Equestrian Order. He correctly guessed that the Senate would not dare oppose the measure: a number of Senatorial judges had just been caught taking bribes. The law passed, and Gaius believed he had broken the power of the Senate once and for all. To the Senators the honor, to the Equites the money. By uniting the Equites and plebeians against the Senate, he had apparently constructed a kind of capitalist democracy at the expense of a landed oligarchy.

Gaius Gracchus then succeeded in bribing the businessmen still further. He put through a program of road-building and other public works most pleasing to contractors and most helpful to jobless plebeians. He planned colonies, or land-grant settlements, to furnish further economic opportunity to plebeians. There remained the question of what to do about the Italians. In 125, Gaius' colleague Flaccus had as consul urged that they be granted

Roman citizenship; the Senate had been outraged. The Italian Allies had helped Rome win the right to govern Cosmopolis. Yet, when public land was distributed, the Italians had habitually received smaller allotments than had Roman citizens.

Gaius had first to go to Carthage, where the land commission was planting a colony. While he was gone, a fellow tribune, Livius Drusus, made himself the tool of the Senate. By offering to buy the plebeians at a higher price than Gaius had already paid, he successfully undermined Gaius and his program. With Senate approval Drusus promised more colonies than had Gaius. Moreover, where Gaius had kept possession of assigned land in the hands of the state to prevent its sale to rich plantation owners, Drusus made the democratic gesture of abolishing the tiny quitrent. The plebeians were delighted.

On his return from Carthage, Gaius attempted to put a broad base under the political structure that his murdered brother had undertaken, perhaps too hastily, to build. He toned down Flaccus' proposal that Roman citizenship be granted to all Italy: he urged cautiously that this be granted only to Latins and that a somewhat smaller voice be granted the rest of Italy. But his opponents quickly convinced the Roman plebeians that it was not to their advantage to share the perquisites of Roman citizenship with either their Latin or their Italian allies. The measure was lost, and when Gaius' term as tribune ended, he was not re-elected. Meanwhile, Papirius Carbo, the third member of the land commission, betrayed him: after visiting Carthage, Carbo sent back fantastic charges to the Senate, especially a charge that Gaius had placed his African colony on the very site that Gaius' brother-in-law, Scipio Africanus the Younger, had solemnly cursed when he destroyed Carthage. The businessmen, who had already got what they wanted, did not rally. In 121 a newly elected tribune, a tool of the Senate, proposed a law to abolish the colony planned for Carthage. There was a scuffle in the Forum, and a supporter of the Senate was killed. Flaccus and some of Gaius' other supporters then occupied the Aventine hill, the traditional rallying ground of a seceding plebs. The Senate instructed the consuls to defend the Republic, and the consul Opimius proclaimed a general levy of citizen-soldiers. Flaccus and Gaius were hunted down and killed. Some 3,000 of their followers were either killed or arrested. Those arrested were quickly tried and executed. The heads of Gaius and Flaccus were brought to Opimius, who paid for them their weight in gold.

The Optimates, or rich oligarchs, who had increasingly ruled the Republic ever since the Second Punic War, had apparently won out against two attempts at social justice. But the Populares, or populists, who had backed reform, did not require any special brilliance to see that it was force and violence which had won. The Optimates were determined to keep the spoils of empire for their own enjoyment. It was by the methodical use of force that the Roman Republic had come to rule directly or dominate indirectly the Hellenistic Cosmopolis and much of its barbarian hinterland. It had first conquered Italy and then had led it against Cosmopolis. The long struggle had transformed the Roman plebs into a multiracial proletariat of freed slaves and uprooted farmers. This struggle had largely pushed the yeomanry off the land, especially in the south, and had replaced them with slave labor, embittered by brutal treatment and watching for a chance to revolt again. It had created an ostentatiously rich new oligarchy, frantically seeking more money, hungry for personal power, position, and prestige. This new oligarchy did not propose to share its power with the Roman knights or with the Roman plebeians or with the Republic's Italian Allies or with the provincials, whom Romans of all classes had together subjected. Although these oligarchs more and more evaded military service and used public office to extort money from provincials, they were confident they could put down rebellion whether of provincials abroad or of the multitude of slaves which war had dumped into Italy and was constantly replacing at cheap prices. True, the soldiers the oligarchy sent out were not as good fighters as their fathers, less willing to face hardship, less tolerant of discipline, and greedier for booty and for generous provisions on discharge; but surely these soldiers would suffice. Conquest had incorporated hordes of barbarians in the Republic's growing empire, as for example in Spain and Illyria. Rome was also breeding her own barbarians: spendthrift sons of the rich whom profligacy was reducing to desperate expedients, sons of the poor who were learning that work was unprofitable when compared with sycophancy, discharged veterans who turned highwayman on the land or pirate on the sea.

All of these elements of a sorely dislocated society wanted to get power. Apparently money could buy power. And the source of money was clearly neither work nor self-denial but force and violence. Force was respected and admired; it was not merely used with regret to support law, to gird right with might. This fact was increasingly demonstrated at Rome and in other cities of Cosmopolis. The characteristic public rite of the Roman people on holiday was the combat of professional gladiators fighting to the death amid the roar of the spectators.

This spirit of violence, fired by the misery and envy of the poor and the greed of the rich, might well have exploded into civil war between the Optimates and the Populares had it not been turned outward once more to defend and enlarge their common conquests. The struggle of the two Gracchi to provide the poor with a means of earning their bread had lasted from 133 to 121. Ten years later, in 111, war broke out with Jugurtha, King of Numidia, a country recently allied with the Republic against Carthage and now the neighbor of Rome's new Province of Africa. For some time Jugurtha had staved off war by bribing leading Roman Senators, for he judged Rome "A city for sale and doomed to speedy destruction if it finds a purchaser!"[189] When war came, in characteristic Roman fashion it got off to a poor start; but a new commander, Gaius Marius, successfully concluded it in 105. At Rome, Marius was granted a formal triumph, and in the procession Jugurtha was led captive. The King was then imprisoned in Rome and died of hunger.

The chief outcome of the war, however, was a keen enmity between Marius, who was an Italian of humble birth, born near Arpinum, and his quaestor, Cornelius Sulla, an impecunious patrician. When Jugurtha had taken refuge with his father-in-law, Bocchus, King of Mauretania, Marius had sent his daring and wily quaestor to wheedle Bocchus into betraying Jugurtha. Sulla's successful mission ended the war and also caused bitter personal rivalry between himself and Marius.

Another important result of the Jugurthine War was that Marius' need for troops had led him to break with the Roman tradition of recruiting legionaries only from the propertied class. Marius had accepted volunteers from among the penniless. He had, perhaps unintentionally, discovered a new lever to gain power. By entering the legions the poor might find themselves in a position to seize by force the land the Optimates had withheld by force against the legal actions of the Gracchi. Moreover, the poor could not desert Marius as easily as they had deserted Gaius Gracchus, because Marius required an oath of loyalty to himself personally, and army discipline obliged them to honor it.

Two years before the Jugurthine War started, a movement of Celtic and Germanic tribes from the north had presented Marius and the Populares with an opportunity to win power. The barbarians had defeated several generals whom the Optimates had sent out. In 105, at Orange, in southern

France, an army of Cimbri and Teutons routed and all but destroyed two large Roman armies. It was Rome's worst defeat since Cannae. The old terror of the Gauls flared up in Rome.

> The Romans of that time . . . believed that all else was easy for their valour, but that with the Gauls they fought for life and not for glory.[190]

Marius, conqueror of Jugurtha, was elected consul. He led his new proletarian army into southern France. Luckily, the Germanic tribes were busy elsewhere. Marius whipped his army into shape, devised new tactics, and in 102 at Aix-en-Provence annihilated a large army of Germanic tribes. Then he crossed the Alps by way of the Brenner Pass, crossed the Po, joined forces with his fellow consul Catulus, and in 101 at Vercelli annihilated a second army of barbarians. The Populares had found their leader, and Marius was hailed as the Third Romulus and as the Second Camillus. He was elected consul for six years in succession.

While Marius was busy in Gaul, Rome was forced to quell a second revolt of slaves in Sicily. The revolt broke out in 103 and took four years of hard fighting to suppress. Concurrently, a slave insurrection broke out in Attica, this time not at the silver mines but at Athens itself, and for the first time in Athenian history. Then, in 100, serious violence erupted again in the very heart of Rome. This was no simple riot; the Optimates and the Populares fought a pitched battle in the Forum. Marius showed little political leadership and in 98 withdrew to the Province of Asia to prepare for a possible war with an Asian king, a war that might yield rich booty and hence power. The Populares managed to get land for his veterans, but the Senate killed another land bill. In 91 a tribune who proposed the right of citizenship for the whole of Italy was assassinated. Ironically, the victim was Livius Drusus, son of the tribune who, though himself convinced that the measures Gaius Gracchus had proposed were urgent business, had served as the Senate's tool against Gaius.

With their Roman spokesmen gone, the Italians took matters into their own hands: they rose, formed a federal republic, named it Italia, and established their capital at Corfinium. They now fought for more than the Roman citizenship they had orginally sought, and their secession united all classes in the Roman Republic and directed their common violence against the Italian cities in a war against the *Socii*, or Allies.[191] But by 89 Rome prudently granted Roman citizenship to all Italians who might apply for it, and the next year the war was substantially over.

Marius fought in the Italian War with some success, but Sulla fought with even more. The Senate despised the Third Romulus and Second Camillus and looked on him as a demagogue and an upstart. They preferred his rival, Sulla, who in 88 was elected consul and immediately prepared to take an army to Asia. There the Asian king whom Marius had hoped to fight, Mithradates VI of Pontus, had taken advantage of Rome's many troubles to build an empire centered in the Crimea and including much of southern Russia; then he had enlarged his domains in Asia Minor. In 88 a Roman general provoked him into war, and Mithradates seized Rome's new Province of Asia in a whirlwind campaign to liberate the Greeks. The Greek cities were more than ready to be liberated: Gaius Gracchus' reform of the courts had put the so-called knights in power, and the publicans, or tax-gatherers, among them had squeezed the Greeks hard. Mithradates ordered a massacre of all the Italians in the province,[192] and the order was carried out with alacrity and considerable thoroughness. As for Manius Aquilius, an ex-consul who had largely instigated the war, "Mithradates poured molten gold down his throat, thus rebuking the Romans for their bribe-taking."[193] Having liberated the Greeks of Asia, Mithradates decided to liberate the Greeks of Europe as well. He engineered a democratic revolution in Athens against the oligarchs favored by Rome and seized much of Greece. He seized the island of Delos, the center of the Mediterranean slave trade, and massacred all the Italian traders there.

Sulla was in Nola, a little west of Naples, about to start for Asia to subdue Mithradates. When the Populares in Rome successfully and violently transferred his command to their hero, Marius, Sulla immediately marched his army to Rome and took the city by storm. Marius escaped to Africa; Sulla re-established the power of the Optimates and left for Asia. But the following year, 87, Marius recaptured Rome and for five days slaughtered the Optimates, confiscated their property, and plundered much of the city. Another year and Marius was dead at the age of seventy-one.

Sulla, now an outlaw, had led his army against Athens in order to overthrow the democratic government that Mithradates had established there. He then proceeded to starve the city into submission. Athens, the road which led to heaven, had always been spared by Roman armies. But the Athenian democracy's collaboration with an Asian despot who had recently ordered the massacre of tens of thousands of Italians would have tested the mercy of any Roman general, and Sulla had never been a merciful man. When Athenian envoys came to treat for peace and spoke loftily of

Theseus and of Athens' heroic actions in the Persian War four centuries earlier, Sulla cried:

> Be off, my dear Sirs, and take these speeches with you; for I was not sent to Athens by the Romans to learn its history, but to subdue its rebels.[194]

> But when he discovered that the defenders of Athens were very severely pressed by hunger, that they had devoured all their cattle, boiled the hides and skins, and licked what they could get therefrom, and that some had even partaken of human flesh, Sulla directed his soldiers to encircle the city with a ditch so that the inhabitants might not escape secretly, even one by one. This done, he brought up his ladders and at the same time began to break through the wall. The feeble defenders were soon put to flight, and the Romans rushed into the city. A great and pitiless slaughter ensued in Athens. The inhabitants, for want of nourishment, were too weak to fly, and Sulla ordered an indiscriminate massacre, not sparing women or children. He was angry that they had so suddenly joined the barbarians without cause, and had displayed such violent animosity toward himself.[195]

By 84 Sulla had driven Mithradates' forces out of Europe and had negotiated a peace with Mithradates requiring him to give up everything he had seized in the war. Then, with an army which the Populares had sent to destroy him but which had instead deserted to him, he hurried toward Rome to put an end to the democratic revolution Marius had begun. He landed his army at Brindisi in 83 and was joined by Gnaeus Pompeius and three legions of volunteers. Pompey was then twenty-three, but already a general. Again Sulla captured Rome, though too late to prevent a final massacre of the Optimates by the Populares. But Sulla quickly outdid the Marians. He herded into the circus at Rome some 6,000 prisoners of war, half of whom had surrendered on his promise that they would be safe. Then he summoned the Senate. As he began to address the Senators, his men began to massacre the prisoners.

> The shrieks of such a multitude, who were being massacred in a narrow space, filled the air, of course, and the senators were dumbfounded; but Sulla, with the calm and unmoved countenance with which he had begun to speak, ordered them to listen to his words and not concern themselves with what was going on outside, for it was only that some criminals were being admonished by his orders.[196]

Sulla posted at Rome lists of names, outlawing certain followers of Marius and putting a price on their heads. List followed list. These proscriptions bore heavily on the Equites, whom Marius, like Gaius Gracchus, had favored. Indeed, it bore on many men who were merely rich enough to make confiscation of their property worthwhile. Several thousands were killed. From among their slaves Sulla formed a bodyguard of 10,000 men. In 82, the Senate named him dictator for an indefinite period and charged him to reform the constitution. Not for a hundred and twenty years had the Senate named a dictator, and formerly it had named dictators only for short, specified periods. The Senate's action was purely *pro forma:* Sulla had already become "king, or tyrant, *de facto,* not elected, but holding power by force and violence."[197] By the end of 80 Sulla had freed Spain, Sicily, and Africa from control by the Populares' armies.

Sulla enlarged the Senate, deprived of much of their power such Equites as remained alive, weakened the popular assembly and its tribunes, made laws against extravagant living, lived extravagantly himself, resigned his dictatorship in 79, retired to a country estate, and died the following year. He had tried by force and violence to restore the Roman Republic to conservative Senatorial rule, and at least temporarily he succeeded.

The Roman Civil War had been, among other things, the most recent episode in the secular struggle between rich and poor. But until the Gracchi attempted their land reform, this struggle had never led to serious street riots and bloodshed. Rome's violence had been great, but it had been largely the cold, controlled violence of political and military power, used to impose her will on her neighbors. That power had expanded her neighborhood to include nearly the whole of Cosmopolis and even many unhellenized or partially hellenized peoples as well. But in expanding her power, Rome had transformed her own political, economic, and social structure. The violence she had once so judiciously controlled had come to control Rome. The Romans, who had eagerly watched professional gladiators fight to the death, now watched the Roman Public Thing itself become a vast gladiatorial combat. Indeed, Rome's internal violence had stirred provincials to revolt, Italian Allies to rebel, an Asian despot to build an empire and liberate the Greeks, the Gallic terror to rise once more in the north. To contemporaries it looked as if Marius and his Populares had overthrown the Optimates, only to have Sulla restore the rule of the rich. But although the Civil War was indeed a war between rich and poor, what it chiefly proved was that the ancient Roman pride in republican government, in constitutional procedure, in obedience to the laws, in devotion unto death to the will of Rome, which was the will of Jove fulfilled here and now in history, had been corrupted by power and pillage. What the Civil War proved was not that Rome had been saved from democracy, nor that democracy would ultimately triumph, but that Rome's deep faith in power and force were pushing her toward the concentration of all power and all force in one man, and that this one man must be whoever could control the army.

On the one hand, extravagant luxury and dissolute living seized Rome and much of Italy when her legions pillaged the wealthy East and the vast booty flowed westward. On the other hand, Greek literature and art evoked in at least some Roman souls a sudden vision of beauty. This vision and this luxury combined to produce a new type in Italian society, the sophisticated, reckless young man or woman, suddenly emancipated from whatever was left of Rome's conservative and repressive morals, morals which Cato the Censor had tried in vain to salvage. Both the corruption of the new wealth and the inspiration of the new Hellenism appeared in the person of Gaius Valerius Catullus.

Catullus was born in Verona, about the year 84, the son of a wealthy army contractor. He came to Rome when he was barely past twenty; formed a liaison with Clodia, the profligate, aristocratic wife of a governor of Cisalpine Gaul, Catullus' home province; and joined a literary coterie of flaming youth. He turned to the writing of lyric poetry. He was Roman enough to produce harshly satirical poems about the kind of life young men of means now often led, poems in which he defied the Mos Majorum or somehow scorned even himself. But his greatest lyrics were love poems to Clodia, whom he addressed, presumably with memories of the poems Sappho had written nearly half a millennium earlier in Lesbos, as Lesbia:

> Come, Lesbia, let us live and love,
> nor give a damn what sour old men say.
> The sun that sets may rise again
> but when our light has sunk into the earth,
> it is gone forever.
> Give me a thousand kisses,
> then a hundrd, another thousand,
> another hundred
> and in one breath
> still kiss another thousand,
> another hundred.

O then with lips and bodies joined
many deep thousands;
confuse
their number,
so that poor fools and cuckolds (envious
even now) shall never
learn our wealth and curse us
with their
evil eyes.[198]

And this:

Do you know, my Lesbia, how many of your kisses
would satisfy my hunger? Count the sands of Africa
from Cyrene, famous for its spices,
from the place where Battus lies,
sepulchred and holy,
to the distant shrine where Jove's eloquence still smoulders;
count the constellations of the stars that rising through the silence
of night look down upon trembling furtive lovers:
then you will know how many times and more
your mad Catullus
could kiss you, kisses ripening beyond the calculation
of the curious eye, nor could a rapid envious tongue
gain speed to count their number.[199]

But he could also show the anger of the lover scorned.

Poor damned Catullus, here's no time for nonsense,
open your eyes, O idiot, innocent boy, look at what has happened:
once there were sunlit days when you followed after
where ever a girl would go, she loved with greater love than any woman
  knew.
Then you took your pleasure
and the girl was not unwilling. Those were the bright days, gone;
now she's no longer yielding; you must be, poor idiot,
more like a man! not running after
her your mind all tears; stand firm, insensitive.
Say with a smile, voice steady, "Good-bye, my girl," Catullus
strong and manly no longer follows you, nor comes when you are calling
him at night and you shall need him.
You whore! Where's your man to cling to, who will praise your beauty,
where's the man that you love and who will call you his,

and when you fall to kissing, whose lips will you devour?
But always, your Catullus will be as firm as rock is.[200]

Catullus was truly Roman in the vividness of his images. If his poetry was
not rich in ideas, yet it was rich in things, things that he could make his
reader see, hear, smell, taste, or touch; and the lapidary Latin words served
him well. But in at least one poem, the longest he ever published, he was
Roman in another way: he turned from the personal to the political.
Starting off with a conventional literary myth, in this case the marriage of
Achilles' parents, he suddenly turned to the horror of the world he had
been born in, a world that had lost its gods and that remembered the
recent butcheries of Marius and Sulla, their proscriptions, the informers, the
betrayals, the greedy head-hunters, the heads suspended in the Forum, all
the brutalities of Rome's first civil war, all the moral confusion of those
who had managed to survive:

> But then followed long years when earth was stained with blood and
>   men released their souls to hell, justice
> a word forgotten; brothers dipped their fingers into brother's blood and
>   sons
> no longer wept over a father's body and fathers ripe with lust would
>   plan the death
> of sons at wedding feasts, their eyes fixed on the bride.
> And mothers slept with sons all ignorant, but for a passion rising from
>   incestuous crime.
> Thus right and wrong became confused; mankind in darkness, bewildered
>   now ignored the gods.
> Never again do gods return to earth or walk with men in the bright
>   sun of noon.[201]

In 57 Catullus went to Bithynia on the staff of Gaius Memmius, son-
in-law of Sulla. While in Asia Minor, he visited near Troy the tomb of his
brother, for whom he wrote this elegy:

> Dear brother, I have come these many miles, through strange lands to
>   this Eastern Continent
> to see your grave, a poor sad monument of what you were, O brother.
> And I have come too late; you cannot hear me; alone now I must speak
> to these few ashes that were once your body and expect no answer.
> I shall perform an ancient ritual over your remains, weeping,
> (this plate of lentils for dead men to feast upon, wet with my tears)

119

O brother, here's my greeting: here's my hand forever welcoming you
and I forever say: goodbye, goodbye.[202]

The next year Catullus became bored with Bithynia and returned on his
own yacht to Italy. He died shortly thereafter, in his thirtieth year.

About this same year another Latin poet died, Titus Lucretius Carus.
Lucretius left but a single poem,[203] though a long one, *On the Nature of
Things*. The poem is essentially an epic on the creation of the world
and all that is in it. It is written in the conventional epic meter, dactylic
hexameter. It begins with the conventional invocation, addressed this time
not to a muse but to Venus, "mother of Aeneas and his race."[204] But
perhaps because Lucretius aimed to destroy religion and the superstitious
fears that religion seemed to him to inculcate, and to explain everything
that exists only as natural science would do, the poet quickly reformulates
his invocation to Venus and restricts her role:

> thee I crave as partner in writing the verses, which I essay to fashion
> touching the Nature of Things.[205]

Lucretius' epic is an Epicurean interpretation of a universe that is purely
material. Though the gods doubtless exist, they neither created nor
concerned themselves with the universe that man sees around him.
Epicurus had therefore rescued man from the fear of death and of divine
wrath:

> When man's life lay for all to see foully grovelling upon the ground,
> crushed beneath the weight of Religion, which displayed her head
> in the regions of heaven, threatening mortals from on high with horrible
> aspect, a man of Greece was the first that dared to uplift mortal eyes
> against her, the first to make stand against her; for neither fables of
> the gods could quell him, nor thunderbolts, nor heaven with menacing
> roar, nay all the more they goaded the eager courage of his soul, so that
> he should desire, first of all men, to shatter the confining bars of nature's
> gates. Therefore the lively power of his mind prevailed, and forth he
> marched far beyond the flaming walls of the heavens, as he traversed
> the immeasurable universe in thought and imagination; whence victorious
> he returns bearing his prize, the knowledge of what can come into
> being, what can not, in a word, how each thing has its powers defined
> and its deep-set boundary mark. Wherefore Religion is now in her
> turn cast down and trampled underfoot, whilst we by the victory are
> exalted high as heaven.[206]

Everything comes from seed, and this seed is nothing but atoms, indivisible particles too small to be sensed. In the beginning was a rain of atoms, falling at equal speed through void. For reasons which Lucretius does not provide his reader, these falling atoms swerve a little in their course. This makes them collide, and the collisions make them form bodies, and sooner or later these bodies or things, which make up the universe, will all disintegrate into atoms again: "all things gradually decay, and go to the tomb outworn by the ancient lapse of years."[207]

By the time Book III begins, Lucretius is ready to apostrophize, not Venus, but Epicurus:

> O thou who first from so great a darkness wert able to raise aloft a light so clear, illumining the blessings of life, thee I follow, O glory of the Grecian race . . .[208]

Mind, as well as body, is composed of atoms, and death is nothing but the dispersion of both. Lucretius repeatedly scoffs at the idea of a purpose in creation and writes therefore that

> nothing is born in us simply in order that we may use it, but that which is born creates the use . . . the tongue came long before speech, and the ear was made long before sound was heard . . .[209]

He laments that it should be so hard

> to make clear the dark discoveries of the Greeks in Latin verses, especially since we have often to employ new words because of the poverty of the language and the novelty of the matters.[210]

But he exults that the nature and rationale of the material things that comprise our world have only recently been discovered, and that "I among the first students am now found the first to describe it in our own mother tongue."[211]

Lucretius wrote in his mother tongue in two different senses. He took a literary form imposed by the mastery of a Greek poet, Homer. The poverty of his native Latin he partially repaired by a strong idiom that echoed earlier Latin poets, especially Ennius. But what he drew on was their language rather than their ideas. Lucretius, with his respect for a culture that had produced Epicurus, would scarcely have retorted as Ennius had to King Pyrrhus' claim to be a descendant of the Greek hero, Aeacus:

That tribe of blockheads, stock of Aeacus
Are war-strong more than wisdom-strong.[212]

He could have responded to Ennius' images: "When the young warriors
of Rome dry themselves from sleep."[213] He could have accepted the view
of death which Ennius expressed in an epitaph he wrote for himself:

Let none embellish me with tears,
Or make a funeral with wailing;
And why? Alive from lips to lips of men I go a-winging.[214]

Despite his conviction that the gods do not intervene in human affairs,
Lucretius was Hellenist enough to have relished an echo of Sappho in
Valerius Aedituus, another early Roman poet:

O Phileros, why a torch, that we need not?
Just as we are we'll go, our hearts aflame.
That flame no wild wind's blast can ever quench,
Or rain that falls torrential from the skies;
Venus herself alone can quell her fire,
No other force there is that has such power.[215]

But in a deeper sense, Lucretius' native tongue made his poem an act of
Roman will; a Roman love of the concrete thing; a paean to the senses,
filled with a sensuous delight but relatively innocent of the idea that
soars; an earthy, earth-bound poem. "What can we find," he asks, "more
certain than the senses themselves to mark for us truth and falsehood?"[216]

Lucretius claimed to bring the reader joy, the quietistic joy of Epicurus.
This joy waived Catullus' sorrow that never again do gods return to earth
or walk with men in the bright sun of noon. In effect, Lucretius declared
that they never had walked on earth with men. What the sun of noon
implicitly illuminates is not gods but eternal atoms, forming into things
and dispersing and forming again into other things. What the sun of
noon discloses is only atoms, moving in void, or nothingness, moved by
the mysterious swerve that allowed the atoms to create, by chance, a
universe. But this account by which Lucretius yearned to bring men
freedom from fear and thereby to bring them joy raised questions almost
as disturbing as those raised by the fear of what may follow death. And
those questions Lucretius' unspeculative Roman mind never went far
enough to answer. He was driven to hammering his theory into his reader:
"you must confess"; "I say therefore"; "Now I will repeat once more";

"Now listen."[217] Such phrases occur again and again: Lucretius insists that we believe him, rid ourselves of superstition, and rejoice. But he himself does not rejoice. His Roman Republic had conquered the City of Man, but the loot from the City had proven an apple of discord. Loot had maddened Rome, had thrown it into its first civil war, which had convulsed much of the City of Man as well. Rome's armies, which had once defended her and preyed on her foes, had followed the booty home and had preyed on Rome herself and Italy. Those armies had started disintegrating and re-forming, like the Lucretian atoms that made up the bodies Lucretius saw and touched and loved. No wonder Lucretius, in the backwash of the Civil War, could predict that the mighty heavens would one day be stormed all round and collapse into crumbling ruin, that the power of life was already broken and an exhausted earth yielded shrunken harvests, and that all things were gradually decaying.[218] The intellectual light that suffuses Lucretius' poem is therefore the melancholy light of late afternoon. But it is a lovely light. For Lucretius loved things, these things created by no god and for no purpose but brought briefly and hopelessly into being by the chance concourse of eternal atoms, these doomed, lovely things that became the thousands of memorable images in his epic *On the Nature of Things*.

The first half of the first century B.C. produced no other Latin literature to compare with the lyrics of Catullus or the epic of Lucretius. Roman drama, for example, could show nothing of consequence. Rome had never produced great tragedy, although she had welcomed the adaptations of Greek comedy by Plautus and Terence. What Rome in the first century wanted of the stage was entertainment: mimes, or farces, preferably indecent. The actors' masks were discarded. For the first time female roles were played not by men but by women, usually by ladies of dubious reputation. There was much improvisation, the plot was generally loose, and if the audience called on the actresses to strip, they gladly obliged.

Since Rome, or rather Italy, had learned to admire the Greek paintings and statues which the Roman armies had brought home as booty, painters and sculptors were kept busy making copies for wealthy patrons. The same wealthy patrons were building more luxurious town houses; and a patron of the Senatorial Order, legally debarred from commercial or financial investment, might buy a considerable number of country estates requiring pleasant houses. Architects, therefore, were kept busy too. The confiscations of the Civil War created a class of newly rich whose one chance of quickly acquiring culture lay in purchase; this brought more orders to painters and sculptors and architects. But Roman society's most authentic work in the plastic arts continued to be what it had always been: the realistic portrait bust, not only the wax ancestral image for funeral processions and official triumphs, but the bust carved in marble or cast in bronze to ornament and glorify the homes of prominent Romans as well as the Roman Forum.

This preference for the concrete individual, who lived or had lived in the Roman state, over the generalized image of man may have been connected with the absence of serious theater: the real drama seemed to be taking place in the Roman Forum and Senate House; the real actors were the orators. Why watch make-believe while the destiny of the world was being decided in full public view, while powerful men engaged in great debates and swayed audiences of immense size? Whether before a court of law or on the hustings or in some vital conflict over policy, the man with power was the orator, unless indeed some millionaire bought up the orator's following or unless some revolutionary general captured Rome, put a price on the orator's head, and eventually suspended it from the rostrum. Yet even the revolutionary general needed to sway the will of crowds in the Forum or at least of his own soldiers in some camp on the eve of battle. A serious citizen, therefore, might justly admire the great orator even more than his favorite gladiator or charioteer or comic actor. Orations became, for such a citizen, his special form of drama.

Into the midst of that exciting drama, early in the first century, there arrived an alert, intelligent boy named Marcus Tullius Cicero. He was born on January 3, 106 B.C., in Arpinum, the town near which Marius had been born some fifty-six years earlier; and their families were connected. Cicero's father was a respectable knight with a literary bent, who moved to Rome in order to give Marcus and his younger brother Quintus a better education than they could hope to receive in Arpinum. At Rome, Marcus heard the lectures of Phaedrus, an Epicurean, and those of the Academic, Philon of Larissa. He was guided also by Diodotus, a Stoic; and he himself became a moderate, eclectic Stoic. In 89 he served briefly in Rome's war with her Italian Allies. He studied law under Mucius Scaevola, the augur. Later he studied under his cousin Mucius Scaevola, the Chief Priest, or *Pontifex Maximus*. Both men were noted jurists. He listened to the famous orators Marcus Antonius and Lucius Crassus. He studied rhetoric under Molon of Rhodes.

When Cicero was fifteen, Sulla seized Rome by storm; and the next year Marius seized it and slaughtered the Optimates for five days. When Cicero was seventeen, Sulla captured and sacked rebellious Athens; when he was twenty-one, Sulla became dictator and started his own reign of terror at Rome. The very next year, Cicero pleaded his first case in court; the year after that, he successfully defended one Sextus Roscius, charged with parricide. In this case he boldly attacked the dictator's favorite freed-man, who had put the name of Roscius' father on Sulla's proscription list in order to buy his confiscated property. Cicero had been most correct in speaking of the dictator himself, but he went abroad the next year for reasons of health and studied at Athens and at Rhodes. When he returned, he again took cases, acquired useful friends, and at twenty-seven was elected to a quaestorship. The next year he served as a sort of deputy governor in the Province of Sicily. Later, at Rome, on behalf of his Sicilian friends he successfully prosecuted in a Senatorial court a governor of Sicily, Lucius Verres, who had plundered that province; Cicero's success made him one of the two leaders of the Roman bar. At thirty-seven he was elected a curule aedile; at forty, a praetor. He was then ready to try for the highest office, a consulship.

Cicero had made his way by hard work, by an eloquence that dazzled and charmed his hearers, by a talent for ingratiating himself with men of influence and for mobilizing their help when needed. He had had but slender financial resources at a time when judicious bribery and expensive public shows had driven up the price of office. He had been without military fame at a time when other men were winning it in the second and third wars against Mithradates; or in the war in Spain, where Sertorius, a general of the Populares, had set up an independent state; or in the bloody suppression of another insurrection of slaves; or in a war to clear the Mediterranean of tens of thousands of pirates who operated a sort of underworld state, preyed on shipping, sacked cities, and kidnaped men, women, and children for the slave markets at Delos and elsewhere.

Cicero was a new man, a man of whose ancestors none had held high office. When he had briefly served in the war with the Italian Allies under the command of Pompeius Strabo, that general's son, three years older than Cicero, had also served. But this son was now officially known as Pompey the Great. For it was Pompey who had suppressed the Spanish rebellion and earned an official triumph. It was Pompey who helped Crassus end the insurrection of the gladiators and slaves. It was he who not only triumphed again but was elected consul at thirty-five. It was he who was said to have killed 10,000 pirates, to have captured 3,000 of their vessels, to have destroyed their fortresses, to have captured 20,000 men and then to have wisely settled them in the interior of Cilicia.

Despite his handicaps, Cicero's boundless ambition to make good in the Roman Republic of his dreams determined him to run for consul in 63. Diligence, influence, and the money of friends might suffice, combined, of course, with the one thing he did best: orate. His basic policy was to unite the Equestrian Order, into which he had been born, with the Senatorial Order, to which a consulship would admit him. The wedge that Gaius Gracchus had driven between these two orders had been replaced by a wedge that Sulla had driven and that still kept them at loggerheads. The Senatorial Order, it is true, had thoroughly demonstrated its inability to govern the huge empire that had been conquered under its guidance. Cicero himself, when prosecuting Verres, had shrewdly urged the judges to find Verres guilty and thereby convince the Roman people that

> our country can be safely guarded by a court composed of senators . . .
> If he is found guilty, people will cease to say that money is the chief
> power in these courts . . .[219]

As for the Equites, they had proven even more dangerously rapacious than the Senators sent out as proconsuls to govern the provinces. But Cicero was confident that, united, the Senators and the Equites could enforce law and order in the Roman Republic and its dominions. It was time to close ranks: in 73 a tribune of the people had even urged plebeians to refuse military service in wars which were profiting only the two higher orders. In a speech this tribune declared:

> I do not advise war or secession, but merely that you should refuse
> longer to shed your blood for them. Let them hold their offices and
> administer them in their own way, let them seek triumphs, let them
> lead their ancestral portraits against Mithridates, Sertorius, and what
> is left of the exiles, but let those who have no share in the profits be
> free also from dangers and toil. . . .

> You have given up everything in exchange for your present slothfulness,
> thinking that you have ample freedom because your backs are spared,

and because you are allowed to go hither and thither by the grace of your rich masters. Yet even these privileges are denied to the country people, who are cut down in the quarrels of the great and sent to the provinces as gifts to the magistrates. Thus they fight and conquer for the benefit of a few, but whatever happens, the commons are treated as vanquished . . .[220]

Cicero's nightmare was subversion, subversion of the civil order by the new-style generals with their new-style proletarian armies, or subversion by proletarian mobs under the leadership of once-rich young men. The former phenomenon he had witnessed when Marius and Sulla had seized power by the sword. The latter he had observed in 66: Lucius Catiline, a former lieutenant of Sulla's, had conspired to murder the two consuls and seize power. Catiline counted, not only on the widespread discontent of patricians like himself, ruined by Sulla's confiscations or by their own profligacy, but on plebeian clamor for the cancellation of debts and the distribution of land.

As a largely self-made man, Cicero loved the social system that would allow him through hard work to achieve at least official equality with members of the oldest and most famous families in the Republic. He was disinclined to see in rebellious speeches to the populace symptoms of economic problems, which could not be solved either by the most brilliant orations or even by what was done in the recent slave uprising when Spartacus and his followers, including free farm workers, fought on

until they all perished except 6000, who were captured and crucified along the whole road from Capua to Rome.[221]

When Cicero detected subversion, he was quick to scent its cause in troublemakers and demagogues, eager to mislead the mob in order to seize power. And such troublemakers did exist. Two of these troublemakers seemed to be Gaius Julius Caesar and Licinius Crassus. Caesar came of an ancient patrician family, but an aunt of his had been the wife of Marius, and he himself favored the Populares. Crassus was perhaps the wealthiest man in Rome.

In 63 Cicero ran for consul. Crassus and Caesar backed, as the candidates of the Populares for the two consulships, Catiline and Gaius Antonius; the former had been tried for conspiracy to murder and had been acquitted. Antonius was successful, but the other consulship went not to Catiline but to Cicero.

From this time Catiline abstained wholly from politics as not leading quickly and surely to absolute power, but as full of the spirit of contention and malice. He procured much money from many women who hoped that they would get their husbands killed in the rising, and he formed a conspiracy with a number of senators and knights, and collected together a body of plebeians, foreign residents, and slaves.[222]

As consul, Cicero three times made speeches against a land bill which Caesar and Crassus had caused to be presented to the popular assembly. It purported to supply land for the poor of Rome. It may well be that Caesar and Crassus were more eager to estrange the plebeians from the Optimates than they were hopeful of passing this bill. But what gave their bill much of its appeal was simple enough: it addressed itself to an urgent public problem. This was the same problem the Senatorial Order had fought against solving when the Gracchi had tried to solve it some seventy years earlier. The ruined farmers and foreign freedmen who made up so large a proportion of the city proletariat could not all hope to find employment. But they could at least sell their votes, and find shelter in one of the so-called islands, five- to seven-story wooden tenements so full of the poor that they often collapsed. These islands also had a way of catching fire. Since there was no public fire department, Caesar's political ally and hopeful creditor, the wealthy Crassus, had made part of his huge fortune by an interesting investment. Crassus organized his own fire brigade, bought up cheaply from its distressed owner any building he saw burning, and then put out the fire. Profits of this kind could eventually be used to buy votes, to bribe key political leaders, and even to raise an army.

Meanwhile Catiline planned his revolt against the conservative Optimates. In the tumult he stirred up, the conservatives saw only an epidemic of political insanity:

> This insanity was not confined to those who were implicated in the plot, but the whole body of the commons through desire for change favoured the designs of Catiline. . . . To begin with, all who were especially conspicuous for their shamelessness and impudence, those too who had squandered their patrimony in riotous living, finally all whom disgrace or crime had forced to leave home, had all flowed into Rome as into a cesspool. Many, too, who recalled Sulla's victory, when they saw common soldiers risen to the rank of senator, and others become so rich that they feasted and lived like kings, hoped each for himself for like fruits of victory, if he took the field. Besides this, the young men who had

maintained a wretched existence by manual labour in the country, tempted by public and private doles had come to prefer idleness in the city to their hateful toil; these, like all the others, battened on the public ills. . . . Moreover, those to whom Sulla's victory had meant the proscription of their parents, loss of property, and curtailment of their rights, looked forward in a similar spirit to the issue of a war. Finally, all who belonged to another party than that of the senate preferred to see the government overthrown rather than be out of power themselves. Such, then, was the evil which after many years had returned upon the state.[223]

When, however, Gnaeus Pompeius had been dispatched to wage war against the pirates and against Mithridates, the power of the commons was lessened, while that of the few increased. These possessed the magistracies, the provinces and everything else; being themselves rich and secure against attack, they lived without fear and by resort to the courts terrified the others, in order that while they themselves were in office they might manage the people with less friction.[224]

A comrade of Catiline's, Gaius Manlius, started raising an army in Etruria. Catiline directed preparations at Rome. In September, 63, Cicero warned the Senate. By October 22 he had secured emergency powers from the Senate, in a decree that amounted to declaring martial law. On November 8, in a thunderous oration in the Senate, he accused Catiline to his face. That night, Catiline fled Rome and joined Manlius at Fiesole. The next day, in a second oration against Catiline, Cicero reported to the popular assembly. Meanwhile, he ferreted out more definite information about the plot. Catiline's associates in Rome had sought out envoys whom the Gallic tribe of Allobroges had sent to Rome and had tried to get that tribe's military support. The envoys reported this effort to Cicero, became his agents, and caused the plotters, together with incriminating sealed letters, to be captured. On December 3 Cicero convoked the Senate, produced the letters, had them identified, opened, and read to the Senate. Confessions followed. Next day, Cicero delivered his third oration against Catiline, this one also to the popular assembly. He reviewed the civil wars that Rome had suffered and then went into his peroration:

And these civil wars, citizens, all aimed, not at the destruction of the state, but at a change in government. These men did not wish that there should be no state at all but that in that state which was to be they should be supreme. They did not wish to burn this city but they wished to have power in this city. Still all these quarrels, none of which sought the destruction of the state, were decided not by a peaceful reconciliation, but by a slaughter of the citizens. In this war, the very greatest and most cruel war within the memory of man, such a war as no barbarous tribe ever waged with its own people, a war in which this rule had been established by Lentulus, Gabinius, Cethegus, Cassius—that all who could be safe while the state was safe should be considered as enemies—in this war I have so conducted myself, citizens, that you all are safe and when your enemies thought that only those citizens would remain who survived an indiscriminate slaughter and only as much of the city as the flames could not envelop, I have preserved both city and citizens safe and sound.

In return for these great services, citizens, I ask from you no reward for courage, no insignia of honour, no monument of praise, except the eternal memory of this day. In your hearts I wish all my triumphs, all decorations of honour, the monuments of glory, the insignia of praise, to be founded and set up. Nothing mute can please me, nothing silent, nothing, finally, that less worthy men can attain. In your memories, citizens, my deeds will be cherished. They will be enhanced by the talk of men. In the monuments of literature they will wax old and strong. I know that the same length of days (I hope it will be eternal) has been destined both for the safety of the city and for the memory of my consulship and that at one time in this state there have been two men one of whom fixed the borders of your empire not by limits of the earth, but by the limits of the sky, the other preserved the home and abiding-place of this empire.

But since the fortune and the lot of the services which I have performed is not the same as the lot of those who have carried on foreign wars—because I have to live with those whom I have overcome and conquered, while they leave their enemies, either killed or subdued—it is your duty, citizens, if others rightly profit by their deeds, to see to it that my deeds may not at some time injure me. I have provided that the criminal and deadly intent of abandoned men shall not injure you; it is your duty to provide that they may not injure me. And yet, citizens, no harm can come to me myself from those men now. For the defence of loyal men counts for much, and that is mine for ever; there is great majesty in the state and it though silent will always defend me; the power of conscience is great, and those who neglect this, wishing to injure me, will be betraying themselves. Such is our spirit, citizens, that we will yield to the effrontery of no man. No, we will even of our own accord ever attack all wicked men. But if all the violence of the traitors, averted from you, shall turn upon me alone, *you* must consider, citizens, in what a situation you wish those hereafter to be who have for your safety exposed themselves to hatred and to dangers of all sorts. As for myself, what is there now which can add to my enjoyment of life, especially when I see no loftier honour that you have to bestow nor any higher pinnacle of glory to which I may wish to ascend? This certainly I will accomplish, citizens: that as a private citizen I may support and dignify the things which I have done in my consulship, so that if odium is incurred in saving the state, it may injure the envious and may redound to my glory. Finally, I will so conduct myself in the state, that I shall always remember what I have done and take care that men will see that it was done by courage and not by chance.

And do you, citizens, since now it is night, give praise to that Jupiter, the guardian of this city and of you, depart to your homes and although the danger is now averted, nevertheless defend them as you did last night with your garrisons and sentinels. I will take care that you shall not have to do this too long and that you may dwell in everlasting peace.[225]

On the next day, December 4, a captured Catilinian named Tarquinius turned state's evidence and declared to the Senate that he had been caught while taking a message from Crassus, urging Catiline to return to Rome and revive the conspiracy:

As soon, however, as Tarquinius named Crassus, a noble of great wealth and of the highest rank, some thought the charge incredible; others believed it to be true, but thought that in such a crisis so powerful a man ought to be propitiated rather than exasperated. There were many, too, who were under obligation to Crassus through private business relations. All these loudly insisted that the accusation was false, and demanded that the matter be laid before the senate. Accordingly, on the motion of Cicero, the senate in full session voted that the testimony of Tarquinius appeared to be false; that he should be kept under guard and given no further hearing until he revealed the name of the man at whose instigation he had lied about a matter of such moment.[226]

The other leader who had certainly had earlier associations with Catiline was Julius Caesar. He, too, was suspected, but nothing was proven. On the morning of December 5 the Senate debated the penalty for the five conspirators who had been seized. A number of senators backed a motion that the five prisoners and four other conspirators, if they could be apprehended, should be put to death. Then it was Caesar's turn:

The greater number of those who have expressed their opinions before me have deplored the lot of the commonwealth in finished and noble phrases . . . the rape of maidens and boys . . . matrons subjected to the will of the victors, temples and homes pillaged . . . in short . . . gore and grief.[227]

Caesar, who commonly made less use than Cicero of finished and noble phrases, pointed out that there were laws against condemning Roman citizens to death and proposed that the convicted men suffer confiscation of goods and imprisonment.

Then Cicero intervened with his fourth and last oration against Catiline. On the surface his speech was an assurance that, whichever sentence might be voted, he as consul would execute it. But it was sufficiently clear that he wanted the death sentence, and he offered a precedent. He was willing to incur the charge of cruelty:

> For I seem to see this city, the light of the whole world and the fortress of all the nations, suddenly involved in one general conflagration. In my imagination I see on the grave of the fatherland the wretched, unburied heaps of citizens. Before my eyes there rises the countenance of Cethegus and his madness as he revels in your death. But when I have pictured to myself . . . Catiline there with an army, then I shudder at the outcries of mothers, the panic of girls and boys, the assault on the Vestal Virgins, and because these acts seem to me pitiful and deserving of pity, therefore I am stern and relentless against those who have wished to bring these things to pass.[228]

He reiterated that it was he who had saved the state. He exploited the occasion to allude to his old dream: if the Senatorial Order and the Equestrian Order retained their new-found political unity, the populace could not be misled. He appealed to religion. There remained only the task of clinching the gratitude which the Senate had expressed for himself: and he went into his peroration:

> Now before I turn to ask your opinions further, I shall speak briefly about myself. I see that I have made for myself as many enemies as there are conspirators—a very large number as you see. But I judge them base, weak and powerless. However if at some time that band, incited by the mad fury of someone, shall have more power than your prestige and the prestige of the state, nevertheless, Conscript Fathers, I will never regret my deeds and my advice. For death which they perhaps threaten awaits all men; no one in his lifetime has attained such praise as you have bestowed on me by your decrees. You have decreed a thanksgiving to others for serving the state well, to me alone for preserving it. Granted that Scipio be famous, by whose wisdom and valour Hannibal

was compelled to leave Italy and return to Africa; granted that the other Africanus who destroyed two cities of our greatest enemies, the cities of Carthage and Numantia, be exalted with especial praise; granted that that noble Paulus be a man renowned, whose triumph the once powerful and noble king Perseus adorned; granted that Marius have eternal glory who twice freed Italy from siege and the fear of slavery; granted that Pompey outrank them all, whose deeds and virtues are limited only by those regions and boundaries that confine the course of the sun: certainly there will be amid the praise of these men some place for my glory, unless perhaps it is a greater thing to lay open for ourselves provinces to which we may go forth than to take care that those who have gone forth may have a place to which they may victoriously return. . . . So I see that I have taken up an unending war with wicked citizens. This I trust can easily be averted from me and mine by your aid and that of all upright men, and by the memory of these great dangers which will always abide, not only among this people who have been saved, but in the words and thought of all nations. And certainly no force will ever be found great enough to break and dissolve your union with the Roman knights, and this complete concord among all upright men. . . .

I ask nothing of you, except that you remember this time and all my consulship. For so long as that remains fixed in your minds, I shall think I am surrounded by an impregnable wall. But if the power of criminals shall disappoint my expectation and shall triumph, I commend to you my little son who will certainly have enough protection, not only for his safety but also for his career, if you will but remember that he is the son of the man who saved the entire state, risking himself alone. Therefore, carefully and bravely, as you have begun, take measures for the protection of yourselves and the Roman people, for your wives and your children, for your altars and your hearths, for the shrines and the temples, for the dwellings and homes of the entire city, for the government and for liberty, for the safety of Italy, for the whole state. You have a consul who does not hesitate to obey your orders, who can uphold your decrees as long as he shall live and who can by himself warrant their accomplishment.[229]

Despite this oration, opinion remained divided. Then Cato the Younger, great-grandson of Cato the Censor, spoke:

In fine and finished phrases did Gaius Caesar a moment ago before this body speak of life and death, regarding as false, I presume, the tales which are told of the Lower World, where they say that the wicked take a different path from the good, and dwell in regions that are gloomy, desolate,

133

unsightly, and full of fears. Therefore he recommended that the goods of the prisoners be confiscated, and that they themselves be imprisoned in the free towns . . . this advice is utterly futile if Caesar fears danger from the conspirators; but if amid such general fear he alone has none, I have the more reason to fear for you and for myself.[230]

Cato voted for death, and his side won. Cicero did not wait until morning. He and the praetors led the five condemned men to a dungeon, where the executioners strangled them. Cicero announced their death to the people in his shortest speech: "They have lived."[231] There remained Catiline's army in Etruria. The three legions that Cicero's colleague, the Consul Antonius, led against it caught it near Pistoia on January 5, 62.

When the battle was ended it became evident what boldness and resolution had pervaded Catiline's army. For almost every man covered with his body, when life was gone, the position which he had taken when alive at the beginning of the conflict. . . . Finally, out of the whole army not a single citizen of free birth was taken during the battle or in flight, showing that all had valued their own lives no more highly than those of their enemies.[232]

The Optimates were overjoyed that the Republic, the Public Thing, which Sulla had restored to them, had been saved from subversion. They hailed Cicero as Father of his Country, that heady title which Camillus had earned when he had saved Rome from the Gauls more than three centuries before. Cicero himself judged that this was his finest hour. But he was soon shocked by the speed with which the conspiracy of Catiline was forgotten, or at least underestimated. He tried to keep green the memory of his consulship by speaking of it in formal orations and by alluding to it in writing his friends. For instance, when Lucius Torquatus had in 65 prosecuted Publius Cornelius Sulla, wealthy nephew of the dictator, for bribery, Sulla was convicted. Three years later, in 62, Torquatus prosecuted him again, this time on the charge of having participated in the conspiracy of Catiline. Cicero undertook the defense, partly, perhaps, because Sulla had lent him 2,000,000 sesterces with which to buy a house on the fashionable Palatine hill; for he had felt it was

quite legitimate to make use of a friend's pocket to buy a place that gives one a social position.[233]

Torquatus, however, had also called Cicero a tyrant, and this gave Cicero a chance to discuss himself. Do not call me a tyrant, he cried,

Unless perhaps it seems to you tyrannical so to live that you are a slave to no man nor even to any passion, to despise all desires, to covet neither gold, nor silver, nor other possessions, to express yourself freely in the senate, to consult the people's need rather than their pleasure, to yield to no one, to oppose many. If you think that is tyrannical, I admit I am a tyrant.[234]

It was then, Cicero reminded his listeners, that

I the consul, by my precaution and my toil, at the risk of my life, without a riot, without a levy, without arms, without an army, by the arrest and confession of five men only, freed the city from conflagration, the citizens from murder, Italy from devastation, the state from ruin. I saved the lives of all the citizens, the peace of the world, this city, the home of us all, the citadel of foreign kings and nations, the light of mankind, the home of empire, by the punishment of five mad, abandoned men.[235]

To forgetfulness and ingratitude the class that Cicero had benefited now added the imputation of vanity. They had used this new man, and now despised his self-praise. Yet to Marcus Cato, who had helped him against Julius Caesar when the Senate debated the death sentence for Catiline and his followers, Cicero wrote, years later:

If ever there was a man who by natural disposition, and even more, as I seem to feel, by reasoned judgment and education, stood aloof from empty plaudits and vulgar talk, that man is assuredly myself. Witness my consulship, in the course of which, as in the rest of my life, I admit that I eagerly pursued whatever might be a source of true glory; glory, in and for itself, I have never thought worth the seeking.[236]

Most annoying of all, perhaps, was Cicero's failure to impress Pompey the Great. In 62 Pompey was completing the reorganization of his extensive conquests in Asia, and was suspected of planning to return in the manner of Sulla and to set up a dictatorship. Cicero's single prescription for the class war that he had temporarily driven underground was still to secure by his own eloquence, prestige, and zeal for political compromise a *concordia ordinum* between Senators and Equites. The Senators based their power publicly on their numerous landed estates; the Equites based theirs on tax collecting, state contracts, and moneylending. It is true that in private Senators and Equites often made deals together: an Eques could discreetly handle a Senator's profits from farming the land and invest them in one of the powerful corporations that farmed the taxes, or invest them in private loans to provincial cities unable to pay their assessed tribute. In return the grateful Senator could use his vote and considerable influence to aid the corporation. Members of both orders were too busy acquiring money and power to serve Cicero's dream of a conservative coalition capable of governing the mob. Cicero, who prided himself on smelling out power, guiding it, and persuading the people to vote for it, distrusted Julius Caesar as a political leader of the Populares; distrusted Crassus, who was placing his millions behind Caesar; and had no other rising political star to hitch his wagon to, except Pompey. Yet Pompey seemed unimpressed by Cicero's suppression of Catiline. In 62 Cicero wrote him:

> As regards your private letter to me, however, in spite of its containing but a slight expression of your regard for me, I assure you I was charmed with it; for generally speaking nothing cheers me up so much as the consciousness of my good services to others; and if, as sometimes happens, they elicit no adequate response, I am quite content that the balance of services rendered should rest with me. Of this I have no doubt at all that, if the proofs of my deep devotion to you have not quite succeeded in attaching me to you, that attachment will be brought about and cemented between us by the interests of the state.[237]

In December, 62, Pompey and his army landed in Brindisi. Here Sulla had landed when he, too, had returned, twenty-one years earlier, from conquest in the East. Here Pompey, then twenty-three, had met him. The next year Sulla had captured Rome and become dictator, charged with restoring the state. But now, in 62, Pompey amazed Rome: after first promising his veterans land, he simply discharged them. He was voted a two-day triumph. He had nearly doubled by his conquests the revenues of the Republic. He had brought to the Treasury immense loot. Even so, the Senate haggled over his Eastern settlement and refused land for his veterans.

Cicero still courted him. In 61, with Pompey present, Cicero spoke to the Senate on his favorite theme. He reported the occasion to Atticus:

> As for me, ye gods, how I showed off before my new listener Pompey! Then, if ever, my flow of rounded periods, my easy transitions, my antitheses, my constructive arguments stood me in good stead. In a word, loud applause! For the gist of it was the importance of the Senatorial order, its unison with the knights, the concord of all Italy, the paralysed remains of the conspiracy, peace and plenty. You know how I can thunder on a subject like that.[238]

About a year after he showed off to Pompey, he defended, with qualifications, Pompey's request that land be distributed to his veterans:

> The Senate was opposed to the whole agrarian scheme, suspecting that Pompey was aiming at getting some new powers. Pompey had set his heart on carrying the law through. I on the other hand, with the full approval of the applicants for land, was for securing the holdings of all private persons—for, as you know, the strength of our party consists in the rich landed gentry—while at the same time I fulfilled my desire to satisfy Pompey and the populace by supporting the purchase of land, thinking that, if that were thoroughly carried out, the city might be emptied of the dregs of the populace, and the deserted parts of Italy peopled.[239]

Cicero's letters to Atticus show how Pompey's title, the Great, could rankle. But he needed Pompey's political support and wrote Atticus that

> For myself, ever since that December day when I won such splendid and immortal glory, though it carried with it much envy and enmity, I have not ceased to employ the same high-minded policy and to keep the position I have won and taken up. But, as soon as the acquittal of Clodius showed me the uncertainty and instability of the law courts, and I saw too how easily our friends the tax-gatherers could be estranged from the Senate, though they might not sever their connection with me, while the well-to-do—your friends with the fish-ponds, I mean—took no pains to disguise their envy of me, I bethought me that I had better look out for some stronger support and more secure protection. So firstly I brought Pompey, the man who had held his peace too long about my achievements, into a frame of mind for attributing to me the salvation of the empire and the world not once only, but time after time and with emphasis in the House. That was not so much for my own benefit—for my achievements were neither so obscure that they required evidence, nor so dubious that they required puffing up—but for the State's sake, for there were some ill-natured persons who thought that there was a certain amount of disagreement between Pompey and myself . . . With him I have formed such an intimate connection that both of us are strengthened in our policy and surer in our political position through our coalition. The dislike which had been aroused against me among our dissipated and dandified youths has been smoothed away by my affability, and now they pay me more attention than anyone. In short I avoid hurting anyone's feelings, though I do not court popularity by relaxing my principles . . .[240]

Pompey countered the Senate's refusal to vindicate his promise of land to his veterans by entering into an informal three-man coalition, a triumvirate, with Caesar and Crassus. The triumvirate controlled the Republic, by bribery, by threats, by reopening the question of distributing public land. Caesar invited the cooperation of Cicero, but Cicero declined. It was the power of the word that Cicero had wanted, not the power of the sword.

Despite Cicero's best efforts to preserve his political influence, his letters to his friend Atticus, an Eques like himself, wealthy owner of estates in Epirus, banker, publisher, patron of the arts, were often melancholy. And in the very year that Pompey returned triumphantly from Asia, Cicero spoke of

> politics, where I dare not make a slip . . . legal work, which I used to undertake for advancement's sake and now keep up to preserve my position through popularity . . .[241]

In 58, Cicero was forced into exile by his personal enemy, Clodius, who was also a tribune and a creature of Caesar's. He was the brother, some said the lover, of that beautiful and wayward Clodia whom the poet Catullus had so loved. Clodius hounded Cicero into exile by charging him with condemning Roman citizens without trial. It was the nighttime executions of the followers of Catiline, the dramatic moment of Cicero's finest hour and indeed of his whole consulship, which had now undone him. He fled to Greece. His fine house on the Palatine was demolished and his country estates at Tusculum and Formiae were ravaged.

By 57 Clodius had been murdered in political gang warfare, and with Pompey's help Cicero found it safe to return to Rome. The triumvirate of Caesar, Pompey, and Crassus still dominated the Republic. As consul in 59, Caesar had wanted to block the aristocratic cabal in the Senate: he had ordered that all debates in the Senate were to be transcribed and published. He had also secured from the popular assembly the land for Pompey's veterans. A term as propraetor in Spain had demonstrated his military skill and had netted him enough booty to pay his large debt to Crassus. Posting soldiers around the Senate House, Caesar put through a measure to distribute public land in Capua to poor men with at least three children. Some 20,000 were assigned allotments. The Optimates, who had lynched the Gracchi for less, were in no position to oppose Caesar. In effect, Caesar was pushing through the Marian revolution that Sulla had thwarted. The personal army, open to volunteers with no property, which was first invented by Marius, now gave the proletarian a chance to get capital by pillage, to get land as a deserving veteran, and to avoid Senatorial vetoes by furnishing the leader of the Populares with force. By the time Cicero, "champion of creditors as I am,"[242] had returned from exile, Caesar had bullied the Senate into assigning to him as proconsul both Cisalpine and Transalpine Gaul. He had defeated the Helvetians near the site of modern Autun and a Germanic chieftain, Ariovistus, in Alsace. In 56 the members of the triumvirate renewed their agreement and used force to get Pompey and Crassus elected consuls. Cicero's brother Quintus, who had served in Sardinia under Pompey, warned him to cooperate with the triumvirate. By 54 Cicero was cooperating enough to persuade Caesar to make Quintus a legate, or staff officer, in Gaul; and in September of that year Cicero wrote Quintus a letter that was presumably intended for Caesar's eyes too:

> Pompey is making a strong effort to become reconciled with me, but as yet has met with no success, and, if I retain a particle of independence, he will never succeed. . . .

> I assure you that, as for "second thoughts," I could have none in my relations with Caesar. He comes next to you and my children with me, and so closely next that he is almost on a par with them. It seems to me that such is my deliberate conviction (and it ought to be so by this time), and yet a strong predilection has its influence upon me.[243]

Cicero explained two months later to his friend Lentulus why it was a good thing to have Quintus on Caesar's staff:

> This enables me to enjoy as though they were my own the advantages both of his influence, which is very powerful, and of his pecuniary resources which, as you know, are very great; indeed I fail to see how otherwise I could have wrecked the intrigues against me of unprincipled scoundrels, than by combining with the safeguards I always possessed the friendliness of men in power.[244]

Meanwhile, Caesar continued to subdue Gaul and to send back clear, terse accounts of his campaigns, accounts that dazzled Rome. He thereby emphasized once more his political alignment with his uncle by marriage, Gaius Marius, who had saved Italy from the Gauls. For the Gauls remained Rome's oldest and most persistent nightmare, so much so that

> in the law which exempted priests and old men from military enrolment a formal exception was made "in case of a Gallic inroad"; for then both priests and old men were required to serve.[245]

Caesar also bridged the Rhine and made a foray into Germany to discourage the Germanic tribes from seeking land in Gaul, and he reconnoitered in force in southern Britain. The next year he campaigned in Britain and brought back hostages. In 52 he quelled a general uprising in Gaul. In 51 he finished pacifying what is now roughly the whole of France; then he pinned it down with ten legions. His fame had grown yearly while Pompey's, like Cicero's, had dimmed. As for Crassus, he had sought military fame commensurate with his vast wealth by leading an army to Asia and attacking Parthia. In 53, at Carrhae, the mounted archers of Parthia outmaneuvered him, surrounded his army, and cut it to pieces. Crassus was taken by treachery and killed. His head was sent to the royal court of Parthia, where the *Bacchae* of Euripides was to be presented. A Greek actor used the severed head of Rome's leading businessman to make the last scene more realistic. By 50 Pompey's relations with Caesar were showing strain, and Pompey was edging back toward the Optimates.

Throughout the troubling years of the triumvirate, Cicero worried about the Populares' threat to the sanctity of private property; about the stupid arrogance of the rich Optimates, less eager to consider the interests of the Republic than to construct new fish-ponds on their numerous estates; about the financial greed of the Equites. But he worried most about the still growing power of Caesar and Pompey, about their threat to constitutional freedom, their threat to government by eloquence and to the sort of decent compromise that Marcus Cato could not tolerate. As to Cato, Cicero had written Atticus as far back as June, 60, that

> the opinions he delivers would be more in place in Plato's Republic than among the dregs of humanity collected by Romulus. That a man who accepts a bribe for the verdict he returns at a trial should be put on trial himself is as fair a principle as one could wish. Cato voted for it and won the House's assent. Result, a war of the knights with the Senate, but not with me. I was against it. That the tax-collectors should repudiate their bargain was a most shameless proceeding. But we ought to have put up with the loss in order to keep their good-will. Cato resisted and carried the day. Result, though we've had a consul in prison, and frequent riots, not a breath of encouragement from one of those who in my own consulship and that of my successors used to rally round us to defend the country. "Must we then bribe them for their support?" you will ask. What help is there, if we cannot get it otherwise?[246]

In the same vein he wrote his brother, Quintus, then propraetor of the Province of Asia, that he could count on support from the Equites, whether tax collectors or traders, since they "consider that the security of the fortunes they enjoy is due to the blessing of my consulship."[247] Still, Cicero made it clear that these publicans did make it hard to govern the provinces justly:

> And yet to all your goodwill and devotion to duty there is a serious obstacle in the *publicani;* if we oppose them, we shall alienate from ourselves and from the commonwealth an order that has deserved extremely well of us, and been brought through our instrumentality into close association with the commonwealth; and yet, if we yield to them in everything, we shall be acquiescing in the utter ruin of those whose security, and indeed whose interest, we are bound to protect.[248]

But even though Cicero more than once declared that he considered honesty was the best policy,[249] he did not urge on Quintus the moral intransigence which Cato affected:

> For it does not at all commend itself to me (especially in view of the distinct bias of modern morality in favour of undue laxity of conduct, and even of self-seeking) that you should investigate every ugly charge, and turn every single one of the charged inside out . . .[250]

And he urged discretion. Before Quintus should leave his province, he should destroy any letters that were "inequitable, eccentric, or inconsistent with others."[251]

Like most Romans in public life, Cicero was constantly worried about money. The political system in which he operated forced men with political ambition to strain their financial resources if they would maintain their prestige. It would have been considered dishonorable for a man in Cicero's position to earn his living except by the very indirect means of practicing law: it was disreputable for a Roman lawyer to accept a fee from a client, though fortunately many grateful clients made gifts. Also, Cicero's wealthy friend Atticus was generous. Cicero's expenses were heavier than such philosophers as Socrates, let alone Diogenes, could have comprehended. He wrote to his brother:

> Now as to that *"opulence"* you so often talk about, I have a longing for it, but quite in moderation—just so far as gladly to welcome my quarry, if it comes my way, but not to hunt it out, if it keeps under cover. Even as it is, I am building in three different places, and refurbishing my

other houses. I am living rather more generously than I used to; I have to do so.[252]

In 51 he was sent as proconsul to govern Cilicia, and that would have lined the pockets of a less scrupulous man. But he took pride in refusing even the customary gift from the provincials, commonly accepted as a bribe not to quarter troops on the inhabitants; nor did he quarter troops. Agents of his aristocratic friend, Marcus Brutus, were trying to persuade him to help them collect interest at forty-eight per cent on a loan Brutus had discreetly made to a city in Cyprus.[253] Yet the legal interest rate was twelve. Here in actual operation was Cicero's harmony between the orders, the patrician landowners and the financier-Equites, a harmony based on the mutual need to extort money from the provincials. It was not the harmony of which he had dreamed when he made his inspiring orations. But, at least in Cilicia, it had sufficed to bleed a province white and to estrange the provincials. Cicero reported ominously to the consuls and Senate that

> there is every danger of our being forced to give up these provinces upon which the revenues of the Roman people depend. But you have no justification at all for basing any hopes upon a levy in this province; there are not many men, and such men as there are scatter at the first approach of danger; and in Asia that very gallant officer, M. Bibulus, has indicated his opinion of this type of soldier by declining to hold a levy when you gave him permission to do so. In fact, owing to the harshness and injustice of Roman rule, the auxiliaries among our allies are either so feeble that they cannot give us much assistance, or else so estranged from us that it looks as though we ought neither to expect anything of them nor to entrust anything to their keeping.[254]

With soldiers like that, what would Cicero do if Parthia, fresh from smashing a Roman army of some 35,000 men and from assigning to Crassus an unexpected role in Euripides, should advance on Cilicia? Cicero did campaign against some troublesome hill tribes; but his modest exploits would not earn him, on his return to Rome, the triumph he longed for. He had written his friend, Publius Lentulus, in 56 when it was Lentulus who was marooned in Cilicia, that

> this is a lesson that even I, devoted as I have been from a boy to all kinds of literature, have still learnt better from practical experience than from books—to be taught while your prosperity is still intact, that we must neither consider our safety to the detriment of our dignity, nor our dignity to the detriment of our safety.[255]

142

Finally, he longed for the bustle, the intrigue, the applause that only Rome could offer: "Rome, my dear Rufus, Rome—stay there in that full light and *live*."[256] He was glad when the end of his term approached, and he wrote Atticus from an army camp in Cappadocia: "Moreover I hope that my justice and restraint may become more famous, if I leave soon . . ."[257]

With all his troubles Cicero heroically preserved his self-respect. In 58, when Clodius, the gangster tribune, drove him into exile, he had written Atticus:

> Did anyone ever fall from such a high estate in such a good cause, especially when he was so well endowed with genius and good sense, so popular and so strongly supported by all honest men? Can I forget what I was? Can I help feeling what I am? Can I help missing my honour and fame, my children, my fortune and my brother?[258]

But, though he had almost never despaired of his own wisdom or rectitude, he had suffered grievous cares. As he wrote from Thessalonica, again to Atticus,

> What about my goods and chattels? What about my house? Will they be restored? If not, how can I be?[259]

As the dangerous fifties wore on and the nightmare image of Caesar challenged Pompey and the Optimates, Cicero gallantly struggled for a political foothold. It was growing steadily harder, in Rome as in Cilicia, to preserve both his safety and his dignity. He lacked the means of both Caesar and Pompey to use force, to appeal to the sword. He lacked the wealth which Pompey had amassed in Asia and which Caesar was squeezing out of the Gauls. He lacked Caesar's loyal and battle-toughened army, or even the handsomely rewarded veterans on whom Pompey believed he could still count. He had never celebrated a triumph, though he had briefly and vainly hoped for one after fighting in his Province of Cilicia. But he could still win thunderous applause in the Forum or in the courts. He lacked the art of wounding with the sword, and in any case his critics charged that he shrank from steel; but his invective was worthy of Demosthenes and his words drew blood. Even in conversation with opponents his words drew blood, as Cato the Elder's had drawn it, and Cicero's invective satisfied a deep Roman need for verbal violence.

But Cicero satisfied another need of the ambitious Optimates and enterprising Equites around him. Now that Rome had conquered the world, there was a loss of social purpose, of function. There was a sense of frustration, of uncertainty, of spiritual insecurity. The common cure for this malaise was flattery, and few Romans could apply it with Cicero's skill. Sometimes it took an intimate, caressing turn, as in a letter to his beloved Atticus:

> You are the only person I know less given to flattery than myself, and, if we both fall into it sometimes in the case of other people, certainly we never use it to one another.[260]

In 56, unable to persuade either Pompey or, indeed, most of the Optimates that he had saved Rome and the world, he sought the help of Lucius Lucceius, a Senator. Lucceius had failed to win an election to the consulship and was now writing a history of Rome, beginning with the war of 91-88 between Rome and her Italian Allies. Cicero wrote him:

> So I frankly ask you again and again to eulogize my actions with even more warmth than perhaps you feel, and in that respect to disregard the canons of history; and—to remind you of that personal partiality of which you have written most charmingly . . . if you find that such personal partiality enhances my merits even to exaggeration in your eyes, I ask you not to disdain it, and of your bounty to bestow on our love even a little more than may be allowed by truth. And if I can induce you to undertake what I suggest, you will, I assure myself, find a theme worthy of your able and flowing pen.
>
> From the beginning of the conspiracy to my return from exile it seems to me that a fair-sized volume could be compiled . . . and if you think you should treat the subject with exceptional freedom of speech, as has been your habit, you will stigmatize the disloyalty, intrigues, and treachery of which many have been guilty towards me.[261]

It was not much to ask. Cicero considered history as closely allied with oratory: why should it not play advocate? The right history would refresh in people's minds the memory of his colossal struggle with Catiline. It would bring him after death the dead's

> peculiar blessings of fame and glory. There is, it may be, nothing in glory that we should desire it, but none the less it follows virtue like a shadow.[262]

Virtue there certainly had been. As he wrote to Lucceius years later,

Yes, I did for my country certainly no less than I was bound to do—
assuredly more than has ever been demanded of the heart or head of any
human being.[263]

But he discovered that he could not count on other men to praise his
consulate adequately: he must do it himself. He reported in a letter to
Atticus with the appropriate defensive note of self-mockery,

> I have sent you a copy of my account of my consulship in Greek. If
> there is anything in it, which to your Attic taste seems bad Greek or
> unscholarly, I will not say what Lucullus said to you—at Panhormus, I
> think—about his history, that he had interspersed a few barbarisms and
> solecisms as a clear proof that it was the work of a Roman. If there is
> anything of the kind in my work, it is there without my knowledge and
> against my will. When I have finished the Latin version, I will send it to
> you. In the third place you may expect a poem, not to let slip any
> method of singing my own praises. Please don't quote "Who will praise
> his sire?" For if there is any more fitting subject for eulogy, then I am
> willing to be blamed for not choosing some other subject. However my
> compositions are not panegyrics at all but histories.[264]

By 50, when Caesar had conquered all Gaul, Pompey had finally cut clear
of the Populares who backed Caesar and was openly siding with the Senate
and the Optimates. Cicero wrote Atticus that he himself was for Pompey but
was advising him not to provoke a clash. Meanwhile, he reported to Atticus,

> Caesar sends me a friendly letter. Balbus does the same on his ac-
> count. Certainly I shall not swerve a finger's breadth from the strictest
> honour; but you know how much I still owe him. Don't you think there
> is fear that this may be cast in my teeth, if I am slack; and repayment
> demanded from me, if I am energetic? What solution is there? "Pay up,"
> say you. Well, I will borrow from the bank. But there is a point you
> might consider. If I ever make a notable speech in the House on behalf
> of the constitution, your friend from Tarshish will be pretty sure to say
> to me as I go out: "Kindly send me a draft."[265]

Atticus' friend from Tarshish was Caesar's friend Balbus. Cicero owed it
to his dignity to save the Republic again. But he owed it to his safety not
to provoke Balbus into calling his loan.

Cicero was later charged with vacillation, but the charge was not wholly
fair. He wanted to preserve constitutional government; and, like most care-

ful observers, he saw military dictatorship approaching. He hated subversion and still believed he had saved Rome from being subverted by murderers, profligates, debtors, and the howl of the needy. He had never understood what economic forces made possible the Gracchi, Marius, Caesar, and indeed, by reaction, Sulla and the new Pompey. He wanted to preserve an harmonious Public Thing, subjecting the rest of the world by force and ruling it by law as justly as might prove practicable. Indeed, he wanted to preserve the kind of society and the kind of polity he had assumed the Roman Republic was when he, a middle-class country boy, had listened with awe to the most famous orators in town, had thrilled to the applause, and had resolved to become what he had since in fact become, the most admired orator in Rome, receiving his clients each morning at his home, stumping the city for votes at election time, buying country houses worthy of his growing fame, and persuading Atticus to send him statues to set off the dignity of such estates. For indeed he had achieved *dignitas*, a word ever on his lips. And now ruthless men, bribing the rabble with other people's land, threatened to overthrow the world he had briefly ruled as consul and still might rule again, if Rome did not fall under tyranny. Since he never grasped the underlying problems of Rome, since he never grasped that the Republic he loved had not existed from the time of the Gracchi, if indeed it had ever existed at all, he could only urge the landed interest and the moneyed interest to unite against anarchy from the lower depths of society.

In all the circumstances, Cicero's program could scarcely be considered a genuine political idea. In default of some political idea as end, he was condemned to a frantic effort to manage what he saw as the means. He was buoyed up by his dream of a conservative, peaceful, prosperous state depending on some sort of Rector or Governor, a man with wisdom and eloquence and complete integrity, perhaps himself. If Caesar and Pompey were each scheming to destroy the Republic and establish a tyranny, then he must scheme faster. He tried to make use of both generals, since great statesmen must use other men and since he was certain that his transcendent wisdom and eloquence made him the Platonic philosopher-king of this great Republic, whether recognized or unrecognized. As for him, he performed those duties which, in his own phrase, his genius and good sense imposed upon him.

Between 52, the year Caesar crushed the Gallic uprising under Vercingetorix, and 46, Cicero seldom spoke in either the Senate or at the bar, although he did what he could behind the scenes. Deprived of a political role, he turned to writing. In his youth he had attempted poetry; but, although his work did not lack virtuosity, it never rose beyond versification. Much of what he now wrote in prose was translation from the Greek. Somewhat inevitably, he translated an oration of Demosthenes'; he also translated Plato's dialogue, the *Protagoras*, and was unperturbed by Socrates' ironical treatment of the sophist. Indeed, though Cicero proudly considered himself a disciple of Plato's, he seemed immune to the Socratic irony that plays like sheet lightning in so many of Plato's dialogues. On the other hand Cicero was a master of sarcasm. What he loved most was oratory, and he delivered all told more than a hundred orations. Understandably, as Caesar's career threw him more and more in the shade, he had turned to the composition of a treatise, *On the Making of an Orator*, which he finished early in 55, the very year that Caesar led an army across the Rhine and later across the Channel to Britain.

On the Making of an Orator was written in the form of a dialogue between several famous Roman orators of Cicero's boyhood days. This dialogue takes place in September, 91, at the villa of Lucius Crassus in Tusculum, and the reader detects that Crassus, who had tutored Cicero in rhetoric, is here Cicero's voice.

> Scaevola, after taking two or three turns, observed, "Crassus, why do we not imitate Socrates as he appears in the *Phaedrus* of Plato? For your plane-tree has suggested this comparison to my mind, casting as it does, with its spreading branches, as deep a shade over this spot, as that one cast whose shelter Socrates sought—which to me seems to owe its eminence less to 'the little rivulet' described by Plato than to the language of his dialogue—and what Socrates did, whose feet were thoroughly hardened, when he threw himself down on the grass and so began the talk which philosophers say was divine,—such ease surely may more reasonably be conceded to my own feet." "Nay," answered Crassus, "but we will make things more comfortable still," whereupon, according to Cotta, he called for cushions, and they all sat down together on the benches that were under the plane-tree.[266]

Neither Cicero nor his Roman readers would have tolerated Roman statesmen lying on the grass. Socrates was a poor man, carefree, and seeking to learn; Cicero's characters were rich, worried, and already knew that they knew; they required chairs and cushions to the same extent that Protagoras, in Plato's dialogue of that name, required pay for teaching what he too already knew.

What the Crassus of Cicero's dialogue loved in oratory was power, power to impose one's will on a free nation:

> "Moreover," he continued, "there is to my mind no more excellent thing than the power, by means of oratory, to get a hold on assemblies of men, win their good will, direct their inclinations wherever the speaker wishes, or divert them from whatever he wishes. In every free nation, and most of all in communities which have attained the enjoyment of peace and tranquillity, this one art has always flourished above the rest and ever reigned supreme."[267]
>
> Who indeed does not know that the orator's virtue is pre-eminently manifested either in rousing men's hearts to anger, hatred, or indignation, or in recalling them from these same passions to mildness and mercy?[268]

Crassus did not like the dialectic of the philosophers he had heard in his youth at Athens, when he was serving as a young officer in Macedonia. He did not like even the author of the most famous of such discussions,

> who spoke with far more weight and eloquence than all of them—I mean Plato—whose *Gorgias* I read with close attention under Charmadas during those days at Athens, and what impressed me most deeply about Plato in that book was, that it was when making fun of orators that he himself seemed to me to be the consummate orator. In fact controversy about a word has long tormented those Greeklings, fonder as they are of argument than of truth.[269]

But when the orator has granted that the philosophers possess knowledge of many things,

> still he will assert his own claim to the oratorical treatment of them, without which that knowledge of theirs is nothing at all.[270]
>
> For never will I say that there are not certain arts belonging exclusively to those who have employed all their energies in the mastery and exercise thereof, but my assertion will be that the complete and finished orator is he who on any matter whatever can speak with fullness and variety.[271]
>
> For example, should our friend Sulpicius here have to speak upon the art of war, he will inquire of our relative Gaius Marius, and when he has

received his teachings, will deliver himself in such fashion as to seem even to Gaius Marius to be almost better informed on the subject than Gaius Marius himself . . .[272]

The orator Marcus Antonius thought even less of philosophers than Crassus did:

> Whenever I light upon your philosophers . . . I do not comprehend a single word, so inextricably are they entangled in closely reasoned and condensed dialectic. Your poets, speaking as they do an altogether different tongue, I do not attempt to handle at all: I divert myself . . . in the company of those who have written the story of events, or speeches delivered by themselves . . .[273]

> And so I am telling you this, Sulpicius, as naturally such a kindly and accomplished teacher would do, in order to help you to be wrathful, indignant and tearful in your speech-making.[274]

And at another point in the discussion Antonius demanded:

> Is there in fact a man among those Greeks who would credit one of us with understanding anything? Not that they worry me so much; I gladly suffer and bear with them all. For they either contribute to my amusement, or contrive to soften my regret at not having been a student.[275]

Crassus and Catulus were likewise annoyed with the Greeks, Catulus remarking,

> Nor do I need any Greek professor to chant at me a series of hackneyed axioms, when he himself never had a glimpse of a law-court or judicial proceeding . . .[276]

And indeed Roman rule had robbed forensic oratory in Greece of most of its practical content.

Crassus remarked that the Greeks, with all their learning, so lacked the virtue of tact that they even lacked a word for tactless. Then he specified:

> But, of all the countless forms assumed by want of tact, I rather think that the grossest is the Greeks' habit, in any place and any company they like, of plunging into the most subtle dialectic concerning subjects that present extreme difficulty, or at any rate do not call for discussion.[277]

This was the kind of tactlessness Socrates would almost certainly have exhibited had he been present at this discussion, which Cicero reported or imagined. Or at least he would have subverted by puzzling questions the delightful combination of a warm, drowsy day in Crassus' garden at peaceful Tusculum, the soothing mutual flattery of important men generously willing to recognize one another's public achievements, and the careful avoidance of controversial ideas or carping doubts. Were not these men, in Crassus' words, "orators, who are the players that act real life"?[278] That charming atmosphere, inviting every reader of Cicero's dialogue into the intimacy of the great, made it easy for Cicero to slip into a speech by the orator Gaius Julius Vopiscus Caesar Strabo a casual remark about Cicero's father as father of "the best man of our time."[279] So much for the envious owners of fish-ponds, who looked on the best man of their time as merely a new man, the parvenu son of a rustic Eques.

Caesar Strabo also spoke in scholarly vein about the kinds of wit the orator may employ; and recalled flatteringly a joke Crassus had made against an opposing advocate in court, one Aelius Lamia, who kept interrupting him. Aelius was a cripple, and finally

> Crassus said, "Let us hear the little beauty." When the laughter at this had subsided, Lamia retorted, "I could not mould my own bodily shape; my talents I could." Thereupon Crassus remarked, "Let us hear the eloquent speaker." At this the laughter was far more uproarious.
>
> Such jests are delightful, whether the underlying thought be grave or gay.[280]

Crassus commended "the discussions of Socrates" because they helped make Critias and Alcibiades "learned and eloquent."[281] Similarly, in another dialogue, Cicero presents himself as praising Plato not so much for his thought as for his style:

> Where will you find a writer of greater richness than Plato? Jupiter would speak with his tongue, they say, if he spoke Greek.[282]

And Cotta, a young follower of Antonius, was pleased when Crassus admitted that it was unnecessary to spend a lifetime in Athens learning the philosophy of the Academics "and that it is possible to gain a complete purview of the system by a mere glance."[283]

Sulpicius, another rising young lawyer, was more impetuous and was all but rude to his elderly host:

> I on the contrary, Crassus, have no use for your Aristotle or Carneades or any other philosopher. You are welcome to assume either that I

have no hope of being able to master those doctrines of yours or that I despise them—as in fact I do; but for my own part our ordinary acquaintance with legal and public affairs is extensive enough for the eloquence that I have in view; though even it contains a great deal that I do not know, and this I only look up when it is necessary for some case that I have to plead.[284]

After exhorting both of these ambitious young orators to diligence in the difficult art of oratory, Crassus decided not to imitate the tactless Greeks by too much talk.

"But now let us rise," he said, "and take some refreshment; this has been a very keen debate, and it is time to give our minds a rest from the strain."[285]

In the last years of the fifties Cicero wrote two philosophic dialogues which bore the titles of two of the most famous dialogues of his master Plato: the *Republic* and the *Laws*. Cicero's *Republic* purports to record a conversation between Scipio Africanus the Younger, who destroyed Carthage, and some of his friends who shared the love of Hellenistic culture which Polybius had instilled in Scipio. Like the *Republic* of Plato, Cicero's dialogue deals with the state. Perhaps few of Cicero's readers would have read Plato's *Republic* and perhaps fewer still would have grasped Plato's meaning. But even had they done so, how could Socrates' ideas about politics compete in interest with those of a Roman patrician, a consul who had destroyed Carthage? This hero, unlike the eccentric Socrates, had exercised power. After all,

the existence of virtue depends entirely upon its use; and its noblest use is the government of the State, and the realization in fact, not in words, of those very things that the philosophers, in their corners, are continually dinning in our ears.[286]

Cicero declared in the introduction to his dialogue the *Republic* that

the citizen who compels all men, by the authority of magistrates and the penalties imposed by law, to follow rules of whose validity philosophers find it hard to convince even a few by their admonitions, must be considered superior even to the teachers who enunciate these principles.[287]

It seemed clear to Cicero that the disinterested philosophic inquiry that Socrates considered as more godlike than ruling a state was in fact nothing of the kind. That was why forcing men to obey the law, as Scipio had done, was a higher function than seeking the truth, as Socrates continually did, and as he had his Guardians of the Republic do when not needed in the sphere of practical government.

> And in fact I note that nearly every one of those Seven whom the Greeks called "wise" took an important part in the affairs of government. For there is really no other occupation in which human virtue approaches more closely the august function of the gods than that of founding new States or preserving those already in existence.[288]

The Scipio of Cicero's Republic, who was a hellenizer, showed deference for astronomy, "yonder realms of the gods,"[289] as well as for "the common law of Nature,"[290] superior even to the decisions of the Roman people or their civil law. He also praised Archimedes for designing a celestial globe when "he appeared to be doing nothing."[291] But he was careful to claim that he was

> speaking to intelligent men who have taken a glorious part, both in the field and at home, in the administration of the greatest of all States . . .[292]

and he therefore proposed, not to set up an imaginary ideal constitution as Socrates had done, but to show why the constitution of the actual, concrete Roman Republic of his day was the best,

> and, using our own government as my pattern, I will fit to it, if I can, all I have to say about the ideal State.[293]

This best of all constitutions was the constitution which, a few years before Scipio expounded its virtues in Cicero's dialogue, Tiberius Gracchus had thought he was trying through reform to salvage. Scipio's friend, Laelius, had already made short work of Gracchus by asking

> why, in one State, we have almost reached the point where there are two senates and two separate peoples? For, as you observe, the death of Tiberius Gracchus, and, even before his death, the whole character of his tribunate, divided one people into two factions.[294]

The refusal of the Optimates of Scipio's day to surrender squatter's rights to public land did not deter Scipio from pronouncing that "res publica res populi, the Public Thing is the People's Thing,"[295] or from adding in the authentic tradition of Greek philosophy, that a people is an assemblage . . . in large numbers associated in an agreement with respect to justice and a partnership for the common good.[296]

As to what this latter definition might mean for Rome when Scipio enunciated it, Gaius Gracchus was yet to be heard from, as were Marius, Sulla, Pompey, and Caesar. So were the plebeians of Rome. Before the year in which this dialogue was supposed to occur had ended, Scipio tried to cripple the land commission, the plebeians turned against him, Scipio prepared one evening to write a speech to deliver to them next day, and during the night died somewhat mysteriously. Here at his villa, however, surrounded by admiring friends, he accepted Manilius' claim that

> we Romans got our culture, not from arts imported from overseas, but from the native excellence of our own people,

and answered:

> Yet you will be able to realize this more easily if you watch our commonwealth as it advances, and, by a route which we may call Nature's road, finally reaches the ideal condition. . . . And you will learn that the Roman people has grown great, not by chance, but by good counsel and discipline, though to be sure fortune has favoured us also.[297]

Plato's ideal republic was small, nor did it actually exist except in the imagination. But Scipio, on the eve of the most ghastly civil wars, which were to last a century and a half, wanted to describe a republic that really existed, that governed millions of men, that was rich and in short a success, "our own commonwealth—the most splendid conceivable."[298] Scipio tried to conscript Plato in his argument:

> As for me, however, I shall endeavour, if I am able to accomplish my purpose, employing the same principles which Plato discerned, yet taking no shadowy commonwealth of the imagination, but a real and very powerful State, to seem to you to be pointing out, as with a demonstrating rod, the causes of every political good and ill.[299]

It might be considered innocent on Cicero's part to retail a conversation extolling the Roman Republic of 129 for his fellow Optimates to read in 51. His was no planned deception, because his dialogue was honestly based on his faith in a dream he had really dreamed, of a republic which, like that of Socrates, existed only in the imagination. The essential difference was that Socrates knew that he was imagining, and Cicero did not know that he also was imagining. Cicero's readers had almost every reason to believe him, and his *Republic* became famous.[300] It offered grateful proof to a political party hovering on the brink of destruction that here was a Roman statesman who understood Greek philosophy; and to any Greek philosopher who read it, a reminder that not many who even pretended to write philosophy had served as consul and made a fortune at the bar.

To top off his philosophical triumph Cicero, like Plato, ended his *Republic* with a dream of human immortality. In Cicero's version Scipio Africanus the Younger, the major participant in the dialogue, visits King Masinissa of Numidia at the beginning of the Third Punic War. They talk of Hannibal's conqueror and Scipio's grandfather through adoption, Scipio Africanus the Elder. That night the elder Scipio appears in a dream to the younger and reveals his future to him. He warns him of what Tiberius will do and urges him to save the Republic from the Gracchi and the Populares. Then, in a speech calculated to reassure the younger Scipio, and for that matter Cicero himself, Scipio the Elder cries:

> all those who have preserved, aided, or enlarged their fatherland have a special place prepared for them in the heavens, where they may enjoy an eternal life of happiness. For nothing of all that is done on earth is more pleasing to that supreme God who rules the whole universe than the assemblies and gatherings of men associated in justice, which are called States. Their rulers and preservers come from that place, and to that place they return.[301]

Then the shade of the elder Scipio produces the shade of Aemilius Paullus, conqueror of Macedonia, the true father of the younger Scipio. Father and son embrace, here in the heaven to which good men go. And the elder Scipio informs the younger that

> if you will only look on high and contemplate this eternal home and resting place, you will no longer attend to the gossip of the vulgar herd or put your trust in human rewards for your exploits. Virtue herself, by her own charms, should lead you on to true glory. Let what others say of you be their own concern; whatever it is, they will say it in any case. But all their talk is limited to those narrow regions which you look upon, nor will any man's reputation endure very long, for what men say dies with them and is blotted out with the forgetfulness of posterity.[302]

The younger Scipio promises he will strive to follow this path to heaven, and the elder replies:

Strive on indeed, and be sure that it is not you that is mortal, but only your body. For that man whom your outward form reveals is not yourself; the spirit is the true self, not that physical figure which can be pointed out by the finger. Know, then, that you are a god, if a god is that which lives, feels, remembers, and foresees, and which rules, governs, and moves the body over which it is set, just as the supreme God above us rules this universe. And just as the eternal God moves the universe, which is partly mortal, so an immortal spirit moves the frail body.[303]

Cicero had now furnished his own generation and posterity with a Republic which they could proudly place beside Plato's Republic or even put in its place. But Plato had later written the *Laws*, which Cicero construed as describing the laws of the state that Plato had described in his Republic.[304] Cicero decided to write on that subject too. Where Plato had made his main speaker an anonymous Athenian Stranger and had laid his scene in Crete, Cicero laid the scene for his own dialogue at his own estate near his native town, Arpinum. For his main speaker, he chose the man whom he had chosen for the second draft of his *Republic* and whom he had later replaced with Scipio the Younger. He chose, that is, himself. For interlocutors he selected his brother Quintus and his wealthy, generous friend, Atticus. In Cicero's *Laws*, it is Atticus who insists that his distinguished friend furnish his idealized Roman Republic with the correct laws. "For I note," he said,

> that this was done by your beloved Plato, whom you admire, revere above all others, and love above all others.[305]

So Cicero discussed law from the point of view of the devoted common-sense Stoic that he himself was. He reversed the view of Socrates in Plato's *Republic*; and instead of deriving law from justice, Cicero announced that

> the origin of Justice is to be found in Law, for Law is a natural force; it is the mind and reason of the intelligent man, the standard by which Justice and Injustice are measured.[306]

He declared that

> out of all the material of the philosophers' discussions, surely there comes nothing more valuable than the full realization that we are born for Justice, and that right is based, not upon men's opinions, but upon Nature.[307]

155

He echoed Zeno's sayings on Cosmopolis. As for Apollo's "Know thyself," he was confident that when the mind

> realizes that it is not shut in by walls as a resident of some fixed spot, but is a citizen of the whole universe, as it were of a single city—then in the midst of this universal grandeur, and with such a view and comprehension of nature, ye immortal gods, how well it will know itself, according to the precept of the Pythian Apollo![308]

Quintus expressed pleasure that Cicero's ideas on law differed from Plato's and that he imitated Plato only in the style of his language; whereupon Cicero tactfully hinted that he could easily have transmitted the intellectual content of one of Plato's more difficult dialogues rather than Plato's style, which he so much admired,

> for who can or ever will be able to imitate him in this? It is very easy to translate another man's ideas, and I might do that, if I did not fully wish to be myself. For what difficulty is there in presenting the same thoughts rendered in practically the same phrases?[309]

Conservative Roman that Cicero was, he was careful, at least on this occasion, being himself an augur, to endorse the science of augury as a means of divining the will of the gods, and to endorse also the Roman practice of furnishing the gods with dwellings in their cities, for "this idea encourages a religious attitude that is useful to States."[310] His discussion of the gods gave him a convenient opportunity, without mentioning names, to denounce the sacrilegious acts of Clodius, who had driven him into exile, and to interpolate without irrelevance,

> I have been vindicated by the judgment of the Senate, of Italy, and indeed of all nations, as the saviour of the fatherland. And what more glorious honour could come to a man?[311]

Cicero believed that

> though the older Stoics also discussed the State, and with keen insight, their discussions were purely theoretical and not intended, as mine is, to be useful to nations and citizens.[312]

He praised Demetrius of Phalerum precisely because, though learned, he also brought his learning down into the arena of politics, and Cicero asked rhetorically:

who can readily be found, except this man, that excelled in both careers, so as to be foremost both in the pursuit of learning and in the actual government of a State?[313]

Atticus seized the opening: "Such a man can be found, I believe; in fact I think he would be one of us three!"[314] Cicero gracefully ignored the implied compliment and proceeded to defend the tribunate of the people, though not certain tribunes like the Gracchi. Quintus objected to the secret ballot, and Atticus declared:

> Certainly no popular measure has ever pleased me, and I think the best government is that which was put in force by Marcus here during his consulship—one that gives the power to the aristocracy.[315]

Unfortunately, replied Cicero, the populace would refuse to return to the voice vote. Give them the ballot. But permit them to show their marked ballots voluntarily to the most eminent citizens and thereby to win the favor of such men. This

> grants the appearance of liberty, preserves the influence of the aristocracy, and removes the causes of dispute between the classes.[316]

The *Laws*, or most of it, was written in 51. Two years later, Caesar had quarreled with the Senate and had crossed the Rubicon, the little river that separated his Province of Cisalpine Gaul from peninsular Italy. To enter Italy from a province with an army, with even a single legion such as Caesar led in, was illegal; and the Senate promptly outlawed him. But Pompey, now the Senate's general, was not yet prepared to defend Rome; he therefore hastily withdrew to Brindisi. Most of the Senate followed. They managed to cross to Macedonia and to transport with them a considerable army.

To wage successful war, Caesar needed not only men but money.[317] To get the money he broke open the public treasury at Rome and even removed funds that were reserved under a curse for one eventuality, a war with the Gauls. Caesar pointed out that, by conquering all the Gauls, he had removed the curse. He then marched his forces to Brindisi. But he lacked ships to take over the six legions he had now collected. He ordered a fleet built, returned to Rome, and convinced the Romans there were to be no proscriptions. Then he and his chief lieutenants between them cleared Pompey's forces from Spain, Sicily, and Sardinia.

In 48 Caesar finally got his army across to Epirus, was cut off from his supplies by Pompey, was defeated near Durazzo, and withdrew into Thessaly with some 22,000 men. Pompey followed him with an army about double the size of Caesar's. But most of Caesar's men had been battle-hardened in Gaul by frontier warfare of a most brutal kind; they included thousands of Gauls and even Germans; they were superbly disciplined; their morale was high; and their general, in whom they had utter confidence, had become the ablest military leader since Alexander the Great. They were fighting against a corrupt and confused government; against functionless economic privilege; against a great general, it is true, but one who was sorely hampered by a plethora of advisers. These advisers assumed that their army would shortly eliminate Caesar's, and as the appearance of victory drew nearer they wrangled over whose turn came next to be consul and how to distribute equitably the houses and estates of Caesar and his principal followers.

Cicero had joined Pompey. He felt duty bound to help put down the democratic tyrant who had destroyed the Roman Republic. He had written Atticus fourteen months earlier, while Caesar was clearing Spain of Pompey's followers, that if Caesar conquered

> I foresee a massacre . . . attack on the wealth of private persons, the recall of exiles, repudiation of debts, high office for the vilest men, and a tyranny intolerable to a Persian, much more to a Roman. Will my indignation be able to keep silence?[318]

Cicero had never really liked Pompey, and of him had written, "I have long known him to be the poorest of statesmen, and I now see he is the poorest of generals."[319] Cicero wandered about Pompey's camp at Durazzo uttering witticisms, which so many of his contemporaries resented when directed at themselves and delighted in when directed at others. Pompey caught up with Caesar near Pharsalus in Thessaly. Caesar's army was still short of provisions and Pompey wisely planned to wait till it got hungrier, but his officers taunted him into a pitched battle. The battle of Pharsalus was fought on August 9, 48. Caesar instructed his veterans to aim their spears at the faces of the wealthy young Romans in Pompey's cavalry. He knew his opponents: they fled. Then Caesar's army fell on the flanks of Pompey's unprotected infantry and Pompey's army broke. Pompey himself sailed to Egypt for protection, but was murdered on arrival.

Caesar remained two days at Pharsalus after the victory, offering sacrifice and giving his army a respite from fighting. Then he set free his Thessalian allies and granted pardon to the suppliant Athenians, and said to them, "How often will the glory of your ancestors save you from self-destruction?"[320]

Cicero was still in Pompey's camp at Durazzo when news came of the catastrophe at Pharsalus. By October he had risked returning to Brindisi and on November 27 he wrote to Atticus:

> I have never regretted leaving the camp. Cruelty was so rampant there, and there was so close an alliance with barbarian nations, that a plan was sketched out for a proscription not of persons but of whole classes; and everybody had made up their minds that the property of you all was to be the prize of his victory.[321]

Caesar proceeded to Egypt and put down a rebellion at Alexandria. Then he went to Asia Minor, defeated a son of Mithradates, and informed Rome that "I came, I saw, I conquered."[322] After a visit to Rome he annihilated an army of Pompeians in Africa in 46; returned to Rome; celebrated four triumphs, for Gaul, Egypt, Asia, and Africa; then in 45 at Munda, near what is now Gibraltar, he conquered an army led by the two sons of Pompey. He returned to Rome and was made dictator for ten years. In 44 he was made dictator for life, with full control of the Republic's army and its finances. In effect he assumed the powers of a Hellenistic king, although Rome's traditional hatred of the word king led him not to accept that title. However, unlike Alexander the Great, he ruled a Cosmopolis that included not only all peoples who spoke Greek but also all those who spoke Latin or who, as in provinces like Spain and Gaul, were learning to speak it. The Roman Public Thing had absorbed Cosmopolis. The Senate became purely advisory, as indeed it had been, except in the matter of royal succession, under Rome's monarchs four centuries earlier. Caesar enlarged the Senate, and to the horror of its patrician members he appointed to it former army centurions, freedmen, Gauls, and Spaniards, a step that made it in some degree represent not merely Rome, not merely Italy, but Cosmopolis itself. In this respect it resembled both the army and indeed the population of Rome. Paradoxically, where Cicero had appealed to Rome's ancient aristocratic traditions, Caesar appealed to her more ancient monarchical traditions, not to Scipio the Younger or even to Scipio the Elder but to

Romulus, who had defended the common people against the patricians and had perhaps for that very reason lost his life.

Caesar out-archaized Cicero, but with a difference, for he was determined to correct the misgovernment of the Optimates. For example, he protected the provincials against the Equites, whom Cicero had felt it necessary to court in order to achieve his harmony between the orders. He protected them against the proconsuls, of whom Caesar himself had been one in Gaul, proconsuls who enriched themselves as governors of provinces. His method was simple. At least in Asia and at least temporarily, he abolished tax farming, and imposed direct taxes payable directly to the state. He carried out the land program of the Gracchi, which the Senate had largely blocked for a century and a half. He colonized the Roman public lands in Italy and also in the provinces, a measure that removed from Rome at least a portion of those citizens who had required a dole to live. If Caesar especially favored veterans as colonists, he was doing what Marius, Sulla, and Pompey had also done; and he was confirming the decision of events that the only way most of the landless could get land was by force, that is by joining the private army of a leader who would get it for them. Rome's oligarchy had tried to monopolize the land that both patrician and plebeian, both rich and poor, had seized as booty in Rome's constant wars. By blocking the attempt of the Gracchi to give the poor their share of the land and thereby afford them a means of earning their bread by their own labor, the oligarchy had merely forced the poor to fight them for it. Whether the Gracchi or Marius or Caesar or for that matter Catiline or Clodius acted from compassion or from greed for power, the fact is that no leader of the Populares could have secured political leverage had not the Gracchi raised the question: were the poor to get their share? When the long series of bloody battles, massacres, and confiscations had ended, a democratic monarchy based in part on populist reforms had replaced by force and violence a plutocratic republic. This, Caesar understood; Cicero never did. So Caesar became dictator, and Cicero feared for his life.

By July, 46, though still anxious, Cicero felt safe enough to indulge his sorrow that his dignity had proven harder to protect than his safety: "I am no longer king of the Forum."[323] Marcus Cato, whose civic morality was too rigid to suit Cicero, had helped defend Africa against Caesar. After Caesar won at Thapsus and slaughtered some 50,000 Pompeian troops, Cato refused to escape. He reread Plato's dialogue on the soul, the *Phaedo*, which recounted the death of Socrates; then he disemboweled himself.

Cicero, too, subscribed to the Stoic philosophy, but he took no such measures. By September, 46, he had recovered enough from his fear of Caesar to write one of his friends that

> It is my intention to make friends with those in closest touch with him, who already have a high regard for me, and are much in my company, and, moreover, to worm myself into familiarity with the great man himself—a familiarity from which I have been hitherto shut out by my own lack of self-assertion . . .[324]

He need not have feared. The massacre Cicero foresaw had not happened, nor the attack on private property, nor the tyranny that even a Persian could not have tolerated. Nobody touched either him or his many villas, perhaps because his indignation did keep silence. Moreover, Caesar, who could be coldly brutal and even cruel if cruelty served a rational purpose, was busy winning a reputation for clemency. In 46 he was appealing to members of the Senate "to love each other without suspicion."[325] He was determined to heal the wounds in the Roman Public Thing and he knew as well as Aristotle that a good polis can exist only where there is friendship between citizens. As for Cicero, he was still admired by many Romans: if he behaved himself, he could be useful. Marcus Cato had once observed that Caesar "was the only man who undertook to overthrow the state when sober."[326] Caesar gave Cicero a free pardon.

But in these years Cicero suffered much worry and grief. In 47 he had divorced his wife Terentia, who had not even joined him in Brindisi after Pompey's defeat when Cicero believed his life was in danger. Also, he seems to have judged her to have been dishonest in money matters during his exile. The next year, at the age of sixty, he married his young ward, Publilia. Yet in the very year of acquiring a rich young wife, he felt abandoned by history. He defended himself for buying a house at Naples and withdrawing from politics. In earlier days he had felt no inclination

> to withdraw for any length of time from the guardianship of the Republic; for I was seated on the poop, and held the tiller, but now there is hardly room for me where the bilge-water is.[327]

In 45 his daughter Tullia died at the age of thirty-three. He wrote to a friend in Athens,

> You remember the bitterness of my grief, in which my chief consolation is, that I saw further than anybody else, when what I desired, however unfavourable the terms, was peace.[328]

He adored Tullia, and now he thought of building a little temple in her memory. How great was his love for her he had suggested thirteen years earlier when, an exile, he wrote to his brother:

> And what of the fact that at the same time I miss a daughter, and how affectionate a daughter, how unassuming, how talented—the very replica of myself in face, speech, and spirit?[329]

But only two months after Tullia's death he was able to write bravely to a friend:

> I have been robbed of every particle of that attractive vivacity of mine which used to delight you more than anybody else. For all that, you will discover my strength of mind and resolution (if I ever possessed those virtues) to be just the same as when you left me.[330]

He proved his strength of mind by writing an extraordinary number of treatises on philosophy and theology in some two years. Atticus wondered how he could hope to write Greek philosophy in Latin, a tongue which did not then possess even a vocabulary adequate to the task. But Cicero's reply was both modest and truthful about his philosophic writings: "They are copies, and don't give me much trouble. I only supply words, and of them I have plenty."[331] Like "our god Plato"[332] Cicero wrote dialogues, and he considered dialectic "a contracted or compressed eloquence."[333] He found philosophy a consolation. He had lost Tullia, who so resembled him; had lost republican freedom, which in his day also resembled him; had lost his political career, which had brought him the fame and adulation he sorely craved. He lived under a military dictatorship, wielded by a tyrant. That tyrant was in turn backed by the turbulent mob that Cicero had always feared and heartily disliked. The force and violence that had conquered the Mediterranean world for the Roman Republic had ended by conquering the republican form of government. That Caesar used this force and this violence to rule the poor of Rome, the poor of Italy, and the conquered, helpless peoples of the provinces better than Cicero, the Senatorial plutocrats, and the usury-loving Equites had ruled them was not a fact that Cicero as self-declared champion of all creditors could readily grasp. He approved of justice in the abstract, but economic justice for the poor he left largely to such subversive demagogues as Catiline and Caesar. The things he loved were political liberty, private property, and freedom of contract.

Caesar's reorganization of the Republic was brilliant, but the remains of Pompey's Senate were not ready to accept his work. Some, like Marcus Brutus and Gaius Cassius, were former Pompeians whom Caesar had pardoned. Some, like Decimus Brutus and Gaius Trebonius, had fought on Caesar's side but now turned against him. Perhaps in part they resented Caesar because he was more modern than they, more Hellenistic, more cosmopolitan, more civilized, less nostalgically Roman and conservative. His willingness to do the necessary, even if the necessary flouted ancient conventions, lacked what Romans called decency. It therefore appeared cynical. The lightning speed of his mind may have impressed slower minds as being a kind of Greek restlessness and instability. Indeed, while Cicero consoled himself for his political inactivity with a not too successful attempt to restate Greek philosophy in Latin idiom, Caesar was transforming Rome into the cultural capital of what was basically a Greek cosmopolis.

In any case, a Senatorial conspiracy was formed; and, on March 15, 44, beside a statue of Pompey in a stone theater which Pompey had built, Caesar was surrounded by Senatorial conspirators and stabbed to death.

Cicero urged in the Senate that the liberated Republic should not try to rescind Caesar's redistribution of property. He wanted no repetition of what he had witnessed in his youth: a Marian revolution followed by a Sullan counterrevolution. He secured amnesty from the Senate for Caesar's assassins. In any case, it shortly became clear that Caesar's lieutenant, Mark Antony,[334] now a consul, was cautiously taking over. But Cicero and Antony quarreled, and suddenly Cicero shook off his philosopher's cloak and attacked Antony in a series of fiery orations, published under a name that recalled Demosthenes' orations against Philip of Macedon: the *Philippics*. Their impact was tremendous. It was as if Caesar's dictatorship had first rung down the curtain on the Roman Forum, that exciting theater of public affairs in which those real-life actors, the orators, had enthralled rich and poor alike; and as if the murder of Caesar had automatically rung up the curtain again. And here Marcus Cicero, the most famous actor the Forum had ever produced, suddenly got his cue. Once more the interrupted play was on. Paradoxically, the man whose death gave the cue had been commonly considered Rome's second greatest orator, though his incisive mind made his speech less elaborate than Cicero's.

But was there any longer room for actor-orators in Rome? The civil war that broke out between Antony and the Senate threatened to take a new form. Antony wanted to wear Caesar's political mantle. But Caesar had named his great-nephew Gaius Octavius his chief heir and his adopted son. Octavius took the name Gaius Julius Caesar Octavianus. Cicero, still hating Antony, persuaded the Senate to back up Octavian. For the sake of expediency, Octavian made a precarious alliance with Antony and with Aemilius Lepidus, another former lieutenant of Caesar's; and of this so-called second triumvirate each member now headed an army of his own. In November, 43, the popular assembly ratified this arrangement. The second triumvirate then proceeded to introduce an era of proscriptions, head money, and confiscations, rivaling in magnitude even the violence of Sulla, now four decades past. The triumvirs bargained with each other over which heads should roll. Antony was determined that Cicero should die, and Octavian reluctantly yielded.

Although Cicero had not joined the conspirators who murdered Julius Caesar, yet after the deed had been done he had congratulated Decimus Brutus on "that achievement of yours, which was the greatest within the memory of man."[335] To Gaius Trebonius he exclaimed:

> How I should like you to have invited me to that most gorgeous banquet on the Ides of March! We should have had no leavings.[336]

The leavings certainly included Antony, whom more than one of the conspirators had wanted to put out of the way. To Gaius Cassius, Cicero had written much the same thing about the same bloody banquet. A month after that banquet he had had time to worry about more trivial matters. He wrote to Atticus:

> Two of my shops have fallen down and the rest are cracking: so not only the tenants but even the mice have migrated. . . . O Socrates and followers of Socrates, I can never thank you sufficiently. Ye gods! how insignificant I count all such things. However . . . I have adopted a plan of rebuilding which will make my loss a profit.[337]

Cicero and his brother Quintus were at Tusculum, where Cicero had recently been writing his philosophic dialogues, when news came that both of them had been proscribed. They promptly decided to join Marcus Brutus, one of the assassins of Caesar. Brutus was collecting an army in Macedonia. The two brothers fled in litters to another of Cicero's dozen or more villas,[338] this one at Astura on the seacoast. There they separated, and Marcus took ship for Circeium; changed his mind and set out on foot for Rome; went again to Astura; was taken by his servants to Gaeta, where he had another estate; then his servants persuaded him to let them carry him in his litter to the seashore. There the headhunters found him and ordered the litter set down.

> Then he himself, clasping his chin with his left hand, as was his wont, looked steadfastly at his slayers, his head all squalid and unkempt, and his face wasted with anxiety, so that most of those that stood by covered their faces while Herennius was slaying him. For he stretched his neck forth from the litter and was slain, being then in his sixty-fourth year.[339]

Some twenty months had passed since that most gorgeous banquet on the Ides of March. Caesar's funeral had been splendid, but Cicero's obsequies lacked the dignity, let alone the glory, which he had always prized. Antony remembered the *Philippics*, in which Cicero with the verbal violence he had so often shown his opponents denounced Antony and Dolabella, Cicero's own son-in-law, as "two creatures, the foulest and filthiest since the creation of human beings."[340] Antony ordered that Cicero's head be exposed on the rostrum from which Cicero had declaimed against him, along with his right hand, which had penned the *Philippics*. Antony's wife, Fulvia, went further. She had been the wife of Clodius, Cicero's bitter enemy who had caused his exile, before she married Antony; so she harbored a double resentment. Before Cicero's head could be exposed, she spat on it, then

> set it on her knees, opened the mouth, and pulled out the tongue, which she pierced with the pins that she used for her hair . . .[341]

It had been neither Cicero's consular chair nor his proconsular sword nor his writings on Greek philosophy that had most brought him the fame and glory he longed for; it was his tongue. The violent word had now been conquered by the violent sword. The Republic, for which violence had won an empire, had itself succumbed to the long, intermittent violence of the civil wars. As republican government lay dying, Rome lost its last great orator, and its most famous. The King of the Forum was gone.

4

THE TOGA-CLAD NATION

ON SEPTEMBER 23, 63, when the Senate was debating whether to give Cicero full powers to deal with the conspiracy of Catiline, a young Senator, C. Octavius, arrived late and gave as excuse the fact that his wife, a niece of Julius Caesar, had that morning borne him a son at his home on the Palatine hill in Rome. The young Senator, despite his alliance with the powerful Julii, was not the son of patrician parents. He came of a wealthy equestrian family in the nearby Latin town of Velitrae. C. Octavius died when his son was four; and the young Octavius, who was sickly, was brought up by his mother and grandmother, largely in the country. When the boy was fourteen, Caesar crossed the Rubicon and marched on Rome; when Octavius was fifteen, Caesar destroyed Pompey's army at Pharsalus and became master of the Republic. In 48 Octavius became a state priest. In 46, when Caesar went to Africa to attack Pompeians like Cato who had assembled an army there, Octavius was ill and could not go with him, but he was able to participate in Caesar's official triumph later. When Caesar left for Spain to attack the army which Pompey's two sons commanded there, Octavius was again too ill to follow him. However, he arrived in March, 45, at Munda, which Caesar had just captured, and he returned with Caesar to Rome, again participating in his official triumph. Caesar also saw to it that his grandnephew should be legally elevated to the patriciate. In 44 Octavius was studying at Apollonia, on the western coast of Macedonia. Like other young Romans of his rank he had already studied Greek literature, the art of rhetoric, and a somewhat softened version of Stoic philosophy. The grand tour of the Greek world would have inevitably followed but for the news that reached him from Rome: the murder of his great-uncle, the will which made him Caesar's heir and adopted son.

Octavius was now eighteen. For most of his lifetime the Roman Republic and many of its provinces had been weakened by political corruption and ravaged by civil war. His great-uncle had fought his way to life dictatorship, had imposed peace, had instituted reforms, and had been struck down as a tyrant by those to whom he had shown mercy and offered friendship. If Octavius now accepted adoption, many powerful Romans would view him as a tyrant's son, armed with a tyrant's wealth, ambitious to destroy Republican government again. He determined, nevertheless, to accept. His intimate friend, Marcus Agrippa, urged him to seek refuge with the army which Caesar had massed in Macedonia with a view to settling the problem of Parthia. Instead, he started for Rome.

From the time Octavius, now Octavian, set foot on Italian soil, he could observe that he had numerous supporters. Soldiers and veterans crowded to him. He thanked them but bade them wait. At Rome, Mark Antony, a consul, was wary. But Cicero, leader of the Senatorial party that saw in Antony another military dictator, tried to use Octavian. Instead, Octavian flattered and used Cicero. Octavian raised a private army and undertook to defend the Senate. Antony's soldiers started deserting to Caesar's son. Octavian

witnessed some military exercises of the two legions that had deserted from Antony, who ranged themselves opposite each other and gave a complete representation of a battle, except only the killing. Octavian was delighted with the spectacle and was pleased to make this a pretext for distributing 500 drachmas more to each man, and he promised that in case of war he would give them 5000 drachmas each if they were victorious. Thus, by means of lavish gifts, did Octavian bind these mercenaries to himself.[342]

After helping two new consuls defeat Antony near Modena and after finding that both of these consuls had been killed, Octavian struck. He had no intention of becoming the tool of the Senate. When it refused to make him consul, he marched on Rome, as his adoptive father had done before him. The Senate's forces deserted to Caesar's son. He seized the Treasury, as Caesar had done. A popular assembly elected him consul. Antony and Lepidus, another of Caesar's followers, brought an army against him out of Gaul. The Senate charged Octavian, as consul, to defend Italy. But he knew the Senate really wanted to get rid of him. He therefore conferred with Antony and Lepidus near Bologna, where they formed the second triumvirate, divided the western provinces among them, and drew up their proscription lists. They listed those like M. Brutus and Cassius who held the East with an army and those in the Senate who opposed them. They all three needed money, and the proscriptions could include confiscations of property.

> To encourage the army with expectation of booty they promised them, beside other gifts, eighteen cities of Italy as colonies—cities which excelled in wealth, in the splendour of their estates and houses, and which were to be divided among them (land, buildings, and all), just as though they had been captured from an enemy in war. The most renowned among these were Capua, Rhegium, Venusia, Beneventum, Nuceria, Ariminum, and Vibo. Thus were the most beautiful parts of Italy marked out for the soldiers. But they decided to destroy their personal enemies beforehand, so that the latter should not interfere with their arrangements while they were carrying on war abroad. Having come to these decisions, they reduced them to writing, and Octavian as consul communicated them to the soldiers, all except the list of proscriptions. When the soldiers heard them they applauded and embraced each other in token of mutual reconciliation.[343]

The triumvirs frightened the Senate into making their triumvirate legal for five years. Not only did the triumvirs' proscription cost Cicero his head, it cost the heads of some three hundred Senators and some two thousand Equites. Not all the murders were purely political, for

> some were not less fearful of their wives and ill-disposed children than of the murderers, while others feared their freedmen and their slaves; creditors feared their debtors and neighbours feared neighbours who coveted their lands.[344]

Then, leaving Lepidus to watch Rome, Antony and Octavian crossed with an army to Macedonia and in 42, in two infantry engagements at Philippi, destroyed the Republican army under Cassius and M. Brutus. More precisely, Antony destroyed it, for Octavian was too ill to fight. Philippi was decisive. Never before

> had such numerous and powerful Roman armies come in conflict with each other. These soldiers were not enlisted from the ordinary conscription, but were picked men. They were not new levies, but under long drill and arrayed against each other, not against foreign or barbarous races. Speaking the same language and using the same tactics, being of like discipline and power of endurance, they were for these reasons what we may call mutually invincible. Nor was there ever such fury and daring in war as here, when citizens contended against citizens, families against families, and fellow-soldiers against each other.[345]

Philippi gave the triumvirs more to divide. It was agreed that Antony would take the opulent East and Octavian would return to Italy. There he had little difficulty in reducing Lepidus' power. But by governing Italy, Octavian now faced the onus of confiscating those eighteen cities which the triumvirs had promised their soldiers. At Ephesus, speaking to the Greeks there of the needs of his and Octavian's victorious soldiers, Antony declared:

> Octavian has gone to Italy to provide them with the land and the cities— to expropriate Italy, if we must speak plainly.[346]

In the event of a conflict with Antony, Octavian would need the veterans: he must give them the cities they had been promised as colonies. His precarious hold on legal power depended on armed force. Was it a force he could control?

> The task of assigning the soldiers to their colonies and dividing the land was one of exceeding difficulty. For the soldiers demanded the cities which had been selected for them before the war as prizes for their valour, and the cities demanded that the whole of Italy should share the burden, or that the cities should cast lots with the other cities, and that those who gave the land should be paid the value of it; and there was no money. . . .

> The soldiers encroached upon their neighbours in an insolent manner, seizing more than had been given to them and choosing the best lands; nor did they cease even when Octavian rebuked them and made them numerous other presents, since they were contemptuous of their rulers in

the knowledge that they needed them to confirm their power, for the five years' term of the triumvirate was passing away, and army and rulers needed the services of each other for mutual security.[347]

However, if Octavian was ever to achieve orderly government for the Roman Republic, he needed the good will of civilians as well as soldiers, and not only of those civilians whose land was being seized for colonizing veterans but of the civilian neighbors of the colonizing veterans. Rome itself was short of food. Sextus Pompeius, son of Pompey the Great, was cutting off imports of grain by sea, and the wars had greatly reduced agricultural production in Italy.

> Whatever food was produced was consumed by the troops. Most of them committed robberies by night in the city. There were acts of violence worse than robbery which went unpunished, and these were supposed to have been committed by soldiers.[348]

Ironically, Antony's brother Lucius and Antony's procurator Manius tried to prevent Octavian from settling these veterans until Antony could get home and share the credit for colonizing. At the very same moment, Italian civilians were supporting the army that Lucius was raising because

> they believed that he was fighting for them against the new colonists. Not only the cities that had been designated for the army, but almost the whole of Italy, rose, fearing like treatment. They drove out of the towns, or killed, those who were borrowing money from the temples for Octavian, manned their walls, and joined Lucius. On the other hand, the colonised soldiers joined Octavian. Each one in both parties took sides as though this were his own war.[349]

Octavian tried to convince the Senate and the Equestrian Order that he wanted to avoid a clash with Lucius Antonius because he was anxious to spare Italy the horrors of another civil war. But when, in 41, the war broke out, the upper classes joined Lucius. Octavian defeated Lucius the next year at Perugia. Luckily, Antony's masterful wife, Fulvia, who had pierced Cicero's tongue and had fought the recent war at her brother-in-law's side, escaped to Greece and died there. Antony conferred at Brindisi with Octavian and there they agreed that the widowed Antony would marry Octavian's sister, Octavia.

> Now Octavian and Antony made a fresh partition of the whole Roman empire between themselves, the boundary line being Scodra, a

city of Illyria which was supposed to be situated about midway up the Adriatic gulf. All provinces and islands east of this place, as far as the river Euphrates, were to belong to Antony and all west of it to the ocean to Octavian.[350]

Octavian did indeed give one province to Lepidus: Africa. It was not till 36 that he maneuvered Lepidus out of the triumvirate and made him *Pontifex Maximus*, or Chief Priest. Octavian's faithful lieutenant, Agrippa, defeated Sextus Pompeius; he thereby lifted the blockade on wheat for Rome and made Octavian's control of the West complete.

The civil war was apparently ended. Octavian was now twenty-eight. It had taken him approximately ten years to maneuver his way from the acceptance of Julius Caesar's legacy and adoption to control of the western, Latin-speaking half of the Graeco-Roman world, leaving Antony control of the eastern, Greek-speaking half. By giving Antony his sister in marriage, Octavian had but imitated Julius Caesar, who had patched up his temporary alliance with Pompey by giving him his daughter Julia. Unfortunately, Antony had already imitated another exploit of Caesar's: he had become the lover of Cleopatra VII, Queen of Egypt, the most remarkable monarch to rule Egypt since Alexander the Great. In 40 Antony left his Roman wife in Athens to return to Cleopatra. His efforts to pacify the East were only partially successful. He was a far better soldier than Octavian, but he was impulsive, generous, with neither the patience nor the talent for statecraft. His mistress, though not unusually beautiful, had immense charm. By blood a Macedonian, she was the first of Egypt's long line of Ptolemies to speak Egyptian, and she was popular with her subjects. She was well educated, in the Greek tradition, of course. She was resourceful. She had tried with only moderate success to use Julius Caesar, but Antony proved easier to use. She had a son whom she declared to be Caesar's, a son who was known as Caesarion. But it was Antony, not Caesar, whom she married, even though in Roman law the marriage was invalid.

Octavian had no intention of sharing with Antony the territory his adoptive father had ruled. On calculation, Antony controlled the wealthy East and Octavian needed money. Though Antony was an abler general than Octavian, Octavian possessed in Marcus Agrippa a general of great loyalty and ability, and Octavian's West produced better fighting men than Antony's East. And Octavian derived moral authority, especially with veterans, from the memory of Julius Caesar. He was also identified with

171

Rome and Italy rather than with the East that Rome had subjected. He had forfeited some of his Roman authority by confiscating the eighteen Italian cities to keep his promise to his veterans. He therefore set about replenishing his authority by robbing Antony of his, through a shrewdly contrived campaign of propaganda. As news of Antony's behavior kept reaching Italy, the Italian view of this swashbuckling general steadily grew less tolerant. The affability he showed his soldiers conquered their hearts but violated the Roman sense of dignity and gravity. His dress sometimes reflected his expansive boasts that he was a descendant of Hercules. He was a winebibber, and his public revels in Alexandria honored Dionysus, the god he proclaimed himself to be, a god whom Rome had long regarded with the gravest suspicion. He was ignoring the authority of Rome and had become in effect the prince consort of an Eastern queen. King of Kings was a title of the ancient Persian, now of the dreaded Parthian, monarchs. Antony had not taken that title, but he had done worse: he was hailing Cleopatra's bastard, Caesarion, King of Kings. In Athens he put off his Roman military insignia and dressed like an Athenian. During the period when he had lived with his Roman bride in Athens he had sometimes held his revels on

> the top of the Acropolis, while the entire city of Athens was illuminated with torches hung from the roofs. And he gave orders that henceforth he should be proclaimed as Dionysus throughout all the cities.[351]

In Alexandria, although he had lost many men in an unsuccessful attempt to carry out Caesar's plan of conquering Parthia, he celebrated a triumph, a thing that should never have been done in any city other than Rome, even after victory.

Then Octavian struck. At the right moment he got hold of Antony's purported will and read it to the Senate. It had already been rumored that Antony was presenting to Cleopatra and to the sons she had borne him provinces that belonged to the Roman Republic. The will ordered that, if Antony died in Rome, his body should be borne in triumph through the Forum and then sent to Egypt for burial. According to report, the will had been deposited with the Vestal Virgins, and Octavian had seized it from them. But would Antony, if indeed he made the will, have expected a Roman court to honor such a testament?

In any case, Octavian was doing more than attacking Antony's character. Ever since Cato's day Rome and Italy had distrusted and feared the

Greek world that Alexander the Great had united and expanded. Romans admired the culture that Alexander's armies carried to Asia and to Egypt, but they were jealous of it too. Scipio the Younger and his friends were fascinated by that culture. Cicero tried to present it in Latin prose; urged Roman orators to study it; but warned them against affronting Roman listeners by appearing to have lost their Roman hearts to it. Many Romans, including Cicero, spoke patronizingly of the *Graeculi*, the Greeklings, degenerate and unworthy descendants of the men who created Greek culture. Some Romans suspected that the Greeks were secretly derisive of sincere, pious, Foursquare Rome. And perhaps the Greeks did have doubts about the She-Wolf whose human nurslings seemed to think they could seize Greek culture by seizing Greek states, about these Western barbarians who thought that Greek culture could be acquired by raping Greece. Moreover, the rape of Greece had led Rome to the rape of half-hellenized Asian states, had led her to Oriental luxury, effeminacy, and vice, and to the corrupting democratic ideas which had misled the Gracchi. The East had thoroughly demoralized Rome, as the seductive Cleopatra had now demoralized Antony and robbed him of his Roman *virtus*, of his manliness, his self-control, his vigor, his loyalty to Rome. Perhaps the capital of Cosmopolis would be moved from Rome to Alexandria, where Alexander the Great had planned it to be. Perhaps Rome, after reuniting the hellenized portions of Alexander's empire and adding to them her far-flung western conquests, would then become a provincial city. Perhaps Italy would lose all her special privileges.

The result of Octavian's propaganda, and even more, of Antony's uncircumspect behavior, was a vast resurgence of *romanitas*, of Romanness, of reaction against all that was un-Roman and rebellious. The emasculation the Roman spirit had suffered at the hands of the seductive East was symbolized by Antony's repudiation of a conspicuously highborn and devoted Roman wife for a woman whose charm and renowned cleverness had enslaved him, a woman who ruled Egypt. And Egypt was a land so degraded that its people worshiped gods who bore the heads of animals. Octavian coolly calculated that the hour had come to destroy Antony altogether. But Rome was thoroughly sick of civil war, and much of Octavian's moral authority would have disappeared had he started one. Skillfully, he engineered a declaration of war, not against his fellow triumvir, Antony, but against the wanton Oriental queen who was bent on acquiring what was Rome's. Octavian demanded, and got, an oath of personal loyalty to himself from most of the municipalities of Italy, the kind of oath which generals ever since Marius had required of their soldiers but had never demanded of civilians. Although Antony expected an attack, he and Cleopatra moved slowly. Octavian had ample time to prepare his final blow, and moved his army to Epirus. His friend Agrippa, who had learned to handle fleets in the course of destroying the power of Sextus Pompeius in Sicily, crossed the Ionian sea and began harassing the ships of Antony and Cleopatra, gathered off the Greek coast around Actium. Meanwhile, Octavian was cutting the supply lines of Antony's army on shore. On September 2, 31, finding his forces weakened by disease and desertion, Antony tried to withdraw them to Asia Minor. In the midst of a naval skirmish Cleopatra suddenly saw her opening and ordered her contingent of sixty ships to escape. Antony and a few of his vessels followed her. The remainder of his ships, deserted by their leader, deserted in their turn to Octavian. Antony's land forces at Actium shortly afterward joined up with Octavian's army.

The battle of Actium was universally recognized as decisive. Egypt was in no position to withstand Octavian, and Antony was a broken man. His forces continued to desert. For the first time since the death of Julius Caesar, nearly all the armed forces of the Graeco-Roman world were in the hands of one man, and that one man was now Caesar's heir indeed. But Egypt, which had never been a Roman province, must be conquered. Cleopatra's treasure was immense, a gold mine; and Octavian was determined, not only to hunt down Antony, but to get his hands on this wealth. Although he now had all the men, that fact only added future debt to the immense obligations he had incurred at home in Italy. Once he had money as well as men, he would have the first prerequisites of political power. The second requirement of such power, authority, was already largely his. For surely the intermittent civil war, which had ravaged the Graeco-Roman world since the lynching of Tiberius Gracchus more than a century before, had at last been brought to a close, and Octavian knew what authority a stable peace would confer on him. The third requirement of power, which was a workable policy, began to take clear shape: peace, prosperity, a religious and moral restoration of the Roman Republic, law and order throughout Rome's empire, the applause of civilized mankind, and a new era of happiness for man. Certainly there was much left to do; but Octavian was barely thirty-two.

Antony and Cleopatra had withdrawn to Alexandria. But, when Octavian's forces approached, desertions again weakened Antony. Moreover, Cleopatra's actions suggest that she was secretly deserting too, though she had probably loved Antony in her fashion. But what she seems really to have loved was power and rule. When Julius Caesar had intervened in Egypt, she was an exile anxious to recover her throne: she became the mistress of the most powerful man in the known world. When Antony shared Roman power with Octavian, the East had fallen to Antony and she had become his mistress. She had meanwhile consolidated her control of Egypt by murdering her brother, whom in royal Egyptian style she had previously married. She had then maneuvered Antony into repudiating Octavia and marrying herself and finally into giving their children Roman lands. With Octavian's invincible army now approaching Alexandria, she began to make overtures to Octavian. Lacking the great beauty that later legend ascribed to her, her wit and charm must still serve as her dynastic weapons for dealing with these uncouth but powerful generals who kept coming out of the West. She was not the wanton Egyptian whom Octavian's propaganda painted her as being. She was one of several royal Macedonian queens stretching back across the centuries to Olympia, the ruthless mother of Alexander the Great, and stretching back in poetry to Aeschylus' terrible and moving Clytemnestra, who welcomed home from Troy, and then betrayed to her lover, her husband Agamemnon. Loving power as Cleopatra did, she may have found it easy to love men who held great power and hard to love adoring bunglers who lost it. If so, she reflected the Greek-speaking Eastern world which Rome had conquered, a Greek world which no longer soared upward or searched inward but which, in its lust for riches and power, had fought its way outward, clear to India. She reflected a Greece that no longer seriously sought to learn the will of Zeus but sought to impose its own will, that in the end collided with the will of Jove, or perhaps with the will of the Roman Public Thing, which claimed to be the will of Jove, incarnate now in human history. This history knocked at Cleopatra's door.

Cleopatra responded: she contrived that Antony should believe she had killed herself. Antony then took his life. She obtained an interview with Octavian and once more tried to beguile a Caesar, but Octavian was cold. She learned through another Roman that Octavian was determined she should grace his forthcoming triumph in Rome. Refusing to accept that fate, she too committed suicide, either by poison or perhaps by means of an asp. In Octavian's later triumph at Rome, only her image could be exposed to public humiliation.

Egypt's immense treasure enabled Octavian, who ruled it as Pharaoh, to

repair many of the injustices he had felt compelled to commit when he
had confiscated the land of innocent persons in order to satisfy his veterans.
Even then, he remained the wealthiest man in the Graeco-Roman world.
Force was his. But this force must be decently veiled: he therefore set
about showing conspicuous deference to the Senate, the traditional source
of authority. He supported the Equites in their business enterprise. As for
the plebs, he purchased their support by an extensive dole and by offering
them frequent and dazzling spectacles: it was the traditional Senatorial
formula. Peace, and the support of all three Orders, made permanent his
authority. Though his policy would be Caesar's, that policy must be re-
shaped to avoid Caesar's failure. Caesar had wanted to be the Hellenistic
monarch of what seemed by his time to have become a Hellenistic world
empire. The Senate and what was left of the Optimates had been outraged.
Octavian knew that if force compelled them to obey one man, at least they
must be allowed to save face. Rome, though she had always believed in
force, preferred her rulers in civilian dress. Moreover, Octavian himself preferred this combination, a combination a thoughtful Greek might call hypocrisy. Caesar had made himself dictator for life; but he had declined the
protection of a group of armed bodyguards, a device that had always symbolized the tyrant. Octavian declined a life dictatorship but retained at
Rome nine cohorts of his Praetorian Guard, although he discreetly stationed some of them outside the city limits and scattered the others in
billets through the city. His person was thus well protected against the fate
of Caesar. Caesar was a patrician. His youth had been prodigal and dissolute. Octavian, though officially elevated to the patriciate, retained an
equestrian soul: he retained a middle-class respect for money, investment,
and trade. Caesar displayed notable physical courage; Octavian was prudent
to the point of timidity when faced with physical danger. Caesar was a
famous orator, both in Latin and in Greek; Octavian generally read his
speeches or had them read by a subordinate. Caesar shared with Alexander
the Great the power to elicit the adoration of his soldiers; Octavian, though
he had paid the usual respects at Alexander's shrine, was followed largely
because he was prudent and because he paid well. Caesar was one of the
greatest military strategists in either Greek or Roman history; Octavian's
strategy was not of the military kind, though it enabled him to choose generals and admirals who used that kind. Caesar was clear-headed, sophisticated, and disinclined to take Roman religion seriously. Octavian, though
born a Roman, was brought up largely in a middle-class, small-town en-

176

vironment, relished the traditional Roman rites, and reserved his clear-headedness for urgent matters like money. Caesar had not always concealed his disdain for a Senate that had proven itself politically bankrupt. Octavian showed the Senate a flattering deference while retaining decisive power. Caesar reduced from 320,000 to 150,000 the number of poor citizens who received the government dole of grain; of those dropped from the list he sent 80,000 to overseas colonies where land was available for them. Octavian longed to abolish the dole and thereby discourage country folk from coming to Rome, but he did not dare. The list of recipients had swelled during the second triumvirate; Octavian managed to prune it down to 200,000. Caesar made extensive grants of Roman citizenship to provincials, and not only as a reward for military service. Octavian confined his grants of Roman citizenship to veterans. Caesar had planned to improve Rome's harbor at Ostia, where grain from Sicily and Africa was received; for some reason Octavian never carried out this plan. He did, however, commission many public works and he established several colonies in Italy. Caesar had planned to attack Parthia; Octavian temporized. Caesar had wanted to codify the jungle of Roman and provincial law, but Octavian presumably judged that the time was not yet ripe.[352] Caesar gave the Graeco-Roman world a rational calendar, which was to stand without revision for sixteen centuries; Octavian attempted a map of Rome's whole empire. Caesar built a new forum in Rome. So did Octavian, and lived to do much more besides. He gave Rome a better water supply and eventually a fire brigade as well as her first police force. He set up a permanent road commission for the growing network of roads and a government courier service throughout Rome's empire.

All in all, Octavian continued Caesar's modernization of the Empire; but, unlike Caesar, he presented his innovations wherever possible as restoration of a golden past. He kept force in his own hands: there must be no third triumvirate, no further civil war. He kept personal control of nearly all the legions; he kept almost the whole of the public Treasury; he retained direct control of those frontier provinces which most needed military protection, retained complete control of grain-rich Egypt as milch cow for his personal treasury, and allowed Senators, now salaried by the state, to govern the remaining provinces. But, holding force, he assiduously sought to consecrate its use. He did this, not only by ostentatiously deferring to a docile Senate, but also by leading the Roman people back to their ancient gods, gods in whom most educated Romans no longer believed. Many moralists were insisting that the horrors of the civil wars had been Rome's punishment for neglecting her gods. Octavian set out, not only to establish a *pax romana* throughout Rome's empire, but to restore the shattered Pax Deorum, the peace of the gods, the peace between gods and men. To that end, he repaired eighty-two temples and revived long-abandoned religious rites and festivals.

Finally, Octavian fostered a renaissance in literature and the arts. Just as he longed for the gods to support his force, his authority, and his policy, he was quick to conclude that culture must support them too. He had successfully asserted against Antony the political authority of Rome and Italy over both the dazzling cultural life of Hellas and the more heady seductions of the ancient Orient, seductions which even Athens in her greatness had to some extent distrusted. Catullus and Lucretius and Cicero had already tried to restate Hellenic culture in the Latin tongue. Architects, sculptors, and painters had also tried to restate Hellenic culture in an Italian idiom. A new generation of poets, prose writers, and artists were a little self-consciously continuing those earlier efforts to provide Roman power with the wisdom and insight of those whom Rome had shorn of power. Power must be made beautiful and wise and lovable, if there was any way to accomplish such a feat. Perhaps money and organization might accomplish just that. In any case Octavian was determined to try.

So far as literature was concerned, Octavian's friend since youth, the wealthy Gaius Maecenas, counselor, diplomatic agent, poetaster, patron of the arts, and unofficial minister of culture, knew where to start. Of all the younger generation of poets, no one seemed better suited to promote Octavian's purposes than Publius Vergilius Maro. Vergilius, or Virgil,[353] was born in 70 in a village near Mantua, the son of a small landowner who sent Virgil to Rome for the usual training in rhetoric. Virgil pleaded one case in court and then turned from the law to study the philosophy of Epicurus. Then he moved to poetry. In 37, during Octavian's war against Sextus Pompeius for Sicily, he published ten *Eclogues,* or *Selections.* The *Eclogues* were bucolics, pastoral poems in the manner of Theocritus. Shepherds competed for prizes in music; both mythological and contemporary allusions abounded; the simple life and the beauties of nature were presented with an enthusiasm somewhat less characteristic of shepherds than of a generation that had migrated from countryside to city and now suffered a sweet nostalgia for rural life. During the years when Virgil composed these *Eclogues,* he met Maecenas, who became one of his patrons. The *Fourth Eclogue* sings the messianic yearnings of the Roman world for a new historic cycle, the return of the golden age of Jove's father, the god Saturn; the wiping away of the guilt acquired in the fearful civil wars. Even so, not all the guilt would be wiped away; enough would remain so that in some distant future agriculture, commerce, navigation, cities, and war would return. Meanwhile, the race of iron was about to disappear, a golden race was to take over the whole world, and Apollo reign. A little boy was about to be born.

Opinions differed as to who this little boy, this savior of mankind, might be; the *Fourth Eclogue* hinted that he might be a baby whom Octavian's wife, Scribonia, was expecting. If so, Virgil's prophetic powers partly failed: the little boy turned out to be a little girl. Octavian named her Julia. He divorced her mother the day Julia was born and immediately married the also divorced Livia, who was pregnant. But the whole poem was veiled in the obscurities peculiar to prophets, and not only on the subject of who the little boy was that would save the world. In any case, Virgil himself considered his *Eclogues* light verse.

In 41, when Virgil was still writing the *Eclogues*, he met Quintus Horatius Flaccus, five years his junior. Horatius, or Horace, was from Venusia, in northwest Apulia, almost due east of Naples. He was of even humbler birth than Virgil: his father was a freedman. Horace, like Virgil, had studied at Rome. Later, as a student at Athens, he had rallied to Brutus and fought at Philippi, "leaving my shield ingloriously behind,"[354] when even those more valorous than he were routed. When he went home, his farm had been confiscated, as Virgil's farm near Mantua probably was. He went to Rome, found work as a treasury clerk, and wrote verse. Two years after he met Virgil, Horace was introduced to Maecenas. His relations with Maecenas ripened into friendship, and his patron presented him with what Horace called his little Sabine farm, some twenty-five miles from Rome. About a year after Octavian won a world at Actium, Horace published his second book of *Satires* and addressed it to Maecenas. Sometimes coarse and bitter, Horace's verse could be gay and humorous, and it abounded in observant glimpses of his time. His conversational tone was charming; but his seemingly effortless charm was the fruit of hard labor, of a faultless ear for meter, of a genius for finding the precisely telling word. The *Satires* were not great poetry, but they were delightful, and Horace's reputation was made.

In 29 Virgil published his *Georgics*, also addressed to Maecenas. Theoretically, the *Georgics* is a poetic treatise on farming, modeled on *Works and Days*, which the Greek, Hesiod of Ascra, had written some seven centuries before; but just as Hesiod's poem was about both farming and justice, so Virgil's was about Caesar Octavianus, who had conquered a world, had imposed law, and had thereby permitted men to farm in peace. The *Georgics* celebrated Rome's oldest art, labor on the land, and abounded in images remembered from farm life. The poem begins:

> What makes the crops joyous, beneath what star, Maecenas, it is well to turn the soil, and wed vines to elms, what tending the kine need, what care the herd in breeding, what skill the thrifty bees—hence shall I begin my song.[355]

But the poem that begins with Maecenas ends with Caesar, son of the deified Julius, a conqueror who took the road to Olympus:

> Thus I sang of the care of fields, of cattle, and of trees, while great Caesar thundered in war by deep Euphrates and gave a victor's laws unto willing nations, and essayed the path to Heaven. In those days I, Virgil, was nursed of sweet Parthenope, and rejoiced in the arts of inglorious ease—I who dallied with shepherds' songs, and, in youth's boldness, sang, Tityrus, of thee under thy spreading beech's covert.[356]

About the time Virgil published the *Georgics*, his friend Horace published his *Epodes*. *Epode 16* had apparently been written before Actium, when civil strife was still raging and when, in Horace's terrible words, a second generation was being ground to pieces by civil wars. The city that not the Etruscans nor the Gauls nor Hannibal nor the Germans could lay low

> we ourselves shall ruin, we, an impious generation, of stock accurst; and the ground shall again be held by beasts of prey. The savage conqueror shall stand, alas! upon the ashes of our city, and the horseman shall trample it with clattering hoof . . .[357]

Recalling the flight of the Greek citizens of Phocaea in Ionia to seek refuge in the western Mediterranean, *Epode 16* urged the Romans to quit Italy and sail to the Islands of the Blest beyond the Atlantic, a land of milk and honey where the earth, unploughed, yet yielded its abundant fruits. "Jupiter," the poem concludes,

> set apart these shores for a righteous folk, ever since with bronze he dimmed the lustre of the Golden Age. With bronze and then with iron did he harden the ages, from which a happy escape is offered to the righteous, if my prophecy be heeded.[358]

Virgil, while addressing the *Georgics* to Maecenas and applauding Octavian's mission to give law to all nations and thereby to mount toward godhood, had, in order to enjoy inglorious ease, escaped from the growing cities to the peace of his boyhood in the country. But Horace, though his *Epodes* also were dedicated to Maecenas, did not find peace by escaping to the little Sabine farm that Maecenas had presented to him. Given the fact that Octavian had not yet brought the nations to heel or started up the path to godhood, the escape Horace chose, both for himself and for Roman civilization, could be achieved only by the un-Roman method of decamping from a polluted land. Could Horace eventually be persuaded not to leave his shield ingloriously behind again but, like Virgil, to help furnish Octavian with the poetry of power?

In the very year, 29, in which the *Georgics* and perhaps the *Epodes* appeared, a thirty-year-old citizen of Padua named Titus Livius also began to write about power: he embarked on a history of Rome from its foundation to his own day. This work was eventually to run to 142 books and to take Livy forty years to write. Ever since their war with Hannibal the Romans had become increasingly preoccupied with history, especially with their own. Although Livy's conviction that history should edify betrayed him sometimes into moralizing, yet his passion for the concrete infused his narrative and made it vivid. The same passion for the concrete did indeed lead him away from those general ideas which might have heightened his sense of relevance and might have better organized his material. Nevertheless, Livy wrote a powerful narrative. It seemed clear to him that what had thrown the Roman Republic into its long series of destructive civil wars was a basic decline of morals. But he never seemed to suspect that behind moral failure there might lie a lack of adequate intellectual life and of aesthetic sensibility. Nor perhaps did he suspect that Rome's successful use of force against her Italian neighbors, against the oligarchy that misgoverned Carthage, against a decadent Hellenistic civilization, against tribal Spain and Gaul, had given Rome such a long training in violence against foreign states that her violence had had to turn inward, that bloody civil strife almost inevitably resulted. As successive books of Livy's history began to appear, they helped build the Roman myth and strengthened Octavian's policy of a revived Romanitas, powerful enough to hold the Greek-speaking provinces in their properly subordinate place.

In 29 Octavian closed the temple of the god Janus as a sign that Rome was everywhere at peace for the third time in the city's long and bellicose history. The next year Octavian set about repairing the disused temples of

Rome. And the year after that, in 27, he undertook, backed up by the increased moral authority which universal peace had earned for him, to redefine his legal authority. He therefore proposed a thing which Julius Caesar never showed any sign of consenting to do: to resign. The offer included the consulship, an office he had held each year since 31, and the censorial powers which had enabled him legally to purge and reorganize the Senate. But the Senate declined to accept his offer, no doubt for many reasons:

> While Caesar was reading this address, varied feelings took possession of the senators. A few of them knew his real intention and consequently kept applauding him enthusiastically; of the rest, some were suspicious of his words, while others believed them, and therefore both classes marvelled equally, the one at his cunning and the other at his decision, and both were displeased, the former at his scheming and the latter at his change of mind. For already there were some who abhorred the democratic constitution as a breeder of strife, were pleased at the change in government, and took delight in Caesar. Consequently, though they were variously affected by his announcement, their views were the same. For, on the one hand, those who believed he had spoken the truth could not show their pleasure,—those who wished to do so being restrained by their fear and the others by their hopes,—and those, on the other hand, who did not believe it did not dare accuse him and expose his insincerity, some because they were afraid and others because they did not care to do so. Hence all the doubters either were compelled to believe him or else pretended that they did. As for praising him, some had not the courage and others were unwilling; on the contrary, both while he was reading and afterwards, they kept shouting out, begging for a monarchical government and urging every argument in its favour, until they forced him, as it was made to appear, to assume autocratic power. His very first act was to secure a decree granting to the men who should compose his bodyguard double the pay that was given to the rest of the soldiers . . .[359]

Moreover, some Senators were under heavy obligations to him, financial or other. Probably, some Senators realized that Octavian could not be dispensed with: his authority had been too shrewdly built into the operation of government. Though the traditional title of *Princeps* already implied that he was leader of the Senate and First Citizen of the Roman Republic, he had skillfully combined Caesar's function of Dictator, a title Octavian had sedulously declined, with the function of Rector, an official that Cicero had thought the Republic required and that he had no doubt longed to become. As unofficial Dictator and Rector, Octavian, on the one hand, protected civilian society from the highly professionalized army as well as from the permanent navy Rome now possessed for the first time in her history; on the other, he protected the armed forces from the incompetence and class interest of the Senate. His position was, to be sure, ambiguous; but that was one of the reasons a highly ambiguous society needed him. His removal would have opened Pandora's box. Finally, even his temperament was right for his post. He could be coldly brutal whenever brutality served his main purpose; wholesale murder and robbery had marked his fight for power. Yet he clothed his ruthless revolutionary radicalism in true Roman fashion with a warm sentimentality about the good old days and Rome's venerable traditions. Since he seemed to have founded Rome for the second time, the Senate inclined to vote him the surname Romulus. But Octavian's own preference was Augustus, and this name was given him.

The adjective *augustus*[360] was most commonly applied to places or things, such as temples, which had been duly consecrated to the gods and therefore deserved to be venerated. For the second time in his life Gaius Octavius had changed his name to suit his past fortune and his purpose for the future, once when he accepted the adoption which Julius Caesar's will had offered him, and now when the Senate voted him, as son of a great-uncle made into a god, a name that gave him a special relation to all gods. Neither the stripling Octavius nor the bloody Caesar Octavian but Caesar Augustus now assumed the burden of empire. But, although he repeatedly held elective office and usually insisted that his grants of special power from the Senate be limited to specified periods of time, the nature of his political functions steadily increased his power regardless of anybody's intention. These same functions increased his heavy burdens. For example, Italy and the provinces taken together now contained between seventy and a hundred million souls.[361] The provinces had been pillaged by the Roman armies which conquered them; had often been bled white by the Equites and others, whether as tax farmers, usurers, or merchants, as well as by Senatorial governors; had been mismanaged by amateur administrators; had been sometimes fought over and pillaged again by rival Roman armies during the civil wars; had sometimes rebelled and been brutally punished; had sometimes been overrun by barbarians from beyond the Imperial frontiers; and had had their commerce preyed on by brigands on the Imperial roads and by pirates on the Imperial seas. Augustus built a salaried Imperial civil service which, though often corrupt, certainly improved on previous Roman rule and often on what the provincials had undergone before the legions conquered them. He legalized exploitation of the provinces by Senators and Equites by absorbing many of them into his civil service, but by the same device he mitigated that exploitation. He also

> forbade all members of the senate to go outside of Italy, unless he himself should command or permit them to do so.[362]

He policed the roads and the seas. He tried to open and protect a trade route through the Red Sea to India, a route that would break the Arabian monopoly of Oriental trade.

The triumph of this descendant of the Equestrian Order, who had been legally transformed into a patrician, did not resuscitate the patriciate, which in any case had been reduced to a fraction of its former self by civil wars and proscriptions. It did benefit the new ruling class of wealthy men, whether equestrian or patrician in origin. Augustus' triumph was the triumph of the bourgeoisie. When Antony fell and the Latin West reconquered the Greek East, Rome once more overthrew whatever revivals of Greek democracy she found in Greek cities, and she followed her traditional policy of establishing oligarchies of the well-to-do, with whom her own well-to-do could deal. Although Augustus did not attack Parthia, as Caesar had hoped to do, he moved an army into Syria. This military pressure, combined with patient diplomacy, induced Parthia to return the Roman prisoners and Roman standards which Parthia had seized when Crassus met his doom at Carrhae. Augustus was also able to establish a friendly king on the throne of Armenia. Finally, at the other end of his empire, his generals pacified northern and northwestern Spain.

Augustus rejected the idea of conquering Britain or even of repeating Caesar's two forays into that island. Instead he fostered trade with British tribes. In 16, German raids into the Province of Gaul provoked punitive operations. In 15 the Raetians, an Illyrian tribe in the central and eastern Alps, were conquered, and before long the Province of Raetia was set up. Between 12 and 7 Augustus' two stepsons, Tiberius and Drusus, warred against the troublesome tribes of Germany clear to the Elbe River; and Pannonia, occupying what is now Austria and western Hungary, was conquered during the same period. There would seem to have been enough wars to lend some irony to Augustus' solemn closing of the Temple of Janus. But these wars were fought on the frontier of empire, on the frontier of law and civilization, and precisely to place a protective shell around the Pax Romana that Augustus had given the Graeco-Roman world. They were fought mostly in far-off places to safeguard the life and property of civilized man. They protected the Roman Public Thing, its hard-won empire, and all the many things which both Republic and Empire enjoyed. Small wonder that, when Horace published in 13 his fourth and last book of *Odes*, the last ode but one should be a hymn to Caesar Augustus, whose reign had restored to farms, including his own Sabine farm,

> their plentiful fruits again,
> Abundant crops, and once more to our own Jove
> Restored those standards torn from haughty
> Parthian portals . . .[363]

His age had called back, too,

> Ways that we once knew, the old-time virtues,
>
> Through which the Latin name and Italian strength
> Have grown, the fame and majesty of our realm
> Have been extended from the Western
> Couch of the sun to his place of rising.[364]

Small wonder that Horace declared himself sure of peace within that vast empire "while Caesar guards the state."[365] Or that, being an Italian and now a distinguished Roman citizen, Horace should express this idea by the phrase *"custode rerum Caesare," rerum* meaning, in its root, neither the state, nor even its powers, but things.

Horace had come a long way since writing certain bitter lines in his *Satires*. He had never become either a hireling or a lickspittle, any more than Virgil had. Or if he had, he was not the hireling or lickspittle of Maecenas, who was his patron, or of Augustus, whom he knew personally. At the worst he was a mouthpiece for a civilization that had reeled, had almost fallen, and had been salvaged. He had not the slightest desire to fight for freedom at another Philippi or to lose his only farm again. When he praised Caesar Augustus for being a custodian of things, or at least when he published his fourth book of *Odes* and his second book of *Epistles*, he was past fifty, a small, stout man with prematurely gray hair, not robust, a contented bachelor of easy morals, free of the powerful passion that Catullus had transmuted into lyric poetry. Augustus called him "a most immaculate libertine," and "his charming little man."[366] When Horace died, he made Augustus his heir, as indeed thousands of other grateful citizens did.

Horace was fond of decent wine but he was no reveler like Antony. He felt no lust for power over other men. Of life he asked only sufficient money to supply him with comfort and enough personal service to supply him with leisure to write. What he called his little Sabine farm was not inconveniently small, since he had five tenant farmers and eight slave laborers to help him live the simple life his poems charmingly described. He was gentle, sensitive, fond of his friends, humorous, and mocking, especially toward himself. As with many men of his period, his love of physical existence, his love of things, and his dependence on money for many things his ancestors had grown or built or woven for themselves condemned him to feel jostled by time, "For fierce time speeds on."[367] His gentle skepticism did not forbid him to show a decent Roman respect for the gods; but his *Odes* betray an unconscious anguish that Lucretius was right and that all we sense and hence all there is will perish. It may have astonished some who knew him that a man who rejoiced so much in indolence as Horace claimed to do should still slave at his little songs as if he were cutting gems. But perhaps he longed to make something of himself endure beyond his death, as Greek poetry had endured so long after those who wrote it had vanished. For in Horace's century many things had vanished.

> More enduring than bronze I've built my monument
> Overtopping the royal pile of the pyramids,
> Which no ravenous rain, neither Aquilo's rage
> Shall suffice to destroy, nor the unnumbered years
> As they pass one by one, nor shall the flight of time.
> I shall not wholly die; no, a great part of me
> Shall escape from death's Queen; still shall my fame rise fresh
> In posterity's praise . . .
> I, grown great though born low, I shall be named as first
> To have spun Grecian song into Italian strands
> With their lyrical modes. . . .[368]

He had retreated from bustling Rome to his Sabine farm. He disliked the rabble: "I hate the vulgar crowd, and I hold it off!"[369] But he disliked also the vulgarity of the rich who wanted to be richer:

> Why should I build a lofty and new-styled hall
> With doors that will arouse only jealousy?
> Why should I change my Sabine valley
> For the more burdening care of riches?[370]

Although he had had his fill of poverty, he had no wish to share the insatiate greed and anxious fears of the powerful and rich:

> Whosoever chooses the golden mean, that
> Man is safe and free from a squalid roof, and
> Soberly is free of a courtly mansion
>   Apt to rouse envy. . . .[371]

> Still the heart, the well-prepared heart keeps hoping
> Change of lot will come to the troubled, fears it
> For the fortunate. . . .
>   Not, if things now go badly,
> Thus will they continue. . . .[372]

In any event, the turbulent decades through which he had lived had left Horace, as it had left many other men of his age, philosophic, at least in the Stoic sense of enduring sudden and unaccountable shifts of fortune.

> A scant, infrequent worshipper of the gods,
> Schooled in a mad philosophy late I strayed,
>   But now I am compelled to turn my
>   Sails and retrace my forsaken courses.[373]

For God has the power of changing

> The low to high, can humble the famous man,
> Bring forth the hidden; Fortune, the spoiler, oft
>   Has snatched away a crown with crackling
>   Rustle of wings, and enjoyed the doing![374]

Horace was a disillusioned and disengaged man who had not only retreated from a world that produced the slaughter of Philippi to his peaceful Sabine farm and its homely comforts, but had also declined Augustus' invitation to become his private secretary: he wanted to write poetry. The recipe for achieving such poetry he gave in his long poem, the *Art of Poetry*. He had been willing in patriotic lyrics to praise the Roman spirit Augustus was attempting to rescue from decay. But when it came to serious business like saying how to write a poem, he did not propose to turn to the old favorites of Latin literature. He turned where Catullus and Lucretius and his own friend, Virgil, had turned: to Greece. For in his candid words, "Greece, the captive, made her savage victor captive, and brought the arts into rustic Latium."[375] In his poem, the *Art of Poetry*, he

187

gave concise counsel to aspiring Roman poets who claimed that Latin ways were best:

> For yourselves, handle Greek models by night, handle them by day. Yet your forefathers, you say, praised both the measures and the wit of Plautus. Too tolerant, not to say foolish, was their admiration of both . . .[376]

Horace knew what the typical Roman child's education was bound to do to that child's poetic insight:

> To the Greeks the Muse gave native wit, to the Greeks she gave speech in well-rounded phrase; they craved naught but glory. Our Romans, by many a long sum, learn in childhood to divide the *as* into a hundred parts. "Let the son of Albinus answer. If from five-twelfths one ounce be taken, what remains? You might have told me by now." "A third." "Good! you will be able to look after your means. An ounce is added; what's the result?" "A half." When once this canker, this lust of petty gain has stained the soul, can we hope for poems to be fashioned, worthy to be smeared with cedar-oil, and kept in polished cypress?[377]

Meanwhile, he did not scorn to write poems that would help Augustus protect his Sabine farm. When his first three books of *Odes* appeared in 23, the fifth ode of Book III declared:

> We have believed that, thundering from the sky,
> Jove reigns; a present god will Augustus be
> When he has added to our realm the
> Troublesome Persians and stubborn Britons.[378]

Four years after these odes appeared, Horace's old friend Virgil died. He had been working for eleven years on an epic poem, the *Aeneid*, and had not finished polishing it. He used, of course, the traditional verse form of Homer's *Iliad* and *Odyssey*, dactylic hexameter. He chose as subject the myth that Romans had long cherished, the myth that Ennius had celebrated in his epic poem, the *Annals*, the legend of how, when Troy fell, the Trojan Aeneas had led a refugee band from the burning city to Italy and, serving the will of Jove, had founded Rome. Of the twelve books of the *Aeneid*, the first six borrowed heavily from the *Odyssey* and recounted the trials and temptations of the refugees as they toilsomely sought the promised land that Jove had given them. The last six books borrowed from the *Iliad*. They narrated the battles these Trojan refugees fought in Latium to enforce the will of Jove: they must found an eternal city that would one day rule the world. Parts of the *Aeneid* were already known to Virgil's friends before his death. Three of the books, indeed, had been read in the presence of Augustus himself. Some of his critics objected to his thefts from Homer. "Why," asked Virgil,

> don't my critics also attempt the same thefts? If they do, they will realize that it is easier to filch his club from Hercules than a line from Homer.[379]

The critics missed the point: Virgil's purpose differed sharply from Homer's. The *Iliad* was a song to sing in a banquet-hall to primitive, fighting nobles, who had invaded and seized Greece. It told them of the tragic pride of Achilles, a man like themselves. It told of man's pride, of the fall that follows pride, and of the understanding that sometimes comes from falling. It told of the life of the immortal gods, and of their interventions, sometimes wrathful, sometimes loving, in the affairs of men. And it declared at the outset that the terrible events it was about to relate took place in order that the will of Zeus might be fulfilled. The *Iliad* may have been made out of many ballads, improvised by many bards. It had many versions. For the generation of Pericles it was already a poem of long ago, and for some of his contemporaries the immortal gods might or might not exist.

The *Aeneid* was a literary epic, planned and toilsomely composed by an already famous literary man for educated readers in a sophisticated and disillusioned society. Compared with the *Iliad*, it was a contrived, a willed poem. Its author did not begin by invoking the Muse to speak through him, as Homer had done in the first line of the *Iliad*. The conventional invocation does not occur in the *Aeneid* until the eighth line, while the first three words of the epic announced what he, Virgil, would sing. Nor did he set out to celebrate failure or exhibit instructive catastrophe and the pitiful limitations of human mortality. On the contrary he set out to celebrate the greatest success of which he had ever heard: how a man, good by serving the will of Jove, founded, not indeed a city of immortal men, but at least a City of Man that would prove to be an eternal city.

To tell the story of Rome's founding, Virgil did not focus on a few days' fighting in a ten-year war, as Homer had done, making those few terrible days forever significant. Virgil felt constrained to interpret in the *Aeneid* the whole long stretch of centuries between the fall of Troy and the restoration of Augustus, to echo Ennius but also the Homeric heritage, to echo the Greek myths that his readers had made their own, to make his readers feel the Roman Empire and its bilingual civilization as the historic continuation of both the She-Wolf that nursed Romulus and the Greeks who fought at Troy. Was it not this purpose of his that dictated thefts from Homer and thefts from whatever other person or thing had produced the Pax Romana, this providential confluence of many cultural streams?

The first human agent of this world-wide order was the founder of eternal Rome, Aeneas of Troy. This *Pius*[380] Aeneas was the son of a goddess, Venus; and she was both a daughter of Jove and an ancestress of Augustus. It was Augustus who had restored Rome's temples and had built next to his own house a temple to Apollo, the reasoning god who gave him victory at Actium against Antony and Dionysiac frenzy. Augustus wanted it understood that only through his piety had he been able to refound the traditionally pious city of Rome. That Rome should be eternal the *Aeneid* made clear; eternal and also Jove's chosen instrument for bringing the whole world under law. It was Venus who reminded Jove of that mission when Aeneas and his men had been driven by storm and had landed on the coast of Africa near Carthage. Venus sought the aid of Jove for Aeneas and his Trojans:

> Firm was thy promise
> That in time to come, as the years went rolling along,
> From them should arise the Romans, a nation of rulers,
> Renewing the line of Teucer, to have in their lordship
> All lands and the sea.[381]

And Jove answered,

> Nothing has changed my mind.
> But since this anguish of thine is eating thy heart,
> I will speak and further unroll the volume of fate:
> This thy son shall in Italy wage great warfare,
> Crush proud tribes, give his people a city, a code. . . .
> Then, proud in the tawny pelt of the she-wolf that nursed him,
> Shall Romulus in his turn take charge of the people,
> Calling them Romans, after his own name,
> And building up the walls of the city of Mars.
> For these have I set no limit of power or time;
> Empire unending I give them. Even fierce Juno,
> Who now in her fear troubles earth and the sea and the sky,

Shall change for the better and cherish, along with me,
The Romans, the lords of the world, the toga-clad nation.
So runs the decree.[382]

Venus soon appeared before Aeneas, disguised as a young huntress, and urged him to proceed to Carthage.

> She had spoken; her neck, as she turned away, was agleam
> With the colour of roses; there breathed from the crown of her head,
> Her immortal tresses, a heavenly perfume; her dress
> Rippled down to her feet, and every step that she took
> Proclaimed her a goddess indeed. When he saw who she was—
> His mother—Aeneas cried after her, even as she went:
> "Art *thou* cruel also? With empty appearances why
> Dost thou make game of thy son so many a time?
> Why dost thou keep me from clasping thy hand in my own
> And hearing thee speak to me truly, and answering so?"[383]

This cry was of course not the cry of Augustus' Romanitas: the gods hardly ever appeared to Romans; instead, they sent them orders through state priests, or through prodigies of nature interpreted by state priests. No, Aeneas' cry was the cry of Hellenistic man, whose Greek ancestors, actual or cultural, had received frequent visits from the gods in the manner familiar to them from Homer's heroes. This is the cry that Lucretius, a hellenized Roman, stifled in his own breast in order to free his readers both from fear of the gods and from fear of an immortality that might bring retribution. The intention of the *Aeneid* was to congratulate Rome on being chosen by the gods; but consciously or unconsciously, in this scene between Venus and her mortal son, Virgil uttered the secret anguish of an entire civilization that true dialogue between god and man had long since been stilled. The loss of that dialogue increased men's *cura*, a word that recurs in the *Aeneid* like the repeated strokes of a tolling bell. Dido, the widowed Queen of Carthage, was led by Venus to fall in love with Aeneas. She was angered by Aeneas' burden of care and scornful of his story that the gods cared too. She would inevitably remind the Roman reader that, centuries after Dido bewitched Aeneas, Carthage would again try to block Rome's divine mission to rule. Dido would also remind the reader of another widowed queen on the same North African coast who later seduced another leader, Antony, from that divine mission, thereby devolving Jove's care upon the shoulders of

191

Augustus. Was this care, this anxiety, then, the just price that Hellenistic civilization, and especially its ruling city, was condemned to pay for assuming the responsibilities of world power and for doing the will of Jove on earth? Or, as Dido suspected, and as some Greeks of Virgil's day must also have suspected, and indeed as Virgil himself may have subconsciously suspected, was this proclaimed will of Jove merely a mask for Roman greed, for Roman lust for power, in fine for the proud She-Wolf of Rome? This was the bitter and scornful cry of Virgil's Dido when Aeneas pleaded that it was an errand from Jove that caused him to leave her:

> A fine sort of task for the gods,
> A fine sort of worry this is to vex their repose!
> I will not keep thee nor prove thy words to be false.
> Go on, then, sail with the wind for Italy's shores,
> Make for this kingdom of thine beyond the seas;
> Yet I hope and pray, if the kindly powers can help me,
> That, cast upon rocks in the midst of the ocean, there
> Thou mayst drink to the dregs the cup of torment, and call
> Aloud upon Dido, many and many a time.[384]

But consciously or unconsciously Virgil may also have known that Venus turned away from Aeneas and avoided full encounter because the care and labor of founding Rome cut him off from love: from Dido's human love and from the divine love which Venus, his own mother, personified. Aeneas was dedicated to power.

Homer's hero, Odysseus, had descended into hell, and in the *Aeneid*, eventually the hero Aeneas did likewise:

> At the very porch, the outermost entry of Orcus,
> Grief and remorseful Care have set up their bed,
> And there dwell pallid Diseases and sad Old Age,
> Fear and ill-counselling Hunger and shameful Want,
> Shapes that are dreadful to look on, and Death and Distress;
> Then Sleep, that is Death's own cousin, and Guilty Joys
> Of the mind, and, against the threshold, death-dealing War,
> With the iron cells of the Furies, and frantic Strife,
> Her viperish hair entwined with blood-dabbled headbands.[385]

First, Apollo's priestess, the Sibyl of Cumae, conducted him to the Mourning Fields, where he saw those who had taken their own lives.

II

IV

V

597
POMPEJUS MAGNUS
d. 48 f. Kr.

VI

VII

VIII

XI

XII

XIII

XV

XVI

XVIII

XIX

XX

There, too, he saw the shade of Dido and knew that the rumor was true: she had killed herself in despair when he had followed duty and had sailed away. Again he tried to justify his desertion; but she turned away, and Aeneas wept. Farther on he met many of the Trojans who had fallen at Troy. Next he entered Tartarus and witnessed the dreadful punishment of notorious sinners. "All dared some terrible crime and did what they dared."[386]

At last the Sibyl led Aeneas to the Elysian Fields, or Joyous Glades, and there he found his father, Anchises, whom he had borne out of burning Troy on his shoulders only to have him die in Sicily. His father explained to Aeneas the transmigration of souls and pointed out to him men who would one day return to earth and make yet-unfounded Rome mistress of nations: Romulus; the two Decii, who would formally devote themselves that the City might be saved; Camillus; Fabius; Cato; the Scipios; Mummius; the Gracchi; Julius Caesar; and "Augustus Caesar, son of a god, who shall again set up the Golden Age."[387] By this prophecy of Trojan Anchises, made not on earth but in heaven, made to the pious hero who had not yet founded Rome, Virgil's readers throughout the Empire of Augustus could feel in their marrow that Roman rule was only incidentally the product of force and violence; essentially it was the product of divine destiny. And before Virgil permitted father and son to break off their dialogue, he had made the father remind the son, and had made the *Aeneid* remind Rome, of the unique contribution that Rome owed Cosmopolis:

> Others, I well believe, into shapelier forms
> Shall hammer the breathing bronze, shall create from marble
> Faces the image of life; they shall plead in the courts
> Better than we can, and trace, with the help of a rod,
> The pathways of heaven, and say when the stars shall arise:
> Do thou, man of Rome, remember to govern the nations—
> These shall be *thine* arts—to stablish the custom of peace,
> To spare the vanquished and break in battle the proud.[388]

When King Latinus of Latium fought Aeneas and the intruders from Troy, they learned, of course, what those learned who fought against Augustus:

> Beneath his burden of grief
> King Latinus sank low; he was shown by the wrath of the gods

> And the fresh graves in front of his eyes that Aeneas
> Was the man of destiny, guided by heaven's clear will.[389]

Virgil allowed Latinus to discover what Hannibal also had discovered and what Roman historians constantly recalled as a peculiar feature of Roman military history:

> Ill-omened this war is, my people, that now we are waging
> With a race that has sprung from the gods, with heroes unconquered.
> No battle can tire them, and even when victory fails them
> They cannot let go of the sword.[390]

The triumph Aeneas sought, to found Rome, seemed to elude him. At the moment of entering the final, decisive battle, Aeneas ordered his son to learn from him *virtus*, courage, and true *labor*, work. For it required grim and dreary work, as well as bursts of courage: "So mighty the task was of founding the Roman race."[391] Yet he worked on, and at the very end of the *Aeneid* he plunged his sword into the breast of his most formidable enemy, Turnus, already fallen to the ground.

> But the other's limbs grew slack and chill, and with a moan life passed
> indignant to the Shades below.[392]

When Juno, who still hated the Trojans, regretted their coming victory over the Latin natives, Jove consoled her:

> Hence shall arise a race—
> From this mingling of Trojan blood with Italy's own—
> Which—thou shalt see it—shall pass all men upon earth,
> Nay, even the gods, in godliness. Never a nation
> Shall do thee worship with like devotion as this.[393]

The tenacity of Pius Aeneas was matched by the tenacity with which Virgil spent the last eleven years of his life recounting Aeneas' labors. In his will he ordered that the manuscript be burned. Augustus authorized Virgil's literary executors to break the will and publish the *Aeneid*. Virgil, of course, may have wanted his work destroyed merely because he had not lived long enough to polish it. Like Horace, he was a painstaking craftsman. But there may have been other, or additional, reasons. Closely as he followed Homer in episode, image, and often in very phrase, the spirit of the *Aeneid*, taken as a whole, could hardly be more different from the spirit of the *Iliad*. Homer was, so to speak, a gay pessimist, where Virgil was a melancholy optimist. How often the *Iliad* comes alive with rosy-fingered dawn! How often in the *Aeneid, nox erat,* it was night; or *nox ruit,* night rushed from the sea. Night falls and deep slumber falls on wearied creatures that breathe. Then their trouble is assuaged, and their hearts are forgetful of woe. Homer remembers dawn with joy, like a child again released to play, while Virgil recalls with a sort of melancholy gratitude how twilight releases weary man from *labor* and *cura,* from work and worry. Naturally, if twilights come, dawns must also break. But

> Dawn in the meantime had lifted her bounteous light
> Upon men and their troubles, renewing their labor and toil. . . .[394]

Surely, among the chief cares of Pius Aeneas was Jove's command "to bring the whole of the world to submit to his laws."[395] Nor was Venus, his mother, though a goddess, exempt from care. When Aeneas reached Africa,

> She was irked by the anger of Juno, and ever at nightfall
> Her care would come back with a rush, again and again.[396]

Not even Jove himself, although he had delegated to Aeneas at least one of the tasks that needed doing, was free from his own imperial care as he watched over mankind.

> And lo! as he stood
> Musing upon the cares that troubled his heart . . .[397]

While the warriors of Aeneas held an anxious nocturnal council, all other living creatures on earth were soothing their cares in sleep; and their hearts were forgetful of their labors. In this epic not only are there cares; there are cares that call the soul in contrary directions: that is, there are dilemmas. Achilles and Odysseus of course suffer cares as other men do; but Homer's heroes, though they suffer quite as much as Virgil's hero does, seem somehow freer both in joy and in sorrow than Pius Aeneas does. Homer's heroes, much more than Aeneas, do what they want to do. Does this partly explain why the stories about them, the *Iliad* and the *Odyssey,* are more spontaneous than the *Aeneid?*

Homer's epics carry a light load of history; Virgil's epic is heavy with history. The *Aeneid* calls to the witness stand the unnumbered years, the flight of time during which the Greeks and Romans had acted and had suffered. And during this flight of time had occurred that last hideous century of civil strife, of proscription, of betrayal, of assassination, and of devastation of the countryside. These things left recent history heavy with the pollution of unatoned crime and with gnawing guilt. These things recurred with unabated fury long after Catullus wrote in anguish that right and wrong had become confused, that bewildered man had ignored his gods, and that "Never again do gods return to earth or walk with men in the bright sun of noon."[398]

Not only had the centuries rolled; they were continuing to roll. Even in the *Georgics*, Virgil's tranquil poem on farming, he had written that "time meanwhile is flying, flying beyond recall."[399] Virgil's century was driven by time, oppressed by time. It was not by chance that Julius Caesar, among his reforms, should have revised the calendar or that his own name and Augustus' name would endure so long as the month of August should succeed July. The City of Rome itself was bustle. Cicero had so loved this bustle that he had imported it into the leisure of his villas in the country, had feverishly dashed off letters from these villas, had made plans to recapture power, to court Caesar, to court Pompey, to use the boy Octavius. Horace withdrew from Rome's bustle only to find himself endlessly polishing odes that extol peace and the absence of bustle. Virgil withdrew also, but only to the immense labor and care of constructing the *Aeneid*. The work and worry that world empire had brought to Rome had increased the strain of living, a strain the most accurate calendar could not measure. Indeed, the calendar seemed to have merely speeded up the once leisurely flow of time. The Roman's conquest of what he proudly called the world had somehow left the world's conqueror crucified on his own sundial. He believed he had made his earthly city Eternal Rome, and he ended by losing the sense of the eternal and leaving himself exposed, like Prometheus, to two rending eagles, in this case constant work and constant worry, the work and worry that are reflected by the troubled frown on the brow of the young Octavian's marble image. Not even the technical skill of Virgil could convert the weight of history or the new torrential rush of time into the sort of epic he had striven to write. Was it Virgil's consciousness of these things that caused him to order the destruction of an epic that was a *tour de force*, narrating a conquest that was also a *tour de force*, melancholy praise of an achievement that was impressive but unexpectedly oppressive too?

Perhaps, when Virgil wrote his will, he was judging that he had failed. Consciously or unconsciously he may have known that his epic contained too many untested answers and too few good questions; that though the rise of Roman power was the biggest success story in recorded history, nobody could tell the story yet, any more than Polybius had been able to, because the human action the *Aeneid* predicted and reflected had not yet ended. Virgil must of course have known that his epic abounded in brief glimpses of poignant beauty, in highly quotable passages. But was the *Aeneid* a *tour de force* to make power lovable? Had Virgil discovered that he did not love it himself? If he did not love it, his imagination would understandably turn toward twilight rather than dawn. Dawn would bring only more labor, and night would bring care; and the tale he told would bring him, despite his optimistic prophecies, not joy but melancholy. Venus, herself the goddess of love, had in Virgil's telling eluded her own son's handclasp and intimate affection.

Again, when Aeneas tried in hell to explain his desertion of her, Dido, and perhaps the heart of the poet, rejected the explanation, although the poet had already furnished a Roman and masculine justification:

> Dido and noble Aeneas made their way
> To the same cave. Primeval Earth gave the signal,
> With Juno, the guardian of marriage. Lightning in heaven
> Flashed to attest the wedding, and high on the hills
> Was heard the wailing of nymphs. That day was the first
> Of those between Dido and death, the beginning of doom;
> No more did she care for appearances, chaste reputation,
> No longer a secret love was that which she dreamed of;
> Marriage she called it; that name was a cloak for her sin.
>
> Straightway did Rumour go speeding through Libya's great cities—
> Rumour, the swiftest of all the evils that are.
> She thrives upon movement and waxes in strength as she goes . . .[400]

Finally, if Aeneas' failure to communicate with his goddess mother and with the shade of his mistress-wife did not sufficiently support the request in Virgil's will, perhaps additional support came from another passage of the *Aeneid*. In this epic of battles won to carry out the will of Jove, one of Aeneas' boldest fighters puts a question to a beloved companion standing nightwatch with him.

> "Is it the gods," said Nisus, "who put in our hearts
> This burning desire, Euryalus? Tell me; or else
> Does each man make of his own wild yearning a god?"[401]

As Dido had exclaimed, a fine sort of task for the gods! The request to burn the *Aeneid*, however well its main theme served Augustus, merely made explicit a murmur of dissent in the *Aeneid* itself.

Whatever Augustus hoped to accomplish by patronage to poets who could clothe in beauty the naked force of men and money, make it lovable, and thereby transmute mere force into moral authority, he needed other men than poets to reach the illiterate. He needed painters, sculptors, and architects. Of these the painters seemed least likely to be useful. Although Rome had long before Augustan times decorated temples and porticos with paintings of public and hence of political interest, most painters now devoted themselves to murals in the houses of the wealthy. Most of these painters were probably imported from the Greek-speaking provinces, and at Rome and in Italy they continued to work in their own tradition, dealing largely with scenes from Greek mythology, as indeed much of Latin poetry did. To please their Roman patrons, they made their work somewhat more sensational and realistic, with plenty of strong color. Much of their work depicted architectural details. It rejoiced in columns and arches and domes and an elaborate use of perspective and shadow to deceive the eye and create the illusion of solid objects. But in one respect Roman patronage largely transformed painting. Like the Hellenistic Greek, the Roman was a nature lover. He loved animals, plants, landscapes, perhaps more than the Greek did. Even the Greek Theocritus' pastoral poetry never caressed such subjects as lovingly as did Virgil's *Georgics* and *Eclogues,* or for that matter the *Aeneid* itself. Painting in the Latin West recorded the same Roman preference, especially for landscape, whether done by a Greek or by his Roman pupil. A favorite genre of mural painting portrayed imaginary windows and the landscape to be seen through them. Moreover, the Roman concern with the flight of time, with specific moments in time, with sequence, and with history led Roman patrons to demand that the brush of the painter narrate, that a fish or an ox or even a man be part of an event, often against the background of specific landscape.

But, more than painting, sculpture and architecture appealed to the Roman and to the man whose Hellenistic view of human existence reached him through the deflecting prism of Roman customs, Roman tastes, and Roman beliefs. And here the Roman tradition dictated orders to the sculptor: the Roman wanted his portrait done. Moreover, he wanted no effort on the sculptor's part to focus on whatever basic humanity the subject had managed to achieve, while neglecting the accidental, the merely specific. The Roman patron, who was likely to be rich if he could afford to get himself immortalized in marble or in bronze, wanted an accurate and detailed likeness. And the sculptor politely obliged him. There resulted a singular outburst of sculptural candor. Sculptors had already recorded for posterity Cicero's and Pompey's vanity, Caesar's hard singlemindedness. They now recorded the aggressive nose, the too small, too self-centered, and slightly scornful mouth, the worried brow[402] of the man whose force, authority, and policy had at last through many cares and much labor refounded Rome and brought peace and prosperity to the nations. These four faces, with the possible exception of Caesar's, were curiously unillumined; what they all displayed was aggressiveness.

Although Augustus made use of the bust, the full-length statue, and always the coin effigy to impress his image on his many millions of subjects or, as he would have preferred to state it, on his fellow citizens and constituents, he used the sculptor more interestingly to identify his person with religion and with Rome's great past. On the one hand he made use of friezes in bas-relief on themes of Augustan history. Greek bas-reliefs dealt almost exclusively with mythology, or with human matters directly concerned with the gods, such as religious processions. It was the great empires like Egypt, Babylonia, Assyria, and Persia that had narrated their annals in stone, and the new Roman Empire, which Augustus ruled, now followed suit. When Augustus built his forum, he did not build it, as Julius had built his, to serve in the old manner as a market. He built it to furnish the people with an outdoor museum of Rome's greatness. Sculptors adorned it with statues of those men who through the centuries had made Rome great, who indeed exemplified Romanitas. This was essentially Virgil's device: Aeneas' father in the Elysian Fields had pointed out the shades of the great men who would return to earth and make Rome great. The content of Augustan art, like the content of Virgil's *Aeneid,* was deeply Roman. Its form, like the form of the *Aeneid,* was Greek. Not that either Virgil or the sculpture that Augustus commissioned continued the Hellenistic tradition on which Rome had drawn for centuries. Virgil went clear back to Homer for his poetic forms, and Augustus went back to Periclean Athens. The result of these decisions was in both cases a certain majesty and serenity as well as a somewhat static purity. After all, Homer and Athens had created their forms out of passionately held beliefs; Augustus and Virgil had borrowed those forms with merely a bow to beliefs no longer held. In place of the often high and urgent dialogue between god and god, between man and man, between god and man, Augustus and Virgil could fall back only on the coin and commerce and common allegiance of Cosmopolis. In place of lost community, they must content themselves with collectivity. And in place of the passionate aspiration of Athens toward justice, they must think first of imposed law and order. Rome's empire was considerably more extensive, considerably richer, more comfortable, and in some sense more civilized. Moreover, Athens flourished but briefly, then swiftly sank to the status of a provincial town, however compelled Roman tourists felt to visit it. But Rome was the Eternal City.

If Roman poets had misgivings about eternal cities, so had sculptors, at least in the Greek-speaking provinces. There was for instance the statue of Laocoön and his sons, illustrative of an episode in the *Iliad* and exhibiting the violence, the sensationalism, and the slightly dreary realism of late Hellenistic art. But this group, significantly, was produced about 50 B.C. and eloquently, if not consciously, symbolized the Hellenistic, Eastern provinces caught in the toils of Roman imperialism. Moreover, it was executed during the dreadful century that preceded the Peace of Augustus, when the Roman civil wars repeatedly ravaged the helpless Eastern provinces. There were also the macabre wine goblets, which, appropriately enough, sculptors from the disillusioned East designed. They carried a bas-relief of human skeletons. A scene on one[403] of them shows the skeleton of Menander holding aloft the torch of life, while another, a tiny skeleton, plays for him on a double flute. A second standing skeleton pours a funeral oblation on a skeleton at his feet, a dead man mourning one even deader; the mourner holds aloft a plate of funeral cakes and garlands. A second tiny skeleton plays for him, on a lyre. An inscription reads: Reverence dung. Above Menander's flute-playing skeleton and beneath his torch of life, another inscription reads: Be gay while you are still alive. It was this dying Hellenistic culture that Augustus faced when he sought to restore to spiritual health the many peoples he had forced to obey his commands. It was this dying culture on which Rome drew for zest and insight, a culture in which the dead honored the deader and sardonically urged the world to be gay.

More than on sculpture and much more than on painting, Augustus relied on massive architecture to convey his message. When he boasted that he had found Rome a city of brick and left her a city of marble, he was talking about public buildings, notably the temples he restored. His normal procedure for making a building marble was to sheathe its brick or rubble and cement walls in marble slabs and perhaps place a row of marble columns in front. Athens, which even in Pericles' time had been poor compared with Rome, built the Parthenon out of solid marble blocks. Ironically, the richer this society became, the more anxiety it felt about the cost of public works. On the other hand, in some of Rome's new buildings, the Athenian method would have been inconveniently expensive, since Rome loved to build big. When she had made sure of her structural engineering problems and her cost accounting, she ornamented. She multiplied blind windows, useless engaged columns. The capitals she chose for her columns tended to be the ornate Corinthian rather than the chaste Ionic or the simple Doric. Often she combined Corinthian and Ionic as if in a panic to capture the beauty she had neglected in her basic building plan; or she built an arcade and placed engaged columns between the arches, as in the Temple of Hercules at Tivoli. That had been Cicero's method for writing: first, argument or invective, then ornament. The art of rhetoric, which had won primacy over the correlative arts of logic and even of grammar, both in the Empire's Greek literature and in its Latin literature, overbore its sister arts in architecture too. If the ornament on Roman buildings sometimes seemed excessive, that may have been because Rome was anxious to be imposing.

Like the muralists, Augustus and others who commissioned Roman buildings loved landscaping. Not for them the sweet confusion of the buildings on the Athenian Acropolis. Augustus was interested in grouping buildings, as he was interested in grouping nations into one empire. And, just as his will imposed order on all provinces, it imposed his own landscape, even if he had to remove a hill to accomplish his purpose. In the old days the Greeks had built their theaters against a slope, as at Epidaurus, just as they had adjusted army encampments to the terrain they found. Roman architects, or Greek architects working for Roman patrons, developed the amphitheater, built on flat ground, its elliptical outer wall often consisting of one arcade placed upon another until the desired height was reached. Similarly, the Roman camp was imposed on the landscape.

Inevitably, one of Rome's most characteristic contributions to architecture was the triumphal arch. The city, which since her earliest days had doled out to her victorious generals the right to triumph, under Augustus developed the monumental stone arch through which the victorious general and his huge procession of soldiers, captives, and other booty might gloriously march. Although this arch might serve as the entrance to a city or a forum or a bridge, it often stood alone. Essentially it was the entrance to fame and to the imortality that fame could bring.

Yet, the immortality was heavily qualified. The slave still whispered to the triumphing general a reminder that the general was but a mortal. The images of his distinguished ancestors were ambiguous: though they immortalized the fame of these ancestors, the ancestors themselves were skeletons in their tombs. And, finally, unless victorious generals were members of Augustus' family, it was Augustus himself who received the honors of a triumph, for Augustus had no intention of enhancing the fame of potentially dangerous military heroes. One of Rome's most bitter memories was the ambush and capture of that Roman army in 321 by the Samnites. The army had been forced to pass beneath the yoke. Three spears at the Caudine Pass had formed an arch of sorts. Some three centuries later, Augustus and other members of his family, mortal in their immortality, triumphed by passing beneath the Virgilian yoke of the labor and care and loneliness of world power. The rich ornamentation, with its implicit triumphalism, failed to give to these arches either the conviction or the beauty which two other typical products of the Roman builder conveyed: the aqueduct and the military road. Neither road nor aqueduct, of course, was a Roman invention. Herodotus, writing in the fifth century, could praise the marvelous aqueduct which the tyrant Polycrates had built for Samos and praise even more memorably the great royal highways, which enabled the Persian kings to govern the most extensive empire the Mediterranean world had then beheld. The relative scarcity of water in that world made it a precious commodity and forced an early interest in hydraulics. The *qanaat* of the Persian plateau had long led water from the mountains for great distances in underground channels to quench the thirst of the dry but fertile plains. The rock cairns of the Nabataeans, who dwelt east of the Jordan, collected the heavy dew and made farming possible. In North Africa the rare, brief torrents that roared down the wadis were not allowed to waste: they were conducted into underground stone cisterns where, protected from evaporation, they awaited man's needs. The canals of Mesopotamia and Egypt had for centuries turned desert into grainfields by distributing the waters of the Tigris, the Euphrates, and the Nile. But the growth of large cities forced on the world of Augustus the collection and concentration of water needed by a denser population, just as it forced government action to guarantee the collection of enough grain to ward off famine. Rome herself had from early days taken measures to bring her growing population the water and grain they had to have or die. So she, too, built aqueducts from the end of the fourth century on. Like Athens she, too, fought to keep the sea lanes open for grain ships—from Sicily or Africa or Egypt.

The peace of the gods and of Augustus promoted the growth of old cities and, especially in Gaul and Spain, the creation of new cities, partly as a means of civilizing tribal peoples, partly as colonies of Roman veterans to stand sentry in the midst of restless subject populations. New cities meant collecting water, as did old cities when they grew. Available technology did not yield pipe strong enough to withstand the pressure these new supplies would have involved; or, rather, not at a feasible cost. Roman builders rarely used the principle of the siphon, which the Greeks had known for many centuries. What the Roman did was to lead water in masonry channels, inclined just enough to keep the water moving. Most of these channels ran underground. But in lower terrain, the aqueduct of masonry might have to be built at a considerable height. This was customarily accomplished by the use of piled arcades such as the builders of theaters used. Moreover, if the water had to cross a river valley, this construction could be enlarged to serve as a bridge. In such a case it would convey both a stream of water and a stream of human traffic, military or commercial, on foot, horse, mule, or in horse-drawn vehicle. The aqueduct known to moderns as the Pont du Gard was just such a double-purpose construction: it brought pure water to the then new city of Nîmes and conveyed traffic across the Gard River. When the water reached Nîmes, it was confronted with a typical Roman theater, built with two-tiered arcades. Unlike the three-tiered Pont du Gard, it had been ornamented. Between each arch and its neighbor stood an engaged column.

All over the Empire, engineers flung these man-made streams, to feed the public fountains and public baths and even some of the homes of the rich in the cities that formed the vital cells of that empire. If the Pont du Gard was more beautiful than many of Augustus' public buildings, it was largely because aqueducts were too palpably utilitarian to invite ornamentation or prettifying afterthoughts; their clarity of purpose apparently cleared their designers' minds. They, too, were as Roman as an army camp. They, too, were imposed on the landscape to defend the Roman people, this time from thirst.

An even better parallel with the camp, however, could be seen in the great military roads that fanned out from Rome like the radii in a spider's web. Like the aqueducts, these roads had a long history, but Augustus' empire used its resources to repair those that had suffered from neglect and to increase their total mileage greatly; the Empire's increasing size required more highway mileage. Like the camp, they defended Rome and her subject cities against human enemies: rebels within, barbarians without. For, expensive as they were to build, they made the army more mobile; without these roads, Augustus would have had to maintain even more legions than those he was struggling to pay for. Like both camp and aqueduct, they were imposed on the landscape, if only because they needed, where possible, to follow a straight line. In the case of an aqueduct, to tunnel through a hill was frequently cheaper than to follow the contour of the land and go the long way around; in the case of the military highway, tunnels were often not only cheaper for the builder but faster for a legion on the march. Mobility required the shortest practicable route, but it also required easy grading for baggage trains and siege machines. To keep her roads as near straight and as near level as possible, Rome's engineers made cuts or tunnels through hills, drove piles into swamps, bridged streams and steep valleys, made fills through low ground. To defend her legionaries against one of the soldier's chief enemies, mud, the engineers paved, preferably with flat stone from a local quarry, or with small stones and gravel, iron slag from mine wastes, or whatever was available locally. Under that pavement might be layers of concrete with occasional layers of earth, extending as much as seven feet down, then another foot of earth and heavy stone. The total effect was that of burying a wall ten feet high, its top flush with the surrounding terrain. Beside this road a paved footpath might run, complete with curb and gutter. Nothing else devised by architect or engineer ever spoke more eloquently of the unity of Augustus' empire than the Roman roads. They were the arteries and veins of empire: through them Rome pumped legions to her frontiers, and through them when the frontier was pacified she drew them back. They were the nerves of empire: out along them went the Imperial courier and back along them came the provincial government's report. If Rome's boast of eternity should ever prove to be futile, and if the Empire should perish, these roads might still endure as the Empire's stone skeleton.[404]

So it was that poets, architects, sculptors, and painters all labored to glorify the power of Imperial Rome, to consecrate the force and authority and policy of Augustus, to help him inaugurate the new Golden Age of peace and prosperity, and to guard civilized mankind from violence. Civilization meant law and order. Inside the Empire, Augustus must prevent any insurrection by barbarous peoples recently annexed, any separatist movements by older provinces, any revolt of the envious poor against the oligarchies Rome supported in cities all over her empire. As for envy from outside the Empire, Augustus patiently sought defensible frontiers. The Desert of Sahara to the south offered no openings except to nomadic bands, which punitive expeditions kept quiet. To the east lay the Atlantic. The north was more complicated. True, no danger threatened from Britain. But repeated raids by Germans into Gaul suggested that the Rhine might prove an inadequate barrier. Augustus therefore annexed German lands from the Rhine to the Elbe. Meanwhile, his biggest conquest had been of the tribes between Macedonia and the Danube. The Elbe and the Danube, although their headwaters left a salient in the northern flank of empire, would have to serve as dikes against Barbaria. There were several impediments to indulging Rome's traditional habit of continual conquest. It required an army of between 250,000 and 300,000 men to defend a frontier line of more than 4,000 miles.[405] Although Augustus was commander-in-chief, he usually commanded from Rome. Remembering the careers of Marius, Sulla, Pompey, Caesar, Antony, and himself, he had to take care that the generals he sent out should not, when victorious, be allowed to challenge his rule with the troops they commanded. The Roman army was a highly trained, professional force, whose size was limited by the money available. Moreover, compulsory military service could gain popular support only in emergencies. By and large, Augustus' subjects did not want to fight. As the historian Velleius Paterculus put it,

> And the recruiting of the army, a thing ordinarily looked upon with great and constant dread, with what calm on the part of the people does he provide for it, and without any of the usual panic attending conscription![406]

Finally, the hope of booty could not be counted on to help pay for war. During the past two centuries, when the Roman Republic was conquering the highly civilized east Mediterranean basin, war meant booty for general and legionary alike. But except on her eastern frontier Rome no longer had neighbors worth assaulting and robbing. Conceivably, a war to wrest Mesopotamia from Parthia might pay for itself: it was a rich portion of Alexander's conquests which the Hellenistic world had been unable to hold. But Parthia had already proved a tough opponent, and Augustus had contented himself with a diplomatic settlement disguised as a military victory. Given the limitations he faced, he had apparently found the necessary frontiers of Cosmopolis, known euphemistically as *orbis terrarum,* the world.

Augustus was anxious that his standing army should remain basically an army of Roman citizens merely supported by auxiliaries from Spain, northern Gaul, Thrace, and Batavia near the mouth of the Rhine. The Romanitas of the army must be preserved; and to preserve it he was concerned to secure a higher birth-rate in Italy. The decay of family life, the easing of divorce laws, the greater independence and easier morals of Roman wives were causing many men to avoid marriage. Increasing luxury in the upper classes and the insatiable desire for money inclined those men who did marry to remain childless or to expose unwanted children.

Augustus was not the first Roman who tried to combat such evils: even in the good old days, making the women behave had been a serious matter. For example, in 295, during the Third Samnite War and hence before Rome had gained complete control of even peninsular Italy, Quintus Fabius Gurges had

> assessed a fine of money against a number of married women who were convicted before the people of adultery, and with this money erected the temple of Venus which is near the Circus.[407]

Augustus had the word of his contemporary, the historian Livy, for this and similar efforts by partriarchal Rome to keep women in order. By the year 19, when Augustus undertook this onerous task, the escapades of Clodia, whom Catullus immortalized as Lesbia, were already past history, and Clodia had since been widely emulated. Augustus legislated to encourage marriage and procreation and to discourage adultery, but the results were disappointing. Not even the support of Horace sufficed to restore the morals of the early Republic. But Horace did what he could:*

> Though guiltless you may be of your fathers' sins,
> You shall atone, O Roman, until at last
>   You have restored the fanes, the falling
>   Shrines of the gods and their smoke-blacked statues.
>
> Because you hold yourselves less than gods, you rule:
> From them trace all beginning, to them each end.
>   The gods, neglected, have brought down on
>   Sorrowing Italy much misfortune. . . .
>
> This generation, fruitful of crime, has fouled

* From *The Odes of Horace,* by Helen Rowe Henze. Copyright 1961 by the University of Oklahoma Press.

Our marriage beds, the blood of our race, our homes;
　　And from this source derived has ruin
　　　　Poured through our land and upon our people.

The ripened maiden revels in being taught
Ionic dances; trained in coquettish arts,
　　Already she is planning guilty
　　　　Loves even now in her tender girlhood.

She later at the feasts of her husband seeks
For younger loves, nor picks one to whom she may,
　　When all the lights have been removed, with
　　　　Eagerness give the forbidden pleasures,

But rises openly when some trader calls—
And not without her husband's awareness why!—
　　Some Spanish vessel's captain, any
　　　　Freehanded buyer of her dishonor.

Not from such parents sprung was our noble youth
Who stained the sea's smooth surface with Punic blood,
　　Felled Pyrrhus, great Antiochus, and
　　　　Vanquished dread Hannibal's force with slaughter:

But manly sons of country-bred soldiery,
Those taught to turn the sod with their Sabine hoes,
　　To cut and carry logs to please the
　　　　Whim of a rigorous mother's judgment.

Until the sun should alter the mountains' shades
And from the weary oxen remove the yoke,
　　Thus, with his chariot departing,
　　　　Ushering in the most welcome hour.

Ah, what does this injurious age not harm?
Our parents' life-span, worse than our grandsires' time,
　　Bore us who are more worthless, and soon
　　　　We shall produce still more sinful offspring.[410]

If Augustus and Horace, his immaculate little libertine, between them quite failed to cleanse Rome, its women might forget their guilt and indulge their illicit joys by heeding the gossip about Augustus himself. Ignoring his divorce of his first wife on the day she gave birth to his only child, Julia, ignoring his somewhat hasty marriage to the divorced Livia, who was later voted the title Augusta by an obliging Senate, as instructed in Augustus' will, the women of Rome might heed with delight the ugly gossip that Augustus himself owed his adoption by Julius Caesar to Caesar's homosexual attachment to him when Augustus was still in his teens. Gossips also reported that, although Augustus now had many women brought to his couch, he showed a pronounced preference for virgins. These, it was spitefully added, Livia herself often procured for him. Nevertheless, when his laws for moral reform failed, he did not despair. He postponed action on the problem.

Augustus was never more Roman than in his determination to make religion serve the state. Besides his punctilious attention to the traditional Roman gods, he became a god himself. That the Greek cities should set up altars to him was no more than they had done for Alexander the Great, for Hellenistic kings, and later for the Roman governors sent out to rule the Greeks. Augustus accepted this customary honor, but he stipulated that the cult be dedicated to both Rome and Augustus. Later he deliberately spread this combined cult to various western provinces too. Altars were set up at Lyons, in Gaul; on the Elbe River, an Imperial frontier; at Tarragona, on the Mediterranean coast of Spain; and indeed by the end of his reign, in most of the provinces. Somewhat hesitantly, he allowed temples to himself or to his *genius*, his soul, even in Italy. Finally, in Rome itself, he permitted no public worship of himself, except by the poor, whose street-corner shrines were supplied with new *Lares*, or household gods, consisting of statues of his ancestors and of his *genius*. But in 28 he allowed a colossal statue of Apollo with Augustus' own features to be set up in a portico of a temple newly built for the god. And by 2 B.C. he had allowed a temple dedicated to his divine ancestors, Mars and Venus, to conduct also a cult to his *genius*.

In 19 and again in 13 Augustus made tours of inspection in various provinces, and after his second tour the Senate erected in thanksgiving for his safe return the *Ara Pacis Augustae*. This altar to the Peace of Augustus was erected on the Field of Mars, the area sacred to Rome's ancient war-god, the area where for centuries the She-Wolf had mustered her human cubs for war. Five years later Lepidus, whom Augustus had converted from a weak but bothersome fellow triumvir to Pontifex Maximus, finally died; and Augustus gladly accepted the vacant office, thereby becoming high priest of his own cult. It was an office for which his constant concern to get the gods' fullest collaboration with his program ideally fitted him.

In between his two tours of inspection, in 17, Augustus had organized the traditional Secular Games, which were held once every hundred years to expiate the Roman People's sins and achieve the Pax Deorum, that peace between the Roman people and its gods which had been the city's constant care. In order to advertise his restoration of peace and to emphasize the arrival of a new Golden Age, Augustus sought and found an oracle of Apollo's Sibyl which authorized Rome to celebrate the Secular Games prematurely, in the year 17. Virgil was dead and Augustus had to turn to Horace for the *Carmen Saeculare*, or Jubilee Hymn, sung antiphonally by a choir of chosen virgins and a choir of chaste young men, not to the nether gods, but to Apollo and Diana. The chaste youths expressed to Apollo the sun-god their hope that the sun might never see a greater city than Rome. Of Diana the chosen maidens asked blessings on Rome's new marriage laws, an abundant increase of grain, cattle, and human offspring. The two choirs prayed that Rome's youth might learn virtuous ways, her aged enjoy peace, and that the race of Romulus might be granted riches and of course offspring again and every glory.

> And what the glorious scion of Anchises and of Venus, with sacrifice of milk-white steers, entreats of you, that may he obtain, triumphant o'er the warring foe, but generous to the fallen![411]

In 2 B.C. new cares were added to Augustus' constant labor. Although the Senate that year voted him officially the appropriate title, Father of his Country, in the same year he banished his only child, Julia, to the island of Pandateria. Julia was then thirty-eight; her imperial father, sixty-one. Her mother, Augustus' divorced wife, voluntarily accompanied her into exile. When Julia was fourteen, Augustus had married her off to her first cousin, Marcellus; and when she was an eighteen-year-old widow, to Agrippa, Augustus' able general who won the crucial sea fight at Actium. Julia bore Agrippa five children. At twenty-seven she was again a widow, and this time Augustus married her to his stepson, Tiberius. All three of her husbands were at one time or another considered likely to be Augustus' choice of a successor. The last two had been required by Augustus to divorce their wives, the mothers of their children, in order to marry Julia. Julia was brought up in Augustus' prescribed simple fashion and taught to spin and weave, like her stepmother Livia, for Augustus wore the home-spun toga to recall Rome's early, virtuous past. He forbade her to say or do anything that she could not record in the household diary he instituted, and he prevented her from meeting young men. Later, as the wife of Tiberius, she displayed a taste for sexual promiscuity worthy of her father and became one of the most notorious women in Rome, accused of nameless vices; but she was a beautiful, cultivated, and witty woman.

Julia's career reached its climax in an orgy one night in the Forum itself. It was too much. Some of the men involved were either executed or banished. Mark Antony's son, Iullus, whom Augustus had spared, was among those who perished. Julia's third husband, the able though morose and suspicious Tiberius, had two years earlier been adopted by Augustus, and Julia had seemed destined to become Empress of the Roman Empire. But her escapade not only deeply shamed Augustus; it angered and outraged him. Whether or not the bacchanalian orgy in the Forum had overtones of political conspiracy, a Claudius, a Scipio, a Gracchus were among the guilty: something like a cultural revolt of the younger aristocracy appeared to be involved. Some of the most famous names in Roman history were desecrated by defiant debauchery on the very spot from which Roman prudence, Roman dignity, and Roman self-control had gone out to conquer, to unite, and to rule a world.

But the descendants of the great Roman patricians who had conquered the world proposed to enjoy the world which their distinguished ancestors had bequeathed them, and they were doing it. They were probably not prepared to challenge the force Augustus disposed of, but they did challenge the moral authority he had painfully accumulated and the policy he had toilsomely hammered out. It was twenty-nine years since Julia's second husband had destroyed Antony's cause at Actium and effectively concluded the long agony of the civil wars. The young patricians saw little reason to be grateful to the inaugurator of the Golden Age, with his Romanitas, his homespun togas, his religious mummery, his laws against adultery, his lap-dog poets praising his name, his Caesarian clemency displayed now that he had murdered everybody who might get in his way, his triumphs for battles other men had won. Pleasure-loving and skeptical, they must have loathed in him what could only appear to them as massive hypocrisy, developed to the point of self-deception. Augustus, the stern wielder of law and order who was himself by law released from obedience to law;[412] the murderer turned Father of his Country; the robber turned protector of the highway and the high sea and the frontier; the adulterer piously outlawing adultery; the Eques turned patrician; the sickly, five-foot-seven statesman, his stature enhanced by thick-soled shoes. The Princeps, or First Citizen, deferring to a Senate he had intimidated and bribed and purged into docility, a Senate whose members he could now scarcely persuade to attend sessions; the ruler who often recommended his grandsons or stepsons for office but always added, "If they be worthy of it."[413] The conqueror of Parthia who had never set foot in Parthia or fought a Parthian army; the champion of the good old days who so disliked fashionable clothes that the sight of a group of men in up-to-date dark cloaks had led him to cry out indignantly and quote his Virgil: "Romans, lords of the world, the toga-clad nation."[414] Always the toga! Always that garment which the skeptical upper-class Roman, knowing as well as did Polybius the political uses of religion, must rearrange to hood discreetly his head and face as he went about his prayers.[415] No doubt, these sophisticated young patricians must have thought, the hungry mob from crowded tenements take Augustus for a god: they are paid to take him for one. Had not the actor Pylades shrewdly remarked: "It is to your advantage, Caesar, that the people should devote their spare time to us"?[416] Had Julia told her friends that the Father of his Country was an impossible father? Or that, when he wanted to discuss some important matter with Livia, the wife to whom he seemed to be devoted after his fashion, he habitually wrote out what he wanted to say and then read it aloud to her?

Augustus appeared to love the few persons he felt really close to, but the concentration of ever-growing power in his hands, the load of work, and the burden of care were inevitably cutting him off from other human beings. True, power had always isolated those who held it; but Augustus, unlike Antony and even unlike Julius Caesar, had been temperamentally egocentric, withdrawn, somewhat imprisoned by self to start with. In early life the seal he used for dispatches and private letters was appropriately a sphinx, although later he adopted an image of Alexander the Great, hailed as son of Zeus, and finally chose an image of himself, also worshiped as a god. To manage the conflicting forces in his vast empire, he who had always manipulated men had been forced to even greater manipulation, until to the unfriendly eye the whole system he had toilsomely constructed could readily appear a massive tissue of lies, the bastard offspring of force and fraud. As a later historian wrote,

> Nevertheless, the events occurring after this time can not be recorded in the same manner as those of previous times. Formerly, as we know, all matters were reported to the senate and to the people, even if they happened at a distance . . . But after this time most things that happened began to be kept secret and concealed, and even though some things are perchance made public, they are distrusted just because they can not be

verified; for it is suspected that everything is said and done with reference to the wishes of the men in power at the time and of their associates.[417]

In sum, to irresponsible, idle, sophisticated young men and women, Augustus cannot have been a hard man to laugh at, at least at night, at a gay party, among trustworthy friends.

Augustus informed the Senate by letter of Julia's misconduct. By a law of his own proposing, Julia was subject to banishment. Even had he not resented what she had done to discredit his role and his mounting honors, not to have enforced the law would have crippled his whole program. Even if his anger were for official reasons feigned, even if he secretly longed to forgive Julia, how could he have flouted the law on adultery that he himself had caused to be passed and that Horace, his immaculate little libertine, had praised?

Whatever pain Augustus may have suffered at finding his own daughter the reigning queen of a high social circle that revolted against his persistent public effort to restore Rome's ancient morality, it may have been even more momentous that Latin poetry on the whole failed to adorn his power or to strengthen his moral authority. Virgil had faithfully tried to support the will of Rome as being truly the will of Jove and therefore lovable; he had tried to supply the poetry of power. Even Horace had tried. But the odes that Horace wrote in praise of Augustan power were not his best. His best odes were small, lovingly carved cameos of the private joys of a Sabine farm: its modest comforts, its moderate pleasures, its tranquil beauties, its charms and little ironies, all of them made possible by the dike of law and order which the work and worry of Augustus had contrived against both civil and foreign war. Horace sang the exquisite little things of civilized existence and gladly left to Virgil the Herculean labor of finding in political power something to which a man might give his whole heart.

Other poets, however, spent even less of their energy than Horace on praising political power. What they praised most was love, not the destroying love that Catullus wrestled with and that Horace half-pretended had also wounded him, but something both pleasanter and safer. They agreed with that early Horace who saw unnecessary difficulties in adultery and thought that a prostitute was often preferable to the matron: the matron's thighs are no softer because she wears pearls and emeralds; besides, in the case of a matron you see in advance only her face, whereas you can see through the other lady's sheer silk precisely what she has to offer.

Also, her husband will not suddenly come back from the country, causing you to flee half-dressed and barefoot.

Albius Tibullus, even more than Horace, eschewed politics for dalliance. Tibullus, who died at thirty-six, in the same year Virgil died, was of equestrian rank. He was a friend of one of Augustus' generals, Messalla Corvinus; was comfortably off, despite the fact that the civil wars had cost him a partial confiscation. His elegiac poems dealt on occasion with country life, but most of them recounted his passion for two women and a boy. The first woman, Plania, whom he calls Delia, was a plebeian and apparently somebody's concubine. He gladly leaves war to Messalla; all he asks for is Delia:

> It suits you, Messalla, to battle on sea and on land
> So that your gates may be showy with enemy trophies;
> A trophy myself, I am bound in the chains of a beauty—
> I sit like a doorman in front of her obstinate doors!
> Praise isn't *my* passion. Delia, only with you
> Let me stay, may the world call me weakling and slack.[418]

There was also a curly-haired boy who betrayed Tibullus with a girl and also with a wealthy old man. Tibullus threatens counterbetrayal, with another boy. And before long, Delia has been replaced with another woman, a freedwoman and apparently a prostitute, whom he appropriately names Nemesis. Tibullus still prefers love to war:

> Macer has joined the army, and what's to become of peaceable Cupid?
> Can't he go alone, like a man pack weapons on his back?
> Though far campaigns take the soldier over land or shifting seas,
> Can't Cupid march beside him with a spear?
> Boy-god, I beg you, brand this rebel who quits your bower.
> Still better, call the deserter back to your ranks.
> However, if you spare soldiers,
>   here's one who'll be a soldier too,
> Even the kind that fetches his water sloshing in his helmet.
> I'm off to enlist, so goodbye Venus, goodbye girls!
> The army's for me, I love the bugle calls!
>
> I talk big, yes, but after I've bragged my biggest bombast,
> A bolted door shakes out all the spunk from my spruced-up words.
> I swore I'd never go near that door again—
>   swore up and down—
> But my feet go right back by themselves.[419]

In one elegy Tibullus sang of "the Eternal City"[420] and made the Sibyl prophesy that "Aeneas never-resting, brother of Cupid"[421] would found Rome, which "is fated to rule the earth"[422] wherever the grain-goddess Ceres looks down from heaven on fields of grain. Then Apollo would bring an idyllic era. So far, Tibullus was writing along Augustan lines. But the elegy then turned into a prayer to Apollo:

> Phoebus, by thy good leave, let bows and arrows perish, so Love may rove unarmed upon the earth. 'Tis an honest craft; but since Cupid took to carrying arrows, how many, ah me, has that honest craft made smart! And me beyond the rest. For a year have I been afflicted from his stroke, and, siding with my malady (for the pain itself is pleasure), I sing unceasingly of Nemesis, apart from whom no verse of mine can find its words or proper feet.[423]

About the same year that Tibullus was born in Latium, at Gabii, a dozen or so miles east of Rome, Sextus Propertius was born at Assisi, in Umbria. Like Horace, Propertius lost land in the confiscations of 41; and like Virgil he went to Rome to make a lawyer of himself and stayed there to make poems instead. Like Tibullus, he was of equestrian rank; and like Tibullus, he met his Nemesis in a prostitute: in this case her name was Hostia; Propertius' poems call her Cynthia. For some five years this passion lasted, despite infidelities on both sides. Her yellow hair, her tapering hands, her tall stately figure, walking in pride and gladness, her transparent robe made of silk from Cos, her naked body when robes were cast away, all these enslaved him and inspired his poems. The force of those poems brought him prompt attention from Maecenas. But could he, filled with so mad a love for a woman, draw inspiration from any other source, even from Caesar Augustus?

> But O Maecenas, if the Fates had made me
> leader of heroes in heroic war,
> I would not sing the Titans, nor the pathway
> Ossa and Pelion make to heaven's door;
> not Thebes, not Troy, the citadel of Homer,
> not Xerxes, joining sea to sundered sea,
> nor Remus' lands, nor the fierce men of Carthage,
> nor Cimbrian threats, nor Marius' bravery.
> No. It would be the deeds of godlike Caesar
> And of yourself my songs would be about.[424]

As sailors talk of wind and wave and sky
so each man has his sphere—the soldier's, warfare;
the ploughman's, oxen; and the shepherd's, sheep.
I am no less an expert on my subject:
the love that binds us, waking or asleep.[425]

So when I die at last, and nothing of me
is left save on a marble slab my name,
Maecenas, you our greatest boast and envy,
whose friendship is my only claim to fame—
if in your carven British chariot you journey
near to my silent dust, O pause beside
that lonely tomb and say, *It was for Cynthia,
for love of heartless Cynthia, that he died.*[426]

But Propertius found support for his true interest even in Greek and Roman annals. Jealousy for a woman caused Troy's fall. And not only in Greece was desire of woman fatal:

Thou, Romulus, nurtured by the milk of the cruel she-wolf, didst give warrant for the crime; thou taughtest thy Romans to ravish unpunished the Sabine maids; thou art the cause that now there is naught Love dare not do at Rome.[427]

In another poem[428] Propertius made a somewhat strained effort to outgrow love and to sing the wars of Augustus: he was angry with Cynthia at the time. But later, when he went to her house to see if she had slept alone, she had; and he was stricken afresh with her beauty. So he wrote a poem[429] that managed to honor Augustus without ignoring Cynthia. He went further. Since he, an equestrian, could not legally marry a prostitute, he would not marry at all. As for Augustus' laws to promote marriage and the offspring the army needed, not Jove himself could part two such lovers as Propertius and Cynthia:

could Caesar? Caesar's glorious in war,
but what to love are all his conquered nations?
Cut off my head—I'd rather that far more:
how could I leave this love to wed another,
and, husband to that other, pass your gate
nor turn back, blind with weeping, to this doorway,
knowing my loss, and knowing it too late?
And of what slumbers would those wedding trumpets
tell you? Their sound would turn into a knell.

I shall beget no sons to swell Rome's glory;
not of my sons shall Rome's historians tell.
But let me follow in your camp, my darling,
and I could bridle Castor's mighty horse—
they know me in the wilds beyond the Dnieper,
so my fame grows and widens in its course.
Let me be your one joy; you at my side
I have no need of sons to feed my pride.[430]

And in another poem, he alluded to the fact that Virgil was already writing the poem Augustus needed, the poem which he, Propertius, stricken by Cupid's arrow, could never write:

Be it for Vergil to sing the shores of Actium o'er which Phoebus watches, and Caesar's gallant ships of war; Vergil that now wakes to life the arms of Trojan Aeneas and the walls he founded on the Lavinian shore. Yield ye, bards of Rome, yield ye, singers of Greece! Something greater than the Iliad now springs to birth![431]

Maecenas must have tried hard to persuade Propertius to adorn Augustus' work. In a poem addressed directly to Maecenas the poet pleaded flatteringly that he, Propertius, was actually following his patron's example. He praised Maecenas for avoiding high public posts and for loyally supporting Augustus' work behind the scenes. Such modesty, he wrote, rivaled the great deeds of Camillus. And men would say that Propertius, whose writings, like those of Callimachus, kindled boys and girls to love, had imitated Maecenas in following his own talents. All this, with a graceful hint that the continued patronage of Maecenas would help the poet do best what he was meant to do.[432]

Also, Propertius believed he knew why Rome had neglected the temples now rebuilt by the piety of Augustus:

But now these shrines lie empty and forgotten.
Piety's lost, and gold's the dream of man.
Gold's banished faith, and made of Roman justice
a mockery, a thing that's bought and sold. . . .
Let me speak, Rome! You'll find me a true prophet.
Gold is your illness; you will die of gold.[433]

Though these lines of Propertius have power, the idea that wealth had corrupted Rome was by this time hackneyed. What was not hackneyed was the implication that nobody could restore the Pax Deorum merely

216

by restoring the gods' temples. So long as men and money, the components of force, were substituted for love, Rome's new power was based on rotten foundations. And by further implication Propertius declined to yield to force, declined to love it or to praise it. Let Virgil praise it.

The primacy of love was reasserted by another poet, a woman. Her name was Sulpicia. She was the niece of Augustus' general, Messalla, whom Tibullus often addressed in his poems. Her revolt against force and hypocrisy and in behalf of love was in some ways more significant than the revolt of Julia, or of Tibullus or Propertius. Nothing in the ancestral customs that Augustus was struggling to restore authorized a young woman, a patrician, to cry out her passionate love for a man. But Sulpicia was not retreating from Roman dignity or Roman patriotism into sensuality. As her uncle's ward she was defying family authority because she loved with her whole soul, and her few brief poems declared love's supremacy. For example,

> At last comes such a love that gossip that I conceal it
>   would be more shame than to some friend reveal it.
> The Cytherean, persuaded by my poetry's charms,
>   has brought him here and placed him in my arms:
> Venus kept her promise. Let those chatter of
>   my joy who never found their own in love.
> I'd wish, in trusting words to letters, never to need
>   them sealed so none before my love might read;
> I'm glad of my guilt; and loathe, for Rumor, to arrange
>   my air. Let's tell that it happened—a fair exchange.[434]

Augustus was to suffer one more assault from poetry and love, this time from Publius Ovidius Naso, or Ovid. Ovid was born at Sulmo, some ninety miles east of Rome. He, too, came of equestrian stock, studied rhetoric and law in Rome, fell in love with poetry. He completed his education at Athens, halfheartedly entered public life in Rome, but soon quit to serve the Muse. Even had Maecenas still been alive, Ovid would have needed no patron: he was comfortably off. He barely met Virgil; he heard Horace recite; but Propertius and Tibullus he knew well and loved. In 16 B.C., three years after the deaths of Virgil and Tibullus, Ovid published his *Amores*, love poems to a probably imaginary lady named Corinna. He opened his work by parodying Virgil's *Aeneid*:

217

Arms, and the violent deeds of war, I was making ready to sound forth—in weighty numbers, with matter suited to the measure. The second verse was equal to the first—but Cupid, they say, with a laugh stole away one foot.[435]

What followed was wit, smooth and skillful versification, little elevation, a titillating sensuality, and an ironical defiance of stuffy Roman decency. Ovid's humorous amorality brought him instant fame.

Augustus had hardly banished Julia when Ovid published *The Art of Love*, which provided with mocking humor and sly gusto advice to men on how to seduce women and advice to women on how to seduce men. It lightly mocked Augustus' Pax Deorum: "Gods are convenient to have, so let us concede their existence."[436] Aside from *The Art of Love's* flamboyant shamelessness, it found no lost paradise in the good old days of high morality:

> Let others rave about those ancient days; I am happy
>   Over the date of my birth: this is the era for me.
> Not because we mine the stubborn gold from the mountains,
>   Not because rare shells come from the farthest of shores,
> Not because the hills decrease as we plunder the marble,
>   Not because sea walls bar raids of the dark-blue sea,
> Not for reasons like these, but because our age has developed
>   Manners, culture and taste, all the old crudities gone.[437]

Augustus was indignant. The poem was defiantly followed by *The Remedies for Love*; it too was erotic, but it ironically claimed to offer a number of cures for the smitten. While among the cares which tormented Pius Aeneas were those cruelest cares of all, dilemmas, cares that pulled Aeneas in contrary directions, Ovid's remedy for the torments of loving a mistress was simple:

> This I do recommend: that you have a couple of sweethearts.
>   If you can manage more, so much the better for you.
> When the distracted mind swings off in either direction,
>   Then the passion is less, troubled divided by two.[438]

So mighty the task was of founding the Roman race, and for Ovid so light the love that knows alternative satisfactions.

But Ovid's masterpiece was the *Metamorphoses*. As its title suggests, its theme is change. Indeed, the poem is a sort of epic on an almost Lucretian universe, or perhaps a universe in which, as Heraclitus had suggested, all things change except the law of change itself. Ovid happened to possess not only great skill in versification but a genius for narrative. Taking for his subject matter the whole range of Greek mythology, which his highly civilized, skeptical mind clearly regarded as preposterous, he managed to string these myths together and to give his readers the illusion that they were reading a connected story. In his erotic poetry he had contrived to suggest the savage power and hence the importance of love. Then, in a deft phrase or two, he had domesticated it as an article of luxury for the consumption of his knowledgeable, civilized readers. In the *Metamorphoses*, in passages of delicate charm, he suggested the eternal majesty of Greek myth while at the same time he gaily cut it down to size and made it a palatable literary commodity for readers who had doubts about both eternity and majesty. Over and over, an added phrase deliciously deflated. For example, when Phaëthon tried to drive the chariot of the sun, only to lose control and crash, for one whole day no sun shone. "The fire supplied what light there was—how useful!"[439] Jupiter turned the lovers, Baucis and Philemon, into a single tree,

> And even to this day
> The peasants in that district show the stranger
> The two trees close together, and the union
> Of oak and linden in one. The ones who told me
> The story, sober ancients, were no liars,
> Why should they be?[440]

Meleager fell in love with Tegea at the crucial moment of a dangerous boar-hunt.

> As soon as he saw her,
> The Calydonian hero longed for her,
> Though the gods willed it otherwise; he felt
> The flame in his heart. "O happy man," he thought,
> "If ever she loves a man!" But neither the time
> Nor his own sense of self-restraint would let him
> Go any further. The greater task was waiting.[441]

A daughter lay with her father, Cynaras.

> The story
> Is terrible, I warn you. Fathers, daughters,
> Had better skip this part, or, if you like my songs,
> Distrust me here, and say it never happened,

Or, if you do believe it, take my word
That it was paid for.[442]

The daughter of Hecuba, Queen of Troy, when she fell under the sword,

kept her look of courage,
And even in her falling she remembered
To keep her body covered, to guard the honor
Of modesty.[443]

As to Virgil's divinely guided war between his hero Aeneas and Turnus, Ovid claimed that

The war went on: both sides brought in their gods
To aid them, and they had another blessing,
As good as any god—they had their courage.[444]

Despite this long, mischievous, and laughing sally against much that Augustus had striven to restore, Ovid, near the end of his poem about how things got turned into other things, slipped in a decent allusion to Augustus as a sort of earthly Jove, and an allusion also to the theological prospects of this Father of his Country, who so much disapproved of Ovid:

Jove rules the lofty citadels of Heaven,
The kingdoms of the triple world, but Earth
Acknowledges Augustus. Each is father
As each is lord. . . .

O gods,

However many, whom the poet's longing
May properly invoke, far be the day,
Later than our own era, when Augustus
Shall leave the world he rules, ascend to Heaven,
And there, beyond our presence, hear our prayers![445]

But since Ovid can hardly have believed a word of this compliment, he added twelve final lines which he did believe but which scarcely strengthened the compliment:

Now I have done my work. It will endure,
I trust, beyond Jove's anger, fire and sword,
Beyond Time's hunger. The day will come, I know,
So let it come, that day which has no power
Save over my body, to end my span of life
Whatever it may be. Still, part of me,

> The better part, immortal, will be borne
> Above the stars; my name will be remembered
> Wherever Roman power rules conquered lands,
> I shall be read, and through all centuries,
> If prophecies of bards are ever truthful,
> I shall be living, always.[446]

This time Ovid had really finished. So had Augustus. In A.D. 8 Augustus exiled his granddaughter, another Julia. She was guilty, like her mother before her, of adultery. In connection with this affair, Ovid and several other persons were also exiled. He himself, in a poem written in exile, claimed that

> My songs made men and women wish to know me, to my cost; my songs made Caesar censor me and my ways . . .[447]

But his songs were not all that Augustus held against him. He was charged with "two crimes, my poems and my error."[448] He did not say what the error was. He was past fifty, a grandfather, and a not-too-likely paramour for a twenty-seven-year-old princess. Perhaps he had obligingly facilitated an assignation. In any event, when Julia was sent to an island in the Adriatic, Ovid was sent to Tomi on the Black Sea. There he spent the last nine or ten years of his life, longing to escape from a cold, half-civilized, frontier fortress town, to return to Rome and to the public that adored him. He knew Rome's weaknesses, of course. Quite as well as Propertius he knew that at Rome gold ruled the law:

> Nowadays nothing but money counts: fortune brings honours, friendships; the poor man everywhere lies low.[449]

Even in exile, Ovid could not stop writing poems. As he himself said in a poem written at Tomi,

> The lover commonly senses his own hurt but clings to it, and pursues the occasion of his own fault. I, too, have delight in my little books, however they have ruined me, and I love the weapon that made my wounds.[450]

Before he left for exile, he dramatically burned his manuscript of the *Metamorphoses*. Luckily, a number of his friends had copies, as surely he must have known. So neither the wrath of Jove nor even the fire that consumed his own copy, neither the sword of Augustus nor the gnawing tooth of time undid his work. Of all the poets who had turned away from

Roma et Augustus to worship Cupid, Ovid had most offended and most suffered for his dissent. He had not only mocked political power and the morality and religion that were expected to buttress power. He had mocked love itself by making it trivial and amusing.

The defeat of Augustus by poetry was not the last of his defeats. In his effort to find defensible frontiers for Cosmopolis, his ambitious choice of the Elbe and the Danube had forced him into dangerous compromises. Neither river was a Chinese Wall. Culturally, the frontier between Cosmopolis and Barbaria had become badly blurred. The western, Latin half of the Empire did indeed transmit some elements of its own version of Hellenistic civilization to the horde of tribally organized barbarians it had now incorporated into the City of Man. But that transmission had its dangers as well as its rewards. What degree of law and taxation would these half-assimilated tribes put up with? The effects of Roman civilization extended even beyond the two great frontier rivers; but the effects of Barbaria, as Roman conquerors sent back German and Balkan prisoners to be sold into slavery, was also not negligible. Moreover, since Augustus needed both men and money, since Barbaria offered little to pillage and was unaccustomed to orderly taxation by a central imperial government, the only way the newly annexed, uncivilized areas could help pay the cost of Imperial expansion was through military recruitment. Army service certainly helped the task of civilizing, but it also transmitted Rome's superior military technique to new subjects of doubtful loyalty. In A.D. 6 this complicated problem of the culturally blurred frontier of empire grew suddenly grave.

Maroboduus, King of the Marcomanni, had led his people out of southern Germany and resettled them in Bohemia, but Rome still feared him. He had raised an army said to number 75,000 men and had disciplined and equipped this army in the Roman fashion. Two Roman armies, one from Roman Germany in the west and one from Pannonia in the south, marched against him in a pincer movement. But Augustus now paid for having incorporated into his empire large numbers of uncivilized tribes. Tiberius, who commanded the army marching northward from Pannonia, had felt forced to make heavy requisitions of supplies as well as recruits for the campaign he planned to fight in Bohemia. The tribes of Pannonia suddenly rose in revolt under a chieftain named Bato and started a general massacre of Romans, merchants as well as army detachments. The revolt immediately spread to Illyria, where another chieftain, also name Bato, took charge. A rumor spread in Rome that a huge force of rebel barbarians was headed for Italy and the Roman She-Wolf's lair. It took Tiberius three years of hard fighting to reconquer these Balkan peoples. In A.D. 8 Pannonia was subdued and in 10 was officially made into a province. In A.D. 9 Illyria was subjected and reorganized as the Province of Dalmatia. When Bato of Dalmatia surrendered, he gave his view of how the trouble had started.

> In the meantime Bato sent his son Sceuas to Tiberius, promising to surrender both himself and all his followers if he obtained pardon. And when he later received a pledge, he came by night to Tiberius' camp and on the following day was led before him as he sat on a tribunal. Bato asked nothing for himself, even holding his head forward to await the stroke, but in behalf of the others he made a long defence. Finally, upon being asked by Tiberius why his people had taken it into their heads to revolt and to war against the Romans so long, he replied: "You Romans are to blame for this; for you send as guardians of your flocks, not dogs or shepherds, but wolves."[451]

Augustus, who had been thoroughly alarmed by the Balkan revolt, learned that his empire still extended to the Danube. His joy and relief lasted precisely five days. Then he was overwhelmed by a message from Germany. From the Rhine to the Danube, Germany had revolted. Publius Quinctilius Varus, an administrator who had gained his experience in Africa and Syria, had been sent by Augustus to govern Germany. He had tried to introduce, perhaps too fast, Roman courts and Roman law. Commerce with other parts of the Empire seemed to be playing its own civilizing role. Then, when the Balkan revolt strained Rome's financial resources, Varus for the first time exacted the head tax from Germany. One of his German friends, a nobleman named Arminius, had served in the Roman army, had been given Roman citizenship, and had even gained admission to the Equestrian Order. Arminius secretly organized a rebellion, ambushed Varus and three Roman legions in the swampy forest of Teutoburg, massacred most of Varus' men, and took the remaining few prisoner. No doubt, to Arminius and his followers the Roman proconsuls, centurions, merchants, and lawyers looked, as they had looked to Bato of Dalmatia, less like dogs or shepherds sent by Rome to guard her German flock than like wolves.

Augustus, who had staked so much on men and money, knew that he now had neither of these components of force in sufficient supply to reconquer his Elbe frontier. Efforts to attract volunteers from Italy had been largely abandoned years ago. Years ago also he had turned his back on large-scale recruitment of non-Italians: he was determined to keep the Italians the master race, commissioned by Jove, who acted through the son of the deified Julius to carry out the divine will. But Jove's vice-regent was now seventy-two, worn down with work and worry. He decided to cut his losses. For a frontier he would have to make do with the Rhone and the Rhine. He contented himself with a few punitive expeditions beyond the Rhine to remind men like Arminius that the She-Wolf still had teeth. The three legions could not for the present be replaced, and later tradition reported that

> for several months in succession he cut neither his beard nor his hair, and sometimes he would dash his head against a door, crying: "Quintilius Varus, give me back my legions!"[452]

But there ought to be more Italians in Italy, and Augustus made one last, dogged attempt to increase the birth rate. In A.D. 9, the very year in which Augustus lost his three legions, he had the two consuls, Papius and Poppaea, pass one more statute, somewhat softening the penalities in force against celibacy and against couples with no children or with fewer than three. At the same time the new law increased the inducements for large families. Moreover, in the same year, after the terrible famine of A.D. 6 and 7, Augustus publicly urged Romans to marry and beget children. Those who refused, he declared, were committing murder.[453] The formal proponents of the law were both bachelors. At one time or another, special dispensations had been granted for infractions of the code of laws governing marriage and childbearing. Virgil, Horace the gay bachelor, and even Livia herself had received exemptions. Besides trying to coax and bully Romans into breeding more potential soldiers to defend the Empire, Augustus tried to coax Italian youth to enlist. Instead of promising the usual grant of land, to be paid at the expiration of the regular term of service, twenty years, he promised something Italians now preferred to land: money. Veterans would receive on discharge a lump sum in cash. The effect of this inducement, however, must have been diminished when veterans frequently were refused discharge when it was due, so dire was Augustus' need of men to defend his long frontiers.

The fact that fewer and fewer Italians were willing to go to war did not mean that the She-Wolf had lost her love of violence. How deeply she loved it was made manifest most clearly by the exciting ritual of the gladiatorial combat. Back of this sort of combat lay atavistic memories: the mysteries of Etruscan religion, funeral games and human sacrifice like those in Homer's *Iliad*, and the long, bloody struggle of the Roman Public Thing from the primitive cattle raid, through the Gallic terror, the shame of the Caudine Pass, bloody Cannae, the fierce civil wars, the sack of the Eastern lands, to the mastery of the Mediterranean world. With war pushed now to the far-away fringes of empire, Romans had all the more reason to crave blood sacrifice. In addition to that deep need for blood, there was the *aficionado*'s love of watching skill act in the face of mortal danger. Finally, there was the curious mixture of conscious excitement and unconscious boredom and anxiety in the rootless, lonely individuals, sucked out of the ancient, familiar countryside by poverty or greed into Rome, Alexandria, Corinth, Marseilles, Cadiz, or dumped into Rome or some other great city by slavery and perhaps subsequent manumission. In Rome and the other large cities, the physical hunger of the unemployed rabble could be eased to some extent by a dole of grain. The boredom was relieved by the chariot race, the display of strange beasts from distant lands, and by human combat: between two men; between two groups of men; between man and beast; on the arena's thirsty sand ready to drink blood; in naval war games on an artificial lake. To win political popularity, Julius Caesar had given huge performances of this sort, but he had not been personally fond of the blood ritual. As host to Rome, he had attended the specatacle; but he had often carried on his correspondence instead of watching. Augustus liked gladiatorial combat. Whenever the pressure of business allowed him to attend, he watched eagerly.

This was as it should have been. Augustus, like his contemporaries, was bored. When he was not working or worrying about future work, he needed distraction. What was this boredom that afflicted Rome, now that she had obeyed Virgil's injunction to rule the nations? What was this boredom that Horace sensed? Was it perhaps loss of purpose and loss of function; was it perhaps the dull pain of living an administered life? Augustus had proved himself the greatest administrator Rome had produced. He had organized the Emipre if only because, with the conglomerate of peoples Rome had conquered, there appeared no choice but one between organization or chaos. Paradoxically, the more Augustus organized the Empire, the more inorganic human existence seemed to become.

Rome's conquests of Hellenistic lands had brought her a measure of unfamiliar ideas and new aesthetic forms. But Hellenism itself was now rapidly running dry. However, the Pax Romana that Augustus had wrested out of civil war opened tremendous possibilities for agriculture, trade, and industry. Taken as a whole, the eastern, Greek half of the Empire quickly rebuilt its wealth, lost during the period of Roman conquest and of the Roman civil wars; western countries like Spain, and especially Gaul, learned Eastern techniques and grew rich too. True, everywhere the cities tended to suck the countryside dry. But the Empire offered ease and pleasure to those with money to spend and golden opportunities to those with money to invest. The Imperial administration was far from perfect, and it was still afflicted with examples of corruption and sloth; but it represented a low overhead for the economy, compared with the numerous, ostentatious royal courts that preceded it in the Eastern provinces.

The empire Augustus ruled offered more to businessmen than to artists or writers if only because Rome never took up the full burden of patronizing the arts, a burden the royal courts in the East had once borne with grace. The decline of patronage would have been more tragic if there had not been so much evidence that in any case writers and artists had less to say. If Augustus was worshiped from one end of the Empire to the other, it was largely because he was, as Horace so justly observed, the guardian of things. His reign was the triumph of the concrete, of the practical, of matter, and of Roman thingness. The coins Augustus successively issued constituted a continuous stream of propaganda for peace, for prosperity, and for Augustus, son of a god, perhaps a god himself, and clearly the savior of civilized man. No more appropriate vehicle could have been devised for the announcement of the new Golden Age than money. Only the literate few could read the new poetry that praised power. The worship of Augustus throughout the Empire might, or might not, deeply move the heart to love Rome and Augustus. But the increasing love of money lent an insistent eloquence to coin, and no other mass medium was available through which Augustus might direct public opinion throughout the Empire.

The labor and cares of Augustus did not grow lighter as he passed into his seventies. But few cares equaled his worry lest the government he had given Eternal Rome might, on his death, collapse. In one of his edicts he had written:

> May it be my privilege to establish the State in a firm and secure position, and reap from that act the fruit that I desire; but only if I may

be called the author of the best possible government, and bear with me the hope when I die that the foundations which I have laid for the State will remain unshaken.[454]

There was no reason to suppose that either the Senate or the popular assembly of Rome could govern the Empire or protect it from both foreign invasion and civil war. The nature of the *Imperium Romanum*, the Roman Empire, determined which of Augustus' many titles would best describe the masked monarchy at its heart: a military title, *imperator*, Emperor. To whom should the monarch's mask be handed down? Hereditary succession was strongly indicated. The eastern, Greek-speaking provinces were accustomed to hereditary monarchy. The Romans, who had long practice in handling political masks, were now ruled by the adopted son of Julius Caesar, who himself had briefly ruled. Augustus, having no sons, turned to adoption. He had thought first of Agrippa, his son-in-law. But Agrippa had died in 12 B.C, during the cruel period that robbed Augustus first of Virgil in 19 and, in 8, of Maecenas and Horace. He had adopted Agrippa's sons by Julia, but Lucius Caesar died in A.D. 2 and Gaius in 4. He had an unsatisfactory relationship with his stepson Tiberius, whom he had forced to divorce his wife in order to marry Agrippa's widow Julia less than a decade before her disgrace and exile. But Tiberius was a brilliant general and a staunch champion of Romanitas against such restless, hellenized Romans as his adulterous wife, his adulterous stepdaughter, and the latter's friend, Ovid. In A.D. 4 Augustus adopted Tiberius, who was recognized as his probable successor.

Some forty years earlier Augustus had built himself a handsome mausoleum. In April of A.D. 13 he deposited his will with the Vestal Virgins, appending directions for his funeral; a businesslike account of the money and men that Rome could count on; and advice to Tiberius and the Senate on the administration of the Empire. He also appended a formal, terse summary of his public achievements:

> At the age of nineteen, on my own initiative and at my own expense, I raised an army by means of which I restored liberty to the republic, which had been oppressed by the tyranny of a faction.   1.
>
> Those who slew my father I drove into exile, punishing their deed by due process of law . . .   2.
>
> Wars, both civil and foreign, I undertook throughout the world, on sea

and land, and when victorious I spared all citizens who sued for pardon.

In my triumphs there were led before my chariot nine kings or children of kings. At the time of writing these words I had been thirteen times consul, and was in the thirty-seventh year of my tribunician power.   4.

The dictatorship offered me by the people and the Roman Senate . . . I did not accept.   5.

I refused to accept any power offered me which was contrary to the traditions of our ancestors.   6.

By decree of the senate my name was included in the Salian hymn, and it was enacted by law that my person should be sacred in perpetuity and that so long as I lived I should hold the tribunician power. I declined to be made Pontifex Maximus in succession to a colleague still living . . .   10.

The Senate . . . ordered the pontiffs and the Vestal virgins to perform a yearly sacrifice on the anniversary of the day on which I returned to the city from Syria, . . . and named the day after my cognomen, the Augustalia.   11.

When I returned from Spain and Gaul, in the consulship of Tiberius Nero and Publius Quintilius, after successful operations in those provinces, the senate voted in honour of my return the consecration of an altar to Pax Augusta.   12.

Janus Quirinus, which our ancestors ordered to be closed whenever there was peace, secured by victory, throughout the whole domain of the Roman people on land and sea, and which, before my birth is recorded to have been closed but twice in all since the foundation of the city, the senate ordered to be closed thrice while I was princeps.   13.

I rebuilt in the city eighty-two temples of the gods, omitting none which at that time stood in need of repair.   20.

Three times in my own name I gave a show of gladiators, and five times in the name of my sons or grandsons; in these shows there fought about ten thousand men . . . on twenty-six occasions I gave to the people, in the circus, in the forum, or in the amphitheatre, hunts of African wild beasts, in which about three thousand five hundred beasts were slain.   22.

I gave the people the spectacle of a naval battle . . . In this spectacle thirty beaked ships, triremes or biremes, and a large number of smaller vessels met in conflict. In these fleets there fought about three thousand men exclusive of the rowers.   23.

Silver statues of me, on foot, on horseback, and in chariots were erected in the city to the number of about eighty; these I myself removed, and from the money thus obtained I placed in the temple of Apollo golden offerings in my own name and in the name of those who had paid me the honour of statue.   24.

I extended the boundaries of all the provinces which were bordered by races not yet subject to our empire.   26.

In my sixth and seventh consulships, when I had extinguished the flames of civil war, after receiving by universal consent the absolute control of affairs, I transferred the republic from my own control to the will of the senate and the Roman people. For this service on my part I was given the title of Augustus by decree of the senate, and the doorposts of my house were covered with laurels by public act, and a civic crown was fixed above my door, and a golden shield was placed in the Curia Julia whose inscription testified that the senate and the Roman people gave me this in recognition of my valour, my clemency, my justice, and my piety. After that time I took precedence of all in rank, but of power I possessed no more than those who were my colleagues in any magistracy.   34.

At the time of writing this I was in my seventy-sixth year.[455]   35.

Not all the statements in this brief biographical note were historically true, but they were true officially and were, no doubt, widely accepted. For fifty-eight years Augustus had created his own facts, many of them from unpromising material. Other facts, those that were harmful to his purpose, he had decently masked. He had masked his naked force behind the Senate, behind the myths of artists and poets, behind the gods. With four traditional Roman weapons, the sword, money, rhetoric, and law, he had refounded Rome and ruled the nations. He had outlived most of those who knew him well when he was young. From private person to public man to all-pervasive myth, from Octavius to Octavian to Augustus, he had withdrawn, ever more thoroughly masked. One final mask he had not yet worn, a mask that Roman sculpture had long known, the death mask. But that mask, too, was approaching, for he was old, ill, increasingly feeble. He saw Tiberius off for Dalmatia: Dalmatia needed pacifying again. Augustus went to the island of Capri to rest for a few days. Then to Naples and on to Nola. Suddenly he became gravely ill. Tiberius was sent for, either by his mother Livia or by the Emperor himself. On August 19, A.D. 14, Augustus died.

On the last day of his life he asked every now and then whether there was any disturbance without on his account; then calling for a mirror, he had his hair combed and his falling jaws set straight. After that, calling in his friends and asking whether it seemed to them that he had played the comedy of life fitly, he added the tag:

> "Since well I've played my part, all clap your hands
> And from the stage dismiss me with applause."[456]

THE KINGDOM OF HEAVEN

THE YEAR 7 B.C. opened with excitement at Sippar, the ancient center of astronomy in Babylonia; it opened with excitement in Egypt. Astronomers in both countries predicted a conjunction of planets that could be witnessed only once in every 794 years. Jupiter, which would be in conjunction with Venus in the spring, would encounter Saturn during the summer and autumn in Pisces, the Sign of the Fishes. But astrologers, whether in Babylon, in Alexandria, or in Rome, had even more reason for excitement than astronomers. Many inhabitants of the Roman Empire identified Augustus, ruler of their world, with the divine ruler of both gods and men, whose Latin name was Jupiter. Since Venus was both the mother of Aeneas and the ancestress of Augustus, the earlier of the two approaching conjunctions was fraught with political signficance for the astrologer. The second was more exciting still. Virgil's *Aeneid* and Horace's *Jubilee Hymn*, and indeed Augustan poetry in general, reflected the belief or hope that the Golden Age of Saturn was about to return.

But another interpretation was possible. In the East, the planet Saturn also signified Palestine; and the Sign of the Fishes signified the last days. Many Jews in Palestine eagerly awaited a Messiah, a descendant of King David, who would liberate them from the bloody oppression of Herod I, the puppet of Augustus, and establish the Kingdom of Heaven on earth. Hebrew prophecy had long proclaimed the intention of Jehovah, or Yahweh, to send such a savior to his chosen people. If the new dispensation was near, the dark days that Palestine still passed through might indeed herald what the Hebrew prophets had predicted: the Son of Man was about to be born. When the Great Conjunction occurred, three Magi, or wise men of the East, set out for Palestine to find the newborn King and worship him. A prominent Alexandrian apparently construed the Great Conjunction in favor of Augustus. On March 8 he set up a tablet on an island in the Nile River in honor of his Emperor, a tablet that hailed Augustus as Zeus Eleutherios, or Jupiter Giver of Freedom.[457] In Palestine itself King Herod made the year 7 memorable by strangling two of his sons, with the sanction of Augustus, for high treason, and by killing numerous other persons in an effort to suppress rebellion. He can scarcely have been ignorant of the traditional prophecies that a descendant of David would be sent by Yahweh to save and to rule Israel. If he heard that such a Messiah had been born, it would be practical to kill all the male children in Bethlehem who were under two years old. For Bethlehem was the traditional home of David's descendants. That, according to later reports, is precisely what he did. Some eighteen years earlier, when conspiracy had threatened, King Herod had slaughtered not only the suspects but their wives and children too. Herod was King of the Jews by the grace of Augustus. With rebellion seething on all sides, he was in no mood to welcome into his kingdom another King of the Jews, one whom the Jewish rebels and fanatics might hail as a savior sent by Yahweh. So he struck.

Augustus would have shared Herod's distrust. Indeed, he distrusted Asians in general, and Egyptians too. As a down-to-earth member of the people of the toga, Augustus needed Asia's taxes, but he feared her enervating luxury, her seductive pleasures, her combination of servility and treachery. Romans found Asians emotionally unstable, visionary, with extravagant religious views, given to exotic ritual and even to orgies. As far back as 205, after thirteen years of exhausting struggle against Hannibal, the Roman Senate had cautiously brought to Rome a black stone representing Cybele, the Great Mother, from her temple in Phrygia: there was a chance she might help against Hannibal. Her fertility cult, as if made to repel Romans, involved ecstasies, prophetic rapture, even self-castration by her priests. But at Rome her cult was prudently hedged in with restrictions.

Twenty years later, the worship of Dionysus, or Bacchus, had so spread in Italy and was so dangerously exciting to his women worshipers that the Senate suppressed the Bacchanalia. Dionysus was, of course, a Greek god and probably reached Rome from Magna Graecia, but many authorities traced him back to Phrygia. Certainly, his worshipers tended toward frenzy, as Cybele's did. The Senate heartily disapproved of religious frenzy, especially in women, whom it considered already hard enough to manage.

By about 100 B.C. Isis and Sarapis entered Italy from Egypt, and their worship was later spread through the Empire by sailors and merchants. The decline of faith in the Olympic gods of Hellas and in the Roman gods identified with them, and the substitution of the Roman Empire for the little polis, the close-knit community of gods and men, left the field open to the new mystery cults like those of the Great Mother and Attis from Asia and of Isis and Sarapis from Egypt. It also spread the traditional mystery cults of Hellas; not only that of Dionysus but also those of Orpheus, of the Cabiri of Samothrace, of Eleusis. In general, these cults involved sacred symbols, purification, asceticism, baptism, and other sacramental acts. In general, they offered men salvation and a life hereafter, sometimes through the aid of a god who had suffered, died, and risen again. They offered community in the midst of a huge, new, impersonal cosmopolis, a cosmopolis that had destroyed many human communities in order to build a single, great, disciplined collectivity. They offered a common bond, freely chosen, in place of the anonymity of the mass in a bondage all had been compelled to enter. They offered a god or gods in whom a man might believe, a better life to hope for, even a god a man might not only obey but love. The West had conquered the East by force and had spread to the East the brutal violence and dark horrors of the Roman civil wars; the East had replied with an offer of light to lighten this darkness. Some of this light came from Egypt. Most of it came, immediately or ultimately, from Asia.

Of all the religions that spread from Asia, the one that posed for Rome the most difficult problem was the Jewish. First, the Jews were strict monotheists. Their one God, Yahweh, forbade them to worship any god other than himself. In general, the Romans were tolerant of the local gods of their subjects and not eager to impose their own gods on the peoples they had conquered. But by the basic tenets of Jewish religion Rome's gods were idols. Secondly, for economic reasons many Jews emigrated from Palestine to Alexandria, to Rome, and to other cities, where their religion tended to set them apart. Judaea had passed from Persian rule to that of Alexander the Great and finally to the rule of his successors in Asia, the Seleucid dynasty. During this period the Jews became somewhat hellenized. Indeed, the Jewish colony in Alexandria largely forgot its Hebrew; its sacred literature was translated into Greek, under the title the *Pentateuch*.[458] This translation enabled Yahweh to speak directly to the Greek-speaking world. What Yahweh said, or the way his followers acted, or both, converted many non-Jews. In 139, only seven years after Rome destroyed Carthage and no longer confronted any serious rival in the Hellenistic world, the Roman Senate was faced with several ominous facts. At least some Roman citizens were deserting the gods who had delivered the Hellenistic world into Roman hands. They began considering these gods as mere idols and were joining a group of Asians whose only ultimate loyalty was to an Asian God with pretensions to the divine government of all mankind. In 139 the Senate met this crisis by evicting all Jews from Rome. When Pompey, in 63, made the Jews tributary to Rome and brought back Jewish prisoners, Rome again permitted synagogues, but insisted on their being outside the city walls along with the temples of Isis and Sarapis.

The expulsion of the Jews in 139 symbolized a clash between the chosen people of Yahweh and the chosen people of Jove, and therefore a clash between Yahweh and Jove. But Yahweh had chosen his people long before Jove had chosen his. According to Hebrew scripture, Yahweh revealed his will to Abraham about 2100 B.C., more than a millennium before Rome was founded. Abraham's grandson, Israel, had twelve sons, the Hebrew founders of the twelve tribes of Israel. One of these sons was sold by his brothers into slavery in Egypt, where he made a career and where he later brought his brothers to share his good fortune. But in Egypt the Hebrews were oppressed, and about 1230 Yahweh appointed a leader named Moses to lead them out of slavery. Moses led them for forty years in the deserts south and east of Palestine, a land which Yahweh had promised would be theirs. During these years Yahweh gave them many laws to follow. Then these Israelites partially conquered Palestine, where they were governed first by an hereditary priesthood and later by so-called judges, who led them in their continuous war with numerous non-Hebraic tribes already settled in or near Palestine. About 1080 the Philistines, descendants of invaders from the Minoan Empire who had settled along the coast, conquered the whole of Palestine. The Hebrews demanded of their judge, Samuel, that he give them a king; and Samuel chose Saul. Saul made a good military leader until Yahweh commanded Samuel to replace him with David. David enlarged his kingdom, until by about 1000 B.C. he directly or indirectly ruled from the Red Sea to Damascus. About 960 his son Solomon succeeded him and built a handsome temple in Jerusalem to Yahweh.

The history of the Hebrews was then written down. It consisted in large part of a sort of dialogue between Yahweh, the one true God, and his chosen people, Israel. But the extraordinary prosperity of Solomon's kingdom brought with it a love of money, a love of power, and a toleration for other gods. After Solomon's death, his kingdom split into the Kingdom of Judah, centered around Jerusalem, and the more northern Kingdom of Israel; and these two kingdoms often fought. A series of prophets arose, through whom Yahweh renewed his dialogue with his people. In 722 the Empire of Assyria conquered Israel, deported many of its inhabitants, and resettled them in Assyria and Media. The Kingdom of Judah fell successively to three great empires, the Assyrian, the Egyptian, and finally, in 586, the Neo-Babylonian or Chaldean. Most of the Judaeans were either killed or taken as slaves to Babylonia. In 538 Cyrus the Great, founder of the Persian Empire and conqueror of Babylonia, allowed the remaining Judaeans, or Jews, to return to Jerusalem; and a portion of them did so. There they rebuilt the temple, which the Babylonians had destroyed. It was completed several years before the Roman nobility drove out Rome's last king and established the Roman Republic. It was built one year before Hippias, son of Pisistratus and, like him, tyrant of Athens, was driven out of the city and took refuge with Darius I of Persia, son and successor of Cyrus the Great.

But where Athens and Rome became self-governing republics, the Jews who returned under Ezra to their holy city remained a religious community, living by the laws which Yahweh had given to Moses, although under Persian royal authority. To the Persian Empire they paid tribute, as they had paid it successively to three other powerful empires. Out of their long history of conquest by foreign empires and of exile, a line of Hebrew prophets forged a body of magnificent religious poetry, the common heritage of the little band of Jews who came home and of the majority who chose to remain in exile in wealthy Babylonia. Those who stayed in exile furnished a kind of model for the many colonies of Jews that would collect in the cities of the Roman Empire. These religious colonies were unlike the colonies which groups of Greek merchant adventurers or land-hungry men had already sown around the edges of the Mediterranean. Nor were they like the colonies of land-hungry veterans with which the Roman Republic would one day peg down Italy and the far-flung provinces of its empire. The Jewish colonies which made up this early diaspora, or dispersion, prospered; but they won no sovereign powers and served no Jewish military purpose. They had in common their one true God; the Law which he had transmitted to them through Moses, and by which he kept them his one, chosen people; the history which recorded their long dialogue with the Holy One of Israel, their disobediences and fallings-away, their repentances and returns; and finally Yahweh's repeated promise to send a Messiah to liberate his people and establish among them a Kingdom of Heaven, a Messiah who perhaps would rule not only the Jews but all the other nations on earth.

In 167 B.C., Antiochus IV of Syria, observing that his tributary, Judaea, was becoming considerably hellenized, decided to speed the process. He attempted to replace the worship of Yahweh in Jerusalem with the worship of Zeus of Olympus. Thereupon a priest of Yahweh named Judas Maccabaeus led an uprising. Not only did Judas, his four brothers, and their successors, all known as the Maccabees, preserve the worship of Yahweh; a new Jewish state, governed by a Maccabean dynasty for almost one hundred years, recovered approximately the territory David and Solomon had ruled nearly a millennium earlier. Eventually a quarrel between two contenders for the throne drew in Pompey to arbitrate. In 63 Pompey captured Jerusalem, abolished the monarchy, greatly diminished its territory, and turned over the government to one of the contenders as High Priest and Ethnarch. Herod I was a king loyal to Rome; and King he still was when the three Magi came out of the east to Jerusalem to find a child who had been born, a child who, according to the best astrology, was born King of the Jews. When the Magi learned that according to the holy writings of the Jews their Messiah would be born in the nearby village of Bethlehem, they immediately went there. In the stable of an inn they found him lying in a manger. His father, Joseph, was a Jewish carpenter in Nazareth, in the district of Galilee. Joseph and Mary, his wife, had come to Bethlehem to register in the Roman census, because Joseph was a descendant of King David, and Bethlehem was the headquarters of the

Davidites. There had been no room for them in the inn itself; their son Jesus was born in the stable. When Herod's soldiers later slaughtered the young children of Bethlehem, Joseph and Mary had already fled with Jesus into Egypt. Three years afterwards Herod died, and Joseph and Mary returned to Nazareth, where Jesus was reared.

Four narratives of what Jesus of Nazareth did and said and suffered were written at various dates after his death by disciples or apostles of his, who either had witnessed much of what they narrated or could have talked with eyewitnesses. But they were not written as histories or biographies in the usual sense. They paid scant attention to chronology. They differed on some details, although they agreed on more. They focused chiefly on the last four years of Jesus' life, those of his ministry, which he began when about thirty-three. By way of preparation Jesus went where a prophet named John was calling on the people to repent their sins, was baptizing in the Jordan River those who repented, and was announcing that the Kingdom of Heaven was at hand. Jesus was baptized. With varying details the accounts report that God there gave signs that Jesus was his Son, with whom he was well pleased.

And now Jesus was led by the Spirit away into the wilderness, to be tempted there by the devil. Forty days and forty nights he spent fasting, and at the end of them was hungry. Then the tempter approached, and said to him, If thou art the Son of God, bid these stones turn into loaves of bread. He answered, It is written, Man cannot live by bread only; there is life for him in all the words which proceed from the mouth of God. Next, the devil took him into the holy city, and there set him down on the pinnacle of the temple, saying to him, If thou art the Son of God, cast thyself down to earth; for it is written, He has given charge to his angels concerning thee, and they will hold thee up with their hands, lest thou shouldst chance to trip on a stone. Jesus said to him, But it is further written, Thou shalt not put the Lord thy God to the proof. Once more, the devil took him to the top of an exceedingly high mountain, from which he shewed him all the kingdoms of the world and the glory of them, and said, I will give thee all these if thou wilt fall down and worship me. Then Jesus said to him, Away with thee, Satan; it is written, Thou shalt worship the Lord thy God, and serve none but him. Then the devil left him alone; and thereupon angels came and ministered to him.[459]

237

The three temptations came to signify to the disciples of Jesus that God had not sent him to bring mere material plenty to society or to test his relation with God or to rule the many societies Augustus had ruled till his death, societies which his successor, the Emperor Tiberius, now ruled, and which some of Jesus' fellow Jews believed that the Messiah, or Christ, would rule. The temptations defined his mission negatively: he came neither as social revolutionary nor as temporal ruler.

What Jesus had come to do revealed itself slowly in the four years that followed. He returned to Galilee, chose out twelve men of humble background like his own, and commanded them to follow him. Each instantly heeded his command. He taught these twelve disciples, preached to crowds in the country around the Sea of Galilee, and healed those of the sick who showed faith in him. He proved himself able to perform miracles, which he seems often to have used as a means of helping others to see something he wanted them to see. He spoke, not in abstract propositions, but in poetic metaphor; in little stories, or parables. Although he made small use of the demonstrative reason that Socrates of Athens had employed over four centuries before, yet he was, like Socrates, concerned to induce insights in others, to move their hearts, to get them to look inward, to enable them to hear something to which they seemed deaf. Like Socrates, he showed gentleness and courtesy to those who appeared to be seeking truth with humble hearts. But he often punctured sharply the pretenses of the arrogant, the self-righteous, the intellectually complacent. He often quoted Hebrew scripture; and he declared that he had not come to do away with the body of law that God had given his people through Moses. Yet it seemed to many that he was breaking that law; to others, that he rejected at least certain literal-minded elaborations and applications of it; to still others, that he believed the law itself was no longer needed. When those who thought he was the Messiah, the King of the Jews, asked him when this kingdom would be established, he answered mysteriously that the Kingdom of Heaven was already among them, or in them. He promised eternal life to those who should believe in him; and he announced that he himself was the way, the truth, and the life.

In private, Jesus taught his disciples that the truly blessed are the humble, the patient, those who know sorrow, those who long for holiness, the merciful, the pure in heart, the peacemakers, those unjustly persecuted. He told them to confront violence with love, not vengeance; to love not only their friends but their enemies, as God did; to be perfect, as God their

Father was perfect. The advice to love one's enemies would have seemed the height of folly to most Romans: their late Emperor Augustus was capable of lying in wait for years to kill or ruin an enemy, and he was praised for acquiring the power which this patient vengeance brought him: did he not rule on earth as Jove ruled in heaven? He wholly worshiped power, and power gave him the kingdoms of the world to rule. Why should not Yahweh, who was no mere Jove but the true God, give his chosen people, or certainly those who followed Jesus, a Messiah to replace the Roman Emperor, as well as the power the Romans held to rule all other nations? This way of being perfect Jesus had rejected in the desert, when the devil tempted him for the third time. Apparently, the only divine power that Jesus wanted his disciples to have they could get only by emptying themselves of the desire for power and by letting God's will work through them; only by subjecting their will completely to the will of God, not by masking their self-will with a claim that their will was really God's. Apparently, perfection lay in loving God first and then loving one's neighbor, as indeed Mosaic law prescribed[460] long before Jesus did; but Jesus also made it painfully clear that a man must love his neighbor even when his neighbor was his enemy.

Jesus' difficult command to his disciples to respond with love when others used violence against them was quite as subversive to the existing political order as Socrates' insistence on questioning everything. What Jesus said when he instructed his twelve disciples in private might have got him into no immediate trouble with the authorities. But month after month, as he and his small band walked the hills of Galilee, he also instructed by means of his simple parables large crowds of people, and on the Sabbath he often taught in some synagogue. Moreover, he directed his disciples to preach the Kingdom of Heaven and to heal the sick.

Meanwhile, knife-men, or resistance fighters, were operating in this hill country, and discontent with Roman rule was widespread. After Herod's death in 4 B.C., Augustus planned to rule through Herod's son, Archelaus: puppet kings often cost Rome less money than direct rule would have done. But Herod's son proved inadequate, and in A.D. 6 Augustus attached Palestine to Syria. Until 1 B.C., Syria had been ruled by a Roman governor, Quinctilius Varus, who "entered the rich province a poor man, but left it a rich man and the province poor."[461] This was the same Varus who later lost three legions in a German forest and cost Augustus his Elbe frontier. The Emperor was represented in Palestine by a procurator, stationed with his troops at Caesarea but retaining the use of Herod's palace at Jerusalem.

The conservative religious forces represented by the priestly council in Jerusalem, known as the Sanhedrin, were shocked by Jesus' attitude toward Jewish religious rules. How could the miracles he worked on the Sabbath, a day when all work was forbidden, be justified by his statement that the Sabbath was made for man, not man for the Sabbath? He made the lame walk and the blind see; he healed lepers; he exorcised demons. His critics complained that he could exorcise demons precisely because he himself was possessed of powerful demons. His critics decided that he was misleading men of Jewish faith: in effect, that he was a Jewish heretic. But by now his large popular following made his case difficult to handle. The most convenient way to silence him might be to embroil him with the Roman provincial administration, perhaps by asking him in public whether Jews should pay the hated tribute.

In the spring of A.D. 30, when Jesus and his disciples went up to Jerusalem for the Feast of the Passover, along with thousands of other Jews, the trap was sprung. With a great show of respect he was asked whether it was "right to pay tribute to Caesar, or not?"[462] He showed that he understood the purpose of the question: if he said No, he would be in trouble with the Roman Imperial administration; if he said Yes, he would lose much of his following. But he said, "Shew me the coinage in which the tribute is paid."[463] He can scarcely have been unfamiliar with it: it was the Roman silver denarius, the precise amount of the Imperial poll tax, or tribute. Unlike the copper coins current in Judaea, it was minted by Rome, probably at Lyons. Probably also[464] the coin showed on its obverse a bust of Tiberius, who had succeeded his adoptive father Augustus as Emperor sixteen years before. The bust was naked, as an Olympian god would most likely be; the head was crowned with laurel, a frequent symbol of divinity. The Latin inscription could be fairly translated either as "Tiberius Caesar Augustus, Son of the Deified Augustus," or as "Emperor Tiberius, August Son of the August God." On the reverse side was one of the Emperor's titles: Pontifex Maximus, or Chief Priest. The reverse also showed an image of Livia, wife of Augustus and mother of Tiberius. She held an Olympian scepter in one hand and in the other hand an olive branch, to symbolize the peace on earth which Augustus claimed to have given man. Rome's coins still propagandized her subjects; her coins now announced worldwide dominion, wielded by men who at death became gods. In the East especially, the coins announced Emperor worship, and in Jewish eyes they could appear only as blasphemy. They even hinted at the triumph of the moneyed class over the poor: everybody knew that Rome favored plutocracy and detested democracy.

"Whose is this likeness? Whose name is inscribed on it?" Jesus asked. Socrates could not have asked questions more dangerous, more dialectical. A trap for trappers was ready to be sprung.

"Caesar's," they said.

"Why then," replied Jesus, "give back to Caesar what is Caesar's and to God what is God's."[465] Perhaps he meant: You are delighted to get the coins Rome issues; you do business with them, and you thereby do business with Rome; you hold we may not worship Caesar, that it is blasphemous to permit the image of Caesar as a god to enter Jerusalem,[466] yet you permit it in the case of money, and thus you show that you yourselves worship money, as indeed Caesar does; that is, you worship power, power based on force and fraud; you cannot then grow squeamish if Rome, the champion of that sort of power everywhere, charges a modest commission. Perhaps he also meant: Your real sin is not that you give Caesar's image back to Caesar, but that you decline to give God's image, your own immortal soul, back to God; you decline daily to do so by worshiping money. When Jesus had given his verdict, there was no answer. Those who had wanted to silence him went away silent.

The verdict was clearly connected with another thing Jesus of Nazareth shared with Socrates of Athens, a deep distrust of money. Both of them voluntarily chose poverty. They did not turn away from things money can buy: both could enjoy feasting. Indeed, Socrates was admired for the amount of wine he could down without becoming in the least confused. The men who charged that John the Baptist was possessed because he fasted so strenuously denounced Jesus for a glutton, who drank wine, and that too with tax collectors and other sinners. But neither Socrates nor Jesus tried to acquire the security that money was supposed to bring. They saw in it slavery. They saw in it the sort of "cares and troubles"[467] that afflicted Martha, the busy housekeeper, annoyed that her sister Mary was not helping her but was sitting at Jesus' feet listening. "The cares of this world and the false charms of riches"[468] cause us to forget the truth even when we have heard it and have understood it. These were the same cares and troubles, the work and worry, that had afflicted Aeneas, busy founding Rome, and that had afflicted Augustus, busy refounding it. Socrates had

declared[469] that money was the chief cause of war. It was extremely difficult, Jesus declared, for a rich man to enter the Kingdom of Heaven. When
a rich young man asked him what he should do to be saved, Jesus reminded
him of the ten commandments, which, being Jews, both men knew well.
The rich young man declared he had kept them. What else? Jesus told
him to give all his riches to the poor and to follow him. But the young man
turned sorrowfully away, "for he had great possessions." When Jesus
taught his disciples in private, he put his finger on the problem: the terrible power of money to preoccupy; to pre-empt first place in a man's
thoughts; that is, to become his god. "A man cannot," he told his disciples,

> be the slave of two masters at once; either he will hate the one and love
> the other, or he will devote himself to the one and despise the other. You
> must serve God or money; you cannot serve both."[470]

His objection to this attempt at dual loyalty was most vividly apparent
when, in Jerusalem, he entered the Temple, within which stood the Holy
of Holies of the Jewish people, and found those who were selling animals
for sacrifice as well as money-changers to accommodate purchasers. He

> began driving out those who sold and bought in the temple, and over-
> threw the tables of the bankers, and the chairs of the pigeon-sellers; nor
> would he allow anyone to carry his wares through the temple. And this
> was the admonition he gave them, Is it not written, My house shall be
> known among all the nations for a house of prayer? Whereas you have
> made it into a den of thieves.[471]

By this act, the only one reported of Jesus that smacks of violence, he
seemed to be saying that money stopped the ears when truth was
spoken, sealed men's eyes from truly seeing, and thereby often enslaved
men. Socrates wanted truth above all things, and Jesus promised those
who believed in him, "you will come to know the truth, and the truth will
set you free."[472] Jesus did indeed talk even more of loving the good
than of seeing the truth, while Socrates talked even more of seeing the
true than of loving the good.[473] But both men taught that seeing and
loving could free men from the prison of care, of toil, of thingness, of
necessity, of death, a prison that hardened the heart and darkened the
inner eye. Both men opened a door and strove lovingly to turn men
around, to con-vert them, so that these men could see the light.[474] Both
men believed that from this particular prison some men can be led but

none can be dragged by force. Both knew that prisoners often come to love prison and to fear freedom. Both knew that each prisoner has to choose: Socrates had seen what happened to men who tried to love equally both truth and material success; and Jesus suggested[475] that it was more practical to serve money and power faithfully than to try to serve two incompatible gods. Finally, both Socrates and Jesus knew that some prisoners would so resent interference with the life they had grown used to that they would be ready to kill those who tried to open their eyes or unstop their ears.[476] Indeed, Jesus predicted to his disciples that in Jerusalem he would be put to death and that they, too, would suffer persecution.

When Socrates was tried for blasphemy, for teaching false religious doctrines, and therefore for subversion, he testified in effect that he had been commissioned by Apollo to question his fellow citizens as he did and that he had no choice but to obey this god, a god who conveyed to men the will of Zeus, father of gods and of men. Socrates asserted also that he was guided by a *daimon*, a sort of inner voice. When Jesus first taught his disciples, he spoke of himself as the Son of Man, a traditional name for the Messiah whom Yahweh had promised to send his people. Later, he asked his disciples who men thought he was. They told him that some said he was Elijah, a prophet who had lived in the days of the kings before the Babylonian capitivity, a prophet who had not died but had been taken up to heaven alive. They told him others believed he was a later prophet, Jeremiah. Others took him for John the Baptist, who had baptized Jesus and had later been beheaded by Herod I. But who did they themselves say he was? Peter answered, "Thou art the Christ, the Son of the living God." Jesus answered that "it is not flesh and blood, it is my Father in heaven that has revealed this to thee."[477] He also forbade them to tell others. Shortly afterward, when Peter and two other disciples were alone with him on a high mountain, perhaps Mount Hermon,

> His garments became bright, dazzling white like snow . . . And a cloud formed, overshadowing them; and from the cloud came a voice, which said, This is my beloved Son; to him, then, listen."[478]

On the way down the mountain Jesus commanded the three disciples to report nothing of what they had seen until the Son of Man should have risen from the dead. But his disciples moved with difficulty from the Jewish hope that Yahweh, their God, would send a human Messiah of the House of David to liberate his people, to establish an independent kingdom, and perhaps even to rule all other nations too, to a belief that God had sent his only-begotten Son to be born of a woman, to live as a man named Jesus among other men, not in order to ascend an earthly throne in Jerusalem but to be killed there, to rise on the third day from the dead, and thereby to save all men who believed that these things were true. Jesus' disciples could not grasp how the eternal, the timeless, could enter at a unique moment into time, into history; or that already, not at some longed-for moment of triumph in the future, the Kingdom of Heaven was among them and in them; or that this penetration of history by eternity, of earth by heaven, would established a new human community on earth, would create a terrestrial province of a Kingdom that was not terrestrial. This theophany would in fact claim from Emperor Tiberius, August Son of the August Son, at least a handful of his subjects for the real Son of the real God, the God of Abraham, Isaac, and Jacob. Might this handful of subjects slowly grow until, as the prophet Isaiah implied, all flesh would come to worship the true God?[479]

In the spring of 32 Jesus was preaching in Jericho and preparing to lead his disciples up to Jerusalem to keep the Feast of the Passover. Even then his disciples could not believe his prediction that in Jerusalem he would be put to death and rise after three days. They were still thinking of success, of triumph; they had recently quarreled about places of honor in the imminent Kingdom of Heaven. They were deaf to his warnings that the Kingdom he had preached was a topsy-turvy affair, a place in which the rulers were servants to the ruled. And, indeed, on the Sunday before Passover when they entered the Holy City, joyful crowds hailed Jesus as the Messiah. True, the Sanhedrin wished to arrest him, but to arrest him by day was dangerous, given the enthusiasm his preaching had stirred up among the many pilgrims who had come up to Jerusalem; his nights he spent outside the city. On Thursday night Jesus and his disciples re-entered Jerusalem and ate their Passover supper[480] together, in private. Mysteriously, he told them that the bread was his body, which was given for them, and the wine was his blood, which was to be shed for them. He also predicted that one of his disciples would betray him. After this last supper together, he went out into a garden and prayed alone, leaving his disciples to keep watch. But the men were tired and they slept. Meanwhile, one of them, bribed with thirty pieces of silver, guided Jesus' enemies to the garden, where they arrested him. In the mêlée Peter drew a sword and wounded a servant of the high priest.

Whereupon Jesus said to him, Put thy sword back into its place; all those who take up the sword will perish by the sword.[481]

Jesus was examined before the Sanhedrin, which was allowed jurisdiction by Rome in cases of religious law. For a while the case against him went poorly. Then

the high priest said to him openly, I adjure thee by the living God to tell us whether thou art the Christ, the Son of God? Jesus answered, Thy own lips have said it. And moreover I tell you this; you will see the Son of Man again, when he is seated at the right hand of power, and comes on the clouds of heaven. At this, the high priest tore his garments, and said, He has blasphemed; what further need have we of witnesses? Mark well, you have heard his blasphemy for yourselves. What is your finding? And they answered, The penalty is death. Then they fell to spitting upon his face and buffeting him and smiting him on the cheek, saying as they did so, Shew thyself a prophet, Christ; tell us who it is that smote thee.

Meanwhile, Peter sat in the court without; and there a maidservant came up to him, and said, Thou too wast with Jesus the Galilean. Whereupon he denied it before all the company; I do not know what thou meanest. And he went out into the porch, where a second maid-servant saw him, and said, to the bystanders, This man, too, was with Jesus the Nazarene. And he made denial again with an oath, I know nothing of the man. But those who stood there came up to Peter soon afterwards, and said, It is certain that thou art one of them; even thy speech betrays thee. And with that he fell to calling down curses on himself and swearing, I know nothing of the man; and thereupon the cock crew. Then Peter remembered the word of Jesus, how he had said, Before the cock crows, thou wilt thrice disown me; and he went out, and wept bitterly.[482]

Presumably, the Sanhedrin had authority to order Jesus stoned for blasphemy. Instead, perhaps because its members still feared the hold he had on a considerable number of people, they turned him over to the Procurator of Judaea, Pontius Pilate, said by the Jewish philosopher, Philo, to be "a man of inflexible, stubborn, and cruel disposition."[483] At this point, according to Luke, the accusers of Jesus charged him with subverting the loyalty of their people, with forbidding them to pay tribute to Caesar, and with calling himself Christ the king.[484] Pilate asked Jesus,

Art thou the king of the Jews? He answered him, Thy own lips have said it. And now the chief priests brought many accusations against him, and

Pilate questioned him again, Dost thou make no answer? See what a weight of accusation they bring against thee. But Jesus still would not answer him, so that the governor was full of astonishment.[485]

Following his custom of pardoning at Passover a condemned criminal chosen by the people, Pilate suggested that he release the King of the Jews. But, incited by the chief priests, the crowd chose for pardon a Jewish resistance fighter guilty of murder rather than the Jew whom the Sanhedrin had judged guilty of blasphemy. Pilate asked what the crowd wanted him to do with the King of the Jews.

And they made a fresh cry of, Crucify him. Why, Pilate said to them, what wrong has he done? But they cried all the more, Crucify him. And so Pilate, determined to humour the multitude,[486]

ordered that Jesus be scourged and then crucified. The Roman soldiers who executed that order evidently took Jesus for a rebel pretender-king rather than for a blasphemer against a religion Rome despised. They put a crown of thorns on his head and a scarlet cloak on his shoulders; then they mockingly greeted him,

Hail, king of the Jews. And they beat him over the head with a rod, and spat upon him, and bowed their knees in worship of him.[487]

Such is the story of the Roman trial and condemnation in the earliest written account. A later record gives a fuller picture of the Roman administrator, faced by what he must have viewed as a typically Asian religious disturbance, perhaps troubled in conscience but fearful of bureaucratic rebuke. Pilate said to Jesus' accusers:

Take him yourselves . . . and judge him according to your own law. Whereupon the Jews said to him, We have no power to put any man to death. . . . [488] So Pilate went back into the palace, and summoned Jesus; Art thou the king of the Jews? he asked. Dost thou say this of thy own impulse, Jesus answered, or is it what others have told thee of me? And Pilate answered, Am I a Jew? It is thy own nation, and its chief priests, who have given thee up to me. What offence hast thou committed? My kingdom, answered Jesus, does not belong to this world. If my kingdom were one which belonged to this world, my servants would be fighting, to prevent my falling into the hands of the Jews; but no, my kingdom does not take its origin here. Thou art a king, then? Pilate asked. And Jesus answered, It is thy own lips that have called me a king. What I was born for, what I came into the world for, is to bear witness of the truth.

Whoever belongs to the truth, listens to my voice. Pilate said to him,
What is truth? And with that he went back to the Jews again, and told
them, I can find no fault in him.[489]

Later he brought him out to the crowd.

Then, as Jesus came out, still wearing the crown of thorns and the
scarlet cloak, he said to them, See, here is the man. When the chief
priests and their officers saw him, they cried out, Crucify him, crucify
him. Take him yourselves, said Pilate, and crucify him; I cannot find any
fault in him. The Jews answered, We have our own law, and by our law
he ought to die, for pretending to be the Son of God. When Pilate heard
this said, he was more afraid than ever; going back into the palace, he
asked Jesus, Whence hast thou come? But Jesus gave him no answer.
What, said Pilate, hast thou no word for me? Dost thou not know that I
have power to crucify thee, and power to release thee? Jesus answered,
Thou wouldst not have any power over me at all, if it had not been given
thee from above. That is why the man who gave me up to thee is more
guilty yet. After this, Pilate was for releasing him, but the Jews went on
crying out, Thou art no friend to Caesar, if thou dost release him; the
man who pretends to be a king is Caesar's rival. . . . See, he said to the
Jews, here is your king. But they cried out, Away with him, away with
him, crucify him. What, Pilate said to them, shall I crucify your king?
We have no king, the chief priests answered, except Caesar. . . .

So Jesus went out, carrying his own cross. . . . And Pilate wrote out a
proclamation, which he put on the cross; it ran, Jesus of Nazareth, the
king of the Jews. This proclamation was read by many of the Jews,
since the place where Jesus was crucified was close to the city; it was
written in Hebrew, Greek, and Latin. And the Jewish chief priests said to
Pilate, Thou shouldst not write, The king of the Jews; thou shouldst
write, This man said, I am the king of the Jews. Pilate's answer was,
What I have written, I have written.[490]

In the earlier account, Pilate emphasized that it would not be his fault
but that of the Sanhedrin and their followers if Jesus were crucified:

Pilate sent for water and washed his hands in full sight of the multitude,
saying as he did so, I have no part in the death of this innocent man; it
concerns you only.[491]

When Pilate consented to crucify Jesus, he pardoned Barabbas, a man
who, according to one account, "was then in custody, with the rebels who
had been guilty of murder during the rebellion."[492] Another says Barabbas

had been imprisoned "for raising a revolt in the city, and for murder."[493] Another merely states that "there was one notable prisoner then in custody, whose name was Barabbas";[494] and yet another, that "Barabbas was a robber."[495] Pilate therefore pardoned the prisoner who had rebelled violently against Roman authority, but a rebel not accused of blasphemy. The pardon no doubt delighted at least the extreme nationalists, the Zealots. Pilate then crucified Jesus. The Sanhedrin had frightened Pilate by implying that if he let Jesus go free they would report him to Rome for condoning the crime of rebellion. Hence the inscription over the cross. The Sanhedrin's fear of the Jewish followers of Jesus, combined with Pilate's fear of his official superiors, had thus led the Roman Empire, in the name of Roman law, to crucify Jesus. The victim of their joint fears showed no fear. Since the man who ordered the crucifixion believed the victim was innocent, he tried to solve the problem by questioning the authority of truth and thereby washing his hands of injustice. Finally, the sign Pilate ordered to be placed over Jesus' cross may have been Pilate's effort to strike back at the Sanhedrin for frightening him into betraying justice.

Augustus had died some eighteen years earlier, in bed, an old man, unchallenged master of the only civilized world he knew, son of a god, widely worshiped as a god himself. Everywhere he was hailed as the benefactor, the savior, of mankind, who had brought peace on earth by doing the will of Jove. There were those who remembered how he had murdered and robbed his way to power, but at least he was successful. He had the ships, he had the men, he had the money too. These gave him the power to impose peace and enforce law on a society in which force had run amuck, had destroyed the basis of peaceful consent to authority: men's faith in the gods and in each other. To make force acceptable, he had always made heavy use of propaganda, although the Roman Empire may not have spread many more lies than other empires, even if it may have spread them farther. In any case, a society grown tolerant of the political lie was willing to applaud him. Augustus might with a tranquil conscience have asked as Pilate asked: "What is truth?" Given Augustus' skepticism about truth, there was a certain candor in his suggestion that he had been the leading actor in a comedy, the comedy of human power. When, on his deathbed, he looked in the mirror while his hair was combed, he may have seen a comic hero on a magnificent scale, willing now to hear one last round of applause.

248

Jesus had started life as a carpenter's son. Then he had been hailed by throngs in his native Galilee and even by throngs beyond the Jordan as that King of the Jews whose coming Hebrew prophets had foreseen. But he had been arrested by the Sanhedrin; he had been turned over to Roman power and falsely accused of being a subversive; he had been scourged, mocked, and spat upon; and he died the ignominious death of the rebellious slaves who had followed Spartacus. He could now be remembered as a good man whose fatal Aristotelian flaw was hybris, the pride that comes before a fall. His life could be seen as the hero's role in a Greek tragedy, suited to arouse pity and terror, to purge those emotions, and to leave in the spectator a healthy recognition that the human condition must never be confused with the divine. His tragedy could appear as more than Promethean, as an attempt to rescue man from man's fated mortality and to bring him eternal life; to rid him of fear and to give him the courage to speak the dangerous truth; to persuade man to love his enemies. Now he was dead, and the Kingdom of Heaven had apparently turned out to be only an exciting dream.

In the face of his death, his disciples seemed to have forgotten his prediction that on the third day he would rise again from the dead. They knew that shortly before Jesus' death Lazarus, whom he loved, had died, and that when Lazarus had been buried for four days, Jesus had raised him from the dead. But it did not follow logically that, once he himself had died, he could also raise himself.

Jesus was buried in a new tomb, cut out of rock and owned by a well-to-do follower; the opening was closed with a large stone. Three of his women followers, who had brought spices with which to anoint the body, visited the tomb.

> And they began to question among themselves, Who is to roll the stone away for us from the door of the tomb? Then they looked up, and saw that the stone, great as it was, had been rolled away already. And they went into the tomb, and saw there, on the right, a young man seated, wearing a white robe; and they were dismayed. But he said to them, No need to be dismayed; you have come to look for Jesus of Nazareth, who was crucified; he has risen again, he is not here. Here is the place where they laid him. Go and tell Peter and the rest of his disciples that he is going before you into Galilee. There you shall have sight of him, as he promised you. So they came out and ran away from the tomb, trembling and awe-struck, and said nothing to anyone, out of fear. But he had risen

again, at dawn on the first day of the week, and shewed himself first of all to Mary Magdalen . . . She went and gave the news to those who had been of his company, where they mourned and wept; and they, when they were told that he was alive and that she had seen him, could not believe it. After that, he appeared in the form of a stranger to two of them as they were walking together, going out into the country; these went back and gave the news to the rest, but they did not believe them either.

Then at last he appeared to all eleven of them as they sat at table, and reproached them with their unbelief and their obstinacy of heart, in giving no credit to those who had seen him after he had risen. And he said to them, Go out all over the world, and preach the gospel to the whole of creation; he who believes and is baptized will be saved; he who refuses belief will be condemned. Where believers go, these signs shall go with them; they will cast out devils in my name, they will speak in tongues that are strange to them; they will take up serpents in their hands, and drink poisonous draughts without harm; they will lay their hands upon the sick and make them recover. And so the Lord Jesus, when he had finished speaking to them, was taken up to heaven, and is seated now at the right hand of God; and they went out and preached everywhere, the Lord aiding them, and attesting his word by the miracles that went with them.[496]

The four earliest accounts differ in detail. But they all agree that the tomb was empty and that those who found it empty reported the fact to the disciples. Most of these accounts report that the disciples could not believe it, and one adds that "to their minds the story seemed madness."[497] All agree that Jesus appeared to the disciples when the eleven who remained were gathered together; two report that his disciples witnessed his final ascension into heaven.

On the day of Pentecost, the fiftieth day after Passover, Jews from many countries and speaking many languages were gathered at Jerusalem. The disciples of Jesus, the Christ or Messiah, were now devoted apostles, or messengers from him, to preach what he had taught them. They, too, were in Jerusalem, "all gathered together in unity of purpose," when there

appeared to them what seemed to be tongues of fire, which parted and came to rest on each of them; and they were all filled with the Holy Spirit, and began to speak in strange languages, as the Spirit gave utterance to each. Among those who were dwelling in Jerusalem at this time were devout Jews from every country under heaven; so, when the noise of this went abroad, the crowd which gathered was in bewilderment; each man severally heard them speak in his own language. And they were all beside themselves with astonishment; Are they not all Galileans speaking? they asked. How is it that each of us hears them talking his own native tongue? There are Parthians among us, and Medes, and Elamites; our homes are in Mesopotamia, or Judaea, or Cappadocia; in Pontus or Asia, Phrygia or Pamphylia, Egypt or the parts of Libya round Cyrene; some of us are visitors from Rome, some of us are Jews and others proselytes; there are Cretans among us too, and Arabians; and each has been hearing them tell of God's wonders in his own language. So they were all beside themselves with perplexity, and asked one another, What can this mean? There were others who said, mockingly, They have had their fill of new wine.[498]

But Peter addressed the crowd and quoted David as prophesying Jesus Christ and his resurrection. "God, then," he said,

has raised up this man, Jesus, from the dead; we are all witnesses of it. And now, exalted at God's right hand, he has claimed from his Father his promise to bestow the Holy Spirit; and he has poured out that Spirit, as you can see and hear for yourselves. . . . Let it be known, then, beyond doubt, to all the house of Israel, that God has made him Master and Christ, this Jesus whom you crucified.[499]

Many who heard Peter were baptized in Christ's name.

The apostles continued their work of conversion. They apparently gave, to those who heard them preach, a sense of immediate encounter with Christ; and they admitted those who felt the encounter, who repented their sins and were baptized, into the Assembly, or Ecclesia, which Christ himself had founded. Traditionally, the Greek polis had been governed by its Ecclesia, its assembly of all its citizens. The new Christian Ecclesia would include all those in Jerusalem, and later in the world, who joined together for love of Christ to do Christ's work in the world. The bond of this Christian Ecclesia was love of Christ, and of his Father through Christ, and love of each member for the others. It confronted the love of power, of money, and of self by choosing to hold all property in common. For those not yet converted, it expressed its love by alms to the poor and by prayers for all men. That its members should pool their property was made easy by their confidence that Christ would come again, that he would bring eternal life to those who believed in him and in his teaching. The joy, the outpouring love, the courtesy, the selflessness of the little Ecclesia, or Church, seemed to draw men and women into itself, there in the ancient city of Jerusalem. The Church rejoiced in its Jewish religious traditions, and it pointed to prophecies in the Hebrew scriptures to support its claims for Christ. It assumed that Jewish religious law still held; the Church therefore not only baptized but also circumcised its Gentile converts.

The majority of Jews in Jerusalem could not accept the teachings of Jesus, nor his interpretation of the Hebrew texts. That God should have a son and that this son should also be God suggested Hellenistic polytheism. As to the promise of eternal life, the Sadducees, the sect of wealth and power in Jerusalem, had never accepted the doctrine of immortality preached by another sect, the Pharisees. Many of those who had hailed Jesus as the Messiah had assumed that he would liberate Judaea from Roman rule, as the Zealots wished to do, and that he would establish a sovereign Jewish kingdom: the crucifixion merely confirmed the doubt that Jesus was the Christ. But conversions continued, not only because, when the apostles preached Christ crucified and risen again, their burning faith and outpouring love seemed contagious, but because they obeyed his charge to heal the sick, and people were flocking into Jerusalem from nearby cities to be cured. The High Priest and the Sadducees tried imprisonment and scourging, but the apostles mysteriously escaped from prison and rejoiced that they too, like the Christ they served, had been scourged. Even some of the priests of Jerusalem were converted. One of the apostles, Stephen, was arrested on a charge of blasphemy. At his trial he rapidly retraced God's long dialogue with Abraham and his descendants. He reminded those present how often the Hebrew prophets, who foretold Christ's coming, had been themselves persecuted. He reminded them of God's command to Abraham that his descendants should be circumcised as a sign of God's covenant with them, and he charged those present with the betrayal and murder of Christ when he had appeared as their own prophets had predicted. Their hearts and ears, he said, were uncircumcised, and they resisted the Holy Spirit. Then Stephen

> fastened his eyes on heaven, and saw there the glory of God, and Jesus standing at God's right hand; I see heaven opening, he said, and the Son of Man standing at the right hand of God. Then they cried aloud, and put their fingers into their ears; with one accord they fell upon him, thrust him out of the city, and stoned him. And the witnesses put down their clothes at the feet of a young man named Saul. Thus they stoned

Stephen; he, meanwhile, was praying; Lord Jesus, he said, receive my spirit; and then, kneeling down, he cried aloud, Lord, do not count this sin against them. And with that, he fell asleep in the Lord.

Saul was one of those who gave their voices for his murder.[500]

Stephen's prayer echoed the prayer that Christ had uttered as he was being nailed to the cross: "Father, forgive them; they do not know what it is they are doing."[501]

Stephen was the first *martyros*, or witness, to die for his faith in Christ. His martyrdom bore immediate fruit. Saul was a young man of Jewish faith, Greek education, and Roman citizenship from the city of Tarsus and an ardent persecutor of the new church in Jerusalem. The persecution had driven many to flee the Holy City; but, in fleeing, they had spread elsewhere the news of Christ's words and deeds. Saul was commissioned by the High Priest to pursue and arrest those who had fled to Damascus. On the road to Damascus

a light from heaven shone suddenly about him. He fell to the ground, and heard a voice saying to him, Saul, Saul, why dost thou persecute me? Who art thou, Lord? he asked. And he said, I am Jesus, whom Saul persecutes. . . . And he, dazed and trembling, asked, Lord, what wilt thou have me do? Then the Lord said to him, Rise up, and go into the city, and there thou shalt be told what thy work is. His companions stood in bewilderment, hearing the voice speak, but not seeing anyone. When he rose from the ground he could see nothing, although his eyes were open, and they had to lead him by the hand, to take him into Damascus. Here for three days he remained without sight, and neither ate nor drank.[502]

When he reached Damascus, a man came to him, announced that he had been sent by the same Lord Jesus who had appeared to him on the road, healed the blindness which his vision on the road had caused, and told Saul he would be filled with the Holy Spirit. Saul lived with Christians in Damascus and preached in the synagogues that Jesus was the Son of God until the Jews who had not become Christians plotted to kill him. He escaped to the apostles at Jerusalem, where he preached to Greek-speaking Jews until his life was again in danger. Then the apostles hurried him to Caesarea, and he went home to Tarsus. From there he proceeded through Asia Minor, preaching to Jew and Gentile alike, and establishing little ecclesias like the one in Jerusalem. He was becoming the most celebrated apostle of all those who preached to the Gentiles.

This expansion of the mother church at Jerusalem into many churches in the Greek cities posed several crucial problems. The Church as a whole had started its life as apparently one more Jewish sect. Its loyalty to one whom it claimed to be both God and man had outraged the Jewish authorities, both in Jerusalem and in the Jewish congregations in the Greek cities. But the new sect, whose adherents were called Christians for the first time at Antioch, thought of Christ and his teachings as the fulfillment of God's covenant with the people he had chosen out to do his will. On the other hand, the Christians not only continued to convert Jews; they accepted Gentiles too. And although they continued to regard the holy scripture of the Jews as theirs, Saul, known to Gentiles by his Roman name, Paul, did not require his Gentile converts to accept circumcision or to follow certain dietary prescriptions of the Law of Moses, even though he did not discourage his Jewish converts from continuing to follow them. That is, if Paul was right, a Gentile could become a Christian without becoming a Jew also. It followed that Jews who had not become Christians could no longer look on Christians as merely misled Jews, or on the Church as merely a Jewish sect. Moreover, if the Christians claimed that Jesus was not only the Messiah but actually the Son of God, then the Jewish authorities could look on Christianity as another Hellenistic myth: Alexander the Great and Caesar Augustus were merely two men in a long line of Gentile heroes who claimed to be sons of a god. But there was only one real God, Yahweh, and although all men were metaphorically his children, not Jesus nor Augustus nor any other man could be divine.

On the other hand, to most Gentiles, the Church looked very Jewish indeed, since, like the Jews, the Christians believed there was only one real God; the other gods were idols or perhaps evil spirits. And while most educated men in Cosmopolis had lost faith in their pantheon, and some of them even leaned toward monotheism, the majority of them looked on temples and sacrifices and the traditional myths about gods as a valuable cement for society and as an aid to law and order. To such a society the denial of all gods but one, whether by the Jew or the Christian, appeared subversive.

The young and growing Church was therefore persecuted by both Jew and Gentile. The tensions between Roman power, the Sanhedrin of Jerusalem, and the Church of Jesus Christ were perhaps more clearly manifest in the apostolate of Paul than in any other man. Teaching and healing, baptizing and organizing, flogged, stoned, imprisoned, shipwrecked, he founded Christian churches in Asia Minor, Macedonia, and Greece, corresponded with them, and revisited them. He spoke as a Jew to Jews, as a man of Greek education to Greeks, as a free-born Roman citizen to officials of the Empire. To the Jews he converted, he taught that the incarnation of God's Son on earth had brought God's people a new covenant with Abraham. As for Jerusalem, that Holy City which so many Jews longed to free from the heavy yoke of Rome, Jerusalem was no eternal city any more than Rome was: "we have an everlasting city, but not here; our goal is the city that is one day to be."[503]

When Paul preached to the Greek-speaking Gentile world, of course he could not appeal to the long Messianic tradition of his fellow Jews or to their centuries-old dialogue with the one true God. On the other hand, he did not need to argue whether the Law of Moses had been superseded by Christ's birth, death, and resurrection. But what of the gods of Hellas? When he and Barnabas preached Christ's word in Asia Minor, they found the old gods had not wholly died. Thus, at Lystra, Paul healed a lame man:

> The multitudes, seeing what Paul had done, cried out in the Lycaonian dialect, It is the gods, who have come down to us in human shape. They called Barnabas Jupiter, and Paul Mercury, because he was the chief speaker; and the priest of Jupiter, Defender of the City, brought out bulls and wreaths to the gates, eager, like the multitude, to do sacrifice.
>
> The apostles tore their garments when they heard of it; and both Barnabas and Paul ran out among the multitude, crying aloud: Sirs, why are you doing all this? We too are mortal men like yourselves; the whole burden of our preaching is that you must turn away from follies like this to the worship of the living God, who made sky and earth and sea and all that is in them.[504]

Yet it was not possible to lead men to Christ merely by denouncing whatever groping religious experience they had already been given. Least of all in Athens, the path to heaven. Athens, her wealth and power sorely shriveled, her income dependent partly on tourists, remained nevertheless the intellectual center of civilization.

And while Paul was waiting . . . in Athens, his heart was moved within him to find the city so much given over to idolatry, and he reasoned, not only in the synagogue with Jews and worshippers of the true God, but in the market-place, with all he met. He encountered philosophers, Stoics and Epicureans, some of whom asked, What can his drift be, this babbler? while others said, He would appear to be proclaiming strange gods; because he had preached to them about Jesus and Resurrection. So they took him by the sleeve and led him up to the Areopagus; May we ask, they said, what this new teaching is thou art delivering? Thou dost introduce terms which are strange to our ears; pray let us know what may be the meaning of it. (No townsman of Athens, or stranger visiting it, has time for anything else than saying something new, or hearing it said.)

So Paul stood up in full view of the Areopagus, and said, Men of Athens, wherever I look I find you scrupulously religious. Why, in examining your monuments as I passed by them, I found among others an altar which bore the inscription, To the unknown God. And it is this unknown object of your devotion that I am revealing to you. The God who made the world and all that is in it, that God who is Lord of heaven and earth, does not dwell in temples that our hands have made; no human handicraft can do him service, as if he stood in need of anything, he, who gives to all of us life and breath and all we have. It is he who has made, of one single stock, all the nations that were to dwell over the whole face of the earth.[505]

The man whom God has appointed to judge all nations everywhere,

he has accredited to all of us, by raising him up from the dead.

When resurrection from the dead was mentioned, some mocked, while others said, We must hear more from thee about this.[506]

From the hill of the war-god Ares where Paul preached love and peace, he could gaze a short distance across to the Acropolis, where stood the Parthenon. But if Paul preached the resurrected Christ and eternal life in this cradle of Graeco-Roman civilization, it was inevitable that he should preach it in Rome, which had organized that civilization and imposed peace on it with the sword. Arrested in Palestine at the urging of the Sanhedrin, Paul demanded of Festus, the Roman governor, the right to appeal to Caesar. He was therefore taken in chains to Rome, where there was already a Christian community.

What did Rome look like to the early Christians? The answer to that question was given in the Apocalypse, or Book of Revelations. This book, which became a part of the Church's holy scriptures, was written on the island of Patmos, according to tradition by the same John who wrote the fourth and latest account.[507] John relates that on Patmos he fell into a trance and heard a voice. In his apocalyptic vision Rome became "the great harlot, that sits by the meeting-place of many rivers."[508] An angel told him that

> These waters in thy vision, at whose meeting the harlot sits enthroned, are all her peoples, nations, and languages.[509]

The harlot herself was "that great city that bears rule over the rulers of the earth."[510]

> There was a title written over her forehead, The mystic Babylon, great mother-city of all harlots, and all that is abominable on earth.[511]

Another angel cried aloud,

> Babylon, great Babylon is fallen . . . The whole world has drunk the maddening wine of her fornication; the kings of the earth have lived in dalliance with her, and its merchants have grown rich through her reckless pleasures.[512]

These kings of the earth would one day stand at a distance for fear of this modern Babylon's punishment and cry out,

> Alas, Babylon the great, alas, Babylon the strong, in one brief hour judgement has come upon thee! And all the merchants of the world will weep and mourn over her; who will buy their merchandise now? Their cargoes of gold and silver, of precious stone and pearl, of lawn and purple, of silk and scarlet; all the citrus wood, the work in ivory and precious stone and brass and iron and marble; cinnamon and balm, perfume and myrrh and incense, wine and oil and wheat and fine flour, cattle and sheep and horses and chariots, and men's bodies, and men's souls. It is gone from thee, the harvest thy soul longed for; all that gaiety and glory is lost to thee, and shall never be seen any more. The merchants that grew rich from such traffic will stand at a distance from her, for fear of sharing her punishment, weeping and mourning; Alas, they will say, alas for the great city, that went clad in lawn and purple and scarlet, all hung about with gold and jewels and pearls; in one brief hour all that wealth has vanished. The sea-captains, too, and all that sail between ports, the mariners and all who make their living from the sea, stood at a distance, crying out, as they saw the smoke rise where she was

257

burning, What city can compare with this great city? They poured dust on their heads, and cried aloud, weeping and mourning, Alas, alas for the great city, whose magnificence brought wealth to all that had ships at sea; in one brief hour she is laid waste.[513]

As for Jerusalem, by rejecting Jesus Christ she entered the vast net of lies and money-making which this modern Babylon had spread over the world from the Atlantic to Parthia, from the Rhine and the Danube to the Sahara. Jerusalem was therefore

an enslaved city, whose children are slaves. Whereas our mother is the heavenly Jersusalem, a city of freedom.[514]

The Christian Ecclesia, this heavenly Jerusalem, this city of freedom, was a new polis, whose citizens were also citizens of many a Greek polis. Where these Greek cities looked wistfully backward to the great days of Hellenic culture and restlessly out toward bodily pleasure and power over others, the citizens of the Christian polis looked exultantly forward to eternal life, and peacefully inward for guidance by the Holy Spirit to do God's will now, in time, wherever their bodies held them. But since bodily pleasure seemed to Paul, as it had seemed to Socrates, a snare to the soul, Paul constantly warned against it. Power over others, backed up by force and propaganda, could impose the Pax Romana with its law and order, its courts and police, its strong rich and weak poor, its masters and its slaves. To the Christian polis, Paul and his fellow apostles preached another kind of peace, based on love, nonviolence, avoidance of litigation, property held in common, and Christ's warning that no man can serve both God and money. Paul was not talking about money as a means of facilitating exchange but about money-getting as the principle of life. No wonder a later tradition ascribed to Paul a letter to the church in Jerusalem declaring that "The love of money should not dwell in your thoughts.[515] He wrote the Thessalonian church that

None of you is to be exorbitant, and take advantage of his brother, in his business dealings. For all such wrong-doing God exacts punishment; we have told you so already, in solemn warning.[516]

To the Christians of Ephesus he wrote

This you must know well enough, that nobody can claim a share in Christ's kingdom, God's kingdom, if he . . . has that love of money which makes a man an idolater.[517]

And to the faithful in Colossae he likewise denounced "that love of money which is idolatry."[518] To his fellow missionary Timothy he declared:

> The love of money is the root of all evil things, and there are those who have wandered away from the faith by making it their ambition, involving themselves in a world of sorrows.[519]

These judgments were not of course new. Paul the Jew had behind him not only the teaching of Christ but a long tradition of Hebrew prophets. Paul, the man of Greek culture, could appeal to Greek philosophy, certainly from Socrates on. Paul, who was born a Roman citizen, could have been under no illusions about the love of money or its role in the Roman Empire.

Given this vast gulf between the purposes of Cosmopolis and the purpose of the Christian polis, Christ had commanded his disciples to be in the world but not of it. Even while Paul and the other apostles schooled the Christian community not to accept the goals Cosmopolis aimed at or to love the things it loved, they nevertheless instructed Christians to obey constituted authority. Like Socrates of Athens, Jesus of Nazareth had refused to meet the violence and deceit of government with either violence or deceit, and Jesus' penalty also had been death. Paul advised Titus, who was preaching the gospel of Christ in Crete, to remind his listeners "that they have a duty of submissive loyalty to governments and to those in authority.[520] To Timothy he wrote:

> This first of all, I ask; that petition, prayer, entreaty and thanksgiving should be offered for all mankind, especially for kings and others in high station, so that we can live a calm and tranquil life, as dutifully and decently as we may.[521]

Similarly, though he warned the Christians of Thessalonica against sharp business practice, he was far from disapproving of honest work for daily bread: "The charge we gave you on our visit was that the man who refuses to work must be left to starve."[522] He did not want Christ's followers to accept the kind of labor or the kind of care that Virgil had allotted to the founder of Rome, since clearly this labor and this care show a distrust in God. But trust in God did not exempt a man from earning his bread. Again to Titus Paul wrote:

> It is well said, and I would have thee dwell on it, that those who have learned to trust in God should be at pains to find honourable employment.[523]

The freedom that the heavenly Jerusalem offered was a deeper freedom, Paul held, than the freedom the legal slave was denied. And it redefined the master-slave relation. This view Paul expounded to the church in Ephesus:

> You who are slaves, give your human masters the obedience you owe to Christ, in anxious fear, singlemindedly; not with that show of service which tries to win human favour, but in the character of Christ's slaves, who do what is God's will with all their heart. Yours must be a slavery of love, not to men, but to the Lord; you know well that each of us, slave or free, will be repaid by the Lord for every task well done. And you who are masters, deal with them accordingly; there is no need to threaten them; you know well enough that you and they have a Master in heaven, who makes no distinction between man and man.[524]

Although Paul taught obedience to law wherever such obedience did not conflict with obedience to Christ, he wanted disagreements between Christians settled, not by law courts backed by force, but by the loving adjudication of the saints, a term that then covered all those who followed Christ. Hence the admonitory question he put to the church in Corinth:

> Are you prepared to go to law before a profane court, when one of you has a quarrel with another, instead of bringing it before the saints?[525]

The stance of Paul, and of the Christian polis in general, presented the Roman Imperial administration and even Hellenistic civilization with a puzzling problem. For the Jews the problem the Christians posed was simpler. Most Jews still rejected the claim of the early Church that Christ came to fulfill, not to abolish, Jewish religious law, and the preaching of Paul especially seemed to justify that rejection. The Jews' real charge against the Christian remained the charge of blasphemy. Rome, acting through her procurator for Judaea, merely chose the easiest way to preserve law and order. Pilate's question, What is truth? expressed not only the Romans' indifference to Jewish squabbles over theological points; it expressed also the self-satisfaction of Hellenistic civilization, or at least of the economic beneficiaries of that civilization. It expressed its knowledge-ability, its disengagement, its dilettantism, its skepticism. Christian congregations did spread rapidly from city to city, but these congregations added up to but a small minority of the total population. Moreover, they attracted especially the poor, the afflicted, the culturally disinherited, in short, persons who felt alienated from the society about them. What was puzzling about the Christians was precisely their Socratic combination of humility and gentleness and courtesy on the one hand, and, on the other, the willingness to die for the truth.

For, like Christ himself, the apostles spoke often of truth. Christ had promised a truth that would set men free, and had promised that his Father would send his Holy Spirit to teach that truth to those who believed in Christ as the Son of God and in his teaching. John reminded those who had never seen Christ that "we have the Spirit's witness that Christ is the truth."[526] Again, John quoted Christ as saying:

> If you have any love for me, you must keep the commandments which I give you; and then I will ask the Father, and he will give you another to befriend you, one who is to dwell continually with you for ever. It is the truth-giving Spirit, for whom the world can find no room, because it cannot see him, cannot recognize him. But you are to recognize him; he will be continually at your side, nay, he will be in you.[527]

Not only love, but this truth, would bind the Christian to his God; not only love, but truth, would bind Christian to Christian. As Paul wrote to the Christians in Ephesus,

> Away with falsehood, then; let everyone speak out the truth to his neighbour; membership of the body binds us to one another.[528]

Not only did John call Christ the light of men which overcomes the darkness around it. To a civilization that depended heavily on half-truths to make its law and order possible, John wrote of Christ's teaching:

> What, then, is this message we have heard from him, and are passing on to you? That God is light, and no darkness can find any place in him; if we claim fellowship with him, when all the while we live and move in darkness, it is a lie; our whole life is an untruth.[529]

Paul wrote the church in Jerusalem,

> Each day, while the word To-day has still a meaning, strengthen your own resolution, to make sure that none of you grows hardened; sin has such power to cheat us. We have been given a share in Christ, but only on condition that we keep unshaken to the end the principle by which we are grounded in him. That is the meaning of the words, If you hear his voice speaking to you this day, do not harden your hearts . . .[530]

Hellenistic civilization felt a certain reverence for cleverness, as the traditional Roman showed reverence for legally constituted authority. But Paul's injunction to the Corinthian church embodied the intellectual humility of Socrates:

> If any of you thinks he is wise, after the fashion of his fellow-men, he must turn himself into a fool, so as to be truly wise.[531]

It was not Virgil who had exhorted the Romans to spare the vanquished and break in battle the proud but Socrates, whom Peter's admonition to various churches in Asia Minor echoed:

> Deference to one another is the livery you must all wear; God thwarts the proud, and keeps his grace for the humble.[532]

For in his own way Socrates had understood that when the son of God spoke God's will to men, it took great humility to listen with the whole soul; it took a certain deference to read the dark, oracular sayings of Delphi; it took practice to acquire that deference; and daily converse with other men gave Socrates the chance to practice such deference. It is true that the god whose will was sought was then called Zeus, and the name of his son, who spoke God's will, was Apollo. But Socrates nevertheless had some of the reasons Peter had for wearing deference as a livery. He wanted truth; he had observed that truth is a hard thing for the proud to find; he had experienced in humility a kind of divine aid, which the Christian would later call divine grace. Of all the philosophers of the great age of Athens, the one whom the Greek world remembered most vividly as a person was the one who died for truth, Socrates. Perhaps the reason Socrates remained a vivid memory was that he not only spoke, but acted, truth. His disciple Phaedo implied this when, reporting his master's execution in prison, he declared:

> Such was the end, Echecrates, of our friend, who was, as we may say, of all those of his time whom we have known, the best and wisest and most righteous man.[533]

Centuries after Phaedo's eyewitness account of the execution of Socrates and during the years when the Christian Ecclesia was establishing a network of little communities, there were still alive eyewitnesses to another execution, to the death of another wise and righteous man. They said this man had risen again from the tomb, had broken bread and had drunk wine with them again, and had ascended into heaven. Eyewitnesses, however, could not testify in all places at once and would in any case die off. Inevitably a demand arose for written testimony, firsthand or nearly firsthand. A number of Christ's sayings had been collected, that men might learn the Gospel, or Glad News. Of several gospels, compiled in the decades that followed Christ's death, the Church eventually chose four as holy writ. These were efforts to convey simply and briefly, in the Greek language, what Christ was, what things he did or said that best told what he was, and what he wanted men to know and do. That the latest gospel, John's, revealed more than the earliest, Mark's, would have been expected by the apostles, since they assumed that the Holy Spirit would steadily open their understanding to what had been at first only implicit. The apostles showed neither fear nor dislike of mystery; the central fact of the incarnation of God as man was itself a divine mystery, not deducible from human knowledge. Nor did they assume that God's most overwhelming intervention in human affairs since the creation of the world could be adequately explained by its historical causes in time.

But this intervention was apparently having daily effects, and Luke's Acts of the Apostles was in some measure a history of the first years of the Church of Christ, a church ordered by Christ to continue his work until his second and final coming. The writings the Church collected for the faithful also included letters, or Epistles, which Paul and other apostles had written either to young growing churches or to one another. To these writings were added the Book of Revelations, with its dark prophecies of the fall of Eternal Rome and the joyful vision of the New Jerusalem, the truly Eternal City. Thus was the Greek New Testament born, and from it passages were read aloud at meetings of Christian congregations. The Old Testament, the Greek version of the Hebrew scriptures habitually read and expounded in Jewish synagogues, was read and expounded in the Christian churches too. In addition, the churches held feasts of love, corporate meals. And finally a liturgy, or service to God, grew up. This liturgy was in Greek, whether at Corinth or in Rome, whether in the other Greek-speaking cities of the East or in the cities of the Latin West.

The central sacrament of the liturgy was the Eucharist, which memorialized the last supper Christ ate with his disciples on the eve of his crucifixion. In the Eucharist, as at the last supper, Christians ate the blessed bread, the substance of life, that he had called his body; they drank the blessed wine, the passion of faith and love, that he had called his blood.

This was not the first time in man's long history that he had eaten his god's body and drunk his blood in order to incorporate him in his life and to obtain some of his divine power. But if the early Christians knew this, it would not have implied to them that the Eucharist was merely an ancient pagan custom borrowed by Christianity to widen its appeal. What they did was done in history; yet in their view it could not be caused by history, but only by God. Their lives were not pointed toward history, as the life of Aeneas was, or for that matter the life of Augustus; their lives were pointed toward an Eternal City, which transcended time and history, even though Christians had to act in time and history.

Since the Church had work to do in the world, growth inevitably brought organization, and organization brought officials. There were elders, or *presbyteroi*,[534] who assumed priestly functions. There were priests who were also overseers, *episcopoi*, or bishops. There were *diakonoi*, or deacons, who were elected by the whole congregation to handle alms for the poor and common meals for the faithful. In the early days the distinction between priest and bishop was vague, but before many decades the bishops alone were overseeing the churches, as the apostles who founded the earliest churches had done. The bishops in the larger cities like Alexandria, Antioch, Carthage, and Rome acquired considerable influence. Peter, who always exercised a kind of leadership in Jerusalem, later visited various churches and finally reached Rome. He was martyred there in 64, and later tradition declared that he was Rome's first bishop. Somewhat slowly, by fits and starts, the bishops of other cities recognized a kind of primacy in that bishopric which was situated in the capital of empire. Ecclesiastical organization, like Christian theology, evolved in those early decades after the crucifixion as the implications of Christ's teachings slowly unfolded. For the Church, this unfolding was only in part the adjustment to historic conditions; it was, more importantly, the work of the Holy Spirit, sent to continue Christ's mission of saving all men everywhere from ignorance and fear, and from sin, which alone brought death to the spirit.

In the early years following Christ's death, the widespread belief that he would shortly return a second time to judge who should enter his Kingdom of Heaven gave a special urgency to the words of his apostles. The race that men were invited to run seemed mercifully short; the prize seemed near. Even before Christ's death his disciples had misunderstood: "they supposed that the kingdom of God was to appear immediately."[535]

Years after the crucifixion, Peter wrote to a group of churches in Asia Minor: "The end of all things is close at hand."[536] James urged his readers to wait patiently and take courage but immediately added that "the Lord's coming is close at hand."[537] "My sons," John wrote, "this is the last age of time."[538] But Peter's second epistle to the churches implicitly warned the impatient of the confusions which afflict the human mind when the eternal bursts in on time and history; on notions like present, past, and future; and on man's anxious attention to calendars. Mockers, wrote Peter, would inevitably ask,

> What has become of the promise that he would appear? . . . But one thing, beloved, you must keep in mind, that with the Lord a day counts as a thousand years, and a thousand years count as a day. The Lord is not being dilatory over his promise, as some think; he is only giving you more time, because his will is that all of you should attain repentance, not that some should be lost.[539]

The feverish anticipation of those early years was bound to pass; one by one, the eyewitnesses to Christ's earthly life disappeared; but the Christian Church continued to grow. Why? From the Church's point of view, the answer was simple: the Holy Spirit inspired the Church, unsealed the eyes and unstopped the ears of those to whom the Church preached, and softened their hearts that they might turn and make the great inward leap from trust in Rome and its Emperor to trust in Jesus Christ.

Seen from outside the Christian faith, the Church greatly attracted those persons who found money and influence beyond their reach. The Church even appealed to some who had got hold of the money and influence, had bought power and pride and pleasure, and yet had somehow remained unfulfilled, imprisoned in themselves, anxious, bored, lonely, unloving, and unloved. Before their eyes was a group of men and women who loved a man, or god, dead but risen, with their whole hearts, a group of men and women who also had learned through him to love each other. Indeed, they loved each other so much that they had pooled their private property. This love they offered others freely and joyfully. The god, or man, or both, of whom they constantly spoke or wrote, had apparently loved in this way and had said to his followers:

> The mark by which all men will know you for my disciples will be the love you bear one another.[540]

To many outside observers the love which the Christians gave to Jesus

Christ and to each other seemed also to bring them a fearlessness and freedom which the tired and disillusioned Roman world had either lost or perhaps had never known. It gave them access to the hearts of other men, who suddenly found themselves confronted by deep conviction and a new meaning for human existence. Many pagans therefore chose baptism and citizenship in a new polis, a city whose citizens conspired to mount no armed rebellion against Cosmopolis and who loyally and even zealously obeyed its laws whenever they could do so without betraying the City of God. When conflict with Cosmopolis occurred, many of them joyfully accepted punishment. In a civilization that was culturally looking back to a glorious Hellenic past, these Christians looked to the future. Yet, whereas those who ruled Cosmopolis thought of the future with the anxiety of Aeneas, these Christians, who accepted persecution, seemed mysteriously free of anxiety. In a society that feared and despised the howl of the needy, these men loved the poor and shared their property with them. They thereby, in some sense, became citizens of the Kingdom of Heaven. As Christ himself reportedly said,

> there will be no saying, See, it is here, or See, it is there; the kingdom of God is here, within you.[541]

Although Christian churches did spring up in many cities of the Greek-speaking provinces of the Empire, only a few cities in the Latin-speaking provinces contained churches. The Church had incorporated into its holy writ the books it had inherited from the Jews, and many pagans doubtless drew no distinction between Jews and Christians; however, the vast majority of Jews rejected Christianity. Jewish treatment of Christians left the Christians looking on the Jews as a people who had indeed been chosen by God but who had rejected his Son. And Christians considered this rejection especially heinous because Christ had preached especially to his fellow Jews. He had explicitly recognized their right to hear, first among all peoples, God's greatest revelation in his long dialogue with his chosen people.

As for the Gentile peoples of the Empire, although the Church did its best to spread the joyful news, many ears inevitably proved deaf. The ambiguity that surrounds all religious experience and had led Homer's gods to appear to men so often in disguise surrounded the written accounts of Christ's life and crucifixion. A young Jew of the laboring class, born in Galilee, a district in Palestine which the Jews of Judaea commonly despised, had wandered through Palestine and nearby areas, preaching rhapsodically in the style affected by Hebrew prophets on what men should do to enter what he called the Kingdom of Heaven. A dozen disciples, like himself simple folk of humble birth, had followed him about. It was claimed that he had healed the sick, or persons who thought they were sick; but in the Asian provinces of the Empire a magician was no new phenomenon. Sometimes large crowds had followed him; but that might be because Palestine longed for freedom from Rome and clung to an ancient Hebrew tradition that a Messiah would come and restore the Kingdom of David. Jesus of Nazareth had claimed to be that Messiah. When Jewish religious authorities had heard that he posed as the son of Yahweh and denounced him to the Roman procurator as a rebel against Rome, his following had melted fast enough. When he was sentenced to die disgracefully by crucifixion, his public miracles had stopped fast enough. The Jews who had opposed him had explained his so-called resurrection: his followers had stolen the body. As to his later appearances and final ascension into heaven, there had been no witnesses except his personal disciples, who either from the hysteria of grief and disappointment or from motives of obvious self-interest would have understandably spread such rumors. There was also a suggestion of hysteria in Paul's account of his vision on the road to Damascus; and even the Christians had admitted that, when the apostles suddenly spoke in many tongues, some of the bystanders judged them to be drunk. Had not Jesus himself been a winebibber and a glutton as well as a bastard[542] with a taste for low company? In fine, there was nothing in the gospels which could not be easily explained away.

As for those who preached the gospel, their exhortations usually caused no public disorder. When they did, a flogging or a jail sentence here and there seemed able to assert the authority of law. In general, Christians behaved well, at least in public. Unfortunately, what they said publicly sometimes angered a local congregation of Jews or stirred the wrath of some special group like the silversmiths of Ephesus. These latter made a living by selling souvenirs to the many who visited Diana's famous temple there, and naturally they objected to any religion that might ruin their business. Since early missionaries like Paul preached primarily in synagogues, the Roman authorities drew no sharp distinction between Christian and Jew. This failure to distinguish characterized the reigns of Augustus' first three successors, Tiberius, Caligula, and Claudius. But during the reign of his fourth successor, Nero, between 54 and 68, the growing Christian community was beginning to arouse general suspicion and dislike among the populace. Paul wrote from Rome to the church at Philippi a letter that ended with greetings from the Christians in Rome, including "those who belong to the Emperor's household."[543] So not all Christians were underdogs. Were Christians deliberately infiltrating the centers of power?

It was becoming clear also that Christians were not in fact Jews; but was the Church, like the Synagogue, in some deep if obscure sense a foreign body in Cosmopolis? Peter, writing from Rome to the churches in Asia Minor, closed a letter with greetings from "The church here in Babylon,"[544] an accepted Christian term for the harlot city on the Tiber. That epithet, Babylon, expressed a spiritual gap. For this reason, should any great public calamity occur, the Church might be exposed to popular demands for a scapegoat. The same question of final loyalty had often exposed the Synagogue, both in Rome and in other cities. When, on July 19 of the year 64, the City of Rome suffered a terrible disaster, it was the Christians' turn and not the Jews'. Writing more than half a century later, the Roman historian Tacitus recorded what happened. Fire broke out in the Circus Maximus, got out of control, raged for six days, and destroyed most of Rome. Temporarily checked by a demolition of buildings, it broke out again and during three more days of horror burned much of what still stood. No fire like it had swept Rome since, 454 years earlier, the Gauls had captured and burned Rome. Following the Gallic fire, the Romans had rebuilt their city in the most haphazard fashion, so that in Nero's day Greek visitors from some of the great Hellenistic cities laid out by city planners were shocked by the disheveled appearance of the mistress of the world. After the fire, Nero, who had a passion for Greek culture, proceeded to do a little city planning of his own. He laid out broader streets, restricted the height of the buildings, paid bounties to builders who used volcanic stone instead of wood, forbade joining neighboring buildings by a partition wall, and provided a more efficient fire service. Then prayers, rituals, and vigils were offered to the gods.

The rumor grew, however, that Nero, who fancied himself as a gifted artist in many fields and frequently appeared in public concerts, had started the fire in order to rebuild Rome more to his own Hellenic taste; that during the fire arsonists had been seen at work spreading it and shouting that "they had their authority";[545] and that Nero himself had mounted the stage in his private theater, or climbed a tower that Virgil's patron Maecenas had built on his own grounds, or gone to his palace roof, and had there sung a poem he had written on the burning of Troy. Tacitus wrote:

> Therefore, to scotch the rumour, Nero substituted as culprits, and punished with the utmost refinements of cruelty, a class of men, loathed for their vices, whom the crowd styled Christians. Christus, the founder of the name, had undergone the death penalty in the reign of Tiberius, by sentence of the procurator Pontius Pilatus, and the pernicious superstition was checked for a moment, only to break out once more, not merely in Judaea, the home of the disease, but in the capital itself, where all things horrible or shameful in the world collect and find a vogue. First, then, the confessed members of the sect were arrested; next, on their disclosures, vast numbers were convicted, not so much on the count of arson as for hatred of the human race. And derision accompanied their end: they were covered with wild beasts' skins and torn to death by dogs; or they were fastened on crosses, and, when daylight failed, were burned to serve as lamps by night. Nero had offered his Gardens for the spectacle, and gave an exhibition in his Circus, mixing with the crowd in the habit of a charioteer, or mounted on his car. Hence, in spite of a guilt which had earned the most exemplary punishment, there arose a sentiment of pity, due to the impression that they were being sacrificed not for the welfare of the state but to the ferocity of a single man.[546]

These fiery crosses in 64 marked the first mass execution of Christians. Tacitus does not record whether the accused were given the option of acquittal by abjuring Christ. According to early Church tradition, among those crucified was Peter. According to a much less trustworthy tradition, Paul died too, but was beheaded. The persecution at Rome may well have had the effect that most persecutions have: that of promoting the cause of the persecuted. The Christian Ecclesia claimed to open a path to heaven beside which that other path to heaven, Athens, was now but a fading memory. This Christian polis was growing in the womb of the Cosmopolis that Rome and Augustus had triumphantly organized, although to Tacitus the Church looked less like an embryo than a cancer. In a sense he was right. Despite his belief that the victims were guilty of hating the human race as well as of other vices, even he admitted that they aroused pity in the spectators. In Athens this pity would have been expected. In the following century, long after gladiatorial butchery spread from Rome to provinces more deeply civilized than Rome, Athens debated whether to institute such spectacles. An orator dissuaded the Athenians from doing so. If they did, he cried, they should first pull down an altar they had erected to Pity.[547] But for more than three centuries the Romans had adored gladiatorial combats; and since Augustus' day the number of victims had steadily increased. Nero had every reason to expect the Roman crowd to applaud the dogs who tore the living flesh, to deride the Christians whose flaming, crucified bodies lighted a Roman holiday. The pity the crowd felt, instead of derision, was getting dangerously close to love. And if the love which the Christians showed for each other and showed, too, for the sick, the imprisoned, the enslaved, the oppressed, whether Christian or not, should ever elicit a response, would this mutual love provide new life for Cosmopolis, or would the new wine prove too heady for the old wineskin?

6

THE EARTHLY PARADISE

THE ROMAN REPUBLIC'S successive conquests in the Eastern Mediterranean during the second and first centuries opened Pandora's box. Along with the military loot, the cash indemnities, the Greek paintings and statues, the taxes which the Equites collected, as well as the usurious interest on loans to half-ruined provinces, there flocked to Rome more Greek philosophers to spread dangerous thoughts, more Greek actors to offer plays that Greeks had written, more astrologers versed in the lore of Babylon, pleasanter vices to weaken Roman energy and will, and new Asian religions to compete with Rome's ancient gods. Out of one tiny country alone had come the Jews, who set up synagogues and formed congregations in city after city throughout the provinces which Rome now ruled, and who mutilated the bodies of their male children[548] at the command of an invisible God, a God of whom no image must be made, and a God whom they seemed to understand "with the mind alone."[549] This God forbade them to worship any of the many other gods worshiped throughout the Mediterranean world. Although both Julius Caesar and Augustus treated their Jewish subjects well, Augustus had been dead for only five years when his successor, Tiberius, a deeply conservative Roman,

> abolished foreign cults, especially the Egyptian and the Jewish rites, compelling all who were addicted to such superstitions to burn their religious vestments and all their paraphernalia. Those of the Jews who were of military age he assigned to provinces of unhealthy climate, ostensibly to serve in the army; the others of that same race or of similar beliefs he banished from the city, on pain of slavery for life if they did not obey.[550]

Tiberius was succeeded in 37 by Caligula. During his reign the large, semi-autonomous Jewish colony in Alexandria was attacked by the Greek population. Synagogues were razed or desecrated, houses pillaged, Jews tormented and lynched. In desperation the Jews sent an embassy to Rome, under the leadership of Philo, a Jewish writer so far from being anti-Gentile that he attempted to reconcile Jewish and Hellenic religious traditions. Meanwhile, Caligula had ordered Petronius, legate of Syria, to have a large gilded statue of Zeus, or Jupiter, placed in the Temple at Jerusalem, under the escort of two legions, to prevent any possible insurrection when it should be installed. Petronius reluctantly marched his legions toward Jerusalem. When they arrived at the Phoenician city of Acre, a little short of Palestine's northern border, a "multitude of Jews suddenly descended like a cloud and covered the whole of Phoenicia,"[551] men, women, and children, weeping. They pointed out that they were unarmed. They offered all their property if the Temple were spared desecration. They offered their lives. They asked for time in order to send an embassy to the Emperor. Petronius and his staff were moved to pity. He wrote Caligula diplomatically on behalf of the Jews.

Caligula thereupon

> appropriated the synagogues in every city, starting with those in Alexandria, and filled them with images of himself. . . . Then he proceeded to adapt and alter the Temple in the Holy City . . . into a shrine of his own, to be called that of "Gaius, the New Zeus made Manifest."[552]

He ordered Petronius to have a second colossal statue of himself disguised as Jupiter made for the shrine. When Petronius reached Tiberias, on the Sea of Galilee, he was again met by a multitude of Jews, this time by tens of thousands. They assured him they would not take up arms against the Emperor and they threw themselves down upon their faces, and stretched out their throats, and said they were ready to be slain; and this they did for forty days together, and in the mean time left off the tilling of their ground, and that while the season of the year required them to sow it. Thus they continued firm in their resolution, and proposed to themselves to die willingly, rather than to see the dedication of the statue.[553]

Fortunately for the Jews Caligula was murdered before he could install a statue of himself in the Temple at Jerusalem. His successor Claudius was reported by a biographer to have expelled the Jews from Rome again. But the reason this biographer gives, that they "constantly made disturbances at the instigation of Chrestus,"[554] suggests that, like so many other Romans, he failed to distinguish the non-Christian Jews from those Jews and Gentiles who followed the teachings of Christus, or Christ, whose Latinized name he garbled. An even later writer[555] believed the Jews were so numerous in Rome that Claudius shrank from expelling them and merely ordered them not to hold meetings.

Agrippa, a Jew whom Tiberius had imprisoned but whom Caligula released and made a puppet ruler in northern Palestine, wrote Caligula during the episode of the statues and the Temple, explaining respectfully that Jerusalem was the spiritual

capital not of the single country of Judaea but of most other countries also, because of the colonies which it has sent out from time to time to the neighbouring lands of Egypt, Phoenicia, and Syria (the so-called Coele Syria as well as Syria proper), to the distant countries of Pamphylia, Cilicia, most of Asia as far as Bithynia and the remote corners of Pontus, and in the same way to Europe, to Thessaly, Boeotia, Macedonia, Aetolia, Attica, Argos, Corinth, and most of the best parts of the Peloponnese. It is not only the continents that are full of Jewish colonies. So are the best known of the islands, Euboea, Cyprus, and Crete. I say nothing about the regions beyond the Euphrates. With the exception of a small district, all of them, Babylon and those of the other satrapies which have fertile land around them, have Jewish settlers. So if my native city has a share in your kindness, it will not be a single city but countless others set in every region of the world as well—in Europe, Asia, and Libya, in continents and islands, in coastal and inland regions —which will enjoy the benefits.[556]

The man who thus described the Jewish Diaspora failed to dissuade Caligula from planning to assert his own godhead in the Holy Temple at

Jerusalem. But when in A.D. 41 Caligula's murder prevented the desecration, Agrippa succeeded in having the Emperor Claudius name him King of Judaea, with the policy of restoring calm there and securing loyalty to Rome. In 44 he died, and Claudius annexed his kingdom.

In 66, twelve years after Nero succeeded Claudius, there were rumblings of an approaching revolt in Jerusalem. Agrippa's son, Agrippa II, pointed out to the would-be rebels with how few legions Rome controlled large and populous countries like Gaul, Spain, Britain, Egypt, and the wealthy Province of Africa.[557] He also thought it unlikely that Yahweh would redress the balance:

> The only refuge, then, left to you is divine assistance. But even this is ranged on the side of the Romans, for, without God's aid, so vast an empire could never have been built up. [558]

Agrippa added that

> all the peoples of the earth either have, or dread the thought of having, the Romans for their masters. The peril, moreover, threatens not only us Jews here, but also all who inhabit foreign cities; for there is not a people in the world which does not contain a portion of our race.[559]

But in that year, 66, the Jews nevertheless revolted, and a Roman army under Vespasian besieged Jerusalem.

A Roman biography of Vespasian, written several decades after the Jewish revolt, asserted that

> There had spread over all the Orient an old and established belief, that it was fated at that time for men coming from Judaea to rule the world. This prediction, referring to the emperor of Rome, as afterwards appeared from the event, the people of Judaea took to themselves; accordingly they revolted . . .[560]

This may have been merely a Roman gibe. On the other hand, the Jewish freedom fighters could always construe Yahweh's choice of Israel as his special people to mean that God expected in good time to assign his chosen people to rule all other nations. In 69 Vespasian left for Rome to take over the Imperial throne, a throne which in that one year three men, Galba, Otho, and Vitellius, successively seized by force and briefly occupied. Tacitus, who disliked Jews, wrote that

> Vespasian had almost put an end to the war with the Jews. The siege of Jerusalem, however, remained, a task rendered difficult and arduous

by the character of the mountain-citadel and the obstinate superstition of the Jews rather than by any adequate resources which the besieged possessed to withstand the inevitable hardships of a siege.[561]

Vespasian's elder son, Titus, took over the siege. The Jewish revolt was the signal for attacks on Jewish colonies outside Palestine. Although most of the Roman emperors, like the Hellenistic kings before them, had found the Jews industrious and hence valuable citizens and had protected them, the protection had often been needed. The pagan neighbors of the Jews were offended by Jewish monotheism and Jewish social exclusiveness. In 66 perhaps the worst outbreak of anti-Jewish feeling had occurred at Damascus. Large numbers of Jews were massacred. Josephus, the historian of the Jewish War of 66–70, claimed that the Gentiles of Damascus had to keep their plans for the massacre secret from "their own wives, who, with few exceptions, had all become converts to the Jewish religion."[562] Three years after the war began, Eleazar, the Jewish guerrilla leader, was still fighting desperately to hold a fortress at Mesada, near the Dead Sea, and telling his followers that

> as you know, there is not a city in Syria which has not slain its Jewish inhabitants . . . As for Egypt, we were told that the number of those who there perished in tortures perhaps exceeded sixty thousand.[563]

In Palestine itself many Jews not killed in battle or captured and sold into slavery had starved to death. Josephus, although he was loyal to the Jewish religion, soon recognized the winning side and gave himself up to Vespasian's army in 67, after entering a suicide pact with a handful of besieged Jews, in which he and one other were left by lot to the last. The Jewish nationalists continued to fight heroically for freedom, while Vespasian correctly observed that

> it becomes even Romans to think of safety as well as victory, since they make war not from necessity, but to increase their empire.[564]

In 70, when Titus was besieging Jerusalem, Josephus, who was with the Roman army, made an appeal to the besieged, an appeal that he later reported in his history of the four-year war. In it he repeated the religious argument of Rome's puppet king, Agrippa II, that

> There was, in fact, an established law, as supreme among brutes as among men, "Yield to the stronger" and "The mastery is for those preeminent in arms." That was why their forefathers, men who in soul and

body, aye and in resources to boot, were by far their superiors, had yielded to the Romans—a thing intolerable to them, had they not known that God was on the Roman side.[565]

After Vespasian left for Rome to assume the crown, his son Titus took Jerusalem. Josephus, who later moved to Rome, reported that:

> The total number of prisoners taken throughout the entire war amounted to ninety-seven thousand, and of those who perished during the seige, from first to last, to one million one hundred thousand.[566]

The treasures of the Temple went to swell the Romans' booty, and

> So glutted with plunder were the troops, one and all, that throughout Syria the standard of gold was depreciated to half its former value.[567]

When Titus succeeded his father as Emperor, he allowed his Jewish subjects to practice their religion but only by paying an annual tax of two drachmas a head. His brother and successor, Domitian, levied this head tax rigorously. Among the many victims of the half-mad, murderous Domitian was a consul who was executed for atheism, "a charge on which many others who drifted into Jewish ways were condemned."[568] There was every incentive for a devout Jew to pay his head tax and hope for the best. Atheism was a favorite Roman charge against both Jews and Christians. Pliny the Elder was merely using a cliché when he characterized the Jews as "a race remarkable for their contempt for the divine powers."[569] More than half a century after Pliny's charge was made, the satirist Juvenal wrote that the Jews

> flout the laws of Rome, they learn and practise and revere the Jewish law, and all that Moses handed down in his secret tome, forbidding to point out the way to any not worshipping the same rites, and conducting none but the circumcised to the desired fountain.

The Jews, he held, were not only too unneighborly to give road directions to a Gentile or help him find water; they were lazy, for they "gave up every seventh day to idleness, keeping it apart from all the concerns of life."[570]

Out of the same tiny country, whose natives Tacitus saw as obstinate and supersititious and whose colonies scattered throughout the Empire he considered as hotbeds of antisocial atheism, there came also the first scattered colonies of Christians. Those pagans who could distinguish at all clearly between the two groups which Palestine had let loose on the civilized world might learn that, whereas the Jews had won their independence from Syria with the sword and had thereby saved holy Jerusalem from Antiochus IV and his blasphemous program of hellenization, and whereas they had vainly tried with the sword to save their Holy City from Pompey, and whereas they had taken the sword against Rome once more in the days of Vespasian and Titus, the Christians presented a different problem. They were not a race, not a nation. Although for them, too, Jerusalem was the Holy City, there was no danger that they would take up the sword to defend it. They looked on Jerusalem as holy not because some of them lived there but because the Son of God had died there, a Jew himself, followed by Jews, denounced by Jews, and crucified by Romans. The allegiance of the Christians was not to Jerusalem but to what they called the New Jerusalem, the Kingdom of Heaven.

Rome tolerated almost any religion, provided its god or gods lived in peace with the other gods of the Empire and provided also that its god did not lead its adherents to revolt, as the Jews of Palestine had done, or to conspire against Rome, as the Druids of Gaul were accused of doing. The Christians did not revolt, but they denied the divinity of all the gods of the Imperial pantheon, including deified Emperors. Moreover, the Christians were more militant proselytizers than the Jews. No wonder Domitian persecuted Christians. An Emperor could do this without believing in the gods whom Christians refused to worship. Vespasian, when he lay dying in 79, remarked gaily, "Alas, I think I'm turning into a god."[571] Domitian was made of sterner stuff, at least theologically. He declined to wait for death to turn him into a god, but wished to be known immediately as "Our Lord and our God."[572]

When Domitian's wife, terrified for her life, arranged to have him lose his own instead, the Senate chose one of their senior members, Nerva, to succeed him. Nerva lived two years, long enough to adopt as son, co-regent, and successor to the throne an able general named Trajan, who ruled from 98 to 117. The Roman upper class breathed freely again, while it recalled with horror the insane tyranny of Domitian. But by that time Emperor worship was in full collision with Christianity. When Trajan sent Pliny the Younger to govern the province of Bithynia on the Black Sea coast of Asia Minor, Pliny reported back that the Christians were a problem. He requested instructions.

> In the meanwhile, the method I have observed towards those who have been denounced to me as Christians is this: I interrogated them whether

they were Christians; if they confessed it I repeated the question twice again, adding the threat of capital punishment; if they still persevered, I ordered them to be executed. For whatever the nature of their creed might be, I could at least feel no doubt that contumacy and inflexible obstinacy deserved chastisement. . . .

These accusations spread (as is usually the case) from the mere fact of the matter being investigated and several forms of the mischief came to light. A placard was put up, without any signature, accusing a large number of persons by name. Those who denied they were, or had ever been, Christians, who repeated after me an invocation to the Gods, and offered adoration, with wine and frankincense, to your image, which I had ordered to be brought for that purpose, together with those of the Gods, and who finally cursed Christ—none of which acts, it is said, those who are really Christians can be forced into performing—these I thought it proper to discharge. Others who were named by that informer at first confessed themselves Christians, and then denied it; true, they had been of that persuasion but they had quitted it, some three years, others many years, and a few as much as twenty-five years ago. They all worshipped your statue and the images of the Gods, and cursed Christ.

They affirmed, however, the whole of their guilt, or their error, was, that they were in the habit of meeting on a certain fixed day before it was light, when they sang in alternate verses a hymn to Christ, as to a god, and bound themselves by a solemn oath, not to any wicked deeds, but never to commit any fraud, theft or adultery, never to falsify their word, nor deny a trust when they should be called upon to deliver it up; after which it was their custom to separate, and then reassemble to partake of food—but food of an ordinary and innocent kind. Even this practice, however, they had abandoned after the publication of my edict, by which, according to your orders, I had forbidden political associations. I judged it so much the more necessary to extract the real truth, with the assistance of torture, from two female slaves, who were styled *deaconesses:* but I could discover nothing more than depraved and excessive superstition.

I therefore adjourned the proceedings, and betook myself at once to your counsel. For the matter seemed to me well worth referring to you,—especially considering the numbers endangered. Persons of all ranks and ages, and of both sexes are, and will be, involved in the prosecution. For this contagious superstition is not confined to the cities only, but has spread through the villages and rural districts; it seems possible, however, to check and cure it. 'Tis certain at least that the temples, which had been almost deserted, begin now to be frequented; and the sacred festivals, after a long intermission, are again revived; while there is a general demand for sacrificial animals, which for some time past have met with but few purchasers. From hence it is easy to imagine what multitudes may be reclaimed from this error, if a door be left open to repentance.[573]

Pliny obviously did not believe the popular stories about the orgies of the Christians, of how, for example, they murdered children ritually and drank their blood. But he and other provincial governors were under pressure from persons who did believe such stories and from those eager to turn informer against any belief or association that an informer could claim was subversive of Roman rule. Pontius Pilate had faced the same problem when he was pressed against his will to crucify Christ as a subversive.

When Pliny appealed for guidance, Trajan had already ruled some dozen years. He had achieved excellent relations with the Senate; had conquered the sizable kingdom of Dacia, north of the lower Danube; had extended the province of Africa; and had annexed the kingdom of the Nabataean Arabs, whose rich trading cities beyond Jordan gave Rome direct access to the caravan trade with the Orient. He would a few years later seize Armenia, Mesopotamia, Assyria, Babylonia, and would by then have added more territory to the Roman Empire than any Emperor since Augustus. He would even place his own candidate on the Parthian throne. Agrippa II's warning to the Jews at Jerusalem that without God's aid so vast an empire could never have been built up seemed now more plausible than ever. Augustus' efforts to continue the military monarchy that Julius Caesar had established, while preserving republican forms, and his efforts to furnish the provinces with a less corrupt administration seemed after Trajan's conquests to have given Eternal Rome, already boundless in time, its proper bounds in space. Men could now forget a century of intermittent violence, of Senatorial conspiracy, of conspiracy within the Imperial family, of military insurrection, of provincial revolt against Rome, of ubiquitous professional informers, of executions and tortures by Emperors, of disgraceful orgies in the Imperial court, of aberrations by the Emperor that sometimes reached sheer insanity, of mad tyranny tempered by timely assassination. Freedom under law seemed at last to have been restored. The gratitude of Trajan's subjects, especially of his propertied subjects, did not solve the problem posed by the Christians and Jews, but it did allow Trajan's administration to be large about it; and accordingly, when Trajan answered Pliny's request for orders, he could write:

> The method you have pursued, my dear Pliny, in sifting the cases of those denounced to you as Christians is extremely proper. It is not possible to lay down any general rule which can be applied as the fixed standard in all cases of this nature. No search should be made for these people; when they are denounced and found guilty they must be punished; with the restriction, however, that when the party denies himself to be a Christian, and shall give proof that he is not (that is, by adoring our Gods) he shall be pardoned on the ground of repentance, even though he may have formerly incurred suspicion. Informations without the accuser's name subscribed must not be admitted in evidence against anyone, as it is introducing a very dangerous precedent, and by no means agreeable to the spirit of the age.[574]

The procedure laid down may not have met the issues which Jesus Christ had raised, but at least it evaded them in a decent Roman fashion. It was in the nature of the Empire that many issues had to be evaded if the spirit of the age were to be preserved. An intransigent Oriental superstition must be ignored where possible, met with exemplary reasonableness when necessary, but not actively prosecuted.

Meanwhile, for any man who found the Roman Empire too big to be a polis, too big to feel like a true community, too highly organized to be truly organic, the local polis, a subject city now shorn of its sovereignty, struggled somewhat vainly to provide a more intimate community. Or a man might join a club, where he could periodically break bread with friends and where he could be sure their common fund would pay for a proper funeral when he died. The members of these clubs, known as *collegia*, or colleges, might be founded to serve a guild interest in a common trade or industry. But the college also diminished the loneliness, the sense of helplessness, of humble men lost in Cosmopolis, lost in an *urbs* which had become an *orbis*, in a city which had become a world.[575] The college became a little polis but one to which all political activity was denied, a republic that might indeed be affectionately called a *respublica collegii*,[576] a college commonwealth. Such clubs were narrowly watched by the Imperial government, ostensibly for fear they would conspire politically against Roman rule but also, perhaps, out of some subconscious fear that, in an empire too big and too impersonal to love, the clubs would drain off loyalty that belonged by rights to the Emperor alone. The same suspicion, of course, lay on the local church and the local synagogue.

In the second century there spread another Oriental religion, this one better adapted to Imperial interests than either Synagogue or Church: the Persian worship of Mithra which supplemented Rome's gods and did not deny their existence. Mithraism also offered advantages over the most convivial club. It offered two things that marked the Greek mystery cults and the Egyptian cults of Isis and Sarapis: purification from the burden of guilt that tormented so many men, and the promise of immortality. Mithraism was apparently restricted to men, and spread very widely in the Imperial army. Mithraism drew heavily on Chaldean traditions of the sun-god, but the Persians had infused it with the dualism that Zoroaster had long ago taught, the struggle between Ahuramazda, god of light and good-ness, and Ahriman, god of evil and of darkness, each followed by an army of lesser spirits. Mithraism made little headway among the Greeks of the Empire, but it made substantial headway in the Latin West. The cosmic struggle it revealed mirrored the human struggle between civilization and barbarism. It had therefore served the ancient Persian Empire well and now served Rome's civilizing mission in Western Europe.

Moreover, infiltrated though the Roman Empire was by the religions of Greece, of Egypt, and of western Asia, it nevertheless remained itself an object of worship. The cult of Rome and Augustus continued, regardless of which Emperor wore the reverential title that Octavian had chosen and regardless too of the skepticism the cult might arouse in a Nero or a Vespasian. The chief economic beneficiaries of the Empire were of course the members of the propertied classes in all Rome's many and diverse provinces. But the poor of Rome looked to the Emperor for the employ-ment which he brought them when he financed public works, for the bread which they bought cheap or which was doled out to them free when work was scarce and famine threatened, for the aqueducts that put clean water in the public fountains and the public baths, for the chariot races and the displays of exotic beasts and the exciting, life-and-death struggles of the gladiators that made a man forget the frustrations begotten in the crowded, unsafe tenement in which he lived, frustrations fostered by the emptiness of his political life. The Emperor still spoke by authority of the Senate and People of Rome. But the Senate no longer held more than subordinate powers and the People were a rootless proletariat, whose only power was the latent power of a city mob. In place of the dialogue between members of a Senate that deliberated and decided, in place of the dialogue between candidate and voters at least at election time, there was now a sort of dialogue at the gladiatorial games between a military autocrat, the Emperor, and a mob inflamed by bloodshed. More than once an Emperor tested his popularity at the games. To keep that popularity he sacrificed many lives.

> And when the games stop for the intermission, they announce: "A little throat-cutting in the meantime, so that there may still be something going on!"[577]

The average citizen was likely to be the son or descendant of a freed slave, himself often a Greek with a better education than his Roman master. In fact the first thing a Greek name in Rome was likely to imply was that the man who bore it was either a slave, a former slave, or the descendant of a slave. But slaves were sometimes barbarians captured in war. Consequently, Rome was now a typical Hellenistic metropolis, though with a thinner cultural tradition than Alexandria, a thinner industrial tradition than Antioch. But there was one thing that made Rome unique: she had built a cosmopolis such as no other polis had ever built. In theory this cosmopolis of hers was a federation of cities like herself, an empire made up of city-states and of tribal territories which might yet grow into city-states. The metropolis that had built this federation had made Latin the lingua franca of the Western provinces. But in the provinces east of the Adriatic, except for those in the northwestern and northern Balkans, Greek was still the language of educated men almost everywhere. It held its own in Egypt and in Cyrenaica. True, the language of the Imperial army and administration was everywhere Latin. But even in the Latin West the leading language of philosophy, literature, and science was Greek.

During the first century B.C. and the first century A.D., Greek culture awoke the West and stimulated it to create a literature in Latin. Thereafter, the quality of Latin literature rapidly declined. To a large extent Cosmopolis remained culturally Hellenistic. Rome's contribution was to build a shell around it and protect it during its long decline, protect it especially from the barbarian tribes which threatened it from the northeast. In the first century A.D. the Parthians built a similar shell around a territory next to Rome's; next to Parthia and eastward, the Kushan Empire built a shell; and next to that, the Han Empire of China. From the Atlantic to the Pacific these four great empires built their shells to hold off the nomadic tribesmen and mounted archers of northern Eurasia who hammered at their gates. But the men who spoke Greek or Latin gave little thought to the three foreign empires that shared their peril. Rome claimed, even while using Chinese silks and Indian spices, to rule the whole Orbis Terrarum, all the countries of the globe: her Emperors held a scepter in one hand and in the other hand an orb. Historically, of course, this claim was nonsense; but as a political myth it was justified.[578] The myth embodied both the Hellenic effort to discover universal truths and the effort of Roman jurisprudence to discover laws applicable to all men. True, it was Stoic philosophy that developed this belief in natural law, and Stoic philosophy was of course Greek, not Roman, in origin. But it was Rome, not Greece, that won with the sword the chance to try to apply natural law to Cosmopolis. The doctrine had already been stated by one of the characters in Cicero's dialogue, the *Republic:*

> There is in fact a true law—namely, right reason—which is in accordance with nature, applies to all men, and is unchangeable and eternal. By its commands this law summons men to the performance of their duties; by its prohibitions it restrains them from doing wrong. Its commands and prohibitions always influence good men, but are without effect upon the bad. To invalidate this law by human legislation is never morally right, nor is it permissible ever to restrict its operation, and to annul it wholly is impossible. Neither the senate nor the people can absolve us from our obligation to obey this law, and it requires no Sextus Aelius to expound and interpret it. It will not lay down one rule at Rome and another at Athens, nor will it be one rule today and another tomorrow. But there will be one law, eternal and unchangeable, binding at all times upon all peoples; and there will be as it were, one common master and ruler of men, namely God, who is the author of this law, its interpreter, and its sponsor. The man who will not obey it will abandon his better self, and, in denying the true nature of a man, will thereby suffer the severest of penalties, though he has escaped all the other consequences which men call punishment.[579]

That an eternal city should discover and enforce one law, eternal and unchangeable, binding at all times upon all peoples, was indeed a proud and Roman dream, a Virgilian dream. In practice, Rome paid less attention to the Stoics' natural law than to the minimal adjustments needed to meet local custom and tradition.

The shell that Rome built around the actual area of law consisted primarily of a highly professional army and its fortifications. During the two centuries that followed the reorganization by Augustus, this army contained from 300,000 to 350,000 men, guarding a population of between 70,000,000 and 100,000,000.[580] Except for Augustus, Claudius, and Trajan, few Roman Emperors made large-scale conquests; the task of the army was to defend the Empire against aggression. Even Augustus' conquest of the northern Balkans and attempted conquest of Germany from the Rhine to the Elbe was defensive in concept: he wanted an Elbe-Danube frontier because it would be shorter and cheaper to defend than the frontier he already had.

During the early Empire the soldier's pay was modest, but he could look forward to some provision at retirement, usually in the form of land in a veterans' colony. If he lacked Roman citizenship, he could expect to receive it on retirement. The Praetorian Guard was long recruited from Italy, but it proved quite impracticable to follow Augustus' dream of recruiting the legions from Roman citizens only. Although morale undoubtedly fell short of the desperate courage of the Roman soldiers who defended the soil of Italy against the genius of Hannibal, the Imperial army of three centuries later partially compensated for this lack by professional skill and improved weapons.

In addition to fighting when the Empire was threatened, Roman soldiers served as a labor force to construct permanent camps, public buildings such as temples, roads, aqueducts, irrigation works, harbors, and canals. Soldiers even manufactured brick for sale to the public. The permanent camps often grew into garrison towns, as merchants, artisans, and women settled just outside the camp proper. Such places might grow into cities or towns like Cologne, Xanten, Nimwegen on or just back of the Rhine; York, in Britain; Lambaesis, now Lambèse, just north of the Aurès range in eastern Algeria. Thus, the hard shell around Cosmopolis gradually thickened into another kind of culture, into a semimilitarized society which spread the Latin tongue and Latin ways along the extreme marches of empire. But it was not Cicero's Latin that the shell of empire spoke; it was soldier's Latin, peppered with soldier's slang. Cicero called his head a *caput*; his mouth an *os*; his horse, an *equus*; and his house, a *domus*. But the soldier in Gaul called his head a *testa*, or box; his mouth, a *bucca*, which really meant a cheek; his horse, his *caballus*; and a house, a *casa*, or hut.[581] The legionaries used such Latin, some of them because they were members of the demoralized proletariat of Rome and many more because

Latin was not even their native tongue. Just beyond the frontier, there were often barbarians who spoke at least some Latin, had acquired a taste for Roman goods and customs, and had even served in the Imperial army. Culturally, therefore, the contrast between Romania and Barbaria was becoming more blurred than ever.

However, the army presented an even graver problem. It was the force and violence that had burst into deadly civil war before Augustus monopolized it. Tiberius complained that to be Emperor was to hold a wolf by the ears.[582] He would have spoken more accurately had he said, to hold the Roman She-Wolf by the ears, the force and violence which the historian Appian detected at the heart of Roman policy. Augustus had used that force to gain complete control of the Roman Republic; he had concealed that violence behind the mask of Jupiter himself. But, like Jupiter, whose vicar on earth he had become, he still held thunderbolts: the Roman legions. Could his successors control these thunderbolts?

The answer to that question came under Nero. Under the first three successors of Augustus, there had been signs of mutiny among the legions, due in part to their envy of the higher pay and higher pensions of the Praetorian Guard at Rome. In 65 a group of Senators and Equites conspired with one of the two commanders of the Guard to assassinate Nero. The conspiracy was discovered and thwarted. But by 69 a series of military revolts had replaced four Emperors within two years and had put Vespasian, the son of an Eques and financier, on the throne. It was now clear that, whatever the theological relation between Jupiter and his thunderbolts might be, the relation between the Emperors and the legions was ambiguous. These military coups merely followed a Roman tradition that antedated the Empire. Marius and Sulla had financed a civil war with each other by looting conquered countries. Julius Caesar and Pompey had financed another by the same method. Octavian and Antony so financed still another. By Vespasian's day, except for the dangerous Parthian Empire, Rome had no near, independent neighbors worth robbing. On the other hand, from Marius to Octavian, generals had looted not only foreigners but Roman citizens too, by proscribing their political opponents and by confiscating their goods in order to get cash for their soldiers or veterans. After Octavian emerged as the sole commander-in-chief, he had hoped to pay the army largely by means of the tribute from the countries Rome had conquered, as well as by the indirect taxes which even Roman citizens had to pay. In a sense, he had planned to contain force and violence by legalizing the process of pillage, to contain the Roman She-Wolf by converting her into a sheep dog fed on her fair share of mutton. But the early Emperors, notably Nero, sometimes neglected the army. By 68 the army had learned that a wolf disguised as a sheep dog can kill the shepherd and follow a new one, one more generous with mutton. When Nero died, there was excitement

> among all the legions and generals; for the secret of empire was now disclosed, that an emperor could be made elsewhere than at Rome.[583]

The Roman legions might have hesitated to turn kingmaker if the rulers of Rome had become hereditary kings, thereby simplifying the problem of succession. Julius Caesar seemed to have this solution in mind. Most of the provinces were accustomed to the idea of monarchy. But Rome, or at least Rome's upper classes, hated the very word king. The Emperor commonly tried either to designate a son as successor or to choose a successor and adopt him as his son. But, although legal adoption had deep roots in Roman tradition, adoption proved insufficient to ensure loyalty to a dynasty. The years 68 and 69 therefore saw a reversion to the late Republican device of letting successful generals fight out the question of who would hold the She-Wolf by the ears.

The ruler of the Roman Empire commanded a choice of masks. He was Princeps, or first among fellow Senators, an old Republican title before Augustus tactfully adopted it. He was *imperator*, or Commander, an ancient title that could be bestowed only by a victorious army on its general. The first Emperor, Octavian, was Caesar by virtue of his adoption by Julius and Augustus by his own choice, in order to suggest a religious sanction for his authority. Both these latter titles were passed on. The custom of deifying an Emperor after his death made his successor the son of a god; and the rapid spread of Emperor worship gave the Emperor the title, God and Son of a God. Precisely how each of these titles was understood varied with time, with place, with individual belief, and with the Emperor. The title *rex*, king, was always avoided.[584] None of the masks the Emperor wore could quite conceal the ultimate source of his power, military force. And what force could protect, it could also replace. Of the first twelve Emperors, at least nine died by violence; and of the first fifteen, every one faced conspiracy. The Emperor commonly answered this constant peril with paid informers, with torture to extort confessions, and sometimes by going mad. The elusive question of loyalty inevitably confused the deed with the word and the word with some possibly disloyal thought.

Under the early Empire the professional army formed a kind of military state within the civilian state, one that both protected and exploited the civilian state by extracting taxes from it. Moreover, as fewer and fewer civilians from the more civilized provinces were willing to face the hardships of military life, the army started recruiting more and more from the least civilized provinces and even from among the barbarians outside the Empire. The Praetorian Guard itself recruited German units. By A.D. 41 the Emperor Caligula maintained a German bodyguard, commanded by Thracian gladiators.[585] This partially barbarized Polis of Force, which had developed a cancerous life of its own within the Roman civilian body politic, commanded the support of the monied classes because the enterprising businessman was often metaphorically, and sometimes literally, the camp follower of the Polis of Force. Indeed, his search for profit often led him to be a scout for this Polis when he ventured beyond the Imperial frontier. Centuries earlier, the farmer-soldiers of the Republic had sometimes as Roman citizens elected a leader who would be their general and who would lead them to booty. Now the legionaries sometimes acclaimed a general Emperor because as Emperor he would loot his civilian subjects, either through taxation or confiscation, and distribute the loot to the Polis of Force as a donative, as higher pay, or as more generous separation pay.

By long practice the Roman Public Thing had learned to extend itself in space. True, its citizens did obey Camillus' urgent advice never to quit permanently the shores of the Tiber. Polybius had noted how the legions on campaign instinctively created, at the end of the day's march, another Rome, walled, moated, with its own streets, its own forum. Moreover, when the first battle had been duly lost by amateur generals and the war duly won by obstinate infantry, Rome exacted land from the vanquished and pinned down her conquest with military colonies. In the early Empire, part of the protective shell Rome built against Barbaria consisted of its permanent camps with their wooden or even brick barracks, set behind a fortified frontier.

Rome's most dangerous frontier, the Rhine-Danube, was defended both by forts along the river bank and by patrol boats. But it was an expensively long frontier, especially where the upper Rhine and upper Danube formed a salient of German tribes in the area of modern Stuttgart and

Freiburg. It was shortened by cutting off the salient with a fortified land frontier. Along this the Romans ran a *limes*, or boundary. When the barbarians attacked, they would first have to cross a zone of cleared land, without the protection of forest cover. For the Romans had learned in the Teutoburg Forest what Germans could do to a Roman legion when trees fought for natives. After this zone of cleared land came blockhouses, large enough to shelter a garrison and furnished with lookout towers. Such blockhouses were at first built of wood, but eventually of stone. A mere fence connected them until the Emperor Hadrian replaced it with a stout palisade of logs. Even the palisade was designed not to defend against serious attack but to help regulate traffic across the frontier. Later a ditch and a rampart with stone towers offered stronger defense. The row of forts behind the *limes* included at intervals larger forts, where larger detachments of troops could be based. In cases of heavy assault additional troops could be quickly shifted by military road from parts of the frontier that were not at the moment threatened. Under Claudius, England, except for the more mountainous parts, was conquered; and by 84, both England and Wales were Roman. Hadrian built a wall and moat at the Scottish border against the wild Picts and Scots; and his successor, Antoninus, ran another wall in Scotland from the Firth of Clyde to the Firth of Forth.

When, between 101 and 107, the Emperor Trajan had conquered and annexed Dacia, roughly the equivalent of modern Romania, the new province of course created a new land frontier, which had to be fortified like the German and Scottish frontiers. The Empire's southern frontier and much of its eastern frontier required protection against desert nomads. But here the shell of Cosmopolis could be thinner. There was, it is true, the same difficulty, as in Germany and Scotland, in finding any organized government to treat with, but these southern and eastern tribesmen, precisely because they lived on the edges of deserts, could not muster the armed forces that the northern tribesmen could. Also in the East, Parthia remained a problem. But, although she could put large and dangerous forces in the field, Parthia at least possessed an organized government with which Rome could treat.

Even without the conquests of his predecessor, Trajan, Hadrian had quite enough trouble finding the men and money to maintain the shell that encased Cosmopolis. Under Rome's next Emperor, Antoninus, a Roman historian could write that the Emperors from Augustus on had finally found the natural limits of Cosmopolis:

> Some nations have been added to the empire by these emperors, and the revolts of others have been suppressed. Possessing the best part of the earth and sea they have, on the whole, aimed to preserve their empire by the exercise of prudence, rather than to extend their sway indefinitely over poverty-stricken and profitless tribes of barbarians, some of whom I have seen at Rome offering themselves, by their ambassadors, as its subjects, but the emperor would not accept them because they would be of no use to him. They give kings to a great many other nations whom they do not wish to have under their own government. On some of these subject nations they spend more than they receive from them, deeming it dishonourable to give them up even though they are costly. They surround the empire with great armies and they garrison the whole stretch of land and sea like a single stronghold.
>
> No empire down to the present time ever attained to such size and duration.[586]

Hadrian could scarcely have succeeded, even after he had jettisoned some of Trajan's conquests, but for the excellent system of military roads that preceding Emperors from Augustus to Trajan had added to those the Roman Republic had built. For an army of from 300,000 to 350,000 to guard so long a frontier, it had to make up in mobility what it lacked in numbers. Although the Empire encircled a two-lobed, inland sea, and although the inhabitants used that sea for the transport of heavy commodities like grain, yet the Mediterranean played only a minor role in the shifting of troops. With the exception of the Rhine delta, most of England, northern and western France, and some of the provinces of North Africa, the Empire was largely a mountainous one. But Roman roads met the challenge, for such was the price of ruling the nations while protecting them from raids by barbarians; while putting down rebellions, especially in mountainous areas like northwest Spain; while protecting the traveler against highwaymen; and while operating a government courier service.

The Imperial navy always remained a stepchild of Roman power, never acquiring either the financial support or the prestige which the legions enjoyed. Since Rome controlled all the shores of the Mediterranean and since no organized foreign navy threatened from the Atlantic or the Black Sea or the Red Sea, Rome's navy functioned chiefly as a coast guard to keep down piracy. In discharging this function it was moderately successful. Navigation and shipbuilding made little headway; but additional harbors were built, and more lighthouses. To guard the grain route to Rome, the Emperor Claudius built an excellent harbor at Ostia, and Trajan added a second. There was a good harbor at the commercial and industrial center of Puteoli, north of Naples. Nero revived Julius Caesar's idea of cutting a canal through the Isthmus of Corinth; the canal was actually begun but it was never completed. Rome did reopen the canal that Darius had built to connect the Nile with the Red Sea, and Egypt's monsoon trade with India and Ceylon was thereby greatly encouraged. Permanent squadrons were stationed at Misenum, near Naples; and at Ravenna, on the Adriatic; also at Seleucia, the port of Antioch; and of course at Alexandria. A fleet was maintained in the English Channel to protect communications with the Province of Britain, and another in the Black Sea to keep in touch with the north coast. There were flotillas on the Rhine and on the Danube. The Channel, Black Sea, and river fleets probably did transport duty when required.

Rome's passion for order had from earliest days driven her to the practice of law. Indeed, the only honorable professions open to a patrician remained law, the army, politics, and farming. With the overthrow of the Roman monarchy in 510 B.C., the nobility monopolized law as they monopolized state priesthoods, religion being a network of contracts between the divine world and the human. As in other primitive societies, law was highly formalistic. Both priestcraft and court practice involved the precise use of traditional formulas, formulas that contained a magical potency. Part of the long struggle of the plebeians to share control of the state was to make law public and write it down as Dracon of Athens had done. From about 450 B.C., when the plebeians forced publication of them, the Twelve Tables remained the original, revered font of Roman law. Many problems which required adjudication were, in this patriarchal society, left to the father of the family, who held absolute rule over his wife, his sons, his grandsons, his unmarried daughters and granddaughters, and the wives of his sons and grandsons, even the right to inflict the death penalty. Outside the family, early legal practice often savored of compulsory arbitration in civil cases and of formally controlled vengeance in criminal cases. Since the Roman was less interested in abstract justice than in public order, law closely conformed to custom.

However, as financial and commercial transactions became more frequent, Roman law developed rapidly in the field of contracts. Court decisions handed down by successive praetors became precedents for lawyers to cite. The result was the growth of a large corpus of praetorian law. Meanwhile, law was growing by the addition of plebiscites, or resolutions of the popular assembly applicable only to plebeians. These plebiscites were finally recognized as applicable to all Roman citizens. When during the early Empire the popular assembly lost practically all of the merely formal powers still remaining to it, the Senate added further laws, increasingly dictated by the Emperor. Both the plebiscites and the later acts of the Senate were interpreted by jurisconsults, men learned in law whom judges and lawyers consulted. In true Roman fashion the jurisconsult worked, less from theoretical principles than from actual court decisions, to bring order out of apparently conflicting cases. Eventually the Emperor's council of jurisconsults monopolized this function, and the edicts and rescripts of the Emperor became the only formal source of new law.

Meanwhile, as the Roman alliance grew, Roman law ceased to regard the non-Roman as without rights; the courts enforced contracts even with foreigners. Moreover, the so-called law of nations, originally concerned only with accepted usage in respect to ambassadors, had come by the time of Cicero to include those laws common to all civilized nations. By Hadrian's day this law of nations covered a whole network of legal relations between citizens of different subject nations as well as that between these citizens and Roman citizens. It was under Hadrian also that C. Salvius Julianus, a native of the Province of Africa and perhaps the ablest jurist the Empire had yet produced, undertook to codify once more the case law developed in the courts and the edicts issued by Roman praetors over the centuries. Julian also wrote commentaries on the works of earlier jurists. He had the genius to move, by means of necessary and brilliant casuistry, from a mass of concrete cases to general principles of justice.

Originally, cases had been pleaded by patrician lawyers without fee, especially as an obligation to their clients or dependents. But as early as 204 B.C. a law had to be passed against the new habit of accepting fees. Even so, lawyers like Cicero generally received gifts from grateful clients and could in that way become rich, though the law of 204 had forbidden gifts too. In A.D. 47 the Senate was trying to revive the old prohibition against fees: the old orators took no fee; fees degraded the fairest of the liberal arts to a mercenary service; they corrupted justice; they fostered litigiousness, because litigation was now as profitable to lawyers as disease was to doctors. But some of the less wealthy Senators loudly objected: it was easy for rich advocates to forego fees; others could not afford to; and if legal studies went unrewarded, the art of advocacy would itself perish. Thereupon the Emperor Claudius,

> who considered that these arguments, if less high-minded, were still not pointless, fixed ten thousand sesterces as the maximum fee to be accepted; those exceeding it to be liable on the count of extortion.[587]

Under Claudius' successor, Nero, the Senate again abolished fees; but Nero apparently revived the law of Claudius, while forbidding the payment of certain court costs.

Although the Emperors from Augustus on had recruited civil servants from the Equestrian Order, Vespasian was the first member of this order to become an Emperor. It was therefore appropriate that it should be Vespasian's chief adviser, Mucianus, who "was for ever declaring that money was the sinews of sovereignty."[588] It is true the businesslike Vespasian did not put an end to corruption: his own mistress sold offices and Imperial decisions.[589] Even later than Vespasian a satirist could write:

> No man will get my help in robbery, and therefore no governor will take me on his staff . . . What man wins favour nowadays unless he be an accomplice—one whose soul seethes and burns with secrets that must never be disclosed?[590]

Bribery and extortion were commonplace, but it is unlikely that they equaled what had happened before Augustus monopolized the political and financial power for which the leading generals of the Republic had contested.

The monopoly of power was handled with varying skill, since the fourteen Emperors from Augustus to Hadrian varied greatly in both purpose and ability. Ten of them came from the Senatorial Order and a few from the patrician families, which the civil wars and the later Imperial executions for treason had all but eliminated by the first century A.D. Eight of them possessed relevant experience in either war or administration or both before reaching the throne. Several, such as the middle-class Vespasian or Trajan or Hadrian, were excellent administrators. Even Domitian and Nerva had had some administrative experience. Only four, or at most six, might be considered to have succeeded their predecessors peacefully. Six were officially deified by the Senate after death, although all of them received some worship before death. At least seven of them died violently by poison or assassination or timely suicide. Ten were of known Italian origin; Trajan and Hadrian were born in Spain of Italian stock; the birthplace of two others is not known. Two, Domitian and Caligula, seem to have gone mad, and three others were quite unbalanced.[591] That most of the fourteen Emperors retained their balance is remarkable: they were all prime targets for assassination, and most of them therefore murdered freely, even members of their own families, out of self-protection. An Emperor's loneliness of power was extreme, and it naturally deformed its victim. The violence that had characterized the Roman community from its earliest days, the deep belief in force, was brought to a focus in and against the person of the Emperor. That relatively competent government should have gone on, even under some of the most morally degraded Emperors, and that most of their violence and madness was restricted to the Imperial palace or at least to the capital of empire were due no doubt to the fact that Augustus had created a military and a civilian bureaucracy that operated under its own momentum regardless of which Emperor might head it. That the paid informer was so omnipresent was due in large measure to the ambiguity that Augustus created when he won control by force, kept control of that force by channeling it through an elaborate bureaucracy, and then cultivated the myth that he held his power by authority of the Senate. Not even his careful cultivation of religion and his patronage of the arts could eliminate that ambiguity. Each of his successors was grossly flattered and at least in some provinces worshiped, as Augustus had been; but a number of them were overthrown by the same means which Augustus had used to rid himself of rivals: an army. Had Julius Caesar succeeded in establishing a Hellenistic monarchy, a certain candor about force might have gained sanction through competent and just rule. But the mask of Senatorial sanction, the mask of religious sanction, the mask of bureaucratic efficiency, and the mask of poetic and artistic sanction sometimes served less to conceal the sword than to tempt other swords from their scabbards. The fear in which the immediate successors of Augustus lived and the greed of the professional informers gave the question of loyalty a new urgency. According to a later writer, who may well have exaggerated,

> Under Tiberius Caesar there was such a common and almost universal frenzy for bringing charges of treason, that it took a heavier toll of Roman citizens than any Civil War . . .[592]

When Caligula succeeded Tiberius,

> he was met by a dense and joyful throng, who called him besides other propitious names their "star," their "chick," their "babe," and their "nursling."[593]

But it was not long before the people turned against him. This so angered him that he cried out, "I wish the Roman people had but a single neck."[594] Caligula, in his madness,

> after giving orders that such statues of the gods as were especially famous for their sanctity or their artistic merit, including that of Jupiter of Olympia, should be brought from Greece, in order to remove their heads and put his own in their place . . . built out a part of the Palace as far as the Forum, and making the temple of Castor and Pollux its vestibule, he often took his place between the divine brethren, and exhibited himself there to be worshipped by those who presented themselves; and some hailed him as Jupiter Latiaris. He also set up a special temple to his own godhead, with priests and with victims of the choicest kind. In this temple was a life-sized statue of the emperor in gold, which was dressed up each day in clothing such as he wore himself. . . . At night he used constantly to invite the full and radiant moon to his embraces and his bed, while in the daytime he would talk confidentially with Jupiter Capitolinus . . . But finally won by entreaties, as he reported, and even invited to live with the god, he built a bridge over the temple of the Deified Augustus, and thus joined his Palace to the Capitol.[595]

Nero, who looked on himself as a great poet and artist, longed to be applauded for his art, not for his political position or his power. Like another tyrant before him, Dionysius I of Syracuse, Nero entered contests at the Greek games. He longed to become Victor in the Grand Tour: that is, to win in the Olympic, Pythian, Isthmian, and Nemean games. So he played the lyre and sang his own poems, competed in the chariot races, acted in Greek tragedies. Not surprisingly, he always won the victor's crown, even when he once fell out of his chariot. On his triumphal return to his palace in Rome,

> the whole population, the senators most of all, kept shouting in chorus: "Hail, Olympian Victor! Hail, Pythian Victor! Augustus! Augustus! Hail to Nero, our Hercules! Hail to Nero, our Apollo! The only Victor of the Grand Tour, the only one from the beginning of time! Augustus! Augustus! O, Divine Voice! Blessed are they that hear thee."[596]

A few months later, when Nero was fleeing a revolution led by Galba and was being pursued by horsemen, he cried, "Jupiter, what an artist perishes in me!"[597] and stabbed himself. Perhaps the whole of Nero's brief, incredible life was a rebellion against the prison of piety, decency, dignity, and ambiguity that Augustus had patiently constructed for the military autocracy of Rome. For trying to break out of that prison, Augustus had punished his own daughter. Nero's reign was marked by sexual perversion in public, fiscal irresponsibility in his last years, nostalgia for Greek culture, impetuous affronts to the *dignitas* of Rome and her code of manners, and a half-mad desire to make aesthetics rather than morals or politics the architectonic science of civilized society. By Nero's suicide in 68, Augustus won.

The very next year, after the struggle that brought Galba, Otho, and Vitellius to the throne in quick succession, Vespasian, who was fighting in Palestine, was acclaimed Emperor by his army. In October of 69 an army loyal to Vitellius and an army loyal to Vespasian fought near Cremona. The women of Cremona brought out food to those who fought for Vitellius. According to later tradition these soldiers knew that whether or not Vespasian succeeded in usurping Vitellius' throne, many men on both sides who fought through the night would never see the dawn. They would die, as so many had already died, in a civil war that often seemed no more significant than a series of gladiatorial combats. The Vitellians took the food. And then,

> One of them would call out the names of his adversary (for they practically all knew one another and were well acquainted) and would say: "Comrade, take and eat this; I give you not a sword but bread. Take and drink this; I hold out to you, not a shield but a cup. Thus, whether you kill me or I you, we shall quit life more comfortably, and the hand that slays will not be feeble and nerveless, whether it be yours that smites me or mine that smites you. For these are the meats of consecration that Vitellius and Vespasian give us while we are yet alive, in order that they may offer us as a sacrifice to the dead slain long since." That would be the style of their conversation . . . [598]

This one battle at least turned out to be both sacramental and politically decisive. The Vitellians were defeated. After they surrendered and all the soldiers had been given leave, both sides plundered Cremona and murdered the inhabitants. In Rome, Vitellius was dragged from hiding and was killed. It was then that Vespasian left the Jewish war for his son Titus to finish, and came west to Rome.

The new Emperor had been born in an Italian village and was the son of a tax collector. He was experienced in both civil administration and military strategy, was skillful with money and accounts, was thrifty, skeptical, and endowed with a salty humor. In manning his civil service, he increased the proportion of Equites, men who knew the Empire's economic problems. He restored the government's financial stability, and in a reign of ten years brought back order and sanity to the Empire. He was famous for his earthy remarks. For example, his son Titus was shocked when Vespasian put a tax on public urinals. Vespasian

> held a piece of money from the first payment to his son's nose, asking whether its odour was offensive to him. When Titus said "No," he replied, "Yet it comes from urine."[599]

The competence and candor of Vespasian, combined with the rude shock of the civil war that he successfully concluded, may well have destroyed some of Augustus' political mythology and clarified the Emperor's function. The Emperor became for the next hundred years, leaving out the tyrannical reign of Domitian, a benevolent despot through whom money ruled the Empire.

It was from the security of this benevolent despotism that the historian Tacitus could write bitterly that the Emperor Tiberius, when he left meetings of the Senate, would ejaculate in Greek,

> "These men!—how ready they are for slavery!" Even he . . . was growing weary of such grovelling patience in his slaves.[600]

Tacitus could recall with shame and horror how, when Piso led a conspiracy against the tyrant, Nero, it was Epicharis, a woman and an emancipated slave at that, who by her example showed up the cowardice of the Senators and Equites whose conspiracy she had entered, and the cowardice of the tyrant himself:

> In the meantime, Nero recollected that Epicharis was in custody on the information of Volusius Proculus; and, assuming that female flesh and blood must be unequal to the pain, he ordered her to be racked. But neither the lash nor fire, nor yet the anger of the torturers, who redoubled their efforts rather than be braved by a woman, broke down her denial of the allegations. Thus the first day of torment had been defied. On the next, as she was being dragged back in a chair to a repetition of

the agony—her dislocated limbs were unable to support her—she fastened the breast-band (which she had stripped from her bosom) in a sort of noose to the canopy of the chair, thrust her neck into it, and, throwing the weight of her body into the effort, squeezed out such feeble breath as remained to her. An emancipated slave and a woman, by shielding, under this dire coercion, men unconnected with her and all but unknown, she had set an example which shone the brighter at a time when persons freeborn and male, Roman knights and senators, untouched by the torture, were betraying each his nearest and dearest. For Lucan himself, and Senecio and Quintianus, did not omit to disclose their confederates wholesale; while Nero's terror grew from more to more, though he had multiplied the strength of the guards surrounding his person.[601]

Tacitus could remember the recovery from tyranny under Vespasian and Titus, and then the reign of Vespasian's second son, Domitian. In those days Domitian had terrified Tacitus and his fellow Senators into voting death sentences against friends and colleagues while he sat and watched their cowardly betrayals. Tacitus wrote of his father-in-law Agricola:

> It was not his fate to see the Senate-house besieged, the Senate surrounded by armed men, and in the same reign of terror so many consulars butchered, the flight and exile of so many honourable women. . . . A little while and our hands it was which dragged Helvidius to his dungeon; we it was who put asunder Mauricus and Rusticus; Senecio bathed us in his unoffending blood. Nero after all withdrew his eyes, nor contemplated the crimes he authorised. Under Domitian it was no small part of our sufferings that we saw him and were seen of him; that our sighs were counted in his books; that not a pale cheek of all that company escaped those brutal eyes, that crimson face which flushed continually lest shame should unawares surprise it.[602]

The Roman Emperors, although they improved the lot of the provincials, could not protect them fully against the rapacity or even the cruelty of the governors they sent out. A Roman governor of the Province of Asia, appointed by Augustus,

> beheaded three hundred persons in one day, and as he strutted among the corpses . . . he cried out in Greek, "What a kingly act!"[603]

While such acts were unusual, the Greek biographer Plutarch, who lived during his mature years under only one tyrannical Emperor, was at pains to warn Greek aspirants to local office that

> when entering upon any office whatsoever . . . you must . . . say to yourself, "You who rule are a subject, ruling a State controlled by proconsuls, the agents of Caesar; 'These are not the spearmen of the plain,' nor is this ancient Sardis, nor the famed Lydian power." You should arrange your cloak more carefully and from the office of the generals keep your eyes upon the orators' platform, and not have great pride or confidence in your crown, since you see the boots of Roman soldiers just above your head. No, you should imitate the actors, who, while putting into the performance their own passion, character, and reputation, yet listen to the prompter and do not go beyond the degree of liberty in rhythms and metres permitted by those in authority over them.[604]

Plutarch's historical allusions to military power in the days when the Romans had only recently conquered Greece reflects the disillusionment in the Greek-speaking provinces of the Empire, in the countries which had seen so many Roman conquerors come and go. In any case, as a Roman satirist observed bitterly, shortly after 100 B.C. when Marius Priscus had been convicted of extortion in Africa,

> Very different in days of old were the wailings of our allies and the harm inflicted on them by losses, when they had been newly conquered and were wealthy still. Their houses then were all well-stored; they had piles of money, with Spartan mantles and Coan purples; beside the paintings of Parrhasius, and the statues of Myron, stood the living ivories of Phidias; everywhere the works of Polyclitus were to be seen; few tables were without a Mentor. . . . Nowadays, on capturing a little farm, you may rob our allies of a few yoke of oxen, or a small stable of mares, with the sire of the herd; or of the household gods themselves, if there be a good statue left, or a single Deity in his little shrine . . . You despise perchance, and deservedly, the unwarlike Rhodian and the scented Corinthian: what harm will their resined youths do you, or the smooth legs of the entire breed? But keep clear of rugged Spain, avoid the land of Gaul and the Dalmatian shore; spare, too, those harvesters who fill the belly of a city that has no leisure save for the Circus and the play: what great profit can you reap from outrages upon Libyans, seeing that Marius has so lately stripped Africa to the skin?[605]

In A.D. 19 the Roman tax collectors and usurers had swarmed into Gaul in such numbers that Rome faced an incipient rebellion among the heavily indebted communities of the Gallic provinces. The most active promoters were Julius Florus . . . and Julius Sacrovir . . . Each was a man of birth, with ancestors whose services had been rewarded by Roman citizenship in years when Roman citizenship was rare and bestowed upon merit only. . . . in assemblies and conventicles they made their seditious pronouncements on the continuous tributes, the grinding rates of interest, the cruelty and pride of the governors . . .[606]

The leaders of revolt had only to point out that the Roman legions were mutinous and that Gauls should note

the poverty of Italy, the unwarlike city population, the feebleness of the armies except for the leavening of foreigners.[607]

In 68 the people of both Gaul and Britain were inflamed by taxes. Julius Vindex, legate of Lyonese Gaul but himself a native of Gaul, led a Gallic revolt against Nero; and the governor of a Spanish province imitated him. The next year a Batavian noble named Civilis secretly planned to exploit the civil war by leading the whole of Gaul in a war of liberation against Rome. The Batavians were a tribe allied with Rome who dwelt near the mouth of the Rhine. Their alliance did not require them to pay taxes to Rome, but it did require them to furnish auxiliary troops. In 69 the ephemeral Emperor Vitellius imposed a military levy on the Batavians.

This burden, which is naturally grievous, was made the heavier by the greed and licence of those in charge of the levy: they hunted out the old and the weak that they might get a price for letting them off; again they dragged away the children to satisfy their lust, choosing the handsomest—and the Batavian children are generally tall beyond their years.[608]

The Batavians revolted. Civilis incited the Gauls to join them. He pointed out that it was with Gallic allies that Rome had subjected Gaul:

"It is by the blood of the provinces that provinces are won. . . . if you consider the matter aright you will see that Gaul owed its fall to its own forces."[609]

But when Civilis' Gallic revolt broke out, the Roman general Cerialis put it down. Then he called an assembly of Gauls and read them a lesson in Roman statecraft:

I have never practised oratory and the Roman people has ever asserted its merits by arms: but since words have the greatest weight with you . . . I have decided to say a few things which now that the war is over are more useful for you to hear than for me to say.[610]

Cerialis pointed out that

you cannot secure tranquillity among nations without armies, nor maintain armies without pay, nor provide pay without taxes . . . You often command our legions; you rule these and other provinces; we claim no privileges, you suffer no exclusion. You enjoy the advantage of the good emperors equally with us, although you dwell far from the capital: the cruel emperors assail those nearest them.[611]

The military struggle of generals who wanted to be Emperor could cause havoc in a province. At Metz, for instance,

though received with all courtesy, the army was struck with sudden panic; the soldiers hurriedly seized their arms to massacre the innocent citizens, not for booty or from a desire to loot, but prompted by wild fury, the cause of which was uncertain and the remedies therefore more difficult. Finally, however, they were quieted by their general's appeals and refrained from completely destroying the community; still about 4,000 had been massacred, and such terror spread over the Gallic provinces that later on, as the army advanced, entire communities headed by their magistrates came out to meet it with appeals, women and children prostrating themselves along the roads, while everything else that can appease an enemy's wrath was offered to secure peace, although there was no war.[612]

How the Pax Romana looked to many of those foreign peoples who were pacified appeared in a speech that the Roman historian Tacitus ascribed to a Briton in Domitian's reign:

Harriers of the world, now that earth fails their all-devastating hands, they probe even the sea: if their enemy have wealth, they have greed; if he be poor, they are ambitious; East nor West has glutted them; alone of mankind they behold with the same passion of concupiscence waste alike and want. To plunder, butcher, steal, these things they misname empire: they make a desolation and they call it peace.[613]

But Tacitus implied that, often, what really prevented pacification was that Rome first conquered by force and then failed to rule justly. Tacitus claimed that his father-in-law, Agricola, after conquering Britain, showed how to hold her:

> Agricola was heedful of the temper of the provincials, and took to heart the lesson which the experience of others suggested, that little was accomplished by force if injustice followed. He decided therefore to cut away at the root the causes of war. He began with himself and his own people: he put in order his own house, a task not less difficult for most governors than the government of a province. . . . he cut off every charge invented only as a means of plunder, and therefore more grievous to be borne than the tribute itself. . . .[614] he began to train the sons of the chieftains in a liberal education and to give a preference to the native talents of the Briton as against the plodding Gaul. As a result, the nation which used to reject the Latin language began to aspire to rhetoric . . . the toga came into fashion, and little by little the Britons were seduced into alluring vices: to the lounge, the bath, the well-appointed dinner-table. The simple natives gave the name of "culture" to this factor of their slavery.[615]

It was obviously the task of the Imperial administration to learn to rule justly after forcing surrender. Rome had, however, besides just rule, one further means of pacification. Although, like Athens, she never evolved any genuine system of elected representatives that would assimilate a conquered people, both Athens and Rome did find means of winning a degree of loyalty. Athens had ruled her League of Delos partly by force and partly by making Athens the cultural capital of all member states. Rome ruled partly by force, partly by extending citizenship and admitting upper-class members of subject races into the Roman Senate. Rome's fourth Emperor, Claudius, insisted, as Julius Caesar had done before him, on admitting leading Gauls to the Senate; and when Roman Senators objected, Claudius gave his reasons:

> "In my own ancestors, the eldest of whom, Clausus, a Sabine by extraction, was made simultaneously a citizen and the head of a patrician house, I find encouragement to employ the same policy in my administration, by transferring hither all true excellence, let it be found where it will. . . . Is it regretted that the Balbi crossed over from Spain and families equally distinguished from Narbonese Gaul? Their descendants remain; nor do they yield to ourselves in love for this native land of theirs. What else proved fatal to Lacedaemon and Athens, in spite of their power in arms, but their policy of holding the conquered aloof as

alien-born? But the sagacity of our own founder Romulus was such that several times he fought and naturalized a people in the course of the same day! Strangers have been kings over us: the conferment of magistracies on the sons of freedmen is not the novelty which it is commonly and mistakenly thought, but a frequent practice of the old commonwealth. . . . All, Conscript Fathers, that is now believed supremely old has been new: plebeian magistrates followed the patrician; Latin, the plebeian; magistrates from the other races of Italy, the Latin. Our innovation, too, will be parcel of the past, and what to-day we defend by precedents will rank among precedents."[616]

The emperor's speech was followed by a resolution of the Fathers, and the Aedui become the first to acquire senatorial rights in the capital: a concession to a long-standing treaty and to their position as the only Gallic community enjoying the title of brothers to the Roman people.[617]

Granted that the power of the Senate had already dwindled; nevertheless Claudius saw its symbolic value and made a beginning toward converting it into a senate of all Cosmopolis. As for Rome's representing Cosmopolis culturally, even that could be partially achieved. All over the Empire, cities of many sizes built their own forums, their own colonnades; imitated the monumental, highly ornamented architecture of Rome, its stately, dignified sculpture, and its portrait statues; duplicated its circuses and theaters; matched on a smaller scale its gladiatorial contests, with their involuntary blood sacrifice to force and violence. And yet, with all its imperial prestige, Rome never attracted the affectionate reverence men still felt for violet-crowned[618] but now shrunken and powerless Athens, the city of ideas and of visions of beauty.

This polarity of Rome and Athens was matched by another polarity, that between political Rome and industrial Antioch or Alexandria. Rome insisted on her right to rule and on its correlative, the duty to defend. Though she charged Cosmopolis a fat fee for ruling and defending, yet, despite more or less frequent revolts in the provinces and occasional clashes between armies each of which championed a candidate for Emperor, the famous Pax Romana did protect fairly well the producer, whether estate owner or small farmer, manufacturer or artisan, overseas trader or retailer. Agriculture, industry, and commerce all profited by the peace Rome imposed. Although Augustan poets had lamented the disappearance of the small farmer and although Columella, who wrote on agriculture a few decades later, joined the lament, and although Pliny the

Elder, in his encyclopaedic *Natural History*, flatly declared that "large estates have been the ruin of Italy, and are now proving the ruin of the provinces too,"[619] the fact remains that under the first thirteen Emperors who succeeded Augustus agricultural output improved, and olives, wine grapes, and animal husbandry predominated.

Once the great wars of conquest ended, there were not enough prisoners of war to supply cheap slave labor, and the improved control of piracy cut down the supply from kidnapping. Even the big estate owners of peninsular Italy fell back on tenant farmers and free wage earners. In Cato's day, with slaves pouring in from the East, slaves had often not been allowed to have children; now they were, and in general they were more humanely treated. Some slaves, therefore, were still available for farm labor.

Tools and methods were improved and spread. Although most crop land was restored by allowing it to lie fallow, landowners began to use leguminous crops. Animal dung was the chief fertilizer, but the Gauls taught the Italians to lime their soil with marl. Wheeled plows with shares capable of turning the soil occasionally replaced the traditional pointed plow, dragged by oxen. The dry interior behind the African coast was irrigated from underground rock cisterns, which caught the runoff and protected it from evaporation till it was needed. In Jordan the Nabataeans learned to conserve the heavy dewfall by erecting stone cairns that collected and allowed it to seep into the ground before the next day's hot sun could steal it. The selective breeding of stock continued. Finally, not only were desirable plants brought in from outside the Empire but they spread from province to province. Cotton from India was naturalized in Egypt, although cotton cloth never competed seriously with either wool or linen. Oriental alfalfa grass was grown in Italy. The peach[620] tree, which had been introduced into Italy from Asia Minor, was acclimatized in Belgica, or northeastern France; and the cherry, which Lucullus had brought back from Armenia in the first century B.C., was now cultivated clear to Britain. As to who profited from this expansion in the quantity and quality of farm production, Pliny was right: capitalistic agriculture had considerably encroached on subsistence farming, and also large estates had encroached on small neighboring farms. But in any case the estate owner's capital did allow improvements in cultivation; and near the Imperial frontiers, as permanent military camps developed into new cities, the market for food expanded.

The Roman peace was also propitious for industry and trade. Italy, it is true, failed to hold its own, because provinces like those in Gaul learned to grow their own grapes just as Spain learned to grow more olives. Italy's export trade in wine and oil and her processings of grapes and olives to feed that trade suffered correspondingly. To protect Italian growers of olives and wine grapes, Roman Emperors sometimes tried to restrict the cultivation of these crops in provinces like Gaul, as the Republic had done. As for industries, those which really profited by Roman law and order were in the Eastern Greek-speaking provinces, where ancient traditions of trade and manufacture existed. A vast new market opened up to the glassmakers of Phoenicia, who had already by Augustus' day learned how to blow glass instead of having to mold it. Alexandria also produced glassware, and exported paper too, made of course from papyrus; even Rome and the cities around Naples as well as Gaul and Spain manufactured glass. The island of Cos and various cities of Asia Minor manufactured textiles, including silk on a linen warp. Gaul, long famous for its metal work, developed textile and pottery works. Spain found tin, and although the supply of silver in Andalusia was declining, the silver deposits contained lead useful for the water pipes, from aqueduct to house, that Rome was making popular in provincial cities. Tin, lead, silver, iron, and coal were mined in Britain. Roman merchants carried metalware down the Rhine and along the coasts to German and Scandinavian buyers, and from the Baltic they brought back the amber which the peoples of the Mediterranean had prized for centuries. Most of the Empire's wholesale trade was carried on by Greeks and Phoenicians and Syrians in the East and by Gauls in much of the West. The Jews dispersed through the Empire were mostly craftsmen or retail merchants.

The considerable trade with Arabia, India, Ceylon, and China was opened up by Greeks. In the second century Ptolemy of Alexandria, best known as an astronomer, published an atlas of maps which included the Malay Peninsula, Sumatra, and Java. The jewels, perfumes, and spices brought from the Orient were largely paid for in precious metals. The argument that the spices were needed in temple worship did not fool the elder Pliny, who wrote that

> by the lowest reckoning India, China and the Arabian peninsula take from our empire 100 million sesterces every year—that is the sum which our luxuries and our women cost us; for what fraction of these imports, I ask you, now goes to the gods or to the powers of the lower world?[621]

The Emperor Vespasian characteristically lamented this disappearance of good money and tried to stop it. In vain: Pliny claimed that the price that Oriental merchandise fetched in the Empire was a hundred times what the merchant had paid for it in the Orient. At no time in recorded history had the merchant and industrialist and banker of the Mediterranean found such golden opportunities as under the protection of the Pax Romana.

The laborers whom these businessmen employed were less fortunate. Although the slaves among them were a minority, there were enough of them to depress wages. Even so, many slaves were emancipated by their masters; of these freedmen, some became factory foremen or even managers, and a few of these managers ended up as millionaires. Compared with the societies the Empire had absorbed and now protected, Cosmopolis was fluid and egalitarian. The test was no longer ancestry but money, and Cosmopolis was less and less fussy about how the money was acquired.

The weakness of Cosmopolis was that it rested on the tired backs of the poor and indeed on the backs of some who labored even lower down than the slave, lower than the roots of vine and olive, lower than the water in African cisterns. The people who labored at this low level worked the Imperial mines. Most of them were convicts, a term that included political offenders and other heretics, like Christians. As for the backs of the weak, Athens had in her most halcyon days also rested on slave labor. But Athens had been, briefly in time and modestly in space, perhaps a lighter load than Eternal Rome, ruling all men everywhere, or everywhere that seemed to matter. Besides, some of Athens' weight was suspended from ideas, and the cables connecting Athens to those ideas were exquisite artistic forms that even slaves, except perhaps in the mines, could scarcely fail to see or hear. Also, in Pericles' days, four centuries before Catullus wrote, the gods, except in the view of a sophisticated minority, had not yet died.

The Romans of course prided themselves on being more practical than the Greeks. Pliny, in his *Natural History*, described the water supply of Rome, furnished his reader with the price of the latest aqueduct, and concluded:

> If we take into careful consideration the abundant supplies of water in public buildings, baths, pools, open channels, private houses, gardens and country estates near the city; if we consider the distances traversed by the water before it arrives, the raising of arches, the tunnelling of

mountains and the building of level routes across deep valleys, we shall readily admit that there has never been anything more remarkable in the whole world.[622]

Frontinus, who served in A.D. 97 as water commissioner of Rome and who wrote a treatise on aqueducts, remarked enthusiastically,

> With such an array of indispensable structures carrying so many waters, compare, if you will, the idle Pyramids or the useless, though famous, works of the Greeks![623]

So much for Pyramid and Parthenon, both useless. The profession of medicine, on the other hand, would seem to be practical, if only because doctors make money. Yet Pliny the Elder observed:

> Medicine alone of the Greek arts we serious Romans have not yet practised; in spite of its great profits only a very few of our citizens have touched upon it, and even these were at once deserters to the Greeks; nay, if medical treatises are written in a language other than Greek they have no prestige even among unlearned men ignorant of Greek, and if any should understand them they have less faith in what concerns their own health.[624]

From the Greek-speaking half of what Rome ruled inventions still came, as the water mill came from Asia Minor in Pliny's own day. Invention and engineering techniques should certainly have appealed even to Romans, too serious to practice medicine. According to the historian Dio Cassius, who came from the Greek world, the Emperor Tiberius wanted to correct the dangerous leaning of one of the largest porticos in Rome. The architect he called in cleverly righted it.

> At the time Tiberius both admired and envied him; for the former reason he honored him with a present of money, and for the latter he expelled him from the city.[625]

The exile returned to ask pardon and purposely let fall what looked like a glass goblet. It was damaged but the architect promptly put it back in shape. Tiberius then put the inventive architect to death. Petronius ascribed the death sentence to Tiberius' fear that if the inventor's secret for manufacturing flexible glass became known, it might depreciate the value of precious metals.[626] Perhaps so; but the envy that Dio Cassius, with his Greek eye for Roman character, ascribed to Tiberius may have escaped the Roman Petronius. The architect was most probably

Greek; Tiberius was an embittered, conservative Roman, and his sort, when faced with clever Greeks, often felt both admiration and resentment.

In a society like that of the Empire, with its powerful tradition of slavery and cheap labor, there was little incentive to develop labor-saving devices. As Seneca pointed out, there was something ignoble about the whole economic process. If Posidonius, the Greek Stoic philosopher, was excited by the discovery of copper and iron and speculated subtly on whether the hammer or the tongs came first into use, Seneca was too contemptuous of manual work to care:

> They were both invented by some man whose mind was nimble and keen, but not great or exalted; and the same holds true of any other discovery which can only be made by means of a bent body and of a mind whose gaze is upon the ground.[627]

Undoubtedly, the Empire could have greatly increased its revenues and hence its means of defense against Barbaria if it had developed systematically its economic resources. For example, a better merchant marine would have given it shorter interior lines for the deployment of its legions as needed. But when the Emperor Claudius furnished marine insurance and shipbuilding subsidies for merchant shipping, he had apparently only one purpose in view: to make sure of the grain supply for Rome.[628] The same purpose led him to build his harbor at Ostia and to complete an aqueduct that would bring Ostia an adequate water supply. Although the Emperors also built a few canals, for either military or commercial purposes or both, more canals would have greatly stimulated the Empire's economic development, since even the marvelous roads which the Republic and then the Empire built did not enable pack animals or animal-drawn vehicles to compete economically with sails and oars. But canals were costly, even with slave labor. On the other hand, river and lake traffic expanded greatly, since it was not only cheaper than traffic by road but safer than traffic by sea. How much safer was eloquently suggested by Nero's plan to cut a canal, 125 miles long, from Rome's port at Ostia to Lake Avernus, which Augustus had already connected with the nearby Bay of Naples.[629] Rivers like the Rhine, the Rhone, and the Danube carried heavier traffic and stimulated the growth of such cities as Cologne, Lyons, Vienna. Smaller rivers brought prosperity to such cities as London, Paris, and Seville. In the Greek East, the Nile, the canal which connected the Nile with the Red Sea, and a magnificent Mediterranean harbor made Alexandria the second greatest city in the Empire.

Nevertheless, the extraordinary scientific advances the Greeks had made never led to the technology the Empire needed. Slavery and the unequal distribution of wealth prevented the growth of a mass market. Greek engineers and Greek architects, like Greek doctors, were impressively good, but the economic exploitation of Greek inventiveness lagged, as it had already lagged in the Greek world before the Romans conquered it. Greek inventiveness tended to provide toys to divert and astound rather than tools which might have fed, clothed, and housed the inhabitants of the Empire. As for Rome, her role was to conquer, to bring order, to appropriate, and to consume, rather than to produce.

In the short run, Rome's program sufficed to organize a paradise on earth for those who had money. The lands the Emperors ruled, at least those lands which lay close to the Mediterranean Sea, were sunny and pleasant. Though some of them could certainly be hot in summer, the heat was usually dry and not enervating. People lived largely outdoors and, except for the tenements of the urban poor and the huts of the rural poor, even their houses were built around the outdoors, in patio style. More and more city streets were paved, and colonnades or arcades projected from the houses to protect pedestrians from sun or rain. The rich won praise for building public baths, theaters, circuses for the races, schools for children, public libraries. Physically, life could be delightful. But Seneca's view of life in Rome on other levels must have been held by many another wealthy man in many another city of the Empire:

> Everyone hurries his life on and suffers from a yearning for the future and a weariness of the present. . . . For what new pleasure is there that any hour can now bring? They are all known, all have been enjoyed to the full.[630]

In quite simple ways wealth conspired with slavery to rob men of their natural functions, as the elder Pliny observed. He served as a cavalry officer in Germany under Claudius; pleaded in the courts; served under Vespasian as procurator in Gaul, Africa, Spain, and Belgium, and as an admiral at Misenum. He used his leisure to compile an encyclopaedia. Pliny observed the rich man carried by slaves in his comfortable litter, while one slave, his *nominator*, was charged with reminding him in advance of the name of any acquaintance who might be approaching. Recalling the masters who had been assassinated by their own slaves, Pliny wrote scornfully:

> We walk with the feet of others, we recognise our acquaintances with the eyes of others, rely on others' memory to make our salutations, and put into the hands of others our very lives; the precious things of nature, which support life, we have quite lost. We have nothing else of our own save our luxuries.[631]

It was perhaps this lack of the precious things that was driving more and more people into Eastern religions. In the century after the poet Catullus had announced in anguish that the gods were dead, a far lesser Latin poet, Lucan, wrote wearily,

> No guardian gods watch over us from heaven:
> Jove is no king; let ages whirl along
> In blind confusion. . . .[632]

The rich and powerful and conservative Roman often retreated into an eclectic Stoicism, a doctrine which itself had somewhat eclectically drawn on the morals Socrates praised and practiced, without accepting the intellectual discipline that Socrates prescribed, and seemingly unaware of his ladder of love.[633] Without this love there was great loneliness in crowded Rome and a certain loss of identity. Many men and many women consequently tried to regain identity, not by seeking the self-knowledge Socrates urged, but by striving to force others to identify and respect them. Nero's passionate longing to be an artist, understood and admired in his own right, was in no way unusual. Well-to-do Roman businessmen and even Roman ladies wanted to perform in public, even in gladiatorial combats. Roman gentlemen wanted especially to write, and then to read or recite to friends what they had written. An upper-class home, therefore, was likely to contain a hearing room, or auditorium. Friends foregathered. They were often bored. But if they did not come, where would they themselves find a captive audience when their turn came to read their own literary attempts? The result of this widespread desire to be known as a writer guaranteed an enormous literary output; and a satirist could say that at Rome a man must

> live in perpetual dread of fires and falling houses, and the thousand perils of this terrible city, and poets spouting in the month of August![634]

The Augustan writers had possessed some sort of hope that seems to have died with their generation. Cross-fertilized by the great literature of an earlier Greece, dazzled by the grandeur of the Pax Romana, the Augustans had achieved a kind of general view of man's destiny. Compared with them, the Latin writers of the next few generations were rarely more than literary men.

For example, there was Seneca, the tutor of the boy-Emperor Nero and for years his chief minister. In many ways he reminds his readers of Cicero, of the Roman man of action who loves money and position but is convinced that he is also a philosopher. Seneca favored the Stoic's detachment; but as underwriting for the good life, he placed such large loans in the new province of Britain that when he suddenly withdrew them, the withdrawal helped provoke a rebellion against Rome.[635] Seneca wrote orations for Nero to deliver; tragedies, mostly Euripidean plots, not to be acted but to be read; familiar essays on moral problems; and many letters, which were clearly either written for publication or revised for publication. His writing abounded in and was greatly admired for that most Roman feature, the *sententia*, a sententious observation, usually in both senses of the word sententious: it was both aphoristic and ponderous. He joined the chorus of lament that Latin was so much less adequate a language than Greek:

> How scant of words our language is, nay, how poverty-stricken, I have not fully understood until to-day. We happened to be speaking of Plato, and a thousand subjects came up for discussion, which needed names and yet possessed none . . .[636]

Stoic that he was, Seneca of course preached the willing acceptance of death and quoted approvingly the words of another Stoic, Hecato: "Cease to hope, and you will cease to fear."[637] "What is the happy life?" Seneca asks, and himself answers: "It is peace of mind and lasting tranquillity."[638]

But Seneca saw no point in false heroism:

> Let us, therefore, see to it that we abstain from giving offence. It is sometimes the people that we ought to fear; or sometimes a body of influential oligarchs in the Senate, if the method of governing the State is such that most of the business is done by that body; and sometimes individuals equipped with power by the people and against the people. It is burdensome to keep the friendship of all such persons; it is enough not

to make enemies of them. . . . Our wise man does the same; he shuns a strong man who may be injurious to him, making a point of not seeming to avoid him, because an important part of one's safety lies in not seeking safety openly. . . .[639]

This millionaire advised men to scorn wealth and "establish business relations with poverty."[640] For "what you hold and call your own is public property—indeed, it belongs to mankind at large."[641] Yet he enjoyed his own wealth: Socrates, it is true, enjoyed leisure largely by ignoring wealth, but Socrates

> lived either in time of war, or under tyrants, or under a democracy, which is more cruel than wars and tyrants.[642]

Seneca wanted the freedom that civilized men want: the freedom of people who are comfortably off; who are considered to have an adequate education, to be knowledgeable and sophisticated; and who are thought to have what is called a philosophy of life. Part of that freedom was the liberty that only a liberal education could give: "I respect no study, and deem no study good, which results in money-making."[643] Toward earlier and less civilized generations, Seneca felt that

> no matter how excellent and guileless was the life of the men of that age, they were not wise men . . . Still, I would not deny that they were men of lofty spirit and—if I may use the phrase—fresh from the gods.[644]

Seneca may have connived with a tyrant; but as the Emperor's first minister, he may also have mitigated the horrors of Nero's reign by bending before the wind. Moreover, the society he lived in exacted a certain courage from a man of his perception. At least, the rich vulgarians who paraded culture did not take him in. He quickly learned that

> it is in the houses of the laziest men that you will see a full collection of orations and history with the boxes piled right up to the ceiling . . . these collections . . . are bought for show and a decoration of their walls.[645]

The wholesale wallowing in sex and food and drink at Rome was quite enough to explain his writing that "one is sometimes seized by hatred of the whole human race."[646] And Seneca must have wondered about the fruits of civilization when he reflected on at least one habit of the rich. For in addition to the auditorium, in which the Roman host read his literary compositions to his defenseless guests, he might also have, just off the banquet room, a smaller room called the *vomitorium*. There his guests might retire with a red feather to tickle their throats. Then, as Seneca wrote his mother from exile,

> they vomit that they may eat, they eat that they may vomit, and they do not deign even to digest the feasts for which they ransack the whole world.[647]

And Seneca reminded his mother of the human blood it had cost to keep these delicacies flowing to the tables of the Roman rich. Pliny, who, as a cavalry officer, had risked shedding some of the blood required, knew that vomiting to eat, or at least to drink, was not confined to the privacy of a *vomitorium* but might occur at the public bath. Some men, he wrote, leap from the bath and

> while still naked and panting, they snatch up huge vessels as if to show off their strength, and pour down the whole of the contents, so as to bring them up again at once, and then drink another draught; and they do this a second and a third time, as if they were born for the purpose of wasting wine, and as if it were impossible for the liquor to be poured away unless by using the human body as a funnel.[648]

Though the bread of the rich and the wine of the rich had indeed cost a great deal of blood, chiefly the blood of the poor, Seneca shared the scorn that men of his class felt, not only for manual labor, but for the men and women whose bodies and minds too much labor had deformed. But, perhaps because he had known eight years of unhappy exile before he was allowed to return to Rome and serve as Nero's tutor, the misfortunes of even the lowly could move him. He wrote in a letter, when his wife's female clown suddenly went blind, that

> she does not know that she is blind. She keeps asking her attendant to change her quarters; she says that her apartments are too dark. . . .
>
> Yet the blind ask for a guide, while we wander without one, saying: "I am not self-seeking; but one cannot live at Rome in any other way."[649]

Seneca once wrote:

> We mortals also are lighted and extinguished; the period of suffering comes in between, but on either side there is a deep peace. . . .
>
> But do you praise and imitate the man whom it does not irk to die, though he takes pleasure in living. For what virtue is there in going away when you are thrust out?[650]

Soon after writing these words, Seneca was put to the test: in 65, when he was sixty-nine, he was accused of taking part in Piso's conspiracy against Nero, and a centurion announced to the old man that he must die.

Seneca, nothing daunted, asked for the tablets containing his will. The centurion refusing, he turned to his friends, and called them to witness that "as he was prevented from showing his gratitude for their services, he left them his sole but fairest possession—the image of his life. If they bore it in mind, they would reap the reward of their loyal friendship in the credit accorded to virtuous accomplishments." At the same time, he recalled them from tears to fortitude, sometimes conversationally, sometimes in sterner, almost coercive tones. "Where," he asked, "were the maxims of their philosophy? Where that reasoned attitude towards impending evils which they had studied through so many years? For to whom had Nero's cruelty been unknown? Nor was anything left him, after the killing of his mother and his brother, but to add the murder of his guardian and preceptor."

After these and some similar remarks, which might have been meant for a wider audience, he embraced his wife, and, softening momentarily in view of the terrors at present threatening her, begged her, conjured her, to moderate her grief—not to take it upon her for ever, but in contemplating the life he had spent in virtue to find legitimate solace for the loss of her husband. Paulina replied by assuring him that she too had made death her choice, and she demanded her part in the executioner's stroke. Seneca, not wishing to stand in the way of her glory, and influenced also by his affection, that he might not leave the woman who enjoyed his whole-hearted love exposed to outrage, now said: "I had shown you the mitigations of life, you prefer the distinction of death: I shall not grudge your setting that example. May the courage of this brave ending be divided equally between us both, but may more of fame attend your own departure!" After this, they made the incision in their arms with a single cut. Seneca, since his aged body, emaciated further by frugal living, gave slow escape to the blood, severed as well the arteries in the leg and behind the knee. Exhausted by the racking pains, and anxious lest his sufferings might break down the spirit of his wife, and he himself lapse into weakness at the sight of her agony, he persuaded her to withdraw into another bedroom. And since, even at the last moment his eloquence remained at command, he called his secretaries, and dictated a long discourse, which has been given to the public in his own words, and which I therefore refrain from modifying. . . .

313

Seneca, in the meantime, as death continued to be protracted and slow, asked Statius Annaeus, who had long held his confidence as a loyal friend and a skillful doctor, to produce the poison—it had been provided much earlier—which was used for despatching prisoners condemned by the public tribunal of Athens.

For Seneca was determined to drink the hemlock, the poison that had killed Socrates.

It was brought, and he swallowed it, but to no purpose; his limbs were already cold, and his system closed to the action of the drug. In the last resort, he entered a vessel of heated water, sprinkling some on the slaves nearest, with the remark that he offered the liquid as a drink-offering to Jove the Liberator. He was then lifted into a bath, suffocated by the vapour, and cremated without ceremony. It was the order he had given in his will, at a time when, still at the zenith of his wealth and power, he was already taking thought for his latter end.[651]

Seneca's twenty-five-year-old nephew, Annaeus Lucanus, was involved in this same conspiracy of Piso's; Lucan, too, took his life, leaving behind him an epic poem on the civil war, called the *Pharsalia*, which dramatized the struggle between Pompey and Caesar. But this struggle could be viewed also as one between a dying republicanism and the military autocracy that succeeded it. There would be "those great rivals biding with us yet, Caesar and Liberty."[652] In Lucan's epic, the battle of Pharsalus overthrew freedom for Rome and for the whole world that Rome ruled. That is why he wrote that on August 9 of 48 B.C. the whole world reeled. Nor should Julius Caesar, who overthrew liberty, begrudge Pompey the immortality that Lucan's epic would bestow, for it spoke of Caesar too. And was not Lucan destined to do for both what Homer had done for the heroes who fought at Troy?

> Long as the heroes of the Trojan time
> Shall live upon the page of Smyrna's bard,
> So shall future races read of thee
> In this my poem; and Pharsalia's song
> Live unforgotten in the age to come.[653]

Lucan planned to write his epic in twelve books, but he broke off in the tenth, presumably to help kill Nero. When Piso's conspiracy was discovered and the conspirators were questioned, Lucan named his mother as one of them.[654] He himself was allowed to open his veins, as his uncle had done. While bleeding to death, he quoted a passage from his epic.

The *Pharsalia* was a remarkable tour de force for so young a poet, but it was nevertheless not likely, despite its author's implication, to rival the works of Homer. Or even of Virgil. In spirit Lucan's epic somewhat resembled the highly polished but not too original *sententiae* of his famous and wealthy uncle, who, being a philosopher, took hemlock and issued his last statement to his public. The *Pharsalia* also was perhaps primarily a statement to the public. Augustus had certainly hoped the *Aeneid* would be such a statement. In some ways it was, but Virgil had been too good a poet to fall into Lucan's declamatory style.

In short, both Nero's minister and the minister's poet-nephew were the victims of rhetoric. Perhaps, therefore, it is not surprising that one of the most admired writers of the time was a professor of rhetoric, Marcus Fabius Quintilianus. Like Cicero and like Isocrates of Athens before him, Quintilian saw rhetoric as the queen of the sciences. Cicero had written his treatise, *On the Making of an Orator*, in the years when Caesar was putting an end to the republican system of government, the system that had made the Forum a stage for Cicero's performances. In the last, terrible years of Domitian's tyranny, Quintilian wrote the *Education of an Orator*. And who is the orator? A good man, answers Quintilian. And philosophy holds no monopoly on ethical principles; those principles are rather a part of the science of rhetoric.

> The man who can really play his part as a citizen and is capable of meeting the demands both of public and private business, the man who can guide a state by his counsels, give it a firm basis by his legislation and purge its vices by his decisions as a judge, is assuredly no other than the orator of our quest.[655]

Indeed, the faculty of speech is Nature's "greatest gift to man, the gift that distinguishes us from other living things."[656] And "rhetoric . . . is the noblest and most sublime of tasks."[657] Where Aristotle had defined man as a *zoon logicon*, a logical animal,[658] Quintilian preferred to define him as a rhetorical animal.

> Reason then was the greatest gift of the Almighty, who willed that we should share its possession with the immortal gods. But reason by itself would help us but little and would be far less evident in us, had we not the power to express our thoughts in speech; for it is the lack of this

power rather than thought and understanding, which they do to a certain extent possess, that is the great defect in other living things.[659]

Where Plato had prescribed years of strenuous philosophic study as the only hope of wise statesmanship, Quintilian asked only that his ideal orator "should be a 'wise man' in the Roman sense."[660] As for eloquence, even a moderate amount will be useful, for

> there is no other source from which men have reaped such a harvest of wealth, honour, friendship and glory, both present and to come.[661]

His orator must never retreat either into specialized legal study or professionalized philosophic quibbling. Of the two escapes, the escape into quibbling is the worse, because "philosophy may be counterfeited, but eloquence never."[662] Like Cicero, Quintilian knew that Latin was a less mellifluous language than Greek and possessed a less rich vocabulary, but he pointed out that Cicero nevertheless solved these problems too by his consummate skill with words.

Quintilian was a Roman Isocrates. But though Isocrates had been a pioneer in the art of public persuasion and of rhetoric, Rome worshiped rhetoric more successfully than the Greeks could ever hope to do. For Rome married rhetoric to power, a rhetoric she had learned largely from the Greeks. In these nuptials Socrates might have seen the marriage of force and fraud. The Hellenistic world had often married force with fraud; yet it never achieved Alexander's dream of unity. It was Rome, the Great Persuader, the Republic of lawyer-soldiers, the Republic of Cicero's courtroom invective and of Caesar's legions, who unified and ruled the nations. It was Rome who persuaded men with words and persuaded them even more with swords. Her success convinced her that the will is what counts and that for a man to have his will he must move the wills of others. Rome never produced an important philosopher; she produced orators like Cicero and Quintilian who thought philosophy was merely a useful tool. She never produced a mathematician of stature. Quintilian posed an interesting rhetorical question when he asked,

> has not man succeeded in crossing the high seas, in learning the number and the courses of the stars, and almost measuring the universe itself, all of them accomplishments of less importance than oratory, but of far greater difficulty?[663]

316

Rome was, in short, not given to listening: either to the gods, whose advice she learned early to manipulate; or to ideas, because she had already made up her mind; or to the forms of beauty that words can lead men to, since with few exceptions her poets and prose writers could will their effects by rhetorical device, by declamation, as Seneca and Lucan did. But a century after the birth of Christ, there were left in the Greek world few philosophers who had not spiritually aligned themselves with Rome. Once, as Horace wrote, captive Greece led her conqueror captive. Could the weary Hellenic spirit do that again?

The Latin literature that suffered least damage from voluntarism was satire. Satire had ancient roots in Latin literature, both oral and written. It formally harnessed the Roman instinct for bluntness. Since it did not try to speculate, it remained unconfused. Since it did not try to communicate love, it remained free of Roman sentimentality. Since it sought out primarily the ugly and abused it, it did not fall into ornamentation and bad taste. One of the writers who cut his arteries when Piso's conspiracy failed was the Roman dandy and satirist, Petronius, the so-called Arbiter of Elegance at Nero's court. According to Tacitus, he was an artist in vice and extravagance, whom Nero had admired and aped. When he died, he issued no public statements to posterity; he declaimed no lines from his writings; he

> did not hurry to take his life, but caused his already severed arteries to be bound up to meet his whim, then opened them once more, and began to converse with his friends, in no grave strain and with no view to the fame of a stout-hearted ending. He listened to them as they rehearsed, not discourses upon the immortality of the soul or the doctrines of philosophy, but light songs and frivolous verses. Some of his slaves tasted of his bounty, a few of the lash. He took his place at dinner, and drowsed a little, so that death, if compulsory, should at least resemble nature. Not even in his will did he follow the routine of suicide by flattering Nero or Tigellinus or another of the mighty,—but prefixing the names of the various catamites and women—detailed the imperial debauches and the novel features of each act of lust, and sent the document under seal to Nero.[664]

Petronius left behind him a picaresque novel, the *Satyricon*,[665] a satirical comedy that parodied the romances so popular in the Greek literature of that period. The most famous episode in this comic tale is a banquet given by a *nouveau riche*, a former slave named Trimalchio, to a crowd of parasitical flatterers hungry for a free meal. Several of them went first to the public baths.

Suddenly we caught sight of an old, bald man in a long red undershirt, playing ball with a bunch of curly-headed slave boys. It wasn't so much the boys who took our eyes—though they were worth looking at—as the old man himself. There he stood, rigged out in undershirt and sandals, nothing else, bouncing a big green ball the color of a leek. When he dropped one ball, moreover, he never bothered to stoop for it, but simply took another from a slave who stood beside him with a huge sack tossing out fresh balls to the players. This was striking enough, but the real refinement was two eunuchs standing on either side of the circle, one clutching a chamber pot of solid silver, the other ticking off the balls.[666]

Suddenly the old man, who was in fact their host Trimalchio,

gave a loud snap with his fingers. The eunuch came waddling up with the chamber pot, Trimalchio emptied his bladder and went merrily on with his game. When he was done, he shouted for water, daintily dipped the tips of his fingers and wiped his hands in the long hair of a slave.[667]

Beside Trimalchio's door, they saw a sign:

ANY SLAVE LEAVING THE PREMISES
WITHOUT AUTHORIZATION FROM THE MASTER
WILL RECEIVE ONE HUNDRED LASHES!

At the entrance sat the porter . . . busily shelling peas into a pan of solid silver. In the doorway hung a cage, all gold, and in it a magpie was croaking out his welcome to the guests.

I was gaping at all this in open-mouthed wonder when I suddenly jumped with terror, stumbled, and nearly broke my leg. For there on the left as you entered, in fresco, stood a huge dog straining at his leash. In large letters under the painting was scrawled:

BEWARE OF THE DOG!

The others burst out laughing at my fright. But when I'd recovered from the shock, I found myself following the rest of the frescoes with fascination. They ran the whole length of the wall. First came a panel showing a slave market with everything clearly captioned. There stood Trimalchio as a young man, his hair long and curly in slave fashion; in his hand he held a staff and he was entering Rome for the first time under the sponsorship of Minerva. In the next panel he appeared as an apprentice

318

accountant, then as a paymaster—each step in his career portrayed in great detail and everything scrupulously labeled. At the end of the portico you came to the climax of the series: a picture of Mercury grasping Trimalchio by the chin and hoisting him up to the lofty eminence of the official's tribunal. Beside the dais stood the goddess Fortuna with a great cornucopia and the three Fates, busily spinning out Trimalchio's life in threads of gold . . .[668]

At last we took our places. Immediately slaves from Alexandria came in and poured ice water over our hands. These were followed by other slaves who knelt at our feet and with extraordinary skill pedicured our toenails. Not for an instant, moreover, during the whole of this odious job, did one of them stop singing. . . . In fact, anything you asked for was invariably served with a snatch of song, so that you would have thought you were eating in a concert-hall rather than a private dining room.

Now that the guests were all in their places, the *hors d'oeuvres* were served, and very sumptuous they were. . . . On a large tray stood a donkey made of rare Corinthian bronze; on the donkey's back were two panniers, one holding green olives, the other, black. Flanking the donkey were two side dishes, both engraved with Trimalchio's name and the weight of the silver, while in dishes shaped to resemble little bridges there were dormice, all dipped in honey and rolled in poppyseed. Nearby, on a silver grill, piping hot, lay small sausages, while beneath the grill black damsons and red pomegranates had been sliced up and arranged so as to give the effect of flames playing over charcoal.

We were nibbling at these splendid appetizers when suddenly the trumpets blared a fanfare and Trimalchio was carried in, propped up on piles of miniature pillows in such a comic way that some of us couldn't resist impolitely smiling. His head, cropped close in a recognizable slave cut, protruded from a cloak of blazing scarlet; his neck, heavily swathed already in bundles of clothing, was wrapped in a large napkin bounded by an incongruous senatorial purple stripe with little tassels dangling down here and there. On the little finger of his left hand he sported an immense gilt ring . . .

He was picking his teeth with a silver toothpick when he first addressed us. "My friends," he said, "I wasn't anxious to eat just yet, but I've ignored my own wishes so as not to keep you waiting."[669]

I turned back to my neighbor to pick up what gossip I could and soon had him blabbing away, especially when I asked him about the woman who was bustling around the room. "Her?" he said, "why that's Fortunata, Trimalchio's wife. And the name couldn't suit her better. She counts her cash by the cartload. And you know what she used to be? Well, begging your Honor's pardon, but you wouldn't have taken bread from her hand. Now, god knows how or why, she's sitting pretty: has Trimalchio eating out of her hand. If she told him at noon it was night, he'd crawl into bed. As for him, he's so loaded he doesn't know how much he has. But that bitch has her finger in everything—where you'd least expect it too. A regular tightwad, never drinks, and sharp as they come. But she's got a nasty tongue; get her gossiping on a couch and she'll chatter like a parrot. If she likes you, you're lucky; if she doesn't, god help you.[670]

While the guests were flattering their host,

servants came . . . and then huge Spartan mastiffs came bounding in and began to gallop around the table. Following the dogs came servants with a tray on which we saw a wild sow of absolutely enormous size. Perched rakishly on the sow's head was the cap of freedom which newly freed slaves wear in token of their liberty, and from her tusks hung two baskets woven from palm leaves: one was filled with dry Egyptian dates, the other held sweet Syrian dates. Clustered around her teats were little suckling pigs made of hard pastry, gifts for the guests to take home as it turned out, but intended to show that ours was a broodsow.[671]

A slave stepped up to carve and

whipped out his knife and gave a savage slash at the sow's flanks. Under the blow the flesh parted, the wound burst open and dozens of thrushes came whirring out! But bird-catchers with limed twigs were standing by and before long they had snared all the birds as they thrashed wildly around the room. Trimalchio ordered that a thrush be given to each guest, adding for good measure, "Well, that old porker liked her acorns juicy all right."[672]

Trimalchio then went to the toilet. He returned,

wiping the sweat from his brow. He splashed his hands in perfume and stood there for a minute in silence. "You'll excuse me, friends," he began, "but I've been constipated for days and the doctors are stumped. I got a little relief from a prescription of pomegranate rind and resin in a vinegar base. Still, I hope my tummy will get back its manners soon. Right now my bowels are bumbling around like a bull. But if any of you has any business that needs attending to, go right ahead; no reason to feel embarrassed. There's not a man been born yet with solid insides.

And I don't know any anguish on earth like trying to hold it in. Jupiter himself couldn't stop it from coming.—What are you giggling about, Fortunata? You're the one who keeps me awake all night with your trips to the potty. Well, anyone at table who wants to go has my permission, and the doctors tell us not to hold it in. Everything's ready outside —water and pots and the rest of the stuff. Take my word for it, friends, the vapors go straight to your brain. Poison your whole system. I know of some who've died from being too polite and holding it in." We thanked him for his kindness and understanding, but we tried to hide our snickers in repeated swallows of wine.[673]

By now Trimalchio was drinking heavily and was, in fact, close to being drunk. "Hey, everybody!" he shouted, "nobody's asked Fortunata to dance. Believe me, you never saw anyone do grinds the way she can." With this he raised his hands over his forehead and did an impersonation of the actor Syrus singing one of his numbers, while the whole troupe of slaves joined in on the chorus. He was just about to get up on the table when Fortunata went and whispered something in his ear, probably a warning that these drunken capers were undignified. . . .

But it was the secretary, not Fortunata, who effectively dampened his desire to dance, for quite without warning he began to read from the estate records as though he were reading some government bulletin.

"Born," he began, "on July 26th, on Trimalchio's estate at Cumae, thirty male and forty female slaves.

"Item, five hundred thousand bushels of wheat transferred from the threshing rooms into storage.

"On the same date, the slave Mithridates crucified alive for blaspheming the guardian spirit of our master Gaius.

"On the same date, the sum of three hundred thousand returned to the safe because it could not be invested.

"On the same date, in the gardens at Pompeii, fire broke out in the house of the bailiff Nasta . . ."

"What?" roared Trimalchio. "When did I buy any gardens at Pompeii?"

"Last year," the steward replied. "That's why they haven't yet appeared on the books."

"I don't care what you buy," stormed Trimalchio, "but if it's not reported to me within six months, I damn well won't have it appearing on the books at all![674]

But Trimalchio suddenly . . . ordered his will brought out and read aloud from beginning to end while the slaves sat there groaning and moaning. At the close of the reading, he turned to Habinnas. "Well, old friend, will you make me my tomb exactly as I order it? First, of course, I want a statue of myself. But carve my dog at my feet, and give me garlands of flowers, jars of perfume and every fight in Petraites' career. Then, thanks to your good offices, I'll live on long after I'm gone. In front, I want my tomb one hundred feet long, but two hundred feet deep. Around it I want an orchard with every known variety of fruit tree. You'd better throw in a vineyard too. For it's wrong, I think, that a man should concern himself with the house where he lives his life but give no thought to the home he'll have forever. But above all I want you to carve this notice:

THIS MONUMENT DOES NOT PASS INTO
THE POSSESSION OF MY HEIRS.

In any case I'll see to it in my will that my grave is protected from damage after my death. I'll appoint one of my ex-slaves to act as custodian to chase off the people who might come and crap on my tomb. Also, I want you to carve me several ships with all sail crowded and a picture of myself sitting on the judge's bench in official dress with five gold rings on my fingers and handing out a sack of coins to the people. For it's a fact, and you're my witness, that I gave a free meal to the whole town and a cash handout to everyone. Also make me a dining room, a frieze maybe, but however you like, and show the whole town celebrating at my expense. On my right I want a statue of Fortunata with a dove in her hand. And oh yes, be sure to have her pet dog tied to her girdle. And don't forget my pet slave. Also I'd like huge jars of wine, well stoppered so the wine won't slosh out. Then sculpt me a broken vase with a little boy sobbing out his heart over it. And in the middle stick a sundial so that anyone who wants the time of day will have to read my name. And how will this do for the epitaph?

HERE LIES GAIUS POMPEIUS TRIMALCHIO
MAECENATIANUS,
VOTED IN ABSENTIA AN OFFICIAL OF THE
IMPERIAL CULT.
HE COULD HAVE BEEN REGISTERED
IN ANY CATEGORY OF THE CIVIL SERVICE AT ROME
BUT CHOSE OTHERWISE.
PIOUS AND COURAGEOUS,

A LOYAL FRIEND,

HE DIED A MILLIONAIRE,

THOUGH HE STARTED LIFE WITH NOTHING.

LET IT BE SAID TO HIS ETERNAL CREDIT

THAT HE NEVER LISTENED TO PHILOSOPHERS.

PEACE TO HIM.

FAREWELL."[675]

At the end Trimalchio burst into tears.

The gaiety in the *Satyricon* is Greek rather than Latin in spirit. Indeed, much of the novel's locale is the formerly Greek area around Naples, "a land," as one of the characters says, "so infested with divinity that one might meet a god more easily than a man."[676] But there are also obscene passages whose filth is more Latin than Greek. When Petronius died in 66, a young poet named Valerius Martialis, who came from Bilbilis, a little southwest of the site of modern Saragossa, had already lived for several years in Rome. Here Martial came to know his fellow Spaniards, Quintilian, Lucan, and Seneca. Martial was far too poor to retreat from the degenerate society he saw about him into the disdainful luxury of Petronius. Comic laughter was impossible. Martial turned to a more traditional Roman defense: the epigrammatic, satirical, and often filthy[677] insult. For some thirty years, from the reign of Nero to the reign of Trajan, he launched poisoned darts into Roman vice. He attended the public spectacles and witnessed what the Roman's love of the concrete could do to Greek myth. Greek poets had sung of the love of Theseus and Ariadne and the dread Minotaur, half man, half bull. The wife of King Minos of Crete, Pasiphaë, had fallen in love with a bull, and the Minotaur was the offspring of their bestial union. When the Emperor Titus offered public spectacles to celebrate the opening of the Colosseum, one performance seized on a single detail in a myth of great beauty and meaning, and staged it:

> That Pasiphaë was mated to the Dictaean bull, believe: we have seen it, the old-time myth has won its warrant. And let not age-long eld, Caesar, marvel at itself: whatever Fame sings of, that the Arena makes real for thee.[678]

But the Colosseum did not always turn to Greek myth for its thrills. A robber named Laureolus had been convicted, crucified, and, while still alive

323

on the cross, had been torn to pieces by wild beasts. In Caligula's day a mime had already represented this horror. But now the Colosseum made it real, made it a Roman thing. Another condemned criminal was forced to die in the arena as the robber Laureolus died:

> As, fettered on a Scythian crag, Prometheus fed the untiring fowl with his too prolific heart, so Laureolus, hanging on no unreal cross, gave up his vitals defenceless to a Caledonian bear. His mangled limbs lived, though the parts dripped gore, and in all his body was nowhere a body's shape.[679]

Martial was poet enough to give to this wretch's agony at least some permanant significance by linking it with the agony of Prometheus. But in general an epigram of Martial's was less an effort to find meaning in another's violence than an effort to mean something violently:

> He who fancies that Acerra reeks of yesterday's wine is wrong. Acerra always drinks till daylight.[680]

> Diaulus has been a doctor, he is now an undertaker. He begins to put his patients to bed in his old effective way.[681]

> That book you recite, O Fidentinus, is mine. But your vile recitation begins to make it your own.[682]

> There was no one in the whole town willing to touch your wife, Caecilianus, gratis, while he was allowed; but, now you have set your guards, there is a huge crowd of gallants. You are an ingenious person![683]

> You complain, Velox, that I write long epigrams, you yourself write nothing. Yours are shorter.[684]

> Paulus purchases poetry, Paulus recites the poetry as his. For what you purchase you may rightly call your own.[685]

> I have often enjoyed Chrestina's favours. Do you ask how generously she grants them? Beyond them, Marianus, nothing is possible.[686]

> That no man willingly meets you, that, wherever you arrive, there is flight and vast solitude around you, Ligurinus, do you want to know what is the matter? You are too much of a poet. This is a fault passing dangerous. No tigress roused by the robbery of her cubs, no viper scorched by tropic suns, nor deadly scorpion is so dreaded. For who, I

ask you, would endure such trials? You read to me while I am standing, and read to me when I am sitting; while I am running you read to me, and read to me while I am using a jakes. I fly to the warm baths: you buzz in my ear; I make for the swimming bath: I am not allowed to swim; I haste to dinner: you detain me as I go; I reach the table: you rout me while I am eating. Wearied out, I sleep: you rouse me as I lie. Do you want to appreciate the evil you cause? Though you are a man just, upright, and harmless, you are a terror.[687]

Whoever can endure to be the guest of Zoilus should dine among the wives by the Walls, and drink, though sober, out of Leda's broken jar; this is a lighter and more decent thing, I maintain. Garbed in green he lies on a couch he alone fills, and with his elbows thrusts off his guests on either side, propped up as he is on purple and on silken cushions. There stands a catamite by him and offers his belching throat red feathers, and slips of mastick, and a concubine, lying on her back, with a green fan stirs a gentle breeze to cool his heat, and a boy flaps away the flies with a sprig of myrtle. With her nimble art a shampooer runs over his body, and spreads her skilled hand over all his limbs. A eunuch knows the signal of a snapped finger, and, being the inquisitor of that fastidious water, guides his boozy master's drunken person. But he himself, bending back to the crowd at his feet, in the midst of his lapdogs who are gnawing goose's livers, portions among his wrestlers the kernel of a boar, and gives his concubine the rumps of turtledoves. And while to us is supplied wine from Ligurian rocks, or must ripened in Massylian smoke, he pledges his naturals in Opimian nectar from crystal and murrine cups.[688]

In A.D. 100, after thirty-five years of denouncing the life of a big city and the vices of Roman society, Martial retired to his native Spain. Retirement sat less well with him than with a Prefect of the Praetorian Guard who retired from busy Rome a few decades later. This official

spent the rest of his life, seven years, quietly in the country, and upon his tomb, he caused this inscription to be placed: "Here lies Similis, who existed so-and-so many years, and lived seven."[689]

Unlike this weary Prefect, the poet sorely missed and needed Rome. He complained of

this provincial solitude, where, unless we study even immoderately, retirement is at once without solace and without excuse. . . . I miss that audience of my fellow-citizens. . . . That subtlety of judgment, that inspiration of the subject, the libraries, theatres, meeting-places, where pleasure is a student without knowing it—to sum up all, those things which fastidiously I deserted I regret, like one desolate.[690]

Martial had time in his provincial solitude to compose and send to Rome one more book of poetic epigrams before he died. Pliny the Younger wrote his friend Cornelius Priscus that Martial had died and that he, Pliny, had paid his way home, both out of friendship and "in return for the little poem which he had written about me." He even attempted in his letter to quote the poem from memory and added:

> Do you not think that the poet who wrote in such terms of me, deserved some friendly marks of my bounty *then*, and that he merits my sorrow *now*? For he gave me the most he could, and it was want of power only, if his present was not more valuable. But to say truth, what higher can be conferred on man than fame, and applause, and immortality? And though it should be granted, that his poems will not be immortal, still, no doubt, he composed them upon the contrary supposition.[691]

Before Martial's retirement to Spain, he had formed an attachment for another satirist, a young man from Aquinum named Junius Juvenalis, who became even better known than Martial. Like Martial, Juvenal turned to the life about him in Imperial Rome and not to Greek mythology. But, in place of Martial's compressed epigrams, the sixteen satires of Juvenal ran for several hundred lines each. In fact, it took him 661 lines merely to dispose of women. For he played the outraged moralist even more than Martial; and he was Roman enough, or at least Italian enough, to denounce real crimes and most newfangled customs with equal vigor. In similar Roman fashion, Pliny the Elder denounced the Greeks for their abominable luxury: "Those parents of all the vices, the Greeks," used olive oil in the gymnasium, on their bodies![692] Juvenal felt, or feigned to feel, anger at the flood of immigrants from the East which Roman conquests and the enslavement of prisoners had dumped into the city of Rome:

> The Syrian Orontes has long since poured into the Tiber, bringing with it its lingo and its manners, its flutes and its slanting harp-strings; bringing too the timbrels of the breed, and the trulls who are bidden ply their trade at the Circus.[693]

He thought the Greeks equally despicable:

they are a nation of play-actors. If you smile, your Greek will split his sides with laughter; if he sees his friend drop a tear, he weeps, though without grieving; if you call for a bit of fire in winter-time, he puts on his cloak; if you say "I am hot," he breaks into a sweat. Thus we are not upon a level, he and I; he has always the best of it, being ready at any moment, by night or by day, to take his expression from another man's face, to throw up his hands and applaud if his friend gives a good belch or piddles straight, or if his golden basin make a gurgle when turned upside down.[694]

Not only were the Greeks flatterers; their boastful histories were full of lies:

We have heard how ships once sailed through Mount Athos and all the lying tales of Grecian history.[695]

At least by the standards of Romans of his class, Juvenal was poor. He was dependent on wealthy patrons, just as the patrons in turn depended for life itself on the Emperor, especially when a bloodthirsty Emperor like Domitian ruled. The intellectual, the teacher of grammar, for example, received nothing as compared with a winning jockey:

And yet, small as the fee is—and it is smaller than the rhetor's wage— the pupil's unfeeling attendant nibbles off a bit of it for himself; so too does the steward.[696]

And yet be sure, ye parents, to impose the strictest laws upon the teacher: he must never be at fault in his grammar; he must know all history, and have all the authorities at his finger-tips. . . . Require of him that he shall mould the young minds as a man moulds a face out of wax with his thumb; insist that he shall be a father to the whole brood . . . "See to all this," you say, "and then, when the year comes round,, receive the golden piece which the mob demands for a winning jockey."[697]

It is no easy matter, anywhere, for a man to rise when poverty stands in the way of his merits: but nowhere is the effort harder than in Rome, where you must pay a big rent for a wretched lodging, a big sum to fill the bellies of your slaves, and buy a frugal dinner for yourself.[698]

In Rome, he adds bitterly, "we all live in a state of pretentious poverty."[699]

But here we inhabit a city supported for the most part by slender props: for that is how the bailiff holds up the tottering house, patches up gaping cracks in the old wall, bidding the inmates sleep at ease under a roof ready to tumble about their ears. No, no, I must live where there are no fires, no nightly alarms. Ucalegon below is already shouting for water and shifting his chattels; smoke is pouring out of your third-floor attic, but you know nothing of it; for if the alarm begins in the ground-floor, the last man to burn will be he who has nothing to shelter him from the rain but the tiles, where the gentle doves lay their eggs.[700]

If you can tear yourself away from the games of the Circus, you can buy an excellent house at Sora, at Fabrateria or Frusino, for what you now pay in Rome to rent a dark garret for one year. And you will there have a little garden, with a shallow well . . .[701]

Who but the wealthy get sleep in Rome? There lies the root of the disorder. The crossing of wagons in the narrow winding streets, the slanging of drovers when brought to a stand, would make sleep impossible for a Drusus—or a sea-calf.[702]

There's death in every open window as you pass along at night; you may well be deemed a fool, improvident of sudden accident, if you go out to dinner without having made your will. You can but hope, and put up a piteous prayer in your heart, that they may be content to pour down on you the contents of their slop-basins![703]

Despite all efforts by the Emperors to prevent provincial governors from exploiting the provinces, corruption continued. Juvenal enjoined one Ponticus:

When you enter your long-expected Province as its Governor, set a curb and a limit to your passion, as also to your greed; have compassion on the impoverished provincials, whose very bones you see sucked dry of marrow . . .[704]

Juvenal castigates the cruelty shown to slaves, the unbridled sexuality of the new woman. Women of the upper class fall in love with gladiators, with comedians, with tragedians, or with flute players. Go to the theater:

Do all the tiers in all our theatres hold one whom you may love without misgiving, and pick out thence? When the soft Bathyllus dances the part of the gesticulating Leda, Tuccia cannot contain herself; Your Apulian maiden heaves a sudden and longing yelp of ecstasy, as though she were in a man's arms; the rustic Thymele is all attention, it is then that she learns her lesson.[705]

328

The moral irresponsibility of Rome blames the goddess Fortuna for everything:

> Thou wouldst have no divinity, O Fortune, if we had but wisdom; it is we that make a goddess of thee, and place thee in the skies.[706]

He knows what rules Rome: it is money, and "unfeigned are the tears which lament the loss of wealth."[707]

Rome the lawgiver did not dazzle Juvenal. Praised as the source of justice for mankind, Rome struck him as enthroning violence. The evidence? Its awesome authority rested securely on naked force, on its army. And the evidence for this? The relation between soldier and civilian:

> Let us first consider the benefits common to all soldiers, of which not the least is this, that no civilian will dare to thrash you; if thrashed himself, he must hold his tongue, and not venture to exhibit to the Praetor the teeth that have been knocked out, or the black and blue lumps upon his face, or the one eye left which the doctor holds out no hope of saving. If he seek redress, he has appointed for him as judge a hobnailed centurion with a row of jurors with brawny calves sitting before a big bench. For the old camp law and the rule of Camillus still holds good which forbids a soldier to attend court outside the camp, and at a distance from the standards. "Most right and proper it is," you say, "that a centurion should pass sentence on a soldier; nor shall I fail of satisfaction if a just complaint is the theme of my prosecution." But then the whole cohort will be your enemies; all the maniples will agree as one man in applying a cure to the redress you have received by giving you a thrashing which shall be worse than the first. . . . Sooner you will find a false witness against a civilian than one who will tell the truth against the interest and the honour of a soldier. . . .
>
> If some rascally neighbour have filched from me a dell or a field of my ancestral estate . . . I shall have to wait for the time of year when the whole world begin their suits, and even then there will be a thousand wearisome delays. . . . But the gentlemen who are armed and belted have their cases set down for whatever time they please; nor is their substance worn away by the slow drag-chain of the law.
>
> Soldiers alone, again, have the right to make their wills during their fathers' life-time; for the law ordains that money earned in military service is not to be included in the property which is wholly in the father's sole control.[708]

If Juvenal loathed oppression by the army and oppression by the rich, he nevertheless saw with such clarity how little one could any longer expect from the Roman plebs that he coined what would become perhaps his most famous single phrase. In A.D. 31 Tiberius, who had withdrawn grimly to the fortified island of Capri, sent a letter to the Senate which doomed Sejanus, his Prefect of the Praetorian Guard. The Roman populace, which by then was formally powerless in politics but had learned to exert mob pressure at the Circus, had once backed Sejanus. But they lightheartedly turned against him,

> And what does the mob of Remus say? It follows fortune, as it always does, and rails against the condemned. That same rabble . . . if the aged Emperor had been struck down unawares, would in that very hour have conferred upon Sejanus the title of Augustus. Now that no one buys our votes, the public has long since cast off its cares; the people that once bestowed commands, consulships, legions and all else, now meddles no more and longs eagerly for just two things—Bread and Circuses![709]

Petronius, Martial, and Juvenal, though all three were satirists, differed greatly. For where Petronius scoffed scornfully but gaily, Martial and Juvenal moralized angrily. Martial's compressed glimpses of his society kept him too busy hating to allow him, except by implication, to show much love or pity. Yet Juvenal longs for what he loves more explicitly than Martial does. For example, Juvenal wrote:

> For what good man, what man worthy of the mystic torch, and such as the priest of Ceres would wish him to be, believes that any human woes concern him not? It is this that separates us from the dumb herd; and it is for this that we alone have had allotted to us a nature worthy of reverence, capable of divine things, fit to acquire and practise the arts of life, and that we have drawn from on high that gift of feeling which is lacking to the beasts that grovel with eyes upon the ground. To them in the beginning of the world our common maker gave only life; to us he gave souls as well, that fellow-feeling might bid us ask or proffer aid, gather scattered dwellers into a people, desert the primeval groves and woods inhabited by our forefathers, build houses for ourselves, with others adjacent to our own, that a neighbour's threshold, from the confidence that comes of union, might give us peaceful slumbers; shield with arms a fallen citizen, or one staggering from a grievous wound, give battle signals by a common trumpet, and seek protection inside the same city walls, and behind gates fastened by a single key.

But in these days there is more amity among serpents than among men . . .[710]

All three of these satirists were artists, beside whom Seneca and Lucan and Quintilian were merely literary men. The satirists were more clear-eyed than the rhetorical statesman, the rhetorical poet, and the professor of rhetoric. They had more to say. To say it, they had to make use, naturally, of rhetoric, but rhetoric rarely made use of them.

A greater Latin writer than these satirists had even more to say. He was a Roman Senator, born about A.D. 55, probably in northern Italy or southern Gaul; and his name was Cornelius Tacitus, whose story of Roman events from Augustus to Vespasian was the most powerful history written in the Latin tongue.[711] He, too, was the product of rhetoric, since rhetoric was the basic subject of liberal education. In fact, when he was still in his twenties and wrote his first work, it was a treatise on rhetoric, done with great rhetorical skill in the form of a dialogue. It was in the tradition of Cicero's dialogue, *On the Making of an Orator*, and of Seneca's, the *Education of an Orator*.[712] Tacitus and Lucan, who were born and lived under military autocracy, rejected the view that the sword of Julius Caesar put an end to a bungling and irresponsible oligarchy, an oligarchy that Pompey and Brutus and Cassius and Cato the Younger fought to restore. For Tacitus, as for Lucan, Caesar's sword put an end to freedom. Yet Tacitus' oversimplified view of the fall of republican government did not invalidate his very sensible judgment that the orator's art had declined precisely because it was too late to talk. The orator's audience, the people, had no political power. Power belonged to the Emperor. Aside from the courtroom, therefore, what was really left was the eulogy, the panegyric. With either Vespasian or Titus on the throne, and the tyrants Caligula and Nero dead, Tacitus could have one of the characters in his dialogue say with some show of truth:

Rhodes has had some orators, Athens a great many: in both communities all power was in the hands of the populace—that is to say, the untutored democracy, in fact the mob. Likewise at Rome, so long as the constitution was unsettled, so long as the country kept wearing itself out with factions and dissensions and disagreements, so long as there was no peace in the forum, no harmony in the senate, no restraint in the courts of law, no respect for authority, no sense of propriety on the part of the officers of state, the growth of eloquence was doubtless sturdier, just as untilled soil produces certain vegetation in greater luxuriance. . . .

If a community could be found in which nobody ever did anything wrong, orators would be just as superfluous among saints as are doctors among those that need no physician. Just as the healing art, I repeat, is very little in demand and makes very little progress in countries where people enjoy good health and strong constitutions, so oratory has less prestige and smaller consideration where people are well behaved and ready to obey their rulers. What is the use of long arguments in the senate, when good citizens agree so quickly? What is the use of one harangue after another on public platforms, when it is not the ignorant multitude that decides a political issue, but a monarch who is the incarnation of wisdom?[713]

In this view, neither the "howl of the needy" that had so disgusted Cicero nor other political protest was a legitimate use of rhetoric. Tacitus remained silent during the savage years of Domitian's reign. About 98, when better days had come, he published an essay, half biography, half eulogy, on his father-in-law, Agricola, who had conquered and wisely administered Britain. The *Agricola* gave Tacitus a chance to speak of the professional informers, the book-burnings, the executions through which he had just lived and to praise the benign rule of Nerva, assisted by his adopted son Trajan:

> Now at last heart is coming back to us: from the first, from the very outset of this happy age, Nerva has united things long incompatible, Empire and liberty; Trajan is increasing daily the happiness of the times; and public confidence has not merely learned to hope and pray, but has received security for the fulfilment of its prayers and even the substance thereof. . . . For the term of fifteen years, a large space in human life, chance and change have been cutting off many among us; others, and the most energetic, have perished by the Emperor's ferocity; while the few who remain have outlived not merely their neighbours but, so to say, themselves; for out of their prime have been blotted fifteen years, during which mature men reached old age and old men the very bounds almost of decrepitude, and all without opening their lips.[714]

Although Tacitus exhibited serious confusion about both the geography of Britain and the military strategy of Agricola, his love for his father-in-law gave his rhetoric work to do. In alliterative, mannered prose it sang a paean to the old-fashioned Roman virtue of a frontier fighter and a just administrator. In the same year he finished a third work, his *Germany*. He knew that the German tribes were the most dangerous of the Empire's foreign foes: in these Germans, as he described them, with their blue eyes, red hair, tall frames, with their dislike of hard work, their inability to bear heat and thirst, their patience under cold and hunger, their beer and drunkenness, he saw a rhetorical foil to the nations Nerva ruled. Germany, with its wild scenery and harsh climate became, as he wrote, a sort of anti-Cosmopolis, held in check largely by intertribal warfare. But while describing the vices of the Germans, he also insinuates that the noble savage of Barbaria in many ways excelled civilized man; in effect, barbarous Germany rebukes a decaying civilization. Its men are warlike, its women are chaste, willing to bear and rear children, and even to breast-feed their babies. Germans are hospitable, they are not money-mad and charge no interest on loans, the members of the lower class are ruled by their betters, and Germans love freedom. In short, despite the barbarian's drunkenness and quarrelsomeness and filth, many of his customs recall the good old days of the early Roman Republic.

Tacitus had served his apprenticeship. He next wrote the *Histories*, an account of Roman history from the civil wars of 69 to, probably,[715] the assassination of Domitian. He then wrote the *Annals*, a narrative of events from the reign of Augustus to 69. His subject was less vast than Livy's: for every decade that Tacitus covered Livy had covered almost a century. But Livy wrote in the triumphal reign of Augustus. Livy told how a tiny republic conquered and ruled the most extensive empire of which either he or his readers had ever heard. He wrote, and indeed died, before the society Augustus tried to restore began to show the more obvious symptoms of decay. It was precisely those symptoms that Tacitus had been forced to witness, and the symptom that caused him to agonize most was tyranny. In one of its dimensions, his history was a kind of poem on the death of political freedom. In a sense, Lucan's literary epic had been that too, but Lucan's *Pharsalia* was written in verse. It was Tacitus' agony that gave his history so many of the qualities of poetry. He was no irresponsible boy, dabbling in conspiracy. He was a Roman official, who lived to serve as proconsul of Asia. Unlike Lucan, he had lived through at least a portion of the horrors he recounted; and, as a Senator, he lived also near to the center of political power. In one respect he resembled the Greek historian, Thucydides, who also had watched social disintegration and the triumph of violence. But, being a Roman under the Empire, he used his rhetorical training to portray rather than to analyze. The freedom he mourned was not the freedom that Periclean Athens had fought for but the freedom of a powerful oligarchy. If he understood why Marius and Julius Caesar had been able to muster the force to fight the oligarchs, he showed little interest in the reckless self-interest of the Senate or its tyranny over most Roman citizens. Theory did not interest him; the fact of a personal tyrant did.

Perhaps it was precisely because Tacitus was so genuine in his hatred of what he saw that not even his rhetorical training ever made him pompous. In this he resembled the satirists Martial and Juvenal. Of the Ciceronian urbanity of his early dialogue no sign remained in his histories. He was terse to the point of occasional obscurity, epigrammatic and biting, ironic with a touch of sarcasm, his prose sometimes twisted by pain and by something close to despair. He may not have been a profound thinker; sometimes indeed he is a superb and impassioned journalist reporting on the collapse of what to him had been a free society. He had a shrewd eye for the practical and specific. His story exhibits a fine tension between pride and disgust. There is the pride caused by what Romans still accomplished in distant climes, and sorrow for her slain, unburied sons abroad. For example, when in A.D. 15, six years after Varus and his three legions were ambushed and destroyed in the Teutoburg Forest, Caesar Germanicus led a punitive expedition beyond the Rhine. On a certain day the Caesar and his army found themselves

> not far from the Teutoburgian Forest, where, it was said, the remains of Varus and his legions lay unburied.
>
> There came upon the Caesar, therefore, a passionate desire to pay the last tribute to the fallen and their leader . . . Survivors of the disaster, who had escaped the battle or their chains, told how here the legates fell, there the eagles were taken, where the first wound was dealt upon Varus, and where he found death by the suicidal stroke of his own unhappy hand. They spoke of the tribunal from which Arminius made his harangue, all the gibbets and the torture-pits for the prisoners and the arrogance with which he insulted the standards and eagles.
>
> And so, six years after the fatal field, a Roman army, present on the ground, buried the bones of the three legions; and no man knew whether he consigned to earth the remains of a stranger or a kinsman, but all thought of all as friends and members of one family, and, with anger rising against the enemy, mourned at once and hated.[716]

The pride and the sorrow expressed in this passage were often in tense and painful conflict with the deep shame Tacitus felt that he and other Senators, in order to save their skins, should have voted against their fellows the unjust sentences which the tyrant Domitian proposed. The self-hate in that shame was the same kind of self-hate that inspired the anger of Martial and Juvenal.

About 120 a Roman official named Gaius Suetonius Tranquillus published a book, the *Lives of the Caesars*, which made him famous. Latin literature had indeed a long tradition of biography, but Latin biography was rooted in the funeral oration and the eulogy, as witness Tacitus' relatively recent life of his father-in-law, Agricola. Suetonius undertook to write brief biographies of Julius Caesar and his eleven successors from Augustus to Domitian. Although the *Lives* inevitably contained much court gossip and although the author was Roman enough to focus more on the morals of his subjects than on their historical function in the political and economic development of the Empire, Suetonius was no mere gossipmonger. As one of the Emperor Hadrian's private secretaries, he may have had access to the Imperial archives;[717] and he was clearly concerned to discover the truth and not merely to edify the reader. Interestingly, although he practiced law briefly and therefore presumably received the stock training in grammar and rhetoric, he wrote several treatises on grammatical problems but little on rhetoric. Among his other works are brief biographies of a number of Latin writers; books on Roman and Greek antiquities; and books on natural history.[718] In short, he was a scholar; and although like Tacitus he lived through the horrors of Domitian's reign, he did not write in agony. He recorded with equal zest the murder, rape, incest, acts of sexual perversion, tortures, and robberies committed by the worst Emperors, along with the good sense and respect for money exhibited by Vespasian. Perhaps Suetonius felt that even under tyrants his own ox was not gored. He was the son of an Eques, and the Empire had been good to the Equites and good for business. Though the freedom of the Senate to govern, which Tacitus longed to go back to, had indeed been lost, or anyhow subordinated to the Emperor, the freedom to do business had increased. It was therefore the Senatorial, not the Equestrian, Order that hatched conspiracies; and the Emperors reacted accordingly. Suetonius was interested in the struggles of the mighty, and he correctly assumed that they would interest his readers.

There were other famous Latin writers in the century that followed Augustus' death. But poets like the Neapolitan Statius or the Etrurian Persius had neither the poetic insight of Virgil and Horace nor the vigor of

335

Martial and Juvenal. And the historian Velleius Paterculus of Campania, for example, was merely a retired officer who had served Tiberius and admired him and was inspired to write an amateurish compendium of Roman history.

In the year 100, Pliny the Elder's nephew and adopted son delivered before the Roman Senate a panegyric to the reigning emperor, Trajan. Pliny the Younger had been about eight years old when the tyrant Nero committed suicide and the Empire was shaken by civil war and when the ephemeral reigns of Galba, Otho, and Vitellius passed in bewildering succession. Vespasian had then brought back order for a decade. Vespasian's elder son Titus had successfully ruled for two years, only to be succeeded by the tyrant Domitian. Pliny had entered government service under Domitian and continued to serve under the good Emperors, Nerva and Trajan. His panegyric to Trajan became a model for future panegyrics, and the resultant literary genre, though it had ancient roots in Roman literature, became peculiarly expressive of the second century, when the system of the Principate had endured long enough to seem secure, successful, and eternal, as Augustan literature had promised. There was no longer either a Virgil or a Horace to praise the Princeps; the rhetorical skill of the younger Pliny came to the rescue. In Augustus' day panegyrists expressed the Empire's thanks to the gods, and to the Emperor; now they thanked Jove's vicar on earth:

> And although until now it might have been uncertain whether rulers were given to the world by fortune, by accident, or by some other *numen*, yet will it be manifest that our Emperor has been appointed by divine providence. For he has been revealed not by the hidden power of the fates but in the public presence by Jove himself: chosen, in fact, among the altars and sacrificial preparations, in the same place which Jove has occupied as presently and as manifestly as he has heaven and the stars. How much more proper and pious it is, O Jupiter Best, that I should beseech you, formerly founder, now preserver of our empire . . . that what I say be as free from the appearance of flattery as my act is from compulsion![719]

Some of the former Emperors had been deified by their successors for the wrong reasons. Not so with Trajan's adoptive father, Nerva:

> Tiberius consecrated Augustus to heaven, but in order to introduce the charge of lèse majesté; Nero, Claudius, but that he might bring ridicule; Titus, Vespasian; Domitian, Titus; but the former that he might appear

336

the son, the latter the brother, of god. You have interred your father among the stars not for a cause of terror to the citizens, not in insolence to the divine powers, not in your own honor, but because you believe him a god.[720]

Then Pliny testified to the assembled Senators:

Often have I silently wondered, Conscript Fathers, of what sort and how great must he be at whose beck and call the seas and the lands are mastered, and peace and war; while I might conceive and imagine an Emperor whom power made equal to the immortal gods, not even in longing did it occur to me to conceive of one like him whom we see.[721]

On the day, Pliny continued, when the Roman populace expected a new Emperor to distribute gifts to the people,

to observe the Emperor's appearance in public, swarms of children, the future populace, used to sit along the wayside. It was the business of the parents to show off their little ones, and having set them on their shoulders to teach them words and cries of flattery and adulation. The children would repeat what they were taught, and very many with vain prayers would bombard the unlistening ears of the Emperor; and ignorant of what they asked and did not receive, they were put off until they should know quite plainly.[722]

By successfully encouraging both the production of goods and their exchange throughout the Empire, Trajan improved on the generosity of the gods. The result was that the provinces preferred the Principate to a Roman Republic that governed itself freely but was rent by destructive civil wars:

How it delights all provinces now to have come under our protection and domination after the advent of an Emperor who transfers and restores, now here, now there, the fruitfulness of the lands, as time and need demand, who sustains and guards a nation separated by the sea as if a part of the people and plebs of Rome! And never even has heaven such liberality as to fecundate and warm all lands at the same time: *he* simultaneously from all dispels, if not sterility, then the evils of sterility; *he* brings in, if not fecundity, then the goods of fecundity; *he* by the exchange of provisions so joins together East and West that all nations in turn learn to know what they produce and what they lack, that they grasp how much more useful it is to serve one master than to serve liberty in discord.[723]

Most of Trajan's predecessors were glad when their subjects lacked virtue.

> And indeed previous Emperors, except for your father and one or two others (and I have said too much) rejoiced rather in the vices of the citizens than their virtues, first because nature enjoys in another what is her own, and finally because they thought those were more patient of slavery to whom it was fitting only to be slaves.[724]

Speaking of the mad and murderous tyrant, Domitian, Pliny declared that

> No one dared to approach him, none to speak to him, that being who chased always after shadows and mystery, who never came out of solitude but to make solitude.[725]

Pliny contrasted the modest bronze statues of Trajan with the gold and silver images of some of the wicked rulers who preceded him:

> And so we see your statue—one or two of them—in the entrance-court of Jupiter Greatest and Best, and that in bronze. But a short time ago every entrance, every step, the whole area shone, here in gold, here in silver—or rather was polluted, since the images of the gods were befouled by their intermingling with the statues of an incestuous Emperor.[726]

If any should ask Pliny why he eulogized his sovereign,

> let them remember that the best way to praise a living Emperor is to censure his predecessors who deserve censure. For when posterity is silent about an evil Emperor, it is clear the actual Emperor is behaving the same way.[727]

In place of the caprice of the tyrant, Trajan had, or so Pliny claimed, restored the rule of law.

> Wherefore now for the first time I hear, now for the first time I learn, it is not "The Emperor above the laws," but "The laws above the Emperor," and when Caesar is consul what is forbidden others is forbidden him.[728]

Before this redefinition of the relation of the Emperor to the Empire,

> We were not accustomed to offer vows for the eternity of the Empire and for the safety of the Emperors, but, on the contrary, for the safety of the Emperors and on *their* account for the eternity of the Empire.[729]

338

No doubt Pliny's *Panegyric* would have struck some members of the Senate during Augustus' reign as the grossest flattery; and as time went on, the panegryics to the Emperors grew more flattering still. But this flattery was a rhetorical device for instructing, just as Pericles more than five centuries earlier, in his oration over the Athenian dead, praised Athens for being what he wished Athens to become. It is true that what Pliny seemed to praise was not a community but an individual; but it is also true that this particular individual, by virtue of the office he held, personified Eternal Rome. By elaborate rhetorical device Pliny was congratulating Rome on having abolished the unashamed tyranny into which certain Emperors had temporarily dragged her and on having restored the Mos Majorum, the customs of the ancestors.

Pliny was typical of those who created second-century Latin literature: the wellborn, wealthy civil servant, famous as a lawyer and an orator, eager to win literary renown. Besides his orations, he dabbled in verse. Like Seneca before him, he was not only a prolific writer of letters; he wrote with an eye to publication. He could describe with careful modesty the luxury of his Laurentine villa on the seashore, an easy horseback ride from his busy life at Rome; but he could also furnish the historian Tacitus with the most detailed account of how his uncle, Pliny the Elder, famous for his encyclopaedic *Natural History,* met his death while commanding the fleet at Misenum. On August 24 in the year 79, Vesuvius erupted. Out of scientific curiosity, Pliny the Elder started for the scene of disaster, joined in the rescue work, and finally died on the seashore, his nephew thought from asphyxiation. Pliny's letters to Trajan dealt not only with the troublesome Christians in his province of Bithynia; Pliny had to cope with a badly planned public bath and begged Trajan to send him an architect. But the Emperor reminded him, a little drily, that Rome usually got architects from the Greek provinces: in effect, that Pliny, not he, was living where the architects were. However, in the same letter, the Emperor spoke impatiently of "these Greeklings."[730]

If the quality of Latin literature declined rapidly after Tacitus, that portion of the literature of Cosmopolis which was written in Greek fared not much better. Greek literature suffered from some of the same diseases that afflicted the Latin writers, notably from an educational system based on rhetoric. Indeed one form which Greek revenge for Rome's conquest and pillage of the Greek world unconsciously took was the stream of Greek professors who moved to Rome to teach rhetoric to their conquer-

339

ors and the Greek schools of rhetoric that upper-class Romans streamed eastward to attend. Decades before the legions for the first time crossed the Adriatic, Isocrates and Demosthenes had won out over Socrates and Plato: rhetoric had dethroned philosophy. Athens was still a holy name, not chiefly because of its orators, but because its philosophers had sought truth and goodness, its artists had sought beauty, its poets had sought all of these, and because a few Greeks had even sought the radiance of grace that only the immortal gods could shed on men. But now Athens sought tourists, purchasers of *objets d'art*. She sought Roman students, both of rhetoric and of enough philosophy to improve rhetoric, and sometimes of enough Stoic philosophy to make bearable the yoke of force which Rome had first placed on others' necks and now wore on her own.

Part of this cultural dilution which Roman rule helped the Greeks to achieve had been the spread of gladiatorial sports eastward. That Corinth should thus celebrate force and death was understandable, since Corinth, sacked by Rome in 146 B.C., had been refounded as a Roman colony. But late in the first century A.D. even Athens had accepted gladiatorial combat, or so an orator reported at Rhodes. At the foot of the Acropolis, in the theater of the god, Dionysus, where the tragedies of Aeschylus, Sophocles, and Euripides had been produced, the gladiators fought. A Greek orator declared to the Rhodians that

in regard to the gladiatorial shows the Athenians have so zealously emulated the Corinthians, or rather, have so surpassed both them and all others in their mad infatuation, that whereas the Corinthians watch these combats outside the city in a glen, a place that is able to hold a crowd but otherwise is dirty and such that no one would even bury there any freeborn citizen, the Athenians look on at this fine spectacle in their theatre under the very walls of the Acropolis, in the place where they bring their Dionysus into the orchestra and stand him up, so that often a fighter is slaughtered among the very seats in which the Hierophant and the other priests must sit. And the philosopher[731] who spoke about this matter and rebuked them they refused to obey and did not even applaud; on the contrary, they were so incensed that, although in blood he was inferior to no Roman, but enjoyed a reputation greater than any one man has attained for generations, and was admittedly the only man who since the time of the ancients had lived most nearly in conformity with reason, this man was forced to leave the city and preferred to go and live somewhere else in Greece. But you, O men of Rhodes, would not tolerate any such thing as that, since among you there is a law which prescribes that the executioner must never enter the city.[732]

The Peloponnesian War had strengthened Greek belief in force and deceit and had helped to prepare her monied class to collaborate with Rome and even to believe in Rome, bringer of peace, queller of the discontented poor. One of Rome's oldest traditions recalled the rape of the Sabine women. But the Sabine women may have partly consented: in any event, Greece did.

Long after Greek tragedy failed, after Greek comedy became trivial and Greek art rhetorical, after Greek history began to exhibit decreasing insight and Greek philosophy turned toward skepticism or moralizing, Greek mathematics and Greek science flourished, notably at Alexandria. By the first century A.D., partly because Rome never adequately replaced the patronage of the Hellenistic kings, the great age of mathematics and science had passed its apogee. But science and mathematics were by no means dead. In the Latin world, of course, writers such as Vitruvius, Columella, and Frontinus confined themselves to the practical. Theoretical work was confined to the Greek East. About A.D. 100 in Gerasa, a city east of Palestine on the fringe of the Arabian Desert, Nicomachus wrote on elementary number theory and on the mathematics of music, two of the sciences Socrates had required of those who would govern his ideal republic. A little later in Smyrna, on the Asian shore of the Aegean Sea, Theon wrote on number theory, on musical harmony, on astronomy. Both of these men worked in the mathematical tradition of Plato. Probably early in the first century A.D., Strabo, who came from the Province of Pontus, had attempted a universal geography in seventeen books; but he too had difficulty getting information, especially from Roman sources. Strabo lived in Rome for eleven years or more and admired the achievement of the Romans. But he was puzzled by the Roman's lack of intellectual curiosity:

> Roman historical writers imitate the Greeks, but not very far. For what they say they take over from the Greeks, but they do not of themselves bring along much love of learning, so that they do very little by way of filling up any gaps left by the others.[733]

In the second century, Ptolemy, a scientist more famous than any of these, wrote on optics, on geometry, on mechanics. He published a treatise on geography along with an atlas of maps. His treatise assumed the sphericity of the earth, and he tried to furnish accurate lines of latitude and longitude; but he lacked adequate knowledge of distant lands. Even more famous than his geography is his *Mathematical Collection*,[734] a treatise on astronomy which he developed from the work Hipparchus had done some three centuries earlier, a work which attempted to explain the movements of both the fixed stars and the planets. Hipparchus, like other Greek scientists, had discarded the hypothesis of Aristarchus of Samos that the planets revolved around the sun. Ptolemy discarded it too, and undertook to explain the apparently retrograde motion of the outer planets by adopting Apollonius of Perga's theory: the planets move in circular orbits whose centers move around the earth in larger orbits. The resulting motion would be that of a point on the rim of a turning wheel whose hub was mounted on the rim of a larger turning wheel. This imagined epicycle, or cycle on a cycle, seemed to explain the phenomena that Ptolemy saw with the naked eye.[735]

What makes Nicomachus and Theon and Ptolemy most notable is that they exemplified the free Greek intellect seeking to understand, not because knowing was a means to practical action, but because, as Aristotle had put it, all men desire by nature to know. This had been the marked characteristic, at least in the fields of mathematics and science, of the Museum at Alexandria during the third century B.C., before the ordeal of Roman conquest had dislocated and largely disintegrated the Eastern, Hellenistic world. But when Trajan and Hadrian were bringing stability to the Imperial system, Hellenic culture was reasserting itself. To a limited extent it was reasserting itself even in the field of philosophy. One of Nero's secretaries, a freedman named Epaphroditus, had a Phrygian slave called Epictetus. Epaphroditus allowed this Asian slave to attend the lectures of the Italian Stoic, Musonius Rufus. Epictetus was later freed, and taught Stoicism himself. In 89, when Domitian banished philosophers from Rome, Epictetus crossed over to Epirus, where he taught for the rest of his life. Stoicism had been founded about 300 B.C. by a Cypriot, Zeno, who may have been of Phoenician rather than Greek extraction; it had been developed at Athens as one of the offshoots of the teachings of Socrates; it had achieved greater success among the Roman oligarchy than any other Greek philosophy; and now, swinging full circle, it was being taught on the western fringe of Greece between Athens and Rome by a former Asian slave, not merely to millionaires but also to the humble and the poor. Epictetus' lack of reverence for wealth and power placed him nearer Zeno, who had once been a Cynic like Diogenes, and also placed him nearer to the barefoot Socrates, whom Stoics liked to quote, than to the Catos and Ciceros and Senecas of Rome.

Perhaps because Epictetus had seen the Roman Empire through the eyes of a slave, he knew from personal observation that power blinds. He loved freedom as passionately as Socrates had; but like Socrates he knew that true freedom resides in the mind and the soul and can exist even under political tyranny. Like Socrates, he knew that the first step toward wisdom is the recognition of one's own ignorance:

> What is the first business of one who practises philosophy? To get rid of thinking that one knows; for it is impossible to get a man to begin to learn that which he thinks he knows.[736]

But then what? Although the Stoics looked on themselves as Socratics, understanding for understanding's sake did not attract them. The Stoics were moralists. For Epictetus as for other Stoics, right action is the goal; philosophy is merely the means.

> The first and most necessary division in philosophy is that which has to do with the application of the principles, as, for example, Do not lie. The second deals with the demonstrations, as, for example, How comes it that we ought not to lie? The third confirms and discriminates between these processes, as, for example, How does it come that this is a proof? For what is a proof, what is logical consequence, what contradiction, what truth, what falsehood? Therefore, the third division is necessary because of the second, and the second because of the first; while the most necessary of all, and the one in which we ought to rest, is the first. But we do the opposite; for we spend our time in the third division, and all our zeal is devoted to it, while we utterly neglect the first. Wherefore, we lie, indeed, but are ready with the arguments which prove that one ought not to lie.[737]

The goal is to achieve moral purpose, *proairesis*, the habit of making right choices:

> Yet, if you enquire of me what is man's good, I can give you no other answer than that it is a kind of moral purpose.[738]

Where Socrates speculated that knowledge is virtue or the source of all virtues, Epictetus was almost saying that morality, the habit of choosing the right act, is the only reason for seeking truth. Epictetus had such faith in the self-reliance of the good man that there is a sense in which he pits this self-reliance not only against the state but against God: "My leg you will fetter, but my moral purpose not even Zeus himself has power to overcome."[739] As for harm from purely human power, how can that hurt the man with right moral purpose?

> "But I can cut off your head." Well said! I had forgotten that I ought to pay attention to you, as to fever or cholera, and set up an altar to you, just as in Rome there is an altar to the God Fever.[740]

It is moral purpose that enables the mind to inquire, the philosopher to philosophize:

> What is that faculty by virtue of which men are curious and inquisitive, or again, unmoved by what is said? The faculty of hearing? No, it is none other than the faculty of moral purpose.[741]

Those who philosophized without that purpose were likely to be one of the professors of philosophy who now sold their wares throughout the Empire. Epictetus did not choose to be one of these. He was indeed trying, as Socrates had done, to achieve direct encounter with the soul of those he taught, and he declined to put on a show:

> Then you will say, "When I met Epictetus it was like meeting a stone, a statue." Yes, for you took a look at me, and nothing more. The person who meets a man as a man is one who learns to understand the other's judgements, and in his turn exhibits his own. Learn to know my judgements; show me your own, and then say you have met me. Let us put one another to the test; if I cherish any evil judgement, take it away; if you cherish one, bring it forward. That is what it means to meet a philosopher. Oh no; but your way is: "We are passing, and while we are hiring our ship, we have a chance to take a look at Epictetus; let's see what in the world he has to say." Then you leave with the remark: "Epictetus was nothing at all, his language was full of solecisms and barbarisms." What else were you capable of judging, when you came in like that?[742]

But even love must be made subservient to philosophic calm:

> if you kiss your child, your brother, your friend, never allow your fancy free rein, nor your exuberant spirits to go as far as they like, but hold them back, stop them, just like those who stand behind generals when they ride in triumph, and keep reminding them that they are mortal.[743]

To gain the Stoic serenity that permits right choice, Epictetus echoes Aristotle's advice in the *Nicomachaean Ethics*:

I am inclined to pleasure; I will betake myself to the opposite side of the rolling ship, and that beyond measure, so as to train myself. I am inclined to avoid hard work; I will strain and exercise my sense-impressions to this end, so that my aversion from everything of this kind shall cease.[744]

In short, Epictetus believed in character training as a bulwark against the mad pleasure-seeking that degraded the upper class. It was a bulwark that had for a time restrained anti-intellectual Sparta and the anti-intellectual patricians of the early Roman Republic. How the bulwark could continue to withstand the internal pressures of a greedy imperialism, Epictetus did not say. It was a bulwark that even Socrates thought appropriate for children. In a sense, the decline of intellectual life, of aesthetic perception, and of mutual trust had left most of the citizens of Cosmopolis like trained children in a new and strange environment. In this new environment, much of their training proved catastrophically inadequate.

Through this dangerous environment, thought Epictetus, a man could find his way to freedom, on one condition:

Give up . . . wanting anything but what God wants. And who will prevent you, who will compel you? No one, any more than anyone prevents or compels Zeus.[745]

Realize that God is the father of men as well as of gods:

Yet, if Caesar adopts you no one will be able to endure your conceit, but if you know that you are a son of Zeus, will you not be elated?[746]

It is up to us to learn not to change the things about us but to accept them and to "keep our wills in harmony with what happens."[747] That Archimedes, the scientist and engineer, could change the things about him a good deal seems not to have interested Epictetus. Other Greeks had for centuries learned how to modify by medical knowledge the part of matter closest of all to man, his own body; but this achievement too seems to have left Epictetus unmoved. Nor was Epictetus, as one might guess, retreating into contemplation. On the contrary, he valued right action above contemplation. But to a world ruled by work, worry, and illusion he urgently preached acceptance of life: we cannot control the moral conduct of others but we can and should control our own. Basically, what we control is our will, whereas in the last analysis a man controls neither his property nor his own body. He quoted Cleanthes' hymn to Zeus:

345

Lead thou me on, O Zeus, and Destiny,
To that goal long ago to me assigned.[748]

The wise man will accept the role assigned him in what Augustus on his deathbed had called the comedy of life:

> Remember that you are an actor in a play, the character of which is determined by the Playwright: if He wishes the play to be short, it is short; if long, it is long; if He wishes you to play the part of a beggar, remember to act even this rôle adroitly; and so if your rôle be that of a cripple, an official, or a layman. For this is your business, to play admirably the rôle assigned you; but the selection of that rôle is Another's.[749]

Whether the Divine Playwright, when Julius Caesar was done to death, really selected for the young Octavian the role of Emperor or whether Octavian himself selected that role and thereby converted the play into a comedy of human power remained a fine theological and historical point. Whether, once this comedy started, Domitian, while pre-empting for himself the role of Divine Playwright, was right to expel the philosophers from Rome remained another point. Cato the Younger was not the only Stoic who objected to seeing an earlier drama end, the drama in which Cicero played in the Forum, the drama of Republican government. Epictetus, of course, would have questioned the moral choices of Octavian, would have despised Domitian's blasphemy, and would have doubted Cato's views on freedom. The stage Epictetus was talking about was not Cicero's forum but the Cosmos ruled by Zeus. If, said Epictetus,

> what is said by the philosophers regarding the kinship of God and men be true, what other course remains for men but that which Socrates took when asked to what country he belonged, never to say, "I am an Athenian," or "I am a Corinthian," but "I am a citizen of the universe"? ... Well, then, anyone who has attentively studied the administration of the universe and has learned that "the greatest and most authoritative and most comprehensive of all governments is this one, which is composed of men and God ..."—why should not such a man call himself a citizen of the universe? Why should he not call himself a son of God?[750]

This Stoic picture of the universe, to which Epictetus here subscribed, might have sounded to a Christian like a groping for the Kingdom of God. To many a non-Christian Roman it might suggest that the Roman Empire accurately reflected God's government as Hadrian reflected Olympian

Zeus or Jupiter. In the tyrannical days of a Nero or a Domitian, many upper-class Roman Stoics were still not sure whether Zeus preferred to have the Res Publica governed by a military autocrat or a Senate full of Catos. But by 135, when Epictetus died, he and Hadrian had come to know each other personally. Custom and the good government of Nerva, Trajan, and Hadrian had settled the problem of whether the Empire was a republic or a monarchy, though unhappily not the question of how one Emperor ought to succeed another. Yet, even if another tyrant like Domitian should reach the throne, and the informer's trade should again thrive, the Stoic need not fear. For Epictetus left open an escape hatch that neither his hero, Socrates, nor the Christians of Epictetus' day permitted men to use: suicide. Nobody, of course, should lightly take his own life. But Epictetus was fond of reminding his pupils that, if a man found life insupportable, then

> remember that the door has been thrown open. Do not become a greater coward than the children, but just as they say, "I won't play any longer," when the thing does not please them, so do you also, when things seem to you to have reached that stage, merely say, "I won't play any longer," and take your departure; but if you stay, stop lamenting.[751]

Despite Socrates' position, the Greek world had always accepted suicide. It was, after all, the Greek world that produced Stoicism and also produced Epictetus. But it was by no mere chance that Rome accepted Stoicism as it had not accepted any other philosophy. The whole history of Rome had been one of perserverance rather than hope, of holding the line in battle, of holding the line in politics. Moreover, Romans had for centuries been fascinated by death, as witness their development of their Etruscan neighbors' funeral rites and human sacrifice into huge gladiatorial carnivals of death. As the Graeco-Roman world grew old, as its educated inhabitants watched both Greek literature and Latin literature flag, along with the other arts that had made the name of Athens a holy name, as they remembered with nostalgia their ancient practice of self-government, those who did not turn to Eastern religions found great consolation in Stoicism, not only because it preached piety and courage but also because it insisted that the door was always open. Stoicism was an embattled fortress, as the Roman Empire was embattled, as the Hellenistic, Romanized soul was embattled.

One of Epictetus' pupils, Flavius Arrianus, was a Greek who came from Bithynia, a province adjacent to Epictetus' native Phrygia. Arrian recorded and published some of Epictetus' lectures. But, unlike Epictetus, Arrian was a successful Roman general, an Imperial governor under Hadrian, a writer of histories and of military treatises, an admirer of the Greek writer, Xenophon. Indeed, the title of his most famous work, a history of Alexander's conquests, imitates the title of Xenophon's *Anabasis*: it is called the *Anabasis of Alexander*. It was as a general who had beaten off the nomadic Alans when in 134 they burst through from southeast Russia to raid Cosmopolis that Arrian wrote. Even so, his *Anabasis* celebrated not his own Roman success but the epic of how the Hellenistic Cosmopolis, before Rome ever conquered it, overthrew its secular foe, the Persian Empire, and extended the cultural influences of Hellas clear to India.

Another Greek who re-created the Hellenic past was Plutarch, born about A.D. 46 in the little town of Chaeronea, where Philip of Macedon nearly four centuries earlier had conquered the Athenian and Theban armies and where, some hundred and thirty years before Plutarch was born, Sulla had defeated the armies of Mithradates. Plutarch studied at Athens, traveled in Greece, Asia Minor, Egypt, and Italy. He visited Rome and formed friendships with many leading Romans, although he never thoroughly mastered Latin. He lived into Hadrian's reign and served that Emperor as procurator of Achaea. Most of his life he spent in Chaeronea, studying and writing. He wrote numerous essays on ethical, religious, and political subjects under the general title, *Morals*. But he earned his most enduring fame as a biographer. Plutarch, like Arrian, loved the Hellenic past but was proud to serve Hadrian. More explicitly than Arrian, he set out as a writer to honor both Greece and Rome. He wanted to prove that Greece had once produced men of action worthy to be set beside Rome's greatest. He decided to write a series of parallel lives, or pairs of biographies, each pair to relate the life of a Greek and the life of some Roman whose career was similar to that of the Greek. To each pair of these biographies, he appended a brief comment, which drew, not always too convincingly, the parallel. He paired Aristides the Just with Cato the Elder, Nicias the businessman politician and soldier with Crassus, Lysander of Sparta with Sulla, Demosthenes with Cicero, Alexander with Julius Caesar, Sparta's reforming kings, Agis and Cleomenes, with Tiberius and Gaius Gracchus. No Roman could exceed Plutarch in his desire to edify. That this characteristic of his mars his biographies so little is due perhaps to his profoundly Greek zest for telling a story, a zest which Latin literature rarely matched. This zest gave Plutarch's *Parallel Lives* some of the magic which, long before, a similar zest had given Herodotus' history.

The period which produced the Latin writings of Seneca, Lucan, Quintilian, Petronius, Martial, Juvenal, Tacitus, and Suetonius and the Greek writings of Epictetus, Arrian, and Plutarch also produced painters and sculptors and architects, though none who immortalized their names. If most were Greeks, yet the profits of empire that flowed in to Rome meant that they often produced their work there or were engaged by Roman governors to ornament provincial cities eager to be little Romes. The temples and triumphal arches and commemorative columns and palaces which the architects built were therefore a continuation of the Augustan theme: they accurately expressed the power of armed might and of money, a power that counted on rich ornamentation to make itself lovable and beautiful. These architectural monuments relied on weight and size to impose a sense of grandeur and splendor on the beholder. They were orations in stone. They expressed will rather than vision, and this gave them the same highly rhetorical character that distinguished the current productions of the orator and the oratorical poet. As in the Augustan period, they were built mostly not of marble but of brick or rubble with a thin veneer of marble to provide an elegant façade. The sculptor still multiplied copies of Greek masterpieces for the houses and gardens of the rich or for public baths and parks. He also carved in stone, or cast in metal, bas-reliefs to celebrate the military glories of empire. Thus the column that Trajan erected in Rome to immortalize his conquest of Dacia narrated the achievements of his armies and recorded for Rome the strange faces and costumes of the barbarians the legions had forced to their knees. In general the bas-reliefs of the period dealt with the vast pageant of human achievement and the victories of organized human will. They were meant to kindle reverence not for the gods but for the god-Emperor, for Rome, for power.

More impressive than the tide of nymphs and fauns and cupids that flooded the private villas of the rich were the portrait busts not only of Emperors and other mighty men but of private citizens eager to remain in men's memories after death. These busts continued the Hellenistic and Roman tradition of furnishing those who paid for them with a good likeness. For neither the Emperors nor the Trimalchios of this empire were ashamed of the way they looked.

The painter, like the sculptor, found a ready market for subjects from Greek mythology, even though that mythology was already by Ovid's time so near death that all Ovid could honestly do with it was to mock it wittily, as in the *Metamorphoses*. To the extent that it remained alive for an artist's brush, it was perhaps more often pretty than beautiful, but it adequately suggested that the owner was both rich and cultured. What led to happier results was the increased love of landscape and of farm animals. This tenderness for animal life beneath the level of human life had already suffused the bucolic poetry of Theocritus and Virgil. The artists of the Empire indulged this tenderness for mindless, joyful life, and not only with the brush. Often they took to mosaics, a form the Hellenistic world had borrowed from the East, at first to produce geometrical designs in pavement but eventually for a caressingly intimate representation of animal and plant on the walls of rooms. Such an art lacked the declamatory chord that public taste or public policy demanded of the architect. In general, the art of the period that followed the reign of Augustus continued the Augustan tradition. It was weighty and ostentatious, as in so many of the great buildings; or interestingly literal, as in the historical bas-reliefs and the portrait busts; or gracefully decorative.

One of the leading inheritors of this somewhat autumnal Graeco-Roman culture was born in the year 76, when the general and business-man, Vespasian, was Emperor. He was born at Italica, some five miles from the site of modern Seville, of an Italian colonial family, and was given the name Publius Aelius Hadrianus. He was a connection of a prominent official and army officer, Ulpius Traianus, who also came from Italica. In 85 Hadrian's father died, and Trajan became the boy's guardian. Hadrian was taken to Rome, where he grew so fond of Greek studies that people called him the Greekling. When he returned a few years later to Spain, he developed a passion for hunting. In 97, when Trajan was governor of Upper Germany, he learned that the Emperor Nerva had adopted him. After Trajan succeeded to the throne in 98, Hadrian held various civil and military posts. In 100, when he was twenty-four, he married Trajan's grandniece, Sabina. He had already served as an army officer on the Danube and Rhine frontiers. He served under Trajan in both of his wars against Dacia; and during Trajan's war with Parthia, Hadrian was governor of Syria. In 117, having won the Parthian War and left for Rome, Trajan died on the southern coast of Asia Minor; and it was announced, though not by Trajan, that he had adopted Hadrian as his successor.

Trajan had operated in the tradition of Julius Caesar. When he had won for Rome the considerable Province of Dacia, beyond the Danube frontiers the gold, silver, and slaves he brought back more than paid for the two wars Dacia had cost him. Moreover, when he had fought Rome's only great military neighbor, Parthia, as Julius Caesar had planned to do before conspiracy struck him down, and had reached the Persian Gulf, direct trade with the Orient opened up for the merchants of Syria and Asia Minor. By conquering Nabataea, a strip of what is now the Kingdom of Jordan, he had already gained for his merchants direct access to the desert caravans and control of those that connected Syria with the merchant ships that plied the Red Sea. But in 116 a revolt in southern Mesopotamia had almost immediately threatened his frontage on the Persian Gulf; a ferocious Jewish revolt broke out in Alexandria, spread to Cyrene, to Salamis in Cyprus, to Mesopotamia; the Moors, the Britons, the Sarmatians were restive; and Parthia was menacing northern Mesopotamia and Armenia. Trajan recovered nearly everything, but at the time of his death he had secured only a precarious peace.

Hadrian shortly thereafter returned from Syria to Rome to claim the throne. He distributed largess to the populace, held gladiatorial shows for a week, gave financial help to needy Senators, and canceled many debts to the state. It behooved him to ingratiate himself: since Trajan had never publicly announced Hadrian's adoption, his widow, Plotina, was suspected of having engineered that adoption, as Livia had been suspected of engineering the adoption of her son Tiberius by Augustus.

If Trajan had patterned himself militarily on Julius Caesar, Hadrian chose the military role of Augustus. The name Caesar had become in effect an Imperial title, but Hadrian's favorite title was Augustus. Although he celebrated a triumph in Trajan's name to signalize the temporary defeat of Parthia, he judged the territories wrested from Parthia to be worth less to the Empire than the cost of protecting them; he accordingly withdrew to the Euphrates; the former frontier, Nabataea, was more readily defensible, and he kept it. Dacia, beyond the Danube, he also decided to keep. True, it gave him an additional land frontier to defend; but Dacia had been partially settled by Roman colonists, and no powerful, near neighbor disputed its possession as was the case with the provinces Trajan had taken from Parthia. Moreover, Dacia served as a bastion against Barbaria. Besides reversing Trajan's imperialist policies in the East, Hadrian succeeded in turning over the civil service more completely to salaried Equites and in strengthening the Emperor's privy council without opening a serious breach with the Senate.

Hadrian followed Augustus in another important act, important both practically and symbolically. Between 120 and 131, he spent most of his time touring various provinces of the Empire. He traveled to Gaul and inspected the vital Rhine frontiers, where he took steps to tighten the discipline of the legions. He lived amongst his troops, ate their soldier's fare with them, and exhibited some of Julius Caesar's flair for remembering the names and exploits of individual soldiers. His public image as the provincials' Emperor slowly took shape. Was he not a provincial himself, and only the second provincial to rule the Empire? He apparently sensed that Italy could no longer impose empire on the many peoples she had conquered; these peoples must wish to belong to their world-state. On this point he tried to realize Julius Caesar's dream, rather than that of Augustus. This Spanish-born Greekling had been tittered at by Senators for his provincial accent in Latin when, as a young man, he had read a message to the Senate from the Emperor Trajan. Now he wished to be head of Cosmopolis, not a Roman Emperor among conquered races. He was moving toward an unwritten constitution that would help justify Aelius Aristides' later boast that the Empire was a federation of free cities. Meanwhile, the coinage Hadrian issued kept his policies before the peoples he ruled: the discipline of Augustus that he was restoring to the legions, the travels he undertook among his subjects, the public works he was ordering.

In 120 or 121 Hadrian went to Gaul, which he had last traversed with Trajan some twenty years earlier. He saw again its broad rivers, navigable at all seasons, so unlike most of the rivers of Italy, now flooding from winter rains, now almost drying up in the parching heat of summer. Gaul was a land of plentiful wheat, barley for beer, magnificent grapes for wine, and in the south, olives for oil. Potentially, Gaul offered Rome more good arable land than any other area of comparable size in her entire empire. Gaul's wide and relatively level valleys contained excellent, deep soil. Her vegetation supplied abundant humus; her flocks and herds, valuable animal manures. In most of Gaul, rainfall or snowfall was rather evenly distributed throughout the year; erosion, therefore, was not the dangerous threat which faced so many Mediterranean farmers.[752] Gaul bred horses, mules, sheep, goats, cattle, pigs, and hounds. Her industrial products included pottery, glass, textiles, jewelry, silver plate, wooden ware; and boats on her numerous rivers distributed these goods. Syrian workmen introduced glassware. Although gold and silver were drawing Romans into Gaul in Julius Caesar's day, underground deposits of precious metals were early abandoned. But excellent deposits of iron and abundant wood stimulated smelting and forging. Both iron and marble were exported to Italy as well as to Britain. For more than a century the Western provinces, which had originally yielded little but agricultural products and raw materials, had increased their production of finished goods. This change was especially marked in Gaul. The great armies that guarded the Rhine still provided hungry markets for Gallic farmers and employment for Gallic artisans.

From Gaul, Hadrian proceeded by boat down the Rhine to what is now Holland, and thence to Britain, where Rome's control of the mountain tribes was loose, as it was in so many other provinces. In the lowlands, cities were springing up, especially around the permanent Roman *castra*, or army cantonments, castra that endowed a later England with place names like Lancaster, Chester, Gloucester. Roman roads were knitting England together militarily. When Hadrian had succeeded Trajan in 117, the Britons had revolted against Roman rule and had wiped out the Ninth Legion, a Spanish legion; Hadrian now established peace firmly. For more than seventy-three miles from coast to coast he ran a wall, paralleled it with a double dike, paralleled the dike with a military road, and built forts at intervals. The wall controlled movement and allowed Roman troops to shift quickly to threatened points. At the same time, the military roads were opening up commerce. Grain, cattle, hides, slaves, hunting dogs, oysters, pearls, and some gold, silver, copper, and lead were exported to Gaul.[753] Back from Gaul came pottery, wine, oil. Iron was abundant, and near the site of modern Exeter there were forges and foundries. Wine, ironmongery, and raw metal were finding their way across Hadrian's Wall or up the coasts to the Scots and Picts. And back from Scotland came cattle, hides, and furs.

News of a riot in Alexandria caused Hadrian to start south, but in Gaul he learned that the disorder in Egypt had been suppressed. In 121 he was in Provence, where he founded the city of Avignon. Plotina, his protectress and Trajan's widow, had died, and he commemorated her by building a basilica at Nîmes. He also erected a handsome tomb bearing a carved inscription; neither tomb nor inscription was for Plotina but for a horse. Despite the cares of empire, Hadrian had remained not only an ardent Hellenist but an ardent huntsman. Near Nîmes his favorite hunter had died. The tomb was for this hunter, and the inscription was a poem that Hadrian himself composed.

Hadrian spent the winter in Tarragona, on the east coast of Spain. There he called a conference of delegates from all over Spain and laid before them plans for putting to an end the raids which Spain sometimes suffered at the hands of the Mauretanians from across the straits. Hadrian's plans called for Spanish levies to bring more order to Mauretania, but even those Spaniards who, like himself, had been born in some one of the Italian colonies of Andalusia were unwilling to serve.

Hadrian built temples and roads in Spain. These roads served to move the army quickly and to get out the gold, silver, lead, tin, copper, and iron from the mines to the harbors and ships. For Spain still remained richer in metals than any other part of the Empire. Nor was her agriculture negligible. Spanish wheat was famous in Italy, as were Spanish olive oil and wines. Spain exported wheat, oil, honey, hams, beeswax, pitch, fine wool, linens; and she had a monopoly on esparto grass, which was used to make rope, baskets, and sandals. Andalusia, known then as Baetica, the province Hadrian and Trajan came from, abounded in highly Romanized cities. There were a few cities elsewhere in Spain. But the rural areas and the northwest still retained their local languages, their local arts, and their ancient gods.

Hadrian found troops outside of Spain, went to Mauretania, and enforced the Roman peace. But this country, which included parts of what are now Algeria and Morocco, was never more than superficially Romanized. Hadrian returned to Spain and shortly sailed for Ephesus, the capital of the Province of Asia.[754] Ephesus was one of the oldest centers of Hellenic culture in the world; and Hadrian, who had been there with Trajan during the Eastern wars, loved it. He now busied himself restoring cities in Asia that recent earthquakes had damaged. He built new cities, and the natives of course insisted on calling them Hadrianopolis, the polis of Hadrian. During the Roman civil wars the Province of Asia had suffered terribly from the exactions of competing generals. But by Hadrian's day it was thriving. It produced wheat, olives, and grapes on the fertile, sunny lowlands along the Aegean. Higher up were splendid pastures for cattle and sheep, and the mountains produced valuable timber. Asia exported wine, oil, wool, leather, textiles, and marble. To support the growing commerce of the Greek cities there, Hadrian authorized at least ten cities to mint new coin. Ephesus, Smyrna, and Pergamum had grown rapidly. Grandiose gymnasiums and baths had sprung up, schools of rhetoric also flourished, and medical schools had been endowed at Pergamum and Ephesus.

Hadrian next set out for the Black Sea province of Bithynia; but, like Alexander and Caesar before him, he stopped off at Troy. The inhabitants showed him what they claimed was the tomb of the Homeric hero, Ajax. It was in ruins; Hadrian restored it. He went to Trebizond, the naval base of his Black Sea fleet. It was here that Xenophon and the Ten Thousand had finally reached the familar sea and friendly Greek cities after their terrible march through the heart of the Persian Empire more than five centuries before, and Hadrian the Greekling and antiquarian must have remembered how the advance guard of those famous mercenaries had cried out exultantly, "The sea! The sea!" Trebizond was a fishing town; the tunny fisheries were especially important. Hadrian built a new harbor and on the roof of a building beside this harbor he mounted a large fish of gilded copper. But the provinces of Pontus and Bithynia produced not only fish. The olive and the grape throve here, as did market gardening. There were pasturage on the hills and on the mountain slopes splendid timber for shipbuilding. The cities on this coast were prospering and were building feverishly. Unhappily, the oligarchies which Rome, as usual, supported in the cities ruled so harshly that the poor were repeatedly driven to revolt. Hadrian understood this problem better than the bluff Trajan had done, and tried to diminish class oppression.

It was in Bithynia that the younger Pliny had served as governor, and here that he had found the Christians a difficult administrative problem, on which he needed the Emperor Trajan's advice. It was from here that Arrian came, the army general and historian of Alexander's conquests; and Hadrian would shortly after his own tour send Arrian to this coast to report in detail on its problems. It was in the town of Bithynium, some hundred miles northwest of Ankara, that Hadrian met Antinoüs, then about eighteen and strikingly handsome in a somewhat feminine fashion. He became Hadrian's constant companion. Their contemporaries assumed that theirs was a full homosexual relationship, a relationship that Hellenic culture had never condemned. Probably it was. But Hadrian was a complex, sophisticated person, who could have had many reasons for loving this young Greek god, symbolic of the ancient Greek culture Hadrian adored, symbolic of the dream that Athens had dreamed when she was young. Not long after their meeting and before leaving for Athens, Hadrian made a pilgrimage to the tomb of Alcibiades, that dashing young Athenian aristocrat, statesman, and soldier whom Socrates had loved, even though he had rejected Alcibiades' invitation to express their attachment physically. Hadrian placed a statue of white Parian marble on Alcibiades' tomb and established annual sacrifices in his memory. Then, in the autumn of 125, he reached his city of cities, Athens.

Hadrian's romantic philhellenism, his genuine administrative ability, and his concern for economic improvement had won the hearts of the people in the Greek cities of Asia Minor. Not far east of Troy, he left a more intimate signature than the city-name Hadrianopolis; this time, Hadrianotherae, Hadrian's Hunts. On the temples dedicated to him, his cult name appeared as Olympian Zeus. Hadrian's forerunner, Augustus, had cultivated an association between himself and the god Apollo. But the Empire had now ripened into a kind of acceptance of autocracy which made the Stoic emphasis on one supreme god, Zeus in the Greek world, Jupiter in the Roman, more relevant than Apollo to the ruler of civilized mankind.

With what excitement Hadrian must have approached Athens again! In 112–113 he had served as honorary Archon of Athens. It was his Holy City, as indeed it was, and for half a millennium had been, the Holy City of cultivated men wherever Greek was spoken. Philhellenes like Hadrian knew that the sculptors Phidias and Praxiteles had been Athenians; that Ictinus had built the Parthenon there at the direction of Pericles; that the three foremost tragic poets of Greece, Aeschylus, Sophocles, and Euripides, had been born in Athens and that most of their tragedies had been first produced there; that the two most famous comic poets, Aristophanes and Menander, had been born there and had written there. The greatest of Greek historians, Thucydides, had been Athenian. Socrates and Plato had been born in Athens and had taught there; Aristotle had come there as a student and remained to teach. Stoicism, Epicureanism, and Cynicism had been born there. The most famous of Greek orators was Demosthenes the Athenian; and so was the most famous of Greek publicists, Isocrates. No other city in the Empire could produce such a roster of genius.

But all these men had long been dead. Although, after the death of Alexander the Great, the Ptolemies of Egypt by judicious patronage had shifted the focus of intellectual life to Alexandria, Athens, along with Rhodes, was the goal of the Romans who streamed eastward for instruction. They were willing to attend lectures on literature and even philosophy, especially Stoicism, with its emphasis on moral action; but their most consistent interest was rhetoric, the art of bending others to their own will, the word as substitute for the sword. Those too who sought merely a certain polish were likely to gravitate to Athens, to take guided tours, and perhaps to buy copies of artistic masterpieces. By Hadrian's time most of the originals, through either pillage or purchase, had flowed to Italy.

Hadrian had never studied in Greece, as Caesar and Cicero had. He had entered active life young and had served Trajan both as a soldier and as an administrator. But he never liked Rome; rather he had always been attracted to the source of the culture which Roman rule transmitted to his native Spain and to the Western provinces in general. Now he was at the source. High on the Acropolis sat the Propylea, which led up to the stately Parthenon and the delicate Erechtheum. Nearby was that second hill where the senate of Athens, the Areopagus, had governed in the days before the unruly democracy, so deplored by upper-class Romans, had seized power. At the foot of the Parthenon was the Theater of Dionysus, where Greek drama had been born. Not far off stood an unfinished temple, which Livy had described as the "only temple on earth of a magnitude worthy the greatness of god."[755] It had been begun, some six and a half centuries before, by Pisistratus, who became tyrant of Athens after Solon's attempt to reform the constitution and laws of Athens. After the tyrant's death, work on the temple had ceased until, more than three centuries later, Antiochus IV of Syria, ardent champion of Hellenism that he was, tried and failed to finish it. By a happy coincidence this temple was planned to worship Olympian Zeus in, to be big enough for the Father of Gods and Men. Hadrian, whose name the Greeks of Asia had just coupled with that of Olympian Zeus, completed the temple. Far larger, if less beautiful, than the Parthenon, it had the tall columns the Romans so much liked, in this case nearly fifty-seven feet high. Whereas Pisistratus had intended to give the columns Ionic capitals, Hadrian followed the plan of Antiochus' Roman architect: the capitals were to be of the more ornate Corinthian type.

Hadrian went further. Sulla's terrible sack of Athens had been hard on statues but had left the temples standing: they were apparently too heavy to carry off to Rome. In addition, the Roman civil wars had greatly impoverished Athens, and much of her residential housing was wretched. Hadrian planned and built a new suburb, centered on his imposing temple to Olympian Zeus. The new town stretched clear to the slopes of Mount Hymettus. It contained, naturally enough, a temple to Hera, Zeus's heavenly consort, since inevitably the Empress Sabina was being assimilated to Hera. It is true that Hadrian had never much liked Sabina, whom he had married to please his patroness, the former Empress Plotina. But then, Zeus did not always seem too devoted to Hera either. Hadrian's new town was furnished also with a temple to Panhellenic Zeus, to serve as religious center for the Panhellenic League he founded; a Pantheon, furnished with a record of the Emperor's good works; and, near the market place, where Socrates had taught, a library. Finally, between the old city and the modern one he erected a gateway, a sort of triumphal arch. On one side was placed an inscription, "This is Athens the former city of Theseus," and on the other side, "This is the city of Hadrian and not of Theseus."

Although he concerned himself with increasing the revenues of Athens and built an aqueduct that would bring it the most Roman of all his gifts, a good water supply, he luxuriated in conversations with learned men, that most Greek of luxuries. These men ranged from the earnest Epictetus, the ex-slave and Stoic, to the clever Favorinus, who came from Arles: a Western provincial like the Emperor, noted for his pure Greek. Favorinus dared argue with Hadrian about whether a certain word was used by reputable authors, but he knew when to yield. Favorinus' friends reproached him for yielding, since Hadrian was clearly wrong. Favorinus retorted:

> You are urging a wrong course, my friends, when you do not suffer me to regard as the most learned of men the one who has thirty legions.[756]

Later Favorinus boasted of three paradoxes in his life: he was a Gaul who lived as a Hellene; he was a eunuch who had been accused of committing adultery with a consul's wife; he had contradicted the Emperor and was still alive. When Favorinus was nominated to be high priest of Athens, he pleaded exemption on the grounds that he was a philosopher. Hadrian jestingly pretended to be outraged that Favorinus should consider himself a philosopher; the city fathers missed the jest and pulled down a statue of

Favorinus. At any rate, said Favorinus laughingly, he had come off better than Socrates.

But all these jests contained unconscious irony. Socrates, when he drank the hemlock, did not think he had come off badly, but knew that Athens had. The Athens Hadrian so much enjoyed was by Socratic standards an intellectual eunuch; or, changing the metaphor, a lovely Greek woman who had lain with many consuls; and though she had sided with Antony against Caesar Octavianus and had even been ravished by Sulla, she was still alive. True, she was alive more in the style of Favorinus than in the style of Socrates; yet she was alive enough to delight Hadrian. To delight and even to assist; for Hadrian needed Athens. Scattered through the Aegean area were statues of Hadrian that exhibited on his breastplate an interesting device. First it displayed that symbol of Roman power, the She-Wolf, nursing Romulus and Remus, the group that long ago had been executed in bronze and adorned the roof of the Capitol. But on Hadrian's breastplate, above this group, appeared the figure of Pallas Athena, the special patroness of Athens. This double device spoke to the world of Hadrian's new version of the policy of Augustus: not the Italian people dominating the peoples she had subjected, but Roman force supporting Hellenistic civilization. This was the policy that was to cause the Greek Aristides to picture the Romans to themselves as he did:

> Taking good care of the Hellenes as of your foster parents, you constantly hold your hand over them, and when they are prostrate, you raise them up. You release free and autonomous those of them who were the noblest and the leaders of yore . . .[757]

Hadrian gave Corinth, too, an aqueduct, and to other cities in Greece he gave roads and baths and temples. At Mantinea he restored the tomb of the great Theban general Epaminondas, who six centuries before had won briefly for Thebes the hegemony over Greece that Athens and Sparta successively had held, that Macedon had later won and, later still, lost to Rome. Like Philip of Macedon, Hadrian was initiated into the Eleusinian mysteries. Before the Emperor left Greece, he consulted the oracle at Delphi. Significantly, he did not ask about the future of Greece but about the past: who, he wanted to know, were Homer's parents?

Indeed, it was not easy to see a future for Greece. Corinth's strategic location, even without the canal that Nero had longed in vain to build, made her prosper. But most of Greece was an economic backwater and a museum. The trade routes of Hadrian's day passed her by. Many cities lay in ruins. The countryside was in many parts depopulated by emigration and by a falling birth rate. The natural resources of Greece, never great, had been in large measure exhausted. Plutarch, the biographer, one of the high priests of Delphi, recognized this exhaustion. He lived in his native Chaeronea and may have been still alive when Hadrian toured Greece. It was here at Chaeronea that Demosthenes of Athens had exulted in the coming battle with Philip of Macedon, had seen Philip triumph, and had flung away his arms and fled. When Plutarch came to write the life of Demosthenes he observed that

> as for me, I live in a small city, and I prefer to dwell there that it may not become smaller still . . .[758]

From Greece, Hadrian went to Sicily and visited Syracuse, Agrigentum, Segesta; and climbed Mount Aetna to watch the sunrise. Then in 123 he went back to Rome, to his reforms of the administration and the law. When he could find the leisure, he wrote poems or played the flute or painted or even designed buildings. It was he who designed a temple to Venus and Rome, although the professional architect who had built Trajan's Forum had to correct the plans. But Hadrian's greatest artistic achievement was a complete rebuilding of Agrippa's Pantheon. Although the pediment and columns of the porch reflected the style of the traditional Greek temple, the great circular Pantheon, its height equal to its diameter, built of the good solid brick that Romans liked and capped with a cup-roof of the brick and concrete they also liked, spoke of the Orbis Terrarum itself, the round earth with all its lands, which, somewhat rhetorically speaking, Eternal Rome now ruled. The dome was the largest ever built.[759] Hadrian secured the majestic height he wanted for his temple without resort to the long columns Rome so often used. For Hadrian's granite columns supported a pediment placed far lower than the great dome. In 135 Hadrian erected another circular brick building, his own mausoleum, modeled after the mausoleum Augustus had built.[760] Augustus had used stone. Hadrian faced his own vast brick drum with marble and crowned it with a roof garden.

After barely more than a year, Hadrian left Rome again. "Your farms," declared Aristides to the Romans, "are Egypt, Sicily and the civilized part of Africa."[761] Hadrian had already visited Sicily; he now inspected another of Rome's farms, Africa, where Tunisia now lies. It was prospering.

In addition to wheat, it raised barley for local stockbreeders. In the south the plow steadily pushed the nomads back toward the Sahara, and not only wheat but the grape, the olive, the fig, other fruit trees, and vegetables like artichokes and beans took over. Africa exported chiefly wheat and olive oil, but also excellent horses and mules, wine, fruit, and vegetables. Moreover, Africa was a principal source of wild beasts for the Roman arena, especially lions, bears, and panthers. Finally, she passed on to the Mediterranean world goods brought her by caravans from the south, notably gold dust, ivory, precious stones, ostrich feathers, and a few Negro slaves for wealthy Roman homes. Of industrial products she exported very few, though some were manufactured for the local market.

At Carthage, where the Latin tongue had not yet eradicated Punic, and in the countryside, where neither had eradicated Berber, Hadrian nevertheless found the Roman armed forces Latinizing native recruits. Hadrian worked hard to improve these armed forces and, following his custom, lived for a while in camp among his soldiers. A palisade of the sort he had built between the Rhine and the Danube could of course not be used here: the border was much too long. The army had to depend on punitive expeditions, and the Roman administrators settled what nomads they could on the newly opened lands.

Hadrian returned to Rome briefly and then escaped again to his beloved Athens, where he could dress and talk like a Greek. He took a higher degree of initiation at Eleusis. He presided at the new Panhellenic Council he had founded. He inspected the handsome gymnasium he had ordered built, his portico, and his public library. He consecrated the huge temple to Olympian Zeus, which was now complete. Then, in March of 129, he and Antinoüs sailed to Ephesus, visited Caria, Phrygia, Lycia, and Cilicia. By June he was in Antioch again, where he had ruled as governor while the Emperor Trajan fought his way to the Persian Gulf. But most people in Antioch, despite centuries of efforts by the Seleucid kings, spoke Aramaic, not Greek, as so many Africans around Carthage had spoken that other Semitic tongue, not Latin. For a romantic philhellene, this was disagreeable; and the fact that his wife Sabina had come with him from Greece also marred his stay at Antioch.

Nevertheless, Hadrian knew that Syria was one of his richest provinces. Northern Syria was good wheat country. Syria's strong wines were exported to the West and also to Persia and India. Her olive oil was good not only for cooking but as a base for perfumes. The figs and damsons of Damascus were famous. Even the fringe of the nearby desert yielded wealth to Syria in the form of meat and wool from the flocks of the nomads. Desert caravans brought gems and perfumes for wealthy Syrian women, and for Syrian temples, myrrh and incense. From the Persian Gulf caravans brought pearls. The Roman navy depended on the magnificent timber from Lebanon, just as the cedars of Lebanon had built the navies of the Pharaohs three thousand years before. From her ports, moreover, still poured manufactured goods, especially textiles: woolens, linens, even silk cloth woven from the raw silk that reached her from China. Damascus was famous for its metal work, its armor, its jewelry. Glass from Sidon and purple dye from Tyre swelled the volume of her exports. If Rome was law and order, Syria was the skilled hand, was enterprise in trade. Syria constantly shipped goods to Puteoli, near Naples. There were now colonies of Syrian traders scattered all over the Empire, as far as Treves in northeastern Gaul. And in Syria itself, including Palestine, there may have been as many as ten million people.

The cultural life of Syria was lively, eclectic in its sources and its styles, and sophisticated, as one would expect of a population dominated by rich traders dedicated to profit and pleasure. With her Semitic traditions of monotheism, Syria could produce Stoics as famous as Posidonius, who went to Rome and numbered both Cicero and Pompey among his pupils; but she could also worship many gods from many lands. Male devotees of the mother goddess, Atargatis, castrated themselves. Temple prostitution continued as of old. Human sacrifice, especially of children, was still practiced until Hadrian officially forbade it, as he did castration.

It was during his visit to Syria that Hadrian negotiated a more stable peace with Parthia, as Augustus had done. Hadrian seemed to realize, as Trajan had not, what the Seleucid dynasty had long ago discovered: it was one thing to liberate the Greek cities as far as the Euphrates and quite another to try to assimilate to Cosmopolis the territory Alexander had conquered between the Euphrates and the Indus. Unlike Western Europe, the East had great cultural memories and had created great empires: the Babylonian, the Assyrian, the Chaldean, the Persian. To people with memories like these, the hellenized world seemed to have little to offer; whereas it had much to offer, even in Romanized form, to the tribes of Britain, Gaul, Spain, and Africa. Hadrian, who felt himself Greek more than Trajan had, may well have sensed this. But centers of exchange between East and West, like Damascus, so near the Anti-Lebanon range, and the wealthy oasis city of Palmyra, less than halfway from Damascus to the Euphrates, were glad to welcome the ruler of a Graeco-Roman empire, and Hadrian visited both cities. Damascus issued coins which showed him as a god and others which showed Sabina as Augusta. Then he went to Beirut, improved the roads in that area, and strictly regulated the lumbering of cedar, pine, cypress, and juniper on the Lebanon range.

From Beirut he went to Rome's newest province, Arabia, and built a paved road from Damascus southward through Philadelphia, now called Amman, to the northern end of the Gulf of Aqaba, the northeastern branch of the Red Sea. He visited the caravan city of Petra, and spent most of the winter of 129–30 at the lovely city of Gerasa, which he entered through a handsome arch built in his honor. In 130 he crossed the Jordan into Palestine.

Hadrian was entering the most explosive province in the Empire. Its people had fought for independence for nine centuries, against Philistines, Assyrians, Egyptians, Chaldeans, Syrians, Romans. They had fought against Vespasian, Titus, Trajan. In 130, Hadrian set about settling the Jewish problem. At Tiberias, on the sea of Galilee, the Greek inhabitants had built a temple in his honor, although the Jewish inhabitants had objected. Hadrian now decided that he would build a new temple to Jupiter Capitolinus on the site of the Temple of Jerusalem, which Titus had destroyed in 70. The new name was equivalent to that other name with which he had strongly associated himself in Greece, Olympian Zeus. But the adjective Capitolinus would remind all comers that the center of political power for every man in the Empire, Jew or Gentile, was the Capitol at Rome and that no god, Semitic or other, could supersede that authority. As for a certain god's mark on his chosen people, circumcision, Hadrian forbade it. This symbol of racial exclusiveness, like castration, doubtless appeared to a hellenized Roman as a maiming, a desecration of the physical form that man shared with the Olympic gods. Jerusalem itself, the Holy City of world Jewry, would be rebuilt; and since his own family name was Aelius, it would be called Aelia Capitolina.

From Palestine, Hadrian set out for Alexandria, founded by another hellenizer and unifier. On the way, by the Egyptian seashore, he stopped at the funeral mound of Pompey the Great, who was the first Roman to conquer Palestine. Pompey had entered into the Holy of Holies in Jerusalem "and saw what it was unlawful for any but the high priests to see."[762] Hadrian built Pompey a tomb. Had he not already built tombs for Ajax, Alcibiades, and Epaminondas?

In Alexandria, Hadrian reported of its inhabitants that "their only god is money." And he added, somewhat defensively, "this the Christians, the Jews, and, in fact, all nations adore."[763] Certainly Italians adored it, though not all of them would have been as candid about adoring it as a certain businessman in Pompeii. In the vestibule of this good man's house, before the ashes of Vesuvius buried it, visitors had once read an inscription in the paving: *Salve Lucrum*, Hail, Profit! Italians of the Senatorial class were less vulgarly candid. The elder Pliny, who died in the same volcanic eruption that discreetly buried the telltale inscription, once wrote loyally:

> The one race of outstanding eminence in virtue among all the races in the whole world is undoubtedly the Roman.[764]

It might be doubted that a race so virtuous could worship money as its god. On the other hand, satirists had often noted how, at Rome, donors judiciously courted the elderly rich with gifts in the hope that they would soon die and would remember them in their wills and how the rich played with such valuable friends as a cat plays with a mouse. The same legacy hunters often avoided having children because it cost money to bring them up, and naturally no Roman child was ever born with money in his hand. Parasites flocked to the tables of the rich for free food, as they did to the table of Trimalchio. They loathed the hosts they toadied to, especially when the hosts drank better wines than they offered their guests. Both men and women married for money and sometimes had recourse to poison in order to collect. Young men and women married the repulsively old, in order to solve the problem of collection more promptly. Successive marriages and divorces often provided a thin legal disguise for what amounted to something like prostitution. During the civil wars the political proscriptions and confiscations had taught Romans to turn informer even against their friends and kindred. Under the early Empire the insecurity felt by a military autocrat had encouraged professional informers to broadcast charges of disloyalty for which the rewards might be considerable. The donatives new Emperors made to the army had taught mutiny-for-profit. Hadrian had done more than most Emperors to mitigate the social evils which the worship of the god, money, had inflicted on the Graeco-Roman Cosmopolis. He probably did not know that the prophets of the Jews' invisible god had denounced economic exploitation and oppression of the poor. Or that the crucified Jew whom Christians proclaimed the Son of God had taught that it is not possible to serve both God and money. Pliny's claim of unique virtue for the Roman race may not have impressed either the Jew or the Christian, and their refusal to worship the Emperor threatened the Empire, which Hadrian was trying to rally around himself and Zeus-Jupiter, an Empire which had already rallied around money.

If Hadrian's charge was true that the Jews and Christians and all nations really worshiped money, there was every reason why Alexandria's worship should be peculiarly fervent. For her money-god had showered blessings on her. In this second largest city in Hadrian's empire, with her Red Sea canal and rich Oriental trade, the recent Jewish revolt had caused widespread devastation; but Alexandria was rapidly recovering. As the leading grain producer of the three countries which Aristides called Rome's three farms, Egypt shipped Rome far more grain than either Africa or Sicily did. In addition, Egypt still had her valuable industries, such as glass, paper, and linen. It was through Alexandria that most Egyptian wheat, industrial products, and goods shipped in from the Orient poured out to Rome and the Empire. And to Hadrian, the lover of Hellenic culture, the city offered a tradition, four centuries old, of intellectual life. Hadrian started up the Nile to inspect the valuable land of Egypt, which had always been ruled directly by the Emperor and not by the Senate, to assess its needs, and also to see its ancient monuments, many of which were old and famous before the Trojan War was fought. When Julius Caesar took this boat trip nearly two centuries before, Queen Cleopatra had accompanied him. Hadrian's companion was Antinoüs. Sabina and one of her women friends also made the journey.

Then came grief. On October 30, 130, Antinoüs drowned in the Nile. How and why? On this point there was disagreement, even in Hadrian's day. But since Hadrian, a deeply superstitious man, was ill at the time, it is quite possible that, when no doctor succeeded in curing him, Antinoüs took his own life as a sacrifice to save that of the Emperor.[765] Hadrian was broken-hearted; but his wife and her friend wanted to visit the Colossi of Memnon. They went, and Sabina's tiresome friend wrote poems to commemorate the event and had them engraved on the left foot of one of the Colossi, the one which, according to Roman tourists, always sang at sunrise. They then sailed back downstream to Alexandria.

At the spot where the beautiful Antinoüs had drowned, Hadrian founded a city and named it Antinoöpolis. Temples were built to Antinoüs throughout the whole Empire. He was assimilated to Hermes, to Apollo, to Osiris, and to Dionysus. Poets praised him. Athens, Argos, and Eleusis gave games in his honor. Hadrian erected an Egyptain obelisk at Rome to commemorate the companion the Nile had ravished from him.

While still in Egypt, Hadrian undertook a visit to the nearby Province of Cyrenaica. Cyrene was the oldest Greek city in Africa, and four centuries earlier had been famous for its Epicurean philosophers and its mathematicians. It drew its wealth from its grain, wool, dates, and, in earlier days, from silphium, a medicinal herb that grew only there. Egypt had ceded Cyrenaica to Rome in 96 B.C., and by the middle of the next century tax farmers had wiped out the production of silphium by causing the land to be overgrazed.[766] Later, despite its lack of good ports, it prospered, if only because Rome fostered Greek and Jewish immigration, protected the Libyan farm workers from desert nomads, and improved irrigation. The Jewish revolt under Trajan caused enormous loss in lives and property. Although Hadrian sent in colonists, the province recovered only a part of its former prosperity.

In the autumn of 131 Hadrian returned to Syria, visited Pontus again, then went to Greece again. But the visit to Greece was interrupted: another fierce nationalist rebellion had broken out in Palestine, probably precipitated by Hadrian's new temple to Jupiter and by his edict forbidding circumcision. Hadrian recalled Julius Severus from Britain, where he was then governor, to put down the Jewish guerrillas, led by a fighter known as Bar Kokba, or Son of the Star, and hailed by many as the long-awaited Messiah. Bar Kokba's guerrillas captured Aelia Capitolina, their desecrated capital, Jerusalem. It took three and a half years for Roman legions, hunger, and thirst to end the heroic revolt. The poll tax on Jews was increased and they were forbidden to enter Aelia Capitolina, which was now handsomely completed, except on one fixed day a year. Where the Holy of Holies had stood, the temple of Jupiter, Father of Gods and Men, now rose. Its great bronze doors were those which had once opened and closed the Temple of the God of Israel. According to a later historian,[767] fifty rebel forts and nearly a thousand villages were destroyed, 580,000 guerrilla fighters were killed in combat, and thousands more perished from starvation or disease. Wolves and hyenas roamed howling through the cities of the Jews. The Romans opened slave markets in Hebron and Gaza to dispose of the huge number of captives.

Hadrian returned to Rome, where he was not popular. For, although in most respects he had imitated Augustus, in one important respect he had imitated Julius Caesar: he had made himself in effect the Hellenistic king of all the peoples of the Roman Empire. Because Caesar had seemed to move in that direction, Senatorial Republicans had assassinated him. Although the ideal of a republic governed by the Senate was dead in Hadrian's day, those Senators who were Italians disliked what he represented. Not only had he been born outside Italy; his heart was clearly in Athens, not in Rome. His love of painting, sculpture, architecture, poetry, music, conversation, perhaps even of ideas, would have been bad enough, even if he had not also painted, written poems, and designed buildings. He protected the provincials against Roman extortion and maladministration. He surrendered provinces that Trajan had conquered because he sensed, as Augustus had done, that the East beyond the Euphrates did not belong culturally to Cosmopolis. Though in his culture he was a Greek, he was also Roman enough to strengthen the wall that Rome had built like a tough shell around the Graeco-Roman world. Part of that wall consisted of stone; part, of earth; part, of wooden palisades. But basically what made the wall strong was the legions. These legions were now in large part local levies, not Italian. They were in large part defending their own homelands and thereby the Empire as a whole. In his long journeys of inspection, Hadrian had made himself intimately their leader, so that not even the Praetorian Guard could have safely backed any Senatorial conspiracy against him. In distant camps on the Scottish border or in Morocco or Tunisia had not the tall, powerful, handsome Emperor, bareheaded in all weather, moved among his polyglot legions, watching their drill and maneuvers, sharing their soldiers' mess, correcting or applauding their performance, making himself their own?

In 126 at Tivoli, some fifteen miles from Rome, a spot beloved by Scipio, Marius, Cicero, Horace, and Maecenas, Hadrian had started to build a villa. He had secured a tract of 750 acres and constructed a palace, baths, theaters, barracks. But he also erected reproductions of the buildings he had loved in Athens: the Academy, the Lyceum, the Painted Porch where Stoicism was born, the town hall. He planted a grove to serve as the Vale of Tempe and even excavated a subterranean Hades. There were colonnades, statues, caryatids that could remind a returned traveler of the Acropolis at Athens, reflecting pools and an island, a little round colonnaded temple to Venus with a copy inside it of Praxiteles' Aphrodite of Cnidus. But his memories went beyond Athens and beyond Greece: he made a Canopus. Canopus was the ancient port of the Nile Delta, and it was in the Nile that his beloved Antinoüs had drowned. Hadrian's villa was in part a villa, in part a park, in part a museum of empire. But the empire it was meant to symbolize was not so much the empire the She-Wolf had won as the empire of Athena, of wisdom, of beauty.

The peace which Hadrian enjoyed in the gardens of his villa epitomized the Pax Romana which the middle class enjoyed during his reign. The Peace of Hadrian would not perhaps have inspired a Virgil; but the issue did not arise, since this sort of society did not produce Virgils. It produced rhetoricians like Dio Cocceianus, known as Chrysostomus, or Golden Mouth, who delivered eulogies of extraordinary virtuosity such as his *Praise of a Gnat, Praise of Baldness,* and *Eulogy of a Parrot.* Hundreds of other rhetoricians delivered similar orations before applauding crowds in the cities of the Empire. But how could this outburst of culture have occurred had not Rome and her legions stood guard against uncultured Barbaria? The triumph of rhetoric over poetry demanded that a rhetorical virtuoso play Virgil to Hadrian's Pax Romana. Pliny the Younger's *Panegyric* to the Emperor Trajan was still the model of what rhetoric could do to fill this need.

Hadrian did not enjoy his villa at Tivoli for long. Though he was still in his fifties, his health was giving way. His life among his troops, his hunting, his mountain-climbing may well have strengthened rather than worn out an already powerful physique. Perhaps more wearing than his physical exertions was the crushing burden of power. Given the means of transportation and communication then available, the empire he governed was enormous. Nor did he merely administer an organization set up by other men: he revolutionized the Imperial administration, both civil and military. In considerable degree he de-Romanized and internationalized both. And he did it in the face of criticism, corruption, conspiracy, and nationalist rebellion. Above all, he experienced all the jealousy, ingratitude, incompetence, and treachery that such a ruler had to face. As he sat or strolled in his gardens among the gracious incarnations of the Hellenic culture he loved, he could hardly escape a sense of disillusionment and futility. There was another way to read the Roman achievement than the way official panegyrics read it. If the vision of Virgil could inspire a panegyric, so could Livy inspire an *Epitome of Roman History*, probably composed during Trajan's reign, by Lucius Annaeus Florus, who proudly wrote about the Roman people that

> those who read of their exploits are learning the history, not of a single people, but of the human race.[768]

Florus, like Livy, found in early Roman history a kind of golden age; then conquest and pillage had brought luxury and civil war. Florus wondered whether it might not have been better for Rome if she had conquered only Italy.

As Hadrian's health deteriorated, he still faced one of the Empire's most persistently dangerous problems, that of succession. He chose, and adopted as his son, Ceionius Commodus, and celebrated the future ruler's adoption by a huge donative to his soldiers and by games and largess for the populace at Rome. But Commodus became ill. Never unconscious of the Empire's fiscal troubles, Hadrian complained,

> We have leaned against a tottering wall and have wasted the four hundred million sesterces which we gave to the populace and the soldiers on the adoption of Commodus.[769]

He was not being heartless; he seems to have had an affection for Commodus; but the labor and care, the work and worry, of empire were growing too much for him. On January 1, 138, Commodus died. Meanwhile, Hadrian's bad health had darkened his mind, and he began to do away with men who seemed too eager to succeed him. On January 24, 138, his sixty-second birthday, he adopted Arrius Antoninus, a member of his Imperial Council.

Hadrian's condition worsened sharply and he tried in vain to persuade a servant to stab him. He drew up his will; and again attempted suicide. His attendants took away his dagger, and he tried to persuade his doctor to poison him. He went to one of his villas, at Baiae, near Naples. There, as he lay dying, he composed one more poem, this one in Latin:

> O blithe little soul, thou, flitting away,
> Guest and comrade of this my clay,
> Whither now goest thou, to what place
> Bare and ghastly and without grace?
> Nor, as thy wont was, joke and play.[770]

He died, on July 10, 138, after ruling the Roman Empire for nearly twenty-one years. As to where his blithe little soul went, he became a god, according to Senatorial decree, although the Senate acted unwillingly and only because Hadrian's successor, Antoninus, insisted.

Some five years after Hadrian's death, his Virgil sang, or, more literally, his rhetorician declaimed, a panegyric on the empire that Hadrian had so largely shaped. The rhetorician was Aelius Aristides, who was born the year[771] Hadrian became Emperor, at Pergamum, and was still a small boy when Hadrian visited that city. He was educated in Pergamum and at Athens. He traveled in Egypt and lectured in Asia Minor in the tradition of the rhetorician Isocrates. Three of his orations were counterattacks on Plato, in answer to the caustic comments on rhetoric that Plato put in Socrates' mouth. For Aristides, rhetoric was "the first, the greatest, and the most perfect achievement among men."[772] It alone made life worth living, repressed violence, and maintained justice. However, he could not refrain from pointing out that he was the only one among the Greeks, so far as he knew, who had

> undertaken oratory not for the sake of riches or fame or honors or marriage or power or for any opportunism whatever, but purely as a lover of the art itself have I received fitting rewards for my lectures.[773]

Probably in 143 at Rome Aristides delivered his *Roman Oration*, in Greek, in his carefully cultivated style. Inevitably there was considerable exaggeration in what he said. When he declared that "for the eternal duration of this empire the whole civilized world prays all together,"[774] he perhaps did not speak for everyone, not for all the poor and certainly not for all the slaves; these would scarcely have shared his enthusiasm for the equality of Roman justice. He was not even speaking for peoples like the Jews of Judaea, who belonged to the Empire only because their attempts to secede had been ferociously crushed, by Titus in 70 and by Hadrian in 135. But Aristides was trying, not to analyze the Empire that existed, but to praise an ideal society which the Empire certainly seemed to reflect. Poetic license, or rather rhetorical license, allowed him to speak as if the ideal had been fully incarnated in history.

The Greek orator tried to make his Roman audience see a league of city states presided over by a unique city, a "civil community of the World . . .

established as a Free Republic."[775] He pictured a sort of gigantic city-state in which Rome bore to its whole empire the relation Athens had borne to Attica, and Sparta to Laconia. By extending Roman citizenship to deserving individuals throughout the whole Empire, Rome had imitated the ideal of the Achaean League and offered equal opportunity to all. Every man willing to serve in Rome's armies automatically gained Roman citizenship. The City of Rome no longer required walls because Rome had walled the whole Federation. "An encamped army like a rampart encloses the civilized world in a ring."[776] And this army was highly disciplined, worthy to "keep watch over the whole world."[777] The Emperor, like Zeus, ruled this world. The Emperor was

> One who holds the most perfect monarchic rule, One without a share in the vices of a tyrant and One elevated above even kingly dignity.[778]

Unlike Tacitus, this second-century orator had never lived under a Nero or a Domitian, but only under three excellent rulers: Trajan, Hadrian, and Antoninus. Unlike Tacitus, he had little reason to look back nostalgically to the days of Senatorial rule at Rome. Was it not the Roman Senate that had first conquered the Greek world, and Senatorial misgovernment that had then let loose upon it Sulla, Lucullus, Pompey, Caesar, Antony, Octavian, and a host of Roman tax gatherers, usurers, and corrupt provincial governors? Was it not Senatorial misgovernment that had sacked Athens and razed Corinth? It was the Emperors who had brought order, abandoned Augustus' dream of a ruling Italian race, opened the army and civil service to talented men of every race, and given Cosmopolis peace, justice, and freedom; or, in Pliny's words, written more than half a century earlier, "the immense majesty of the Roman peace."[779]

Aristides briefly reviewed the Persian Empire's failure to subject and organize the Greek cities; the successive failures of Athens, Sparta, and Thebes to subject and organize them; the conquest of Alexander and the speedy breakup of his empire when he died. Where all had failed, Rome had gloriously succeeded:

> As on a holiday the whole civilized world lays down the arms which were its ancient burden and has turned to adornment. . . . All localities are full of gymnasia, fountains, monumental approaches, temples, workshops, schools, and one can say that the civilized world, which had been

sick from the beginning, as it were, has been brought by the right knowledge to a state of health. Gifts never cease from you to the cities . . .[780]

It is you again who have best proved the general assertion, that Earth is mother of all and common fatherland. Now indeed it is possible for Hellene or non-Hellene, with or without his property, to travel wherever he will, easily, just as if passing from fatherland to fatherland. Neither Cilician Gates nor narrow sandy approaches to Egypt through Arab country, nor inaccessible mountains, nor immense stretches of river, nor inhospitable tribes of barbarians cause terror, but for security it suffices to be a Roman citizen, or rather to be one of those united under your hegemony.[781]

Homer said, "Earth common of all," and you have made it come true. You have measured and recorded the land of the entire civilized world; you have spanned the rivers with all kinds of bridges and hewn highways through the mountains and filled the barren stretches with posting stations; you have accustomed all areas to a settled and orderly way of life. . . . Though the citizens of Athens began the civilized life of today, this life in its turn has been firmly established by you, who came later but who, men say, are better.[782]

For

now a clear and universal freedom from all fear has been granted both to the world and to those who live in it.[783]

The picture this Greek orator painted of universal disarmament, except for the professional forces which formed a wall around the Empire, of a sick world healed by Roman peace, by Roman law, and by freedom from fear, was of course in many ways as applicable to Augustus as to Hadrian. However, when Aristides, early in the reign of Antoninus Pius, praised the empire that Hadrian had ruled and molded for twenty-one years, he could rightly see that the She-Wolf's function was to protect Athena. Thus, somewhat tardily and ambiguously, Hadrian had vindicated Flamininus' claim to have liberated the Greeks.

7

THE PHILOSOPHER KING

THE REIGN of Antoninus Pius vindicated Hadrian's second choice of a successor. For twenty-three years, from 138 to 161, Antoninus ruled the Empire benignly. He was not a product of the army, but a methodical administrator who staffed it with capable generals. These defended Britain from the wild tribes in Scotland and built a second, shorter wall to cover the thirty-seven miles from the Firth of Forth to the Clyde; or put down rebellion in Mauretania or Egypt or Palestine or Greece; or fought back German raiders. As a condition of his adoption, Hadrian had made Antoninus promise to adopt Marcus Aurelius Verus, Antoninus' nephew by marriage, and also Lucius Verus, son of the tottering wall on whom Hadrian had leaned and whose death had cost him four hundred million sesterces in wasted donatives to the populace and soldiery.[784] To Marcus Aurelius Verus, Hadrian had taken an immense liking; punning on the boy's name, Hadrian called him *Verissimus,* the most sincere of the sincere. The boy was not only sincere and serious, but somewhat timid and not physically strong. He partially repaired this second weakness by boxing, wrestling, hunting, and playing at ball.

He was educated by private tutors in music, geometry, and Greek and Latin literature. He studied Latin rhetoric under Cornelius Fronto, a celebrated rhetorician from Cirta, in what is now Algeria; Greek rhetoric under Herodes Atticus; law under several jurisconsults.

Even at twelve, Marcus had reacted against the pleasant corruption of his native Rome. His imagination was so fired by the traditional philosopher's scorn of physical luxury that he wore a rough Greek cloak and slept on the ground until his mother persuaded him to use a couch with skins for cover. He reacted against the Roman's passionate love of money and more than once surrendered to others some of his testamentary expectations. He was seventeen when his adoptive grandfather Hadrian died and his adoptive father Antoninus Pius came to the throne. The next year he was made a quaestor, and Antoninus further formalized his position as heir apparent by conferring on him the additional name Caesar. In 140, at the age of nineteen, he served as Antoninus' fellow consul. Further to bind Marcus to the future responsibilities of rule, Antoninus Pius made this adoptive son his son-in-law. Marcus Aurelius was twenty-four when he married Faustina, his first cousin; she was sixteen or seventeen. The young bridegroom, in the very year of his marriage, began the study of Stoicism under Apollonius of Chalcedon, and Stoic philosophy deeply satisfied his somewhat solemn, studious nature. Stoicism also turned him away from rhetoric. His arranged marriage with Faustina and his conversion from rhetoric, queen of the sciences, to the half-religious philosophy of Stoicism may[785] have occurred only a year after Aelius Aristides had harnessed rhetoric to declare the glory of the Pax Romana and the age of the Antonines. It is even possible that the clear-eyed young heir apparent, who would most likely have heard Aristides' declamation, was so struck by the discrepancy between what he saw about him and the world the famous rhetorician was conjuring into being that he could never again content himself with rhetoric as a guide to life. Within a year or two a sign of his conversion marked his personal appearance: he began to wear a beard. True, Hadrian had introduced the fashion after centuries of clean-shaven Republican leaders and Emperors, centuries during which the beard suggested the Greek East and especially the Greek philosopher. But Hadrian's beard consisted only of glorified sideburns, and these were defended by some on the grounds that they concealed a disfiguring scar he had received while hunting. In short, the people of the toga were a clean-shaven people. Antoninus' beard was more pronounced. But Marcus' beard, at least in his later years, was of the long, full sort that professional Greek philosophers wore.

In matters more important than the cut of their beards, there were great differences between Hadrian and the man whom he had chosen to succeed his own successor. Well educated by the standards of his day, Marcus was an ascetic where Hadrian had been a sensualist, a civilian where Hadrian had been a soldier, a moralist where Hadrian had been something of an artist, a believer where Hadrian had been a skeptic. But like Hadrian he was spiritually a Hellenist.

In 161 Antoninus Pius died, and the learned Stoic became Emperor. Although he had held various offices, he was unschooled in war. Thirty-seven of his forty years had been passed in Rome. The successive reigns of Nerva, Trajan, Hadrian, and Antoninus Pius had in sixty-five years rescued the office of Emperor from the tarnish it had acquired under some of the tyrants and madmen of the first century A.D., men like Caligula, Nero, and Domitian. No doubt Antoninus Pius' power had rested ultimately on men and money, on the taxes and the legions; but he had been careful to display deference to the Senate. Marcus Aurelius had never shown the slightest desire to be Emperor: it was his duty to rule, and he had long schooled himself to do his duty. He was responsible for governing a territory of some 1,700,000 square miles. He was the head of an immense bureaucracy. Obviously, the burden would be a heavy one: he had scarcely become Emperor when he induced the Senate to make Lucius Verus, Antoninus' other adopted son, his co-Emperor. Verus was ten years younger than Marcus, much more robust, better able to take the field in time of war. Unhappily, Verus tended to construe his elevation as an invitation to share the pleasures of power rather than its burdens, which may be the reason Antoninus Pius had given the rank of Caesar to Marcus Aurelius but not to Verus. For the first time in its history the Empire officially possessed two Emperors neither of whom had reached the throne by force.

One of these Emperors, Marcus, must inevitably have reminded his more literate and more hopeful friends of Plato's philosopher king.

> Ever on his lips was a saying of Plato's, that those states prospered where the philosophers were kings or the kings philosophers.[786]

But the polis which Socrates wanted to see ruled by a philosopher or group of philosophers was the city-state, and a small city-state at that.

Socrates imagined it to contain some five thousand citizens, not the million or so that Rome contained, much less the seventy to one hundred millions that Marcus ruled. This fact alone would have justified Marcus' exhortation to himself, after years of exhausting rule: "Hope not for Plato's commonwealth."[787]

Moreover, though Socrates would have applauded when Marcus outgrew rhetoric and turned to philosophy, yet Marcus' philosophic studies had little in common with the studies Socrates prescribed for the guardians of his imaginary republic. The Stoic curriculum contained too much character-training and too little dialectic, too little high, rigorous, disinterested inquiry to make a philosopher-king. The fact remains that Marcus Aurelius loved reason, not force; truth, not political rhetoric; honest and just administration, not bribery and corruption; self-mastery, not self-indulgence; forgiveness, not revenge.

The troubles of the would-be philosopher-king began soon: in 162 there was revolt in Britain; the Chatti, who were one of the more obstinate German tribes, were raiding the provinces of Upper Germany as well as Raetia, an area lying in what are now parts of Switzerland, Austria, and northern Italy; the Parthians seized Armenia and defeated two Roman armies. Marcus' generals quelled the British rebellion, beat back the Chatti. His junior colleague, Verus, he sent east against the Parthians. But the lighthearted Verus, for whom Imperial rule was always a lark, took his time: Antioch was a pleasure lover's paradise. At Rome, Marcus labored. Although he dutifully attended the public games, he sat reading Stoic philosophy. Or he dictated letters, as Julius Caesar had done. A more instinctively political Emperor might have recognized that, now that the popular assembly had disappeared, the gladiatorial and other public games provided almost the only chance for dialogue between himself and the populace. Admittedly, this dialogue was often rough. As a Christian apologist of his period pointed out to the pagan world,

> I will . . . remind you of the irreverence of your own lower classes, and the scandalous lampoons of which the statues are so cognizant, and the sneers which are sometimes uttered at the public games, and the curses with which the circus resounds. If not in arms, you are in tongue at all events always rebellious.[788]

But Marcus detested Rome's traditional blood sacrifice to violence, the gladiatorial combats, and he annoyed the populace by ordering that the points of the gladiators' swords be dulled. A current farce went so far as to imply subtly that, while Marcus sat imperturbably in the audience, his young Empress, Faustina, was cuckolding him, as her mother, also named Faustina, had reportedly cuckolded Antoninus Pius.

One of Marcus' generals, Priscus, recovered Armenia, and a Roman candidate was placed on the throne. Another general, Avidius Cassius, overran Parthia's province of Mesopotamia and even raided Media, the farthest east that a Roman army had ever penetrated the Parthian Empire. Rome also annexed enough territory east of the Euphrates to straighten and shorten her frontier at the point where the Euphrates bends westward. In 165 Verus negotiated peace with Parthia. Thanks to this war, Rome's army brought back to the Empire two gifts from Asia: a victorious peace and a devastating plague. The plague quickly spread to Egypt, Greece, and finally Italy.

In addition to this deadly pestilence, Marcus Aurelius faced a new problem: Roman merchants operating beyond the Danube frontier reported that powerful German tribes were on the march there. Notwithstanding raids by the Chatti across the Rhine, it soon became clear that, whereas for the Emperors of the first century the Rhine had been the most vulnerable frontier, the Danube had now taken its place. Pressed by tribes from the east, the Marcomanni, the Quadi, and other German tribes crossed the Danube and entered Raetia. Then most of the middle Danube frontier, from which many troops had been borrowed for the Parthian War, buckled. The Germans fought their way south and besieged the important city of Aquileia at the head of the Adriatic. Verus had unwillingly returned to Rome from the delights of Antioch, followed by Egyptian slaves, by Syrian actresses of comedy, and by Syrian dancing girls. To celebrate his triumph he had brought also elephants, camels, and prisoners from the Caucasus and the Arabian desert. The Romans, bored by the austerities of Marcus, were delighted. But the Eastern plague had at last reached Rome; it raged especially in the tenements of the poor; meanwhile Verus gave mad parties in his palace.

In 166 Marcus prepared to relieve Aquileia. Lacking sufficient forces, he raised two new legions. By May of 167 the Germans attacked Dacia, and the Romans had to abandon the gold mines they were working in Transylvania at a moment when the government had rarely needed money more. The Danube line was forced, in what are now Austria, Hungary, Yugoslavia. For the first time in his life Marcus himself, now forty-six, led an

army. He made Verus go with him to Aquileia. As the two Emperors and
their hastily mustered army approached the city, the Germans abandoned
the siege and evacuated northern Italy, fighting rear-guard actions. Marcus
and his unwilling colleague spent the winter of 168–169 at Aquileia collecting soldiers from distant provinces.

About 167, Fronto, Marcus' principal tutor in rhetoric, died. Despite
Marcus' desertion of rhetoric for Stoic philosophy, he had always loved
Fronto. Some four years before his death Fronto was still trying by letter
to win Marcus back to the glories and grandeurs of rhetoric, of eloquence:

> I have heard you say sometimes, *But indeed, when I have said some-*
> *thing rather brilliant, I feel gratified, and that is why I shun eloquence.*
> Why not rather correct and cure yourself of your self-gratification, in-
> stead of repudiating that which gratifies you. For acting as you now do,
> you are tying a poultice in the wrong place. What then? If you gratify
> yourself by giving just judgment, will you disown justice? If you gratify
> yourself by shewing some filial respect to your father, will you despise
> filial duty? You gratify yourself, when eloquent: chastize yourself then,
> but why chastize eloquence?[789]

Again, in the same year, Fronto wrote Marcus in sorrow that

> you seem to have deserted the pursuit of eloquence, and to have turned
> aside after philosophy, in which there is no exordium to be carefully
> elaborated, no marshalling of facts concisely and clearly and skilfully, no
> dividing of a subject into heads, no arguments to be hunted for, no
> amplification . . .[790]

In a letter to Marcus' brother, Verus, whom he had also taught, Fronto
made the stock Roman claim for rhetoric as the queen of the sciences:

> Therefore, if you seek a veritable sovran of the human race, it is your
> eloquence that is sovran, eloquence that sways men's minds. It inspires
> fear, wins love, is a spur to effort, puts shame to silence, exhorts to
> virtue, exposes vices, urges, soothes, teaches, consoles. In fine, I chal-
> lenge boldly and on an old condition—give up eloquence and rule; give
> up making speeches in the Senate and subdue Armenia. . . . Nerva
> commended his acts in the Senate with words requisitioned from others.
> Moreover, most of the emperors that preceded your progenitors were
> virtually dumb and inarticulate, and were no more able to speak of their
> military achievements than could their helmets.[791]

Fronto, less troubled by self-doubt than Marcus, wrote to him:

> I have held the pursuit of learning higher than the acquisition of wealth.
> I preferred to be poor rather than indebted to another's help, at the worst
> to be in want rather than to beg.
>
> In expenditure I have never been extravagant, sometimes earned only
> enough to live upon. I have spoken the truth studiously, I have heard
> the truth gladly. I have held it better to be forgotten than to fawn, to be
> silent than insincere, to be a negligent friend than a diligent flatterer. It
> is little I have sought, not a little I have deserved.[792]

It is unlikely that this former tutor, and later friend, of Emperors should
have written letters to them like this one to Marcus and should also have
been in danger of want. Verus, who cared less for the stringent truth
than Marcus did, counted on Fronto's proposed history of his Parthian
campaign to magnify his role:

> I am ready to fall in with any suggestions as long as my exploits are set
> in a bright light by you. . . .
>
> In short, my achievements . . . can be made to seem as great as you
> would have them seem.[793]

It was no more than Cicero had asked of an historian, and Fronto considered Cicero "the chiefest and supreme mouthpiece of the Roman
tongue."[794] From Fronto, Verus according to his own written testimony
had "learnt simplicity and the love of truth far before the lesson of polite
phrasing."[795] But Verus knew he could count on the rhetoric of a man
commonly considered the foremost Roman orator of his day; nor did
Fronto disappoint him. In the preamble to his history, addressed to Verus,
he spoke of

> these great exploits wrought by you such as Achilles himself would
> fain have wrought and Homer written . . .[796]

Neither did this eloquent man forget to remind the reader that, while other
men lie, writers must be truthful. Except for lovers,

> all other mortals tell present-day lies, but the lies of writers deserve a
> reprobation as everlasting as their memory . . .[797]

At the time that Fronto left this testimony to his love of truth, he did
not know or prudently chose not to know that Avidius Cassius, the able
Syrian-born general who had really won the Parthian War, may well have

considered Verus a lazy, dissipated clown, unfit to direct any war. Verus valued Fronto, the chiefest and supreme mouthpiece of the Roman tongue in his day. Men would know better than to read a masterpiece of eloquence by a court historian as if it were testimony before a judge. For eloquence was sovereign, at least in the orator's world that Fronto invited his readers to enter. Meanwhile, the real world that Rome governed was perhaps beyond the Homeric powers of Verus to save.

In 169, on his way from Aquileia to Rome, Verus died of a stroke. Marcus felt some measure of relief at his death. The horror of the German invasions continued in Macedonia, Thrace, Bithynia. A few war bands penetrated even Greece, and the holy city of Eleusis was sacked. By 172 or 173 Marcus was so desperately short of men that, like the Romans after Hannibal's victory at Cannae, he pieced out his army with slave volunteers.[798] For good measure he recruited gladiators, brigands from Dalmatia and Dardania, men from the police forces of the Greek cities in Asia Minor, Germans, Scythians. In 169 he was driven to a desperate expedient: in the forum built by the great conqueror Trajan, he auctioned off the furniture from his own palace and from Hadrian's villa. Meanwhile, his health reflected the strain he was under; there were stomach pains, frequent fevers, insomnia. But already in 166 he had provided for the succession by making his son Commodus, then five years old, his Caesar. In October of 169 Marcus marched against the Quadi and Sarmatians, who were again warring on the Danube frontier; and from 170 to 175 he fought barbarians on the Danube front, while at night, alone in his quarters, he wrote parts of *Marcus Aurelius Antoninus, the Emperor, to Himself,* now commonly called the *Meditations.*

The *Meditations* show no evidence that they were written for the public of his day or for posterity. They are scattered notes, artless, direct. Sometimes they are repetitious, because more than once Marcus found an ugliness or pettiness in his soul that needed correction. In various camps in what is now southern Czechoslovakia, a little east of the site of modern Vienna, Marcus engaged in that inner dialectic of which Socrates had spoken five centuries before: the dialogue with one's own soul. In his army quarters was placed a bust of Socrates but none of Alexander and none of Julius Caesar. For Marcus hated war. If he was nevertheless engaged now in a most desperate war, this was not because the Roman She-Wolf had for centuries followed war. He was far too steeped in Greek tradition to settle ethical problems by blindly imitating the great Romans of old. On the contrary, he exhorted himself, as he sat writing to himself in Greek, to

> bear in mind . . . that there should be nothing of the *children from parents* style, that is, no mere perfunctory *what our fathers have told us.*[799]

As for rounding up these Sarmatians,

> A spider prides itself on capturing a fly; one man on catching a hare, another on netting a sprat, another on taking wild boars, another bears, another Sarmatians. Are not these brigands, if thou test their principles?[800]

Frequently in bad health, weary of his burden, Marcus often noted the apparent futility and repetitiousness of human history, a history in which he must actively play out the role that history had assigned him:

> Think by way of illustration upon the times of Vespasian, and thou shalt see all these things: mankind marrying, rearing children, sickening, dying, warring, making holiday, trafficking, tilling, flattering others, vaunting themselves, suspecting, scheming, praying for the death of others, murmuring at their own lot, loving, hoarding, coveting a consulate, coveting a kingdom. Not a vestige of that life of theirs is left anywhere any longer.

> Change the scene again to the times of Trajan. Again it is all the same; that life too is dead. In like manner contemplate all the other records of past time and of entire nations, and see how many after all their high-strung efforts sank down so soon in death and were resolved into the elements. But above all must thou dwell in thought upon those whom thou hast thyself known, who, following after vanity, neglected to do the things that accorded with their own constitution and, cleaving steadfastly thereto, to be content with them. And here it is essential to remember that a due sense of value and proportion should regulate the care bestowed on every action. For thus wilt thou never give over in disgust, if thou busy not thyself beyond what is right with the lesser things.[801]

> He, who sees what now is, hath seen all that ever hath been from times everlasting, and that shall be to eternity; for all things are of one lineage and one likeness.[802]

> Pass in review the far-off things of the past and its succession of sovranties without number. Thou canst look forward and see the future also. For it will most surely be of the same character, and it cannot but carry on the rhythm of existing things.[803]

What are they like when eating, sleeping, coupling, evacuating, and the rest! What again when lording it over others, when puffed up with pride, when filled with resentment or rebuking others from a loftier plane! Yet but a moment ago they were lackeying how many and for what ends, and anon will be at their old trade.[804]

Nevertheless, Marcus managed to defend this bullying, lackeying civilization by formalizing his relationship to it. He was determined to comport himself as if the Roman Empire were indeed what many Roman Stoics thought it: Cosmopolis, the world-city, the City of Man, ruled ultimately by Zeus:

> Thou hast but a short time left to live. Live as on a mountain; for whether it be here or there, matters not provided that, wherever a man live, he live as a citizen of the World-City.[805]

Reason made all men citizens of one world.

> If the intellectual capacity is common to us all, common too is the reason, which makes us rational creatures. If so, that reason also is common which tells us to do or not to do. If so, law also is common. If so, we are citizens. If so, we are fellow-members of an organised community. If so, the Universe is as it were a state—for of what other single polity can the whole race of mankind be said to be fellow-members?[806]

Not even Athens, city of the mythical King Cecrops, which largely created the culture that Marcus, adoptive son of Antoninus, was fighting to save from barbarism, was the ideal community the Stoic longed for:

> There is one who says *Dear City of Cecrops!* Wilt thou not say *O dear City of Zeus?*[807]

> But my nature is rational and civic; my city and country, as Antoninus, is Rome; as a man, the world. The things then that are of advantage to these communities, these, and no other, are good for me.[808]

Zeus, or God, was incarnated in him and in his neighbors all over the planet; Zeus was incarnated as their common reason and intelligence:

> And thou forgettest this too, that each man's intelligence is God and has emanated from Him; and this, that nothing is a man's very own, but that his babe, his body, his very soul came forth from Him; and this, that everything is but opinion. . . .[809]

> Enter into every man's ruling Reason, and give every one else an opportunity to enter into thine.[810]

Through his years of hardship on the northern edge of empire, the philosopher-king fought off melancholy and the sense of futility by looking inward at a polis his precariously guarded empire ill reflected, a polis of all men, ruled by Zeus through the reason of all men, living in freedom under what the Stoics called natural law, and able to enter each other's minds in a community of understanding,

> a state with one law for all, based upon individual equality and freedom of speech, and of a sovranty which prizes above all things the liberty of the subject . . .[811]

That vision sustained him in his labor of Sisyphus, as barbarian inroads, internal rebellions, and ruinous pestilence often undid the work he strove to finish. Meanwhile, at Rome the rich escaped satiety and boredom and the poor forgot their misery at the gladiatorial combats. When Marcus had mustered even gladiators into his army,

> there was talk among the people that he intended to deprive them of their amusements and thereby drive them to the study of philosophy.[812]

But other gladiators were found, both at Rome and in the cities throughout the Empire, to celebrate blood, to celebrate violence and power and death, to celebrate the strife that was absent from Marcus' vision of the City of Zeus. Marcus wrote:

> As the shows in the amphitheatre and such places grate upon thee as being an everlasting repetition of the same sight, and the similarity makes the spectacle pall, such must be the effect of the whole of life. For everything up and down is ever the same and the result of the same things. How long then?[813]

The immense melancholy of the *Meditations* measured the abyss that yawned between the polity Marcus loved and the empire he was fated to rule and defend. He exhorted himself to act his part neither unwillingly nor against the grain but as

> a Roman, and a ruler, who hath taken his post as one who awaits the signal of recall from life in all readiness, needing no oath nor any man as his voucher. Be thine the cheery face and independence of help from without and independence of such ease as others can give. It needs then to stand, and not be set, upright.[814]

383

He was sure that the post he had taken was predestined, that "Whatever befalls thee was set in train for thee from everlasting."[815] But acceptance was not easy: "Seeds of decay in the underlying material of everything—water, dust, bones, reek!"[816]

The Empire's burden of memories weighed him down, its memories of ceaseless labor, of never-ending care, of force and violence, of skepticism, blindness, and boredom. He must support, not only his own aging body, but also an aging body politic, assaulted from within and without. When he applied to himself Epictetus' warning, "Thou art a *little soul bearing up a corpse*,"[817] Marcus might have applied it also to the aging civilization whose northern frontier he defended. For Graeco-Roman civilization now derived most of its fading significance from a culture that had long ago flowered and had once made human existence in Athens a kind of dance, often tragic, often grossly comic, but a dance fraught with meaning. That culture had expanded until it suffused Cosmopolis, but it was no longer a dancing matter:

> The business of life is more akin to wrestling than dancing, for it requires of us to stand ready and unshakeable against every assault. . . .[818]

Ready and unshakable Marcus stood, but

> all the things of the body are as a river, and the things of the soul as a dream and a vapour; and life is a warfare and a pilgrim's sojourn, and fame after death is only forgetfulness.[819]

Besides the assaults of German tribesmen, who in a sense were merely German brigands fighting Roman brigands for power and plunder, he bore the intimate assaults of private grief for Fronto's death, for other deaths, even the deaths of his own children. Remember, he told himself, that

> Such are the races of men as the leaves that the wind scatters earthwards.
>
> And thy children too are little leaves.[820]

Marcus reflected that, had his destiny not assigned him to save an empire and an ancient civilization, he might have continued the studies he so loved:

> This too serves as a corrective to vain-gloriousness, that thou art no longer able to have lived thy life wholly, or even from thy youth up, as a philosopher. Thou canst clearly perceive, and many others can see it too, that thou art far from Philosophy. So then thy life is a chaos, and no

longer is it easy for thee to win the credit of being a philosopher; and the facts of thy life too war against it. . . .

Thou canst not be a student. But thou canst . . . forbear to be angry with the unfeeling and the thankless, aye and even care for them.[821]

In true Stoic style, he commanded himself: "Put an end once for all to this discussion of what a good man should be, and be one."[822] Granted that even as a youth he had found neither Hadrian's court nor the court of Antoninus a fit place for study, yet at least in his actions he had tried to live in accordance with philosophy. And so, all these years later, he wrote:

Where life is possible, there it is possible also to live well. *But the life is life in a Court.* Well, in a Court too it is possible to live well.[823]

No doubt Marcus' effort to live well irritated many, but he tried not to resent his critics:

For we have come into being for co-operation, as have the feet, the hands, the eyelids, the rows of upper and lower teeth. Therefore to thwart one another is against Nature; and we do thwart one another by shewing resentment and aversion.[824]

And the soul wrongs itself then again, when it turns away from any man or even opposes him with intent to do him harm, as is the case with those who are angry.[825]

He held with Socrates that "wrong-doing is involuntary."[826] He therefore adjured himself not to judge harshly

the characters of thine associates, even the most refined of whom it is difficult to put up with, let alone the fact that a man has enough to do to endure himself.[827]

Over and over again, his thoughts turned to the necessity to forgive, not to be angry, not to hate:

Suppose that a competitor in the ring has gashed us with his nails and butted us violently with his head, we do not protest or take it amiss or suspect our opponent in future of foul play. Still we do keep an eye on him, not indeed as an enemy, or from suspicion of him, but with good-humoured avoidance. Act much in the same way in all the other parts of life. Let us make many allowances for our fellow-athletes as it were.

385

Avoidance is always possible, as I have said, without suspicion or hatred.[828]

How intolerant it is not to permit men to cherish an impulse towards what is in their eyes congenial and advantageous! . . . *But they are mistaken.* Well, then, teach and enlighten them without any resentment.[829]

Does a man do thee wrong? Go to and mark what notion of good and evil was his that did the wrong. Once perceive that and thou wilt feel compassion not surprise or anger.

See that thou never have for the inhuman the feeling which the inhuman have for human kind.[830]

When men blame or hate thee or give utterance to some such feelings against thee, turn to their souls, enter into them, and see what sort of men they are. . . . Yet must thou feel kindly towards them, for Nature made them dear to thee. The Gods too lend them aid in divers ways by dreams and oracles, to win those very things on which their hearts are set.[831]

But above all, when thou findest fault with a man for faithlessness and ingratitude, turn thy thoughts to thyself. For evidently the fault is thine own, whether thou hadst faith that a man with such a character would keep faith with thee, or if in bestowing a kindness thou didst not bestow it absolutely and as from the very doing of it having at once received the full complete fruit.[832]

If a man makes a slip, enlighten him with loving-kindness, and shew him wherein he hath seen amiss. Failing that, blame thyself or not even thyself.[833]

Wilt thou then, O my Soul, ever at last be good and simple and single and naked, shewing thyself more visible than the body that overlies thee? Wilt thou ever taste the sweets of a loving and a tender heart? . . . Wilt thou ever at last fit thyself so to be a fellow-citizen with the Gods and with men as never to find fault with them or incur their condemnation?[834]

Marcus was convinced that

to be wroth is not manly, but a mild and gentle disposition, as it is more human, so it is more masculine. Such a man, and not he who gives way to anger and discontent, is endowed with strength and sinews and manly courage. . . . As grief is a weakness, so also is anger. In both it is a case of a wound and a surrender.[835]

386

Marcus risked, of course, a certain frigidity and even priggishness by keeping himself aloof from the wounding passions to which most of his subjects had surrendered. But he was not merely saving himself from the self-inflicted wounds and surrender that he saw back of his own anger and his hatred of the viciousness about him. He knew that to be a citizen of the world Zeus ruled implied more than his own reasonableness, more than purging himself of anger or hatred; it implied actually loving his fellow citizens, no matter how unlovable their vices might prove. From Plutarch's grandson, Sextus, he had learned that he should be "full of natural affection,"[836] and from Fronto he had learned that

> as a general rule, those amongst us who rank as patricians are somewhat wanting in natural affection.[837]

He was grateful for both lessons. He wrote:

> See thou be not *Caesarified.* . . . keep thyself a simple and good man, uncorrupt, dignified, plain, a friend of justice, god-fearing, gracious, affectionate, manful in doing thy duty. . . . Revere the Gods, save mankind. Life is short. This only is the harvest of earthly existence, a righteous disposition and social acts.[838]

But he told himself reassuringly that

> We are all fellow-workers towards the fulfilment of one object, some of us knowingly and intelligently, others blindly; just as Heraclitus, I think, says that *even when they sleep men are workers* and fellow-agents in all that goes on in the world.[839]

The Christian apologist Justin, who sent Marcus Aurelius a defense of Christianity and was martyred early in his reign, would surely have read with a kind of recognition Marcus' admonition to himself to remember that

> A branch cut off from its neighbour branch can not but be cut off from the whole plant. In the very same way a man severed from one man has fallen away from the fellowship of all men. Now a branch is cut off by others, but a man separates himself from his neighbour by his own agency in hating him or turning his back upon him; and is unaware that he has thereby sundered himself from the whole civic community. But mark the gift of Zeus who established the law of fellowship. For it is in our power to grow again to the neighbour branch and again become perfective of the whole. But such a schism constantly repeated makes it

difficult for the seceding part to unite again. . . . Be of one bush, but not of one mind.[840]

Of one bush, but not of one mind. The two phrases suggest that Marcus had somehow grasped the important double message of Socrates on the nature of high philosophic dialectic: that a common love of truth could join men even while a sharply distinguished intellectual difference could fructify their love. The possibility that Marcus did in fact grasp this opposition and this union perhaps lends a special poignancy to the lament of a studious Emperor torn from his studies by the responsibilities of Imperial rule and frontier war, the lament Marcus expressed when he wrote,

> nor because thou hast been baulked in the hope of becoming skilled in dialectics and physics, needest thou despair of being free and modest and unselfish and obedient to God.[841]

His frequent command to himself to "love the men among whom thy lot is thrown, but whole-heartedly"[842] might suggest that he found it difficult to love the men about him. But in fact he loved not only many persons but also the simplest objects he saw about him, including those that some men scorned as being imperfect or spoilt. He wrote that

> the accessories too of natural operations have a charm and attractiveness of their own. For instance, when bread is in the baking, some of the parts split open, and these very fissures, though in a sense thwarting the bread-maker's design, have an appropriateness of their own and in a peculiar way stimulate the desire for food. Again when figs are at their ripest, they gape open; and in olives that are ready to fall their very approach to over-ripeness gives a peculiar beauty to the fruit. And the full ears of corn bending downwards, and the lion's beetling brows, and the foam dripping from the jaws of the wild-boar, and many other things, though, if looked at apart from their setting, they are far from being comely, yet, as resultants from the operations of Nature, lend them an added charm and excite our admiration.[843]

Faced with the rains of the distant north frontier, this Roman could quote Euripides: "The earth is in love with showers and the majestic sky is in love,"[844] and add:

> And the Universe is in love with making whatever has to be. To the Universe I say: *Together with thee I will be in love.*[845]

By 175 the Marcomanni and Quadi had been driven back and Marcus was preparing a counterattack: he planned to set up two new provinces in order to carry his frontiers to the Carpathians and to the Erzebirge Mountains of what is now Bohemia. However, his hard war with the Marcomanni had weakened his frontier garrisons elsewhere. Moorish brigands[846] appeared in Spain. Rome's puppet king of Armenia was overthrown. Once more the Germans on the Rhine were making trouble. The rural population of Egypt started rioting and finally formed a peasant army under the leadership of an Egyptian priest. The Prefect of Egypt had to get military help from Avidius Cassius, whom Marcus had stationed at Antioch to govern the Eastern provinces.

In March, 175, at the Roman colony of Sirmium, near the site of modern Belgrade, Marcus fell seriously ill. A rumor reached Avidius Cassius that the Emperor was dead, and some of the detractors of the Empress later claimed that Faustina had conspired with Cassius. In any case, at Antioch Cassius was proclaimed Emperor, and Egypt and most of the Asian provinces rallied to him. But by May, Marcus had recovered. To free his army for a march east against Cassius, he made peace at the old Danube frontier and abandoned or postponed his plan for new buffer provinces beyond that river. Then he marched east. But Marcus and Cassius did not have to fight it out: some of Cassius' officers had murdered him and sent his head to Marcus. Marcus ordered it buried. The next year Faustina died. She was suspected by some of treason: would her correspondence inculpate her? Marcus burned it without reading it. For about thirty years she had held the title of Augusta. Notwithstanding Roman gossip, she had borne him some thirteen children and was deeply loved by him. For several years she had followed Marcus on campaign: the soldiers had called her Mother of the Camp. Now that she was dead, the Senate, at Marcus' request, deified her.

Before returning to Rome, Marcus visited Egypt, Palestine, Syria, Smyrna. His was an Imperial Eastern tour, reminiscent of Hadrian's. At Smyrna he sent for the orator Aelius Aristides and asked,

Why have you been so slow in letting me see you? And Aristides said, "A professional problem, O King, occupied me, and the mind, when so engaged, must not be detached from the prosecution of its enquiry." The Emperor, charmed by the man's character, his extreme naïveté and studiousness, said, When shall I hear you? And Aristides replied, "Suggest a subject to-day and hear me to-morrow; for I am not of those who 'throw up' what is in their minds but of those who speak with precision. But grant, O King, that my pupils also may be present at the hearing." *Certainly*, said Marcus, *they may, for it is free to all*. And on Aristides saying, "Permit them, O King, to cheer and applaud as loud as they can," the Emperor smiling said, *That depends on yourself*.[847]

From Smyrna Marcus crossed the Aegean to Athens. He and his son Commodus, like Hadrian and Antinoüs, followed the Sacred Way from Athens to Eleusis, where they were initiated into the Mysteries. At Eleusis the Emperor could inspect the ruins of the ancient temple of the Mysteries, burned some six years before by barbarian invaders. Marcus set up professorships at Athens not only in Stoicism but in the peripatetic philosophy founded by Aristotle, in the philosophy of the Cynics, and Epicureanism. In November, 176, he passed through Macedonia and Epirus and crossed to Brindisi. There he touched Italian soil for the first time in eight years; he characteristically ordered the Imperial Guard to change from soldier's dress to the toga. Rome celebrated his return noisily and gratefully. At the amphitheater officials paraded the golden statue of the now dead Faustina, the woman the gossips claimed had been fond of sleeping with sailors and gladiators. The crowd was respectfully silent. Finally, on December 23, 176, the official triumph was held. Marcus' son Commodus, a handsome youth who hated study and loved personal combat, took part and was given the title of Imperator.

The next year, 177, at Lyons there was a popular outbreak against Christians, and mobs cried, "The Christians to the lions!" Suspects were questioned under torture, as were their slaves, some of whom were pagan. The slaves were tortured until they confessed that Christians really did hold secret orgies, commit incest, and eat the flesh of murdered children. Forty-seven persons were thrown to the lions. Marcus shared a widespread fear and distrust of Christians and probably accepted the charges of debauchery that Fronto had made against them. In any case he approved the legal sentence, capital punishment, for those Christians who refused to recant. On Stoic grounds he followed many precepts that Christians followed too, but apparently the Christian attitude to martyrdom did not move him. Of the readiness to die, Marcus wrote later that it

> must spring from a man's inner judgment, and not be the result of mere opposition [as is the case with the Christians]. It must be associated with

deliberation and dignity and, if others too are to be convinced, with nothing like stage-heroics.[848]

It was in this same year, 177, that Marcus fell ill again. He recovered, only to be confronted with more German raids across the Danube, this time into the Province of Pannonia. Once more history condemned him to the futile labor of Sisyphus in Hades. The pestilence from Asia had decimated large areas and had thereby dangerously reduced, not only his military manpower, but his agricultural manpower too, at a time when famines were inviting pestilence. The pestilence in turn demoralized the population and increased the brigandage. The area around Ravenna was so short of men to till the land that Marcus resettled it with conquered Marcomanni. They revolted. Repeated rebellions aggravated his shortage of troops. In 177 also, Marcus gave Commodus the title of Augustus. Then, leaving him as co-Emperor in Rome, Marcus started north once more, and once more drove out the perennial invaders. In that single year the Empire witnessed a moral victory inflicted by a still young church upon an aging empire; another illness of an heroic Roman Emperor during what seemed an endless struggle to ward off or drive out barbarian invaders; and another return of this Emperor, now in his old age, to man the frontiers.[849] Marcus again planned to do what illness and the revolt of Avidius Cassius had prevented a few years earlier: to advance the frontier northward from the Danube to include two new provinces. But in March, 180, at his winter quarters in Vienna, he again fell ill. Had Cassius, a second time and posthumously, thwarted his grand design? It was Cassius' army that had brought back to the Empire the devastating Eastern plague, and this time the illness that felled Marcus may have been the plague.[850] He wrote, during this same general period,

> Despise not death, but welcome it, for Nature wills it like all else. . . . A man then that has reasoned the matter out should not take up towards death the attitude of indifference, eagerness, or scorn, but await it as one of the processes of Nature. Look for the hour when thy soul shall emerge from this sheath, as now thou awaitest the moment when the child she carries shall come forth from thy wife's womb.[851]

Now at last a death that might prove to be a birth seemed imminent. He shared the hope of Socrates as well as his lack of certainty that the soul of a good man is immortal. Understandably, he expressed both the hope and the uncertainty through a more complex rhetoric:

How can the Gods, after disposing all things well and with good will towards men, ever have overlooked this one thing, that some of mankind, and they especially good men, who have had as it were the closest commerce with the Divine, and by devout conduct and acts of worship have been in the most intimate fellowship with it, should when once dead have no second existence but be wholly extinguished? But if indeed this be haply so, doubt not that they would have ordained it otherwise had it needed to be otherwise. . . . Therefore, from its not being so, if indeed it is not so, be assured that it ought not to have been so. For even thyself canst see that in this presumptuous enquiry of thine thou art reasoning with God. But we should not thus be arguing with the Gods were they not infinitely good and just. But in that case they could not have overlooked anything being wrongly and irrationally neglected in their thorough ordering of the Universe.[852]

Marcus' view of death differed from that of Socrates. Socrates attached more importance to truth and to doing the will of Zeus as conveyed to him, however darkly, by that god's son, Apollo of Delphi, than he attached to preserving his body; this choice did indeed lead to his execution. But Socrates rejected suicide as morally wrong; the Stoicism of Marcus did not. Indeed, the lectures which Epictetus had delivered in Epirus and which the historian Arrian had transcribed, repeatedly sanctioned suicide; and the copy of these lectures, which Marcus had received from his beloved tutor Rusticus some thirty years before Marcus lay ill at his camp in 180, was listed in the *Meditations* as among his chief blessings. Granted that Marcus disapproved of indifference toward death, or eagerness for it, or scorn of it, yet his problem was complicated by his duty to rule the Roman Empire. That task was his first responsibility. He may well have felt, as once more he lay ill, this time in his sixtieth year, that he was no longer adequate to the task of ruling the Graeco-Roman world. Part of this inadequacy was the fact that he was a good and gentle man, cultivated, studious, a ruler whose courtiers may well have found him unfitted for power, too scrupulous in its uses, too merciful toward rebels, too romantic about the common good. Above all, his daily life rebuked them, as the daily life of his hero Socrates had rebuked the Athenians. These things Marcus knew and noted in his *Meditations*:

There is no one so fortunate as not to have one or two standing by his death-bed who will welcome the evil which is befalling him. Say he was a worthy man and a wise; will there not be some one at the very end to say in his heart, *We can breathe again at last, freed from this schoolmaster, not that he was hard on any of us, but I was all along conscious that he tacitly condemns us?* So much for the worthy, but in our own case how many other reasons can be found for which hundreds would be only too glad to be quit of us. Think then upon this when dying, and thy passing from life will be easier if thou reason thus: I am leaving a life in which even my intimates for whom I have so greatly toiled, prayed, and thought, aye even they wish me gone, expecting belike to gain thereby some further ease. Why then should anyone cling to a longer sojourn here?[853]

The knowledge that he was trying to govern through men who did not understand his purposes may have freed Marcus from any duty to keep his body alive. In a sense, the choice of whether he ought to live was theirs, not his; as the choice of whether Socrates ought to accept the cup of hemlock from his jailer's hands, voluntarily raise the cup, and drain it, had been even more clearly the choice of an Athenian court and not that of Socrates. So Marcus simply refused food for six days until death came.

Marcus had ruled just over nineteen years. Perhaps his chief claim to the bust of Socrates, which he kept in his quarters, was his determination that he also should learn to listen:

Train thyself to pay careful attention to what is being said by another and as far as possible enter into his soul.[854]

Marcus had once given himself the command, "Revere gods, save men."[855] But Marcus, whom many of his subjects revered as a god, was a god-man and savior armed with a sword, with the power to tax and the power to raise armies in a vast empire. With these weapons he had, at least temporarily, saved his empire from destruction. But for how long? On the other hand, because he listened to other men and entered into their souls, his *Meditations*, the only really significant book a Roman Emperor ever wrote, promised to outlast Eternal Rome.[856]

Commodus, who saw his father in his last week, was left sole Emperor at the age of nineteen. He abandoned Marcus' project of advancing the northern frontier, bribed the troublesome Germans with a subsidy, returned to Rome to celebrate a brilliant triumph. He soon played the tyrant, became deranged, and decided that he was an incarnation of the god Hercules. In 192, in the thirteenth year of his reign as sole Emperor, he insisted on fighting personally in the gladiatorial combats; his advisers were outraged and had him strangled. He had proven to be a much less worthy legacy than the *Meditations*. Why did Marcus choose him as successor rather than adopt one of his abler generals? Probably because the army preferred hereditary succession.[857] True, the Senate preferred the system of adoption, which Nerva, Trajan, Hadrian, and Antoninus Pius had used. But in their case the army's preference was irrelevant: none of these Emperors had sons of their own. Moreover, while there were signs that Marcus had begun to doubt the wisdom of his choice, it was too late: Commodus was already his co-Augustus and extremely popular with the army.

Commodus' successor, Pertinax, might have been a good Emperor, but the Praetorian Guard, although they had put him in power, found him stingy and too stern a disciplinarian: in three months he was murdered. There were two candidates for the empty throne, and the Praetorian Guard held an auction. A rich Senator named Didius Julianus bid in the Empire. It was not the first time money had played a decisive role in filling the Imperial throne, but a public auction was an innovation. The frontier armies in Britain, Pannonia, and Syria remembered what the historian Tacitus had called the secret of empire: in the last analysis the army could make an Emperor. Each of the two armies in Pannonia and Syria promptly acclaimed one, but Pannonia was of course a good deal nearer Rome than either Britain or Syria. Septimius Severus, a native of Leptis Magna, a city on the coast of what is now Libya, was Governor of Upper Pannonia. When his army acclaimed him Emperor, he marched on Rome and seized it, and thereby become the fourth man to rule in barely six months. He made a possible claimant from Britain his Caesar; marched east in 193 and put down his Syrian competitor; later, his Caesar revolted, crossed to Gaul, and established himself at Lyons, and there in 197 Severus attacked and defeated him. Once he had disposed of his two rivals he made no pretence of deferring to the Senate. He packed his bureaucracy with former military men. In 211, as he lay dying at York, he reportedly said to his two sons, Caracalla and Geta, whom he had designated to rule jointly: "Be harmonious, enrich the soldiers, and scorn all other men."[858] The next year Caracalla murdered Geta in their mother's arms.

This act of fratricide occurred in 212, thirty-two years after the great plague, or some other illness, struck down Marcus Aurelius. To the generation brought up during his reign and later exposed to the madness of Commodus, the murder of Pertinax, the auctioning of the Empire, Severus' seizure of the throne, and Caracalla's despotism, the preceding Age of the Antonines seemed a lost paradise.

Although the literature produced in the Age of the Antonines lacked the quality of that written under Augustus, some of it was nevertheless memorable. Suetonius, the biographer of Rome's first twelve Emperors, did not die until about the year in which Marcus mounted the throne, and Marcus is almost certain to have read him. Aulus Gellius, the author of *Attic Nights*, flourished during Marcus' reign; but his literary chitchat is likely to have interested Fronto more than Marcus. Perhaps the same thing is true of such cultural dilettantes as Athenaeus of Naucratis in Egypt, who wrote, probably after Marcus' death, the *Sophists at Dinner*, a long symposium on literature, stuffed with quotations. The author dealt with the philosophers of his day by quoting a Greek epigram:

> Sons-of-eyebrow-raisers, noses-fixed-in-beards, beards-bag-fashion-trimmed, and casserole-pilferers too, cloaks-over-shoulders-slinging, barefoot-shambling-with-eyes-cast-down, night-birds-secretly-feeding, night-sinners-in-deceit, puny-lad-deceivers, and silly-babblers-of-sought-syllables, wise-in-their-vain-conceits, degenerate-sons-of-seekers-after-good.[859]

In this same dialogue a participant attacks Plato's *Symposium* and *Republic* with knowing iconoclasm:

> Plato, I say, ridicules Agathon's balanced clauses and antitheses, and also brings on the scene Alcibiades, who avows that he is consumed with lust. Nevertheless, while writing that kind of stuff, they banish Homer from their states![860]

Another feaster at Athenaeus' learned banquet points out that in any case Plato's banquet, the *Symposium*, is anachronistic:

> But Plato's *Symposium* is nonsense pure and simple. For when Agathon won his victory, Plato was only fourteen years old.[861]

If Plato had pictured himself as participating in the banquet, the point might have been accurate, though scarcely relevant to Plato's thought. But perhaps this latter-day literary critic had read Plato only in excerpt or in digest form, or had not read him at all but had read a book about the books which Plato wrote. Anyhow, his point provoked a learned discussion of Plato's anachronisms. These civilized, metropolitan banqueters were doubtless well enough traveled to use Athenaeus' epithets for the best-known cities: Rome was "the populace of the world"; Alexandria was the "golden" city; Antioch, the "beautiful"; Nicomedia, the "very lovely"; and Athens was "the most radiant of all the towns that Zeus created."[862]

Marcus Aurelius would have found more useful than either Gellius or Athenaeus such writers in Greek as Appian, a friend of Fronto's, who probably wrote his history of Rome under Marcus' predecessor, and Arrian, the transcriber of Epictetus' lectures, who died about the same time as Marcus.

It was, however, during the reign of Marcus that two really great masters of fiction appeared: Apuleius wrote a satirical novel in Latin and Lucian wrote a large number of satirical sketches in Greek. The world that these two writers portrayed bore little resemblance to the City of Zeus. About 123, when Marcus Aurelius was a small child, Lucius Apuleius was born of wealthy parents in Madauros, in what is now Algeria. A quarter of a century before, some sixty miles west of Madauros, the city of Cirta had won renown by producing the rhetorician Fronto. Apuleius, too, became a rhetorician, as well as a lawyer. He studied at Carthage and then at Athens. On a trip to Egypt he met and married at Oea, now Tripoli, a wealthy widow. Her relatives sued him on a charge of using magic to win her. His defense, written in a style not unworthy of Fronto himself, was successful. But, unlike Fronto, Apuleius made a major contribution to Latin literature. His *Metamorphoses*, now commonly called *The Golden Ass*, is no epic of change such as Ovid meant his own *Metamorphoses* to be. Yet changes there are in this picaresque novel. The plot is built around a young man's transforming himself by accident into a donkey and being rescued by the Egyptian goddess Isis, who instructs him how to change himself back into a man. The reader can scarcely fail to see behind the events of the plot a young man who made a lecherous ass of himself and recovered his manhood by religious conversion. But the adventures of the young hero are so utterly fortuitous and absurd that Apuleius' novel often seems to be saying one of the things Ovid's poem says: that all is chance and change. Apuleius possessed Ovid's uncanny gift for narrative, which made all these rapid changes delightfully plausible.

Even in this novel Apuleius' style resembles Fronto's. The difference is that in Apuleius' case the rhetoric serves a more genuine, more universal purpose: to tell a good yarn, or what critics in his day called a Milesian tale. The novel purports to be written in the first person by a Greek, who bore Apuleius' first name, Lucius, and who had some of the experiences the author had. The world through which this imaginary Lucius moves is a world of violence. There are bandits; dangerous magic and sorcery in Thessaly; witches and necromancers; debauchery in Corinth; misers, beautiful and obliging slave girls, oppressive centurions, eunuch priests, murder and adultery, abandoned love-making, instruments of torture such as foot scorchers and the wheel, floggings and crucifixions, hairbreadth escapes, the agony and tribulations of a man's soul inhabiting the body of a cruelly treated ass. There are the starving slum dwellers of Plataea and the condemned criminals waiting to be fed to wild beasts in the arena.

In the midst of these horrors comes a charming tale of Cupid and Psyche. Cupid visits Psyche by night. And then, as Apuleius adds in the manner of Ovid,

> He left her hastily just before daybreak, and almost at once she heard the voices of her maids reassuring her that though she had lost her virginity, her chastity was safe.[863]

The hero of the whole tale, the human donkey, delights a new owner by doing tricks. The new owner, named Thyasus, has just been appointed Lord Chief Justice of Corinth and is expected to mark the occasion with gladiatorial shows. The ass's fame has spread; a rich noblewoman has fallen in love with him, has even spent several blissful nights with him. "I began," says the hero in recounting this amour,

> to appreciate the story of Pasiphaë: if she was anything like this woman she had every reason to fix her affections on the bull who fathered the Minotaur on her.[864]

Then the new Chief Justice hears of this unnatural liaison.

> "Splendid, splendid!" cried Thyasus. "That's the very act we need to liven up our show. But what a pity that his sweetheart is a noblewoman: her family would never allow her to perform in public."[865]

So Thyasus searched the brothels for which Corinth had long been famous, but found no volunteer. Then he selected a murderess, who had been sentenced to be torn by wild beasts in the arena. Here Apuleius recounts with gusto her hideous crimes, so hideous indeed that Apuleius achieves the miracle, largely by skillful understatement, of making the story of her crimes amusing. As to her punishment,

Doubtless she deserved a still worse fate than merely to be thrown to the wild beasts; still, this was the most appropriate sentence that occurred to the Governor at the time.[866]

The human ass was horrified by the projected exhibition,

> which almost amounted to a legal marriage. It was with extreme anguish that I waited for the day of the show. I was tempted to commit suicide rather than defile myself and be put to everlasting shame by bedding down with this wicked creature before the eyes of the entire amphitheatre.[867]

The day came and the shamefaced ass was led through the cheering crowds to the theater. First, he was privileged to witness a ballet, then a representation of the Judgment of Paris, in which Venus, wearing only a little gauze apron and that on a pleasantly breezy day, was "greeted with a roar of welcome by the audience."[868] While Juno and Minerva stood hopefully by, Venus danced for Paris, especially with her eyes, and "Young Paris gladly handed her the golden apple in token of her victory."[869]

At this point in his narrative, Apuleius, the lawyer, bursts with feigned rage into an apostrophe to all lawyers on the corruption of justice by bribes. But hastily returning to his story he reports that

> After this, a soldier ran along the main aisle and out of the theatre to fetch the murderess who, though condemned (as I have already explained) to be eaten by wild beasts, was destined first to become my glorious bride. Our marriage bed, inlaid with fine Indian tortoise shell, was already in position, and provided with a luxurious feather mattress and an embroidered Chinese coverlet. I was not only appalled at the disgraceful part that I was expected to play: I was in terror of death. It occurred to me that when she and I were locked in what was supposed to be a passionate embrace and the wild beast, whose part in the drama would be to eat her, came bounding into our bridal cage, I could not count on the creature's being so naturally sagacious, or so well trained, or so abstemious, as to tear her to pieces as she cuddled close to me, but leave me alone.[870]

When Juvenal reported, or invented, in one of his epigrams a literal-minded representation of the Pasiphaë myth in the Roman arena, it was with the moral indignation that commonly inspired his satires. Apuleius displays no moral indignation whatever; he is thoroughly amused that an

398

ass should feel so mortified by a show staged to delight a human audience and by the ass's sudden terror that at the crucial moment he would share his glorious bride's fate and be eaten up. Anyhow, Apuleius prevents both the act of sexual bestiality and the double death from occurring: in the nick of time the ass manages to escape, is rescued by Isis, and is restored to human shape. He then is initiated into the religion of this goddess, and the High Priest addresses the initiate:

> "Lucius, my friend," he said, "you have endured and performed many labours and withstood the buffetings of all the winds of ill luck. Now at last you have put into the harbour of peace and stand before the altar of loving-kindness. Neither your noble blood and rank nor your education sufficed to keep you from falling a slave to pleasure; youthful follies ran away with you. Your luckless curiosity earned you a sinister punishment. . . . Rest assured that you are now safe under the protection of the true Fortune, all-seeing Providence, whose clear light shines for all the gods that are."[871]

It was characteristic of Apuleius that his hero then went to Rome and practiced law; and that, though he found Rome expensive, yet once he had luckily got himself initiated into the mysteries of Isis' divine consort, Osiris, the latter,

> as the God of Good Fortune, put briefs in my way and I made quite a decent living as a barrister, even though I had to plead in Latin, not Greek.[872]

No wonder Lucius became a Temple Councillor for five years, kept his head shaved, and "displayed it without shame on all occasions."[873] With this statement the racy, entertaining, morally detached novel ends.

Within a few years of the birth of Apuleius, another second-century writer, Lucian, was born at the other end of the Empire, at Samosata, a fortress town on the west bank of the Euphrates; at about this time the Emperor Hadrian, upon abandoning Trajan's conquest of Mesopotamia, moved his frontier back to this city. Unlike Apuleius, Lucian was born in moderate circumstances, and the career of professional rhetorician seemed to be the only possible escape from apprenticeship to a statuary. He studied in Ionia and became a lawyer, like Apuleius; but turned to the profession of public orator, like Aelius Aristides. He passed to Greece, to Italy, and then Gaul, where he may have held for a while a professorial chair in rhetoric. When he was in his middle thirties he returned to his native Syria and lived in Antioch, where he delivered a panegyric on Panthea, mistress of the Emperor Verus, Marcus Aurelius' lighthearted brother. Then he went to Athens, there he gave up rhetoric to study philosophy. But Lucian became disillusioned with the Athenian dialecticians of his day and began to parody them. His own dialogues became less rhetorical and more like comic conversations.

It was Lucian's love of truth that first caused his strong disgust for the sophistry, the pomposity, the double-talk, of the rhetoricians who swarmed across the face of the Roman Empire, declaiming nothings with a virtuosity that won them applause, fame, and a good income. The same love of truth made him detest the skillful but shallow dialectic that he believed characterized the professional philosophers of Athens. And finally his love of truth led him to use the written dialogue, not for philosophic exploration, but as Aristophanes had used it: to laugh at man's follies and especially at his peculiar zest for lying.

Lucian did not attempt to revive comic drama. Having quit sculpture to seek fame and fortune, rhetoric to seek the truth, he now quit professional philosophy because, not having found the truth, he could still enjoy a long laugh at the pompous shams of every sort that enclosed and protected and infected the golden age of the Antonine Emperors, as the hard shell of frontier legions enclosed and protected, and eventually infected with militarism, the complacent society the Antonines governed. Being a clever Syrian by origin, he wrote satire which was singularly free of the resentment and hate, perhaps self-hate, that embittered the satires of Martial and Juvenal, even though all three writers often touched on the same subjects. For Lucian was troubled by no sentimental attachment for the lost moralities of the Roman Republic. As a sophisticated Greek Oriental, he could take seriously neither the vaunted majesty of Roman law nor the warmed-over culture of Hellas. He held up a mirror in which the Graeco-Roman world appeared as a ludicrous fraud. He laughed at the rhetorical historian who aped Herodotus or Thucydides, or the historian who packed his narrative with irrelevant word paintings of places, or who needlessly philosophized; or the historian who boasted that he wrote only of what he had seen, and then quickly proved himself a liar by his stupid blunders. To these he preferred even the man who has

> compiled a bare record of the events and set it down on paper, completely prosaic and ordinary, such as a soldier or artisan or pedlar following the army might have put together as a diary of daily events. However, this amateur was not so bad—it was quite obvious at the beginning

what he was, and his work has cleared the ground for some future historian of taste and ability.[874]

What he asked of the historian above all was that he be frank, free from flattery, and truthful; and this was a great deal to ask when history had become a branch of rhetoric.

The question of truth haunted him. He wrote a dialogue called *The Lover of Lies*, which expressed bewilderment that men should so love to lie. He wrote a fantasy called *A True Story*, in which he starts off by mentioning certain books of travel, obviously packed with lies. And he adds:

> Well, on reading all these authors, I did not find much fault with them for their lying, as I saw that this was already a common practice even among men who profess philosophy. I did wonder, though, that they thought that they could write untruths and not get caught at it. Therefore, as I myself, thanks to my vanity, was eager to hand something down to posterity, that I might not be the only one excluded from the privileges of poetic licence, and as I had nothing true to tell, not having had any adventures of significance, I took to lying.[875]

So he claims he once sailed with a crew of fifty through the Pillars of Hercules to explore the Atlantic Ocean. A waterspout sucked his ship up and a high wind carried her to the moon, where they helped the Moonfolk make war on the Sunfolk. Later they passed Cloudcuckooland, and Lucian remembered Aristophanes, "the learned and veracious poet whose statements had met with unmerited incredulity."[876] The ship returned to earth, and to the Ocean; but a huge whale swallowed her. Finally, always inside the whale, they so to speak made land. Another war, this time between local tribes inside the whale. Later in this true story, Lucian visited the Isle of the Blest, met Homer, and tried out on the poet some of the questions raised by centuries of literary criticism, questions not much more exciting than the one the Emperor Hadrian had put to the Delphic oracle.

> I next asked him why he began with the wrath of Achilles; and he said that it just came into his head that way, without any study.[877]

Lucian also met Odysseus, who, when Penelope was not looking, slipped him a letter to give to Calypso. But before delivering it Lucian opened it and read:

Soon after I built the raft and sailed away from you I was ship-wrecked, and with the help of Leucothea managed to reach the land of the Phaeacians in safety. They sent me home, and there I found that my wife had a number of suitors who were living on the fat of the land at our house. I killed them all, and was afterwards slain by Telegonus, my son by Circe. Now I am on the Isle of the Blest, thoroughly sorry to have given up my life with you and the immortality which you offered me. Therefore, if I get a chance, I shall run away and come to you.[878]

On this same Isle of the Blest, Lucian found most of the philosophers, even the great ones, acting as they had acted on earth, as indeed he found philosophers of his own day acting at Athens. Rhadamanthus, ruler and judge of the dead, had his hands full:

It was said that Rhadamanthus was angry at Socrates and had often threatened to banish him from the island if he kept up his nonsense and would not quit his irony and be merry. Plato alone was not there: it was said that he was living in his imaginary city under the constitution and the laws that he himself wrote. . . . None of the Stoics was there—they were said to be still on the way up the steep hill of virtue. With regard to Chrysippus, we heard tell that he is not permitted to set foot on the island until he submits himself to the hellebore treatment for the fourth time. They said that the Academicians wanted to come but were still holding off and debating, for they could not arrive at a conclusion even on the question whether such an island existed. Then too I suppose they feared to have Rhadamanthus judge them, as they themselves had abolished standards of judgment. It was said, however, that many of them had started to follow people coming thither, but fell behind through their slowness, being constitutionally unable to arrive at any-thing, and so turned back half-way.[879]

In one of Lucian's dialogues Menippus the Cynic, who had lived in the third century B.C., found himself after his death escorted by Hermes and ferried by Charon in Hades, along with various other souls of the departed who were filled with self-importance and trying to take with them the signs of their fame on earth. Menippus spotted a professional philosopher:

Menippus: A philosopher, Hermes, or rather an imposter, full of talk of marvels. Strip him too, and you'll see many amusing things covered up under his cloak.

Hermes: You there, off first with your clothes, and then with all this here. Ye gods, what hypocrisy he carries, what ignorance, contentiousness, vanity, unanswerable puzzles, thorny argumentations, and complicated conceptions—yes, and plenty of wasted effort, and no little nonsense, and idle talk, and splitting of hairs, and, good heavens, here's gold too, and soft living, shamelessness, temper, luxury, and effeminacy! I can see them, however much you try to hide them. Away with your falsehood too, and your pride, and notions of your superiority over the rest of men. If you came on board with all these, not even a battleship would be big enough for you. . . .

Menippus: But he ought to take off that beard as well, Hermes; it's heavy and shaggy, as you can see. He has at least five pounds of hair there.

Hermes: Well spoken. Off with that too.

Philosopher: Who will be my barber?

Hermes: Menippus here will take a shipwright's axe and cut it off; he can use the gangway as his block.

Menippus: No, Hermes, pass me up a saw. That'll be better fun. . . . Shall I take a little off his eyebrows as well?

Hermes: By all means; he has them rising high over his forehead, as he strains after something or other. What's this? Crying, you scum? Afraid to face death? Get in with you.

Menippus: He still has the heaviest thing of all under his arm.

Hermes: What, Menippus?

Menippus: Flattery, Hermes, which was often most useful to him in life.

Philosopher: What about you then, Menippus? Off with your independence, plain speaking, cheerfulness, noble bearing, and laughter. You're the only one that laughs.

Hermes: Do nothing of the sort, but keep them, Menippus; they're light and easy to carry, and useful for the voyage. But you, rhetorician, throw away your endless loquacity, your antitheses, balanced clauses, periods, foreign phrases, and everything else that makes your speeches so heavy.[880]

In more than one of his dialogues Lucian displayed to advantage the Cynic's refusal to join the mad scramble for wealth and power and position. A Cynic character of Lucian's says:

Now you others are like the greedy unrestrained person who lays hands on everything; local productions will not do for you, the world must be your storehouse; your native land and its seas are quite insufficient; you purchase your pleasures from the ends of the earth . . . Give a moment's thought, if you will, to the gold you all pray for, to the silver, the costly houses, the elaborate dresses, and do not forget their conditions precedent, the trouble and toil and danger they cost—nay, the blood and mortality and ruin; not only do numbers perish at sea on their account, or endure miseries in the acquisition or working of them; besides that, they have very likely to be fought for, or the desire of them makes friends plot against friends, children against parents, wives against husbands.[881]

Menippus was so anxious to find the truth that in another dialogue Lucian had him visit Hades before his final trip, this time to consult the shade of the blind Theban seer Tiresias, who had told Oedipus the truth and had not been believed. He saw countless shades of the departed:

It was not at all easy, though, to tell them apart, for all, without exception, become precisely alike when their bones are bare. . . .

So as I looked at them it seemed to me that human life is like a long pageant, and that all its trappings are supplied and distributed by Fortune, who arrays the participants in various costumes of many colours. Taking one person, it may be, she attires him royally, placing a tiara upon his head, giving him body-guards, and encircling his brow with the diadem; but upon another she puts the costume of a slave. Again, she makes up one person so that he is handsome, but causes another to be ugly and ridiculous. I suppose that the show must needs be diversified.[882]

When Menippus too was dead, two of those beings who looked so precisely alike because their bones were bare could apparently not forget their former beauty and urged Menippus to judge between them. But he answered: "Dreams, dreams. I am looking at what you are. What you were is ancient history."[883] For Menippus had learned that "Neither you nor anyone else is handsome here. In Hades all are equal, and all alike."[884] This important truth Menippus had learned when he visited Hades earlier, if only by watching a formal assembly of all the souls pass a most interesting decree. It concerned the behavior of the rich on earth above, who were accused of violence, ostentation, pride, and injustice. The decree read,

Whereas many lawless deeds are done in life by the rich, who plunder and oppress and in every way humiliate the poor,

Be it resolved by the senate and people, that when they die their bodies be punished like those of other malefactors, but their souls be sent back up into life and enter into donkeys until they shall have passed two hundred and fifty thousand years in the said condition, transmigrating from donkey to donkey, bearing burdens, and being driven by the poor; and that thereafter it be permitted them to die.[885]

Even without this decree, death had always been a fearful thing for the rich, especially when they discovered that Charon refused to overload his ferry with the clutter of possessions they had accumulated. But death was not necessarily feared by the poor. When a poor man's hour came, he might well be glad. Micyllus the cobbler, for instance, reported to Menippus in Hades:

But as for me, having nothing at stake in life, neither farm nor tenement nor gold nor gear nor reputation nor statues, of course I was in marching order, and when Atropos did but sign to me I gladly flung away my knife and my leather (I was working on a sandal) and sprang up at once and followed her, barefooted as I was and without even washing off the blacking. In fact, I led the way, with my eyes to the fore, since there was nothing in the rear to turn me about and call me back. And by Heaven I see already that everything is splendid here with you, for that all should have equal rank and nobody be any better than his neighbour is more than pleasant, to me at least. And I infer that there is no dunning of debtors here and no paying of taxes, and above all no freezing in winter or falling ill or being thrashed by men of greater consequence. All are at peace, and the tables are turned, for we paupers laugh while the rich are distressed and lament.[886]

According to one of Lucian's satires the poor who were still on earth wrote in desperation a letter to Cronus, or Saturn, as the Saturnalian feast approached. Cronus accordingly wrote to the rich, urging them to be more merciful if they wished to forestall a demand that property be redistributed. But the rich, who thereupon tried a little kindness, professed to be shocked by the result:

The Rich to Cronus—Greetings!

Do you really think that you are the only one written to by the poor in this vein, Cronus? Isn't Zeus already quite deaf from the din of their demands for just that, a redistribution of wealth, and of their charges against fate for inequality in distribution and against us for not considering giving them any share? But he, being Zeus, knows who is to blame and for that reason takes no notice of most of their complaints. Nevertheless we shall defend ourselves to you, since you are our lord at present.

We for our part have set before us all you have written—that it was a fine thing to succour the needy out of our plenty, and that it was more agreeable to mix and feast with the poor. This is what we always used to do, putting ourselves on an equal footing with them so that not even our guest himself could find anything to complain of. Now in the beginning they said that they asked for very little, but once we had opened our doors to them they never stopped making demand after demand; and if they didn't get it all immediately and on demand then there was bad temper and ill-feeling and maledictions came readily enough. And if they told a lie about us then those who heard them believed them, for they supposed their knowledge to be accurate because they had been with us. So we had the choice either not to give and inevitably be their enemies or to throw everything away and be straightway very poor and enter the ranks of the beggars ourselves. Now all the rest isn't so bad compared with these very dinners you mention. For themselves they do not care so much about filling their bellies, but when they've drunk more than enough they either nudge the hand of a pretty page when he gives the cup back to them or make attempts on your mistress or your wedded wife. Then, after being sick all over the dining-room, next day back at home they abuse us, saying that they were thirsty and well acquainted with starvation.[887]

Lucian himself figures in this sketch of his and quotes a letter he purportedly wrote Saturn about the problem of poverty:

You ought, my dear Cronus, to have abolished this inequality, made the good things accessible to everyone, and then bid the festival begin. As we now are it is a case of "ant or camel," as the saying has it.[888]

In Hades, Tiresias' whispered advice to Menippus on how to live on earth was that

The life of the common sort is best, and you will act more wisely if you stop speculating about heavenly bodies and discussing final causes and first causes, spit your scorn at those clever syllogisms, and counting all that sort of thing nonsense, make it always your sole object to put the present to good use and to hasten on your way laughing a great deal and taking nothing seriously.[889]

But Lucian, who reported this conversation, still had a problem. In the civilized world he inhabited, something lay back of the stupid wars, the philosophers' sectarian quarrels and the tension between the gorging rich and the hungry poor or between the condescending rich and the toadying poor: the lack of unity of spirit and sense of community. The cleavages in the community did not seem greatly to bother Apuleius; but Apuleius came of a family with property and wrote in the tongue of empire, while Lucian, a Syrian by birth and a Hellene by cultural inheritance, came of poorer parents. Both writers laughed and ridiculed. But beneath Lucian's ridicule there was a pity for the dispossessed and a craving for the mutual understanding without which a polis could not be wholly human. And though he laughed as much as Ovid at the foibles of the gods in Greek mythology, he was considerably more concerned than Ovid with the injustice and hypocrisy of men. He reported that when Menippus visited Zeus in Heaven, Zeus rejected his polite assurance that the world of men still reverenced him. There had indeed been a time, Zeus retorted, when he had been men's prophet, their healer, and their all; and Zeus quoted the poet Aratus:

> Yea, full of Zeus were all the streets
> And all the marts of men.[890]

What could Menippus in all honor answer? He had come up to Heaven where the gods dwelt precisely because the conflicting theologies of the philosophers had confused him.

As for the gods, why speak of them at all, seeing that to some a number was god, while others swore by geese and dogs and plane-trees? Moreover, some banished all the rest of the gods and assigned the governance of the universe to one only, so that it made me a little disgusted to hear that gods were so scarce. Others, however, lavishly declared them to be many and drew a distinction between them, calling one a first god and ascribing to others second and third rank in divinity. Furthermore, some thought that the godhead was without form and substance, while others defined it as body. Then too they did not all think that the gods exercise providence in our affairs; there were some who relieved them of every bit of responsibility as we are accustomed to relieve old men of public duties; indeed, the part that they give them to play is just like that of supers in comedy. A few went beyond all this and did not even believe that there were any gods at all, but left the world to wag on unruled and ungoverned.

When I heard all this, the result was that I did not venture to dis-
believe "high-thundering" gentlemen with goodly beards. . .[891]

When Menippus listened in Heaven to the prayers that ascended from the
earth, he discovered that those who uttered them were clearly not interested in the will of Zeus but in what they themselves willed and in somehow bribing Zeus to serve their petty material interests.

Had Lucian ever been drawn to two communities now scattered in
synagogues or churches all over the Greek East and even, to a lesser
extent, over the Latin West? The Jews and the Christians both worshipped, not Zeus indeed, but a God; and for both alike, full of God were
all the streets and all the marts of men, and indeed all the universe. Both
were committed to achieving dialogue with that God and with each other,
a dialogue of love. In the Hebrew scriptures shared by both groups, it was
written: "Though he slay me, yet will I trust in him."[892] And in the
Christian scriptures,

> God so loved the world, that he gave up his only-begotten Son, so that
> those who believe in him may not perish, but have eternal life.[893]

Both Jewish and Christian scripture taught that neighbor must love neighbor.[894] Perhaps Lucian's revulsion from the shallow religiosity about him
prevented him from inquiring so far into the Christians' belief. He reported through the mouth of an unnamed character that a wandering
prophet named Proteus, or Peregrinus, briefly preyed on the Christians'
credulity. Peregrinus

> learned the wondrous lore of the Christians, by associating with their
> priests and scribes in Palestine. And—how else could it be?—in a trice he
> made them all look like children; for he was prophet, cult-leader, head of
> the synagogue, and everything, all by himself. He interpreted and ex-
> plained some of their books and even composed many, and they revered
> him as a god, made use of him as a lawgiver, and set him down as a
> protector, next after that other, to be sure, whom they still worship, the
> man who was crucified in Palestine because he introduced this new cult
> into the world.
>
> Then at length Proteus was apprehended for this and thrown into
> prison, which itself gave him no little reputation as an asset for his future
> career and the charlatanism and notoriety-seeking that he was enamoured
> of. Well, when he had been imprisoned, the Christians, regarding the
> incident as a calamity, left nothing undone in the effort to rescue him.

Then, as this was impossible, every other form of attention was shown him, not in any casual way but with assiduity; and from the very break of day aged widows and orphan children could be seen waiting near the prison, while their officials even slept inside with him after bribing the guards. Then elaborate meals were brought in, and sacred books of theirs were read aloud, and excellent Peregrinus—for he still went by that name—was called by them "the new Socrates."

Indeed, people came even from the cities in Asia, sent by the Christians at their common expense, to succour and defend and encourage the hero. They show incredible speed whenever any such public action is taken; for in no time they lavish their all. So it was then in the case of Peregrinus; much money came to him from them by reason of his imprisonment, and he procured not a little revenue from it. The poor wretches have convinced themselves, first and foremost, that they are going to be immortal and live for all time, in consequence of which they despise death and even willingly give themselves into custody, most of them. Furthermore, their first lawgiver persuaded them that they are all brothers of one another after they have transgressed once for all by denying the Greek gods and by worshipping that crucified sophist himself and living under his laws. Therefore they despise all things indiscriminately and consider them common property, receiving such doctrines traditionally without any definite evidence. So if any charlatan and trickster, able to profit by occasions, comes among them, he quickly acquires sudden wealth by imposing upon simple folk.[895]

Lucian's sketch, *The Wisdom of Nigrinus*, reflected his preference for Athens, foolish as her professional philosophers might be, over Rome. In this sketch he reported a trip to Rome to see an oculist. But he had struck unexpected good fortune. He visited Nigrinus, a noted Platonic philosopher, and it was his mind's eye that was healed, not his body's eyes. Nigrinus contrasted Rome and Athens, and he

mentioned a millionaire who came to Athens, a very conspicuous and vulgar person with his crowd of attendants and his gay clothes and jewelry, and expected to be envied by all the Athenians and to be looked up to as a happy man. But they thought the creature unfortunate, and undertook to educate him, not in a harsh way, however, nor yet by directly forbidding him to live as he would in a free city. But when he made himself a nuisance at the athletic clubs and the baths by jostling and crowding passers with his retinue, someone or other would say in a low tone, pretending to be covert, as if he were not directing the remark at the man himself: "He is afraid of being murdered in his tub! Why, profound peace reigns in the baths; there is no need of an army, then!" And the man, who never failed to hear, got a bit of instruction in passing. His gay clothes and his purple gown they stripped from him very neatly by making fun of his flowery colours, saying, "Spring already?" "How did that peacock get here?" "Perhaps it's his mother's" and the like. His other vulgarities they turned into jest in the same way—the number of his rings, the overniceness of his hair, the extravagance of his life. So he was disciplined little by little, and went away much improved by the public education he had received.[896]

Nigrinus thought that

a serious man who has been taught to despise wealth and elects to live for what is intrinsically good will find Athens exactly suited to him. But a man who loves wealth and is enthralled by gold and measures happiness by purple and power, who has not tasted liberty or tested free speech or contemplated truth, whose constant companions are flattery and servility; a man who has unreservedly committed his soul to pleasure and has resolved to serve none but her, fond of extravagant fare and fond of wine and women, full of trickery, deceit and falsehood; a man who likes to hear twanging, fluting and emasculated singing—"Such folk," said he, "should live in Rome, for every street and every square is full of the things they cherish most, and they can admit pleasure by every gate—by the eyes, by the ears and nostrils, by the throat and reins. Its ever-flowing, turbid stream widens every street; it brings in adultery, avarice, perjury and the whole family of the vices, and sweeps the flooded soul bare of self-respect, virtue, and righteousness; and then the ground which they have left a desert, ever parched with thirst, puts forth a rank, wild growth of lusts."

That was the character of the city, he declared, and those all the good things it taught. "For my part," said he, "when I first came back from Greece, on getting into the neighbourhood of Rome I stopped and asked myself why I had come here, repeating the well-known words of Homer: 'Why left you, luckless man, the light of day'—Greece, to wit, and all that happiness and freedom—'and came to see' the hurly-burly here—informers, haughty greetings, dinners, flatterers, murders, legacy-hunting, feigned friendships?"[897]

Nigrinus

told about the uproar of the city, the crowding, the theatres, the races, the statues of the drivers, the names of the horses, and the conversations in the streets about these matters. The craze for horses is really great, you know, and men with a name for earnestness have caught it in great numbers.[898]

Nigrinus added

that sons of Rome speak the truth only once in their whole lives (meaning in their wills), in order that they may not reap the fruits of their truthfulness![899]

Nigrinus, if challenged to give an example of this indulgence in truthfulness, would perhaps have cited the case of Petronius Arbiter, the author of the *Satyricon*, who spoke in his will of Nero's appalling vices and then calmly sent him the document. Nigrinus also pictured the arrogant rich and their toadies, the latter including the so-called philosophers who disgraced Nigrinus' own vocation:

Our rich men are an entertainment in themselves, with their purple and their rings always in evidence, and their thousand vulgarities. The latest development is the *salutation by proxy*; they favour us with a glance, and that must be happiness enough. By the more ambitious spirits, an obeisance is expected; this is not performed at a distance, after the Persian fashion—you go right up, and make a profound bow, testifying with the angle of your body to the self-abasement of your soul; you then kiss his hand or breast—and happy and enviable is he who may do so much! And there stands the great man, protracting the illusion as long as may be. (I heartily acquiesce, by the way, in the churlish sentence which excludes us from a nearer acquaintance with their *lips*.)

But if these men are amusing, their courtiers and flatterers are doubly so. They rise in the small hours of the night, to go their round of the city, to have doors slammed in their faces by slaves, to swallow as best they may the compliments of "Dog," "Toadeater," and the like. And the guerdon of their painful circumambulations? A vulgarly magnificent dinner, the source of many woes! They eat too much, they drink more than they want, they talk more than they should; and then they go away, angry and disappointed, grumbling at their fare, and protesting against the scant courtesy shown them by their insolent patron. You may see them vomiting in every alley, squabbling at every brothel. The daylight most of them spend in bed, furnishing employment for the doctors. Most of them, I say; for with some it has come to this, that they actually have no time to be ill. . . . If by common consent they would abstain, were it only for a few days, from this voluntary servitude, the tables must surely be turned, and the rich come to the doors of the paupers, imploring them not to leave such blessedness as theirs without a witness, their fine houses and elegant furniture lying idle for want of some one to use them. Not wealth, but the envy that waits on wealth, is the object of their desire. . . . But that men who call themselves philosophers should actually outdo the rest in degradation,—this, indeed, is the climax. Imagine my feelings, when I see a brother philosopher, an old man, perhaps, mingling in the herd of sycophants; dancing attendance on some great man; adapting himself to the conversational level of a possible host! One thing, indeed, serves to distinguish him from his company, and to accentuate his disgrace;—he wears the garb of philosophy. It is much to be regretted that actors of uniform excellence in other respects will not dress conformably to their part. For in the achievements of the table, what toad-eater besides can be compared with them? There is an artlessness in their manner of stuffing themselves, a frankness in their tippling, which defy competition; they sponge with more spirit than other men, and sit on with greater persistency.[900]

Lucian, in another of his dialogues, *The Dependent Scholar*, had some things to say about the "salaried intellects,"[901] especially Greek, who adorned the staffs of wealthy Romans. Such a cultural prostitute is eventually turned off, is accused by the public of nameless crimes, and for his pains gets called "a loose-principled, unscrupulous *Greek*. That is the character we Greeks bear; and it serves us right. . ."[902] But Lucian listened with pleasure to Nigrinus' account of the wealthy Romans, who displayed the queer dependence on their servants that Pliny the Elder had noted. Nigrinus

had much to say about their behaviour in the baths—the number of their attendants, their offensive actions, and the fact that some of them are carried by servants almost as if they were corpses on their way to the graveyard. There is one practice, however, which he appeared to detest above all others, a wide-spread custom in the city and in the baths. It is the duty of certain servants, going in advance of their masters, to cry out and warn them to mind their footing when they are about to pass something high or low, thus reminding them, oddly enough, that they are walking! He was indignant, you see, that although they do not need the mouths or the hands of others in eating or the ears of others in hearing, they need the eyes of others to see their way in spite of the soundness of their own, and suffer themselves to be given directions fit only for unfortunates and blind men. "Why," said he, "This is actually done in public squares at midday, even to governors of cities!"[903]

In a deep sense, the freedom that upper-class Romans loved to praise belonged no more to the wealthy than to the poor: the poor were imprisoned by hunger and deprivation; the rich, by their own power and the pretentious role it imposed upon them. Perhaps it was Rome, the power center of Lucian's world, that Lucian himself had in mind when, in his dialogue, *A True Story*, he described the victory that he and his companions won over the enemy tribes inside the whale and of the pleasant life that victory brought. Pleasant, except for one thing:

> In short, we resembled men leading a life of luxury and roaming at large in a great prison that they cannot break out of.[904]

Was the city of Rome by any chance the same sort of prison to the men whose wealth had conquered it for them? Or was the whole Empire the belly of a whale that had swallowed all rich men and now permitted them to roam at large in luxury but never to escape? From that belly Lucian escaped by laughing at its luxury, at its pretensions to freedom, and at its claim to be a home for man. Lucian knew it for a belly. Even the less subtle Apuleius knew it as such, though perhaps less explicitly.

Moreover, Lucian knew that Eternal Rome itself, which was still the administrative center of this vast prison, the Empire, would some day inevitably perish. When the god Hermes took the ferryman of Hades, Charon, on a guided tour of the earth, he showed Charon Cyrus the Great of Persia; King Croesus of Lydia, talking with Solon of Athens; Tomyris, Queen of Scythia, who was to kill Cyrus; Cambyses, son of Cyrus, who was to conquer Egypt and die a madman; Polycrates, the cruel tyrant of Samos, who was fated to be crucified. Then the common people: usurers here, beggars there. "Their cities," observes Charon gazing about him,

> remind me of bee-hives. Every man keeps a sting for his neighbour's service; and a few, like wasps, make spoil of their weaker brethren.[905]

Charon wanted Hermes to show him the really great cities, those that "we hear talked about in Hades; Nineveh, Babylon, Mycenae, Cleonae, and Troy itself." But Hermes answered:

> Why, as to Nineveh, it is gone, friend, long ago, and has left no trace behind it; there is no saying whereabouts it may have been. But

there is Babylon, with its fine battlements and its enormous wall. Before long it will be as hard to find as Nineveh. As to Mycenae and Cleonae, I am ashamed to show them to you, let alone Troy. You will throttle Homer, for certain, when you get back, for puffing them so. They were prosperous cities, too, in their day; but they have gone the way of all flesh. Cities, my friend, die just like men . . . [906]

More than three centuries before Lucian was born, Carthage had died; and Scipio Africanus had watched her death and had wept at the thought that Rome also must some day die. But Scipio's tears were perhaps the somewhat philosophic tears of a hellenized Roman. Since then Roman arms and Roman law had merged the cities of the world from the Scottish lowlands to the Sahara, from Lucian's birthplace on the Euphrates to the Atlantic Ocean, into a single empire that dwarfed the empires of Nineveh and Babylon so that these seemed mere Roman provinces. It had transformed the globe into one City of Man, the orbis into an urbs; it had given all men a Pax Romana under the wise guidance of Eternal Rome. Or so Rome's poets had suggested; so Rome's rhetoricians had proclaimed; so Rome's mintmasters had guaranteed on the coins they designed.

In this late second century, Apuleius told a tale that showed a somewhat seamy side of the Imperial power that official panegyrics glorified. Lucian, more analytical than Apuleius, raised serious questions about the law and order that his cobbler so joyfully relinquished in favor of Hades. Lucian pictured a world full of brigands or of rebels he called brigands; of wealthy men, like wasps, making spoil of their weaker brethren; of lying sophists and professional philosophers wrangling, contentious, and venal. He surveyed the culture about him and transmuted the ugliness that wounded him into loud satiric laughter. As for Eternal Rome, Hermes told Charon that cities die just like men.

The serial publication of Pausanias' antiquarian *Description of Greece* apparently coincided with Marcus' reign, and the astronomer Ptolemy lived into his reign, but there is no evidence that Marcus read the works of either man. However, a scientist as important as Ptolemy was writing medical treatises in Rome from Marcus' second year as Emperor until long after Marcus' death, except for one absence of three years. His name was Claudius Galenus.[907] Born in Pergamum about 129 and about the time the Emperor Hadrian visited that city, Galen received an excellent education during the reign of Antoninus Pius. He studied Plato, Aristotle, the Stoics, and the Epicureans; only after acquiring this foundation did he proceed to medicine, which he studied at Pergamum, Alexandria, and other cities. He gained clinical experience as surgeon to the gladiators of Pergamum and, when he was still in his early thirties, he established a medical practice at Rome. In the late sixties he returned to Pergamum, only to be recalled shortly thereafter by the Emperor, who wanted him to accompany him on his Danube campaign against the Germans. But Galen was excused, became court physician, and devoted his time largely to writing treatises on medicine. An imposing corpus resulted. His achievement was partly a synthesis of what Greek medicine had accomplished to date, comparable with Ptolemy's great synthesis of Greek astronomy and Euclid's earlier synthesis of Greek geometry. But he was far from merely summarizing; like Euclid and Ptolemy, Galen brought imagination, quick intuition, and rigorous analysis to his task. Along with his clinical observation, he also brought to it diligent experimentation on living animals. Finally, he brought to it the elegant and forceful Attic style of a man too preoccupied with truth to indulge in rhetorical virtuosity.

Behind Galen lay a great tradition, which he had thoroughly assimilated: the god Asclepius, the Asclepiades, their temple cures, their ancient herbal medicine. But above all he had behind him the work of Hippocrates of Cos, who had lived and practiced some six centuries before Galen's time. To Hippocrates were commonly ascribed a copious number of small treatises and acute word pictures of the various stages of many diseases. Galen turned back to that unity of the human organism on which Hippocrates had insisted, a unity of which the Alexandrian anatomists five centuries earlier, and indeed many of Galen's professional contemporaries, had often lost sight in their ardor for specialization. He turned back to Hippocrates, and Plato too, for the profoundly Greek notions of function and purpose. Like Hippocrates, he thought of the living organism as struggling to perform its proper *ergon*, its appropriate work; like him, he observed the organism's uncanny powers to heal itself if only impediments to this power could be removed by wise medical care. Finally, he shared Hippocrates' love of his profession and his passion to heal.

Hippocrates had seen the human body whole in order to make it truly whole; the Alexandrian anatomists had dissected out its parts. Galen, although he was a patient anatomist, anatomized under the formality of physiology. As to those doctors whom Democritus and Epicurus had misled into thinking that the universe, including the human bodies it contains, is only a chance concourse of atoms, Galen presumably knew Aristotle's very Platonic doctrine of the final cause as distinguished from the material cause, the purpose at work in the universe as distinguished from the matter which limits that purpose. Galen's causal analyses of what he dissected, of what he observed, of what experiments he performed were profoundly teleological. It was because he was philosophically competent as well as rigorous in experiment that the treatises he wrote, including such a masterpiece as *On the Natural Faculties*, not only summarized and synthesized Greek medical science; they were landmarks in medical science which rose to the level of genuine literature.

Between the death of Marcus Aurelius in 180 and the accession of Diocletian in 285, an interval of scarcely more than a century, thirty-two Emperors reigned.[908] Of these thirty-two Emperors, only two certainly died a natural death. A third was either struck by lightning or killed by his own Prefect. Two of the Emperors were children. Nine, perhaps ten, of those murdered were killed by their own soldiers. Eight Emperors claimed the throne by heredity. Three were elected by the Praetorian Guard. Fourteen were chosen by other army units. Only three were formally chosen by the Roman Senate. In this dangerous century some reigns were extremely brief. Just as Rome had in 69 witnessed all or parts of three reigns, in 193 she witnessed all or parts of four reigns. The year 238 witnessed parts of two single reigns and all of two double reigns, involving a total of six Emperors, of whom one was killed in battle while fighting rebellious legions, one committed suicide, and four were murdered. The year 253 saw parts of two double reigns and all of a single reign, five Emperors in all. One of these five died a prisoner in Persia; the other four were murdered. During 276 there occurred three single reigns: two Emperors were murdered and the third was either murdered or died of fear that he shortly would be murdered. Some of the thirty-two Emperors came from Africa, Syria, Arabia, Thrace, Pannonia, or Dalmatia. Some were of humble origin. Maximinus the Thracian had been a herdsman, leader of a band organized to hunt brigands, then a centurion. The father of Philip the Arab, a sheik from the hill country south of Damascus, was said to have led a band of brigands.[909]

This reduction to absurdity of the solution Augustus had offered for the problem of Imperial succession might have done little damage if it had applied only to Rome, leaving the provinces to their more or less peaceful pursuits. But many of these Emperors reached the throne only after fighting their way from distant provinces. The armies that fought these civil wars often caused widespread ruin, and often they oppressed helpless civilians. Moreover, since successful contenders had to satisfy the soldiers who won their thrones for them, high taxation, official extortion, and monetary inflation took their toll even after nominal peace was restored. From the reign of Marcus on, famines and outbreaks of pestilence occurred repeatedly, causing a grave shortage of manpower in many areas. This shortage made it more difficult to defend the frontiers, and led not only Marcus but many of his successors to hire barbarians as mercenaries. This custom of course tended to barbarize the army. Also, land that pestilence or public disorder had left untenanted in a period of famines was settled with barbarians, which further barbarized the civilian population. The famine, pestilence, and disorders of civil war of the third century also gravely weakened industrial production. In 262, after twelve years of plague throughout the Empire,

> amid so many calamities of war, there was also a terrible earthquake and a darkness for many days. . . . This disaster, indeed, was worst in the cities of Asia; but Rome, too, was shaken and Libya also was shaken. In many places the earth yawned open, and salt water appeared in the fissures. Many cities were even overwhelmed by the sea. . . . For so great a pestilence, too, had arisen in both Rome and the cities of Achaea that in one single day five thousand men died of the same disease.[910]

By this same year 262, Alexandria, the second largest city of the Empire and a busy center of both industry and trade, had lost some three-fifths of her population. When natural disasters like earthquakes occurred, the impoverished Imperial treasury was less able to extend the customary assistance to rebuild devastated cities. Nor was it simple to replenish the Treasury through taxation in a period when citizens sometimes fled their city rather than face higher taxes. Moreover, an epidemic of plague could profoundly demoralize people whose mutual confidence was already at low ebb. For instance, the historian Dio Cassius, recording both natural disaster and mutual distrust, wrote that nine years after Marcus Aurelius' death,

> a pestilence occurred, the greatest of any of which I have knowledge; for two thousand persons often died in Rome in a single day. Then, too, many others, not alone in the City, but throughout almost the entire empire, perished at the hands of criminals who smeared some deadly

drugs on tiny needles and for pay infected people with the poison by means of these instruments.[911]

Even under the benign Antonine Emperors of the second century, when the Empire seemed well and strong, issues of silver coin were debased in order to make ends meet. But in the early third century Caracalla debased gold coins also, though not those destined for payments beyond the frontier. To force acceptance of this debased coin he prescribed that the same punishment inflicted on counterfeiters should be inflicted on any citizen who refused payment in coin bearing the Emperor's sacred image. Meanwhile, the trade that had once bound the provinces together diminished sharply, partly because there was less surplus to exchange, but also because in the prevailing political disorder it was less safe to transport goods. Each of these problems made it harder to solve the others: the Empire was caught in a vicious circle. It was a circle that nobody but the Emperor was in a position to break, assuming that even he could break it. The decision of Caracalla's immediate predecessor, Septimius Severus, to ignore the Senate was based on the brutal fact that the army belonged to the Emperor. Some of his third-century successors exhibited more respect for the myth Augustus had created, the myth that even though the Emperor controlled the army, yet religion and the immemorial authority of the Roman Senate controlled the Emperor. But the Senate remained far too weak to initiate any program to break the vicious circle. The Emperor for his part always faced possible assassination by a Senator or a Senatorial faction, or an army mutiny led by a Senatorial aspirant. Naturally, professional informers flourished, and Dio Cassius witnessed scenes in the Senate similar to those which his fellow historian Tacitus had reported about a century earlier. For example, in 205, Apronianus, Proconsul of Asia,

> was accused because his nurse was reported to have dreamed once that he should be emperor and because he was believed to have employed some magic to this end; and he was condemned while absent at his post as governor of Asia. Now when the evidence concerning him, taken under torture, was read to us, there appeared in it the statement that one of the persons conducting the examination had inquired who had told the dream and who had heard it, and that the man under examination had said, among other things: "I saw a certain bald-headed senator peeping in." On hearing this we found ourselves in a terrible position; for although neither the man had spoken nor Severus written anyone's name,

yet such was the general consternation that even those who had never visited the house of Apronianus, and not alone the bald-headed but even those who were bald on their forehead, grew afraid. And although no one was very cheerful, except those who had unusually heavy hair, yet we all looked round at those who were not so fortunate, and a murmur ran about: "It's So-and-so." "No, it's So-and-so." I will not conceal what happened to me at the time, ridiculous as it is. I was so disconcerted that I actually felt with my hand to see whether I had any hair on my head. And a good many others had the same experience. And we were very careful to direct our gaze upon those who were more or less bald, as if we should thereby divert our own danger upon them; we continued to do this until the further statement was read that the bald-head in question had worn a purple-bordered toga. When this detail came out, we turned our eyes upon Baebius Marcellinus; for he had been aedile at the time and was extremely bald. So he rose, and coming forward, said: "He will of course recognize me, if he has seen me." After we had commended this course, the informer was brought in while Marcellinus stood by, and for a considerable time remained silent, looking about for a man he could recognize, but finally, following the direction of an almost imperceptible nod that somebody gave, he said that Marcellinus was the man. Thus was Marcellinus convicted of a bald-head's peeping, and he was led out of the senate-chamber bewailing his fate. When he had passed through the Forum, he refused to proceed farther, but just where he was took leave of his children, four in number, and spoke these most affecting words: "There is only one thing that causes me sorrow, my children, and that is that I leave you behind alive." Then his head was cut off.[912]

Occasionally, catastrophe might give the Senate momentary power. Thus, when the Emperor Aurelian, a stern but effectual handler of both would-be barbarian invaders and domestic rebels, was murdered in 275,

the army referred to the senate the business of choosing an emperor, for the reason that it believed that no one of those should be chosen who had slain such an excellent ruler. The senate, however, thrust this selection back on the army, knowing well that the emperors whom the senate selected were no longer gladly received by the troops. Finally, for the third time, the choice was referred, and so for the space of six[913] months the Roman world was without a ruler, and all those governors whom either the senate or Aurelian had chosen remained at their posts, save only that Faltonius Probus was appointed proconsul of Asia in the place of Arellius Fuscus.[914]

When the Senate finally ventured to choose Marcus Tacitus, one of its members, to succeed Aurelian,

> so great was the joy of the senate that the power of choosing an emperor had been restored to this most noble body, that it both voted ceremonies of thanksgiving and promised a hecatomb and finally each of the senators wrote to his relatives, and not to his relatives only but also to strangers, and letters were even despatched to the provinces . . .[915]

But the new Emperor, chosen by the Senate though he was, kept a firm grip on the army until he was murdered by his own troops. When he died, his Praetorian Prefect, who was also his half brother, seized the Empire as if it were a family heirloom. Three months later, when he too was murdered by his own troops, another general seized the throne.

Back of the monotonous violence of the third century lay the fact that Rome's habit of conquest, which enabled her to take over first peninsular Italy and finally the many peoples and great wealth that Augustus controlled, had become a sort of reflex action. Rome had gobbled up many countries; and once the habit of violence and the respect for force and the love of pillage had been thwarted by the sea or the desert or by the uninviting poverty of Barbaria, the Roman Empire started gobbling up itself. Otherwise stated, the problem of who would succeed a dead or weak Emperor was somewhat brutally solved by some Roman army's reconquering and plundering the Roman Empire. For plunder had been built into the Roman political system. Was that perhaps why Caracalla, like other Emperors, turned his predatory soldiers' faces outward beyond the frontiers and dreamed of repeating the epic march of Alexander the Great, of annexing by force the Empire's only civilized neighbor, Parthia, the only neighbor any longer left that was worth plundering?

But Caracalla failed; and after 224, when the Persian dynasty of the Sassanids won back Persian control of the Iranian plateau from the Median dynasty of the Arsacids, a vigorous New Persian Empire replaced the Parthian Empire. It was a few decades later that the Emperor Valerian, trying to beat off a Persian invader, was taken prisoner by King Sapor and died in captivity. The New Persia remained, not a promise of plunder, but a military and hence a financial threat.

Inevitably, the Empire's professional soldiery, with the Emperor of the moment at its head, continued to operate as a sort of state within the state, controlling and exploiting the civilian population, as the wealthy class had long controlled and exploited the poor, and as both the wealthy and the moderately well-to-do had exploited the slaves. Soldiers had long served as police, as detectives and spies to ferret out conspiracy, and as a local militia to suppress brigands and highway robbers. They had accompanied the tax collector to enforce collection from recalcitrants. In Egypt, where the Emperor inherited the immense powers of the Macedonian monarchs, themselves the heirs of the Pharaohs, it was soldiers who certified Roman citizens and later began to serve as judges. During the first third of the third century the army took over from civilians many other bureaucratic functions; and by the middle decades it was the soldiers whom the taxpayer most dreaded. Because these new-style bureaucrats were armed, accustomed to make quick decisions, used to being obeyed, and often not above extorting bribes, they brutalized and barbarized the population. An increasing number were indeed barbarians, and their rule and their example contributed not a little to the barbarization of the whole culture of the Empire. They were less exclusively massed on the frontiers than had been the case in the first and second centuries. More than two centuries had passed since the Pannonians, whose land had been recently annexed by the Empire, had complained that the watchdogs were devouring the sheep. The watchdogs had now turned back from the frontiers to devour fatter, more civilized sheep. By A.D. 300 Egypt alone contained at least sixty military posts.

Not only did the soldiers govern civilians more and more; they also tended, especially in the frontier provinces, to set the social standards of the Empire. It was veterans who formed the aristocracy of Aquincum, the modern Budapest, and of small towns in the eastern provinces as well. For centuries Rome, of course, had planted military colonies, but after the reign of Hadrian, Emperors frequently assigned single farms as well. As for the working capital a veteran needed in order to farm, officers were extremely well paid; both officers and men normally received substantial donatives on the accession of a new Emperor, a practice that must have provided considerable funds in the third century. True, the wild tribes of Scotland and Germany yielded meager plunder compared with the wealth the Roman Republic had won in the days when it was still conquering the highly civilized, Greek-speaking world. But in the frequent civil wars there was plenty of plunder to be snatched. Nor need a soldier always await discharge before farming. After 197, when Septimius Severus permitted soldiers to marry, they could even house their wives and children on their farms.

Architecture, too, reflected the militarization of society. As public order declined, the interior provinces of the Empire increasingly took on the customs and appearance of frontier provinces. Fort-towers appeared, as a defense not only against foreign invaders but against cattle rustlers and other robbers. Country houses looked less and less like the luxurious villas of a Cicero or a Pliny and more and more like fortresses or military camps, including courtyard space in which peasants and their livestock could take refuge. City architecture, too, reflected the anarchy of the third century. Cities that had never been walled, or had torn down their walls, were now walled and fortified. And if civilians aped soldiers in civil life, in army life soldiers aped civilians: they lived a more settled life and more often lived it in their native province. Naturally, their military discipline slackened, and the quality of strategy and even of siege machinery deteriorated along with discipline. Rome's ancient Virgilian sense of mission, no longer stimulated by the expectation of foreign booty, had declined. The Imperial army, even in times of peace, mustered all the way from 250,000 to 500,000, but its skill and morale had greatly fallen off along with the skill and morale of the civilian.

During the middle of the third century the Roman legions were frequently stationed wherever there were sufficient crops to feed them. A legion then bought locally, or requisitioned, the food it needed. In what are now Syria and Algeria, to make sure that sufficient food was grown, army engineers helped to improve the system of irrigation. Moreover, now that the legions were stationed for generations in one spot, they could acquire nearby farms, place civilian tenants on them, and sometimes even protect those tenants from meddlesome civil authorities. Sometimes, instead of buying its provisions or renting its own land to civilians, a legion might have its soldiers work army land themselves: since the army increasingly recruited from the peasantry, green thumbs were plentiful. This last method of provisioning a legion might pin down a frontier like those in Africa in a somewhat more organized way than a colony of veterans could do, and in a somewhat less expensive way than by quartermaster's corps and difficult transport. A legion could become a highly organized body of soldier-farmer frontiersmen, fighting, as the armies of the early Roman Republic had fought, for the soil they tilled. Organizationally, the army was thus experiencing a sort of second childhood.

The army, however, did not produce only food. It often made the industrial products it required: it baked brick or sawed lumber to build with, or turned pottery for table use. It sometimes quarried stone, or mined iron or lead and refined its own ore. For refining, it burned wood or in some places, as in Britain, coal. It might manufacture its own weapons and armor. It might even sell or barter surplus brick. As in Augustus' day, the army continued to be used often as a labor force to build public works such as temples, arches, porticos, basilicas; to construct underground cisterns for use in irrigation, as well as roads and aqueducts; and even to build canals, although nowhere near as many as the Empire could have profitably used.

It may have been this general militarization of the peoples the Emperor and his army governed which stimulated an increase in honorific titles. Although Roman law, which owed so much to Greek jurisprudence, had never been guided by Athens' dream of *isonomia*, equality of all citizens before the law, nevertheless the early Empire had witnessed an impressive social leveling. The largely defunctionalized Senatorial Order had been forced to share with the Equestrian Order whatever military and administrative functions it still preserved. The activity of the Equites, or businessmen, had continued to increase, as had the powers and functions of the Emperor's freedmen. The gulf between rich and poor had largely replaced differences of birth, but Trimalchio was not the only man to bridge that gulf. Many millionaires had started life as poor men, and the Roman hunger for status asserted itself in the competition for the new honorific titles. If a man were convicted in court, the judge was required to consider both his wealth and his rank before deciding on the severity of the penalty. Thus, for the same crime, one man might be exiled while another might be crucified. This legal stratification, however, can have offended few men of property. Rome practiced an *isonomia* of its own, not concerned with the rights of the poor, and this practice culminated in 212, when an edict of Caracalla's extended full Roman citizenship to almost all free subjects within the Empire.

The cultural blurring of the frontiers continued. The ancient civilization of the Roman Empire and the tribal culture beyond the German frontier interpenetrated each other. The hard shell that had protected the Empire was melting as if it were metal. Since the Imperial government could less and less protect lives and property from violence and extortion, the panegyrics which professional rhetoricians delivered to successive monarchs, in the tradition of Pliny's panegyric to Trajan and of Aelius Aristides' praise of Rome, must have rung somewhat hollow even for some of the well-to-do, like the debased coin they were legally forced to accept. Moreover, since armed violence was the usual road to power, the Emperor could not call on the moral authority that had been available to rulers like Nerva, Trajan, Hadrian, Antoninus Pius, and Marcus Aurelius in the previous century. Indeed, Marcus Aurelius may have been the last Roman Emperor to bear within his own breast the civilization of Greece and Rome and to defend it with his sword. Some of his successors, such as Septimius Severus and Aurelian, were strong men, perhaps more suited to their actual task than Marcus was to his, but they were concerned not so much to defend Hellenistic civilization as to preserve Roman military power. With depopulation and monetary inflation threatening both the production of needed food and the manufacture and distribution of other necessities, the later Emperors had to impose harsh taxation on their subjects, even on those whom their soldiers had already plundered, if a greedy army was to be satisfied. To defend the northern frontier, the Emperors used subsidy to tribal chiefs as well as the enlistment of barbarians. That is, they paid some of the tribes outside the Empire not to attack it and, in case the tribesmen broke their treaties and attacked it anyway, the Emperors paid other tribes to help defend it. They bribed their own soldiers to fight by giving them higher pay, laxer discipline, and free land on the frontier, although finally on condition that the sons of soldiers could inherit such land only by serving in the army. Meanwhile, if the habits of frontier life spread back into the Roman Empire, militarized it, and barbarized it, Roman traders did nevertheless carry some degree of civilization into Barbaria, as did refugees from Roman oppression and barbarians who had served in the Roman army. Many barbarians acquired Roman discipline and even the ability to speak a little Latin at the very time that Roman legions were losing their traditional discipline and that the gap between the Latin of educated Romans and the Latin the populace spoke was widening. So far had this gap widened even by Marcus' day that Marcus had found it difficult to talk to some of his own officers:

> One of the prefects of Marcus was Bassaeus Rufus, who was a good man in other respects, but was uneducated because of his rustic origin and had been reared in poverty in his youth. . . .
>
> Once when Marcus was talking to someone in Latin and not only the man addressed but no one else of the bystanders, either, knew what he

had said, Rufus, the prefect, exclaimed: "No wonder, Caesar, that he does not know what you said; for he does not understand Greek either.[916]

Caracalla, who preferred German and Scythian bodyguards to Roman ones,

> would often converse with the envoys sent to him from time to time by the nations to which these soldiers belonged . . . instructing them, in case anything happened to him, to invade Italy and march upon Rome, assuring them that it was very easy to capture . . .[917]

If such an idea could occur to the head of the Empire, small wonder that in several provinces, notably in Thrace, the mine workers, normally slaves or condemned persons at the other end of the social scale from Caracalla, should look on barbarian invaders as rescuers and should help them all they could. As for the classes in between the Emperor and the miners, they were arming and barricading themselves against barbarian and Imperial soldiery alike.

Although the problem of rebellion still persisted, it was not always easy for historians to discover whether a given rebellion was caused by wounded religious sentiment, as happened so often in Egypt and Judaea; or by the economic discontent in, say, the Danube provinces; or by memories of lost independence, as in Britain or Gaul or the German provinces west of the Rhine. Often, no doubt, all of these causes operated in combination. The problem of keeping the peace would have been a great deal easier had the territory Rome governed been a little less mountainous. It was always costly in men and money and nearly impossible with the weapons at Rome's disposal to clear the mountains of guerrilla fighters. The major wars of the Roman Republic had of course paid for themselves in plunder; but, except for known metal deposits or valued trade routes or, more rarely, timber in regions where timber was scarce, mountain tribes were not worth the cost of conquest. Their poverty, combined with their courage and skill, left such areas as Wales, Cornwall, Brittany, Galicia, the Atlas Mountains, and Cilicia in southern Asia Minor centers of recurrent trouble. But mountainous areas also provided redoubts for a social element, or conglomerate of elements, which the Roman authorities and Roman historians called simply *latrones*, brigands. *Latrones*, under the pressure of the military anarchy of the third century, became an epithet with which the party in power could designate the losers, an epithet to

425

demolish the claim of an unsuccessful claimant to the crown or even of a deposed Emperor, such as Maximinus.[918] Flavius Vopiscus, the biographer of the pretender Firmus, wrote explicitly of the use of the term brigand as a political epithet:

> For you know, my dear Bassus, how great an argument we had but recently with Marcus Fonteius, that lover of history, when he asserted that Firmus, who had seized Egypt in the time of Aurelian, was not an emperor but merely a brigand . . . Fonteius, on the other hand, in his contention against us, had only the argument that Aurelian wrote in one of his edicts, not that he had slain a pretender, but that he had rid the state of a brigand—just as though a prince of such renown could properly have called so obscure a fellow by the name of pretender, or as though mighty emperors did not always use the term of brigand in speaking of those whom they slew when attempting to seize the purple! I myself, indeed, in my Life of Aurelian, before I learned the whole story of Firmus, thought of him, not as one who had worn the purple, but only as a sort of brigand . . .[919]

In his life of Aurelian, to which he here alludes, Vopiscus had written that Firmus

> laid claim to Egypt, but without the imperial insignia and as though he purposed to make it into a free state.[920]

Apparently the brigand had then appeared to Vopiscus as the leader of a nationalist revolt. But, writing at a later time, Vopiscus quoted a purported proclamation by the Emperor Aurelian which suggests that hungry peasants who could be called barbarians had first backed Zenobia, Queen Regent of Palmyra, a woman so shameless as to threaten the Emperor with the loss of many provinces, and had then backed Firmus; and that they had done so in an effort to prevent so much of the wheat they produced from flowing annually into the vast maw of Rome. Aurelian announced to the Roman people that

> Firmus, that brigand in Egypt, who rose in revolt with barbarians and gathered together the remaining adherents of a shameless woman . . . we have routed and seized and tortured and slain. There is nothing now, fellow-citizens, sons of Romulus, which you need fear. The grain-supply from Egypt, which has been interrupted by that evil brigand, will now arrive undiminished. Do you only maintain harmony with the senate, friendship with the equestrian order, and good will toward the praetorian

guard. I will see to it that there is no anxiety in Rome. Do you devote your leisure to games and to races in the circus. Let me be concerned with the needs of the state, and do you busy yourselves with your pleasures.[921]

Vopiscus reported that when Aurelian marched against Zenobia's wealthy oasis-kingdom of Palmyra, after she had revolted against Rome and had overrun Syria, Egypt, and all but one province in Asia Minor,

> frequently on the march his army met with a hostile reception from the brigands of Syria, and after suffering many mishaps he incurred great danger during the siege. . . . [922]

In what Vopiscus offers his readers as being a letter from Zenobia to Aurelian, the Queen taunts the Emperor: "The brigands of Syria have defeated your army, Aurelian. What more need be said?"[923] Was Zenobia scoffing because a band of robbers had defeated Aurelian's army or because Aurelian had denounced as brigands guerrillas who were warring against Roman power and Roman taxation and who longed to free their country? For by this time indigent veterans, farmers who had been sold out, and poor men in general had turned to brigandage for a livelihood and in order to rob the wealthy men, who, they felt, had first robbed the poor. Sometimes, like the miners and those Syrian brigands or guerrillas who defeated an Imperial army, they revolted against an Imperial city that had for centuries protected plutocracy everywhere. Or as Trebellius Pollio, the biographer of the Emperor Gallienus, put it:

> Last of all, when all parts of the Empire were thrown into commotion, as though by a conspiracy of the whole world, there arose in Sicily also a sort of slave-revolt, for bandits roved about and were put down only with great difficulty.[924]

Pollio's impression of a world conspiracy must have been shared by more than one upper-class Roman citizen. After all, the famous jurisconsult, Ulpian, who served as Praetorian Prefect under the Emperor Severus Alexander, wrote on the duties of a provincial governor:

> A good, serious-minded governor ought to see that the province he rules is peaceful and quiet. This he will accomplish without difficulty if he acts with zeal to clear the province of bad men and searches them out; for he is bound to search out the sacrilegious, brigands, kidnappers, and thieves, to punish each according to his offense, and to repress those who shelter them, without whom a brigand cannot long be hid.[925]

For the fact is that many of the men whom Roman historians called brigands were being sheltered from the special military police by the rural population. No wonder that Pollio detected a whiff of conspiracy. At a minimum, those peasants who suffered most from Eternal Rome had aligned themselves with robbers, rebels, and even invading barbarians. Yet Ulpian was murdered by his own mutinous Praetorians in 228, before the full horror of the third century had dawned. Or consider that other famous jurisconsult, Papinian. He too served as Praetorian Prefect, under Caracalla, who executed him when Papinian disapproved of his murdering his brother and co-Emperor, Geta. Dio Cassius, a more dependable historian than the biographers Vopiscus and Pollio, wrote that already in the reign of Septimius Severus, Papinian too confronted this curious problem of the third-century brigand. Severus had

> abolished the practice of selecting the body-guard exclusively from Italy, Spain, Macedonia and Noricum,—a plan that furnished men of more respectable appearance and of simpler habits,—and ordered that any vacancies should be filled from all the legions alike. Now he did this with the idea that he should thus have guards with a better knowledge of the soldier's duties, and should also be offering a kind of prize for those who proved brave in war; but, as a matter of fact, it became only too apparent that he had incidentally ruined the youth of Italy, who turned to brigandage and gladiatorial fighting in place of their former service in the army, and in filling the city with a throng of motley soldiers most savage in appearance, most terrifying in speech, and most boorish in conversation.[926]

Perhaps it was some of these younger Italians who, no longer able to find employment in the Praetorian Guard, helped produce a notable case of a state within the state. The brigand citizens of this smaller state could live by plundering the citizens of the larger, plundering Empire which Severus ruled and the laws of which Papinian expounded. Nor could the brigand-citizens have easily eluded for two years Severus' efforts to kill or capture them were it not, in Ulpian's words, for "those who shelter them, without whom a brigand can not long be hid." The leader of these bandits, Bulla Felix, Lucky Bulla, seemed to think he could make as good a moral case for living off the civilian population illegally as the learned jurisconsult Papinian could make for the Imperial government's living off the same population legally.

428

At this period one Bulla, an Italian, got together a robber band of about six hundred men, and for two years continued to plunder Italy under the very noses of the emperors and of a multitude of soldiers. For though he was pursued by many men, and though Severus eagerly followed his trail, he was never really seen when seen, never found when found, never caught when caught, thanks to his great bribes and his cleverness. For he learned of everybody that was setting out from Rome and everybody that was putting into port at Brundisium, and knew both who and how many there were, and what and how much they had with them. In the case of most persons he would take a part of what they had and let them go at once, but he detained artisans for a time and made use of their skill, then dismissed them with a present. Once, when two of his men had been captured and were about to be given to wild beasts, he paid a visit to the keeper of the prison, pretending that he was the governor of his native district and needed some men of such and such a description, and in this way he secured and saved the men. And he approached the centurion who was trying to exterminate the band and accused himself, pretending to be someone else, and promised, if the centurion would accompany him, to deliver the robber to him. So, on the pretext that he was leading him to Felix (this was another name by which he was called), he led him into a defile beset with thickets, and easily seized him. Later, he assumed the dress of a magistrate, ascended the tribunal, and having summoned the centurion, caused part of his head to be shaved, and then said: "Carry this message to your masters: 'Feed your slaves, so that they may not turn to brigandage.' " Bulla had with him, in fact, a very large number of imperial freedmen, some of whom had been poorly paid, while others had received absolutely no pay at all. Severus, informed of these various occurrences, was angry at the thought that though he was winning the wars in Britain through others, yet he himself had proved no match for a robber in Italy; and finally he sent a tribune from his body-guard with many horsemen, after threatening him with dire punishment if he should fail to bring back the robber alive. So this tribune, having learned that the brigand was intimate with another man's wife, persuaded her through her husband to assist them on promise of immunity. As a result, the robber was arrested while asleep in a cave. Papinian, the prefect, asked him, "Why did you become a robber?" And he replied: "Why are you a prefect?" Later, after due proclamation, he was given to wild beasts, and his band was broken up—to such an extent did the strength of the whole six hundred lie in him.[927]

Lucky Bulla's counterquestion to Papinian was reported by Dio presumably because of its impudent wit. But there the promising dialogue stopped; to Lucky Bulla's counterquestion the beasts who tore his flesh in the arena made the only answer recorded for posterity. A Thucydides or a Polybius might have continued the dialogue, if not with Lucky, perhaps with Papinian, or only with the readers of the history he was writing. But the Imperial government could not have very well tolerated a question so fundamentally ironic, least of all in the third century: the government was far too busy putting down violence with violence to consider so basic a question as economic justice. Its frantic efforts to prevent or suppress rebellion were helping to change the whole character of Graeco-Roman civilization, and the government's name for rebels of all varieties remained brigands. That is, its reaction to incipient revolution was to enforce order, partly with the sword and partly with the rhetorical epithet. Since the number and varied nature of the revolts which it hastened to quell were merely symptoms of a disease, and since apparently nobody seriously analyzed the disease itself, historians could give no genuinely intelligible account of the third-century ordeal through which the She-Wolf doomed herself to pass.

This failure to understand afflicted not only the historian Dio Cassius but the group of biographers such as Herodian, Vopiscus, Pollio, and Capitolinus, who continued the work of writing the lives of the Emperors which Suetonius had begun. Dio Cassius of Nicaea in Bithynia, who was a provincial governor's son, himself became a member of the Roman Senate. Dio spent ten years of research preparing to write in Greek a history of Rome from its origins to A.D. 229. His history,[928] which is full of revealing anecdote, took him twelve years to write. It has little organic structure. It is essentially chronicle, based largely on Polybius, Livy, and either Tacitus or perhaps sources used by Tacitus; his views are sometimes anachronistic and his narrative sometimes inaccurate. Far less competent than Dio is Herodian of Syria, who wrote the lives of the Emperors from 180 to 238. Herodian's love of rhetoric and his lack of love of accuracy combined to betray him.[929] As for those latter-day Plutarchs, Pollio and Vopiscus, not even Herodian was sufficiently ingenuous to write, as Pollio did:

> I seem to have gone on further than the matter demanded. But what am I to do? For knowledge is ever wordy through a natural inclination.[930]

Imagine a Tacitus indulging in the unconscious humor of Vopiscus:

These details may perhaps seem to someone to be paltry and over trivial, but research stops at nothing.[931]

Or again:

There is still in existence a letter, which for the sake of accuracy, as is my wont, or rather because I see that other writers of annals have done so, I have thought I should insert . . .[932]

This charming excuse suffices to explain why so much historical writing from the third century impresses the reader as the work of an automaton or, at best, of a compiler. It suffices to explain also the increasing love of excerpts and digests and literary tags. Writers too empty of ideas to think for themselves could still cannibalize earlier writers who had had ideas; they could still publish condensations or digests of these earlier writers' works. These capsule editions afforded their readers a short, if misleading, road to culture.

The rhetorical spirit that had increasingly affected literature showed itself also in art: in overemphasis, in exaggeration for effect, in painful efforts to catch the eye of any viewer whose aesthetic sense suffered from wandering attention. The confusion of political and military events and the general loss of any high and intelligible public purpose were reflected in the increased confusion of the crowded bas-reliefs which sculptors were designing. Fashions in sculpture began to shift faster as if in a frantic attempt to find some language by which communication might be restored. Much of the energy of sculptors went into carvings on sarcophagi, those stone coffins that furnished a last retreat from pestilence, famine, rebellion, invasion, plundering soldiers, and official extortion. Nor did these carved figures seem to fear death. Whereas the portrait busts of the times often showed either animal brutality or a kind of discontent with life or even terror, the bas-reliefs on sarcophagi were changing from lion hunts and traditional Amazons to groups of philosophers. Bas-reliefs showed another interesting tendency, a tendency toward frontality. Whereas earlier groups of persons were engaged with each other in activities which the viewer was merely allowed as spectator to observe, now the persons shown, or perhaps one among those persons, faced out toward the viewer as if escaping from his carved stone world into some other world. During the decades from 230 to 250, as sculpture declined, there seems to have been an increase of miniature portraits executed on glass with gold leaf.

In general, third-century art was most successful when the artist viewed

431

a fragment of his world only, and least successful when he tried to see it as an organic whole. This was especially evident in architecture, which tended toward arbitrary combination as well as heavy ornamentation and lack of function. These characteristics were combined with considerable emphasis on size, as in the Temple of Jupiter at Heliopolis in Syria, the site of Baalbek in modern Lebanon. The three temples of Baalbek were indeed begun in the second century, but they were not completed until the early third. Except for Syria and Africa, the Empire was too torn by war to do much new building; but perhaps the day of great architecture, especially civilian architecture, had passed. One sign of exhaustion, whether artistic or financial, or both, was that new buildings cannibalized old ones. Why attempt an original bas-relief, for example, if a reasonably apposite one could be appropriated from another building?

Perhaps more impressive than anything the third century added to Greek art, and more important than anything in science since Galen, was a new development in Greek mathematics. Galen died in 199. But as late as the middle of the third century, when Greek culture was being submerged by anarchy and violence, Greek mathematics incredibly produced, not a summarizer, but a pioneer. Diophantus of Alexandria devised an algebraic notation capable of handling unknown quantities up to the sixth power and of dealing with negative numbers. He found ingenious algebraic solutions of quadratic equations. It is not surprising that Diophantus' work led to no full-fledged Greek algebra. Not only was the intellectual energy of his civilization running down; the mathematical tool he proposed was deeply un-Hellenic. Generally the Greek mathematician preferred to abstract his mathematical concepts directly from spatial images; they were the conceptual distillations of sculptural imaginings. Hence geometry was the Greek's preferred tool, whether he pondered conic sections, mechanics, or astronomy. In the absence of a high technology, he was less interested in the practical convenience of such devices as algebraic notation than in the plastic beauty of the so-called perfect solids. He was not trying to save time so much as to contemplate what was timeless. Similarly, although Nicomachus' *Introduction to Arithmetic* had insisted that arithmetic was logically prior to geometry, the theory of numbers it set forth reflected an image of groups of dots geometrically arranged. It is perhaps primarily because the Greek's attention was fixed on finding truth through embodied beauty that the algebraic tool which Diophantus fashioned dropped from listless Greek hands.

In the middle of the third century, when the chaos and horrors of that century were in full swing, the great philosophic tradition of Hellas incredibly began to bloom a second time. For in that period Plotinus started putting on paper the most imposing corpus of philosophic writings that Hellenic culture had produced since Plato and Aristotle some six centuries before. Plotinus was born in 205 in Egypt, bore a Roman name, and probably spoke Greek as his native tongue. At twenty-eight he turned to philosophy, and went to Alexandria to study. His professors he found disappointing until he heard the mystic, Ammonius, a former Christian; he studied under him for eleven years. When Gordian III launched an expedition against the New Persian Empire in 242–43, Plotinus joined the army in order to learn something of Persian and Indian philosophic thought. The expedition failed, Gordian was killed in Mesopotamia, and Plotinus escaped to Antioch. The next year, when Plotinus was forty and his fellow African, Philip the Arab, ruled the Empire, he settled in Rome; there he taught for fifteen years. His powerful mind, his kindness, his gentleness, and his freedom from pedantry and pomposity soon attracted a considerable group of disciples, including Porphyry of Tyre, to whom Plotinus later entrusted the task of editing his writings. Plotinus wrote nothing until he was fifty: he shared the distrust that his master, Plato, felt for writing about important philosophic matters, given the difficulty of achieving in writing the dialectical give-and-take of discussion. Plotinus' writings are not in dialogue form, though his use of the rhetorical question often suggests dialogue. He lived ascetically and followed the Pythagorean injunction against eating flesh. Although he scorned his own body and declined to celebrate the anniversaries of his birth, he always celebrated the birthdays of Socrates and Plato by giving a banquet to his disciples at which he invited each to speak, in memory no doubt of that other banquet, Plato's *Symposium*, to which he may have owed many of his insights. Those chosen to rule in Plato's Republic achieved, by arduous dialectical ascent and the habit of contemplation, the ineffable vision of the Good. Plotinus believed that four times in his life he had experienced complete escape from self into union with the One, with God:

> We must advance into this sanctuary, penetrating into it, if we have the strength to do so, closing our eyes to the spectacle of terrestrial things, without throwing a backward glance on the bodies whose graces for-

433

merly charmed us. If we do still see corporeal beauties, we must no longer rush at them, but, knowing that they are only images, traces and adumbrations of a superior principle, we will flee from them, to approach Him of whom they are merely reflections. Whoever would let himself be misled by the pursuit of those vain shadows, mistaking them for realities, would grasp only an image as fugitive as the fluctuating form reflected by the waters, and would resemble that senseless (Narcissus) who, wishing to grasp that image himself, according to the fable, disappeared, carried away by the current. Likewise he would wish to embrace corporeal beauties, and not release them, would plunge, not his body, but his soul into the gloomy abysses, so repugnant to intelligence; he would be condemned to total blindness; and on this earth, as well as in hell, he would see naught but mendacious shades.

This indeed is the occasion to quote (from Homer) with peculiar force, "Let us fly unto our dear fatherland!" . . .

Our fatherland is the region whence we descend here below. It is there that dwells our Father. But how shall we return thither? What means shall be employed to return us thither? Not our feet, indeed; all they could do would be to move us from one place of the earth to another. Neither is it a chariot, nor ship which need be prepared. All these vain helps must be left aside, and not even considered. We must close the eyes of the body, to open another vision, which indeed all possess, but very few employ.[933]

Plotinus did not suppose any more than did Socrates or Plato that most persons could live the life of philosophy or even that all who had the intellectual power to do so would choose that path. The sage

knows that there are two kinds of life; that of the virtuous who achieve the supreme degree (of perfection) and the intelligible world, and that of common earthly men. Even the latter life is double; for though at times they do think of virtue, and participate somewhat in the good, at other times they form only a vile crowd, and are only machines, destined to satisfy the primary needs of virtuous people.[934]

Even before Plotinus reached Rome about 245, the Romans had witnessed eight reigns in twenty-seven years, not counting co-Emperors, and four in the single year 238. During his Roman years, the Emperor Philip and his son were killed in battle by Decius, who succeeded to the throne. There followed a stream of Emperors, of claimants to the throne, of assassinations, of betrayals, of civil wars, and invasions by barbarians. From 250 to 265 another outbreak of plague racked the whole of the

Empire. So many pretenders to the throne arose that their biographer, Pollio, padded the list somewhat and published their lives under the title *The Thirty Tyrants*, in obvious allusion to the so-called Thirty Tyrants who governed Athens after her defeat in the Peloponnesian War. Plotinus serenely surmounted the unimaginable turmoil of his times. By purification and disengagement, he sought to make his soul inviolably free and to find in rigorous dialectic and quiet contemplation those virtues which alone could sustain the moral virtues so praised by ancient Rome. By implication, he stated, more mystically than Aristotle but with equal conviction, that the intellectual virtues were a prerequisite to any genuine moral virtues and that intuitive knowledge was supreme over logic-chopping.

> The good of the soul is to remain united to her sister intelligence; her evil, is to abandon herself to the contrary things. After purifying the soul, therefore, she must be united to the divinity; but this implies turning her towards Him. Now this conversion does not begin to occur after the purification, but is its very result. The virtue of the soul, therefore, does not consist in her conversion, but in that which she thereby obtains. This is the intuition of her intelligible object; its image produced and realized within herself; an image similar to that in the eye, an image which represents the things seen. It is not necessary to conclude that the soul did not possess this image, nor had any reminiscence thereof; she no doubt possessed it, but inactively, latently, obscurely. To clarify it, to discover her possessions, the soul needs to approach the source of all clearness. As, however, the soul possesses only the images of the intelligibles, without possessing the intelligibles themselves, she will be compelled to compare with them her own image of them. Easily does the soul contemplate the intelligibles, because the intelligence is not foreign to her; when the soul wishes to enter in relations with them, all the soul needs to do is to turn her glance towards them. Otherwise, the intelligence, though present in the soul, will remain foreign to her. This explains how all our acquisitions of knowledge are foreign to us (as if non-existent), while we fail to recall them.[935]

To the Stoic's claim that the only purpose of thinking was right action, and even more to the centuries-old Roman claim that the ancestral mores sufficed for right action, Plotinus had a reply:

> Dialectics . . . is only one part of philosophy, but the most important. Indeed, philosophy has other branches. First, it studies nature (in physics), therein employing dialectics, as the other arts employ arithmetic,

though philosophy owes far more to dialectics. Then philosophy treats of morals, and here again it is dialectics that ascertains the principles; ethics limits itself to building good habits thereon, and to propose the exercises that shall produce those good habits. The . . . rational virtues also owe to dialectics the principles which seem to be their characteristics; for they chiefly deal with material things (because they moderate the passions). The other virtues also imply the application of reason to the passions and actions which are characteristic of each of them. However, prudence applies reason to them in a superior manner. Prudence deals rather with the universal, considering whether the virtues concatenate, and whether an action should be done now, or be deferred, or be superseded by another. . . . Now it is dialectics, or its resultant science of wisdom which, under a general and immaterial form, furnishes prudence with all the principles it needs.

Could the lower knowledge not be possessed without dialectics or wisdom? They would, at least, be imperfect and mutilated. On the other hand, though the dialectician, that is, the true sage, no longer need these inferior things, he never would have become such without them; they must precede, and they increase with the progress made in dialectics.[936]

The true human virtues, those which are formed and guided by the light of intellect, possess a beauty greater than any sensuous beauty:

Let us now propound a question about experiences to these men who feel love for incorporeal beauties. What do you feel in presence of the noble occupations, the good morals, the habits of temperance, and in general of virtuous acts and sentiments, and of all that constitutes the beauty of souls? What do you feel when you contemplate your inner beauty? What is the source of your ecstasies, or your enthusiasms? Whence come your desires to unite yourselves to your real selves, and to refresh yourselves by retirement from your bodies? Such indeed are the experiences of those who love genuinely. What then is the object which causes these, your emotions? It is neither a figure, nor a color, nor any size; it is that . . . invisible soul, which possesses a wisdom equally invisible; this soul in which may be seen shining the splendor of all the virtues, when one discovers in oneself, or contemplates in others, the greatness of character, the justice of the heart, the pure temperance, the imposing countenance of valor, dignity and modesty, proceeding alone firmly, calmly, and imperturbably; and above all, intelligence, resembling the divinity, by its brilliant light. What is the reason that we declare these objects to be beautiful, when we are transported with admiration and love for them? They exist, they manifest themselves, and whoever beholds them will never be able to restrain himself from confessing them to be veritable beings. Now what are these genuine beings? They are beautiful.[937]

Consider temperance, or self-control; courage; magnanimity, the habit of acting as men of great soul act:

And indeed, what would real temperance consist of, if it be not to avoid attaching oneself to the pleasures of the body, and to flee from them as impure, and as only proper for an impure being? What else is courage, unless no longer to fear death, which is mere separation of the soul from the body? Whoever therefore is willing to withdraw from the body could surely not fear death. Magnanimity is nothing but scorn of things here below.

And consider the role of beauty:

Restored to intelligence, the soul sees her own beauty increase; indeed, her own beauty consists of the intelligence with its ideas; only when united to intelligence is the soul really isolated from all the remainder. That is the reason that it is right to say that "the soul's welfare and beauty lie in assimilating herself to the divinity," because it is the principle of beauty and of the essences; or rather, being is beauty, while the other nature (non-being, matter), is ugliness. . . . The first rank is to be assigned to beauty, which is identical with the good, and from which is derived the intelligence which is beautiful by itself. The soul is beautiful by intelligence, then, the other things, like actions and studies, are beautiful by the soul which gives them a form. It is still the soul which beautifies the bodies to which is ascribed this perfection; being a divine essence, and participating in beauty, when she seizes an object, or subjects it to her dominion, she gives to it the beauty that the nature of this object enables it to receive.

We must still ascend to the Good to which every soul aspires. Whoever has seen it knows what I still have to say, and knows the beauty of the Good. Indeed, the Good is desirable for its own sake; it is the goal of our desires. To attain it, we have to ascend to the higher regions, turn towards them, and lay aside the garment which we put on when descending here below; just as, in the . . . mysteries, those who are admitted to penetrate into the recesses of the sanctuary, after having purified themselves, lay aside every garment, and advance stark naked.[938]

When Plotinus wrote of the perfect functioning of the human soul, his disciples could recognize Aristotle's views on human happiness, the one thing that all men desire above all other things:

Could any one say that there was, for any being, any good but the activity of "living according to nature?" For a being composed of several parts, however, the good will consist in the activity of its best part, an action which is peculiar, natural, and unfailing.[939]

The distinction between spirit and matter is as sharp as it was in Plato. To reduce the soul to a species of matter, composed of finer atoms than those which form the material objects we sense, struck Plotinus as absurd:

> how could you explain the operations and affections of the soul by movements of atoms? How could atomic shock, whether vertical or oblique, produce in the soul these our reasonings, or appetites, whether necessarily, or in any other way? What explanation could they give of the soul's resistance to the impulsions of the body? By what concourse of atoms will one man become a geometrician, another become a mathematician and astronomer, and the other a philosopher? For, according to that doctrine we no longer produce any act for which we are responsible, we are even no longer living beings, since we undergo the impulsion of bodies that affect us just as they do inaminate things.[940]

The Platonic ideas, or forms, of which material objects were in some sense images, were for Plotinus more like spiritual forces. The universe was a system of emanations from the One, like an overflow of energy which descends through the World Mind and the World Soul until it animates all nature. Yet all these low grades of Being and of Good and of Beauty yearn toward their source. The world is full of evil because of the limitations matter imposes on spirit when spirit infuses and forms and animates it. It is when we forget man's divine source and fix our attention on these limitations of man that he seems to be mere animal.

Despite Plotinus' very Platonic insistence that right action, which seemed to the Stoic the proper end of man, depends on an even higher human end and that this end can be reached only through philosophy and dialectic, yet when Plotinus talked of the practical world in which man has to act, much of what he said sounded thoroughly Stoic. What he did was to add a philosophic and theological top to the practical advice of the Stoic. He was thereby enabled to accept life's pain and grief with a certain confidence, a confidence the Stoic often seemed to achieve only by a grim act of will. For Plotinus substituted intelligibility for the somewhat military orders the Stoic steeled himself to carry out, and gave richer meaning to the Stoic precepts that all men are citizens of one city, ruled providentially by one God, and that the evils which man suffers can be transformed by God, and even by the wise man, into goods. The evil that the soul experiences when it is mired in matter is therefore not only to be borne but is to be seen as useful to Providence:

> Indeed, when a being is dissolved into its elements, the Reason of the universe uses it to beget other beings, for the universal Reason embraces everything within its sphere of activity. Thus when the body is disorganized, and the soul is softened by her passions, then the body, overcome by sickness, and the soul, overcome by vice, are introduced into another series and order. There are things, like poverty and sickness, which benefit the persons who undergo them. Even vice contributes to the perfection of the universe, because it furnishes opportunity for the exercise of the divine justice. It serves other purposes also; for instance, it increases the vigilance of souls, and excites the mind and intelligence to avoid the paths of perdition . . . Of course, such utilities are not the cause of the existence of evils; we only mean that, since evils exist, the divinity made use of them to accomplish His purposes. It would be the characteristic of a great power to make even evils promote the fulfilment of its purposes, to cause formless things to assist in the production of forms. In short, we assert that evil is only an omission or failure of good.[941]

As for the crisis and anguish that characterized the third century, Plotinus refused to condemn Providence for these. Spirit still ruled matter, even though on earth souls, being united to bodies, were not pure. Even before the world existed, the souls

> were already disposed to form part of it, to busy themselves with it, to infuse it with life, to administer it, and in it to exert their power in a characteristic manner, either by presiding over its (issues), and by communicating to it something of their power, or by descending into it, or by acting in respect to the world each in its individual manner. . . .

> But how shall we explain the difference that is observed between the lot of the good and the evil? How can it occur that the former are poor, while others are rich, and possess more than necessary to satisfy their needs, being even powerful, and governing cities and nations? . . .

> It remains for us to explain how sense-objects are good and participate in the (cosmic) Order; or at least, that they are not evil. In every animal, the higher parts, such as the face and head, are the most beautiful, and are not equalled by the middle or lower parts. Now men occupy the middle and lower region of the universe. In the higher region we find

the heaven containing the divinities; it is they that fill the greater part of
the world, with the vast sphere where they reside. The earth occupies the
centre and seems to be one of the stars. We are surprised at seeing
injustice reigning here below chiefly because man is regarded as the most
venerable and wisest being in the universe. Nevertheless, this being that
is so wise occupies but the middle place between divinities and animals,
at different times inclining towards the former or the latter. Some men
resemble the divinities, and others resemble animals; but the greater part
continue midway between them.[942]

Plotinus knew that, if the Empire was in many ways sinking back into
the barbarism from which Hellenic culture had centuries ago emerged, this
relapse could not all be charged to the wickedness of those who ruled and
exploited:

The evil rule only because of the cowardice of those who obey them; this
is juster than if it were otherwise.

Nor should the sphere of Providence be extended to the point of
suppressing our own action. For if Providence did everything, and Providence alone existed, it would thereby be annihilated. To what, indeed,
would it apply? There would be nothing but divinity! It is indeed incontestable that divinity exists, and that its sphere extends over other beings
—but divinity does not suppress the latter. For instance, divinity approaches man, and preserves in him what constitutes humanity; that is,
divinity makes him live in conformity to the law of Providence, and
makes him fulfil the commandments of that law.[943]

Plotinus, the peaceful and contemplative philosopher, was undismayed
that beast preyed on beast or that armies of men should fight senseless
wars. The separation of spirit from matter, of soul from body, is temporary: he accepted the ancient Pythagorean doctrine of the transmigration
of souls, the doctrine that interested Plato too, as witness the last book of
the *Republic*. Of course what happens to the soul is of the utmost impor-
ance; but not what happens, or may happen, to the body in battle.

The principle of things is, therefore, the Logos, or Reason (of the universe), which is everything. By it were things begotten, by it were they
co-ordinated in generation.

What then . . . is the necessity of this natural internecine warfare of
animals, and also of men? First, animals have to devour each other in
order to renew themselves; they could not, indeed, last eternally, even if
they were not killed. Is there any reason to complain because, being

440

already condemned to death, as they are, they should find an end which is useful to other beings? What objection can there be to their mutually devouring each other, in order to be reborn under other forms? It is as if on the stage an actor who is thought to be killed, goes to change his clothing, and returns under another mask. Is it objected that he was not really dead? Yes indeed, but dying is no more than a change of bodies, just as the comedian changes his costume, or if the body were to be entirely despoiled, this is no more than when an actor, at the end of a drama, lays aside his costume, only to take it up again when once more the drama begins. Therefore, there is nothing frightful in the mutual transformation of animals into each other. Is it not better for them to have lived under this condition, than never to have lived at all? Life would then be completely absent from the universe, and life could no longer be communicated to other beings. But as this universe contains a multiple life, it produces and varies everything during the course of its existence; as it were joking with them, it never ceases to beget living beings, remarkable by beauty and by the proportion of their forms. The combats in which mortal men continually fight against each other, with a regularity strongly reminding of the Pyrrhic dances . . . clearly show how all these affairs, that are considered so serious, are only children's games, and that their death was nothing serious. To die early in wars and battles is to precede by only a very little time the unescapable fate of old age, and it is only an earlier departure for a closer return. . . . Murders, massacres, the taking and pillaging of towns should be considered as in the theatre we consider changes of scene and of personages, the tears and cries of the actors.

In this world, indeed, just as in the theatre, it is not the soul, the interior man, but his shadow, the exterior man, who gives himself up to lamentations and groans, who on this earth moves about so much, and who makes of it the scene of an immense drama . . . [944]

There are a heaven and a hell in the cosmos of Plotinus, and it is reasonable that both of them should exist. In what he called "the drama of the world," the actors, "the souls themselves run to meet" their "punishments and rewards."

In the universe everything is good and beautiful if every being occupy the place he deserves, if, for instance, he utter discordant sounds when in darkness and Tartarus; for such sounds fit that place.[945]

Some of the philosophic system of Plotinus is reminiscent of Christian theology as well as of the religious views of Homer and Hesiod, and this suggests that Plotinus' master, Ammonius, who once taught the Christian theologian, Origen, may have taken some Christian teachings with him when he turned away from Christianity. But Plotinus never saw in Christianity a solution to his philosophic problem; and his disciple and editor, Porphyry, wrote a tract *Against the Christians.* Nevertheless, Plotinus' philosophy remains in large part a theology, one of the many responses to an increased spiritual anguish. Of course, he was far from revolting against intellect, though revolt he did against the arid rationalism and logic-chopping that repelled Lucian even at Athens and repelled Plotinus himself in his Alexandrian professors before he met Ammonius. It was because he loved his neighbor and even more because he loved the One that Plotinus could think as he did:

> there are two Venuses. The second . . . is daughter of Jupiter and Dione, and she presides over earthly marriages. The first Venus, the celestial one, daughter of Uranus . . . has no mother, and does not preside over marriages, for the reason that there are none in heaven. The Celestial Venus, therefore, daughter of Kronos, that is, of Intelligence, is the divine Soul, which is born pure of pure Intelligence, and which dwells above. As her nature does not admit of inclining earthward, she neither can nor will descend here below. She is, therefore, a form of existence . . . separated from matter, not participating in its nature. This is the significance of the allegory that she had no mother. Rather than a guardian, therefore, she should be considered a deity, as she is pure Being . . .
>
> In fact, that which is immediately born of Intelligence is pure in itself, because, by its very proximity to Intelligence, it has more innate force, desiring to unite itself firmly to the principle that begat it, and which can retain it there on high. The soul which is thus suspended to Intelligence could not fall down, any more than the light which shines around the sun could separate from the body from which it radiates, and to which it is attached.
>
> Celestial Venus (the universal Soul, the third principle or hypostasis), therefore, attaches herself to Kronos (divine Intelligence, the second principle), or, if you prefer to Uranus (the One, the Good, the first Principle), the father of Kronos. Thus Venus turns towards Uranus, and unites herself to him; and in the act of loving him, she procreates Love, with which she contemplates Uranus. Her activity thus effects a hypostasis and being. Both of them therefore fix their gaze on Uranus, both the mother and the fair child, whose nature it is to be hypostasis ever

turned towards another beauty, an intermediary essence between the lover and the beloved object. In fact, Love is the eye by which the lover sees the beloved object; anticipating her, so to speak; and before giving her the faculty of seeing by the organ which he thus constitutes, he himself is already full of the spectacle offered to his contemplation. Though he thus anticipates her, he does not contemplate the intelligible in the same manner as she does, in that he offers her the spectacle of the intelligible, and that he himself enjoys the vision of the beautiful . . . [946]

It is true that, when men directed their weapons against each other in war and under doom of death and when they lined up neatly as if in a pyrrhic sword dance, Plotinus could not feel strongly about either side. But that was not from fear of action nor from that hatred of mankind of which the Jews and Christians were both accused. Rather it was from the love of a more real kind of life and for the source of all real life on earth. Plotinus, as much as Lucian or perhaps far more than he, sought the dialogue of man with God and the dialogue that flows from this, the one of man with man. Seeing no present way of forwarding that dialogue in public life, he felt freed for the highest form of action, namely contemplation and teaching. He was never called, as Plato felt called, to go to some Syracuse or to teach geometry and philosophy to some half-contrite tyrant and thereby to help create a genuine human community. The nearest he came to such a venture was a project he mentioned to the Emperor Gallienus and the Empress Salonina, who honored and venerated him.

Counting on their good will, he besought them to have a ruined town in Campania rebuilt, to give it with all its territory to him, that its inhabitants might be ruled by the laws of Plato. Plotinos intended to have it named Platonopolis, and to go and reside there with his disciples. This request would easily have been granted but that some of the emperor's courtiers opposed this project, either from spite, jealousy, or other unworthy motive.[947]

Plotinus was no nostalgic antiquary, though for guidance he went back seven centuries to Plato. But although the Peloponnesian War justified a certain melancholy apprehension in Plato that the Hellenic world was straying, Plotinus wrote when that world was collapsing. He thereby performed an enormous act of faith in intellect. It was this faith in intellect and not a tired or timid need to syncretize that led Plotinus to accept truth either from Athens or Jerusalem, and to long for truth even from dimly distant India. On the other hand, although Plotinus' mind had the same universal thrust as Plato's, he never wrote on one of Plato's major themes, politics. Perhaps he felt certain that to speak of the political order during the anarchy of the third century was to talk against the wind.

In 270 Plotinus died. One of his disciples, remembering perhaps how a disciple of Socrates had consulted the oracle of Apollo at Delphi as to whether any man was wiser than Socrates, also consulted Apollo as to where the soul of Plotinus had gone; and the god answered:

> Sacred choir of Muses, let us together celebrate this man,
> For long-haired Apollo is among you!
>
> O Deity, who formerly wert a man, but now approachest
> The divine host of guardian spirits, delivered from the narrowing bonds
> of necessity
> That enchains man . . . and from the tumult caused by the
> Confusing whirlwind of the passions of the body,
> Sustained by the vigor of thy mind, thou hastenest to swim . . .
> to land on a shore not submerged by the waves,
> With vigorous stroke, far from the impious crowds.
> Persistently following the straightening path of the purified soul,
> Where the splendor of the divinity surrounds you, the home of justice,
> Far from contamination, in the holy sanctuary of initiation,
> When in the past you struggled to escape the bitter waves,
> When blood-stained life eddied around you with repulsive currents,
> In the midst of the waters dazed by frightening tumult,
> Even then the divinities often showed you your end . . .
> No deep slumber closed your eyelids, and when shaken by the eddies . . .
> You sought to withdraw your eyes from the night that pressed down
> upon them . . .
>
> And you, blessed man, after having fought many a valiant fight . . .
> you have achieved eternal Felicity.
>
> Here, O Muses, let us close this hymn in honor of Plotinos;
> Cease the mazes of the dancing of the graceful choir;
> This is what my golden lyre had to say of this eternally blessed man![948]

8

CASTRA AND ECCLESIA

By THE YEAR 284 more than two and a half centuries had passed since the Emperor Augustus died near Naples; since then some forty-five Emperors had governed or tried to govern the Roman Empire, but twenty of these Emperors had been crowded into the last forty-nine years. The life expectancy of a newly crowned ruler had shrunk to two and a half years. The system Augustus had founded had clearly broken down. In this year 284 an army fresh from a successful war against Persia discovered its young leader, the Emperor Numerian, lying dead in the closed litter in which he was traveling. Only the year before, his father, the Emperor Carus, had disappeared, reportedly struck by lightning. In the death of each, there was suspicion of foul play. The army leaders, ignoring not only the Senate but also Numerian's elder brother and co-Emperor, Carinus, proceeded to elect as Emperor Diocles, whose Roman name was Diocletianus. Diocletian promptly killed with his own hand the dead Emperor's Praetorian Prefect, who was also that Emperor's father-in-law; then he announced that he had done this because the Prefect had murdered the Emperor Numerian. Next, Diocletian marched west to confront the Emperor Carinus, whose army he fought on the banks of the Morava River in what is now eastern Yugoslavia. Fortunately for Diocletian, Carinus was murdered by one of his own officers. Diocletian, now sole ruler of the Roman Empire, showed mercy to those who had fought against him.

A good half-century of experience, however, suggested that the Empire had become a Public Thing which no man, certainly no one man, could rule. The Roman army's habit of conquering the Roman Empire had indeed become a reflex, like the habit the Hellenistic kings had taught the Roman Republic: that of liberating the Greeks. Diocletian was a Dalmatian of humble birth. He was not well educated: he was a product of the army. True, he was better at administration than at strategy; but the kind of administration he understood was military. The religion, philosophy, art, and literature that made up what men called Hellenism had now sharply declined. Indeed there were signs that a new kind of culture, either Christian or at least Graeco-Oriental, was taking shape, especially in the Eastern, Greek-speaking Mediterranean world. Politically, the capital of this Hellenistic world was still Eternal Rome and the citizens of the eastern provinces still called themselves *Romaioi*, Romans. They lived under Roman law, although that law had absorbed much from the more mature East. The Romaioi still heard Latin in the army, the administration, and the courts, but Latin had never become the language of literature or philosophy or science. In the East the Emperor's edicts had long been issued in both tongues.

In the Latin West, barbarization had of course proceeded even further than in the East. Latin was still the common tongue of educated men, but among the uneducated it continued to break up into local dialects. Similarly, while the common artistic forms of the Empire were losing their vitality, there were signs in the provinces of new, more vital forms, local dialects of art in which the artist could speak with conviction. Many of the tribes of Spain, Gaul, Britain, the northern Balkan area, and the coasts of northwest Africa had learned to live in cities and to model their social life on that of Rome; yet incursions by barbarians from beyond the frontiers, as well as the civil wars provoked by claimants to the Imperial throne, had seriously diminished the civilizing effect of the cities. Some of these Western cities, notably those in what is now southern France, had received Hellenistic influences directly from the Greek East by way of roads that Rome had built. Nevertheless, by Diocletian's day relatively few educated

446

men in the Latin West could speak or read Greek. Economically, although the Greek East was in decline, the Latin West had declined further. The Greek world had always had deeper-rooted skills, whether in agriculture or commerce or industry. By the time of Diocletian's accession, economic growth was largely confined to those areas near the frontier where army cantonments created new and hungry markets. Rome, having first conquered, pillaged, and organized the Greek world, and having lived by exploiting it, now found that its military grip on the Greek world had loosened. Since the army, which Augustus had hoped to keep Italian, was no longer either Latin and Western, or Greek and Eastern, as much as it was barbarian, Diocletian had no reason to base his power on the Latin West rather than on the Greek East.

Whereas Augustus had masked his power as military autocrat by inventing the Principate, a system in which theoretically he was merely the Princeps or leader of a senate to which he made a point of deferring, Diocletian formally discarded the mask Augustus had worn. He recognized the constitutional right, so to speak, by which the army leaders had chosen, in Alexander's phrase, the best, or strongest, to rule Cosmopolis. He thereby formally founded the Dominate, a system in which the Emperor was absolute ruler. Augustus had masked his power also by appearing to restore Roman religion. Although Diocletian formally worshiped the gods of Rome and Greece, he would have gained nothing from an ostentatious piety or from a campaign to restore the Mos Majorum. What Diocletian was determined to restore was law and order. It was the army of the East that, in September of 284, elected him Emperor. And it was not in Rome but in the Greek city of Nicomedia, on the shore of Asia, that he took up his reign as sole Emperor. He did not even visit Rome.⁹⁴⁹ The Principate was dead and the Dominate that now succeeded it was created by a half-barbarian professional soldier who accepted the traditional title of Augustus but whose coins advertised that he was also *Dominus et Deus*, Lord and God. Diocletian might hope that this resurrected title, briefly worn by the mad Domitian, would place his power beyond the reach of the Roman army, with its long-ingrained habit of creating Emperors, including himself.

Meanwhile, there was more constructive work for the army to do. Diocletian appointed as his Caesar a fellow officer and comrade, Maximian, a Pannonian, born near the site of modern Belgrade, uneducated but able; and sent him to Gaul to defend the Rhine frontier and especially to put down an insurrection of peasants who called themselves Bagaudae. Since 253, when the Franks had breached the Rhine frontier, there had been repeated inroads of barbarians. In 276 the Franks broke in again; peace was restored by settling some of them inside the Empire to help defend it. But even those barbarian troops who served in the Imperial army sometimes sacked Gallic cities. Such cities hastily walled themselves, using the débris of their own temples and amphitheaters. The wall often enclosed only a fraction of the city. Once the city's commerce and industry had been largely destroyed, its population shrank. The new wall protected chiefly government troops and government personnel. Lacking adequate siege machinery and seeking more exposed booty, barbarian war bands swirled past such cities and pillaged or wasted the suburbs and the countryside. The peasants, driven from the land, rose in insurrection and, driven by hunger, they too pillaged. Indeed, after Maximian had quelled the Bagaudae and Diocletian had promoted him to the rank of Augustus charged with governing the Latin West, and after Diocletian had assumed the additional title, Jovius, and had accorded the lesser title, Herculius, to his junior colleague, a panegyrist likened Maximian's action in overcoming the Bagaudae to Hercules' helping Jupiter to overcome the Giants. This orator suggested that just as the Giants were half man, half serpent, so these monstrous Bagaudae might be described as

> peasants ignorant of soldiery who have got a taste for it; laborers who would be infantry; herdsmen who would be cavalry; rustics become devastators of their own way of life in imitation of the barbarian enemy.[950]

The Giants whom the Hercules of the West, the Emperor Maximian, put down, were Roman citizens bearing arms against Rome. A kingdom of the Gauls had been set up in 260 and had functioned for a decade. But this had been less a separatist, nationalist movement than a region of the Empire forced to provide its own military defense during a period when the Emperor Gallienus was too preoccupied elsewhere to reassert the unity of the Empire. Functionally, there were signs of an independent Western empire within the Graeco-Roman empire that Diocletian headed, as witness the fact that Britain and Spain had joined the new kingdom of the Gauls. Must not some of the Bagaudae have thought of themselves as winning freedom from Rome, whose taxation had oppressed them and whose protection against invasion had repeatedly failed them?

Even after the Bagaudae had been suppressed, a barbarian named Carausius, from what is now northern Belgium, seemed on the verge of forming another Western state within the Empire. Carausius had been charged by Diocletian with clearing the North Sea and the Scheldt River of Frankish and Saxon pirates. He ended by controlling with his navy both sides of the English Channel and the whole Gallic coast from the Rhine to the Loire, with garrisons at Boulogne and Rouen. From his capital at London in 286 he declared himself an Emperor. The coins he issued announced that he had brought the Peace of Augustus and that Jupiter was his savior; the sun-god was his companion; Minerva, Neptune, and Apollo were his protectors. His coins also showed Maximian and himself ranged on either side of Diocletian. He clearly meant to be one of two junior, or Herculian, Augusti. Diocletian, however, intended to have only one Herculian Augustus rule the Western provinces, and he never recognized Carausius as such, although efforts to destroy his power had to be postponed. He countered Carausius' self-nomination by appointing two Caesars, one to help him govern the Greek East and one to help Maximian govern the poorer, more turbulent Latin West and to reverse its centrifugal tendencies. He chose as his own Caesar a professional soldier, Galerius Valerius, son of a peasant by a Dacian mother. Galerius' task was to defend the Danube and if necessary to fight off attacks from the east by the Persian Empire. Galerius put away his wife and duly married a daughter of Diocletian. As Caesar of the West, Diocletian chose Constantius Chlorus, an officer and provincial governor, an Illyrian of Dardanian stock, but better educated than his three Imperial colleagues. Constantius' first task was to put down Carausius, and by a brilliant campaign he captured Boulogne, cut off the potential German allies of Carausius, built a large fleet, and crossed to Britain. There he found Carausius had been assassinated by one of his own subordinates. By 293 Constantius had reconquered Britain. He beat off the Scots and Picts, who threatened from the north. He fortified the British coast of the North Sea against German pirates. He again sealed the Channel against the Frankish pirates, always eager to ravage the coasts of Gaul and Spain. In 297 the Caesar of the East, Galerius, fought off an attack by Persia, destroyed a Persian army, and threw a chain of forts around Mesopotamia, now once more the Roman Empire's.

Indeed, the Tetrarchy, or rule by four, that Diocletian had established, was basically a military device. It distributed the labor and care of defending the various frontiers and of suppressing internal rebellions. Few of its chief characteristics were new. Already in 161, Marcus Aurelius had made Verus his co-Augustus. It was said that as early as 212 Caracalla and Geta toyed with the idea of taking, one the provinces of Europe, the other the provinces of Asia.[951] Again, for an Augustus to choose a Caesar and make him his son-in-law was a familiar device. That all four tetrarchs should be professional military men was dictated by the task of defending the Empire's long frontiers; but in any case the military profession had long offered the commonest road to the throne. As for the danger of rivalry, that danger could perhaps be handled better by establishing four domains of sovereignty than by entrusting large armies to generals whose only chance of finding a crown was by rebelling and fighting for one. Besides, Diocletian remained the senior, or Jovian, Augustus and fortified his special authority by issuing coins that broke all precedent. So far as is known, he was the first Emperor ever portrayed on a coin dressed in the costume of Jupiter himself. He was the first to make the title Lord and God both official and apparently acceptable. No Roman army seemed able to create an Eternal Augustus or even a Perpetual Caesar; and one of these titles each of the four crowned soldiers from the Balkan Peninsula now wore.[952] If Caesar Augustus had masked his power behind the indisputable authority of the gods, Diocletian, Lord and God, came close to covering his face with the mask of Jupiter himself. An orator celebrating an anniversary of Jovius and Herculius even dared point out with satisfaction that the two Augusti, Diocletian and Maximian, were of more immediate help to the Empire than their divine fathers, or patrons, and were therefore more worth worshiping:

> Jupiter in person is invoked, not as transmitted by opinion but visible and present; Hercules is adored, not as a stranger but as Emperor![953]

As for the ancient authority of the Senate, Diocletian had little need of that. It sufficed that the Roman Senate should exist: its actual function was rapidly diminishing to that of town council of the City of Rome, although it still recruited its ranks from the wealthier landowners of the whole Empire.

The invasions, civil wars, famines, and plagues of the third century had severely decreased the manpower on which Diocletian could draw. Between 250 and 265 the Empire had been ravaged by a plague even more devastating than the plague Marcus Aurelius had faced in the last fifteen years of his reign. Not only was there a smaller population from which to draw recruits; it was also harder now to find citizens willing to serve in the army. Landowners were therefore required to supply quotas of conscripts from among their *coloni*, or serfs; they naturally sent their least able-bodied ones. Neither such soldiers as these nor for the most part the barbarians whom Diocletian could hire possessed the willingness to acquire skill through discipline and hard work or the willingness to die fighting that had enabled the Roman legions to defeat Hannibal and then to conquer the Greek East. Diocletian tried to compensate for this loss of quality by quantity. During the third century the army had expanded to some 400,000 men; Diocletian increased it to at least 500,000.[954] Even then, the frontiers had to be more heavily furnished with fortresses if the shell of empire was to hold. And often the tribes outside the shell had still to be held off with bribes disguised as free gifts. What with these bribes and the wages earned by German barbarians recruited into the Imperial army, the fringe of Barbaria that inhabited both sides of the frontier now lived off the Empire as surely as if they had conquered it. Moreover, this fringe tended to develop its own hybrid culture, a culture partly akin to the tired civilization upon whose declining production it battened and partly akin to the rough, tribal culture it kept at bay.

In place of Rome, capital of the Orbis Terrarum, the fringe of hybrid culture had established what from many points of view amounted to four capitals. Diocletian, Jovian Augustus, Lord and God, ruled at Nicomedia on the Asian coast of the Propontis. His special jurisdiction was known as the Prefecture of the East and included Roman Asia, the islands of the eastern Aegean, Egypt, and Cyrenaica. His Eastern Caesar, adopted son and son-in-law, Galerius, ruled at Sirmium, conveniently close to the lower Danube. Galerius' Prefecture of Illyricum included most of the Balkan peninsula clear north to the Danube, east to the Bosphorus, and west far enough to cover all of what is now Albania. Maximian, the Western Augustus, ruled at Milan. Of the four capitals his was farthest from the frontier, as if he were unwilling to go too far from Rome, yet wanted to remain reasonably convenient to the upper Danube, to the desert frontier of Africa, and even to the Rhine and the Scottish border. Maximian's Prefecture of Italy ran from the Danube south to include the northwestern part of what is now Yugoslavia, all of what is modern Italy and its islands, and the Roman provinces in what are today the western coastlands of Libya, Tunisia, and northern Algeria. The Western Caesar, Constantius, based himself at Treves, closer than his Augustus to the Rhine and closer to the troublesome Scottish border. His Prefecture of Gaul included what are now England, France clear to the Rhine, Spain, Portugal, and northern Morocco. Nearly all of this westernmost prefecture had not so very long ago been composed of tribal lands. The Roman Republic and Empire had successively conquered these lands, had largely Romanized them, had thinly urbanized them, had very thinly hellenized them, and until the third century had defended their cities with success from Pict, Scot, German, and Moor, as well as from each province's own least civilized mountain tribes.

Two of the four Imperial capitals were based inside the hybrid cultural fringe, and all four rulers, or tetrarchs, were in varying degrees themselves products of that fringe. By the standards of a Marcus Aurelius they had little understanding of what the Roman Empire and, even less, Athens had meant. But the flattery a panegyrist aimed at Diocletian and Maximian was not ill aimed:

> For you were not born and brought up in a part of the world corrupted by leisure and luxuriousness, but in those provinces where the frontier, always with weapons at the ready although opposite an enfeebled enemy, nevertheless exacts the indefatigable habit of labor and endurance, where all of life is military service, and where even the women are more courageous than the men of other countries.[955]

Finally, the cultural fringe even developed its own economy: not only three of its political capitals but a number of other army bases had their own arms industries and produced many of the other supplies they needed without either the cost of transport from the rear or the danger of their being intercepted by raiding barbarians, by armed rebels, or by brigands. Moreover, the economy of the fringe stimulated the growth of population at a time when the population of the Empire, taken as a whole, was declining along with its economy. It was symbolic that the population of the City of Rome itself was declining.

Nevertheless, to support the barbarian military fringe still required money from the Empire it encircled. In the days of the Republic and also of the early Empire, Rome had of course financed her armies first from conquest and pillage and then through the tribute her tax collectors and moneylenders could force out of her subject provinces. During Hadrian's reign, agriculture, industry, and commerce had prospered under the Pax

Romana and had yielded a relatively good tax base. But the crisis of the third century had wrecked or badly damaged these three sources, and the Empire's tax base suffered proportionally. If Diocletian was to protect the Empire from outside aggression and to maintain law and order inside, he would have to raise taxes, either by persuasion or by force. Since the population of the Empire was by this time distinguished by a lack of public spirit, a lack that was ill reflected in the panegyrics the professional rhetoricians addressed to the Emperors, there was in a sense no community to persuade. Diocletian therefore reorganized and tightened taxation by force.

Taxation, however, was already beginning to eat into capital. The once prosperous middle class was steadily diminishing. The military, half-barbarian ring that encircled and protected the Empire must also help govern it, enforce its laws, and suppress numerous local rebellions; and these services cost money. But the monetary system was now failing, and galloping inflation continued to make the money that could be squeezed out of taxpayers less worth collecting. At Hadrian's death in 138, the denarius, the basic silver coin of the Empire, contained 75 per cent silver. A hundred years later, when a single year saw six Emperors, the silver content had dropped to 28 per cent. And in thirty more years it dropped to one-fiftieth of 1 per cent. The denarius had become a base-metal coin washed in silver or indeed sometimes in tin. Diocletian therefore tried with some success to reform the currency. But prices went on rising. Diocletian had to appeal to force again: in 301 he issued a price list for both goods and services and provided a penalty of death for those who either offered or demanded more than the official rate. Even so, the edict of 301 proved unenforceable, and he was constrained to let it lapse except in those transactions in which the government itself was either the buyer or the seller. The fate of those who engaged in such commerce vindicated the statement of Jesus that no man could serve both God and money. But at least the choice of those who served money was masked by the image and superscription of a human Lord and God, closely identified with Jove. Now even this device failed. The subjects of the human God were offered coin scarcely worth serving. Both religious faith and financial credit had successively collapsed; and, like stateless barbarians, the citizens of the Empire more and more often bartered their goods and services.

If debasement of the coinage during the third century had inflated prices, that other currency, words, by means of which men had once written immortal poems and had once, in dialectical combat, sought philosophic truth, had also been largely ruined by an equally dangerous sort of inflation: the triumph of rhetoric over all the other liberal arts. Again, especially in the Latin West, language was no longer the adequate currency of a civilized community, and the local dialects into which it had crumbled served primarily animal needs. The more specifically human needs, which men had once met by reasoning together, were partly or wholly forgotten; and the search for an ideal Republic, for the common good, which Socrates and Plato and other Greeks had led, gave way largely to the control of human animals by force and fear. A sort of primitivism, economic as well as cultural, was growing beneath the surface of the Graeco-Roman culture.

Diocletian, despite his reputed admiration for Marcus Aurelius,[956] was himself the product of this world of inflated coinage, of inflated words, of lost faith, of lost hopes, of diminished mutual confidence among men, of general disillusionment. He made yet another try at salvaging the empire he had seized. He too would turn to barter. He proceeded to systematize a whole host of emergency measures, which had sprung up like rank weeds during the decades of chaos preceding his reign. He replaced the land tax in cash with taxes in kind so that, even if his reformed currency underwent another inflation, the government would not lose. The landowner must also pay a land tax on the men and women who labored for him and, in some areas, for the livestock he raised. The land was divided into standard taxable units, the size of which varied with the fertility of the land and the nature of the crop grown. In each city-state the members of the curia, or local senate, which governed the city and its territory, continued to be responsible for collecting the total tax assessed against the city. In contrast to the economic development of the military cultural ring, fostered by the needs of the increased frontier defenses with their governmentally operated arms industry, many cities in the interior became ghost towns, and their new, necessary, and shorter walls mocked the memory of the Antonine frontiers, once considered a common wall for all cities. As city life declined, the great landowners moved out and retreated to their estates, which eventually became the prototypes of the medieval manors that would one day spread across Western Europe. Their villas evolved into castles, as their laborers evolved into serfs. Owners managed to seize illegally a good deal of land from small and helpless farmers; in other cases small farmers sometimes chose to place themselves under great landowners able to protect them against armed marauders and even against rapacious extortion by Imperial tax collectors.

The shift from a money tax to harsher taxes collected largely in kind necessitated a much enlarged civil service to assess, collect, store, and transport the supplies the government required of its subjects, as well as a secret service to watch over the honesty of the civil servants. The genuine threat of invasion by barbarian tribes apparently did not cause the population to close ranks, to rally to the Public Thing, to cooperate with the tax collector in order to support the common defense. This failure to rally made the collection of taxes more difficult to effect. To squeeze out of his subjects what was needed, Diocletian gave each provincial governor a smaller area to squeeze: by 305 he had raised the number of provinces from forty-eight to more than a hundred, though in some cases he may have had as additional motive the desire to diminish the military power of each governor and thereby to diminish the chances that he might try to seize a throne. These hundred-odd provinces he grouped in fourteen dioceses; the Greek word *dioikesis*, which had originally meant housekeeping, now meant also a government or public administration. Each diocese was placed under a *vicarius*, a vicar or deputy of the ruler. Finally, the dioceses were grouped in the four prefectures. Of the four, the East and Illyricum still spoke Greek as the lingua franca of the educated, except in the northern Balkans and the south side of the lower Danube, which had never been subjected by Alexander the Great and had later learned Latin from their Roman masters. Men of the upper class in the two Greek-speaking prefectures learned the Latin language if they sought careers in the army or civil service or law, but tended to feel only contempt for Latin literature.

The two western prefectures used Latin, which by Diocletian's day had more or less replaced Greek even in Magna Graecia and Sicily, as it had more or less replaced Phoenician in the area around Carthage. Administratively at least, a formal fissure had begun to appear between the Greek and Latin worlds, each with its own Augustus and its own Caesar, each of these with his own capital and his own élite mobile corps, ready to reinforce those of the Empire's frontier forces which fell within his jurisdiction. The Prefecture of the East, which Diocletian retained for himself, was the most populous and wealthy. It contained the homes of great, ancient, half-forgotten cultures, such as that of the Nile Valley and that of the upper valleys of the Tigris and Euphrates. It contained Palestine, the home of Judaism and the birthplace of Christianity. The Christians could no longer be considered a Jewish sect; they were an organized church that rejected the gods of the Empire for a belief in the one, invisible God of the Hebrews. This church now had many branches, most highly concentrated in Diocletian's prefecture. Most of its local churches worshiped in Greek; most of its theologians and apologists thought and wrote in Greek. During the third century, as knowledge of Greek died out in the Latin West, the churches there adopted a Latin translation of the liturgy so that it could be better followed by the worshipers. Shortly after 150 a Latin translation of the New Testament had been undertaken.[957] Successive bishops of Rome showed a truly Roman talent for organization and administration, although the Latin Christian West, as one would expect, exhibited both less taste and less talent for theological debate than did the Greek Christian East. Moreover, since its clergy less and less often understood Greek, especially the technical terms of Greek theologians, they could not always follow the discussions which successive heresies provoked, discussions which supplied the Eastern Church with at least the possibility of a valuable inner dialogue.

The conquered Greek world had shown a vitality which the Latin West lacked. It had first accepted Roman conquest; had, as Horace pointed out, conquered its conquerors culturally; had in some sense used the Romans to bring itself unity, a common legal system, and military protection against both the ancient Persian foe and the unruly barbarians in the north. As for law, Diocletian strove to keep it Roman and to protect it from absorbing Greek legal usages. But clearly the East was now, as it were, patiently outsitting Rome; it was even, given Diocletian's choice of prefectures, in a sense ruling Rome. Again, having long ago conquered Rome culturally, the Greek world had exported to Rome a religion from one of its own eastern provinces, was now working out for Rome a theology from that religion, and had begun once more to conquer the Latin West, although this time not for Homer nor for Socrates, but for Christ. Thus the Greek East in some sort cast Rome aside, as a man would cast away a garment he no longer needed. Should the frontiers of the Empire give way, might not the Greek East then be salvaged, even if the less civilized and now sorely battered Latin West should have to be jettisoned?

In East and West alike the spiritual alienation from the Public Thing, which the chaos of the third century had greatly accelerated, long before

Diocletian had seized power, was increased by the compulsion he felt constrained to use against his subjects. As Diocletian intensified the pressure upon these subjects in an effort to finance their defense, they somehow slipped out from under that pressure. The *curialis*, or member of a municipal curia, would try to shift the tax load from his own shoulders to the shoulders of the poor. The member of a trade or craft guild, once called a college but now a corporation, found his corporation legally responsible for heavy public duties. He tried to shift to another occupation; his membership was thereupon made legally binding and also hereditary. The farm laborer or sharecropper who worked for some great landed proprietor was often so oppressed by his employer or landlord that he attempted to escape to the very city life from which the great proprietors were withdrawing. The government, fearing that the landlord could not for lack of workers meet his taxes, not only bound his laborers legally to the soil but made their serflike status hereditary. In effect, Diocletian and his three colleagues conscripted almost the whole population, some into the army, the rest into supporting the government. By making many occupations legally hereditary, Diocletian was creating a caste system. Small wonder that, when barbarians invaded, few subjects of the Empire were ready to risk their lives to defend the Public Thing; some subjects even joined the invaders or escaped into Barbaria. Rome had once offered men, especially propertied men, freedom through law; and by and large the offer had been accepted. But somehow, somewhere, the freedom seemed to have disappeared and a sense of all-pervading compulsion appeared in its place. To use the metaphor of Lucian of Samosata, all were swallowed and imprisoned in the belly of a whale; and the biblical name of the whale was Leviathan.

Or perhaps the prison was not a whale but a seaside fortress, which Diocletian had built stone by stone with his own hands, not according to a blueprint, but forced by a sea of troubles to add each stone as the waves grew higher. When the fortress stood complete, it may have surprised and shocked Diocletian himself. Certainly, nobody was more imprisoned by it than he was. He was a tough soldier and a simple, unpretentious man. But his determination to be no mere general against whom other generals might be tempted to rebel led him to reign as the King of Persia reigned. All who approached Jovian Augustus must first prostrate themselves. In addressing his subjects, he spoke of himself by a title such as Our Serenity and of them by a title such as Your Devotion. He lived aloof from other men and even when he went out from his palace it was with diadem on head, body clothed in purple and gold. By sharply separating the civil administration from the military, he prevented the civil authority and the military force from falling into the same hands and thereby enabling some rebel to supplant him. The same separation protected the taxpayer from the rapacious soldiers who had recently collected taxes. It was not Diocletian's fault that extortion continued anyhow or that, from his reign on, the Emperor's palace was called the *castra*, the camp, and the entire Imperial government was known as the *militia*. He had not built his system according to some preconceived theory of government; his system was rather the sum of his successive efforts to meet emergencies. For example, though he revolutionized the Roman army, it was to meet an immediate problem. He vastly expanded his cavalry forces and equipped them with heavy armor for the same reason Persia had done so: both empires faced nomadic horsemen, and the time had passed when Roman infantry could hold its own against such horsemen. The Tetrarchy, his oriental court ceremonial, his currency reform, his price-fixing, his exaction of taxes in kind, his laws forbidding his subjects, or their descendants, to quit certain occupations, were all emergency measures. He ended by wagering all on force, and at least officially on the ancient gods of Rome. For some fourteen years his regime of force seemed to work; no other Roman Emperor had reigned so long since Marcus Aurelius, except Septimius Severus, who had died at York eighty-seven years before. The historian Flavius Vopiscus understandably described Diocletian as "a man indispensable to the state."[958]

But this indispensable Emperor was quite intelligent enough to know that the Empire commanded little positive loyalty. No doubt many or most of Diocletian's subjects were glad that he had rescued them from the decades of horror that preceded his reign, but there were few signs of enthusiasm in the population he ruled. He could scarcely avoid knowing that scattered throughout that population were two human communities, within each of which the members were bound together by strong religious ties, and these members had repeatedly shown themselves willing to die for their religion. These two communities were, of course, the Christian and the Jewish. Indeed, Tertullian had chosen to describe the Christians as "a race of men ever ready for death."[959] Many Christians now occupied high places in the civil service and even in Diocletian's official family. Many served in the army. The Christian Church was now a far more numerous group than Jewry, and its members were overwhelmingly of

Gentile extraction. Moreover, the Jews had all but ceased to proselytize, whereas proselytizing was one of the prime purposes of the Christian Church.

During the first fourteen years of his reign, Diocletian apparently refrained from religious persecution. In 297, when he suppressed a revolt in Egypt, he had indeed let loose there a severe persecution of the Manichaeans, believers in an ascetic religion that had invaded the Roman Empire from Persia. But Diocletian had evidence that these Manichaeans had acted as agents of Persia, with whom he was then at war. Christians he continued to tolerate. On a certain occasion, probably in 298, Diocletian and his pagan priests were attempting to read the future by slaying victims and examining their livers. Lactantius, a Christian convert and an eloquent writer, whom Diocletian had appointed a professor of rhetoric at Nicomedia, reported that while Diocletian sacrificed,

> some attendants of his, who were Christians, stood by, and they put the *immortal sign* on their foreheads. At this the demons were chased away, and the holy rites interrupted. The soothsayers trembled, unable to investigate the wonted marks on the entrails of the victims. They frequently repeated the sacrifices, as if the former had been unpropitious; but the victims, slain from time to time, afforded no tokens for divination. At length Tages, the chief of the soothsayers, either from guess or from his own observation, said, "There are profane persons here, who obstruct the rites." Then Diocletian, in furious passion, ordered not only all who were assisting at the holy ceremonies, but also all who resided within the palace, to sacrifice, and, in case of their refusal, to be scourged. And further, by letters to the commanding officers, he enjoined that all soldiers should be forced to the like impiety, under pain of being dismissed the service.[960]

Diocletian's sudden anger perhaps reflected an equally sudden realization of the hopelessness of his fourteen-year struggle to protect and govern the population of the Empire. Indeed, that population must often have felt to him like an apathetic, uncooperative, conquered people in whose land his army was an army of occupation. Worse, a growing fraction of the Empire's subjects served an Oriental God who forbade them to sacrifice to the gods of the Empire, gods whom the Christians seemed to consider evil spirits. Here, on this day of sacrifice, Christians were by Christian magic preventing the gods of the Empire from aiding the Empire. Many other Christians, who served in the Imperial army, refused to make the custom-

459

ary sacrifices. The scene at the altar was the last straw for a man who had striven against odds for fourteen years to save the Empire from destruction. Given his burden, his orders to the army and to his palace staff seemed not unreasonable: either those who served him would lend him their full moral support by sacrificing to the gods of the Empire or he would dismiss them. Against those Christians who were neither soldiers nor palace officials he took no steps. Then he went to Bithynia, presumably to his capital Nicomedia, for the winter.

There his Caesar, Galerius, joined him. Lactantius later wrote that Galerius out of hatred for the Christians urged Diocletian to burn alive all persons who refused to sacrifice to the Emperor's divinity. For five years Diocletian rejected this advice. Even when at last he yielded, his orders were that no blood should be shed. In February of 303 a general persecution began. The Christians had boldly built one of their churches opposite the palace; while Diocletian and Galerius looked on, the church was demolished.

> Next day an edict was published, depriving the Christians of all honours and dignities; ordaining also that, without any distinction of rank or degree, they should be subjected to tortures, and that every suit at law should be received against them; while, on the other hand, they were debarred from being plaintiffs in questions of wrong, adultery, or theft; and, finally, that they should neither be capable of freedom, nor have right of suffrage. A certain person tore down this edict, and cut it in pieces, improperly indeed, but with high spirit, saying in scorn, "These are the triumphs of Goths and Sarmatians." Having been instantly seized and brought to judgment, he was not only tortured, but burnt alive, in the forms of law; and having displayed admirable patience under sufferings, he was consumed to ashes.[961]

Next, a fire broke out in the Imperial palace; a part of it burned; and the Christians were accused of setting the fire in order to destroy Diocletian and Galerius. Lactantius later reported that Galerius had ordered the fire set. In any case, Diocletian flew into another rage, questioned all his domestics under torture, but learned nothing. Fifteen days later another fire broke out in the palace. Galerius, announcing that he did not propose to be burned alive, left. Diocletian's own wife and daughter seem to have had close relations with Christians: he forced them to make the pagan sacrifice. A large number of Christians were rounded up and burned alive, and the persecution spread. Maximian, the Western Augustus, and his

Caesar, Constantius, were ordered to carry out the edicts of persecution. Maximian gladly obeyed; Constantius dared limit his obedience to the destruction of churches.

In November of 303 Diocletian made his first visit to Rome in order to celebrate the commencement of the twentieth year of his reign. But he disliked the Roman's unlicensed tongue, and immediately after the celebration he left. He returned to Nicomedia, his arrival delayed by a serious illness. On May 1, 305, he and his co-Augustus abdicated and were succeeded by their two Caesars, Galerius in the East and Constantius in the West, each supplied by Diocletian with a new Caesar. Lactantius later charged the ambitious persecutor, Galerius, with having persuaded both former Augusti to step down. But it is possible that the abdication was Diocletian's idea and that it was he who persuaded Maximian to resign at the same time. Diocletian had reasons enough for such a decision. His health was poor. For more than twenty years it was he who had borne the heaviest burden of holding the Empire together and defending it. His desperate lunge at the Christians suggests that he recognized as a somewhat hollow success the bureaucratic fortress into which he had turned the Roman Empire. The results of the persecution also turned out somewhat hollow. Many of his officials in the provinces enforced only spasmodically his edicts on Christianity: Constantius never completely enforced them in Britain or Gaul; the first edict was enforced in Italy, Africa, and Spain, but only for about a year; in the two Greek prefectures, the edicts were better enforced but failed to get much popular support from Diocletian's pagan subjects. The historian Eusebius, Bishop of Caesarea, reported:

> Then indeed, then very many rulers of the churches contended with a stout heart under terrible torments, and displayed spectacles of mighty conflicts; while countless others, whose souls cowardice had numbed beforehand, readily proved weak at the first assault; while of the rest, each underwent a series of varied forms of torture: one would have his body maltreated by scourgings; another would be punished with the rack and torn to an unbearable degree, whereat some met a miserable end to their life. But others, again, emerged from the conflict otherwise: one man was brought to the abominable and unholy sacrifices by the violence of others who pressed round him, and dismissed as if he had sacrificed, even though he had not; another who did not so much as approach or touch any accursed thing, when others had said that he had sacrificed, went away bearing the false accusation in silence. A third was taken up half-dead and cast aside as if he were a corpse already; and, again, a

certain person lying on the ground was dragged a long distance by the feet, having been reckoned among those who had voluntarily sacrificed. One cried out and with a loud voice attested his refusal to sacrifice, and another shouted aloud that he was a Christian, glorying in his confession of the saving Name. Another stoutly maintained that he had not sacrificed, and never would. Nevertheless these also were struck on the mouth and silenced by a large band of soldiers drawn up for that purpose, and with blows on their face and cheeks driven forcibly away.[962]

Many churches were destroyed, along with the sacred furnishings; many copies of the Christian scriptures were burned, along with manuscripts which pious fraud or bureaucratic connivance claimed were the scriptures. The object of the edicts was not to kill Christians but to force them to transfer their first loyalty from their Kingdom of Heaven to the Roman Empire, from Jesus Christ to the Empire's Lord and God and to his patron, Jove. But Diocletian's bureaucracy was often willing to settle for an allegiance that was nominal or even fictitious, provided the bureaucrat's paper work could report compliance.

After his abdication Diocletian retired to his native Dalmatia, where he built a palace on the shore of the Adriatic near the city of Salona.[963] Unlike the villa that Hadrian built at Tivoli, Diocletian's palace was built in the form of a foursquare Roman camp, fortified with powerful masonry walls and with numerous towers and huge gates. He who had tried hard to convert an empire into a fortress retired now to something smaller than an empire: to a country seaside estate. And, this time literally, he made his domain into a fortress. In doing so, he did no more than many a wealthy subject of his had already done. They had left the city life that had for centuries characterized Graeco-Roman culture and had retired to fortified estates, able to withstand soldiery, brigands, and tax collectors alike. Diocletian's retirement brought him disillusionment: his most famous invention, the Tetrarchy, collapsed. So long as he retained his power, he had successfully prevented civil war among the four tetrarchs. Now that he had retired, a struggle over the succession broke out. By 306 there was civil war, and in that year there were three Augusti and three Caesars; by 307 there were six Augusti. Once, in 308, Diocletian emerged from retirement in a brief effort to help Galerius restore order. This effort failed, but when Galerius tried to persuade him to resume his reign,

> then, as if warding off some pestilence, he responded in this wise: "If only you could see the cabbages cultivated by our own hands you would certainly never suggest that such a thing should be attempted."[964]

462

When Diocletian died in his fortress-palace in 313, the wars of succession had not ended.

A little more than eight years after Diocletian's persecution began in earnest, Galerius too fell ill. His disease was painful, and he appears to have decided that the god of the Christians might be punishing him. In his own name and in those of the two other Augusti then reigning he issued an edict of partial religious toleration:

> Among the other measures that we frame for the use and profit of the state, it had been our own wish formerly that all things should be set to rights in accordance with the ancient laws and public order of the Romans; and to make provision for this, namely, that the Christians also, such as had abandoned the persuasion of their own ancestors, should return to a sound mind; seeing that through some reasoning they had been possessed of such self-will and seized with such folly that, instead of following the institutions of the ancients, which perchance their own forefathers had formerly established, they made for themselves, and were observing, laws merely in accordance with their own disposition and as each one wished, and were assembling various multitudes in divers places: Therefore when a command of ours soon followed to the intent that they should betake themselves to the institutions of the ancients, very many indeed were subjected to peril, while very many were harassed and endured all kinds of death; And since the majority held to the same folly, and we perceived that they were neither paying the worship due to the gods of heaven nor honouring the god of the Christians; having regard to our clemency and the invariable custom by which we are wont to accord pardon to all men, we thought it right in this case also to extend most willingly our indulgence: That Christians may exist again and build the houses in which they used to assemble, always provided that they do nothing contrary to order. In another letter we shall indicate to the judges how they should proceed. Wherefore, in accordance with this our indulgence, they will be bound to beseech their own god for our welfare, and that of the state, and their own; that in every way both the well-being of the state may be secured, and they may be enabled to live free from care in their own homes.[965]

In 311, a few days after this edict was issued, Galerius died. But Maximinus Daza, or Daia, an uneducated kinsman of his, whose soldiers had in 308 proclaimed him an Augustus, soon renewed the persecution, which did not end until the spring of 313.

Behind all the immediate causes of the worst persecution the Christians had yet undergone lay a much more fundamental cause. Within the womb of a decaying pagan civilization, a young and vital human community was growing fast. The relation of this community to the civilization of which it was part posed difficult problems for both Empire and Church. The Church's founder had taught that his followers must be both in the world and not of it: those who governed the Church construed this command to mean that they were first and foremost citizens of a City of God, or Kingdom of Heaven, but that this citizenship carried with it a subordinate duty to be good citizens of the temporal state; and in the case of nearly all Christians the temporal state was the Roman Empire. In the concurrent jurisdiction that resulted, there would be conflicts, and in case of conflict the Christian was obligated, of course, to obey God's law rather than Caesar's. His loyalty to Caesar was therefore from the point of view of the Imperial administration conditional. By what must have then seemed a paradox, within this limit the Christian was committed to love not only other Christians but all other men, including those who persecuted him with the greatest violence, and to obey his ruler. To the extent that he obeyed, he made a better citizen, always with the one reservation, than the vast majority of his pagan neighbors. His support of government was active where theirs was often apathetic at best, and at worst an evasion of civic responsibilities. Diocletian valued diligent, honest, intelligent service, and he knew that the Christians made good citizens. As one of their apologists had written for pagan readers:

> So I have a right to say, Caesar is more ours than yours, appointed as he is by our God. He is mine; and so I do more for his safety . . . [966]

Yet the Christian could not worship the gods of the Empire, gods in whom the pagan, or at least the uneducated pagan, still believed, gods toward whom the educated and skeptical pagan displayed a decent reverence when the state required it. A writer who described himself as having been a disciple of the apostles and a teacher of the Gentiles and who described the Christians as willingly sharing the burdens of society, admitted that the Christians

> dwell in their own countries, but simply as sojourners. As citizens they share in all things with others, and yet endure all things as if foreigners. Every foreign land is to them as their native country, and every land of their birth as a land of strangers.[967]

This formula could scarcely satisfy a patriotic pagan, or even a pagan equally willing to sacrifice to society's gods and to evade his more mun-

dane civic duties. Still another Christian writer had spoken in language
Marcus Aurelius might at least in part have used, suggesting that man is
not only a political or social animal, and ultimately a citizen in a polis
which includes all mankind, but that to be a good citizen of the world he
must know God:

> Nor can you well perform your social duty unless you know that com-
> munity of the world which is common to all, especially since in this
> respect we differ from the wild beasts, that while they are prone and
> tending to the earth, and are born to look upon nothing but their food,
> we, whose countenance is erect, whose look is turned towards heaven, as
> is our converse and reason, whereby we recognise, feel, and imitate God,
> have neither right nor reason to be ignorant of the celestial glory which
> forms itself into our eyes and senses.[968]

The Hebrew myth of the garden of Eden before man's separation from
God found an analogue in the Hellenistic tradition. For Homer reported,
as did Hesiod, how the gods had once walked and talked with men long
before Catullus' lament that never again did gods "return to earth or
walk with men in the bright sun of noon." From Augustus to Diocletian
many Emperors had built or restored temples or had admitted new Oriental gods into the divine pantheon in an effort to bring the gods back to
earth or at a minimum to persuade them to protect the power of Rome
and permit it to bring men peace and prosperity.

In the second century a professional philosopher named Justin, born in
the Palestinian city of Nablus was converted to Christianity and taught
Christian theology in Rome. There, at some time between 163 and 167,
he was denounced as a Christian by a jealous fellow lecturer who was a
Cynic philosopher. He was tried before the City Prefect, Junius Rusticus,
who as tutor had turned Marcus Aurelius from rhetoric to Stoic philosophy. Justin declined to sacrifice to the pagan gods and was condemned,
flogged, and executed. But though he was an ardent enough believer to die
for his faith and though he thought that many pagan doctrines had been
inspired by demons, he could also recognize religious insight in pre-
Christian Greece and could therefore say that "Christ . . . was partially
known even by Socrates."[969] For "Whatever things were rightly said
among all men, are the property of us Christians."[970] Justin Martyr
suspected that Plato had known the Hebrew scriptures since he "manifestly held the correct opinion concerning the really existing God."[971]
Justin sought to show how the Logos of Greek philosophers, the Word,

was made manifest in Christ; he sought to build a bridge from the philosophic tradition of Hellenistic culture to the Oriental religion he had
embraced. Of baptism he wrote that

> this washing is called illumination, because they who learn these things
> are illuminated in their understandings.[972]

But he was certain that the eternal life which this illumination promised
remained more important to him than the philosophic understanding it
made possible:

> The Word exercises an influence which does not make poets: it does not
> equip philosophers nor skilled orators, but by its instruction it makes
> mortals immortal, mortals gods . . . [973]

Justin died in the belief that his martyrdom would make him quite as
immortal as any Hellenistic god had ever been assumed to be; that is, that
his death would not be a lasting death; that he would rise again, not just to
life but to life eternal.

Soon after Justin, as the terrible third century approached, another
Christian convert, a bishop of Alexandria named Clement, appealed to
Hellenistic man's growing fear that his dialogue with the divine was
broken and could not be restored. Clement assured him that not the gods
he had once believed in but the one true and invisible God so loved the
world that in the reign of Rome's first Emperor he had sent his only Son
to be born of a woman and to walk with men in the bright sun of Palestine, a divine man among other men, talking with them and teaching
them how to re-enter a long-lost polis, the polis of God and man:

> There was an innate original communion between men and heaven,
> obscured through ignorance, but which now at length has leapt forth
> instantaneously from the darkness, and shines resplendent.[974]

> Thou art a man, if we look to that which is most common to thee and
> others—seek Him who created thee; thou art a son, if we look to that
> which is thy peculiar prerogative—acknowledge thy Father.

> . . . So, placing our finger on what is man's peculiar and distinguishing
> characteristic above other creatures, we invite him—born, as he is, for
> the contemplation of heaven, and being, as he is, a truly heavenly plant
> —to the knowledge of God . . . [975]

Since Clement himself had undergone the wrench of conversion from
Hellenism to the Christian vision of God's unique intervention in human

466

history, he was fitted in the light of that conversion to urge others to make the same leap of faith:

> Let us then avoid custom as we would a dangerous headland, or the threatening Charybdis, or the mythic sirens. It chokes man, turns him away from life: custom is a snare, a gulf, a pit . . .[976]

But Clement was a gentle man, a writer of great charm, and far too good a teacher and dialectician to scorn the religious insights which the civilization that produced him had received in the days when it was more nearly, in Seneca's words, fresh from the gods. Like that other Alexandrian, the Jewish Philo, who had tried to show how much Hellenic religious insight shared with Judaism, Clement sought not to destroy Hellenism but to consecrate it and build upon it. For Clement, Jewish law and Greek philosophy were alike part of God's revelation, premonitions of the greater revelation by Jesus Christ. He quoted his contemporary Numenius, an intellectual forerunner of Plotinus, who had written: "For what is Plato, but Moses speaking in Attic Greek?"[977]

For several years Clement directed in Alexandria a school for converts to Christianity, but in 202 he fled the persecution that occurred under the Emperor Septimius Severus and was succeeded by one of his pupils, Origines. Origen was only about eighteen or nineteen when he became the school's official head. Himself of Christian background, he felt the need of understanding pagan philosophy and therefore studied under Ammonius Saccas, who later taught Plotinus. Origen wrote voluminously and brilliantly, of course in Greek. He was ordained a priest but, his relations with his bishop becoming strained, he was relieved of his priestly duties and withdrew to Palestine. During the persecution of 250–51, under the Emperor Decius, he was arrested and repeatedly tortured, but he refused to deny his faith. However, the ordeal appears to have broken his health, and four or five years later he died at the age of sixty-nine.

A very different Christian apologist, an elder contemporary of Origen's, was Quintus Tertullianus. Though he was born in the province of Africa and therefore normally wrote in Latin rather than Greek, Tertullian published books in both tongues. His parents were pagans; his training was rhetorical and legal, not philosophic. His talent, as might be expected from a man of the Latin West, was not speculative. Once he was converted to Christianity, he set out to persuade others. His most famous work, the *Apology*, was published in 197; it was addressed to those in

political power and arraigned their persecutions of the Christians. In praising Christ he had at his disposal the same sort of rhetorical training as had
the panegyrists who praised the Emperors but he had and used one enormous advantage over these rhetoricians. The striking difference between
a decaying Cosmopolis that looked sadly backward and a smaller but
more vigorous polis that looked joyously forward gave the rhetoric of
Tertullian a genuine function. Yet though the Christians, especially in
Tertullian's Latin West, were but a modest fraction of the Empire's population, like a lawyer at the bar he knew how to put his client's best foot
foremost:

> Men proclaim aloud that the state is beset with us; in countryside, in
> villages, in islands, Christians; every sex, age, condition, yes! and rank
> going over to this name.[978]

And again:

> We are but of yesterday, and we have filled everything you have—cities,
> islands, forts, towns, exchanges, yes! and camps, tribes, decuries, palace,
> senate, forum. All we have left to you is the temples![979]

As for Rome's ancient claim to be eternal, Tertullian knew that cities die
just like men and that what endures is not of this world but is only, for a
brief time, in it:

> Look to it then, lest it prove that He dispenses the kingdoms, Whose is
> the world that is reigned over and the man who reigns; lest it be He that
> has ordained the progression of empires each at its time in the world's
> story, He who was ere time was, who made the world's story of all the
> times; lest it be He who extols the cities or brings them low, He under
> whom mankind was once without cities at all.[980]

As for Rome's frequent if merely rhetorical claim to rule the world, he
invited the official imagination to picture what it would mean if the secession of the Christian polis had become physical as well as spiritual:

> For if so vast a mass of people as we had broken away from you and
> removed to some recess of the world apart, the mere loss of so many
> citizens of whatever sort would have brought a blush to your rule—yes,
> that it would, and punished you, too, by sheer desertion! Beyond doubt,
> you would have shuddered at your solitude, at the silence in the world,
> the stupor as it were of a dead globe. You would have had to look about
> for people to rule. You would have had more enemies left than citizens.

For, as things are, you have fewer enemies because of the multitude of Christians, when nearly all the citizens you have in nearly all the cities are Christian. But you have preferred to call us enemies of the human race rather than of human error.[981]

Having played on Hellenistic man's sense of alienation from the community of gods and men, Tertullian tried to describe the mysterious beauty of the one true God:

> What we worship is the One God; who fashioned this whole fabric with all its equipment of elements, bodies, spirits; who by the word wherewith He commanded, by the reason wherewith He ordered it, by the might wherewith He could do it, fashioned it out of nothing, to the glory of His majesty. Hence the Greeks also have given to the universe the name *cosmos*, "order." He is invisible, though He is seen; incomprehensible, though by grace revealed; beyond our conceiving, though conceived by human senses. So true is He and so great. But what in the ordinary sense can be seen, comprehended, conceived, is less than the eyes that grasp it, the hands that soil it, the senses that discover it. The infinite is known only to itself. Because this is so, it allows us to conceive of God—though He is beyond our conceiving. The power of His greatness makes Him known to men, and unknown.[982]

And later in his work Tertullian wrote of the act by which the one inconceivable and unknown God had most dramatically made himself both known and lovable to all men:

> We, too, to that Word, Reason and Power (by which we said God devised all things) would ascribe Spirit as its proper nature; and in Spirit, giving utterance, we should find Word; with Spirit, ordering and disposing all things, Reason; and over Spirit, achieving all things, Power. This, we have been taught, proceeds from God, begotten in this proceeding from God, and therefore called "Son of God" and "God" because of unity of nature. For God too is spirit. When a ray is projected from the sun, it is a portion of the whole; but the sun will be in the ray, because it is the sun's ray, nor is it a division of nature, but an extension. Spirit from Spirit, God from God—as light is lit from light. The source of the substance remains whole and undiminished even if you borrow many offshoots of its quality from it. Thus what has proceeded from God, is God and God's Son, and both are one. Thus Spirit from Spirit, God from God—it makes in mode a double number, in order not in condition (*status*), not departing from the source but proceeding from it. This ray of god, as was ever foretold in time past, entered into a certain

virgin, and, in her womb fashioned into flesh, is born, man mingled with God. The flesh informed by the spirit is nourished, grows to manhood, speaks, teaches, acts—and is Christ.[983]

In the world, but not of it: this hard command by Christ led the Christian between the Scylla of avoiding his pagan neighbor, for whom he was expected to be willing to give his very life, and the Charybdis of being swallowed again by the whale men called the Roman Empire: of worshiping its false gods, including its god-Emperor; of worshiping money and force and pomp and power; of participating in its ruthless exploitation of the poor and weak, its flattery of the rich and strong, its bribery and usury, its gluttony and drunkenness, its perverted sexuality, and the sadism of gladiatorial combat and of wild beasts tearing condemned persons in the arena to make a Roman holiday.

Christians condemned gladiatorial combats on two counts. In the first place, these combats, since they had grown out of Etruscan funeral games, were rooted in the worship of pagan gods. Tertullian pointed out that

> in that most religious of all cities, the city of the pious race of Aeneas, is a certain Jupiter, whom they drench with human blood at his own games. . . .
>
> To-day and here, when men are dedicated to Bellona, the thigh is cut, the blood is caught in a little shield, and given them to consume—as a sign. Again, those who, when a show is given in the arena, with greedy thirst have caught the fresh blood of the guilty slain, as it pours fresh from their throats, and carry it off as a cure for their epilepsy—what of them? Again, those who dine on the flesh of wild animals from the arena, keen on the meat of boar or stag? That boar in his battle has wiped the blood off him whose blood he drew; that stag has wallowed in the blood of a gladiator. The bellies of the very bears are sought, full of raw and undigested human flesh. Man's flesh goes belching, fattened on man's flesh. You who eat these things, how far are you from those Christian banquets?
>
> Let your error blush before the Christians, for we do not include even animals' blood in our natural diet.[984]

In the second place, gladiatorial combats were a sort of legal lynching, a fact that led the Christian in Minucius Felix's dialogue *Octavius* to say to his pagan friend that "in the arena you clamour for the bloodshed for which upon the stage you weep."[985] It was this fact of participating in murder that made Lactantius repeat a century later Tertullian's attack.

470

For, like Tertullian, Lactantius held that the Christian ought not to participate in even the legal killing of other human beings, as when condemned
men fought as gladiators or when men or women or children were devoured by wild beasts in the arena:

> I ask now whether they can be just and pious men, who, when they
> see men placed under the stroke of death, and entreating mercy, not only
> suffer them to be put to death, but also demand it, and give cruel and
> inhuman votes for their death, not being satiated with wounds nor
> contented with bloodshed. Moreover, they order them, even though
> wounded and prostrate, to be attacked again, and their carcases to be
> wasted with blows, that no one may delude them by a pretended death.
> They are even angry with the combatants, unless one of the two is
> quickly slain; and as though they thirsted for human blood, they hate
> delays. They demand that other and fresh combatants should be given to
> them, that they may satisfy their eyes as soon as possible. Being imbued
> with this practice, they have lost their humanity. Therefore they do not
> spare even the innocent, but practise upon all that which they have
> learned in the slaughter of the wicked. It is not therefore befitting that
> those who strive to keep to the path of justice should be companions and
> sharers in this public homicide.[986]

Although such Christians as Tertullian and Lactantius condemned attendance at gladiatorial combats as taking part in ritual murder, pagans continued to charge the Christians with meeting at night for the precise purpose of committing ritual murder. In Minucius Felix's dialogue the pagan
repeats that charge:

> Is it not then deplorable that a gang—excuse my vehemence in using
> strong language for the cause I advocate—a gang, I say, of discredited
> and proscribed desperadoes band themselves against the gods? Fellows
> who gather together illiterates from the dregs of the populace and credu-
> lous women with the instability natural to their sex, and so organize a
> rabble of profane conspirators, leagued together by meetings at night and
> ritual fast and unnatural repasts . . . a secret tribe that shuns the light,
> silent in the open, but talkative in hid corners . . . [987]

Despite Justin's and Clement's awareness of the Hellenic contribution
to Christianity, the great literature of Hellas presented the educated Christian with problems. Like Hellenic sculpture and painting, it of course
teemed with false gods, though Christians were not alone in rejecting the
gods as pictured by the poets: Socrates had rejected them four centuries

before Christ did and Plotinus rejected them two centuries after Christ was crucified. Yet the very textbooks that schoolboys read [988] related the somewhat sensational amours of Zeus. It was in this world of pagan cultural debris that the Christian was ordered to follow Christ. It is no wonder that by the third century some Christians fled from Greek cities to the desert, as Lot had fled from Sodom, or that others compromised with paganism. For those who stayed, the old expectation of Christ's imminent return faded and along with it the voluntary communism practiced by the Christian Ecclesia in its infancy. The Ecclesia still gave to the poor, of course, but it was organizing itself now for a period of unknown length; it was fully entering history. The faithful might make considerable gifts to their local church, legally incorporated under Roman law as a funeral society. Some gifts of this sort still went to the poor, but some went to providing a permanent place of worship, a dwelling for God, worthy of his power as well as of his love. Handsome basilicas were therefore erected, worthy rivals of the Greek temples which housed Zeus. The Christian Ecclesia was acquiring economic power in place of its early Christ-like poverty. By the third century, Cyprian, Bishop of Carthage, was claiming that many bishops were involved personally in the world of business: they managed property, practiced usury, legally evicted tenants. The Bishop of Antioch held a high post in public finance. Late in the third century a Christian priest in Antioch managed the government factory that made purple dye. Some Christians served as actors, as gladiators, as soldiers, and some served even in pagan priesthoods. The government made tempting accommodations: a Christian might serve as high priest at the shrine of Rome and Augustus, yet be excused from offering sacrifices to these official deities. Clearly, such cases involved an accommodation that was mutual. The Christian polis was partially assimilating itself to the civilization from which it had seceded. Having bravely accepted its responsibility to be in the world, in increasing degree it found itself also of the world, a state that Christ had forbidden it to accept.

Throughout the history of the Roman Empire, from the days of the Emperor Tiberius and his procurator, Pontius Pilate, to the days of the Great Persecution, which began under Diocletian, the dilemma of the Christian Ecclesia continued. The Christian apologists sought to love their pagan neighbors while denying their gods, to adapt to Christ's service whatever in their civilization could be reinterpreted and consecrated while rejecting whatever could not be adapted. Not adaptable, according to

472

Clement of Alexandria, were the pagan gods whom even pagan literature mocked, such as the doctor-god, Asclepius, "greedy of gold."[989] Tertullian, by drawing on the titles of sophisticated comedies, in effect added to the list: *Anubis the Adulterer, The Gentleman Moon, Diana Lashed* and *Three Hungry Herculeses,* along with *The Will of the Late Jove, deceased.*[990] He ironically congratulated pagans on fearing the Emperor more than they feared Jove.[991] Minucius Felix asserted that the great pagan philosophers, such as Plato, rejected these imaginary gods in favor of one God,[992] and scoffed at one of the Romans' most ancient and cherished convictions: that

> their strength lay not so much in valour as in religion and piety. . . .
>
> All that the Romans hold, occupy and possess is the spoil of outrage; their temples are all of loot, drawn from the ruin of cities, the plunder of gods and the slaughter of priests.
>
> It is an insult and a mockery to serve vanquished religions, first to enslave and then worship the vanquished. To adore what you have seized by force is to hallow sacrilege, not deities. Each Roman triumph has meant a new impiety, and all trophies over nations new spoliations of the gods. The Romans then have grown great not by religion, but by unpunished sacrilege; for in their actual wars they could not have had the assistance of the gods against whom they took up arms. A triumph over trampled gods is the preliminary to their worship; yet what can such gods do for Romans, when they could not help their own votaries against the arms of Rome? . . .
>
> And after all, under God's dispensation, before Romans existed, Assyrians, Medes, Persians, Greeks too and Egyptians ruled great empires, although they had no Pontiffs, no Arval Brothers, no Salii Vestals or Augurs, no cooped chickens to rule the destinies of state by their appetite or distaste for food.[993]

Lactantius wrote, mostly after Diocletian's abdication, a defense of Christian doctrine. In this defense an apocalyptic passage predicted that

> the Roman name, by which the world is now ruled, will be taken away from the earth, and the government return to Asia; and the East will again bear rule, and the West be reduced to servitude. Nor ought it to appear wonderful to any one, if a kingdom founded with such vastness, and so long increased by so many and such men, and in short strengthened by such great resources, shall nevertheless at some time fall. There is nothing prepared by human strength which cannot equally be

473

destroyed by human strength, since the works of mortals are mortal. Thus also other kingdoms in former times, though they had long flourished, were nevertheless destroyed. For it is related that the Egyptians, and Persians, and Greeks, and Assyrians had the government of the world; and after the destruction of them all, the chief power came to the Romans also. And inasmuch as they excel all other kingdoms in magnitude, with so much greater an overthrow will they fall, because those buildings which are higher than others have more weight for a downfall.[994]

So much for Eternal Rome, said to have been founded by the piety of Aeneas and refounded by the piety of Augustus, although in fact it had been founded by the *vis*, the strength, or force, of the She-Wolf, and would therefore be overthrown by force when its hour should come. Even while Lactantius wrote, Cosmopolis was struggling by hideous tortures and executions to force the citizens of the Christian polis to give at least nominal adherence to the gods of Rome. But Cosmopolis, Lactantius warned, was doomed like every earlier human polis to vanish. Only the Kingdom of Heaven was truly eternal, and of that Kingdom the one province visible to pagan Rome was the persecuted Christian Ecclesia. Christ himself had diagnosed the illness of the world about him as a blindness and a deafness:

> And if I talk to them in parables, it is because, though they have eyes, they cannot see, and though they have ears, they cannot hear or understand. Indeed, in them the prophecy of Isaias is fulfilled, You will listen and listen, but for you there is no understanding; you will watch and watch, but for you there is no perceiving.[995]

Centuries before Christ, the Stoics' hero, Socrates of Athens, watching his polis learn war and violence and forget attentive inquiry, had surpassed all comers in his power to listen closely, lovingly, and understandingly. Centuries after Socrates, during the reign of the Emperor Trajan, Ignatius, Bishop of Antioch, had been arrested for his faith and had been sent under guard to Rome to be devoured by wild beasts. He was able to visit several local churches on his route, including the church at Ephesus. When he reached Smyrna, he wrote a letter to the Ephesians, in which he alluded to this problem of listening and spoke of the incarnation of the Son of God as a mysterious *krauge*, a Greek word that means a crying, screaming, shrieking, or shouting. But this particular *krauge* could be heard only by those who listened in quietude of spirit:

474

And the virginity of Mary, and her giving birth, were hidden from the Prince of this world,[996] as was also the death of the Lord. Three mysteries of a cry which were wrought in the stillness of God. . . . Hence all things were disturbed, because the abolition of death was being planned.[997]

Then Ignatius left Smyrna and proceeded joyfully toward Rome and the wild beasts.

During the first two centuries Christian opinion seems to have held that a man who professed Christ could not enlist in the army. Since, during those centuries, the Emperors rarely exercised their authority to conscript but counted on money to secure the forces needed, the Christians had only to refrain from joining a profession that was often lucrative. They thereby avoided shedding blood in battle. If a convert was already a soldier, he was advised to refrain from bloodshed as far as possible or, if he could do so, to leave military service. Neither Origen nor Tertullian preached against military service by non-Christians. On the contrary, Christian thinkers recognized that the Pax Romana facilitated the spread of Christianity. About A.D. 200 Tertullian asked whether a Christian had the moral right to enlist in the army and whether a pagan soldier might join the Christian Church but remain a soldier:

> But now this very matter is under question, whether a believer may turn to military service, and whether the military may be admitted to the faith, at least the common or inferior soldier, who is not under the necessity of making sacrifices or capital judgments. . . . But how shall he make war, how even in peace shall he serve as a soldier without the sword, which the Lord has taken away? For . . . the Lord in disarming Peter ungirded every soldier. No dress is lawful among us which is appropriate to an unlawful act.[998]

In another work, written probably a few years later, Tertullian was even less tentative. The converted soldier must refuse to serve, even if refusal should mean martyrdom.

> Will it be lawful to occupy himself with the sword, when our Lord declares that he who uses the sword shall perish by the sword? Shall the son of peace engage in combat when he may not even engage in litigation? And shall he who is not the avenger of his own injuries administer chains and imprisonment and tortures and executions? . . . Clearly the case is otherwise for those whose faith comes after they are in military

service, as it was for those whom John admitted to baptism and those most believing centurions whom Christ approves and whom Peter catechizes; nevertheless, once the faith has been embraced and confirmed, either the service must be instantly abandoned, as it has been by many, or all sorts of excuses must be used that nothing be done to offend God which is also forbidden outside the service, or, finally, that suffering must be endured for God's sake which the faith of the civilian has accepted. For military service will not promise impunity of sins or immunity of martyrdom. Nowhere is a Christian any other thing.[999]

It was positions like this that had led the pagan Celsus, when Marcus Aurelius was desperately trying to defend the Danubian frontier, to attack the Christians for placing loyalty to their God above their loyalty to the Emperor, himself delegated to carry out the will of Jove on earth:

For if all were to do the same as you, there would be nothing to prevent his being left in utter solitude and desertion, and the affairs of the earth would fall into the hands of the wildest and most lawless barbarians; and then there would no longer remain among men any of the glory of your religion or of the true wisdom.[1000]

But Origen replied that

if all the Romans, according to the supposition of Celsus, embrace the Christian faith, they will, when they pray, overcome their enemies; or rather, they will not war at all, being guarded by that divine power which promised to save five entire cities for the sake of fifty just persons.[1001]

Origen was as sure as Tertullian that the Christian was committed not to bear arms:

In the next place, Celsus urges us "to help the king with all our might, and to labour with him in the maintenance of justice, to fight for him; and if he requires it, to fight under him, or lead an army along with him." To this our answer is, that we do, when occasion requires, give help to kings, and that, so to say, a divine help, "putting on the whole armour of God." And this we do in obedience to the injunction of the apostle, "I exhort, therefore, that first of all, supplications, prayers, intercessions, and giving of thanks, be made for all men; for kings, and for all that are in authority"; and the more any one excels in piety, the more effective help does he render to kings, even more than is given by soldiers, who go forth to fight and slay as many of the enemy as they can. . . . And we do take our part in public affairs, when along with righteous

476

prayers we join self-denying exercises and meditations, which teach us to despise pleasures, and not to be led away by them. And none fight better for the king than we do. We do not indeed fight under him, although he require it; but we fight on his behalf, forming a special army—an army of piety—by offering our prayers to God.[1002]

The passage of Lactantius in which he denounced gladiatorial combats also denounced both military service and accusations in court that could lead to the execution of the accused:

For when God forbids us to kill, He not only prohibits us from open violence, which is not even allowed by the public laws, but He warns us against the commission of those things which are esteemed lawful among men. Thus it will be neither lawful for a just man to engage in warfare, since his warfare is justice itself, nor to accuse any one of a capital charge, because it makes no difference whether you put a man to death by word, or rather by the sword, since it is the act of putting to death itself which is prohibited. Therefore, with regard to this precept of God, there ought to be no exception at all; but that it is always unlawful to put to death a man, whom God willed to be a sacred animal.[1003]

It is of course true that the Roman Empire normally practiced religious toleration and was even more willing than the Republic to absorb strange gods into the Graeco-Roman pantheon, while formal sacrifice to the god-Emperor was retained for social cement. But the exclusive monotheism of both Jew and Christian confronted official tolerance with what looked like intolerance. The refusal of both Jew and Christian to participate in countless pagan festivities, half religious, half patriotic, still subjected both Church and Synagogue to the charge that they hated the human race. That an increasing number of subjects in a beleaguered empire should refuse to defend it with the sword on the grounds that men were sacred animals looked like both madness and treason. If, on the whole, the Imperial administration was inclined to be lenient with both of these religious minorities, pagan neighbors were less so. This difference had been reflected in the instructions which Pliny the Younger, Governor of Bithynia, had received from the Emperor Trajan; in Trajan's remark about the spirit of the times; and in his orders not to hunt out Christians, not to hear anonymous informers, and even when confronted with an accused Christian, to let him choose between making the required sacrifice and facing punishment. The solution reflected the solution of Pontius Pilate: look the other way normally, but yield, when necessary, to popular clamor or local pressure. How many Jews and Christians lost their lives under this cautious policy of law and order is simply not known. Hadrian continued Trajan's tolerant policy toward Christians, although he of course put down the Jewish war for an independent Palestine with great severity. From the time of that event onward, the Jews presented few problems; it was the growing Christian community that provided the challenge. Justin Martyr in his *Apology* tried to make it clear to Hadrian's successor, Antoninus Pius, that the Christian polis presented no political threat to an Emperor:

> And when you hear that we look for a kingdom, you suppose, without making any inquiry, that we speak of a human kingdom; whereas we speak of that which is with God, as appears also from the confession of their faith made by those who are charged with being Christians, though they know that death is the punishment awarded to him who so confesses. For if we looked for a human kingdom, we should also deny our Christ, that we might not be slain . . .[1004]

When the Common Assembly of Asia reacted to destructive earthquakes by ascribing them to Christian impiety toward the gods, and when the Assembly appealed in that vein to Antoninus, the Emperor replied:

> I should have thought that the gods themselves would see to it that such offenders should not escape. For if they had the power, they themselves would much rather punish those who refuse to worship them; but it is you who bring trouble on these persons, and accuse as the opinion of atheists that which they hold, and lay to their charge certain other things which we are unable to prove. But it would be advantageous to them that they should be thought to die for that of which they are accused, and they conquer you by being lavish of their lives rather than yield that obedience which you require of them. And regarding the earthquakes which have already happened and are now occurring, it is not seemly that you remind us of them, losing heart whenever they occur, and thus set your conduct in contrast with that of these men; for they have much greater confidence towards God than you yourselves have. And you, indeed, seem at such times to ignore the gods, and you neglect the temples, and make no recognition of the worship of God. And hence you are jealous of those who do serve Him, and persecute them to the death.[1005]

More earthquakes in the same Province of Asia, where the Christian churches had gone on multiplying, brought petitions to the Emperor, now Marcus Aurelius, but this time from Christians who were being persecuted. And Marcus, though he was capable of sanctioning the martyrdoms at Lyons in 177, was not impressed by the piety of these pagans who wished to appease the gods by persecuting Christians. He therefore wrote to the Common Assembly of Asia that

> I for my part indeed know that the gods also are careful that such persons should not escape detection. For theirs it is, much rather than yours, to punish such as will not worship them. Whom if ye bring into trouble, accusing them as atheists, ye will but confirm in the opinion which they hold. For when accused it were preferable in their eyes to appear to die for their own god rather than to live. Wherefore also they come off victorious when they give up their own lives rather than obey your behests. But as to the earthquakes which have taken, and are still taking, place, it is not improper to admonish you who lose heart whensoever they occur, and compare our condition with theirs. They indeed become the more confident towards their god; but ye during all the time (in which ye are seemingly ignorant) neglect both the other gods and the worship of the Immortal. And the Christians, because they worship Him, ye harass and persecute unto death. Now, with regard to such persons, many also of the provincial governors wrote in times past to our divine father too; to whom also he sent a rescript that they should in no wise annoy such persons, unless they were mainfestly making some attempt upon the government of the Romans. And to me also many have given information concerning such persons; to whom also I sent a rescript in agreement with my father's decision. But if anyone persist in bringing to trial any of such persons as such: let him who is accused be acquitted of the charge, even though he be manifestly such; but the accuser shall be liable to be punished.[1006]

Certain other Emperors, notably Septimius Severus at the beginning of the third century, Decius and Valerian in its middle, and of course Diocletian just after its close, persecuted the Christians. Severus went so far as to forbid conversion to Judaism "under heavy penalties and enacted a similar law in regard to the Christians."[1007] Decius organized the first systematic persecution that covered the whole Empire. However, even in the cases of these Emperors it was not usually the central government that initiated persecution. The Christians were subject constantly to local outbreaks, which involved anything from mild harassment, through destruction or confiscation of their property, to imprisonment and excruciating physical torture. Punishment by death, in whatever form, rather than torture aimed at forcing them to deny Christ or at least to sacrifice to the

Empire's gods, may have been relatively rare.[1008] Thus Tertullian wrote the magistrates of the Empire:

> How often, too, without regard to you, does the unfriendly mob on its own account assail us with stones and fire?[1009]

Half a century later, the Bishop of Alexandria wrote to the Bishop of Antioch that

> It was not with the imperial edict [of Decius] that the persecution began amongst us, but it preceded it by a whole year; and that prophet and creator of evils for this city, whoever he was, was beforehand in stirring and inciting the masses of the heathen against us, fanning anew the flame of their native superstition. . . .
>
> First, then, they seized an old man named Metras, and bade him utter blasphemous words; when he refused to obey they belaboured his body with cudgels, stabbed his face and eyes with sharp reeds, and leading him to the suburbs stoned him.
>
> Then they led a woman called Quinta, a believer, to the idol temple, and were for forcing her to worship. But when she turned away and showed her disgust, they bound her by the feet and dragged her through the whole city over the rough pavement, so that she was bruised by the big stones, beating her all the while; and bringing her to the same place they stoned her to death. Then with one accord they all rushed to the houses of the godly, and, falling each upon those whom they recognized as neighbours, they harried, spoiled and plundered them, appropriating the more valuable of their treasures, and scattering and burning in the streets the cheaper articles and such as were made of wood, until they gave the city the appearance of having been captured by enemies. But the brethren gave way and gradually retired, and, like those of whom Paul also testified, they *took joyfully the spoiling of their possessions.* And I know not if there be any—save, it may be, a single one who fell into their hands—who up to the present has denied the Lord. . . .
>
> And, what is more, the edict arrived . . . And of many of the more eminent persons, some came forward immediately through fear, others in public positions were compelled to do so by their business, and others were dragged by those around them. Called by name they approached the impure and unholy sacrifices, some pale and trembling, as if they were not for sacrificing but rather to be themselves the sacrifices and victims to the idols, so that the large crowd that stood around heaped mockery upon them, and it was evident that they were by nature cow-

ards in everything, cowards both to die and to sacrifice. But others ran eagerly towards the altars, affirming by their forwardness that they had not been Christians even formerly . . . Of the rest, some followed one or other of these, others fled; some were captured, and of these some went as far as *bonds and imprisonment*, and certain, when they had been shut up for many days, then forswore themselves even before coming into court, while others, who remained firm for a certain time under tortures, subsequently gave in.

But the firm and blessed pillars of the Lord, being strengthened by Him, and receiving power and stedfastness in due measure according to the mighty faith that was in them, proved themselves admirable martyrs of His kingdom.[1010]

Even though Christians were forbidden to join their pagan neighbors in sacrifices to the Emperor, Tertullian rejected the inference that they were therefore public enemies:

If . . . we are bidden love our enemies, whom have we to hate? Again, if when a man injures us, we are forbidden to retaliate, that the action may not make us alike, whom then can we injure?[1011]

Pagans, wrote Tertullian, lamented the spread of Christianity and considered it an evil. Yet, if it were evil, the Christian would exhibit shame and fear. The contrary, he declared, is the case:

If he is denounced . . . he glories in it; if he is accused, he does not defend himself; when he is questioned, he confesses without any presure; when he is condemned, he renders thanks. What sort of evil is that which has none of the native marks of evil—fear, shame, shuffling, regret, lament? What? is that evil where the criminal is glad, where accusation is the thing he prays for, and punishment is his felicity?[1012]

Tertullian no doubt gave an idealized picture of the Christian. When the Graeco-Roman world experienced during the third century unprecedented disasters such as invasions, rebellions, famine, pestilence, declining population, declining production, appalling inflation, and military tyranny, these disasters, as in the case of the earthquakes in Asia, were frequently ascribed by pagans to the Christian's refusal to reverence the gods who had made Rome great. The result, of course, was the local outbreaks of persecution. Though many Christians denied their faith, Eusebius in his history of the Christian Church would later record with pride such cases of courage as one that occurred in Palestine where, as Bishop of Caesarea, he was well placed to collect information on the Great Persecution under Diocletian. A Christian named Paul was brought to trial and confessed his faith.

> Now after this Paul, a confessor, was brought forward to the conflict: and he also strove bravely. And in that hour he was condemned by the impious judge to be crowned, and receive sentence of decapitation by the sword. And when he was at the place of his departure, where the blessed one was to pass from this life, he requested the executioner who was about to cut off his head to have patience with him for a brief space of time. And when the executioner granted him this desire, with sweet and resonant voice, first of all, he offered up praise and worship and honour and prayer to God who had accounted him worthy of this victory; and then he besought God for the tranquillity and peace of our people, imploring Him to bestow deliverance upon them with all speed; and after this he *prayed for the enemies,* the Jews (for many of them at that time stood around him); and proceeding further in his intercession, he also prayed for the Samaritans, and for those among the nations who were in ignorance—he prayed that they might *come to the knowledge of the truth*; nor did he leave unheeded those who surrounded him: for them also he prayed. Oh, unspeakable guilelessness!—for the judge also who sentenced him to death, and for all rulers in every place did he pray; and not only for them, but also for the executioner who was about to cut off his head. And while he made supplication to God the executioners heard him with their own ears, praying for them and earnestly entreating God that He would not reckon to them that which they did to him; and as he prayed for all men with a voice of yearning he brought the whole multitude of spectators who stood around him to sadness and tears; and then he voluntarily bowed his body and stretched out his neck to be severed by the sword.[1013]

Looking back on this same persecution, which had begun in 302 toward the end of Diocletian's reign, Lactantius saw in the terror and torture an act of God to convert pagan bystanders. And, indeed, the pity that according to Tacitus many people felt for the crucified and flaming bodies of Nero's victims was repeated: many pagans hid Christians from the authorities. Moreover, the spectators who shed tears when Paul prayed God to forgive his executioners and then joyfully accepted death may well have felt more than pity. Such martyrs as Paul gave their pagan neighbors a pledge of faith that preachment could not give. Eusebius, also looking back, knew this about martyrdom, but he believed he saw in the catastrophe of the Christian Ecclesia another dimension of God's providence: the Church was being purged of the pride and sloth and hypocrisy it had too often shown, especially during the prosperous periods between persecutions. It was being punished for the disgraceful theological disputes which rent its clergy and caused them to turn words into weapons against each other. This spirit of violence often afflicted the Church in the third century. It was being assimilated to the Empire and hence to force and fear, away from love and humility. The spirit of violence which infected it was shown in the behavior of some of the faithful toward their persecutors. Thus Procopius, a Christian of Scythopolis, by implication assailed the Tetrarchy in open court and quoted Homer to prove that there should be only one monarch. In Caesarea a Christian named Apphianus rushed to a pagan temple, where the pagan governor was preparing to sacrifice, seized his hand, and then in what Eusebius reports was "a truly gentle manner and with a divinely-given assurance exhorted him to cease from his error."[1014] The governor's military guards assaulted him, imprisoned him, and finally tortured him. Asked who he was, he answered that he was the slave of Christ. All other questions he refused to answer. He was tortured again, refused to answer questions, was imprisoned again, then drowned. But a brother of Apphianus, condemned to the mines for his Christian faith, escaped from the mines, fled to Alexandria, heard an official condemn some Christian virgins to be raped, and understandably was indignant. He thereupon berated the official,

> dealt him blows on the face, threw him to the ground, and as he lay there on his back kept hitting and warning him not to dare to act in a manner contrary to nature towards the servants of God.[1015]

This determined Christian too was tortured, then drowned. The soldiers of Christ were multiplying along with the economic power of the Church and along with those words like weapons which Christian theologians hurled at each other.

The indignation that led some persecuted prisoners to insult or even assault their pagan persecutors was matched by the strain of sarcasm that runs through Tertullian's *Apology* and the indignation many Christians felt against the Jews, a people to whom Christ had especially come, only to be rejected by them. Justin Martyr charged that the Jews of Jerusalem sent chosen men through all the land to tell that the godless heresy of the Christians had sprung up, and to publish those things which all they who knew us not speak against us.[1016]

The Jews, Justin charged in his *First Apology*, addressed to the rulers and people of Rome,

count us foes and enemies; and, like yourselves, they kill and punish us whenever they have the power, as you can well believe. For in the Jewish war which lately raged, Barchochebas, the leader of the revolt of the Jews, gave orders that Christians alone should be led to cruel punishments, unless they would deny Jesus Christ and utter blasphemy.[1017]

But Bar Kokba had been leading a nationalist rebellion against the army of Hadrian. When the members of a small Jewish sect, a sect he would naturally regard as heretical and blasphemous, refused to fight for the national cause, when they also withdrew eastward from the Jews' holy city and abandoned it to destruction and desecration by the Romans, Bar Kokba might well have felt that the Christians of Palestine were not only blasphemous heretics but wartime traitors as well. Bar Kokba needed help so desperately that he had even said to his God, "We pray Thee, do not give assistance to the enemy; us Thou needest not help!"[1018] The Christians could scarcely agree with the gentle Rabbi Akiba, who said of this courageous leader, born of the House of David: "This is the King Messiah."[1019] For the Christians believed that another Jew, also of the House of David, had already been sent as Messiah, had taught men not to take the sword, and had freely given his life both for the Jews and for all other men. Decades before the Christians refused to join the Jewish revolt in Palestine, the many synagogues of the Diaspora presumably knew of the malediction in *Birkath-ha-Minim* against the Christians and had been warned to have no dealings with them. There had been wide Jewish expectancy that the Messianic Age would open about the middle of the first century, but relatively few Jews had ever accepted Christ as the Messiah. By the second century the Christian Church was overwhelmingly Gentile both in membership and in leadership. On the one hand, although the Church still made use of Hebrew scripture, the Apostle Paul's view that the Christian need not observe the whole of Mosaic law had won out. On the other hand, Christians interpreted the Hebrew prophets' predictions of a Messiah as predictions that Jesus Christ, the Son of God, would walk among men, teach them God's will, and give his life upon the cross in

484

order to redeem from sin and permanent death those who believed in him. Indeed, the controversy between Jew and Christian had shifted its focus from Jewish law to the interpretation of these predictions by the prophets.

While Tertullian claimed that the synagogues were "the seed-plot of all the calumny against us," the Jews of the Diaspora might truthfully retort that the Christians had used the synagogues as places to teach a dangerous blasphemy. Origen did indeed report that in his day Jews complained that

> having no altar, no temple, no priest, and on account of this offering no sacrifices, our sins . . . remain in us; and therefore no forgiveness ensues.[1020]

The natural Christian answer was that the Christian Church offered them all these things; but those who complained to Origen might well have been bemoaning the destruction of their Holy of Holies and Hadrian's construction on its site of a temple to the idol called Jupiter. As for Christ's being the mediator between God and man, in the second and third centuries the Jews sought an alternative mediator, an alternative Messiah. Meanwhile, the bad blood between these two religious minorities continued. It affected the last words of Pionius of Smyrna. He addressed these words to spectators in the city's forum, who had witnessed his refusal to make the sacrifice that the Emperor Decius had ordered all his subjects to make:

> You who rejoice in the beauty of the buildings of Smyrna, and delight in its adornment, you who are proud of your poet Homer, and you Jews also, if any of you are present, listen to these few words. For I hear that you laugh at those who have sacrificed, whether they have done it voluntarily, or yielded to compulsion, and in both cases you condemn what is weakness as deliberate infidelity. You should obey rather the words of your teacher and master Homer, who says that it is a sin to insult the dead, and that none should war against the blind or the dead. And you who are Jews should obey the precepts of Moses, who tells you that if the animal of your enemy fall, you should help it and not pass by. And Solomon likewise says that you should not rejoice over the fall of your enemy or the misfortune of others. Wherefore I would rather die and suffer any torment, however awful, than renounce either what I have learnt or what I have taught. I say this to you Jews who dissolve in laughter and mockery at those who voluntarily or involuntarily sacrifice, and who laugh at us also and shout insultingly that we have been given too much licence, I say to you that if we are enemies, we are also men.

Have any suffered loss through us? Have we caused any to be tortured? Whom have we unjustly persecuted? Whom have we harmed in speech? Whom have we cruelly dragged to torture? Such crimes are very different from those of men who have acted in fear of the lions. There is an immense difference between voluntary and involuntary sin. There is this difference between him who is forced, and him who of his own free will does wrong. There it is the will, here it is the occasion which is responsible. And who compelled the Jews to foul themselves with the worship of Belphegor, with heathen rites and sacrifices? Who forced them into fornication with strange women, or into sensual pleasures? At whose compulsion did they make burnt offerings of their own sons, murmur against God, and secretly speak ill of Moses? At whose behest did they forget so many benefits? Who made them ungrateful? Who compelled them to return in heart to Egypt, or, when Moses had ascended the Mount to receive the Law, to say to Aaron: "Make us Gods, and a calf to go before us"; and to commit all their other sins? You pagans, perhaps, they may deceive, but they will never impose upon us.[1021]

Having thus spoken, Pionius was burned to death. His speech was of course a rebuke to both pagans and Jews and perhaps moved his listeners less than the last, loving words of the Palestinian martyr, Paul. But Pionius' speech was at least free of the anger that the Christian community and the Jewish often felt toward each other, and perhaps they were turned into loving words, at least in intention, by his voluntary acceptance of death for the sake of Christ, who had commanded his followers to love even their enemies and persecutors.

As the apostolic period receded in time and as churches sprang up all over the Greek East and to some extent even in the Latin West, it was inevitable that they should seek some common organization. As eyewitnesses to Christ's ministry died off, the churches had of course collected and disseminated accounts of his doings and sayings, along with the doings and sayings of the early apostles. With organization came a more complicated distribution of function, a hierarchy of priesthood, a development of sacraments judged to be implicit in Christ's own words and actions. Appropriate discipline for the clergy was worked out: for example, the authority of the bishops grew; groups of bishops exercised a collegial responsibility; successive Bishops of Rome increasingly exercised, especially in the Latin West, the authority they had always claimed over other bishops. Provincial cities had been accustomed to look to Rome for final political authority; provincial bishops, especially in the Latin provinces, turned to the Bishop of Rome. Political Rome had been wealthy and the Emperors had usually helped other cities of the Empire when they had suffered misfortunes like fire, famine, or earthquake; the Bishop of Rome did the same for his fellow bishops. The Bishop of Rome asked for obedience: he did not always get it, but he frequently did. Before the Roman Republic annexed the Greek East, quarreling Greek states had often turned to Rome for help and her interventions had increased her authority and power. Centuries later Greek bishops or Greek theologians appealed to the Bishop of Rome, and his interventions increased his authority too. But all these historical pressures aside, the power of the bishops of Rome seemed to be sanctioned by the special responsibility that Christ had laid on the Apostle Peter; and was not Peter the first Bishop of Rome? Why should those elected to his office not inherit his special authority?

Rome's great contribution to the Church was its constant effort to secure and maintain unity and order. The Roman bishops were conspicuously less concerned with theological speculation than with settling the sometimes acrimonious disputes these speculations bred. On the other hand, about 190 Bishop Victor tried in vain to persuade the Asian bishops to celebrate Easter on a Sunday rather than on the Jewish Passover. When his Asian colleagues balked, he threatened excommunication; but even some of his Western bishops would not support him, and apparently he desisted. Tertullian was capable of sarcasm about "The *Pontifex Maximus* —that is, the bishop of bishops";[1022] and about three decades later, Cyprian, Bishop of Carthage, defied a threat of excommunication from Rome. At a council in Carthage attended by eighty-seven bishops from what are now Tunisia, Algeria, and Morocco, and presided over by Cyprian, he declared pointedly that each bishop should express his views on the matter under dispute, since

> no one of us setteth himself up as a Bishop of Bishops . . . inasmuch as every Bishop, in the free use of his liberty and power, has the right of forming his own judgment, and can no more be judged by another than he can himself judge another.[1023]

All present voted against Rome's position on the matter. A new Bishop of Rome adopted a more lenient policy; a few weeks later Cyprian was martyred by the Roman government; and fifty-seven years later the Council of Arles adopted the original Roman solution of the problem.

Despite the efforts of the Bishop of Rome to conciliate theological differences and preserve unity, heresies inevitably developed. True, by Tertullian's day a statement of belief very much like what is now called the Apostles' Creed had already been formulated, and during the third century this or similar creeds spread throughout the Christian Church. But the creeds were in some ways as mysterious as were some of Christ's own statements. Indeed, they briefly stated those essential facts that Christ had revealed to his apostles, facts that human reason could not deduce from what man himself already knew. But from these revealed premises, combined with insights that human experience brought, what else followed? It was the work of philosophers and metaphysicians, whose faith had turned them into theologians, either to develop the implications of creed and holy scripture alike or at least to speculate responsibly on such implications. In each century of Christianity speculation gave rise to heresies. Indeed, heresies, no matter how idle or empty they might sound in Rome, or for that matter how idle or dangerous they might sound to simple believers, provided the Church with a dialectical process which took account of man's intellectual powers. Unfortunately, as Socrates had so well understood, the dialectical combat that leads toward greater understanding could often give way to eristic, to the litigious, to violent controversy aimed at winning victory rather than at discovering truth. Thus, like the Empire, the Church fought off assault from without, in her case by pagan critics, only to find herself engaged in theological civil war and rebellion within. When theological dialectic did maintain itself successfully, understanding grew and with it the peace and unity of the Church. Witness, for example, what happened when Dionysius, Bishop of Alexandria, a former pupil of Origen's, learned that the Christians in the district of Arsinoe were understanding the Apocalypse as prophesying a millennium on this earth devoted to bodily indulgence. Instead of hurling anathemas at these Christians, Dionysius went to Arsinoe. In this district, he writes, where

> this doctrine had long been prevalent, so that schisms and defections of whole churches had taken place, I called together the presbyters and teachers of the brethren in the villages (there were present also such of the brethren as wished), and I urged them to hold the examination of the question publicly. And when they brought me this book . . . I sat with them and for three successive days from morn till night attempted to correct what had been written. On that occasion I conceived the greatest admiration for the brethren, their firmness, love of truth, facility in following an argument, and intelligence, as we propounded in order

488

and with forbearance the questions, the difficulties raised and the points of agreement; on the one hand refusing to cling obstinately and at all costs (even though they were manifestly wrong) to opinions once held; and on the other hand not shirking the counter-arguments, but as far as possible attempting to grapple with the questions in hand and master them. Nor, if convinced by reason, were we ashamed to change our opinions and give our assent; but conscientiously and unfeignedly and with hearts laid open to God we accepted whatever was established by the proofs and teachings of the holy Scriptures. And in the end the leader and introducer of this teaching, Coracion . . . in the hearing of all the brethren present, assented, and testified to us that he would no longer adhere to it, nor discourse upon it, nor mention nor teach it, since he had been sufficiently convinced by the contrary arguments.[1024]

In the collision between Diocletian and the Church, Diocletian had possessed the biggest army in Rome's entire history; the Church had possessed none. He had possessed more money, even though, as Eusebius recorded, the Church was no longer poor. Certainly, her increasing property made her more vulnerable than the primitive Church had been. But most citizens of the Empire were born to citizenship, while the citizens of the Christian polis had willed to be citizens. Tertullian had written to the pagans, "We are from among yourselves. Christians are made, not born!"[1025] Pagan soldiers who died for Eternal Rome were not rewarded later by enjoying Rome's eternity. Countless Christians died in the faith that physical death was the threshold to fuller citizenship in a City of God that really was eternal and a citizenship which they themselves would eternally enjoy.

Although the panegyrists of Rome insisted that she ruled the whole world, no informed person imagined that Rome ruled Persia, or India, or China. At best this rhetorical claim reflected the Stoic view that Marcus Aurelius held, the view that mankind by nature comprised one polis, Cosmopolis, the City of Zeus. In Aristotelian terms mankind was potentially one state under one government, while Rome had actualized only a modest portion of such a state. Formally, her Virgilian mission was to bring all nations under law, the law she had already adapted to the needs of many nations. The Imperial government, perhaps by the very nature of sovereignty, faced this obligation to extend law to all mankind, either by the tried Roman method of conquest or by the application of the earlier Hellenic dream of federation. In practice Diocletian was struggling to

maintain the Imperial government against pressure from those unactual-
ized citizens, the barbarians, and against rebellion and civil war. For these
threatened to reduce to its original state of mere potentiality that part of
the City of Zeus which Rome had already actualized.

The Empire's formal relation to the *oikoumene*, the ecumene or inhabited world, was duplicated in the Church. As the Christian participant in
Minucius' dialogue pointed out, men "distinguish nations and tribes: to
God the whole world is a single household."[1026] From the Christians'
point of view all men belonged to God's household; all men were potentially Christian. Christ had assigned Christians the task of drawing all men
everywhere into his Church, of actualizing their citizenship in the Christian polis, a citizenship that was theirs for the claiming. In a sense the
Church was as imperialistic as the Empire. But Christ had designated
the weapons the Christian could use: to love God, to love each other, and
to love all other men, always including the Christians' own enemies. The
weapons they were forbidden to use, or at least to substitute for love and
work, were force and the power of accumulated money. If the Church
should turn to these forbidden substitutes, it would to that extent become
imperialistic in another and more literal sense.

Whereas the citizen of the Empire was forced to pay taxes, originally in
money and then in kind, the Church could not properly exact a tax of any
man. Tertullian pointed out the Church's proper relation to money:

> Even if there is a chest of a sort, it is not made up of money paid in
> entrance-fees, as if religion were a matter of contract. Every man once
> a month brings some modest coin—or whenever he wishes, and only if
> he does wish, and if he can; for nobody is compelled; it is a voluntary
> offering.[1027]

Although the first claim on this money was to meet the needs of the poor
and sick and not to build the handsome basilicas which began to multiply
soon after Tertullian's death, the Christian owed the afflicted not only his
money but his service and if necessary his life. A Christian apologist,
describing the Christians either to Hadrian or to his successor, had written
that

> if there is among them any that is poor and needy, and if they have no
> spare food, they fast two or three days in order to supply to the needy
> their lack of food.[1028]

When plague raged in Alexandria, Bishop Dionysius contrasted the fear-
less love shown by the Christians with the fear of death that demoralized
the non-Christian community:

> The most, at all events, of our brethren in their exceeding love and
> affection for the brotherhood were unsparing of themselves and clave to
> one another, visiting the sick without a thought as to the danger, as-
> siduously ministering to them, tending them in Christ, and so most
> gladly departed this life along with them . . . In this manner the best at
> any rate of our brethren departed this life, certain presbyters and dea-
> cons and some of the laity . . . . So, too, the bodies of the saints they
> would take up in their open hands to their bosom, closing their eyes and
> shutting their mouths, carrying them on their shoulders and laying them
> out; they would cling to them, embrace them, bathe and adorn them
> with their burial clothes, and after a little receive the same services
> themselves . . . . but the conduct of the heathen was the exact opposite.
> Even those who were in the first stages of the disease they thrust away,
> and fled from their dearest. They would even cast them in the roads half-
> dead, and treat the unburied corpses as vile refuse, in their attempts to
> avoid the spreading and contagion of the death-plague . . . [1029]

But it was not only bishops and not only Christians in general who
often testified to the love that bound their Ecclesia together, freed them
from fear of death, and overflowed in loving service to their pagan neighbors. This willingness to give their property, their service, their love, and
their lives to others often enabled the Christians to touch the hearts of
many. The same powerful sense of community and the commitment of
many Christians not to use force against others enabled the Christian
Ecclesia to survive the persecution of Diocletian and his fellow-tetrarchs
and to continue to draw pagans into itself. Despite the indubitable increase of corruption in the Church, despite the apostasy of those who
could not face torture or could face no more of it, and despite the violence
that sometimes marred agument between Christian theologians, enough
spiritual strength remained to defeat the purpose of the persecution. What
Justin claimed before his martyrdom in 165 was still sufficiently true of
enough Christians to attract to the Christian polis a devotion the Empire
could no longer command. What Justin had written in the *Apology*, which
he addressed to Antoninus Pius, remained true of many Christians in
Diocletian's day: that

we who formerly delighted in fornication . . . now embrace chastity alone; we who formerly used magical arts, dedicate ourselves to the good and unbegotten God; we who valued above all things the acquisition of wealth and possessions, now bring what we have into a common stock, and communicate to every one in need; we who hated and destroyed one another, and on account of their different manners would not live with men of a different tribe, now, since the coming of Christ, live familiarly with them, and pray for our enemies, and endeavour to persuade those who hate us unjustly to live conformably to the good precepts of Christ, to the end that they may become partakers with us of the same joyful hope of a reward from God the ruler of all.[1030]

Marcus Aurelius' court physician, Galen, testified from outside the Christian Ecclesia to a fearlessness and a physical self-control that a doctor's eye would tend to perceive. He observed that the Christians'

contempt of death . . . is patent to us every day, and likewise their restraint in cohabitation. For they include not only men but also women who refrain from cohabiting all through their lives; and they also number individuals who, in self-discipline and self-control in matters of food and drink, and in their keen pursuit of justice, have attained a pitch not inferior to that of genuine philosophers.[1031]

And Ignatius, Bishop of Antioch, had spoken of his impending death in the arena as "the pains of birth."[1032]

Some two centuries after the martyrdom of Ignatius, when Diocletian was living in retirement and news kept coming that one civil war after another was tearing apart the Empire he had held together for nineteen years, did the ill, exhausted old soldier wonder if the Roman Empire was at last dying? There was little in his education or experience to suggest to him that a death can also be a birth; or that, while the City of Zeus really was dying, within it another and different civilization was struggling to be born.

When Diocletian in 293 chose Constantius Chlorus to be Caesar of the West and required him to divorce Helena and marry Theodora, daughter of the new Augustus of the West, he had brought to his own court Constantine, Constantius' son by Helena. Constantine, then perhaps twenty years old,[1033] had been born in Nish, in what is now southeastern Yugoslavia. He was hence a product of the half-barbarian cultural fringe, and his language, despite his Eastern origin, was Latin. His education was not elaborate. While his father was reconquering Britain or defending the Rhine frontier or rebuilding ravaged cities in Gaul, the young Constantine was with Diocletian in Egypt or was fighting Persians, or following Diocletian's itinerant court and watching Diocletian's desperate efforts to restore the Empire. Constantine witnessed that fateful sacrifice when the Christians in attendance made the sign of the cross and were charged with causing the omens to fail, and when Diocletian's sudden anger started the Great Persecution. Constantine watched that persecution as it showed signs of failing, and he presumably knew that in Britain and Gaul his own father enforced the edicts against Christianity unwillingly and halfheartedly. In 305 at Nicomedia, he watched Diocletian and Maximian abdicate, ceding their posts to Galerius as Eastern Augustus and to Constantius as Western Augustus. To replace them, two new Caesars had to be found. Galerius had no son, but Constantius had. Constantine was passed over; Severus, a soldier of peasant origin and a friend of Galerius', was chosen as Western Caesar. Galerius' soldier-kinsman, Maximinus Daza, was chosen as Eastern Caesar.

Soon afterward Constantius wrote Galerius that he was ill and asked that his son be sent to him. Galerius played for time: suppose Constantius died and his army proclaimed Constantine not just Caesar but Augustus? Nevertheless, he at last gave permission. Next morning he repented, but it was too late; Constantine had ridden off rapidly during the night. The horsemen who were sent after him discovered at successive posting stations that all the horses had been removed, and the pursuit failed. Constantine found his father at Boulogne, about to leave for Britain's north frontier to fight the Picts. Constantine helped him win victory. But after they withdrew to York, Constantius died, and his army proclaimed the young Constantine Augustus. Britain and Gaul recognized him; Spain refused. He sought recognition from the Eastern Augustus, but Galerius recognized him only, and, at that, grudgingly, as Western Caesar and raised Severus, already Western Caesar, to the rank of Augustus and to the command of the Prefecture of Italy. But in October, 306, the Praetorian Guard at Rome revolted against Severus and proclaimed Maxentius, son of Diocletian's co-Augustus Maximian, as Western Augustus in Severus' place. By the summer of 312 Maxentius was making himself the champion of paganism against the Christians and was destroying statues of Constantine in Rome and other Italian cities. Constantine led an army across the Alps, captured Susa, spared the city from pillage, defeated a

493

contingent of cavalry clad in mail-armor in the Persian manner, captured Turin, accepted the surrender of Milan, routed more cavalry at Brescia, took Verona, won Aquileia and Modena without battle. Constantine, who ever since 307 had claimed the title of Augustus, now marched on Rome.

On October 28, 312, Maxentius ventured beyond the great walls of Rome, crossed the Tiber by the Milvian Bridge, marched northward, and faced the army of Constantine. He observed that the shields of Constantine's men were marked with a mysterious monogram,[1034] a monogram composed of the Greek letters, Chi and Rho, the first two letters of the Greek word for Christ. Though the army opposing Constantine was probably at least double the size of his, he engaged confidently. He forced the enemy back against the Tiber River and routed him. Maxentius lost his life in the Tiber, but his body was recovered and his head was borne on a lance through Rome as the signal that Constantine was Rome's new ruler. The Senate elected Constantine senior Augustus.

Two of Constantine's Christian contemporaries who knew him personally agreed later that his daring victory outside Rome followed a conversion to Christianity, but they disagreed on the assurances of victory that God had given him. Lactantius wrote that shortly before the victory Constantine

> was directed in a dream to cause *the heavenly sign* to be delineated on the shields of his soldiers, and so to proceed to battle.[1035]

Eusebius wrote in his *Life of Constantine* that Constantine knew before he marched south toward Italy that he lacked the manpower to overthrow Maxentius without help from God; that, lacking confidence in the pagan gods, he prayed to the one God, apparently the one the Christians worshiped, to reveal himself and to help him. Then, according to an account Constantine later gave Eusebius on oath, one afternoon, when he was leading his army on some expedition, he saw in the heavens

> lying over the sun the sign of the cross, composed out of the light, and bearing the inscription, CONQUER BY THIS.[1036]

He was, he said, amazed by the miracle, and so was his whole army. Moreover, that night in a dream

> the Christ of God appeared to him with the same sign he had seen in the heavens, and commanded him to procure a standard made in the likeness

494

of that sign, and to use it as a safeguard in all engagements with his enemies.[1037]

Constantine obeyed. He also sought instruction in Christianity and appointed Christian priests as counselors. It was only then, according to Eusebius, that he prepared to conquer the prefecture of his neighbor, Maxentius.[1038]

When Constantine obeyed the Christ of God whom he saw in his dream and when Eusebius in his history accepted the cross in the heavens and also the dream as communications from Christ, both were doing what Homer in his way had done when he believed that the Achaeans and Trojans had fought in order that the will of Zeus might be fulfilled.[1039] They were doing as Homer had done when he recounted that Athena appeared repeatedly to Odysseus. Or as Hesiod did when he reported that the Muses, the daughters of Zeus, had appeared to him and instructed him as he was shepherding his lambs under holy Helicon. It is true that Athena had appeared to Odysseus' son disguised as one of his friends and that when she appeared to Odysseus himself in his swineherd's hut the swineherd had not noticed her. Hesiod admitted that the Muses, who were in the habit of going about at night, were veiled in thick mist; that the thrice ten thousand spirits whom Zeus sent all over the earth as watchers of mortal men were also clothed in mist when on duty. Homer and Hesiod at the birth of Greek culture, like Constantine and Eusebius when Graeco-Roman civilization lay prostrate and dying, believed that divine intervention was one of the causes of human events. All four, therefore, were alert to detect such interventions, alert to those miracles and divine symbols whose meaning mist conceals from the inner eye of most men. Did this alertness mean that Constantine's real mission was, not to revive Graeco-Roman civilization, but to help bring to birth a different culture, with a different religion, a different art, another kind of literature albeit one written in Greek words? The fact is that the violent third century, which produced Plotinus, Eusebius, and Constantine, had so destroyed in the citizens of Cosmopolis the confidence that they could control their fate by human means that they turned either to religion or superstition, either to religion or magic. They became more primitive, more childlike, more hopeful, more trustful. They became men fresher from the gods than the men of Pericles' day and certainly than the men of Plato's generation.

Before Constantine invaded Italy, his coinage had proclaimed allegiance to Mars. Sometimes it was to Hercules, the official patron of whoever was Western Augustus. After his somewhat dubious claim to be a descendant of the Emperor Claudius Gothicus, his coins gave allegiance to the Unconquered Sun, a deity whom both Claudius and Constantine's late father had held in special honor. But political reasons would amply explain the allegiances of Constantine's coins. Indeed, they would explain his father's and his own toleration for the Christians. If the Christians threatened the political and social order of Graeco-Roman civilization, it was less in the Latin West, where the Christian minority was very small, than in the Greek East, where the Christian minority was large and growing. There, persecution continued. Indeed, in 311, shortly after Galerius and Maximian had issued their edict of toleration and Galerius had died, Maximinus Daza, who had been proclaimed Augustus by his troops in 308, renewed the persecution in the Prefecture of the East, and of course his predecessor, Galerius, had persecuted Christians almost up to his death. Maximinus even organized paganism on the model of church organization in his effort to revive faith in the old gods. In the Prefecture of Italy, Maxentius, though a pagan, had refrained from persecution and even restored much confiscated church property. But so long as Christians in the Greek East died for their faith, Constantine could not but appear as a hero to the Christian minority at Rome. Whether or not, as Eusebius later claimed, Maxentius really had violated the wives of important men, killed Senators in order to seize their estates, and oppressed the populace, it is certain that his reign was not a popular one. A rebellion in Africa had recently cut off the supply of African wheat, and the Roman populace had suffered from famine. The Senate presented a somewhat different problem from that of feeding the populace. As a panegyrist pointed out in 321, Rome had become "the leader of all peoples and the queen of the world" when she had admitted to the Senate "the leading citizens of every province . . . from the élite of the whole world."[1040] These leading citizens were almost all pagans, but they were conservatives in many matters besides religion and Maxentius' reign can have done little to endear him to them. Constantine had therefore been able to approach Rome as the deliverer of pagan and Christian alike. And he could hold a successful triumph as ruler of both Latin-speaking prefectures. As deliverer of the Christians he erected in Rome a statue of himself holding a long spear in the form of a cross, but the pagans could hardly be much offended by the inscription:

BY VIRTUE OF THIS SALUTARY SIGN, WHICH IS THE TRUE SYMBOL OF VALOUR, I HAVE PRESERVED AND LIBERATED YOUR CITY FROM THE YOKE OF TYRANNY. I HAVE ALSO SET AT LIBERTY THE ROMAN SENATE AND PEOPLE, AND RESTORED THEM TO THEIR ANCIENT GREATNESS AND SPLENDOUR.[1041]

The Senate, three years later, built a triumphal arch in Constantine's honor, but the inscription placed on the arch discreetly skirted any religious difference between Senators and Emperor:

> To the Emperor Caesar Flavius Constantine, the Greatest, the Pious, the Fortunate, Augustus, because by the prompting of the Divinity and the greatness of his soul, he with his forces avenged the commonwealth with just arms both on the tyrant and on all his faction, the Senate and people of Rome dedicated this triumphal arch.[1042]

Constantine answered discretion with discretion. He accepted the post of Pontifex Maximus, official Chief Priest of the pagan religion, although he undoubtedly regarded himself by now as a Christian. Moreover, for eight years after his capture of Rome his issues of new coin continued to honor Hercules, or Mars, or Jupiter, and for three more years after that an issue of coin proclaimed the Unconquered Sun.

Constantine's possible identification of Christ with the Unconquered Sun, over which he had seen the miraculous cross of light appear, was matched by his identification of Christ as the chief source of military power. For Constantine was an ambitious general, with the Latin Westerner's love of action and dislike of Greek hair-splitting, love of order and unity, and belief in force. He believed he had seen the pagan gods fail Diocletian. He believed he had seen what Christ could do on the battlefield against great odds. Might Christ not also restore internal unity to the Empire, loyalty to its Emperor, and concord among its subjects? Constantine had received what looked like clear proof that Christ had chosen him to preserve his Church from persecution and to defend the Empire from its foes, both foreign and domestic. In the circumstances he established complete religious toleration in his two prefectures, probably within the year of his great victory. But he went further. He subsidized the Christian Church with public funds, exempted the clergy from holding any public office that involved pagan religious duties, and restored to them all property that had been confiscated.

Within six months of Constantine's victory, the Donatist schismatics of

Africa were appealing to him for help; within a year, Constantine had called a number of bishops to a council in Rome to heal the schism. The schism dragged miserably on. Eventually, of course, Constantine aligned himself with the Catholic bishops in Africa against the schismatic bishops of the Donatists, with their perfervid love of those whom the recent persecution had martyred and with their refusal to obey those clerics who had been frightened by persecution into surrendering copies of the holy scriptures or had gone into hiding. In general, the poor tended to follow the Donatists, while the rich followed the Catholics. In siding with the rich, Constantine acted of course in the tradition of the Empire. But his chief concern was the unity of the Church. The Donatists were out of step not only with the Bishop of Rome but with the solution of the problem of apostasy in most provinces of the Empire. That would have been enough for Constantine. He did not see in either heresy or schism an invitation to dialectic but only to eristic, to idle and destructive dispute. Christ was clearly Lord of the Christian Ecclesia, as Constantine was Lord of the Empire, and Constantine intended to maintain both his own authority and Christ's. For that reason he salaried no schismatic clergy. That is, he undertook to defend the authority of Christ with money. But Constantine used money also to distribute to the poor of Rome, along with food and clothing. Finally, in February, 313, Constantine persuaded Licinius, now Augustus of the Prefecture of Illyricum, to meet him in Milan. There they agreed on a joint policy of toleration for all religions and sealed their agreement by the marriage of Constantine's half sister, Constantia, to Licinius.

Maximinus Daza, who ruled the Prefecture of the East and had since 308 claimed the title of Augustus, had at first counted on a protracted struggle between Constantine and Maxentius, a struggle into which Licinius would be drawn. Maximinus Daza had been a secret ally of Maxentius and had planned to strike Licinius from the rear when Licinius was engaged in the West. That project had been ruined by Constantine's swift victory and Maxentius' death in battle. Then came the alliance of Licinius and Constantine: Maximinus Daza expected to be attacked. He had continued intermittently his persecution of the Christians. By contrast, at least in the judgment of one of his subjects, Eusebius, Bishop of Caesarea, both Constantine and Licinius were already converted to Christianity; and presumably many Christians in the East would look on them both as rescuers. Most of Licinius' troops were on the Italian frontier, too far to recall in time if Maximinus attacked first and quickly. Maximinus therefore struck. Byzantium cost him eleven days of siege; Heraclea, several days more. By the time he reached Hadrianople, Licinius was almost upon him. On April 30, 313, Maximinus was defeated; he fled back to Asia Minor, and at Tarsus committed suicide. Licinius also crossed to Asia, took possession of his opponent's capital, Nicomedia, and on June 15, 313, issued an edict of religious toleration in the Prefecture of the East.

There were now only two Augusti left and no Caesars. Licinius ruled the two Greek-speaking prefectures and officially tolerated their large Christian minority. His brother-in-law, Constantine, ruled the two Latin-speaking prefectures and actively protected and patronized their much smaller Christian minority, while trying not to offend the pagan Senate. The two Augusti soon quarreled, and after Constantine had successfully crushed an effort by the Franks to invade Gaul and had spent twelve months at Treves restoring order, he attacked Licinius northwest of the site of modern Belgrade and soundly defeated his superior forces. In 315, to secure peace, Licinius surrendered all his European territory except Thrace. Later in the year Constantine visited both Rome and Gaul. Then in the autumn of 316 the Danube frontier, which was no longer his defeated rival's responsibility, engaged him; he campaigned there for eight years. In 322 he crossed the Danube and made war on the Sarmatians, but in 323 the Goths invaded and pillaged his own diocese of Moesia and Licinius' diocese of Thrace.

When Constantine attacked the Goths in both dioceses, Licinius protested the trespass; Constantine declined to give satisfaction; and in 324 the two Augusti fought a second war. This one was carried on by land and sea. Licinius had the larger navy, but it was mismanaged. He even had a slightly larger army, but his soldiers were inferior to the tough fighters whom Constantine had trained in eight years of frontier service against barbarians. Moreover, Licinius had inherited the problem of morale that his victim, Maximinus Daza, had faced. During the years when Constantine was fighting on the Danube, his loyalty to the Christian faith had made him the hero of the Church. Licinius seems to have suspected that his own far more numerous Christian subjects were secretly praying for Constantine. He himself had looked like a Christian when he had rescued the churches of the East from strenuous persecution by Maximinus Daza; later, however, the Christians no longer contrasted him with Maximinus

499

but with that ardent champion of Christianity, Constantine. The distrust Licinius felt for the Christians led to annoying regulations aimed at weakening the Church, to renewed demands upon them for pagan sacrifice, and finally to the destruction of church buildings in some cities, arrests, and executions.

It is most probable that Constantine had long desired to be sole Emperor. The new persecution in the East gave him his chance. In 320 he had eliminated all pagan gods from new issues of coin, except the god whom the Balkan peasantry from which he recruited his army especially adored: the Unconquered Sun. That his new mint at Sirmium should praise this deity reminded his subjects not only that he was son of a previous senior Augustus but that he claimed descent from another one, Claudius Gothicus, and that both Constantius and Claudius had ardently worshiped the sun. Whether Licinius' father or forebears did so mattered little: there was neither an Augustus nor a Caesar among the lot of them. Moreover, Constantine seemed to believe that there was some special connection between Christ and the sun. Perhaps for this reason in 321 he decreed that Sunday, the day the Romans had dedicated to the Unconquered Sun, rather than Saturn's day, which coincided with the Jewish Sabbath, should be a holy day of prayer. He excused from duty those soldiers who were Christians that they might worship on that day. He prescribed for his other soldiers a Sunday prayer in Latin, which was addressed to "Thee the only God," through whose help they had "gotten the victory."[1043] The prayer did not mention Christ. Indeed, his pagan soldiers may well have considered it a prayer to the Unconquered Sun on the Sun's holy day.

By 324 Constantine was preparing for what would literally be a crusade against Licinius. He summoned Christian bishops to help him prepare to meet the enemy of Christ in battle. Fifty soldiers were detailed to protect and to take turns bearing the sacred labarum or standard which Christ himself had reportedly taught him how to design. With his Christian soldiers granted time on Sundays to worship the true God and his pagan soldiers required on Sundays to recite in unison a prayer to a single if unspecified god, Constantine was ready to defend Christ's flock with the sword. Licinius accepted the war on Constantine's terms. He informed his council that he was making war to defend the ancestral gods against the atheist who worshiped a strange god. He had already purged his court and civil service of Christians. Licinius implied that if he won, and he was sure

500

that he would, he would make war on all Christians. On September 18, 324, at Chrysopolis, a city on the Asian side of the Bosphorus opposite Byzantium, Constantine won a victory so decisive that Licinius fled to Nicomedia and sued for his life. Constantine granted him his life, dined him, and interned him at Thessalonica. For the first time in thirty-eight years one Augustus ruled the whole Empire, this time with three of his own sons as Caesars.

Constantine naturally announced that he had rescued the East from Licinius' misrule and he blamed all the recent wars and famines on those who had persecuted the Church. He made it clear that Christianity was the only true faith but that his government would guarantee freedom of religion to those who were still blinded by error, on the grounds that their freedom might lead them into the path of truth. He of course released all Christians in Licinius' prefecture who had been imprisoned and restored all confiscated property, as he had done in Maxentius' former prefecture. But he found the Church itself rent by theological quarrels which centered on the precise meaning of the divinity of Christ and by a schism between the Catholic Church and the Church of the Martyrs. This latter, Novatian, schism strongly resembled the Donatist schism he had struggled with in Africa. Ten years earlier he had convened a council of bishops at Arles, and this council had taken strong if not too successful action against the Donatists. Now that he was sole head of the Roman Empire he convened a council of bishops from the whole Empire to meet on May 20, 325, at Nicaea in Bithynia, conveniently close to Constantine's palace at Nicomedia. It was the first ecumenical council the Christian Church ever held. According to Eusebius, more than 250 bishops attended, mostly from the Greek-speaking provinces. Out of the Latin West came one bishop from Italy, one from Gaul, one from Illyria, one from Africa, none from Britain, none from Spain except the Emperor's adviser, Bishop Hosius. The Bishop of Rome was too old to make the journey, but sent two deacons to represent him. As usual, the Western bishops were not much interested in theological dispute; besides, it is likely that not many of them could speak Greek, the language in which the debates were naturally held. Even had these debates been carried on in Latin, the philosophic vocabulary of Latin could hardly have borne the burden. The meagerness of representation from the West was partly counterbalanced ecumenically by the presence of one Persian bishop and one Scythian. The Emperor, erect, powerfully built, clad in resplendent purple, opened the proceedings with a speech that pleaded for unity and harmony. Since he did not speak Greek well and perhaps since the language of government would lend more authority to the occasion, he used Latin. When he had finished, an interpreter read a Greek translation of the speech.

On at least some occasions Constantine presided. He also entered freely, if somewhat blindly, into the debates, commended speakers who pleased him, reproved others. He even did the bishops the courtesy of commenting in Greek on their discussions. He made seemingly successful efforts to get peace and uniformity in the Christian polis and to secure thereby the power of Christ as a sure bulwark against the internal political dissension and external aggression that threatened the Empire Christ had chosen him to rule. The churches of the Greek East had never recognized the canons agreed on by the churches of the Latin West, nor had the West recognized the canons on which Eastern councils had agreed. Under Constantine's respectful but persistent pressure, the Council of Nicaea passed canons which were subsequently recognized by churches everywhere. Among the canons which East and West accepted, one alluded to the many clerics who through love of gain lent money at 12 per cent, and another prescribed the penance for soldier-converts who,

> put off their belts, but afterwards, like dogs, ran back to their own vomit, as some have even expended money and have reinstated themselves in the army by favors . . . [1044]

For Constantine permitted soldiers who were converted to Christianity to quit military service in accordance with the doctrine of nonviolence, which many Christians still followed.[1045] The Novation schismatics were apparently reconciled and the schism was healed. The charge of heresy against the Alexandrian priest, Arius, that he denied that Christ had the same divinity as God the Father, led to the formulation of the so-called Nicene Creed, which was adopted, albeit with many misgivings by some of the bishops. There had been disagreements about the correct date on which to celebrate Easter. Constantine was especially annoyed that some churches made the date depend on that chosen by the Jews for their feast of the Passover. In reporting the results of the Council of Nicaea to all the churches of the Empire, he reflected the anti-Semitism that had long afflicted the Church. "Let us then," he wrote,

> have nothing in common with the detestable Jewish crowd; for we have received from our Saviour a different way. A course at once legitimate

and honorable lies open to our most holy religion. Beloved brethren, let us with one consent adopt this course, and withdraw ourselves from all participation in their baseness. For their boast is absurd indeed, that it is not in our power without instruction from them to observe these things. For how should they be capable of forming a sound judgment, who, since their parricidal guilt in slaying their Lord, have been subject to the direction, not of reason, but of ungoverned passion, and are swayed by every impulse of the mad spirit that is in them?[1046]

Constantine's apparent triumph in healing the dissensions in the Church occurred some nineteen years after his father's army at York had proclaimed him as Augustus. There were celebrations throughout the provinces, but Constantine celebrated his success at Nicaea by feasting the bishops, now ready to return to their respective dioceses. So splendid was this feast that Bishop Eusebius of Caesarea wrote in his biography of the Emperor: "One might have thought that a picture of Christ's kingdom was thus shadowed forth . . ."[1047]

It was not until the following year that Constantine made one of his rare visits to Rome, to celebrate his vicennalia, the twentieth year of his reign, at the capital itself. His relations with the Senate had become more and more strained. He tried to conciliate Rome with brilliant games; he also appointed the first Christian ever to serve as its governor. When his troops were scheduled to march to the Capitol to perform the customary rites of a pagan festival, he planned to attend. However, when he saw the procession, he exploded into a sudden fury, cursed, swore, and thereby further estranged both Senate and people in this capital of the pagan world.

What caused the nervous strain that provoked this unexpected explosion? The most obvious explanation is that the recalcitrance of Rome, and especially of the Senate, as the Emperor moved further and further away from paganism, had placed him in an intolerable position. He had no ready way to convert the pagan majority of his subjects. And he had no intention of yielding his throne in order to follow Christ. He firmly believed that Christ had given him the Empire to rule and by implication to Christianize. Yet he was still Pontifex Maximus, high priest of Rome's pagan gods. His army was strongly pagan. All the forces in the conflict between the dying pagan Cosmopolis and the young, vigorous, growing Christian polis which formed inside it converged in the breast of this one, energetic, earnest man of action; and the conflict was tearing him in two.

Added to this anguish, which history had imposed on him, was perhaps another and more private anguish. Recently, on his way to Rome, he had suddenly murdered his eldest son Crispus, whose brilliant naval victory off what is now Gallipoli had forced Licinius to abandon Byzantium and had greatly contributed to Constantine's final victory. Then, shortly after murdering his son, he had murdered his wife, Fausta, whom he had married eighteen years before, after divorcing Crispus' mother. The reasons for this double murder are uncertain, though somewhat later it was asserted by historians that Fausta had accused her stepson of trying to seduce her; that after the hasty execution of the stepson, Constantine's mother, Helena, convinced him that the guilt was Fausta's; and that he therefore murdered Fausta. In any case the two murders were on Constantine's conscience when he lost control of himself at Rome. Perhaps something else was on his conscience. After promising to spare Licinius' life and interning him at Thessalonica, he had accused him of a plot and had got the Roman Senate to have him executed.

A hundred years after the event the pagan historian Zosimus asserted that Constantine's explosion made him so unpopular at Rome that he decided at that time to make Byzantium a rival capital. But Constantine's friend Eusebius reported that, immediately after he defeated Licinius, God had appeared to him in a dream and had ordered him to make Byzantium his residence. Perhaps both reports are true. In any case, he cannot have found the order uninviting: Byzantium was pre-eminently fitted to be the capital of a new, Greek, Christian empire. The city stood on a high and hence easily fortified site endowed with magnificent harbors. It stood where Europe and Asia almost met and it guarded the narrow strait that connected two seas. It guarded the Bosphorus even better than did Nicomedia, Diocletian's choice. Constantine had never really lived in Rome or liked it: his various temporary capitals had been Cologne, on the Rhine; Treves and Lyons, back of the Rhine; Sirmium, near the Danube; Sardica, today called Sofia, which was farther down the Danube valley and somewhat farther from the river; Thessalonica, on the Macedonian coast of the Aegean; Milan, which guarded Italy; and Antioch, the rear base for defense against Persia. He had especially liked Sardica and had playfully declared, "Sardica is my Rome."[1048] He had once considered making it his capital, but God, or his dream of God, was right: Sardica was of course much closer to the Danube, but Byzantium would make the better capital. He therefore rebuilt it and called it Second Rome, but it quickly became known as the Polis of Constantine, Constantinopolis.[1049]

Constantinople, far more than Diocletian's Nicomedia, symbolized the fact that the center of gravity of the Roman Empire had shifted from the poorer, less civilized Latin West to the richer, more deeply cultivated Greek East, an East that was by no means merely Greek but rather a palimpsest of high civilizations. In the Graeco-Roman Cosmopolis, now grown old and ill, the conquered Greek East had outlasted the conquering Latin West: its civilization was deeper-rooted; its shrunken cities were less impoverished; and it bore within itself not only disillusionment and a sense of defeat but also the greater portion of a younger, growing, hopeful polis, the Christian polis.

Perhaps the real reason Byzantium had to be transformed into Constantinople was not to reassert the will of Zeus but to carry out the will of the one true God. Constantine destined his Second Rome to be the Christian capital of a Cosmopolis that not only was already partly Christian but would become, he was certain, wholly Christian. From Constantine's point of view, the truly Holy City of Cosmopolis was neither Athens nor Rome but Jerusalem. Its true founder was not Cecrops, Athens' legendary ruler, not Alexander of Macedon, not Romulus but Christ. Its truest literature had been written not by Homer or Aeschylus or Plato or Virgil but by the Hebrew prophets, by those who wrote the Gospels, and by those New Testament writers who later chronicled in Greek the acts of the Ecclesia that Christ had founded or who wrote epistles instructing the local churches or who expressed a prophetic vision.

Since Constantinople must be not only Christian but a capital, a Rome, and since for centuries the idea of an Imperial capital implied a Senate as well as a People, a *Populus Romanus*, Constantine built splendid residences for those Roman Senators who could be induced to move to the new Rome, and he set up a free bread ration for the People. Since Rome was built on seven hills, Constantine enlarged the walls of Byzantium to include seven hills. The Imperial palace had to be as large as the one in Rome; a hippodrome for horse races was constructed, although gladiatorial combats were forbidden;[1050] and of course a forum was laid out and was surrounded by public buildings. Rome-on-Tiber possessed a mystical name, Flora; Rome-on-Bosphorus was given the same mystical name translated into Greek, Anthusa. Rome was filled with statues and other works of art; Constantine ransacked the provinces to beautify Constantinople. He patronized philosophers and rhetoricians who could give his new Rome the cultural life of an imperial capital. He gave its citizens the same legal rights as the citizens of Rome had, and also freed the city of several important taxes. True, where the Senators of old Rome continued to wear the honorific title *clarissimus*, Most Illustrious, those of new Rome had to be content with *clarus*, Illustrious; and such differences acknowledged the primacy of prestige that Rome continued to enjoy. But Constantinople enjoyed another kind of prestige: it was Christ's capital, not Jove's. Bishop Eusebius was probably correct when he implied that public worship of the pagan gods never polluted Constantinople. Pagan Rome still had but few churches; Constantinople was planned as a city of churches. In Rome Constantine had built the Church of the Lateran and he later built the church of St. Peter and that of St. Paul. He had also built a church at Cirta, the African city he had renamed Constantine; a handsome cathedral at Nicomedia; the Golden Church at Antioch. At Second Rome he built, among others, the Church of the Holy Apostles and matched Augustus' Altar of Peace in Rome with the Church of the Holy Peace.[1051] Although pagan worship was allowed elsewhere, the temples and holy places of the old gods, including Delphi, were forced to disgorge their treasures of gold and silver in order to finance the magnificent churches of the one true God that Constantine was building in Christ's capital. Bronze doors were removed from temples, gold and silver plates were stripped from the statues of gods. This enormous treasure from the ancient fanes of Hellenistic civilization not only went to Christ's new churches but helped to pay the soldiers who had fought successfully under Christ's banner and to bring a long-lost stability to the Imperial currency which his chosen Emperor issued. Somewhat as those who built in Rome the triumphal arch to Constantine had cannibalized other works of art in an effort to achieve maximum splendor, Constantine and his architects cannibalized both the art works and the capital endowments of pagan Hellas to give the new Christian city the proper degree of splendor, the obvious symbols of Christ's power.

In the sore travail of transforming Jove's empire into Christ's, Constantine cannibalized still further. His mother, Helena Augusta, in her old age made a pilgrimage to Palestine, where either she or her son built a church at Christ's birthplace in Bethlehem, another on the site of the Holy Sepulcher, and a third on the Mount of Olives whence Christ had ascended into heaven. Also, she reported finding Christ's cross with the nails still intact. Constantine was ever grateful that Christ, who had renounced force and violence and had rejected worldly power, had repeatedly led Constantine's crusades to victory. Therefore, according to a Christian historian of the next century,

> the nails with which Christ's hands were fastened to the cross . . . Constantine took and had made into bridle-bits and a helmet, which he used in his military expeditions.[1052]

The conversion of Byzantium into the Christian capital of a powerful empire took six years. On May 17, 330, Constantine celebrated the twenty-fifth anniversary of his accession by dedicating Constantinople, as he was to celebrate in the same city his thirtieth.

Two years after capturing Rome, Constantine had spoken of dissensions in the African church

> by which the highest divinity may perhaps be roused not only against the human race but even against me myself, to whose care he has, by his heavenly will, committed the governance of all things . . . [1053]

He had thereby defined his relationship to the Empire, when he still controlled only its Latin half; to the rest of mankind, of which the whole Empire contained but a fraction; and perhaps to the Christian Ecclesia, not yet a majority in the Greek half of the Empire. Bishop Eusebius wrote approvingly that Constantine

> assumed as it were the functions of a general bishop constituted by God, and convened synods of His ministers.[1054]

To a group of bishops, Constantine declared:

> You are bishops of those within the church, while I, appointed by God, would be bishop of those outside.[1055]

For he believed he had been converted not by the bishops but directly by Christ himself. Since he bore the weight of converting those outside the Church, both inside his predominantly pagan Roman Empire and far beyond its frontiers, he may well have felt some impatience with ecclesiastics who appeared to be too preoccupied with those already converted. At least he was impatient with the doctrinal disputes of these ecclesiastics. Had not the Apostle Paul, who also was Christ's convert and not that of the apostles in Jerusalem, shown impatience with their Jewish scruples over circumcising his Gentile converts? To quarrel over the precise definition of Christ's divinity, Constantine thought, was to argue over "truly insignificant questions," "trifling and foolish verbal difference," points that were "trivial and altogether unessential."[1056] The proper date of Easter, on the other hand, was "so sacred a question" that disagreement about it was clearly "unbecoming."[1057]

All these quarrels were gravely inconvenient to an Emperor who, "appointed by God, would be bishop of those outside" the Church, and even outside the Empire. That was why he convened the Council of Nicaea, took part in its debates, and personally proposed that the Nicene Creed describe Christ as *homoousios,* having the same essence as God the Father. This Greek philosophic term had long been familiar to Western theologians; indeed, Hosius, Bishop of Cordova, who had for years advised Constantine, may well have taught it to him. He was of course in no intellectual position to understand its implications. But his plans for the pagan, as well as the Christian world depended, he believed, on church unity. To Arius, the Alexandrian priest who had started most of the trouble, and to Arius' bishop, who had deposed him, Constantine had once written:

> My design then was, first, to bring the diverse judgments formed by all nations respecting the Deity to a condition, as it were, of settled uniformity; and, secondly, to restore a healthy tone to the system of the world, then suffering under the malignant power of a grievous distemper. Keeping these objects in view, I looked forward to the accomplishment of the one with the secret gaze of the mental eye, while the other I endeavoured to secure by the aid of military power. For I was aware that, if I should succeed in establishing, according to my hopes, a common harmony of sentiment among all the servants of God, the general course of affairs would also experience a change correspondent to the pious desires of them all.[1058]

With this program in mind and without depending wholly on the secret eye of thought, he not only pressed for a single statement of faith but sought to provide adequate spiritual support to military force and authority in order to encourage his Christian subjects to serve in the army of their Christian Emperor. He therefore

> removed the stigma of dishonor from those upon whom it had been cast, and permitted those who had been deprived of high appointments in the army, either to reassume their former place, or with an honorable discharge, to enjoy a liberal ease according to their own choice . . .

When he engaged in war, he caused a tent to be borne before him, constructed in the shape of a church . . . Priests and deacons followed the tent. . . . From that period the Roman legions, which now were called by their number, provided each its own tent, with attendant priests and deacons.[1059]

Constantine backed up the Nicene Creed by an edict aimed at suppressing heretics. He even wrote a personal and abusive letter addressed to the various groups whose members were considered heretical or schismatic. His letter forbade them to assemble, whether in public or in private; it also confiscated their churches for the benefit of the Catholic or universal Church. As to his responsibilities to the pagan majority of his subjects, although he despoiled their temples, he did not systematically confiscate them for Christian use. Three pagan temples he utterly destroyed. Two of these were temples to Venus, in which ritual prostitution was practiced, a custom that outraged Constantine, one of them at Heliopolis in what is now Lebanon and the other on nearby Mount Lebanon. The third temple he razed was one in Cilicia dedicated to Asclepius, where the ill went to pass the night and be healed by the god. Finally, since he had assumed responsibility for converting the barbarians, he found a simple and characteristic method for converting them. As he reported to the Synod of Tyre in 335,

the barbarians have, through my instrumentality, learnt to know genuinely and to worship God; for they perceived that everywhere and on all occasions, his protection rested on me; and they reverence God the more deeply because they fear my power.

At this point he found it desirable to add a warning against further dissension over the matter of Christ's divine nature:

But we who have to announce the mysteries of forbearance (for I will not say that we keep them), we, I say, ought not to do anything that can tend to dissension or hatred, or, to speak plainly, to the destruction of the human race.[1060]

For how could Constantine convert the whole human race to the true faith, even by the sword, even with the nails from the true cross incorporated into his helmet and bridle-bit, unless the bishops could agree on what the true faith was? Soldier and ruler that he was, he seems to have inferred little from certain peaceful encounters between Christians and barbarians. During the second half of the third century many barbarians had embraced Christianity:

> For when an unspeakable multitude of mixed nations passed over from Thrace into Asia and overran it, and when other barbarians from the various regions did the same things to the adajcent Romans, many priests of Christ who had been taken captive, dwelt among these tribes; and during their residence among them, healed the sick, and cleansed those who were possessed of demons, by the name of Christ only, and by calling on the Son of God; moreover they led a blameless life, and excited envy by their virtues. The barbarians, amazed at the conduct and wonderful works of these men, thought that it would be prudent on their part, and pleasing to the Deity, if they should imitate those who they saw were better; and, like them, would render homage to God. When teachers as to what should be done, had been proposed to them, the people were taught and baptized, and subsequently were gathered into churches.[1061]

Although the fear of Constantine's military power may have converted more barbarians than the captive Christian priests had converted, there may also have been a considerable difference in the depth of the conversion. According to Constantine himself, when Diocletian and later Emperors unleashed successive persecutions, many Christians fled to the barbarians for refuge and found it.[1062] This, too, made for genuine encounter. Similarly, the Persians whom the Christians also converted may have found it harder than before to convert others, once Constantine had written their emperor, Sapor, on their behalf: henceforth they might well appear to other Persians as tools of Roman military power. Again, Constantine's well-meant, if sometimes heavy-handed, patronage of the Church inside the Empire made it not only safe but more profitable than ever for his pagan subjects to become Christians. Membership in the Church no longer seemed to promise scorn, petty persecution, and perhaps torture and death, but honor, privilege, and perhaps advancement, power, and riches. No wonder converts, of whatever conviction, multiplied rapidly.[1063]

Like some chivalrous knight Constantine had ridden out of the West, had rescued the Church from the dragon Persecution, had married the fair maiden and endowed her with the slain dragon's treasure. Within little more than a century the church historian Socrates could report that

> whenever the affairs of the state were disturbed, those of the Church, as if by some vital sympathy, became disordered also. . . . We have con-

tinually included the emperors in these historical details; because from the time they began to profess the Christian religion, the affairs of the Church have depended on them, so that even the greatest Synods have been, and still are convened by their appointment.[1064]

This symbiosis of Church and Empire, which enabled them to pass on to one another the disorders that afflicted them, seems to have encouraged in the Church an authoritarianism that viewed heretics as unruly subjects to be silenced rather than as fellow believers to be engaged in fruitful dialectic. Thus, in a synod convoked at Antioch a group of bishops deposed the Bishop of Antioch, and the historian Socrates commented that

> this is a matter of common occurrence; the bishops are accustomed to do this in all cases, accusing and pronouncing impious those whom they depose, but not explaining their warrant for so doing.[1065]

Some twenty years after the Council of Nicaea had seemingly brought unity to the Church, another church historian, Sozomen, wrote that the bishops of the West were deposing various bishops of the East and that those of the East answered by deposing those of the West, including Julius, Bishop of Rome. In such ecclesiastical wars, the bishops of course found it convenient to appeal to the Emperor.[1066]

The same vital sympathy that was assimilating the Church to the Empire in these various ways facilitated the Church's fuller acceptance of war. Athanasius, a principal leader in the war of words against Arius and in his final excommunication, accepted also the war men fight with swords. In effect he handed back to the soldier the weapons he had lost when, according to Tertullian, Christ ungirded every soldier. Athanasius wrote that

> it is not right to kill, yet in war it is lawful and praiseworthy to destroy the enemy; accordingly not only are they who have distinguished themselves in the field held worthy of great honours, but monuments are put up proclaiming their achievements. So that the same act is at one time and under some circumstances unlawful, while under others, and at the right time, it is lawful and permissible.[1067]

The cooperation between Empire and Church turned out less well than Constantine had hoped when he rescued the Church from persecution. When he marched against Licinius he had cherished the hope that the older and wiser Greek Church would help him with the bitter Donatist schism in the Church of North Africa. But he had found an analogous schism in the East and many more charges and countercharges of heresy than the Latin Church had ever heard of. Hence his impulsive convocation at Nicaea of the First Ecumenical Council of the Christian Church; hence his impulsive assumption of the Council's presidencies, his bold interventions in its debates, his impatience with arguments he could not follow, his insistence on a common creed for all Christians, and his daring proposal of the term, homoousios, of one essence. When at last he had seemed to get the agreement of all the bishops, some of them were sorely troubled, but they were grateful to him for his rescue of the Greek Church from a long and terrible and in some ways demoralizing ordeal. They were touched, perhaps, by his childlike audacity, by his very real modesty, and by his deference to their authority. They were fearful of alienating him by seeming to him merely obstinate. They were perhaps a little dazzled by his deference and by the splendor of their surroundings. Constantine must have tasted the sweets of complete triumph when he tendered them a final banquet and when

> Detachments of the body guard and other troops surrounded the entrance of the palace with drawn swords, and through the midst of these the men of God proceeded without fear into the innermost of the imperial apartments, in which some were the emperor's own companions at table, while others reclined on couches arranged on either side.[1068]

The triumph turned out to be an illusion of hybris. The bishops of Nicomedia and of Nicaea were deposed by the Church for sympathizing with Arius' views on the very point that the Emperor's proposal of homoousios was designed to settle. Constantine exiled both bishops. Then the two exiles petitioned their fellow bishops to reinstate them, insisting that they had never in fact followed the heresy ascribed to Arius, but only opposed excommunicating him for taking a position they did not believe he had taken.[1069] The Church reinstated the two bishops and Constantine recalled them from exile. They informed Constantine that, in signing the Nicene Creed,

> they had not assented to those doctrines from conviction, but from the fear that, if the disputes then existing were prolonged, the emperor, who was then just beginning to embrace Christianity, and who was yet unbaptized, might be impelled to return to Paganism, as seemed likely, and to persecute the Church. They assert that Constantine was pleased

with this defense, and determined upon convening another council; but that, being prevented by death from carrying his scheme into execution, the task devolved upon his eldest son, Constantius, to whom he represented that it would avail him nothing to be possessed of imperial power, unless he could establish uniformity of worship throughout his empire . . . 1070

The wrangling over homoousios, however, continued to afflict the Church. Constantine indeed got the date of Easter fixed, and this point had always seemed to him more important than questions of theology which he could not understand. But his was a Pyrrhic victory: the theologians considered their differences in doctrine a great deal more important than the date for celebrating Easter. This judgment of theirs prevented the unity of purpose, the *philia*, or friendship, between citizens which Aristotle had declared necessary to a good polis. Constantine, who is unlikely ever to have read Aristotle, instinctively knew that the Christian polis, around which he had planned to rebuild Cosmopolis, must achieve this unity of spirit if his plans were to succeed. He was left to reconstruct Cosmopolis as best he could, his work punctuated by gusts of anger at the intransigence, first of one side of the quarrel, now of the other. The thirtieth year of his reign, 335, was marred by the failure of two successive Church councils to put an end to the theological wrangle, one council held in Tyre and a second in Jerusalem. In the West the Donatists of Africa were still in rebellion and were insulting Constantine's Praetorian Prefect of Italy and Africa.

Meanwhile, Constantine tried to strengthen the Empire. He increased the size of the field army Diocletian had established: he could thus more readily hasten emergency reinforcements to frontier garrisons. This redeployment of his troops would have dangerously weakened his frontier garrisons had he not strengthened them with German recruits. When, in 312, he captured Rome he disbanded the Praetorian Guard, which had so often played kingmaker, and assigned its prefects to the civil service. He replaced the Guard itself with an Imperial bodyguard composed of Germans. He tried to control extortion on the part of his civil service. His currency reform was so successful that two generations later the Imperial government commuted payments in kind to cash and Roman coin was once more acceptable in foreign lands. Constantinople became the richest city in the Empire and possibly in the world. But he was so lavish in expenditure that he was forced to increase taxes on large estates and to impose one on merchants.[1071] Moreover, the harsh realities of a decaying Empire made many of his reforms of Diocletian's system so unworkable that they had to be rescinded. Indeed, the problems Diocletian had tried to meet forced Constantine in some cases to go even further than Diocletian had gone.

Constantine's last years were years of disillusionment. Controversy was still raging in the Christian Ecclesia when in 337, shortly after Easter, nearly thirty-one years after the army at York had proclaimed him Western Augustus, he fell ill. Near Nicomedia he summoned a number of bishops. He had never been baptized. There was much blood on his hands, including the blood of his wife and his son Crispus. It was not unusual for converts to Christianity to postpone baptism and thereby leave themselves little time to commit the only sins from which, in their belief, they had not already been washed clean. Although the Church disapproved of such nice calculation, its bishops seem not to have urged baptism on Constantine earlier. But now he expected death. He was baptized by the Bishop of Nicomedia, the same bishop whom the Church had once deposed on the charge of heresy and Constantine had once exiled. He had already assigned to his three surviving sons the parts of his empire they were to inherit. And he had already prepared his own sarcophagus in the church which he himself had built and had dedicated to the Holy Apostles. On either side of this sarcophagus stood six others. The twelve empty sarcophagi memorialized the twelve apostles of Christ. Was this arrangement meant to suggest that Constantine was the Thirteenth Apostle?[1072] On the day of Pentecost, May 22, 337, he died.

Some 300 miles west of Constantine's tomb, long ago at Aegae, Philip of Macedon had entered a public theater preceded by a pompous procession. This procession had borne twelve images representing the twelve great gods of Hellas;

> the image of Philip, clothed like the gods in every respect, made the thirteenth, hereby arrogating to himself a place, as if he would be enthroned among the gods.[1073]

Then a dagger had flashed, and Philip had fallen dead. That had happened in 336 B.C. Now, in A.D. 337, another monarch, also from the fringe of Hellenic culture, had used his sword to unite and rule Hellas, but this time a largely Christian Hellas. He had built his tomb between the two sets of symbolic tombs, the tombs of Christ's immediate followers, who were already thought of as the first bishops, whom Christ had appointed to guide his Church. Had not Christ himself converted Constantine, the first Roman Emperor to become a Christian? And did not this Emperor declare that he too would be a bishop, charged with all those as yet outside the Church, including those as yet outside the Empire? For he had won that empire, sword in hand, Christ's monogram on his banner.

Perhaps, however, Alexander the Great, rather than his father, the Thirteenth God, most vividly foreshadowed the Emperor who seemed to nominate himself the Thirteenth Apostle of the one true God's only begotten Son, whom God had lovingly sent to save all men, whether Greek or barbarian. Alexander the Great and Constantine the Great had suffered the same overweening thirst for power; had displayed the same shrewd grasp of politics and war, the same respect for dreams and portents, the same efficacious use of symbols. A fateful reading, or misreading, of a symbol led both men into the excruciating ambiguities of human power. Alexander was reported to have consulted Delphi on an inauspicious day and had tried by force to drag a recalcitrant priestess into the temple to give him Apollo's version of the will of Zeus concerning his plan to attack the Persian Empire. It was reported that the priestess had cried out, "Thou art invincible, my son!" And that Alexander had chosen to construe these words as Apollo's and as thereby bringing the will of Zeus into proper conformity with the will of Alexander. When Alexander was challenged to untie the subtle knot at Gordium and thereby to become the lord of Asia, he cut it instead with the sword; and the sword led him through battle and bloody massacre beyond the liberation of the Greek world, into the vast Iranian mountains, through the barbarous destruction of Persepolis, through the terrible battles of northwest Afghanistan, through the Khyber Pass to India, back through the ghastly Desert of Baluchistan to Babylon, fever, and death. But, before that, the ambiguities of his position as King of the Macedonians, as elected leader of the Greek city-states, Pharaoh of Egypt, Emperor of Persia, and commander of an imperiled army moving through strange and dangerous lands had led him to murder, or to order murdered, some of his closest companions. He had struggled to convert his sprawling, half-organized empire into a human community: he had dressed like a Persian; he had enlisted 30,000 Asians into his army, trained to fight in the Macedonian manner; he had married a daughter of the Persian Emperor whom he had overthrown and had married off

10,000 of his soldiers to their native concubines. And at Opis on the Tigris River he had feasted 9,000 men of many nations and had

> bade them all consider as their fatherland the whole inhabited earth . . .
> as akin to them all good men, and as foreigners only the wicked . . .[1074]

and he had prayed for Harmony and Fellowship. But the sword that had cut the Gordian knot had somehow taken on a life of its own; it had first carved out an empire; and after his death, had slashed it into separate pieces.

When the cross appeared to Constantine, he too had read his symbol and leapt to the conclusion that the Prince of Peace would fight at his side. The whole Latin West came under Constantine. He became Pontifex Maximus of Rome, Chief Priest of a predominantly pagan empire, and convert of Christ himself. He watched for his moment to seize the Greek East from Licinius, by the sword and by Christ's power; to rescue the Greek Christians from torture and death. He expropriated the pagan temples to endow and ornament the Church of Christ, and punished the heretics who threatened the Harmony and Fellowship he was determined to restore to the Church. He too held his feast of Opis, the banquet concluding the first session of the Ecumenical Council of Nicaea, at which he urgently pleaded for concord. He convoked the Council of Nicaea himself, presided over it, and crucially intervened in the debates in order to secure the unity of the Church and to build on that unity the unity of a Christian empire. No priest of Ammon had half-convinced him that he was the son of Zeus, destined like Heracles to save mankind: he was spared the hybris that threatened Alexander. But he suffered his own hybris: he was the divinely chosen agent of God's will to do what he himself seems to have pretty clearly willed before either God or the Son of God had spoken, whether by cross over the sun or by dreams or by any other sign.

Constantine, like Alexander, had built a city that would perpetuate his name down to the present day. Both Alexandria and Constantinople were strategically placed to become wealthy and powerful capitals, marts for the exchange of commodities, cities in which scholars and teachers would also exchange ideas. But the real city that each man vainly strove to found, first by the sword and then by the Word, was a universal City of Man, a Cosmopolis, a true community of spirit, a City of Zeus, a City of God.

516

EPILOGUE

OF ATHENS AND ROME, what was handed down as legacy? In the Byzantine Empire, the ancient literature of Hellas continued to be cultivated, if in a somewhat Mandarin spirit. The literature which the Byzantines themselves produced never attained the level of their art or their architecture. Technology, and notably military technology, developed in response to continued pressure on the Imperial frontiers. Commerce and industry throve. Rome's organizational technique was carried over and somewhat Orientalized.

But of all that Rome bequeathed, it is the corpus of Roman law that has most dazzled Western civilization in modern times. From the Twelve Tables, which the plebeians wrested from the patricians in the middle of the fifth century B.C., to the great legal compendia under Justinian in the sixth century A.D., Roman law was slowly and toilsomely built. Rooted firmly in custom, at first concerned overwhelmingly with property rights, including the father's outright ownership of wife, children, and slaves, it was forced by grim necessity to include a measure of plebeian rights; and then, as the Roman Public Thing steadily expanded, of the rights accorded to the peoples annexed by Rome. By court interpretation, legal precedent, legal casuistry, and legal fiction it adapted itself to the problems of empire. Civil law was modified by the law of nations, which in turn under the influence of Greek Stoicism came to be thought of as a sort of natural law, law dictated supposedly by the very nature of man. The courts of the praetors adapted it to foreign needs, and under Hadrian the praetorian edicts were in some measure harmonized and unified. The Roman mind, which had always disliked abstractions and clung to the concrete, was forced, as Roman rule expanded, toward a degree of abstraction in the field of law. True, in this intellectual crisis Rome frequently had to commandeer legal minds from the Greek-speaking provinces. Thus Papinian was most probably a Syrian; Ulpian was certainly born in Tyre. The pooled effort of such jurisconsults spoke through the mouth of the reigning Emperor. And at last Justinian's legal advisers summed up the work of more than a thousand years.

Yet even after a thousand years, despite the ameliorating influence of Hellenic civilization, despite the rapid spread of Christianity, Roman law retained some of the harshness of the Twelve Tables. "The maintenance of the integrity of the government," states the Second Preface to the Code of Justinian,

> depends upon two things, namely, the force of arms and the observance of the laws: and, for this reason, the fortunate race of the Romans obtained power and precedence over all other nations in former times, and will do so forever, if God should be propitious; since each of these has ever required the aid of the other, for, as military affairs are rendered secure by the laws, so also are the laws preserved by force of arms.[1075]

In these words an Emperor, even a Christian one, declared that what made Rome, or might make Rome, eternal was the law behind Roman force and the force behind Roman law. The concern of Hellenic thought with the search for justice and its concern that positive law express that justice were submerged by the passion for law and order and the firm guarantee of property rights. Did not notions of justice lead to subversive movements like the agrarian reforms of those dangerously hellenized Gracchi? The Gracchi had been suppressed by violence. In any case the long war with Hannibal had already destroyed the class of small farmers for whom the Gracchi sought justice. The class war led by Marius had failed; the concern of his nephew by marriage, Julius Caesar, to find land for the landless had ended with his death at the hands of the Senatorial class. And, although Caesar's nephew, Octavian, had found confiscated land for his veterans, the Augustan settlement basically favored the estate owner and the financier. The triumph of the Roman plutocracy enabled Rome to suppress Greek liberalism throughout her growing empire, and

Roman law faithfully reflected the plutocracy's decided preference for the property rights of men of substance over the howl of the needy. Revolution was staved off partly by the dole, which the rich always preferred to basic economic reforms, partly by public games to divert discontent, and partly by the ostentatious benevolences of the rich: free public baths, parks, and other such amenities.

The Imperial codes of law abound in separate penalties for the rich and the poor for the same crime. Thus,

> When accused persons are to be placed in custody, the Proconsul should determine whether they should be sent to prison, delivered to a soldier, or committed to the care of their sureties, or to that of themselves. This is usually done after taking into consideration the nature of the crime of which the defendant is accused, or his distinguished rank, or his great wealth, or his presumed innocence, or his reputation.[1076]

Though torture was a common device for soliciting evidence, it was decided in the reign of Marcus Aurelius

> that the descendants of men who are designated "Most Eminent and Most Perfect," to the degree of great-grandchildren, shall not be subject either to the penalties or the tortures inflicted upon plebeians if no stigma of violated honor attached to those of a nearer degree, through whom this privilege was transmitted to their descendants.[1077]

True, there were limits, even for the poor:

> No one can be condemned to the penalty of being beaten to death, or to die under rods or during torture, although most persons, when they are tortured, lose their lives.[1078]

Crimes were carefully graded with respect to rank:

> The following is the gradation of capital crimes. The extreme penalty is considered to be sentence to the gallows, or burning alive. Although the latter seems, with good reason, to have been included in the term "extreme penalty," still, because this kind of punishment was invented subsequently, it appears to come after the first, just as decapitation does. The next penalty to death is that of labor in the mines. After that comes deportation to an island.[1079]

> (1) Other penalties have reference to reputation, without incurring the danger of death; as, for instance, relegation for a certain term of years, or for life, or to an island; or sentence to labor on the public works; or where the culprit is subjected to the punishment of whipping.

(2) It is not customary for all persons to be whipped, but only men who are free and of inferior station; those of higher rank are not subjected to the penalty of castigation.

This is especially provided by the Imperial Rescripts. . . .

(5) And, generally speaking, I should say that all those whom it is not permitted to punish by whipping are persons that should have the same respect shown to them that decurions have. For it would be inconsistent to hold that anyone whom the Emperors have, by their Constitutions, forbidden to be whipped, should be sentenced to the mines.

After pointing out that "the laws afford security to all men," the *Digest* continues to exemplify this principle:

(11) Slaves who have plotted against the lives of their masters are generally put to death by fire; sometimes freemen, also, suffer this penalty, if they are plebeians and persons of low rank.

(15) It has been held by many authorities that notorious robbers should be hanged in those very places which they had subjected to pillage, in order that others might be deterred by their example from perpetrating the same crimes, and that it might be a consolation to the relatives and connections of the persons who had been killed . . . Some also condemned them to be thrown to the wild beasts.[1080]

The poor suffered the further liability that they were usually unable to muster witnesses whom the court would trust, for not only a witness's reputation for veracity but also his social standing had to be duly weighed:

The rank, the integrity, the manners, and the gravity of witnesses must be taken into consideration . . .

(3) The integrity of witnesses should be carefully investigated, and in consideration of their personal characteristics, attention should be, in the first place, paid to their rank; as to whether the witness is a Decurion or a plebeian . . . whether he is rich or poor, lest he may readily swear falsely for the purpose of gain . . .[1081]

This is why Hadrian instructed a provincial governor that

You are best qualified to ascertain how much faith should be placed in witnesses, who they are, what is their rank and reputation . . . [1082]

Presumptuous behavior by members of the lower class toward those of rank often led to the horrors of work in the mines:

It has been decided that a freedman who aspires to marry his patroness, or the daughter of the wife of his patron, shall be sentenced to
the mines, or to labor on the public works, according to the dignity of
the person in question.[1083]

The difference between those who are sentenced to the mines, and
those who are sentenced to labor in the mines, is only a matter of chains;
for those who are sentenced to the mines are oppressed with heavier
chains, and those who are sentenced to work connected with the mines
wear lighter ones.[1084]

For committing any one of a long list of more serious acts, the rich were
constrained to live on a penal island, often in considerable comfort; the
poor were led off to the mines, or perhaps to death. A law that may well
have concerned Christian believers before the reign of Constantine is
typical:

Those who introduce new religious doctrines which are unknown to
use or reason, and by which the minds of men are influenced, if they are
of higher rank, shall be deported, if of inferior station, they shall be
punished with death.[1085]

Since the relation of rich to poor could easily undermine the loyalty the
poor might feel for the state, subversive activity by the poor required harsh
treatment:

The authors of sedition and tumult, or those who stir up the people,
shall, according to their rank, either be crucified, thrown to wild beasts,
or deported to an island.[1086]

The same desperate need for law and order that prescribed terrible
punishments for the oppressed when they dared challenge their oppressors
also prescribed the absolute power of the Emperor to protect himself
against rich and poor alike. As commander of the army he monopolized
military force, unless one of his generals overthrew and replaced him.
Actually or potentially he controlled, though he did not monopolize, the
power of money. As patron of arts and letters, he was master of the power
of propaganda. Emperor worship gave him the power of religious sanction. He therefore symbolized in his person the rights of might, reflected in
the Roman codes of law, and to weaken the Emperor was to weaken the
rights of might. In such a case, by about A.D. 200, a lesser right of might
was canceled and the accused of any social rank whatever could be put

to the question: that is, tortured. The Empire's first Christian Emperor provided, in addition, that

> If one person should accuse another of the crime of treason, he who is accused, no matter what his rank or privileges may be, cannot protect himself from torture, and whoever brings the accusation . . . also shall be put to the question . . . [1087]

And this although in fact most persons, when they were tortured, lost their lives, without the law's intent.

Although the patriarchal rigors of early Roman law towards women were mitigated during the Empire, there was no question of giving them the same legal status as men. This was notably true in the case of sexual misdemeanors. In A.D. 326 the Emperor Constantine proclaimed:

> When a woman is convicted of having secretly had sexual intercourse with her slave, she shall be sentenced to death, and the rascally slave shall perish by fire.[1088]

A female slave was subject to her master in the matter of concubinage. But even if he freed her and she entered marriage, "It is evident, when the freedwoman ceases to be married, that her services can be demanded. . . ." [1089] And Paulus, who flourished around A.D. 200, reported that

> Where a freedwoman, who has two or more patrons, marries with the consent of one of them, the other will continue to have the right to her services.[1090]

Moreover, Ulpian judged early in the third century

> that a concubine should not have the right to marry if she leaves her patron without his consent, since it is more honorable for a freedwoman to be the concubine of a patron than to become the mother of a family.[1091]

How firm a legal control the patron had over his concubine is reflected by the provision, cited by Paulus, that

> Where a patron, who has a freedwoman as his concubine, becomes insane, it is more equitable to hold that she remains in concubinage.[1092]

Of course the freedwoman-concubine labored under the double handicap of being a woman as well as an ex-slave; the stain of slavery was not wholly cleansed by emancipation. Neither the Greeks of the great age nor the rulers of the Roman Empire did much more for the slave than occasionally lament his misfortune. Not even the Christian Church forbade slavery. In this matter of slavery the jurist Ulpian, a native of the Greek East and the legal adviser of the ruling Latin West, measured the philosophic failure of Roman law when he wrote,

> So far as the Civil Law is concerned, slaves are not considered persons, but this is not the case according to natural law, because natural law regards all men as equal.[1093]

And again, "We, to a certain extent, compare slavery with death."[1094] Only, however, to a certain extent. Elsewhere in the *Digest,* drawn up under Justinian, a very old law was cited as placing

> in the same category with slaves animals which are included under the head of cattle, and are kept in herds . . .[1095]

Thus the law placed the slave in the same category as a hog but not in that of a dog. On the other hand, lest a slave make the mistake of assuming that self-preservation was the first law of both slaves and hogs, slaves were required by a Rescript of Hadrian's to make their master's preservation their first law, a distinction that would have been hard to explain to a hog:

> Whenever slaves can afford assistance to their master, they should not prefer their own safety to his. Moreover, a female slave who is in the same room with her mistress can give her assistance, if not with her body, certainly by crying out . . . and this is evident even if she should allege that the murderer threatened her with death if she cried out. She ought, therefore, to undergo capital punishment, to prevent other slaves from thinking that they should consult their own safety when their master is in danger.[1096]

The slave was unlike a hog in another particular. Because slaves and other human beings look somewhat alike, mistakes occurred: a slave might turn out to be a freedman. Thus Marcus Aurelius provided that in such event a slave might even file an accusation in court:

> when a slave complains that a will in which freedom was granted him has been suppressed, he should be allowed to file an accusation for suppressing it.[1097]

Although the severity of Roman law underwent occasional mitigations in favor of women, of the poor, and even of slaves, it remained throughout the history of Roman supremacy a law to conserve the interests of the strong, and it exhibited a distrust and even a hatred for the egalitarianism of Greek democracy.[1098]

When the Franks had occupied northern Gaul, when the Goths had invaded Italy and sacked Rome, when the West Goths had settled in southern Gaul, when the Vandals had occupied northern Africa and made Carthage their capital, when pagan subjects of the shrinking Western Empire could ascribe its collapse to its desertion of the old gods who had led Rome to power, and when Christian subjects lamented that their own God seemed unwatchful of his people's welfare, a Christian Gaul launched a homiletic work entitled *On the Government of God*. Salvian was born of upper-class parents about 400 in the general neighborhood of Treves and witnessed the sack of Treves by barbarians. He and his wife retired to monastic life in Lérins, an island opposite Cannes to which many Christian refugees had withdrawn. At that time Lérins and Marseilles were perhaps the two main centers of Christian influence in Gaul. Salvian was ordained a priest, moved to Marseilles, and became famous for his Christian writings. The burden of his book, *On the Government of God*, was that the inhabitants of the Roman Empire, including many Christians, had brought on its collapse by their own behavior. He was especially critical of the main beneficiaries of the Empire, the rich:

> Meanwhile the poor are being robbed, widows groan, orphans are trodden down, so that many, even persons of good birth, who have enjoyed a liberal education, seek refuge with the enemy to escape death under the trials of the general persecution. They seek among the barbarians the Roman mercy, since they cannot endure the barbarous mercilessness they find among the Romans.

> Although these men differ in customs and language from those with whom they have taken refuge, and are unaccustomed too, if I may say so, to the nauseous odor of the bodies and clothing of the barbarians, yet they prefer the strange life they find there to the injustice rife among the Romans. So you find men passing over everywhere, now to the Goths, now to the Bagaudae, or whatever other barbarians have established their power anywhere, and they do not repent of their expatriation, for they would rather live as free men, though in seeming captivity, than as captives in seeming liberty. Hence the name of Roman citizen, once not only much valued but dearly bought, is now voluntarily repudiated and shunned, and is thought not merely valueless, but even almost abhorrent.

What can be greater proof of Roman injustice than that many worthy noblemen to whom their Roman status should have been the greatest source of fame and honor, have nevertheless been driven so far by the cruelty of Roman injustice that they no longer wish to be Romans?

The result is that even those who do not take refuge with the barbarians are yet compelled to be barbarians themselves; for this is the case with the greater part of the Spaniards, no small proportion of the Gauls, and, in fine, all those throughout the Roman world whose Roman citizenship has been brought to nothing by Roman extortion.

I must now speak of the Bagaudae,[1099] who, despoiled, afflicted, and murdered by wicked and bloodthirsty magistrates, after they had lost the rights of Roman citizens, forfeited also the honor of the Roman name. We transform their misfortunes into crime, we brand them with a name that recalls their losses, with a name that we ourselves have contrived for their shame! We call those men rebels and utterly abandoned, whom we ourselves have forced into crime. For by what other causes were they made Bagaudae save by our unjust acts, the wicked decisions of the magistrates, the proscription and extortion of those who have turned the public exactions to the increase of their private fortunes and made the tax indictions their opportunity for plunder? . . .

How does our present situation differ from theirs? Those who have not before joined the Bagaudae are now being compelled to join them. . . .

Such is the case among almost all the lower classes . . .

Frequently there come from the highest imperial officials new envoys, new bearers of dispatches, sent under recommendation to a few men of note, for the ruin of the many. In their honor new contributions and tax levies are decreed. The mighty determine what sums the poor shall pay; the favor of the rich decrees what the masses of the lowly shall lose; for they themselves are not at all involved in these exactions. . . .

As the poor are the first to receive the burden, they are the last to obtain relief . . . the poor are not reckoned as taxpayers at all, except when the weight of taxation is being imposed on them; they are outside the number when remedies are being distributed.

Under such circumstances can we think ourselves undeserving of God's severe punishment when we ourselves continually so punish the poor? Can we believe that God ought not to exercise his judgment against us all, when we are constantly unjust? For where, or among what people, do these evils exist save only among the Romans? Who commit such grave acts of injustice as ours? Take the Franks, they are ignorant of this wrong; the Huns are immune to it; there is nothing of the sort among the Vandals, nothing among the Goths. For in the Gothic country the barbarians are so far from tolerating this sort of oppression that not even Romans who live among them have to bear it. Hence all the Romans in that region have but one desire, that they may never have to return to the Roman jurisdiction. . . .[1100]

Salvian's attack on the social injustice of an empire already famous for its achievements in law was no doubt written off by the rich as the rantings of a Christian fanatic. But Salvian could hardly have pictured as he did the attitude of so many Roman citizens toward the barbarian invader unless this attitude was known to exist. Besides, Salvian was not the only writer to speak out in this period; Orosius, Paulinus of Pella, Sidonius, and Priscus gave similar testimony. The historian Priscus bears witness to the fact that it was not only in the crumbling Western Roman Empire but also in the Greek East that men fled from the Graeco-Roman world to live among barbarians. In 448 he served on an embassy from Constantinople to the court of Attila, the King of the Huns. He reported that there he met a Greek who had fled the Empire and preferred life among the Huns. The Huns, this Greek argued,

> live in inactivity, enjoying what they have got, and not at all, or very little harassed. The Romans, on the other hand, are in the first place very liable to perish in war, as they have to rest their hopes of safety on others, and are not allowed, on account of their *tyrants*, to use arms. And those who use them are injured by the cowardice of their generals, who cannot support the conduct of war. But the condition of the subjects in time of peace is far more grievous than the evils of war, for the exaction of the taxes is very severe, and unprincipled men inflict injuries on others, because the laws are practically not valid against all classes. A transgressor who belongs to the wealthy classes is not punished for his injustice, while a poor man, who does not understand business, undergoes the legal penalty, that is if he does not depart this life before the trial, so long is the course of lawsuits protracted, and so much money is expended on them. The climax of the misery is to have to pay in order to obtain justice. For no one will give a court to the injured man except he pay a sum of money to the judge and the judge's clerks.

Priscus, according to his account, defended Roman law until the Greek wept and confessed that the laws and constitution of the Romans were fair, but deplored that the governors, not possessing the spirit of former generations, were ruining the State.[1101]

Whether or not Roman laws were fair to the poor, life among the Huns certainly offered protection against the officials who administered those laws. Ulpian, living a little before the worst period of the third century, wrote that

> There is no one who is not aware how frequently appeals are employed, and how necessary they are to correct the injustice or the ignorance of judges . . .[1102]

Ulpian also wrote that "There is no one who is not aware of the audacity and insolence of farmers of the revenue. . . ."[1103] A century later Constantine publicly proclaimed that

> As the receivers of taxes in cities, acting in collusion with powerful people, are in the habit of transferring the greater part of the burden of taxation to persons of inferior rank, everyone who is able to prove that he has been imposed upon in this way shall only be required to pay the amount originally allotted to him.[1104]

Nor did Constantine trust the provincial governor's courts to defend the weak:

> Governors of provinces must neither hear nor determine cases in which any powerful person is interested whom they cannot punish, but must report him to Us, or give notice of the case to the Praetorian Prefecture, by which provision may be made for the maintenance of public order, and for the redress of wrongs inflicted upon persons who are weak.[1105]

The Emperor Justinian might later be right that the laws were preserved by force of arms, but Constantine knew enough about Roman armies to conclude that armed men could also make a mockery of law, and ordered that

> Soldiers stationed in garrisons shall not venture to extort more taxes than are due, nor put anyone into prison, nor, themselves, keep anyone in custody, even though he may be clearly guilty of crime.[1106]

Soldiers not only extorted a supplement on taxes due; they were behind illegal military requisitions:

> No one in the name of counts, tribunes, officers, or soldiers shall, under the pretext of supplies, extort from their hosts mattresses, wood, or oil, nor shall he take anything of this kind, even with the consent of his hosts . . .[1107]

Perhaps Justinian, who ruled the Byzantine Empire nearly two centuries after Constantine had died, understood how deeply Roman faith in force corroded both the making and the administration of just law; how war, to which Rome had so long and with such triumphant success applied herself, could vitiate the Greek Stoics' ecumenical vision of natural law that so long haunted the Roman legal mind:

> The Law of Nations, however, is common to the entire human race, for all nations have established for themselves certain regulations exacted by custom and human necessity. For wars have arisen, and captivity and slavery, which are contrary to natural law, have followed as a result, as, according to Natural Law, all men were originally born free; and from this law nearly all contracts, such as purchase, sale, hire, partnership, deposit, loan and innumerable others have been derived.[1108]

Captivity and slavery, contrary to natural law, should have had ample scope under Justinian, for wars certainly arose. He fought off Persia, fought off barbarian pressure in the Balkans, and temporarily recovered North Africa, Sicily, Italy, and even a part of eastern Spain from rule by barbarian invaders. Yet his real monument was the codification of Roman law, which he caused to be undertaken and published. When Constantinople's Western conquests were lost, when the tradition of Greek culture faded from men's memories in the Latin West, Roman law remained. It was taken over, as canon law, by the Western Church; it was used by the secular authorities under the Holy Roman Empire; and, later, when the Renaissance had revived the study of Latin literature and even of Greek literature by Western scholars, Roman law was used by the monarchs of the new nation states.

Why has Western man so warmly extolled Roman law, so rarely analyzed its shortcomings? Perhaps because of certain real achievements. In the first place, it was grounded in long and deep experience of human altercations. If it was largely blind to the concern of both Hellas and the Christian Ecclesia about what a just society would be like and how good law might help lead men into such a society, it was also free of a foolish utopianism. It specialized in defining and punishing the injuries which

Romans did to one another, especially in the matter of property. As Roman law extended its experience of the many races of men, some of them more highly civilized than Rome and some of them barbarian, which conquest incorporated into their empire, it came to reflect the minimal standards of behavior that might be successfully imposed on a sizable fraction of mankind. It enforced this standard with some success on a Greek world that the Greeks, though the intellectual superiors of the Romans, had signally failed to organize. It even tried to correct the bribery and extortion that afflicted Roman administration. If its scale of punishments was harsher on the poor and weak than on the rich and strong, this inequality merely reflected the Romans' observation that poverty tended to breed crime, that the poor became desperate, and that only terrifying punishments could be expected to deter the desperate from crime. Finally, those who wrote of Roman law before the Empire grew feeble and those who wrote of it when the Western Empire had disintegrated were normally not the sons of poverty and misery and were rarely concerned with equal justice in court. What the professional panegyrists of the late Empire saw was precise, predictable law, protecting them and their class, and extending over a great area for centuries. What the modern panegyrist sees is perhaps the same thing. And, indeed, the legend of Roman law today, regardless of the things the law conveniently overlooked, could not have come into existence had not Rome actually extended its jurisdiction both in time and place so magnificently far.

In 416, six years after the West Goths had sacked Rome, a poet named Rutilius Namatianus traveled from Rome to his native Gaul. The broken bridges and ruined roads of Italy and the desolated fields of Gaul caused him to weep, but his tears could not dim his vision of Rome's concrete achievements in time and space:

> Hear, loveliest Queen of all the world, thy world,
> O Rome, translated to the starry skies!
> Hear, Mother of Men, and Mother of Gods!
> We, through thy temples, dwell not far from heaven.
> Thee sing we, and, long as Fate allows, will sing;
> None can forget thee while he lives and breathes. . . .
> Far as the habitable climes extend
> Toward either pole thy valour finds its path.
> Thou hast made of alien realms one fatherland;
> The lawless found their gain beneath thy sway;

Sharing thy laws with them thou hast subdued,
Thou hast made a city of the once wide world.[1109]

If the fall of Rome cannot cause us, too, to weep, nevertheless she can rightly demand the homage of any generation that loves power and believes deeply in force. Rome ruled a collectivity of competitive individuals held together largely by respect for power, rather than a community based on understanding between persons. Is it not with an unerring instinct that modern man admires Rome and the law and order Rome imposed?

Some of those modern readers who find the Roman Empire a brutal degradation of the Hellenic culture that it partly adopted have found relief in Cicero as a true Roman and as also the expounder of that culture. They have rejected Mommsen's judgment that he was merely a phrasemaker and a journalist. They have rejected even that gentler critic, Montaigne, who wrote: "Boldly to confess the truth . . . his way of writing appears to me tedious . . . most of the time I find nothing but wind . . ."[1110] Nor need they accept, even if the Roman Empire seems to them brutal, Simone Weil's comparison of Roman conquest and rule with those of Hitler's totalitarian Reich:

> The Romans conquered the world because they were serious, disciplined, and organized; because their outlook and methods were consistently maintained; because they were convinced of being a superior race, born to command. And also because they successfully employed the most ruthless, premeditated, calculated, systematic cruelty, combining or alternating it with cold-hearted perfidy and hypocritical propaganda. With unswerving resolution, they always sacrificed everything to considerations of prestige; they were always inflexible in danger and impervious to pity or any human feeling. They knew how to undermine by terror the very souls of their adversaries, or how to lull them with hopes before enslaving them by force of arms; and, finally, they were so skilful in the policy of the big lie that they have imposed it even on posterity, and we still believe it today. Can anyone fail to recognize this character?[1111]

And now the tale has ended. It has been a tale of two cities, of two ideas of a City of Man, both embodied in a single, great culture, Hellenic culture. One of them was personified in the Homeric hero, Achilles, who counted on physical force and courage to give man's life significance; the other, in the Homeric hero, Odysseus, who was also a warrior but who persistently and restlessly inquired. Athens embodied both ideas. She was a city of gods and men, of gods who taught men the arts of civilization, who inspired her sculptors and painters and architects, her tragic and comic poets, and finally her speculative thinkers. Having led her sister cities against Persian invaders, she formed a confederacy of free cities. But Odysseus, though more inquiring than Achilles, not only sought the truth but was also wily. Athens converted her confederacy into a commercial and naval empire, ruled it by force, put down rebellion, and collided with an Achillean Sparta. The Peloponnesian War taught her violence until she, who had so loved inquiry, silenced in death her most acute inquirer. She lost her chance to federate in a common freedom the many cities that shared her Hellenic culture. Sparta tried by force to lead them, and failed. Thebes tried. Macedonia tried. And this cultural decrescendo ended when Alexander of Macedon tried to lead all Hellas against Persia and to establish an Hellenic Cosmopolis. This story *The Will of Zeus* sought to tell.

Where both Alexander and the successor-dynasties who ruled the Hellenistic world failed to unite Cosmopolis, Rome succeeded by cutting with the sword a Gordian knot, which Rome, like Alexander, lacked the wit to untie. The sword Rome used turned on its user and converted Rome into a military despotism. Rome had raped Hellas, as a looting Roman soldier might rape and enslave a Greek woman captured from a vanquished city. This rape of Hellas, which seemed in the days of Virgil to have produced a marriage, was disclosed in the end as a concubinage, in which the concubine was admired, enjoyed, but never really understood. In the end, when the conqueror's love of force and money and mastery had confused him, had alienated his own household, and had left him a prey to his enemies, she eluded his control: the Greek East was transformed into a single Byzantine Empire with another religion and another art, albeit with a Roman code of law and with forms of administration learned from Rome.

Behind the fall of the Roman Empire in the West and the triumph of Byzantine culture in the East lay the mortal illness of Hellenism, a Hellenism that played whore to Roman force and Roman money, accepting a world in which force and money were incarnated in her Lord and God, the Roman Emperor.

Into that world a man came whose words and deeds were directed straight to the hearts of his hearers though they confounded the dishonest and the arrogant. The power he spoke of was the power of love and of truth and of purity of heart. His was a City, not indeed of the fading gods of Hellas, but of one true God, who would help men enter his City. There was profound poetic justice in the fact that it was Rome who crucified him.

Since Graeco-Roman civilization never really recovered from the horrors of the third century, since Diocletian's increased use of force failed to restore a sick empire, and since Constantine refounded the Empire as the political expression of a nascent Christian culture, half Greek but half Oriental, Byzantine civilization emerged. But the Byzantine Empire lacked the means to defend the Latin West, which, bereft of its richest provinces, could count on neither enough money nor enough loyalty from its subjects to protect the Rhine-Danube line. It was invaded and settled by successive war bands of barbarian tribesmen.

The Byzantine Empire still called itself Roman; but the cultural chasm that separated it from its parent culture may be measured by the chasm on the one hand between Zeus-Jove and the single, triune god of the Christians, and on the other hand by the chasm between the sculpture of Phidias and a Byzantine mosaic, or between the Parthenon and Santa Sophia. The Western, Latin part of the Empire disintegrated into various barbarian kingdoms, and when these were later cut off from commerce with the wealthier East by Islamic invasions of North Africa, Spain, and southern France and by an Islamic closure of the Mediterranean, the commercial cities of the West withered. Western Europe then entered a Dark Age not unlike the Dark Age that separated Mycenaean civilization from Hellenic. Subsistence agriculture and local industry took over; government also became essentially local. The great network of Roman roads fell into disuse and disrepair. Europeans could not even guess the purpose of these roads. The English called one of them the Devil's Causeway and called another the Maiden Way. In Serbia peasants related of another Roman road that it was made for a princess so that she need never touch the ground with her feet.[1112] Only religion, the Church organization, and the loose-knit Holy Roman Empire preserved some semblance of a cosmopolis. The Roman Empire of Augustus and Hadrian became a legend. It had seemingly solved the chief practical problem of Hellenic man, although at enormous human cost. It had created a political unity.

But in addition to creating a legend of all mankind living in peace under law, the Roman Empire left a record of how not to attempt the construction of a genuine City of Man. This, perhaps, is no paltry legacy.

CHRONOLOGICAL SUMMARY

533

264-241	First Punic War. Annexation of Carthaginian Sicily.
238	Rome seizes Sardinia and Corsica from Carthage.
218-201	Second Punic (Hannibalic) War. Carthaginian Spain annexed.
215-205	First Macedonian War.
212	Death of Archimedes at Syracuse.
200-196	Second Macedonian War: Flamininus "liberates" the Greeks.
190	Death of Apollonius of Perga, Greek mathematician.
171-167	Third Macedonian War: Greece passes effectually under Roman control.
161-126	Hipparchus, Greek astronomer, *floruit*.
149	Death of Cato the Elder.
147-146	Third Punic War.
146	Destruction of Carthage and Corinth by Rome.
c. 135-132	Slave revolts in Sicily, Laurium, Delos, Pergamum, Italy, Rome.
133	Tiberius Gracchus secures passage of land-reform law. Murdered. Scipio Africanus the Younger pacifies Spain.
121	Gaius Gracchus killed.
120	Death of Polybius, historian of Rome.
111-105	Jugurthine War, in North Africa.
c. 103—c. 99	Slave revolt in Sicily. Athens' first slave revolt.
91	Italian cities form a federal republic independent of Rome.
89	Rome grants citizenship to Italians on application.

88	Greek cities of Asia murder Italian inhabitants. Sulla marches on Rome.
88-84	First Mithradatic War.
87	Marius captures Rome.
86	Death of Marius. Sulla slaughters inhabitants of Athens.
82-79	Sulla Dictator.
78	Death of Sulla.
63	Pompey captures Jerusalem. Conspiracy of Catiline.
60	First Triumvirate formed.
55(?)	Death of Lucretius.
c. 54	Death of Catullus.
49	Caesar crosses Rubicon.
48	Caesar conquers Pompey at Pharsalus. Pompey assassinated.
44	Caesar made Dictator for life. Assassinated.
43	Caesar Octavian marches on Rome. Second Triumvirate formed. Cicero executed.
42	Antony and Octavian defeat republican army at Philippi.
36	Octavian controls Western part of Roman Empire.
31	Octavian defeats Antony at Actium. Sole ruler of Roman Empire.
19	Death of Virgil.
8	Death of Horace.
6(?)	Birth of Jesus.

A.D.

14	Death of Augustus.
17	Death of Livy and probably Ovid.
32(?)	Jesus crucified.
64	First mass persecution of Christians.
65	Death of Seneca, Lucan, and Petronius.
66	Jewish rebellion in Palestine.
70	Destruction of Jerusalem by Titus, son of Vespasian.
c. 104	Death of Martial.
post 115	Death of Tacitus.
post 120	Death of Plutarch.
post 127	Death of Juvenal.
132-135	Revolt of the Jews in the East.
c. 135	Death of Epictetus.
c. 140	Death of Suetonius.
143(?)	*Roman Oration*, by Aristides.
post 161	Death of Ptolemy, Greek astronomer.
post 161	Death of Apuleius.
165(?)	Death of Appian, historian.
c. 167	Death of Fronto, rhetorician.
c. 180	Death of Arrian, biographer of Alexander the Great.
post 180	Death of Lucian.
197	Tertullian's *Apology*.
193	Praetorian Guard auctions off Roman Empire.
199	Death of Galen, Greek medical scientist.

202	Edicts of persecution against Christians and Jews.
212	Roman citizenship extended to free subjects throughout Roman Empire.
226	New Persian (Sassanid) Empire established.
250-251	Persecution of Christians under Decius.
250-265	Great Plague throughout Roman Empire.
c. 254	Death of Origen, Christian theologian.
257	Persecution of Christians renewed.
270	Death of Plotinus, Greek philosopher.
303-313	The Great Persecution.
312	Constantine takes Rome.
313	Constantine and Licinius tolerate all religions.
320-321	Persecution of Christians in the East.
324	Constantine becomes sole ruler of Roman Empire.
325	First ecumenical council at Nicaea.
330	Byzantium rebuilt as Constantinople, capital of Roman Empire.
337	Death of Constantine.

BIBLIOGRAPHICAL NOTE

I WOULD HOPE this book might serve at least two purposes: that it might incite those readers who come to it without much knowledge of the subject to explore further; and that it might also convincingly transmit even to those who know the subject well certain questions that the recent course of our own Christian civilization has urgently raised. The reader who belongs to the first group may welcome suggestions for further reading. If he wants greater factual detail than the plan of this book has permitted me to present, I urge him to read Max Cary, *A History of the Greek World from 323 to 146 B.C.* (2nd Ed., reprinted, London, 1959), and the same author's *A History of Rome* (London, 1938). These two works, taken together, cover the same period as *The Mask of Jove*. They were written by a highly competent scholar, not unwilling to put together the work of many specialists in an intelligible whole. Since these two books of Cary's were originally published in 1932 and 1935 respectively, and therefore before the Second World War and its revolutionary aftermath, both of them reflect assumptions about the nature of civilization that now seem somewhat dated. If the reader will accept an even less present-day account of Roman history, there is greatness still to be found in Theodor Mommsen's *The History of Rome*. Naturally, some of our most agonizing questions never arose in Mommsen's mind. And of course historical and archaeological research since his day has supplied factual data to which he could have no access. Both of these qualifications apply, and naturally with even more force, to Edward Gibbon's magnificent work, *The Decline and Fall of the Roman Empire*. Again, Mommsen's work ends with the dictatorship of Julius Caesar. In effect Gibbon begins his study with the Antonine Emperors, scarcely glancing at the century and a half that followed the assassination of Caesar. And only the first eighteen of his seventy-one chapters fall within the narrative scope of *The Mask of Jove*. Since his unifying theme is the legal entity that called itself the Roman Empire, his story cannot stop until Constantinople has fallen in 1453. Living in the autumnal culture of the late eighteenth century, Gibbon responded the more readily to the autumnal culture of Antonine Rome. Living also in the capital of a growing, modern empire, he felt no qualms about colonialism. A rationalist and a skeptic, he was not attracted to the Christian community that proved such a nuisance to the Roman

539

Imperial administration. As a cultivated, conservative English gentleman, he was unlikely to see in the Roman Empire the few rich riding the many poor and weak, as a camel might ride an ant. This analogy is Lucian's (*Saturnalia*, 19), who actually lived under the Antonines, while Gibbon only praised their reigns. Nevertheless, Gibbon possessed the wit, the irony, the scorn for obfuscation and maudlin enthusiasm that marked his class and his period. These, together with a certain solidity of verbal architecture, which he and Mommsen both achieved, serve as a salutary reminder that, while the diligence and care that both men exhibit are necessary conditions for good history, they are never its sufficient cause, and that bad writing usually reflects muddled thinking. In addition to such general works as those mentioned, there are of course many excellent books, too numerous to list here, that treat of various special periods, areas, or problems of Hellenistic or Roman history. Without such special studies, no useful general history could be undertaken.

In my Bibliographical Note to *The Will of Zeus* I urged the reader not to content himself with what historians of our own day said that the Greeks said but to let the Greeks speak for themselves, even if only through translations. Unfortunately, few of the Greek writers who lived in the period which this second volume of my history covers spoke as well as an impressive number of their ancestors. And none of the authors who wrote in Latin, including those our Western world has most often praised and so long cherished, ever in my judgment produced as inspired works as some of the Greeks produced in the fifth and fourth centuries B.C. On the other hand, Latin literature remains in some respects more immediately accessible to Western man than Greek, and especially to American readers of the twentieth century: the problems it deals with and the society it depicts are in many ways so much more similar to his own.

I would urge those readers who wish to experience directly the alienation and anxiety of Graeco-Roman civilization during the period covered by this book to read or reread some of the principal works I have discussed in the text. If they know enough Latin or Greek to prefer to have the original text on the left-hand page while reading an English translation on the right, I recommend the Loeb Classical Library, now published in this country by the Harvard University Press. Not all the translations in it are equally felicitous, but this fact is partly compensated for by the inclusion of useful explanatory footnotes.

I have not discussed any work of either Latin or Greek literature merely as an historical document, as source material. Every work I discussed seems to me either a voice that speaks to the modern reader from another world than ours or a remark overheard and equally revealing to the ironic ear.

540

NOTES

CHAPTER ONE

1. Arrian: *Anabasis of Alexander* VII, 26, 3. Author's trans.
2. Homer: *Iliad* XX, 291 ff.
3. Ibid., XX, 307-8. Loeb.
4. Ibid., XX, 325.
5. Ibid., V, 311 ff.; 344 ff.
6. Plutarch: *Lives* II, Camillus xxii, 2. Loeb.
7. Ennius: *Satires* II, 3-4. In *Remains of Old Latin*, Loeb.
8. Throughout this book I shall speak of the popular assembly as if there were only one such body. Actually, there were several different kinds of popular assembly at Rome and these exercised various functions at various periods of Roman history, but it would not, I believe, aid the reader to tell him each time I speak of the popular assembly which one I mean. For all practical purposes popular assemblies lost their power when the Republic fell and was succeeded by the principate of Augustus.
9. Livy: *From the Founding of the City* I, xvi, 4. Loeb.
10. Aulus Gellius: *Attic Nights* XX, 1, 48. His interpretation is sometimes challenged. The law reads: "When debt has been acknowledged, or judgment about matter has been pronounced in court, 30 days must be the legitimate time of grace. After that, then arrest of debtor may be made by laying on hands. Bring him into court. If he does not satisfy the judgment, or no one in court offers himself as surety on his behalf, creditor may take defaulter with him. He may bind him either in stocks or in fetters; he may bind him with weight not less than 15 pounds, or with more if he shall so desire. Debtor if he shall wish may live on his own. If he does not live on his own, person [who shall hold him in bonds] shall give him one pound of grits for each day. He may give more if he shall so desire. On third market-day creditors shall cut pieces. Should they have cut more or less than their due, it shall be with impunity." Translator's brackets. (Table III of the Twelve Tables. In *Remains of Old Latin*, Loeb.)
11. Livy: *From the Founding of the City* V, xxxvii, 8. Loeb.
12. Ibid., V, xlviii, 8-9.
13. Ibid., V, l, 8.
14. Ibid., V, li, 5.
15. Ibid., V, lii, 2.
16. Tertullian: *Apology* XXXIII, 4. Loeb.
17. The reader should be warned that we possess no account of the Roman triumph dating from the period in which Camillus triumphed, the early fourth century B.C. The account given here is based on Livy and Appian. Given the Romans' profound conservatism in matters of religious ritual, it is most doubt-

ful that the ceremony of the official triumph had substantially changed by the time of either of these two writers.

18. Livy: *From the Founding of the City* II, xii, 13. Loeb.

19. Ibid., VII, vi, 4-5.

20. Ibid., VIII, ix, 4-9.

21. Ibid., VIII, ix, 13.

22. Ibid., X, xxviii, 15-18.

23. Ibid., I, lvi, 6.

24. Cicero: *De Inventione* II, 66. Loeb.

25. Author unknown. Ascribed to Neleus in *Remains of Old Latin* II, 629, Loeb.

26. Xenophon: *Anabasis* III, i, 4-7. See also Stringfellow Barr: *The Will of Zeus*, New York, 1961, pp. 299-300.

27. See Stringfellow Barr: *The Will of Zeus*, pp. 239 ff., for Socrates' distinction between eristic and dialectic. See ibid., p. 46, for the way a great Greek poet had made the same distinction centuries earlier, in his epic *Works and Days*, lines 11-26, where Hesiod speaks of Eris, goddess of strife, and insists that there were two Erises, not one: the good Eris and the evil Eris. From the philosophical poet and the poetic philosopher we can gather that the good Eris presides over the Socratic dialectic in Plato's dialogues and that the evil Eris presides over what contemporary journalism calls eyeball-to-eyeball, or sometimes belly-to-belly, confrontations. Eristic, a word of course derived from Eris, is Socrates' name for such disputes. The confrontations of dialectic are mind-to-mind. They can be excitingly engaged in, even with eyes closed and bellies decorously far apart.

28. Tenney Frank: *Economic Survey of Ancient Rome*, Baltimore, 1937, Vol. I, p. 40.

29. Appian: *Roman History* VI, The Wars in Spain 21. Loeb.

30. Plutarch: *Lives* IX, Pyrrhus xix, 5. Loeb.

31. This date is in dispute.

32. Livy: *From the Founding of the City* V, ii, 1. Loeb.

33. Cicero: *De Re Publica* II, 40. Loeb.

34. Livy: *From the Founding of the City* III, xix, 12. Loeb.

35. Ibid., IV, ii, 2-7.

36. Ibid., IV, iii, 1-9.

37. Ibid., IV, iv, 4-12.

38. Ibid., IV, v, 5-6.

39. Ibid., IV, lviii, 12.

40. Ibid., VI, xxvii, 7.

41. Ibid., VI, xxxi, 4.

42. Ibid., V, iii, 6-7.

43. Ibid., X, vi, 7-11.

44. Ibid., X, viii, 3-4.

45. According to Suetonius, (*The Deified Augustus* XXII, Loeb) the temple was closed only twice before Augustus closed it in 29 B.C.

46. Livy: *From the Founding of the City* XLII, lxii, 11. Loeb.

47. Ibid., XLII, lxii, 7.

48. Unfortunately for this tradition, Rome expelled her last king about a century and a half before Pythagoras taught at Croton.

49. Livy: *From the Founding of the City* I, xix, 1. Loeb.
50. Ibid., II, i, 1.
51. Ibid., III, xxxi, 8.
52. Ennius: *Annals* 467. In *Remains of Old Latin*, Loeb.
53. Livy: *From the Founding of the City* IX, xi, 6-8. Loeb.
54. Ibid., VIII, v, 5-6.
55. Ibid., VIII, v, 8-10.
56. This statue is thought to have been cast in the sixth century B.C. The statue as it now appears shows suckling twins that were added in the sixteenth century.
57. Polybius: *The Histories* I, 22, 3. Loeb.
58. Pliny: *Natural History* VII, lx, 214. Loeb.

CHAPTER TWO

59. Athenaeus: *The Deipnosophists* 652f. Loeb.
60. Many modern scholars believe that the name of the Cynic school derived from its site, at the "Place of the Dog," outside Athens.
61. Diogenes Laertius: *The Lives of Eminent Philosophers* VI, 54. Loeb.
62. Ibid., VI, 63. Author's trans.
63. Athenaeus: *The Deipnosophists* 254c. Loeb.
64. Epicurus: "Letter to Monoeceus" 124. Tr. Cyril Bailey, Oxford, 1926.
65. Ibid., 128. Translator's brackets.
66. Ibid., 132. Translator's brackets.
67. Epicurus: "Principal Doctrines" XXVII, 148. Tr. Cyril Bailey, Oxford, 1926.
68. In the third century A.D., Diophantus of Alexandria did invent the beginnings of algebraic notation. But by then Greek mathematics had largely lost its impetus.
69. See T. L. Heath: *Greek Mathematics*, Oxford, 1921, Vol. II, pp. 81-85, for Archimedes' notation. See Vol. I, Chap. 2, for the numerical notation the Greeks used.
70. Aristotle: *The Metaphysics* I, 1.
71. This toy engine is often ascribed to Heron, who described it in his *Pneumatica*.
72. In the view of modern scholars, many of the Hippocratic writings were not written by Hippocrates himself but by his followers.
73. Heraclitus had entitled a book of his poems *Nightingales*.
74. Callimachus: *To Heracleitus*. Tr. William Cory. In Edward Capps: *From Homer to Theocritus*, New York, 1901, p. 153.
75. As to those cocks of the Muses, the contemporaries of Theocritus were unlikely not to be reminded especially of those subsidized cocks whom Theocritus would have met at the Museum of Alexandria, as described by Athenaeus. See p. 54.
76. *The Idylls of Theokritos* VII. Tr. Barriss Mills. West Lafayette, Ind., 1961, p. 28.
77. Ibid., XIX, p. 72.
78. Theocritus: *Epigrams* XVI. Tr. A. S. F. Gow, Cambridge, 1950.
79. Ibid., XX.

80. Ibid., XVIII.
81. Athenaeus: *The Deipnosophists* 22d. Loeb.
82. Polybius: *The Histories* V, 88, 2-5. Loeb.
83. Sallust: *The War with Catiline* LI, 37-38. Loeb. Sallust ascribes these words to Julius Caesar, in a speech before the Roman Senate in December, 63.
84. Polybius: *The Histories* II, 24, 17. Loeb.
85. Author's translation of *Unus homo nobis cunctando restituit rem*. (Ennius: *Annals* II, 360. In *Remains of Old Latin*, Loeb.) E. H. Warmington, the Loeb translator of Ennius, quite justifiably understands *rem* to be the *rem publicam*, or Republic, and translates it as "the state."
86. Polybius: *The Histories* III, 78, 2-3. Loeb.
87. Ibid., XI, 19, 4-5.
88. Ibid., V, 101, 6 – 102, 1.
89. Ibid., V, 104.
90. Ibid., V, 105, 4-8.
91. Livy: *From the Founding of the City* XXIV, ii, 8. Loeb.
92. Plutarch: *Lives* V, Marcellus xix, 4. Loeb.
93. Livy: *From the Founding of the City* XXIV, xxxiv, 1-2. Loeb.
94. Polybius: *The Histories* IX, 37, 7 – 38, 1. Loeb.
95. Appian: *Roman History* VI, The Wars in Spain 23. Loeb.
96. Polybius: *The Histories* XV, 8, 2. Loeb.
97. Ibid., XV, 10, 2.
98. Ennius: *Annals* 312. In *Remains of Old Latin*, Loeb.
99. Polybius: *The Histories* VI, 24, 9. Loeb.
100. Ibid., VI, 26, 10.
101. Ibid., VI, 31, 10.
102. Ibid., VI, 41, 10-12.
103. Livy: *From the Founding of the City* XLIV, xxxix, 5. Loeb.
104. Polybius: *The Histories* VI, 37, 1 – 38, 4. Loeb.
105. Ibid., VI, 39, 9-11.
106. Ibid., X, 16, 6 – 17, 2.
107. Ibid., VI, 47, 7-10.
108. Ibid., VI, 50, 3-6.
109. Livy: *From the Founding of the City* XL, xlvii, 5. Loeb.
110. Lucilius 1271. In *Remains of Old Latin*, Loeb. Author's translation of '*Vis*' est '*vita*,' vides, '*vis*' nos facere omnia cogit.
111. Ennius: *Annals* 485. In *Remains of Old Latin*, Loeb.
112. Livy: *From the Founding of the City* XL, xxv, 3. Loeb.
113. Polybius: *The Histories* I, 37, 7. Loeb.
114. Ibid., XVIII, 37, 7.
115. Ibid., XVIII, 37, 9.
116. Ibid., XVIII, 37, 12.
117. Ibid., XVIII, 34, 7 – 35, 2.
118. Plutarch: *Lives* X, Titus Flamininus xii, 6. Loeb.
119. Ibid., Titus Flamininus xii, 7.
120. Appian: *Roman History* XI, The Syrian Wars ii, 7. Loeb.
121. Livy: *From the Founding of the City* XXXVI, xli, 5. Loeb.
122. Ibid., XXXIX, li, 9-12.
123. Polybius: *The Histories* III, 11, 7. Loeb.

124. Livy: *From the Founding of the City* XLII, xlv, 4. Loeb.
125. Polybius: *The Histories* XXVII, 8, 7-10. Loeb.
126. Ibid., XXVII, 9, 1.
127. Ibid., XXVII, 10, 3-5.
128. Ibid., XXVIII, 9, 6-8.
129. Livy: *From the Founding of the City* XLII, xxx, 2-7. Loeb.
130. Polybius: *The Histories* XXX, 10, 2. Loeb.
131. Ibid., XXX, 10, 6.
132. Livy: *From the Founding of the City* XLV, xxviii, 5. Loeb.
133. Ibid., XLV, xxvii, 11.
134. Ibid., XLV, iv, 7.
135. Ibid., XLV, xii, 4-6.
136. Polybius: *The Histories* XXX, 18, 1-7. Loeb.
137. Plutarch: *Lives* II, Marcus Cato xxvii, 1. Loeb.
138. Ibid., Marcus Cato xxiii, 1.
139. Ibid., Marcus Cato ii, 4.
140. Ibid., Marcus Cato xxi, 8.
141. Ibid., Marcus Cato ix, 5.
142. Ibid., Marcus Cato xv, 4.
143. Appian: *Roman History* VI, The Wars in Spain 39. Loeb.
144. Iulius Victor: *Ars Rhetorica* I, i. In Carolus Halm: *Rhetores Latini Minores*, Leipzig, 1863, p. 374. Author's trans.
145. Appian: *Roman History* VIII, The Punic Wars 76. Loeb.
146. Ibid., The Punic Wars 77.
147. Ibid., The Punic Wars 78.
148. Ibid., The Punic Wars 79.
149. Ibid., The Punic Wars 81.
150. Ibid., The Punic Wars 85.
151. Ibid., The Punic Wars 86-89.
152. Polybius: *The Histories* XXXI, 25, 2-7. Loeb.
153. Appian: *Roman History* VIII, The Punic Wars 132. Loeb.
154. Ibid., The Punic Wars 134.
155. Polybius: *The Histories* XXXVI, 9, 1-10. Loeb.
156. Antipater of Sidon IX, 151. In *The Greek Anthology*, Loeb.
157. Polybius: *The Histories* XXXIX, 2, 2. Loeb.
158. Ibid., XXXVIII, 16, 6-10.
159. Ibid., I, 4, 4.
160. Justin: *Epitome* XXVIII, i. Bohn Library. M. Holleaux (*Rome, la Grèce et les Monarchies Hellénistiques*, Paris, 1912, pp. 7 ff.) regards the episode as fictitious. Even if he is right about this particular statement, it would be strange if no Greeks either shared or pretended to share the belief that Aeneas of Troy founded Rome.
161. Dionysius of Halicarnassus: *Roman Antiquities* I, 4, 2-3. Loeb.
162. Livy: *From the Founding of the City* XL, v, 7. Loeb.
163. Polybius: *The Histories* XXX, 22, 1-12. Loeb.
164. Livy: *From the Founding of the City* XLI, xx, 10-13. Loeb.
165. Polybius: *The Histories* VI, 56, 6-15. Loeb.
166. Ibid., VI, 53, 5-10.
167. Ibid., XXXI, 26, 9.

168. Ibid., XXXI, 27, 10-11.
169. Ibid., XXIV, 13, 1-6.
170. Livy: *From the Founding of the City* XXIX, xix, 11-12. Loeb.
171. Lucilius 87-93. In *Remains of Old Latin*, Loeb.
172. Naevius: *Epitaph*. In *Remains of Old Latin*, Loeb.
173. Cicero: *De Legibus* I, xx, 53. Loeb.
174. Cicero: *De Oratore* II, 57. Loeb. Written, of course, in the first century, but by a man who had listened as a boy to the orations of Antonius and Crassus.
175. Ibid., II, 4.
176. Ibid., II, 153.
177. Athenaeus: *The Deipnosophists* 250f. Loeb.
178. Ibid., 254b. Athenaeus lived centuries after Rome annexed Greece, but his phrase well expresses the attitude of philhellenes even before Roman armies entered Greece.
179. Cicero: *De Oratore* III, 43. Loeb.
180. Cicero: *Pro Flacco* VII, 16-17.
181. Ibid., VII, 15.
182. Ibid., VII, 19.
183. Ibid., X, 23.

CHAPTER THREE

184. Plutarch: *Lives* X, Tiberius and Caius Gracchus ix, 4-5. Loeb.
185. Appian: *Roman History*, The Civil Wars I, 14. Loeb.
186. Ibid., I, 16.
187. Ibid., I, 17.
188. In this volume the *equites*, or knights, will frequently be called "businessmen." However, it should be remembered that, as time went on, many freedmen, who were not Equites, made their living out of business operations, and even some slaves did so with the consent of their masters.
189. Sallust: *The War with Jugurtha* XXXV, 10. Loeb.
190. Ibid., CXIV, 2.
191. Historians often call this war the Social War, a literal translation of *bellum sociale*, itself a term used by Livy, or at least by an ancient summarizer of his history of Rome. Livy: *From the Founding of the City*, Summaries LXXI. Loeb.
192. No stable figures are available for the number massacred, but 80,000 seems to be the lowest estimate. See Max Cary: *History of Rome*, London, 1938, p. 333.
193. Appian: *Roman History* XII, The Mithradatic Wars 21. Loeb.
194. Plutarch: *Lives* IV, Sulla xiii, 4. Loeb.
195. Appian: *Roman History* XII, The Mithradatic Wars 38. Loeb.
196. Plutarch: *Lives* IV, Sulla xxx, 3. Loeb.
197. Appian: *Roman History*, The Civil Wars I, 98. Loeb.
198. *The Poems of Catullus* 5. Tr. Horace Gregory, New York, 1956. Because Catullus is one of the least translatable of Latin poets, I have chosen a freer translation of his poems than I have done in the case of other writers quoted in this book.
199. Ibid., 7.

200. Ibid., 8.
201. Ibid., 64.
202. Ibid., 101.
203. At least, so far as modern historians know.
204. Lucretius: *De Rerum Natura* I, 1. Loeb.
205. Ibid., I, 24-25.
206. Ibid., I, 62-79.
207. Ibid., II, 1173-74.
208. Ibid., III, 1-3.
209. Ibid., IV, 834-40.
210. Ibid., I, 136-39.
211. Ibid., V, 336-37.
212. Ennius: *Annals* VI, 175-76. In *Remains of Old Latin*, Loeb.
213. Ibid., VI, 480.
214. Ennius: *Epigrams* 9-10. In *Remains of Old Latin*, Loeb.
215. Quoted in Aulus Gellius: *Attic Nights* XIX, ix, 12. Loeb.
216. Lucretius: *De Rerum Natura* I, 699-700. Loeb.
217. Ibid., V, 376; IV, 42; VI, 936; IV, 176.
218. Ibid., II, 1148 ff.
219. Cicero: *The Verrine Orations* II, 4-6. Loeb.
220. Sallust: *The Speech of Macer, Tribune of the Commons to the Commons*, 17-18, 26-27. From the *Histories*. Loeb.
221. Appian: *Roman History*, The Civil Wars I, 120. Loeb.
222. Ibid., II, 2.
223. Sallust: *The War with Catiline* XXXVII, 1-11. Loeb.
224. Ibid., XXXIX, 1-2.
225. Cicero: *In Catilinam* III, 25-29. Loeb.
226. Sallust: *The War with Catiline* XLVIII, 5-6. Loeb.
227. Ibid., LI, 9.
228. Cicero: *In Catilinam* IV, 11-12. Loeb.
229. Ibid., IV, 20-24.
230. Sallust: *The War with Catiline* LII, 13-16. Loeb.
231. Plutarch: *Lives* VII, Cicero xxii, 2. Loeb.
232. Sallust: *The War with Catiline* LXI, 1-6. Loeb.
233. Cicero: *Letters to Atticus* I, 16. Loeb.
234. Cicero: *Pro Sulla* 25. Loeb.
235. Ibid., 33.
236. Cicero: *The Letters to His Friends* XV, iv, 13. Loeb.
237. Ibid., V, vii, 2.
238. Cicero: *Letters to Atticus* I, 14. Loeb.
239. Ibid., I, 19.
240. Ibid., I, 19.
241. Ibid., I, 17.
242. Ibid., II, 1.
243. Cicero: *Letters to His Brother Quintus* III, i, 15-18. In *The Letters to His Friends*, Loeb.
244. Cicero: *The Letters to His Friends* I, ix, 21. Loeb.
245. Appian: *Roman History*, The Civil Wars II, 150. Loeb.
246. Cicero: *Letters to Atticus* II, 1.

247. Cicero: *Letters to His Brother Quintus* I, i, 6. In *The Letters to His Friends*, Loeb.

248. Ibid., I, i, 32.

249. Cicero: *Letters to Atticus* VII, 3. In *The Letters to His Friends* V, xix, 1 and 2. Loeb.

250. Cicero: *Letters to His Brother Quintus* I, i, 11. In *The Letters to His Friends*, Loeb.

251. Ibid., I, ii, 8.

252. Ibid., II, iv, 3.

253. Cicero: *Letters to Atticus* V, 21; VI, 1; VI, 2. Loeb.

254. Cicero: *The Letters to His Friends* XV, i, 5. Loeb.

255. Ibid., I, vii, 10.

256. Ibid., II, xii, 2.

257. Cicero: *Letters to Atticus* V, 17. Loeb.

258. Ibid., III, 10.

259. Ibid., III, 15.

260. Ibid., XII, 3.

261. Cicero: *The Letters to His Friends* V, xii, 3-4. Loeb.

262. Cicero: *Tusculan Disputations* I, 109. Loeb.

263. Cicero: *The Letters to His Friends* V, xiii, 4. Loeb.

264. Cicero: *Letters to Atticus* I, 19. Loeb.

265. Ibid., VII, 3.

266. Cicero: *De Oratore* I, 28-29. Loeb.

267. Ibid., I, 31.

268. Ibid., I, 53.

269. Ibid., I, 47.

270. Ibid., I, 54.

271. Ibid., I, 59.

272. Ibid., I, 66.

273. Ibid., II, 61.

274. Ibid., II, 196.

275. Ibid., II, 77.

276. Ibid., II, 75.

277. Ibid., II, 18.

278. Ibid., III, 214.

279. Ibid., II, 265.

280. Ibid., II, 262.

281. Ibid., III, 139.

282. Cicero: *Brutus* 120-21. Loeb. "Of greater richness" – *uberior in dicendo*, which could have been translated as "more fruitful" or as "more fertile." But I agree with Professor G. L. Hendrickson, the translator, that Cicero is talking about *style* rather than intellectual content.

283. Cicero: *De Oratore* III, 145. Loeb.

284. Ibid., III, 147.

285. Ibid., III, 230.

286. Cicero: *De Re Publica* I, 2. Loeb.

287. Ibid., I, 3.

288. Ibid., I, 12.

289. Ibid., I, 26.

290. Ibid., I, 27.
291. Ibid., I, 28.
292. Ibid., I, 38.
293. Ibid., I, 70.
294. Ibid., I, 31.
295. Cicero: *De Re Publica* I, 39. Author's trans.
296. Cicero: *De Re Publica* I, 39. Loeb.
297. Ibid., II, 29-30.
298. Ibid., II, 42.
299. Ibid., II, 52.
300. It has remained so. Perhaps Western man has always read Cicero far more than he has read Plato, certainly since the Renaissance.
301. Cicero: *De Re Publica* VI, 13. Loeb.
302. Ibid., VI, 25.
303. Ibid., VI, 26.
304. Cicero: *De Legibus* II, 14. Loeb.
305. Ibid., I, 15.
306. Ibid., I, 19.
307. Ibid., I, 28.
308. Ibid., I, 61.
309. Ibid., II, 17.
310. Ibid., II, 26.
311. Ibid., II, 42.
312. Ibid., III, 14.
313. Ibid., III, 14.
314. Ibid., III, 14.
315. Ibid., III, 37.
316. Ibid., III, 39.
317. Dio Cassius: *Roman History* XLII, 49, 4. Loeb.
318. Cicero: *Letters to Atticus* X, 8. Loeb.
319. Ibid., VIII, 16.
320. Appian: *Roman History*, The Civil Wars II, 88. Loeb.
321. Cicero: *Letters to Atticus* XI, 6. Loeb.
322. Suetonius: *The Deified Julius* XXXVII, 2. Loeb.
323. Cicero: *The Letters to His Friends* IX, xviii, 1, Loeb.
324. Ibid., IV, xiii, 6.
325. Dio Cassius: *Roman History* XLIII, 17, 5. Loeb.
326. Suetonius: *The Deified Julius* LIII. Loeb.
327. Cicero: *The Letters to His Friends* IX, xv, 3. Loeb.
328. Ibid., VI, iv, 4.
329. Cicero: *Letters to His Brother Quintus* I, iii, 3. In *The Letters to His Friends*, Loeb.
330. Cicero: *The Letters to His Friends* IX, xi, 1. Loeb.
331. Cicero: *Letters to Atticus* XII, 52. Loeb.
332. Ibid., IV, 16.
333. Cicero: *Brutus* 309. Loeb.
334. Grandson of Marcus Antonius, the orator, who appears as a character in Cicero's *On the Making of an Orator* (*De Oratore*).
335. Cicero: *The Letters to His Friends* XI, v, 1. Loeb.

336. Ibid., X, xxviii, 1.
337. Cicero: *Letters to Atticus* XIV, ix. Loeb.
338. The number of Cicero's villas is unknown but the estimates run as high as nineteen. He also held various city properties.
339. Plutarch: *Lives* VII, Cicero xlviii, 3-4. Loeb.
340. Cicero: *Philippics* XI, 1. Loeb.
341. Dio Cassius: *Roman History* XLVII, 8, 4. Loeb.

CHAPTER FOUR

342. Appian: *Roman History*, The Civil Wars III, 48. Loeb.
343. Ibid., IV, 3.
344. Ibid., IV, 13.
345. Ibid., IV, 137.
346. Ibid., V, 5.
347. Ibid., V, 12-13.
348. Ibid., V, 18.
349. Ibid., V, 27.
350. Ibid., V, 65.
351. Athenaeus: *The Deipnosophists* IV, 148c. Loeb.
352. Roman law was not fully codified until Justinian's day, half a millennium later.
353. Many modern scholars for obvious reasons insist on rendering this name in English as Vergil. In this volume I have chosen the more familiar English spelling.
354. Horace: *The Odes and Epodes*, Ode II, vii, 10. Loeb.
355. Virgil: *Georgics* I, 1-5. Loeb.
356. Ibid., IV, 559-66.
357. Horace: *The Odes and Epodes*, Epode XVI, 9-12. Loeb.
358. Ibid., Epode XVI, 63-66.
359. Dio Cassius: *Roman History* LIII, 11, 1-5. Loeb.
360. Professor Lily Ross Taylor (*The Divinity of the Roman Emperor*, Middletown, Conn., 1931, pp. 159-60) connects *augustus* through *augere* with *auctoritas*, and points out that Augustus himself later claimed in his *Res Gestae* that he was given more authority, not more power, than his fellow magistrates. Dr. Taylor also considers *augustus* a synonym for "holy" and "divine."
361. No dependable estimate of the Empire's population exists. The *Res Gestae* of Augustus, however, gives the number of *citizens* at different periods of his reign. The number steadily increased.
362. Dio Cassius: *Roman History* LII, 42, 6. Loeb.
363. Horace: *Odes* IV, 15. Tr. Helen Rowe Henze, Norman, Okla., 1961.
364. Ibid.
365. Horace: *The Odes and Epodes*, Ode IV, xv, 17. Loeb.
366. Suetonius: *Life of Horace*. Loeb.
367. Horace: *Odes* II, v, 13-14. Author's trans. of *currit enim ferox aetas*.
368. Horace: *Odes* III, 30. Tr. Helen Rowe Henze, Norman, Okla., 1961.
369. Ibid., III, 1.
370. Ibid.
371. Ibid., II, 10.

372. Ibid.

373. Ibid., I, 24.

374. Ibid.

375. Horace: *Satires, Epistles, Ars Poetica,* Epistle II, 1, 156-57. Loeb.

376. Ibid., Ars Poetica 268-72.

377. Ibid., Ars Poetica 323-32.

378. Horace: *Odes* III, 5. Tr. Helen Rowe Henze, Norman, Okla., 1961.

379. Suetonius: *The Life of Virgil* 46. Loeb.

380. Virgil's regular epithet for Aeneas. Since its English derivative, pious, has fallen on evil days, I have generally preserved the Latin spelling in speaking of Aeneas.

381. Virgil: *The Aeneid* I [234-37]. Tr. Michael Oakley, New York, 1957, pp. 7-8.

382. Ibid., I [260-83], pp. 8-9.

383. Ibid., I [402-9], pp. 12-13.

384. Ibid., IV [379-84], p. 77.

385. Ibid., VI [273-81], p. 121.

386. Ibid., VI [624], p. 130.

387. Virgil: *The Aeneid* VI, 792-93. Loeb. "Son of a god"—*divi genus.*

388. Virgil: *The Aeneid* VI, [847-53]. Tr. Michael Oakley, New York, 1957, p. 137.

389. Ibid., XI [231-33], p. 249.

390. Ibid., XI [305-7], pp. 251-52.

391. Ibid., I [33], p.2.

392. Virgil: *Aeneid* XII, 951-52. Loeb.

393. Virgil: *The Aeneid* XII [838-40]. Tr. Michael Oakley, New York, 1957, pp. 294-95.

394. Ibid., XI [182-83], p. 248.

395. Ibid., IV [231], p. 72.

396. Ibid., I [662], p. 20.

397. Ibid., I [227], p. 7.

398. *The Poems of Catullus* 64. Tr. Horace Gregory, New York, 1956.

399. Virgil: *Georgics* III, 284. Loeb.

400. Virgil: *The Aeneid* IV [165-75]. Tr. Michael Oakley, New York, 1957, pp. 70-71.

401. Ibid., IX [184-85], p. 194.

402. The face of Augustus' statue reproduced in his volume (see Plate X) does less justice to his worried brow than the Prima Porta statue.

403. Boscoreale Goblet, Louvre. See Plate I.

404. Up to the time of McAdam in the eighteenth century, the best roads England possessed had been built when she was still a Roman province. Some of these are still important highways.

405. Estimate given in Max Cary: *History of Rome,* London, 1938, p. 505.

406. Velleius Paterculus: *Compendium of Roman History* II, cxxx, 2. Loeb.

407. Livy: *From the Founding of the City* X, xxi, 9. Loeb.

408. A king of the Parthians.

409. A son of Orodes, King of Parthia, the conqueror of Crassus.

410. Horace: *Odes* III, 6. Tr. Helen Rowe Henze, Norman, Okla., 1961.

411. Horace: *The Odes and Epodes,* Carmen Saeculare 49-52. Loeb.

412. Dio Cassius: *Roman History* LIII, 18, 1-2; 28, 2. Loeb.

413. Suetonius: *The Deified Augustus* LVI, 2. Loeb.

414. Virgil: *The Aeneid* I [282]. Tr. Michael Oakley, New York, 1957, p. 9. Cf. Suetonius: *The Deified Augustus* XL, 5. Loeb.

415. Plutarch: *Moralia* IV, 266C. Loeb.

416. Dio Cassius: *Roman History* LIV, 17, 5. Loeb.

417. Ibid., LIII, 19, 1-3.

418. Tibullus I, 1, 53-58. In L. R. Lind: *Latin Poetry*, Boston, 1957, p. 219.

419. Ibid., II, 6, 1-14, pp. 230-31.

420. Tibullus II, v, 23. Loeb. It is claimed that this is the earliest appearance in extant Latin literature of the phrase *aeterna urbs*, Eternal City.

421. Ibid., II, v, 39.

422. Ibid., II, v, 57.

423. Ibid., II, v, 105-12.

424. *The Poems of Propertius* II, i, 17-26. Tr. Constance Carrier, Bloomington, Ind., 1963, pp. 57-58.

425. Ibid., II, i, 43-45, p. 58.

426. Ibid., II, i, 71-78, p. 59.

427. Propertius II, vi, 19-22. Loeb.

428. Ibid., II, x.

429. Ibid., II, xxxi.

430. *The Poems of Propertius* II, vii, 5-20. Tr. Constance Carrier, Bloomington, Ind., 1963, p. 67.

431. Propertius II, xxxiv, 61-66. Loeb.

432. For this poem to Maecenas, see Propertius III, ix. Loeb.

433. *The Poems of Propertius* III, xiii, 47-60. Tr. Constance Carrier, Bloomington, Ind., 1963, pp. 139-40.

434. Sulpicia IV, 7. In L. R. Lind: *Latin Poetry*, Boston, 1957, p. 239. The six poems from Sulpicia's hand appeared after Tibullus' death, in Book III of Tibullus' poems, and were ascribed to his pen.

435. Ovid: *Amores* I, i, 1-4. Loeb.

436. Ovid: *The Art of Love* I, 637. In *The Art of Beauty, The Remedies for Love, and The Art of Love*. Tr. Rolfe Humphries, Bloomington, Ind., 1957.

437. Ibid., III, 121-28.

438. Ovid: *The Remedies for Love*, 441-44. In *The Art of Beauty, The Remedies for Love, and The Art of Love*. Tr. Rolfe Humphries, Bloomington, Ind., 1957.

439. Ovid: *The Metamorphoses* II, 331-32. Tr. Rolfe Humphries, Bloomington, Ind., 1955.

440. Ibid., VIII, 719-22.

441. Ibid., VIII, 324-28.

442. Ibid., X, 299-303.

443. Ibid., XIII, 478-80.

444. Ibid., XIV, 568-69.

445. Ibid., XV, 858-70.

446. Ibid., XV, 871-79.

447. Ovid: *Tristia* II, 5-8. Author's trans.

448. Ibid., II, 207.

449. Ovid: *Fasti* I, 217-18. Loeb.

450. Ovid: *Tristia* IV, 33-37. Author's trans.
451. Dio Cassius: *Roman History* LVI, 16, 1-3. Loeb.
452. Suetonius: *The Deified Augustus* XXIII, 2. Loeb.
453. Dio Cassius: *Roman History* LVI, 5, 1. Loeb.
454. Suetonius: *The Deified Augustus* XXVIII, 2. Loeb.
455. *Res Gestae Divi Augusti* 1-35. Loeb. Augustus must have drafted this document earlier than his seventy-sixth year if Suetonius, in *The Deified Augustus* CI, is correct in his report that Augustus wrote his will on April 3, A.D. 13. For the will mentions this document. On the other hand, the document itself (8) mentions his third census, which was completed only a hundred days before his death. Augustus or an editor must have revised or at least retouched it.
456. Suetonius: *The Deified Augustus* XCIX, 1. Loeb.

CHAPTER FIVE

457. On the whole question of the star the Magi followed, see Ethelbert Stauffer: *Jesus and His Story*, New York, 1960, pp. 32-35. For the much disputed chronology of Jesus' life, I have chosen to follow Stauffer.
458. The *Pentateuch* comprised the five books of the Torah, which are also the first five of the Old Testament.
459. Matthew 4, 1-11. In *The New Testament*, tr. Ronald Knox, New York, 1945. (Hereafter cited as Knox.)
460. Leviticus 19, 18. The great Hebrew prophets not only had harsh things to say on the subject of social injustice; they also, like Jesus, preached compassion.
461. Velleius Paterculus: *History of Rome* II, cxvii, 2. Loeb.
462. Matthew 22, 17. Knox.
463. Ibid., 22, 19.
464. On this probability see Ethelbert Stauffer: *Christ and the Caesars*, London, 1955, pp. 124 ff.
465. Matthew 22, 20-21. Knox.
466. When Pilate's troops had entered Jerusalem bearing standards that portrayed their god-Emperor, the Jews had rioted. See Ethelbert Stauffer: *Christ and the Caesars*, London, 1955, pp. 118-19.
467. Luke 10, 41. Knox.
468. Matthew 13, 22. Knox.
469. Plato: *Republic* II, 373D-E.
470. Matthew 6, 24. Knox. In the King James version, "Ye cannot serve God and mammon." But mammon is an attempt to translate a Syriac word for money.
471. Mark 11, 15-17. Knox.
472. John 8, 32. Knox.
473. But on the role of love in Socrates' teaching, see Simone Weil: *Intimations of Christianity among the Greeks*, Boston, 1958, Chap. IX, "The Symposium of Plato."
474. On this mysterious process of turning around, of being converted, Socrates spoke in his allegory of the cave or den. Plato: *Republic* VII, 514-517A.

475. Luke 16, 1-9. Knox.
476. For this view of Socrates', see Plato: *Republic* VII, 517A.
477. Matthew 16, 17. Knox.
478. Mark 9, 1-6. Knox.
479. Isaiah 66, 23.
480. Not to be confused with the Passover Feast. See Ethelbert Stauffer: *Jesus and His Story*, New York, 1960, pp. 113-18.
481. Matthew 26, 52. Knox.
482. Matthew 26, 63-75. Knox.
483. Philo: *The Embassy to Gaius* 38. Tr. E. Mary Smallwood, Leiden, 1961.
484. Luke 23, 2. Knox.
485. Mark 15, 2-5. Knox.
486. Mark 15, 13-15. Knox.
487. Mark 15, 18-19. Knox.
488. This statement apparently contradicts the unanimous judgment of the Sanhedrin that Jesus had blasphemed and that "the penalty is death." But note that their charge to Pilate was not that Jesus was a blasphemer but that he was a political subversive. The Sanhedrin really was powerless to punish subversion with capital punishment.

It would appear that the Jewish religious oligarchy was even more responsible for the crucifixion of Jesus than Pilate, at least morally. In any case the many Jews who followed Jesus were not responsible, much less the Jewish race. Yet one of the cries of Christian anti-Semitism has long been the cruel and absurd one of "Christ killers."

489. John 18, 31-38. Knox.
490. John 19, 5-22. Knox.
491. Matthew 27, 24. Knox.
492. Mark 15, 7. Knox.
493. Luke 23, 19. Knox.
494. Matthew 27, 16. Knox.
495. John 18, 40. Knox.
496. Mark 16, 3-20. Knox.
497. Luke 24, 11. Knox.
498. Acts 2, 1-13. Knox.
499. Acts 2, 32-36. Knox.
500. Acts 7, 55-59. Knox.
501. Luke 23, 34. Knox.
502. Acts 9, 4-9. Knox.
503. Hebrews 13, 14. Knox.
504. Acts 14, 10-14. Knox.
505. Acts 17, 16-26. Knox.
506. Acts 17, 31-32. Knox.
507. That the John who wrote the Apocalypse is the same John who wrote the fourth gospel is widely disputed by modern biblical scholars.
508. Apocalypse 17, 1. Knox.
509. Apocalypse 17, 15. Knox.
510. Apocalypse 17, 18. Knox.
511. Apocalypse 17, 5. Knox.

512. Apocalypse 18, 2-3. Knox.
513. Apocalypse 18, 10-19. Knox.
514. Galatians 5, 25-26. Knox.
515. Hebrews 13, 5. Knox.
516. I Thessalonians 4, 6. Knox.
517. Ephesians 5, 5. Knox.
518. Colossians 3, 5. Knox.
519. I Timothy 6, 10. Knox.
520. Titus 3, 1. Knox.
521. I Timothy 2, 1-2. Knox.
522. II Thessalonians 3, 10. Knox.
523. Titus 3, 8. Knox.
524. Ephesians 6, 5-9. Knox.
525. I Corinthians 6, 1. Knox.
526. I John 5, 6. Knox.
527. John 14, 15-17. Knox.
528. Ephesians 4, 25. Knox.
529. I John 1, 5-6. Knox.
530. Hebrews 3, 13-15. Knox.
531. I Corinthians 3, 18. Knox.
532. I Peter 5, 5. Knox.
533. Plato: *Phaedo* 118A. Loeb.
534. From which the English word priest is derived, via the Latin *presbyter*.
535. Luke 19, 11. Knox.
536. I Peter 4, 7. Knox.
537. James 5, 8. Knox.
538. I John 2, 18. Knox.
539. II Peter 3, 4-9. Knox.
540. John 13, 35. Knox.
541. Luke 17, 21. Knox.
542. On this charge, see Ethelbert Stauffer: *Jesus and His Story*, New York, 1960, pp. 16-18.
543. Philippians 4, 22. Knox.
544. I Peter 5, 13. Knox.
545. Tacitus: *The Annals* XV, xxxviii. Loeb.
546. Ibid., XV, xliv.
547. Lucian: *Demonax* 57.

CHAPTER SIX

548. The Romans insisted on regarding the religious rite of circumcision as mutilation.
549. Tacitus: *The Histories* V, 5. Loeb.
550. Suetonius: *Tiberius* XXXVI. Loeb.
551. Philo: *The Embassy to Gaius* 226. Tr. E. M. Smallwood, Leiden, 1961.
552. Ibid., 346.
553. Josephus: *Antiquities of the Jews* XVIII, viii, 3. Tr. William Whiston, New York, 1897.
554. Suetonius: *The Deified Claudius* XXV, 4. Loeb.

555. Dio Cassius: *Roman History* LX, 6, 6. Loeb.
556. Philo: *The Embassy to Gaius* 281-83. Tr. E. M. Smallwood, Leiden, 1961.
557. Josephus: *The Jewish War* II, 372-87. Loeb.
558. Ibid., II, 390.
559. Ibid., II, 397-98.
560. Suetonius: *The Deified Vespasian* IV, 5. Loeb.
561. Tacitus: *The Histories* II, iv. Loeb.
562. Josephus: *The Jewish War* II, 560. Loeb.
563. Ibid., VII, 367-69.
564. Ibid., III, 210.
565. Ibid., V, 367-68.
566. Ibid., VI, 420.
567. Ibid., VI, 317.
568. Dio Cassius: *Roman History* LXVII, 14, 2. Loeb.
569. Pliny: *Natural History* XIII, 46. Loeb.
570. Juvenal: *Satires* XIV, 100-6. Loeb. In a note to his Loeb translation, Dr. G. G. Ramsay suggests that "the desired fountain" may allude to baptism, a rite which John the Baptist, for example, practiced before there was a Christian church. But Juvenal, like many Romans, might have seen no difference between the Jew and the Christian and might have thought that the Christian rite of baptism was Jewish and open only to the circumcised.
571. Suetonius: *The Deified Vespasian* XXIII, 4. Author's trans.
572. Suetonius: *Domitian* XIII, 2. Loeb.
573. Pliny: *Letters* X, xxcvi. Loeb.
574. Ibid., X, xcvii.
575. *The Home-coming of Rutilius Claudius Namatianus* I, 66. Ed. C. H. Keene, tr. George F. Savage-Armstrong, London, 1907. *Urbem fecisti, quod prius orbis erat.*
576. *Inscriptionum Latinarum* 4068. Ed. Johann Kaspar von Orelli and W. Henzen, Turici, 1828-56.
577. Seneca: Epistles (*Ad Lucilium epistulae morales*) VII, 5. Loeb.
578. Reputable modern historians sometimes casually repeat that Rome ruled the civilized world. This extraordinary statement can be made by careful scholars if they themselves live in one of Rome's western provinces, where well into the twentieth century "civilization" meant the civilization of modern Europe and was identified as the latest, highest form of the civilization which Rome once organized politically.
579. Cicero: *On the Commonwealth* III, xxii. Tr. George Holland Sabine and Stanley Barney Smith, Columbus, Ohio, 1929.
580. No firm population statistics for the whole Empire exist. Some modern historians estimate a total even lower than 70,000,000.
581. The soldier's four words became, through the phonetic changes operative in northern France, *tête, bouche, cheval,* and *chez.* Similar linquistic shifts occurred in Spain, Portugal, Rumania, and in Italy itself. Modern Romance languages did not, of course, develop from literary Latin but from the Latin the Italian populace spoke and brought from Italy.
582. Suetonius: *Tiberius* XXV, 1.
583. Tacitus: *The Histories* I, iv. Loeb.

584. Some of these titles have, of course, endured to the present: *princeps* as prince; *imperator* as emperor; *Caesar* as kaiser and tsar. *Caesar* became the Empire's commonest designation of its ruler, regardless of his lineage, as the word emperor became the more general modern usage.

585. Suetonius: *Caligula* LV, 2. Loeb.

586. Appian: *Roman History*, Preface 7-8. Loeb.

587. Tacitus: *The Annals* XI, vii. Loeb.

588. Dio Cassius: *Roman History* LXV, 2, 5. Loeb.

589. Ibid., LXV, 14, 3-4.

590. Juvenal: *Satires* III, 46-50. Loeb.

591. Both of these last estimates are charitable, even when allowance has been made for the torrent of slander to which absolute power is exposed.

592. Seneca: *Moral Essays* III, 26, 1. Loeb.

593. Suetonius: *Caligula* XIII. Loeb.

594. Ibid., XXX, 2.

595. Ibid., XXII, 2-4.

596. Dio Cassius: *Roman History* LXII, 20, 5. Loeb.

597. Ibid., LXIII, 29, 2.

598. Ibid., LXIV, 13, 3-5.

599. Suetonius: *The Deified Vespasian* XXIII, 3. Loeb.

600. Tacitus: *The Annals* III, lxv. Loeb.

601. Ibid., XV, lvii.

602. Tacitus: *Agricola* 45. Loeb. Modern historians tend to discount as prejudiced Tacitus' portrait of Domitian.

603. Seneca: *Moral Essays* II, v, 5. Loeb.

604. Plutarch: *Moralia* 813D-F. Loeb.

605. Juvenal: *Satires* VIII, 98-120. Loeb.

606. Tacitus: *The Annals* III, xl. Loeb.

607. Ibid., III, xl.

608. Tacitus: *The Histories* IV, xiv. Loeb.

609. Ibid., IV, xvii.

610. Ibid., IV, lxxiii.

611. Ibid., IV, lxxiv.

612. Ibid., I, lxiii.

613. Tacitus: *Agricola* 30. Loeb.

614. Ibid., 19.

615. Ibid., 21.

616. Tacitus: *The Annals* XI, xxiv. Loeb.

617. Ibid., XI, xxv.

618. An epithet of Pindar's which had wide currency in the ancient world: "Oh! the gleaming, and the violet-crowned, and the sung in story; the bulwark of Hellas, famous Athens, city divine!" Pindar: *Dithyrambs* 76 (46). Loeb.

619. Pliny: *Natural History* XVIII, 35. Loeb.

620. Our word peach comes from the French word *pêche*, which is in turn derived from the Latin *Persicum* (*malum*), or Persian apple.

621. Pliny: *Natural History* XII, 84. Loeb.

622. Ibid., XXXVI, 12-13.

623. Frontinus: *The Aqueducts of Rome* I, 16. Loeb.

624. Pliny: *Natural History* XXIX, 17. Loeb.

625. Dio Cassius: *Roman History* LVII, 21, 6. Loeb.
626. Pliny: *Natural History* XXXVI, 196; Petronius: *Satyricon* 51.
627. Seneca: *Epistles (Ad Lucilium epistulae morales)* XC, 13. Loeb.
628. Suetonius: *The Deified Claudius* XVIII, 2. Loeb.
629. Suetonius: *Nero* XXXI, 3. Loeb.
630. Seneca: *Moral Essays* VII, 8-9. Loeb.
631. Pliny: *Natural History* XXIX, 19. Loeb.
632. Lucan: *Pharsalia* VII, 527-29. Tr. Sir Edward Ridley, New York, 1905, p. 215.
633. Plato: *Symposium* I, 211C.
634. Juvenal: *Satires* III, 7-9. Loeb.
635. Dio Cassius: *Roman History* LXII, 2, 1. Loeb. This politico-financial venture of Seneca's has been contested as being merely the usual slander that the powerful attract. In the case of Seneca, it was at least mud likely to stick.
636. Seneca: *Epistles (Ad Lucilium epistulae morales)* LVIII, 1. Loeb.
637. Ibid., V, 7.
638. Ibid., XCII, 3.
639. Ibid., XIV, 7-8.
640. Ibid., XVIII, 12.
641. Ibid., LXXXVIII, 12.
642. Ibid., CIV, 27.
643. Ibid., LXXXVIII, 1.
644. Ibid., XC, 44.
645. Seneca: *Moral Essays* IX, ix, 7. Loeb.
646. Ibid., IX, xv, 1.
647. Ibid., XII, x, 3.
648. Pliny: *Natural History* XIV, 139. Loeb.
649. Seneca: *Epistles (Ad Lucilium epistulae morales)* L, 2-3. Loeb.
650. Ibid., LIV, 5; 7.
651. Tacitus: *The Annals* XV, lxii-lxiv. Loeb.
652. Lucan: *Pharsalia* VII, 813-14. Tr. Sir Edward Ridley, New York, 1905, p. 215.
653. Ibid., IX, 1163-67.
654. Tacitus: *The Annals* XV, lvi.
655. Quintilian: *Institutio Oratoria* I, Preface 10. Loeb.
656. Ibid., XII, i, 2.
657. Ibid., II, xvii, 3. Loeb. Although few Americans any longer study the formal art of rhetoric, surely all Americans recognize the primary role of rhetoric in present-day society. It goes of course by other names than rhetoric. It can take the form of white papers, state papers, state department bulletins, overseas information programs, recruiting posters, press releases, ghost-writing, opinion polls, image-making, public relations, sloganeering, and advertising of all sorts, whether hard-sell, soft-sell, whisper-copy, or subliminal. Even those who denounce such devices are often silenced by the explanation that what is called the system, including the national economy and international relations, rests precariously on the skillful management of public opinion. The Roman's name for this management was rhetoric, not Madison Avenue. It should not seem odd to us that he considered rhetorical skill the chief purpose of liberal education, the prerequisite to success in life. The difficulty with this pre-

requisite is stated succinctly by Plato, in an imaginary conversation written by a great Greek satirist: "All this, good sir, is quite according to the principles of rhetoric; that is to say, it is clean contrary to the facts . . ." (Lucian: *The Fisher* 7. Tr. H. W. and F. G. Fowler, Oxford, 1939.)

658. For Greek philosophers like Socrates or Plato or Aristotle, man was an animal who could deal with the *logos*, a word that meant both word and thought. The art of rhetoric mediated between thought and word; hence, between logic and grammar. It governed neither.

659. Quintilian: *Institutio Oratoria* II, xvi, 14-15. Loeb.

660. Ibid., XII, ii, 7.

661. Ibid., XII, xi, 29.

662. Ibid., XII, iii, 12.

663. Ibid., XII, xi, 10.

664. Tacitus: *The Annals* XVI, xix. Loeb.

665. Unhappily, only a fragment of the *Satyricon* has survived to modern times. Some scholars have questioned whether the Petronius who wrote the *Satyricon* was in fact Nero's courtier, Gaius Petronius. The consensus of modern scholars, however, identifies them as the same man.

666. Petronius: *The Satyricon*, pp. 25-26. Tr. William Arrowsmith, Ann Arbor, 1959.

667. Ibid., p. 26.

668. Ibid., p. 27.

669. Ibid., pp. 29-30.

670. Ibid., pp. 33-34.

671. Ibid., p. 37.

672. Ibid., pp. 37-38.

673. Ibid., p. 45.

674. Ibid., pp. 50-51.

675. Ibid., pp. 71-72.

676. Ibid., p. 17.

677. In the Loeb edition, the British translator discreetly publishes some of Martial's foulest epigrams in Italian translation rather than English. If the reader can handle either Italian or Latin, he will be slow to snort at what might seem British hypocrisy.

678. Martial: *Epigrams* V. Loeb.

679. Ibid., VII, 1-6.

680. Ibid., I, xxviii.

681. Ibid., I, xxx.

682. Ibid., I, xxxviii.

683. Ibid., I, lxxiii.

684. Ibid., I, cx.

685. Ibid., II, xx.

686. Ibid., II, xxxi.

687. Ibid., II, xliv.

688. Ibid., III, lxxxii, 1-25.

689. Dio Cassius: *Roman History* LXIX, 19, 2. Loeb.

690. Martial to Priscus, in Preface to Book XII of *Epigrams*. Loeb.

691. Pliny: *Letters* III, xxi. Loeb.

692. Pliny: *Natural History* XV, 19. Loeb.

693. Juvenal: *Satires* III, 62-65. Loeb.

694. Ibid., III, 100-108.

695. Ibid., X, 173-75. If Xerxes had really tried to dig his canal through towering Mount Athos instead of through the low-lying isthmus which connected Athos with the mainland, the Greek historian Herodotus would have lied indeed.

696. Ibid., VII, 216-19.

697. Ibid., VII, 229-43.

698. Ibid., III, 164-67.

699. Ibid., III, 182-83.

700. Ibid., III, 193-202.

701. Ibid., III, 223-26.

702. Ibid., III, 235-38.

703. Ibid., III, 272-77.

704. Ibid., VIII, 87-90.

705. Ibid., VI, 61-66.

706. Ibid., X, 365-66.

707. Ibid., XIII, 134.

708. Ibid., XVI, 7-54.

709. Ibid., X, 72-81. I have changed the last word of *panem et circenses* from "Bread and Games" to "Bread and Circuses," because the latter translation is commoner usage in English, having had immense success in modern times as a political slogan of the conservative.

710. Ibid., XV, 140-59.

711. This judgment is subject to provisos. Not all of Tacitus' history has survived to modern times, nor have all the works of his competitors survived.

712. Tacitus' dialogue would have made the Socrates of Plato's dialogue, the *Gorgias*, smile. Clearly Gorgias, by making rhetoric the architectonic liberal art, had appeared to Socrates as one who worked his will on audiences by flattery. And this flattery struck Socrates as bearing the same relation to true deliberation as cookery bears to medicine, and as costume and cosmetics bear to health-giving gymnastic. This is why Cicero's dream for the Roman Republic would have suggested merely a deal between the Senatorial landholders and the financier Equites, with a Rector to persuade the plebeian assembly that the resultant law and order were the fruit of a just republic. Not Cicero nor Seneca nor any of Plato's other imitators, whether Greek or Roman, ever achieved the dramatic, dialectical tension of Plato's best dialogues, in which genuine ideas as well as persons genuinely encounter each other. In comparison with these dialogues of Plato's, Hellenistic and Roman dialogues are either interrupted monologues or oratorical contests made possible by conventional courtesy, forbearance, and absent-mindedness.

713. Tacitus: *A Dialogue on Oratory* 40-41. Loeb.

714. Tacitus: *Agricola* 3. Loeb.

715. This conjecture is necessitated by the fact that much of both the *Histories* and the *Annals* has not survived to modern times.

716. Tacitus: *The Annals* I, lx-lxii. Loeb.

717. It seems doubtful whether Suetonius was appointed secretary early enough to help him do more than revise the *Lives*, if that. The dates of his service are uncertain.

718. Only his *Lives of the Caesars,* the lives of a few Latin writers, and some fragments have survived.

719. Pliny: *Panegyric* 1, 4-6. Author's trans.

720. Ibid., 11, 1-2.

721. Ibid., 4, 4.

722. Ibid., 26, 1-2.

723. Ibid., 32, 1-2.

724. Ibid., 45, 1.

725. Ibid., 48, 5.

726. Ibid., 52, 3.

727. Ibid., 53, 6.

728. Ibid., 65, 1.

729. Ibid., 67, 3.

730. Pliny: *Letters* X, xl. Loeb. *Graeculi* is translated in Loeb as "these paltry Greeks."

731. It has been guessed from Dio Chrysostom's description of the philosopher who protested that he was Musonius Rufus, from whom the Greek-speaking Asian freedman, Epictetus, first learned Stoicism, a Greek philosophy.

732. Dio Chrysostom 31, 121-22. Loeb.

733. Strabo: *The Geography* III, 4, 19. Author's trans.

734. Commonly called the *Almagest,* a name the Arabs gave it when they acquired Greek science, which they later transmitted to Western Europe.

735. The geocentric system of Ptolemy remained supreme in West European astronomy until in the sixteenth century A.D. Copernicus revived the heliocentric theory of Aristarchus. Galileo and Kepler confirmed this theory with the aid of the telescope.

736. Epictetus: *The Discourses* II, xvii, 1. Loeb.

737. Epictetus: *Manual* 52. Loeb.

738. Epictetus: *The Discourses* I, viii, 16. Loeb.

739. Ibid., I, i, 23.

740. Ibid., I, xix, 6.

741. Ibid., II, xxiii, 10.

742. Ibid., III, ix, 12-14.

743. Ibid., III, xxiv, 85.

744. Ibid., III, xii, 7.

745. Ibid., II, xvii, 22.

746. Ibid., I, iii, 2.

747. Ibid., I, xii, 17.

748. Ibid., IV, i, 131.

749. Epictetus: *Manual* 17. Loeb.

750. Epictetus: *The Discourses* I, ix, 1-6. Loeb.

751. Ibid., I, xxiv, 20.

752. On the other hand, in Roman times much of Gaul's level land was swamp; the art of draining such land was not applied there until centuries later. Meanwhile farmers cultivated high ground, where the soil was less deep but the slope took care of drainage.

753. Although for centuries the Carthaginians traded for tin in Cornwall, the writers in Hadrian's day make little mention of tin in Britain. Extant in-

scriptions, however, show that British tin was mined in the period of the Empire.

754. Some modern historians believe it was at this time that he visited Cyrenaica, now northeastern Libya. The chronological sequence of his visits to various provinces is uncertain.

755. Livy: *From the Founding of the City* XLI, xx, 8. Author's trans.

756. *Scriptores Historiae Augustae*, Hadrian XV, 13. Loeb.

757. Aelius Aristides: *The Roman Oration* 96. Tr. James H. Oliver, in *Transactions of the American Philosophical Society*, Vol. 43, Pt. 4, Philadelphia, 1953.

758. Plutarch: *Lives VII*, Demosthenes ii, 2. Loeb.

759. Its diameter exceeds the diameter of the dome of St. Peter's in Rome.

760. Hadrian's tomb still stands, now known as the Castel Sant' Angelo.

761. Aelius Aristides: *The Roman Oration* 12. Tr. James H. Oliver, in *Transactions of the American Philosophical Society*, Vol. 43, Pt. 4, Philadelphia, 1953.

762. Josephus: *Antiquities of the Jews* XIV, 72. Loeb.

763. *Scriptores Historiae Augustae*, Saturninus VIII, 6-7. Loeb.

764. Pliny: *Natural History* VII, 130. Loeb.

765. On this point, see Dio Cassius: *Roman History* LXIX, 11. Loeb.

766. Pliny: *Natural History* XIX, 38 ff. Loeb.

767. Dio Cassius: *Roman History* LXIX, 14, 1. Loeb.

768. L. Annaeus Florus: *Epitome of Roman History*, Introduction I, 2. Loeb. E. S. Forster, who translated the *Epitome* for the Loeb edition, thinks its author may in fact have been P. Annius Florus, a poet friend of Hadrian's, but follows most recent scholars in ascribing it to Lucius Annaeus Florus.

769. *Scriptores Historiae Augustae*, Hadrian XXIII, 14. Loeb.

770. It is not certain that this poem is Hadrian's. Even his biographer, Aelius Spartianus, about whose accuracy there are many doubts, writes merely that Hadrian "is said, as he lay dying, to have composed the following lines . . ." (*Scriptores Historiae Augustae*, Hadrian XXV, 9. Loeb.) On the other hand, from the far too little we know of Hadrian, the poem is completely in character.

771. That is, if he really was born in 117 and not, as some scholars believe, in 129. Professor James H. Oliver, whose translation of the *Roman Oration* I use, leans toward 117. See *Transactions of the American Philosophical Society*, Vol. 43, Pt. 4, Philadelphia, 1953, p. 886.

772. Aelius Aristides: *Against Plato on Rhetoric* XLV, 47, 15. Ed. William Dindorf, Lipsiae, 1829. Author's trans.

773. Aelius Aristides: *Against Those Who Censure Him for not Declaiming* LI, 421, 5. Ed. William Dindorf, Lipsiae, 1829. Author's trans.

774. Aelius Aristides: *The Roman Oration* 29. Tr. James H. Oliver, in *Transactions of the American Philosophical Society*, Vol. 43, Pt. 4, Philadelphia, 1953.

775. Ibid., 60.

776. Ibid., 82.

777. Ibid., 84.

778. Ibid., 90.

779. Pliny: *Natural History* XXVII, i, 3. Loeb.

780. Aelius Aristides: *The Roman Oration* 97-98. Translated by James H.

Oliver, in *Transactions of the American Philosophical Society*, Vol. 43, Pt. 4, Philadelphia, 1953.
781. Ibid., 100.
782. Ibid., 101.
783. Ibid., 104.

CHAPTER SEVEN

784. Antoninus' full name was Titus Aurelius Fulvius Boionius Antoninus. His wife's nephew, Marcus Annius Verus, became on adoption Marcus Aelius Aurelius Verus Caesar, and is commonly called Marcus Aurelius. Ceionius Commodus' son, Lucius Ceionius Commodus, became on adoption Lucius Aurelius Verus, and is now commonly called Lucius Verus.

785. Whether Aelius Aristides delivered his eulogy of Rome in 143, the date toward which Professor James H. Oliver leans (*The Ruling Power, Transactions of the American Philosophical Society*, Philadelphia, 1953, Vol. 43, Pt. 4, pp. 886-88), or twelve years later, the eulogy was part of a solemn occasion, the celebration of the refoundation of Eternal Rome. It is unlikely that, either as Antoninus Caesar or as Emperor, Marcus would have been absent from this state occasion. In the latter case, of course, Aristides' eulogy came too late to help cause Marcus' conversion from rhetoric to Stoicism.

786. *Scriptores Historiae Augustae:* Marcus Antoninus XVII, 7. Loeb.
787. Marcus Aurelius Antoninus: *Meditations* IX, 29. Author's trans.
788. Tertullian: *To the Nations* I, xvii. In *The Ante-Nicene Fathers*, American Reprint, Grand Rapids, Mich., 1951.
789. Marcus Cornelius Fronto: *Correspondence*, Fronto to Antoninus Augustus, A.D. 162, 1, 10. Loeb II, 63.
790. Ibid., 3, 4. Loeb II, 75.
791. Ibid., Fronto to Lucius Verus, A.D. 165, 5. Loeb II, 137.
792. Ibid., Fronto to Antoninus Augustus, A.D. 165, 8-9. Loeb II, 231.
793. Ibid., Lucius Verus to Fronto, A.D. 165 Loeb II, 197.
794. Ibid., Fronto to Lucius Verus, A.D. 163, 13. Loeb II, 143.
795. Ibid., Lucius Verus to Fronto, A.D. 165. Loeb II, 119.
796. Ibid., Fronto to Lucius Verus, A.D. 165, 1. Loeb II, 199.
797. Ibid., 4. Loeb II, 201.
798. The sources are confused as to the time at which this nondescript force was raised. It may have been when Marcus and Verus had led an army to the relief of Aquileia.
799. Marcus Aurelius Antoninus: *Meditations* IV, 46. Loeb.
800. Ibid., X, 10.
801. Ibid., IV, 32.
802. Ibid., VI, 37.
803. Ibid., VII, 49.
804. Ibid., X, 19.
805. Ibid., X, 15.
806. Ibid., IV, 4.
807. Ibid., IV, 23.
808. Ibid., VI, 44.
809. Ibid., XII, 26.

810. Ibid., VIII, 61.
811. Ibid., I, 14.
812. *Scriptores Historiae Augustae:* Marcus Antoninus XXIII, 5. Loeb.
813. Marcus Aurelius Antoninus: *Meditations* VI, 46. Loeb.
814. Ibid., III, 5.
815. Ibid., X, 5.
816. Ibid., IX, 36.
817. Ibid., IV, 41.
818. Ibid., VII, 61.
819. Ibid., II, 17.
820. Ibid., X, 34. See Homer: *Iliad* VI, 147.
821. Ibid., VIII, 8.
822. Ibid., X, 16.
823. Ibid., V, 16.
824. Ibid., II, 1.
825. Ibid., II, 16.
826. Ibid., IV, 3.
827. Ibid., V, 10.
828. Ibid., VI, 20.
829. Ibid., VI, 27.
830. Ibid., VII, 65.
831. Ibid., IX, 27.
832. Ibid., IX, 42, 4.
833. Ibid., X, 4.
834. Ibid., X, 1.
835. Ibid., XI, 18, 10.
836. Ibid., I, 9, 3.
837. Ibid., I, 11.
838. Ibid., VI, 30.
839. Ibid., VI, 42.
840. Ibid., XI, 8.
841. Ibid., VII, 67.
842. Ibid., VI, 39.
843. Ibid., III, 2.
844. Ibid., X, 21 (quoting Euripides: *Fragments* 890).
845. Ibid.
846. The tribesmen of Mauretania had rebelled twice under Hadrian and once under Antoninus. The brigands who now appeared in Spain may have been as much interested in independence from Rome as in loot. In either case, Roman historians would have called them brigands, the word Romans commonly applied to any of their subjects who, with whatever motive, used force against the law.
847. Philostratus: *The Lives of the Sophists* (16) ii, 9. Quoted in Loeb ed. of Marcus Aurelius Antoninus.
848. Marcus Aurelius Antoninus: *Meditations* XI, 3. Mr. C. R. Haines, whose translation of the *Meditations* has been used throughout this chapter, believes that the phrase in brackets was not written by Marcus but added as a gloss by the hand of another writer. However, he thinks that Marcus may have had the Christians in mind when he wrote this passage, that he would have

approved of the Christian martyrs' willingness to die cheerfully, and that he would have disapproved of those martyrs who seemed to him to substitute stage-heroics for deliberation and dignity. I agree with all three judgments. See Mr. Haines's discussion of this problem in the Loeb edition of Marcus Aurelius, pp. 381-85.

849. Unless, as some think, Marcus did not return to the frontiers until the next year, 178.

850. The evidence that Marcus' illness was caused by the plague is inconclusive. Dio Cassius (*Roman History* LXII, 33) says that Marcus' doctors did away with him to please Commodus. Again, although Aurelius Victor in his *Caesares* XVI, 12, Épitome XVI, 12, writes that he died at Vienna, Tertullian, *Apology* XXV, 5, claims he died at Sirmium. (See *Scriptores Historiae Augustae*, Marcus Antoninus XXVIII, 4 and 8, where Marcus on his deathbed rebukes his friends for not thinking about the pestilence and later sent his son away at once "in fear that he would catch the disease." Loeb.)

851. Marcus Aurelius Antoninus: *Meditations* IX, 3, 1.

852. Ibid., XII, 5.

853. Ibid., X, 36.

854. Ibid., VI, 53.

855. Author's trans. of ἀιδοῦ θεούς, σωξε ἀνθρώπους. The Loeb translation appears on p. 387 of this book.

856. Julius Caesar was no mean writer. But Augustus, not Caesar, is reckoned the first Roman Emperor.

857. On this problem, see A. H. M. Jones: *The Late Roman Empire*, Norman, Okla., 1964, Vol. I, p. 7.

858. Dio Cassius: *Roman History* LXXVII, 15, 2. Loeb.

859. Athenaeus: *The Deipnosophists* IV, 162a. Loeb.

860. Ibid., V, 187c.

861. Ibid., V, 217a.

862. Ibid., I, 20b.

863. Apuleius: *The Golden Ass*. Tr. Robert Graves, Harmondsworth, Eng., 1951, p. 121.

864. Ibid., p. 256.

865. Ibid.

866. Ibid., p. 261.

867. Ibid., p. 262.

868. Ibid., pp. 264-65.

869. Ibid., p. 265.

870. Ibid., p. 267.

871. Ibid., p. 279.

872. Ibid., p. 291.

873. Ibid., p. 293.

874. Lucian: *How to Write History* 16. Loeb.

875. Lucian: *A True Story* I, 4. Loeb.

876. Lucian: *The True History* I, 29. Tr. H. W. and F. G. Fowler, Oxford, 1905.

877. Lucian: *A True Story* II, 20. Loeb.

878. Ibid., II, 35.

879. Ibid., II, 17-18.

880. Lucian: *The Dialogues of the Dead* 20 (10), 368-74. Loeb.
881. Lucian: *The Cynic* 8. Tr. H. W. and F. G. Fowler, Oxford, 1905.
882. Lucian: *Menippus, or the Descent into Hades* 15-16. Loeb.
883. Lucian: *The Dialogues of the Dead* XXV. Tr. H. W. and F. G. Fowler, Oxford, 1905.
884. Lucian: *The Dialogues of the Dead* 30 (25), 433. Loeb.
885. Lucian: *Menippus, or the Descent into Hades* 20. Loeb.
886. Lucian: *The Downward Journey, or the Tyrant* 15. Loeb.
887. Lucian: *Saturnalia* 36-38. Loeb.
888. Ibid., 19.
889. Lucian: *Menippus, or the Descent into Hades* 21. Loeb.
890. Lucian: *Icaromenippus, or the Sky-Man* 24. Loeb. (Aratus: *Phaenomena* 2-3.)
891. Ibid., 9-10.
892. Job xiii, 15. King James.
893. John 3, 16. In *The New Testament*, tr. Ronald Knox, New York, 1945.
894. Leviticus xix, 18. Matthew 22, 39.
895. Lucian: *The Passing of Peregrinus* 11-13. Loeb.
896. Lucian: *The Wisdom of Nigrinus* 13. Loeb.
897. Ibid., 14-17.
898. Ibid., 29.
899. Ibid., 30.
900. Lucian: *The Wisdom of Nigrinus* 21-25. Tr. H. W. and F. G. Fowler, Oxford, 1905.
901. Lucian: *The Dependent Scholar* 3. Tr. H. W. and F. G. Fowler, Oxford, 1905.
902. Ibid., 40.
903. Lucian: *The Wisdom of Nigrinus* 34. Loeb.
904. Lucian: *A True Story* I, 39. Loeb.
905. Lucian: *Charon* 15. Tr. H. W. and F. G Fowler, Oxford, 1905.
906. Ibid., 23.
907. Galen's medical writings were destined to dominate Greek medicine, then Byzantine, then Arabian, and finally West European for a total of some fourteen centuries and were not seriously challenged until the Renaissance.

Many persons, enamored of modern science and convinced that *nous avons changé tout cela*, will smile knowingly at my assessment of Galen. They are urged to read Galen, *On the Natural Faculties*, which is available, incidentally, in an excellent English translation by A. J. Brock, M.D., a long-time student of Hellenic medicine and pupil of Sir Arthur Thomson. Dr. Brock's translation was made with the encouragement of the late Sir William Osler. It is published in the Loeb Classics. It is supplied with an excellent introduction, which gives what is known of Galen's life and assesses his scientific achievement.

Just as a second-rate modern astronomer can, by looking through a telescope, observe relevant phenomena that Ptolemy could never see, so a second-rate modern medical scientist with a microscope, not to mention X-ray, can see phenomena Galen never saw. These two facts conclusively prove the superiority of our scientific instruments over those of the Greeks. How much do they prove about the relative intellectual achievements of those scientists of whatever period who carefully observe what it is in their power to observe and think about what they observe? In my comments on Galen I am speaking, not of his equipment, but of his mind. The same warning applies to my comments on other Greek scientists.

908. Fourteen of these were paired as co-Augusti for at least a portion of their reigns.

909. But as usual, the word brigand may here again refer to freedom fighters against Rome or against economic oppression or both.

910. *Scriptores Historiae Augustae:* The Two Gallieni V, 205. Loeb.

911. Dio Cassius: *Roman History* LXXIII, 14, 3-4. Loeb.

912. Ibid., LXXVII, 8, 1—9, 2.

913. Modern historians estimate this interval to be considerably shorter than six months.

914. *Scriptores Historiae Augustae:* The Deified Aurelian XL, 2-4. Loeb.

915. Ibid., Tacitus XII, 1.

916. Dio Cassius: *Roman History* LXXII, 5, 2-3. Loeb.

917. Ibid., LXXIX, 6, 2.

918. Julius Capitolinus, in his biographies of Maximus, now generally identified as Pupienus, and Balbinus, has a consul congratulating these joint Emperors on restoring the state from the hands of *latrones improbos,* wicked brigands, and alluding to Maximinus as a *sceleratus latro,* criminal brigand (*Scriptores Historiae Augustae* XVII, 1; 2. Loeb translates the two phrases respectively as "wicked bandits" and "impious bandit.") True, documents quoted in *Scriptores* are viewed with suspicion by modern scholars, but there is nothing improbable about the usage itself. Maximinus did usurp the throne by force of arms, but in his day that was the usual method.

919. *Scriptores Historiae Augustae:* Firmus II, 1-3. Loeb. Fonteius is not elsewhere mentioned in available sources, and the editor of the Loeb *Scriptores* writes that both he and the argument here alluded to are probably fictitious. If this should be the case, the point Vopiscus implicitly makes might still hold good: that an Emperor who has killed a would-be usurper could be expected to use the epithet brigand on his rival. The public knew the pretender Firmus had failed to win in a show of force. But the successful claimant still had the problem of persuading the public that the pretender deserved to lose anyhow. Proof? His claim was morally invalid: he was a brigand.

920. Ibid., The Deified Aurelian XXXII, 2.

921. Ibid., Firmus V, 3-6.

922. Ibid., The Deified Aurelian XXVI, 1.

923. Ibid., XXVII, 5.

924. Ibid., The Two Gallieni IV, 9. The reader should be warned that Pollio, like Vopiscus, had a marked prejudice against Gallienus and often exaggerated. But even if the phrase "all parts" is challenged, conditions in the Empire at this period might easily suggest world conspiracy to Pollio.

925. Justinian: *Digest* I, 18, 13 pr. Author's trans.

926. Dio Cassius: *Roman History* LXXV, 2, 4-6. Loeb.

927. Ibid., LXXVII, 10.

928. Much of it now exists only in the form of summaries made centuries later by Xiphilinus and Zonaras.

929. Because Dio Cassius and Herodian are often our only literary sources, they are of practical value to the historian; but this value need not be confused

with the intellectual value of what they wrote. Under judgment here is their caliber as historians, not their apparent lack of competition as purveyors of information not elsewhere to be found.

930. *Scriptores Historiae Augustae:* The Thirty Pretenders XXXII, 7. Loeb.
931. Ibid., The Deified Aurelian X, 1.
932. Ibid., XVII, 1.
933. Plotinos: *Complete Works* I, 6, 8. Tr. Kenneth Sylvan Guthrie, Alpine, N.J., 1918.
934. Ibid., II, 9, 9.
935. Ibid., I, 2, 4.
936. Ibid. I, 3, 6.
937. Ibid., I, 6, 5.
938. Ibid., I, 6, 6.
939. Ibid., I, 7, 1.
940. Ibid., III, 1, 3.
941. Ibid., III, 2, 5.
942. Ibid., III, 2, 7-8.
943. Ibid., III, 2, 8-9
944. Ibid., III, 2, 15.
945. Ibid., III, 2, 17.
946. Ibid., III, 5, 2.
947. Ibid., Porphyry's Life of Plotinos xii.
948. Ibid., xxii.

CHAPTER EIGHT

949. I have followed, on this point, William Seston: *Dioclétian et la Tétrarchie*, Paris, 1946, p. 54.
950. Mamertine's Panegyric to Maximian Augustus, IV. A.D. 289. In *Panégyriques Latins*, ed. Edouard Galletier, Paris, 1949, Vol. I. Author's trans.
951. Herodian: *History of the Roman Empire* IV, Caracalla iii, 5-9. Tr. Edward C. Echols, Berkeley and Los Angeles, 1961.
952. Apparently, by the end of Dioletian's reign, only an Augustus was eternal. A Caesar could merely be perpetual.
953. Mamertine's Anniversary Panegyric to Maximian Augustus, III, x. A.D. 291. In *Panégyriques Latins*, ed. Edouard Galletier, Paris, 1949, Vol. I. Author's trans.
954. According to Max Cary: *History of Rome*, London, 1938, p. 738. But Arthur E. R. Boak, in *A History of Rome to 565 A.D.*, 4th ed., New York, 1955, p. 451, doubts if the army was increased to much more than 450,000.
955. Mamertine's Anniversary Panegyric to Maximian Augustus, III. A.D. 291. In *Panégyriques Latins*, ed. Edouard Galletier, Paris, 1949, Vol. I. Author's trans.
956. *Scriptores Historiae Augustae:* Marcus Antoninus XIX, 12. Loeb.
957. About 180, at least some of the New Testament had been put into Syriac; in the third century, it was translated into Coptic (*Cambridge Ancient History* XII, 492 ff.)
958. *Scriptores Historiae Augustae:* Carus, Carinus, and Numerian X. Loeb.
959. Tertullian: *De Spectaculis* I. Loeb.

960. Lactantius: *Of the Manner in Which the Persecutors Died* X. In *The Ante-Nicene Fathers*, American Reprint, Grand Rapids, Mich., 1951. (Hereafter cited as *The Ante-Nicene Fathers*.) Though this book was probably written by Lactantius, the authorship is disputed.

961. Ibid., XIII.

962. Eusebius: *The Ecclesiastical History* VIII, 3, 1-4. Tr. H. J. Lawlor and J. E. L. Oulton, New York and Toronto, 1927.

963. Barbarians sacked Salona in the seventh century and its inhabitants fled. When these inhabitants later returned, they built their homes inside Diocletian's massive palace. This second settlement has since overflowed the palace and has become the modern city of Split in Yugoslavia.

964. Sextus Aurelius Victor: *Epitome* XXXIX, 6. Author's trans.

965. Eusebius: *The Ecclesiastical History* VIII, 17, 6-10. Tr. H. J. Lawlor and J. E. L. Oulton, New York and Toronto, 1927.

966. Tertullian: *Apology* XXXIII, 2. Loeb.

967. Anonymous: *Epistle to Diognetus* V. In *The Ante-Nicene Fathers*. The epistle was probably written early in the second century A.D.

968. Minucius Felix: *Octavius* XVII. In *The Ante-Nicene Fathers*.

969. Justin Martyr: *Second Apology* X. In *The Ante-Nicene Fathers*.

970. Ibid., XIII. In *The Ante-Nicene Fathers*.

971. Justin Martyr: *Hortatory Address to the Greeks* XX. In *The Ante-Nicene Fathers*.

972. Justin Martyr: *First Apology* LXI. In *The Ante-Nicene Fathers*.

973. Justin Martyr: *Hortatory Address to the Greeks* V. In *The Ante-Nicene Fathers*.

974. Clement of Alexandria: *Exhortation to the Heathen* II. In *The Ante-Nicene Fathers*.

975. Ibid., X.

976. Ibid., XII.

977. Clement of Alexandria: *Stromata* I, xxii. In *The Ante-Nicene Fathers*.

978. Tertullian: *Apology* I, 7. Loeb.

979. Ibid., XXXVII, 4.

980. Ibid., XXVI, 1.

981. Ibid., XXXVII, 6-8.

982. Ibid., XVII, 1-3.

983. Ibid., XXI, 11-14.

984. Ibid., IX, 5; 10-13.

985. Minucius Felix: *Octavius* XXXVII, 12, Loeb. Minucius was a Christian apologist who lived probably between the mid-second and mid-third centuries. He was probably a native of the province of Africa. Of his writings, only the *Octavius* survives.

986. Lactantius: *The Divine Institutes* VI, xx. In *The Ante-Nicene Fathers*.

987. Minucius Felix: *Octavius* VIII, 3-4. Loeb.

988. And read clear down to the sixth century.

989. Clement of Alexandria: *Exhortation to the Heathen* II. In *The Ante-Nicene Fathers*.

990. Tertullian: *Apology* XV, 1. Loeb.

991. Ibid., XXVIII, 2.

992. Minucius Felix: *Octavius* XIX, 15—XX, 2. Loeb.

993. Ibid., XXV, 1; 5-7; 12.

994. Lactantius: *The Divine Institutes* VII, xv. In *The Ante-Nicene Fathers*.

995. Matthew 13, 13-14. In *The New Testament*, tr. Ronald Knox, New York, 1945.

996. Literally, the three mysteries "escaped the notice of the ruler of this age," the temporal power, who, at the time of Christ's birth, was of course the Emperor Augustus and, at the time of his death, Tiberius. The Greek is ἔλαθεν τὸν ἄρχοντα τοῦ αἰῶνος τούτου.

997. St. Ignatius: *Epistle to the Ephesians* XIX, 1-3. In *The Apostolic Fathers*, Loeb.

998. Tertullian: *Opera* II (*On Idolatry* 19, 1; 3). In *Corpus Christianorum, Series Latina*, Turnholti, 1954. Author's trans.

999. Ibid., (*On the Military Crown* XI, 2; 4-5).

1000. Quoted in Origen: *Against Celsus* VIII, lxviii. In *The Ante-Nicene Fathers*.

1001. Ibid., VIII, lxix-lxx.

1002. Ibid., VIII, lxxiii.

1003. Lactantius: *The Divine Institutes* VI, xx. In *The Ante-Nicene Fathers*.

1004. Justin Martyr: *First Apology* XI. In *The Ante-Nicene Fathers*.

1005. Ibid., LXVIII.

1006. Eusebius: *The Ecclesiastical History* IV, 13, 1-7. Tr. H. J. Lawlor and J. E. L. Oulton, New York and Toronto, 1927. The authenticity of this document has been questioned. Some scholars hold that at the least it contains Christian emendations.

1007. *Scriptores Historiae Augustae*: Severus XVII, 1. Loeb.

1008. Edward Gibbon, in his great work, *The Decline and Fall of the Roman Empire*, wittily estimates that the total number of martyrdoms under Diocletian and his successors "might consequently amount to about fifteen hundred, a number which, if it is equally divided between the ten years of the persecution will allow an annual consumption of one hundred and fifty martyrs." (P. 503, Modern Library ed.) Gibbon's remark would have been less witty had it recognized, first, that the Christians were normally in more danger from local mobs than from Imperial edicts; second, that his statistics on the number of Christians killed might not include lynchings, or deaths which followed when one of Tertullian's "unfriendly mobs" assailed the Christians with "stones and fire"; and, third, that death was less terrible than the tortures they faced, tortures which perhaps few upper-class Englishmen of the eighteenth century had accurately imagined, much less sampled. In this respect, our century, less witty than Gibbon's, has been more instructive, especially on concentration camps, institutions which Gibbon clearly did not foresee. Moreover, suicide, through which many inmates of Nazi camps escaped further physical agony, was forbidden to the Christian. Gibbon of course forestalled criticism from his contemporaries by somewhat gratuitously assuming that "vague descriptions" of torture are "so easily exaggerated" that we had better stick to calculating reported deaths. And this although, as a later wit has pointed out, death too can be much exaggerated.

1009. Tertullian: *Apology* XXXVII, 2. Loeb.

1010. Eusebius: *The Ecclesiastical History* VI, 41, 1-4; 10-14. Tr. H. J. Lawlor and J. E. L. Oulton, New York and Toronto, 1927.

1011. Tertullian: *Apology* XXXVII, 1. Loeb.

1012. Ibid., I, 12-13.

1013. Eusebius: *Martyrs of Palestine* 8, 9-12. Tr. H. J. Lawlor and J. E. L. Oulton, New York and Toronto, 1927.

1014. Ibid., 4, 8.

1015. Ibid., 5, 3.

1016. Justin Martyr: *Dialogue with Trypho* XVII. In *The Ante-Nicene Fathers.*

1017. Justin Martyr: *First Apology* XXXI. In *The Ante-Nicene Fathers.*

1018. See *The Jewish Encyclopedia,* article on Bar Kokba.

1019. Ibid.

1020. Origen: *Homily on Numbers* X, 2. In Migne: *Patrologiae Graecae* XII. Author's trans.

1021. *Acta Sanctorum,* Feb. 1. Tr. James Parkes in his *The Conflict of the Church and the Synagogue,* London, 1934, pp. 137-38.

1022. Tertullian: *On Modesty* I. In *The Ante-Nicene Fathers.*

1023. St. Cyprian at the Council of Carthage, A.D. 256. In *A Library of the Fathers of the Holy Catholic Church,* Vol. 17, p. 286. Tr. members of the English Church, Oxford and London, 1844.

1024. Eusebius: *The Ecclesiastical History* VII, 24, 6-9. Tr. H. J. Lawlor and J. E. L. Oulton, New York and Toronto, 1927.

1025. Tertullian: *Apology* XVIII, 4. Loeb.

1026. Minucius Felix: *Octavius* XXXIII, 1. Loeb.

1027. Tertullian: *Apology* XXXIX, 5. Loeb.

1028. Aristides the Philosopher: *Apology* XV. From the Syriac version in *The Ante-Nicene Fathers.*

1029. Eusebius: *The Ecclesiastical History* VII, 22, 7-10. Tr. H. J. Lawlor and J. E. L. Oulton, New York and Toronto, 1927.

1030. Justin Martyr: *First Apology* XIV. In *The Ante-Nicene Fathers.*

1031. Quoted by R. Walzer: *Galen on Jews and Christians,* London, 1949, p. 15. Preserved only in Arabic quotations.

1032. St. Ignatius to the Romans VI, 1. In *The Apostolic Fathers,* Loeb.

1033. The year of Constantine's birth is unknown. See A. H. M. Jones: *Constantine and the Conversion of Europe,* New York, 1949, pp. 1-2.

1034. The coin reproduced at the beginning of this chapter shows the monogram Constantine used.

1035. Lactantius: *Of the Manner in Which the Persecutors Died* XLIV. In *The Ante-Nicene Fathers.*

1036. Eusebius: *Life of Constantine* I, xxviii. In Migne: *Patrologiae Graecae* XX. Author's trans.

1037. Eusebius: *Life of Constantine* XXIX. In *The Greek Ecclesiastical Historians,* London, 1845.

1038. Needless to say, the dream and the cross of light in the heavens reported by Eusebius are subject to very different interpretations by modern historians. Constantine was a shrewd and ambitious man, who needed the political support of the Christian population in the Empire; it is impossible to prove he did not invent the dreams along with the fact that the whole army saw the cross. However, what he did and what he said, so far as our knowledge goes, suggest that he believed his own account. As to the two dreams, Christians of

571

his day shared with pagans the belief that dreams are among the means by which the divine communicates with the human, although there had for centuries been skeptics who rejected this interpretation. Many moderns would prefer to see in Constantine's dreams a Freudian wish fulfillment.

As to the more famous cross of light in the heavens, those who accept miracles are spared at least one problem. Those who do not will perhaps be satisfied with assuming hallucination and self-deception: that is, Constantine thought he saw the cross and mistakenly assumed his army did too. A. H. M. Jones (*Constantine and the Conversion of Europe*, New York, 1949, p. 96) thinks Constantine probably saw a form of the halo phenomenon that is sometimes caused by the fall of ice crystals across the rays of the sun. Professor Jones observes that "a cross of light with the sun in its centre has been on several occasions scientifically observed." By implication he renders 'ὑπερκείμενον τοῦ ἡλίου as "superimposed on the sun" rather than "above the sun." In English the word "over" might carry either meaning. But although his explanation furnishes us with a nonmiraculous cross of light, it seems to leave the inscription, *Conquer by this*, without benefit of modern science, and we are thrown back on the familiar choice, hallucination or miracle.

1039. Homer: *Iliad* I, 5.

1040. Nazarius' Panegyric to Constantine Augustus XXXV, A.D. 321. In *Panégyriques Latins*, ed. Édouard Galletier, Paris, 1949. Author's trans.

1041. Eusebius: *Life of Constantine* I, xl. In *The Greek Ecclesiastical Historians*, London, 1845. Professor Andrew Alföldi (*The Conversion of Constantine and Pagan Rome*, tr. Harold Mattingly, Oxford, 1948, p. 42) contends that the statue bore a standard, not a cross, and that on the standard was the monogram of Christ which had won him the battle against Maxentius.

1042. Quoted in A. H. M. Jones: *Constantine and the Conversion of Europe*, New York, 1949, p. 91.

1043. Eusebius: *Life of Constantine* IV, xx. In *The Greek Ecclesiastical Historians*, London, 1845.

1044. Council of Nicaea, Canon XII. In *Authoritative Christianity*, ed. James Chrystal, Jersey City, 1891.

1045. Canon III of the Synod of Arles had some ten years before apparently sanctioned military service by Christians, but its text is disputed and may indeed refer to gladiators, not soldiers.

1046. Eusebius: *Life of Constantine* III, xviii. In *The Greek Ecclesiastical Historians*, London, 1845.

1047. Ibid., III, xv.

1048. K. Müller: *Fragmenta historicorum graecorum* IV, 199. (Anonymus, qui Dionis Cassii Historias continuavit, Frag. 15, 1), Paris, 1868. Author's trans.

1049. English corrupted the name to Constantinople; Turkish, to Istanbul. Turkish corrupted the name of Nicomedia to Isnikmid and later to Izmit, its present name.

1050. It was not, however, until the next century that gladiatorial combats finally disappeared from the Roman Empire.

1051. The Church of the Holy Wisdom, now commonly called St. Sophia, was built after Constantine's reign.

1052. Socrates: *Ecclesiastical History* I, 17. In *A Select Library of Nicene and Post-Nicene Fathers of the Christian Church*, 2nd Series, Grand Rapids, Mich., 1952.

1053. *S. Optati Milevitani Librii* VII, Appendix III, 15. Ed. Carolus Ziwsa, Prague, Vienna, and Leipzig, 1893. Author's trans.

1054. Eusebius: *Life of Constantine* I, xliv. In *The Greek Ecclesiastical Historians*, London, 1845.

1055. Eusebius: *Life of Constantine* IV, xxiv. In Migne: *Patrologiae Graecae* XX. Author's trans.

1056. Eusebius: *Life of Constantine* II, lxxi. In *The Greek Ecclesiastical Historians*, London, 1845.

1057. Ibid., III, xix.

1058. Ibid., II, lxv.

1059. Sozomen: *Ecclesiastical History* I, viii. In *A Select Library of Nicene and Post-Nicene Fathers of the Christian Church*, 2nd Series, Grand Rapids, Mich., 1952.

1060. Ibid., II, xxviii.

1061. Ibid., II, vi.

1062. Eusebius: *Life of Constantine* II, liii. In *The Greek Ecclesiastical Historians*, London, 1845.

1063. Indeed, by the fifth century there were more Christians in the Eastern Empire than pagans; by the sixth, paganism had all but disappeared there.

1064. Socrates: *Ecclesiastical History*, Introd. V. In *A Select Library of Nicene and Post-Nicene Fathers of the Christian Church*, 2nd Series, Grand Rapids, Mich., 1952.

1065. Ibid., I, xxiv.

1066. The bishops had moved a long way from Dionysius, Bishop of Alexandria, who had humbly listened to heretics and had lovingly reached agreements with them. The increasing acerbity of theological debate and the substitution of power for discussion and mutual understanding may well have been one of the causes of a tendency by the fifth century to shift the emphasis of church missions from converting persons to converting tribes. For if a tribal chieftain could be converted, his tribe often followed him, at least nominally.

1067. Athanasius: Letter XLVIII, to Amun. In *A Select Library of Nicene and Post-Nicene Fathers of the Christian Church*, 2nd Series, Grand Rapids, Mich., 1952. In a few decades, Bishop Ambrose of Milan and Bishop Augustine of Hippo were defending the right of a Christian to use the sword in defense of a just cause. Before the fourth century was over, bishops were leading troops, and churches were being fortified in Antioch, Alexandria, and Cyrene. Eastern monasteries, founded by men who had fled from the life of the Empire in order to live a more purely Christian life, were likewise being fortified. If, as is now thought, the Emperor Valentinian to whom Vegetius dedicated his treatise on military science was Valentinian II, then it was in the late fourth century that he described the ceremony of enlisting recruits in a fashion that would have startled theologians of an earlier day: "They swear by God, by Christ, and by the Holy Spirit, and by the majesty of the Emperor, which, next to God, must be loved and revered. For once he has received the name of Augustus, to the Emperor as to God, present and incorporated, sincere devotion and ever-watchful servitude must be openly rendered. And he preserves God either in a private or a military station when he faithfully loves him who rules by God's authority." (*De re militari* II, v, ed. N. Schwebelius, Argentoratum, 1806. Author's trans.) By 416 the Code of Theodosian forbade non-Christians to serve in the army. (*Codex Theodosianus* XVI, x, 21.)

1068. Eusebius: *Life of Constantine* III, xv. In *The Greek Ecclesiastical Historians*, London, 1845.

1069. Socrates: *Ecclesiastical History* I, xiv. In A *Select Library of Nicene and Post-Nicene Fathers of the Christian Church*, 2nd Series, Grand Rapids, Mich., 1952.

1070. Sozomen: *Ecclesiastical History* III, 19. In A *Select Library of Nicene and Post-Nicene Fathers of the Christian Church*, 2nd Series, Grand Rapids, Mich., 1952. Sozomen calls this story, or at least the part about convening the council, "a gross fabrication," on the grounds that the council Constantius was said to have convened at Rimini did not occur until twenty-two years after Constantius succeeded to the Empire. However, in IV, 12, Sozomen himself reports that Constantius "wished to establish uniformity of doctrine throughout the Church, and to unite the priesthood in the maintenance of the same sentiments."

1071. From a purely secular point of view, Constantine's new Christian capital proved its worth. When he established this Second Rome, the real Rome claimed to be 1,083 years old. But Constantine's new Rome was destined to remain the capital of the Eastern Empire for 1,123 years. It would hold off Avars and Persians in the early seventh century, the Moslem Caliphate in the late seventh, an Arab attack in the early eighth. True, in 1203 the commercial Republic of Venice managed to divert the Fourth Crusade from rescuing Christ's Sepulcher to sacking Venice's trade rival, Constantinople. But it recovered and remained the capital of the Romaioi until the Turks seized it in 1453 and made it the capital of their Moslem empire. Even then it was permitted to remain the religious capital of the Eastern churches and the Orthodox churches of Russia and other Slavic lands.

1072. P. Franchi de' Cavalieri (*I funeriali ed il sepolcro di Constantino Magno*, in *Mélanges d'archéologie et d'histoire*, Vol. XXXVI, 1916-17, pp. 242-43) contends that Constantine's sarcophagus was in the middle only because he had founded the Church of the Holy Apostles, and that the empty sarcophagi were intended to receive the mortal remains of those who would succeed him on the throne.

1073. Diodorus Siculus XVI, 92. Tr. G. Booth, London, 1814.

1074. Plutarch: *Moralia* 329C-D. Loeb.

EPILOGUE

1075. Tr. S. P. Scott: *The Civil Law*, Cincinnati, 1932. (Hereafter cited as Scott: *The Civil Law*.)

1076. Justinian: *Digest* XLVIII, iii, 1. In Scott: *The Civil Law*.

1077. Justinian: *Code* IX, xli, 11. In Scott: *The Civil Law*.

1078. Justinian: *Digest* XLVIII, xix, 8 (3). In Scott: *The Civil Law*.

1079. In Roman law not all "capital crimes" were punishable by death; some entailed civic death only, a loss of all rights of Roman citizenship.

1080. Justinian: *Digest* XLVIII, xix, 28. In Scott: *The Civil Law*.

1081. Ibid., XXII, v, 2.

1082. Ibid., XXII, v, 2 (3).
1083. *The Opinions of Paulus* II, xix. 9. In Scott: *The Civil Law.*
1084. Justinian: *Digest* XLVIII, xix, 8 (6). In Scott: *The Civil Law.*
1085. *The Opinions of Paulus* V, xxi (2). In Scott: *The Civil Law.*
1086. Ibid., V, xxii (1).
1087. Justinian: *Code* IX, viii, 3. In Scott: *The Civil Law.*
1088. Ibid., IX, xi, 1.
1089. Justinian: *Digest* XXXVIII, i, 14. In Scott: *The Civil Law.*
1090. Ibid., XXXVIII, i, 28.
1091. Ibid., XXV, vii, 1.
1092. Ibid., XXV, vii, 2.
1093. Ibid., L, xvii, 32.
1094. Ibid., L, xvii, 209.
1095. Ibid., IX, ii, 2 (2).
1096. Ibid., XXIX, v, 1 (28).
1097. Ibid., XLVIII, x, 7.
1098. Many Americans of our generation, taught that our aim is equality for all before the law, may be troubled by discovering that Roman jurisprudence made few pretenses on this score. But recent work by the Vera Foundation of New York and recent public statements by the Attorney General of the United States have doubtless apprised many readers of this book that a rich or influential American, charged with crime, can face his charge with an equanimity quite inappropriate to a poor man. The problems of posting bond while awaiting trial, of securing competent legal counsel, and sometimes even of avoiding torture by the police, inflicted to elicit confession, are now publicly known to be quite different problems for the poor and the rich. An Ulpian or a Papinian might urge that Roman legal theory was merely less hypocritical than our own. Perhaps this inequality in our system of justice has led many a modern historian to overlook the explicit, brutal inequalities of Roman jurisprudence recorded in Justinian's *Digest* and to write panegyrics on the moral majesty of Roman Law.
1099. Maximian Herculius had of course been sent by Diocletian Jovius to Gaul to quell the revolt of the Bagaudae and had apparently solved the Bagaudae problem by force in 285. Force was duly crowned by rhetoric when the rhetorician Mamertine addressed a panegyric to Maximian, inevitably likening his triumph to Hercules' helping Jupiter overcome the Giants, whom Mamertine eloquently described as being half men, half serpents. But the problem proved not susceptible to solution by force. Since the same economic conditions which made these peasants half men before constituted the real problem, they had again turned half serpent and again become guerrilla rebels against Roman law and order.

Salvian, the Christian looking at them not as monsters but as whole men, saw the whole problem. He also objected to the familiar precaution taken by the oppressor against freedom fighters: branding them with a dehumanizing epithet "contrived for their shame." No loyal citizen will protest the subjection, or even the extermination, of monsters.

The precise meaning of Bagaudae is unknown. It is thought to be a Celtic word.

1100. Salvian: *On the Government of God* V, 5; 7-8. Tr. Eva M. Sanford, New York, 1930.

1101. K. Müller: *Fragmenta historicorum graecorum* IV, 86-88. (Priscus Panites, Frag. 8) Paris, 1868. Tr. J. B. Bury: *History of the Later Roman Empire* I, 218-19, London and New York, 1889.

1102. Justinian: *Digest* XLIX, i, 1. In Scott: *The Civil Law.*

1103. Ibid., XXXIX, iv, 12.

1104. Justinian: *Code* XI, lvii, 1. In Scott: *The Civil Law.*

1105. Ibid., I, xli, 2.

1106. Ibid., XII, lviii, 1.

1107. Ibid., XII, xlii, 1.

1108. Justinian: *Institutes* II (2). In Scott: *The Civil Law.*

1109. *The Homecoming of Rutilius Namatianus* I, 47-66. Tr. G. F. Savage-Armstrong, London, 1907.

1110. Michel de Montaigne: *Selected Essays* [II, 10], "On Books," Modern Library, New York, 1949, p. 159.

1111. Simone Weil: "The Great Beast." In *Selected Essays 1934-43*, ed. and tr. Richard Rees, London, 1962, p. 102.

1112. This Serbian legend is mentioned by Martin P. Nilsson: *Imperial Rome*, New York, [1926], p. 222. I have been unable to get further information about this legend, a legend that perhaps unconsciously reflects the wisdom of the Greek myth of the giant, Antaeus.

ABOUT THE ILLUSTRATIONS

I.   COCK FIGHT, 3rd century B.C., Hellenistic, from Amisus, terra cotta. *Reproduced by permission of the Walters Art Gallery, Baltimore. Museum photo.*

II.   OLD MARKET WOMAN, 2nd century B.C., Hellenistic, found in Rome, marble. *Reproduced by permission of the Metropolitan Museum of Art, Rogers Fund, 1909, New York. Museum photo.*

III.   LATE HELLENISTIC SILVER GOBLET, found at Boscoreale, Italy, from Smyrna. *The Louvre. Reproduced with permission from a photo by Réunion des Musées Nationaux.*

IV.   HEAD OF AN UNKNOWN ROMAN, 1st century B.C., *The Vatican Museum. Photo by Alinari.*

V.   CICERO, probably from the reign of Augustus, found on the Appian Way. *The Vatican Museum. Photo by Alinari.*

VI.   POMPEY, probably a copy made in the reign of Claudius of a bronze executed during Pompey's lifetime. *Ny Carlsberg Glyptotek, Copenhagen. Museum photo.*

VII.   JULIUS CAESAR, part of a statue or bust in marble, the nose restored. *Palazzo dell'Opera della Primaziale, Pisa. Photo by Alinari.*

VIII.   AUGUSTUS, from his reign. *The Roman National Museum, Rome. Photo by Alinari.*

IX.   MAECENAS, from the reign of Augustus, south frieze of Ara Pacis. *Photo by Alinari.*

X.   SENECA, from a double herm in marble, a copy found in Rome, made in the 3rd century A.D., of a 1st-century work. *Statliche Museen, Berlin. Museum photo.*

XI.   VESPASIAN, from his reign, found in Ostia, Italy. *The Roman National Museum, Rome. Photo by Alinari.*

XII.   HADRIAN, done shortly after his death, found in the Castel Sant'Angelo. *The Vatican Museum. Museum photo.*

XIII.   SOLDIERS OF THE PRAETORIAN GUARD, reign of Hadrian. *The Louvre. Photo by Arthaud.*

XIV.   THE ROMAN EMPIRE UNDER HADRIAN. Boundary line super-imposed on Rand McNally Geo-Physical Globe Transparency. Global Map copyright by Rand McNally & Co., © Time Inc.

XV.   HADRIAN'S WALL ACROSS BRITAIN. *Photo by Aerofilms and Aero Pictorial Ltd.*

XVI.   ROMAN ROAD AT PETRA, Jordan. *Photo by Arthaud.*

XVII.   AQUEDUCT IN GAUL, commonly known as the Pont du Gard, built in the reign of Augustus. *Photo by Yan.*

XVIII.   MARCUS AURELIUS, entering Rome in triumph, done during his reign. *Museo dei Conservatori, Rome. Photo by Alinari.*

XIX.   COMMODUS, attired as Hercules. Marble bust done during his reign. *Museo dei Conservatori, Rome. Photo by Alinari.*

XX.   CARACALLA. Marble bust, early 3rd century. *The Art Museum, Princeton University, Princeton. Museum photo.*

XXI.   DECIUS. Bust done during his reign. *The Capitoline Museum, Rome. Photo by Anderson.*

XXII.   CONSTANTINE. Marble head from a colossal statue done c. 312. *In the courtyard of the Museo dei Conservatori, Rome. Photo by Anderson.*

INDEX

579